Cynthia Harrod-Eagles is the author of the contemporary Bill Slider Mystery series as well as the Morland Dynasty novels. Her passions are music, wine, horses, architecture and the English countryside.

Visit the author's website at www.cynthiaharrodeagles.com

Also in the *Dynasty* series:

DYNASTY

20

The Winter Journey

Cynthia Harrod-Eagles

sphere

SPHERE

First published in Great Britain in 1997
by Little, Brown and Company

This edition published by Warner Books in 1998
Reprinted in 2000
Reprinted by Time Warner Paperbacks in 2004
Reprinted by Sphere in 2007, 2009, 2011, 2012, 2014

A CIP catalogue record for this book
is available from the British Library.

ISBN 978-0-7515-2023-1

Typeset by Palimpsest Book Production Limited,
Polmont, Stirlingshire
Printed and bound in Great Britain by
Clays Ltd, St Ives plc

Papers used by Sphere are from well-managed forests
and other responsible sources.

Sphere
An imprint of
Little, Brown Book Group
100 Victoria Embankment
London EC4Y 0DY

An Hachette UK Company
www.hachette.co.uk

www.littlebrown.co.uk

To Tony, who gets me through, with love and thanks

SELECT BIBLIOGRAPHY

Anglesey, Marquess of	*A History of the British Cavalry*
Battiscombe, G.	*Shaftesbury, A Biography, 1801–1885*
Burton, Elizabeth	*The Early Victorians at Home*
Briggs, Asa	*The Age of Improvement*
Calthorpe, S.J.G.	*Cadogan's Crimea*
Cardigan, Earl of	*Eight Months on Active Service*
Chesney, Kellow	*The Victorian Underworld*
Ffrench, Yvonne	*The Great Exhibition 1851*
Finer, S.E.	*Life and Times of Sir Edwin Chadwick*
Gernsheim, H. and A.	*Roger Fenton, Photographer of the Crimean War*
Goldie, S.	*Florence Nightingale in the Crimean War*
Hamley, Sir E.	*The War in the Crimea*
Hammond, J.L. and B.	*Lord Shaftesbury*
Hibbert, Christopher	*The Destruction of Lord Raglan*
Hibbert, Christopher	*The English: A Social History 1066–1945*
Huxley, Elspeth	*Florence Nightingale*
Mayhew, Henry	*Mayhew's London*
McCreevy, T.R.	*A History of Nursing 1845–1945*
Reader, W.J.	*Victorian England*

Russell, W.H.	*The British Expedition to the Crimea*
Stone, Lawrence	*The Road to Divorce*
Webb, R.K.	*Modern England*
Woodham Smith, Cecil	*Florence Nightingale*
Woodham Smith, Cecil	*The Reason Why*
Woodward, Llewellyn	*The Age of Reform 1815–1870*
Young, G.M.	*Early Victorian England*

THE MORLAND FAMILY

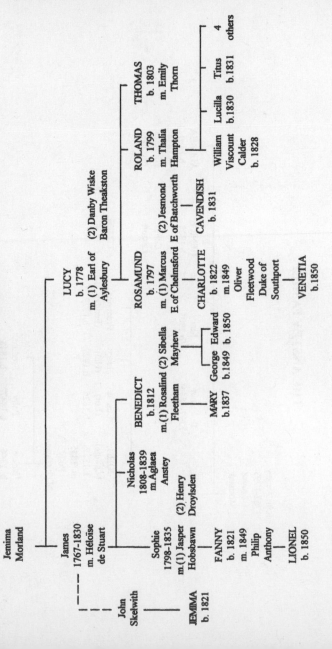

THE ANSTEY FAMILY

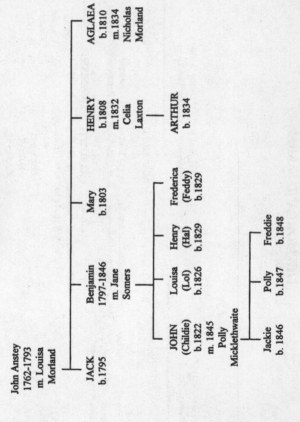

John Anstey
1762-1793
m. Louisa
Morland

JACK
b.1795

Benjamin
1797-1846
m. Jane
Somers

Mary
b.1803

HENRY
b.1808
m.1832
Celia
Laxton

AGLAEA
b.1810
m.1834
Nicholas
Morland

JOHN
(Childie)
b.1822
m. 1845
Polly
Micklethwaite

Louisa
(Lol)
b.1826

Henry
(Hal)
b.1829

Frederica
(Feddy)
b.1829

ARTHUR
b. 1834

Jackie
b.1846

Polly
b.1847

Freddie
b.1848

THE AMERICAN COUSINS

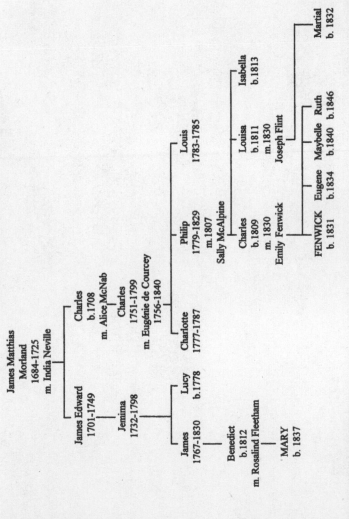

James Matthias
Morland
1684-1725
m. India Neville

James Edward
1701-1749

Charles
b.1708
m. Alice McNab

Jemima
1732-1798

Charles
1751-1799
m. Eugénie de Courcey
1756-1840

Lucy
b.1778

James
1767-1830

Charlotte
1777-1787

Philip
1779-1829
m.1807
Sally McAlpine

Louis
1783-1785

Benedict
b.1812
m. Rosalind Fleetham

MARY
b. 1837

Charles
b.1809
m. 1830
Emily Fenwick

Louisa
b.1811
m.1830
Joseph Flint

Isabella
b.1813

FENWICK
b. 1831

Eugene
b.1834

Maybelle
b.1840

Ruth
b.1846

Martial
b. 1832

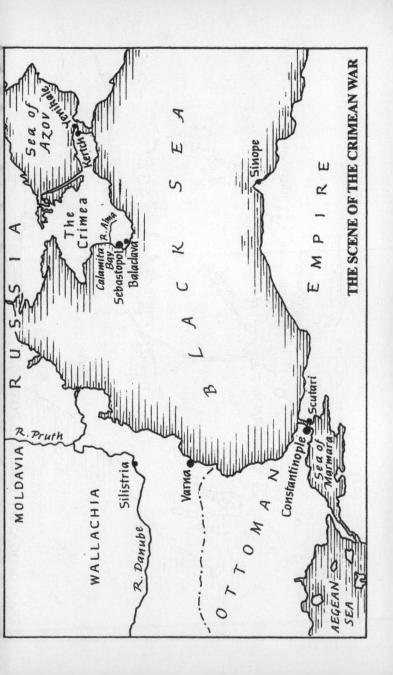

THE SCENE OF THE CRIMEAN WAR

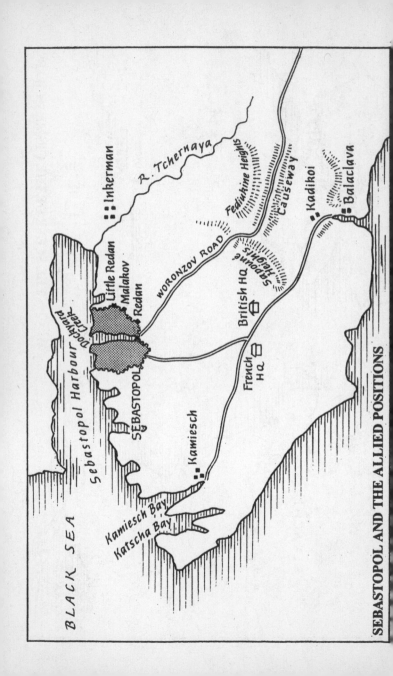

SEBASTOPOL AND THE ALLIED POSITIONS

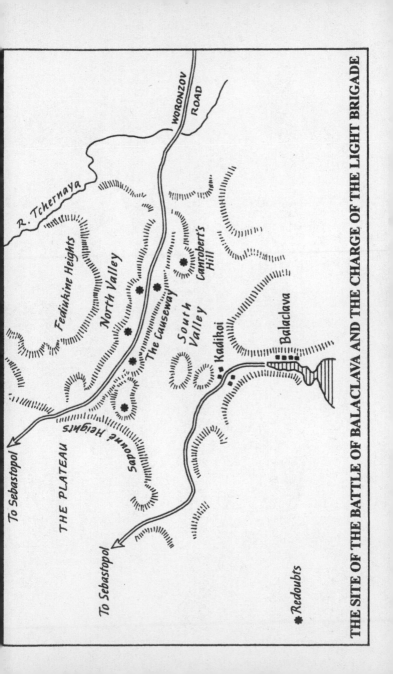

THE SITE OF THE BATTLE OF BALACLAVA AND THE CHARGE OF THE LIGHT BRIGADE

To Sebastopol

To Sebastopol

THE PLATEAU

Sapoune Heights

R. Tchernaya

Fediukine Heights

North Valley

The Causeway

South Valley

Canrobert's Hill

Kadikoi

Balaclava

WORONZOV ROAD

* Redoubts

BOOK ONE

In the Shadows

I saw a gradual vision through my tears:
The sweet, sad years, the melancholy years –
Those of my own life, who by turns had flung
A shadow across me.

Elizabeth Barrett Browning:
Sonnets from the Portuguese

CHAPTER ONE

1851

It was cool when they rode out in the morning, with that pale, clear coolness of a June day that is going to be hot. The dew was thick, and darkened the horses' legs as they brushed through the long grass; the sky was almost white, the sun still below the trees. The dogs ran ahead, noses deep in the hedgerows, pausing now and then to look back encouragingly. They never stayed the whole ride. Sooner or later they would turn aside after something that simply *had* to be investigated; then finding the master and mistress gone out of sight they would give up and work their way slowly home.

Benedict and Sibella rode in silence, glad just to be alone together. It had been a crowded year, and times like these had been rare. Morland Place always kept them busy, but Benedict had been away from home a great deal too, helping shape the Great Exhibition in London. This most troublesome brain-child of Prince Albert had finally opened to the public on the first of May, in Paxton's glorious great greenhouse in Hyde Park, which a newspaper had dubbed 'the Crystal Palace'.

Benedict's former colleague Robert Stephenson had been involved with the Exhibition from the beginning, and he had been quick to call on the services of old friends. Benedict had been summoned to London every other week, not only for his engineering expertise, but for his persuasive powers, which had been honed in the service of the York and North Midland Railway. Stephenson said no-one could get into a pocket like Benedict Morland, and still leave the victim smiling.

Benedict had enjoyed his involvement. The business of creating the Exhibition was interesting in itself, and there was always a great deal going on in London. And he had met up with old friends – Stephenson, Charles Vignoles, Brunel and Lyon Playfair – and made lots of new ones. The disadvantage was that it interfered with the work of the estate, and took him away from Sibella.

It was a glorious day for a ride. The horses were happy to be out, swinging along at an eager walk, ears and eyes everywhere, nostrils fluttering, absorbing the morning with infectious delight. The country was beautiful, the grass dense and juicy, the hedges and trees in glossy full-leaf and stiff with birdsong. As they rode past Low Field, the mares lifted their heads only briefly from the serious business of grazing, but the new foals raced down to the fence to goggle and snort. They cat-jumped with excitement, flirted their teeth at each other in mock ferocity, and stilted away up the pasture again at full gallop, mad with with the joy of their own speed.

Sibella met Benedict's eyes and they both smiled. 'What pleasure could be superior to this: riding about one's own land, with one's own wife?' he said.

'I take it that is a rhetorical question,' Sibella said. Her happiness was so profound she could almost taste it. She had been in love with Benedict since she first met him, when she was fifteen years old and he was a railway engineer – grown-up, handsome, dashing, and with all the gypsy romance that hung about the great men of the Workings. She had been just a school-room miss in pigtails to him, then: he was in love with someone else. When he married the someone else, hope went out of life for Sibella; so that when later a business colleague of her father's offered for her, she accepted, thinking nothing mattered any more. Sir Samuel Mayhew was very rich, and forty years her senior; but he was madly in love with her, and Sibella thought that he would be like an indulgent father. She would be comfortable, have her own establishment, and be free of her mother, which was a great object.

She had not reckoned on Mayhew's insane jealousy: he set his servants to spy on her, and fell into wild rages if she so much as spoke to a groom or a porter. She had not reckoned on the misery of being under constant suspicion, of enduring false accusations. And she had not reckoned – how could she? – on the horrors of physical intimacy with an elderly man she neither liked nor respected.

She blamed no-one but herself: the match was convenient to her father but she knew he would not have forced her to marry against her will. She had done her best to be a good wife, to live in conformity with her husband's freakish rules; and schooled her mind never, never even to think of his dying, for fear she might come to hope for it. But it was his death, of course, which released her, a few years after the death of Benedict's wife. Benedict, miserably married to a woman who deceived and cuckolded him, had learned belatedly to value Sibella's translucent qualities. As soon as she was free, he went to find her, to claim her and carry her away like St George of old.

In her memory, Sibella's first marriage was not so much a dragon as a dark cave, from which she had emerged, blinking, into brilliant sunshine. And now, surprisingly quickly – for they had been married not quite three years – the whole Mayhew business had receded in into unreality, like something ugly glimpsed from a railway train and left instantly far behind. She glanced at Benedict as they rode, and he seemed so familiar and dear they might have been married for thirty years instead of three. Their lives together were simple and satisfying. There was the Morland estate to run and the children to raise, and they did these things in partnership, sharing the duties and the pleasures equally.

By the time they turned homewards the sun was high, and the promised heat lay like crystal over the land, holding it in a spell of stillness. The birds had fallen silent; only a little breeze moved shadows about beguilingly under the leaves, with a sound like water. And the horses' hooves thudded a soft heartbeat as they trod their short shadows, their heads nodding now, and their ears eloquent of *home* and *feed*. When they passed through Ten Thorn Gap they found Kai, Benedict's old bitch, lying in the cool of the hedge waiting for them, her yellow eyes glowing strangely in the shadow. The young bitch Brach, Mary's wolfound Dog and Sibella's pointer Dancer were nowhere to be seen.

'Superior loyalty,' Benedict said, pleased, as Kai fell in at Monarch's heels.

'She's too old to run as far as the others, that's all.'

'Don't listen, Kai. Missus is just jealous.' Kai smiled and waved her tail, perfectly in agreement. They rode on. After a little, Benedict glanced at Sibella, and asked, 'What is it?'

'I'm sorry – what did you say?'

'I wondered what you were thinking about. You looked so serious.'

'Oh, I was thinking about how nice and cool it will be inside the house. And about lemonade straight from the cold-house. And how hungry I will feel when I've stopped being so horrid thirsty.'

He laughed. 'God bless your appetites! Is all your happiness rooted in the here and now?'

'It's enough for me at present,' she said. 'I'll think of

6

heaven nearer the time. Oh, look!' They had come over the rise and the house lay before them at the foot of the shallow slope. 'There's a carriage just leaving.'

It had come out from under the barbican, over the drawbridge, and was turning onto the track in the direction of York.

'It's Harry Anstey's barouche,' Benedict said.

'How can you tell from this distance?'

'I recognise the horses, of course – I sold them to him. Mary must be home!' And he pushed Monarch abruptly into a trot, making Ebony toss his head as he tried to follow and was checked by Sibella in the interests of good equine manners. Benedict's eagerness to see his daughter was such that he had disappeared into the yard before Sibella had even reached the drawbridge; and Mary had only been away a week.

She was still in the great hall when Benedict entered, shedding her gloves and trying to fend off the overjoyed hounds, who threatened to knock her over: Dog was as tall as her when he stood on his hind legs to wash her face. Malton, the butler, was waiting to receive her mantle, as was his duty; but Father Moineau, the chaplain-tutor, had beaten everyone to the post and was untying Mary's ribbons with his own hands, while several servants who had no real duty there were hovering about the hall, beaming.

Everyone adored Mary, and none more than her father, who had a moment, unnoticed in all the fuss, to look at her unobserved. At a week less than fourteen years old, she was still as small as a child, no more than four feet and ten inches tall; but in every other way she was a woman. In her tight-waisted, full-skirted, three-flounced gown, her plaid mantle and fashionably small bonnet, she looked like a miniature of a grown-up lady. And she was

7

not just pretty, but truly beautiful, with lovely features, wide violet eyes and a skin like blush-roses, framed with long curls of shining gold. She was the image of her mother, Benedict thought painfully. Many of her little gestures and expressions she must have caught from her mother in early childhood. They had been very fond of each other.

But Mary's face had an animation and expressiveness which Rosalind's had never had. Rosalind had been a pretty doll, but Mary was intelligent beyond the norm. Father Moineau cherished her mind, and it was for her sake that he had given up his wandering life and settled at Morland Place, to spend his sunset years in contemplation of a miracle. With him Mary did lessons that would have taxed most adult men; and she enjoyed the exercise of her own intellect so much she would play with Latin epigrams as other children played with balls and hoops.

This great intelligence, which had made it impossible for the last two years to treat her as a child, she did not get from her mother. Rosalind could read and write, but never troubled herself with either. No, Benedict believed that the extraordinary qualities of Mary's mind came from her father.

Now she had seen him. Her face lit and she ran to him, her arms wide with unselfconscious joy. 'Papa!'

'How is my angel?' he enquired tenderly, bending to receive her kisses. 'You look rosy enough. Are you well again?' She had had one of her troublesome colds, which Dr Holland said had been made worse by excessive studying. To get her away from her books, Benedict had sent her to stay with friends in York.

'I'm *perfectly* well,' she said emphatically. 'It was only a little cold, Papa. You didn't need to send me away.'

'But did you have a pleasant time, all the same?'

'Oh yes, very pleasant! I always do, you know. Aunt Celia is so kind, and I have such interesting talks with Uncle Harry. But I'm glad to be home.' She looked round her with satisfaction. 'Home is best.'

'I'm glad you think so. Is that a new bonnet?'

'Aunt Celia bought it for me. And look, she's shown me how to put up my hair.' She pulled off her bonnet and turned to show him the back of her head. The back hair had been drawn into a neat, braided chignon: only the side hair was in the long, loose curls he loved. 'Don't you like it?' she asked anxiously, turning again to see why he was silent.

'Oh yes, very much,' he said; but he could not fob her off. 'I wish you wouldn't grow up so quickly.'

'I am nearly fourteen,' she reminded him gravely. 'Juliet was *married* at fourteen.'

'You, however,' he said firmly, 'will not be.'

'I don't think I want to be,' she said judiciously. 'Boys are so very silly. They don't know anything, and they roar and push and go red in the face and say stupid things.' This, Benedict reflected, was an accurate description of the effect she had on lads of her own age. 'And anyway,' Mary added, 'I shall always love you best.'

He made himself laugh. 'I'll remind you of that when you have a husband!'

Sibella arrived at that moment, and Mary went to kiss and greet her; the same questions and answers were exchanged; and then Mary exclaimed, 'Goodness, I'm hungry! Will luncheon be soon? Is there time to go and see my darling babies first, Mama?'

It was a piece of the purest kindness that Mary had always called Sibella *Mama* without being asked.

'There's time, if you're quick,' Sibella said. 'Papa and I have to change, in any case.'

'Come with me,' Mary begged. 'I'm sure they must want to see you *almost* as much as me.'

'Well, as it happens, some messages came in while we were out which I ought to attend to,' Benedict said. 'Malton, can we postpone luncheon by half an hour?'

So Sibella and Mary went upstairs together, while Benedict and Father Moineau walked away towards the steward's room. Mary chatted about her stay in York and Sibella studied her as she listened. Mary was a lovely girl, in every sense: lovely, loving, and lovable. If there had been anything about her to dislike it might have made it easier for Benedict; but he had adored her since the moment of her birth, and not until it was too late to take back his heart had he found out that she was not his own flesh and blood. From the very beginning, Rosalind had cuckolded him. This shining jewel of a child had in fact been fathered by Rosalind's lover, Sir Carlton Miniott, and *that* was where Mary had her intelligence – for Miniott had an extraordinary mind, while Benedict was no more than clever.

Mary was not Benedict's daughter and there was nothing of him in her; but he loved her, and had dedicated himself to making sure she never discovered what her mother had done. Only Father Moineau and Sibella knew the truth. Sometimes Sibella wished Benedict had not told her. Knowing was like trying to sleep in a bed in which you've lost a sewing-needle: you never knew quite when it might run into you, but you were sure that sooner or later it would.

Sibella brought her mind back to what Mary was telling her, the details of a legal problem that 'Uncle Harry' was dealing with. Harry Anstey was a solicitor, Benedict's man of business as well as his childhood friend. 'Do you really understand all that?' Sibella asked at last. It seemed immensely complicated to her.

'Oh yes,' Mary said, with faint surprise. 'It isn't difficult to follow. You see—'

'No, don't tell me again,' Sibella protested, laughing. 'It sounds like one of those fiendish conundrums! I don't think I have a legal mind.'

'Probably I don't explain it properly,' Mary said tactfully. 'Uncle Harry has such a clear way of putting things.'

'He talks to you a great deal about such things, doesn't he?'

'Well, I do find it interesting,' Mary said almost apologetically. She knew it was not what was expected of females. 'He said yesterday it was a great pity I wasn't born a boy, so that I could go into the law.'

'Should you have liked to?'

'I don't *think* so,' she said judiciously. 'A great deal of it is dreadful nonsense – things done a certain way because they always have been, not because it makes sense. Often it doesn't even work.'

'Work?'

'I mean, it doesn't achieve the desired result. One thinks of justice, I suppose; but after all, it's more a matter of maintaining the structure as it is.' She frowned, away on a train of thought. Sibella waited patiently for her to come back. 'But,' Mary went on at last, and with an unconscious sigh, 'I do often wish I'd been a boy, because there doesn't seem to be anything a girl can do. I wonder sometimes—'

'Yes?'

'Why God bothered to give us brains at all. When I see how little females are expected to think about anything. And,' she added as if this were more to the point, 'how difficult it is to *have* intelligence when there's nothing you can do with it. It's like – like being shut in a tiny room with a huge restless dog.'

Sibella thought the illustration very striking. She searched about for comfort. 'You have your studies. Aren't they a pleasure?'

'Yes, but they don't lead anywhere. One ought to be useful as well,' Mary said with childlike certainty. 'But a girl can only be a wife and mother.'

'Isn't it useful to be a wife and mother?'

'I suppose so; but one doesn't need any brains for it. Look at cows and sheep.'

'Thank you,' said Sibella drily.

'Oh,' Mary said, disconcerted, 'I didn't mean you.'

'It's all right. I know what you meant. But you can use your brains to educate your children, can't you?'

'Only if they're boys,' Mary said.

'I can't argue with you,' Sibella laughed. 'You always have the last word.'

They reached the nursery. George, Sibella's firstborn, was almost two – his birthday was two days before Mary's. He was beginning lessons with Mary's former governess, Miss Titchell, who was painstakingly teaching him to make his loops and tails. He was a solemn, chubby boy, very like Benedict to look at, except that his hair was darker and straighter and his eyes, surprisingly, were blue; and like Benedict in early childhood he had a passion for animals, preferably those small enough to be carried about in his pocket. George adored Mary, and as soon as she appeared he rushed to tell her in a breathless babble about a nest of earwigs he had discovered in the garden since she went away. The long-suffering Miss Titchell had learned to be wary about any small boxes she found lying about in the nursery.

Little Edward – Teddy, as he was known – was as yet no trouble to anyone: ten months old, a happy baby, arms held out indiscriminately to anyone who would pick him up and make a fuss of him. He was really still the province of the nursery-maids, but sometimes when they had a lot to do they left him with Miss Titchell, to sit on the floor and play with his toys while she taught Georgie. She accepted his presence with surprising equanimity, making the excuse that it would 'prepare him for the discipline of learning'. Sibella suspected, however, that Miss Titchell had felt rather hurt when Mary grew too clever to be taught by her, and was trying to make up quality with quantity.

When they left the nursery again, Sibella asked Mary, 'By the way, wasn't Arthur there, at Uncle Harry's?'

'Oh yes, he was there,' Mary said neutrally.

'You didn't mention him at all.' Sibella looked at her closely. It was unlike Mary to say so little about any subject, and Arthur – Harry and Celia's only son – had been a friend and playmate all her life. He was three years older than her, but because of her intelligence they had always seemed much of an age. 'You haven't quarrelled with him, have you?'

'We don't quarrel,' Mary said. She slid her eyes sidelong. 'He's got awfully *silly*,' she explained.

'Silly?' Sibella queried. Mary seemed unwilling to say more, but Sibella thought she understood. Arthur was seventeen, after all, and Mary was very, very pretty. 'Never mind, darling, he'll grow out of it,' she said, suppressing a smile. 'And if he doesn't, in a year or two you might be glad of a devoted swain, to dance with at parties and fetch you ices and pick up your shawl.'

Mary's reply was an unfeminine snort of derision.

The following day business caught up with Benedict and he was forced to disappear into the steward's room. It amazed Sibella, who had been brought up in a house which had nothing more than pleasure-grounds, how much work the owner of a large estate had to do, even

13

with the help of bailiffs and agents. One day a month was all her father had had to dedicate to such matters.

The weather was too good to waste by staying indoors, and she did not care to ride alone. Her mind turned naturally to Mary. Mary's outside tutors would not be coming again until next week: she was studying with Father Moineau, and Sibella did not feel guilty about interrupting him with a request that Mary be released.

'You know Doctor Holland said she mustn't study for too long at a time. She needs fresh air and exercise. And what's more,' she added, meeting the priest's eyes across Mary's bent head, 'so do you.'

'I hope you do not propose to get me up on a horse,' Moineau said. He patted his circumference. 'God did not design this body with horses in mind.'

'Oh no,' Sibella said. 'I have a picture in my mind of you walking slowly round the moat with a book in your hand, and then discovering that sitting on a bench and watching the swans is really more to your taste this morning than Socrates.'

'Sophocles,' Mary corrected, looking up from the book at last.

'It's all the same to me,' Sibella said with perfect truth.

Moineau smiled. 'You are a wise woman. At my age, one ought not to waste such a lovely day as this. Well, Mary, what do you think?'

Mary hardly hesitated. 'I haven't had a good gallop for a week,' she said wistfully. 'Has someone been exercising Linnet for me, or will he buck me off the moment he sees grass?'

'He had leading exercise yesterday. And I had him out for an hour the day before.'

'Oh, is that all? We'd better go out on the moor, then, hadn't we, and get it over with. May I, Father?'

'Go, child. Sophocles will wait another day.'

Linnet, Mary's chestnut, was fresh, and communicated his bad manners to Ebony, so they had a lively ride of it until they could get out onto Marston Moor and let them gallop. Then when the horses had got the itch out of their feet they rode a wide circle home, walking side by side and chatting pleasantly: Sibella always found Mary good company when they were alone together.

When eventually they came in sight of the house again, Sibella had a strange feeling of reliving the past, for there was a carriage standing at the end of the drawbridge. 'Now who can that be?' she said. 'We weren't expecting anyone.'

'It's a hired phaeton. And one of Willans's jobs,' Mary said, recognising the horse with an unerring horseman's eye. 'It's that wall-eyed roan that kicks. You remember it almost caused an accident in Micklegate last week?'

'Well, the visitor must be a stranger, then,' Sibella said. 'Everyone in York knows better than to let Willans fob them off with that beast.'

'Oh, yes, there he is,' Mary said. 'I don't recognise him, do you? It must be someone come to see round the house.'

Yes, now Sibella saw him, a man standing with his hands in his pockets and his head thrown back, gazing up at the barbican with the rapt air of the practised tourist.

'I think you're right,' she said, with a sigh. 'What a nuisance, when your papa is so busy.'

She was not particularly surprised at the circumstance. Morland Place had been included in the latest edition of the local guide book, and two or three times a week parties would arrive, drawn by the promise of a 'fine and most rare example of a fortified manor house', complete

15

with moat, drawbridge and portcullis, fifteenth century chapel, Exceptional Cantilevered Staircase, and collection of family portraits by Leading Artists of Every Age.

Benedict had decreed that visitors should be shown only the hall, dining room, chapel and long saloon: Morland Place was a comparatively small house, and there would otherwise be no end to the disruption of normal daily business. Even so he had been known to bolt wildly for the steward's room at the first sound of strangers' voices at the door.

'Fancy going to look at houses all alone,' Mary said. 'Do you suppose he hasn't any friends?' Visitors always came in parties.

'Perhaps he's studying architecture,' Sibella suggested.

Mary stared. 'Isn't there something strange about his clothes?'

'The cut is odd, perhaps,' Sibella agreed. 'And there's something very queer indeed about his hat.'

Mary giggled. 'Perhaps he's a lunatic escaped from his keeper.'

'I hope your father has had time to go into hiding.'

'Poor man,' Mary said, suddenly sorry for him. 'Are we going to avoid him too?'

'Malton can show him round, or Mrs Hoddle,' Sibella said firmly. 'What does one keep servants for?'

'They don't mind, anyway,' Mary said. 'They nearly always get a half crown for it.'

'Do they?' Sibella was often surprised at the things Mary knew.

'Oh yes,' said Mary. 'It's quite the usual fee. But in some houses the master makes them give it up to him. Malton told me,' she added, seeing the question in Sibella's eye.

'I suppose Malton doesn't mean to offer it to your father?'

'He's saving. He wants to make Mrs Hoddle an honest woman.'

Sibella burst out laughing. 'Mary! The things you say!'

'Oh, it's only what Malton told me. Shall we go round to the back door, then?'

'Too late. He's seen us.'

The stranger had turned and was doffing his peculiar headgear in automatic courtesy. Sibella saw that he was young – about eighteen or nineteen, perhaps – and well-built, though the loose fit of his clothes had made him look scrawny from a distance. His hair was blond and wiry, his face weather-tanned, his eyes pale blue, with thick sun-bleached lashes – like an albino horse, Mary thought. His straight nose was freckled, his wide mouth seemed designed for smiling. He scanned their faces eagerly as though he hoped he might recognise them.

'Good morning,' Sibella said politely.

'Good morning, ma'am,' the stranger replied. He bowed to Sibella, taking sidelong glances, like little sips, at Mary. 'Would this be Morland Place?' he said, but without waiting for an answer shook his head and went on, 'No, I guess that's a stupid question. There can't be two places like this, not even in England. And besides, here it is, right where it's supposed to be.' He tapped the guide book triumphantly.

His accent was strange, and Sibella couldn't place it. 'Have you come to look round the house?' she asked.

'Oh, Lord, have I just?' the young man said fervently. He clasped his hands together at chest-level as though he were about to pray. 'I've been looking forward to this moment the whole of my life – well, since I was five years old at any rate. I just can hardly believe I'm really here. May I ask, ma'am, would you be the lady of the house?'

17

Sibella admitted that she was.

The youth beamed. 'Well, ma'am, I am mighty proud to meet you! Just how proud I guess you'll understand when I tell you that my great great grandfather was born in this very house, a hundred and fifty years ago, give or take a year. And my great grandfather was born exactly one hundred years ago this year, which makes it kind of special for me being here at this particular time, although he wasn't actually *born* in Morland Place. But he stayed here a lot, and I guess he looked on it as his home.'

Sibella could only stare at him helplessly, bemused by the flood of words. Mary, however, had managed to follow him.

'Your great great grandfather lived here?' she asked.

He turned towards her with an eagerness which suggested he had only been waiting for an excuse.

'Yes indeed. He was a Morland and a son of this house – which makes us kind of cousins, I guess.'

'You are no cousin to me, sir, I'm afraid,' Sibella said. 'I'm only a Morland by marriage.'

The young man's smile wavered, he looked disconcerted, and turned his hat rapidly round and round by the brim. 'I beg pardon, ma'am. I hope I haven't said anything to offend. I didn't mean to be forward.' He coloured under his tan, and lowered his gaze. 'Naturally the connection being so distant, I shouldn't expect to be noticed by the family. But I did understand that the house was open to visitors—'

Sibella felt as though she had kicked a puppy. 'Indeed, sir, you did not offend. Mr – er?'

'Morland, ma'am.'

'Of course,' Sibella said, supressing a smile. 'I am Mrs Benedict Morland. This is my daughter, Miss Mary Morland.'

He bowed to Mary. 'Fenwick Morland, of Twelvetrees, near Dorchester, South Carolina – at your service, ma'am.'

'Oh, but our stud is called Twelvetrees,' Mary exclaimed with interest.

'I guess ours is named after yours,' he said. 'There was an avenue of ten lime trees when Pa took it over, so he planted two more and called it Twelvetrees. It was just called the Smithson place before that.'

'Where is South Carolina?' Sibella queried, getting left behind.

'It's in America, Mama,' Mary supplied.

'Ah!' Sibella said. She had never met an American before. 'I did hear there was a branch of the family went to America – oh, a long time ago. It must be an interesting country.'

Fenwick Morland's smile widened. 'It surely is, ma'am. And South Carolina's the best darned State in the whole Union.'

'But that means you're a long-lost cousin,' Mary exclaimed. 'Just like a story!'

He turned to her. 'In a story, however,' he said, 'it's always a long-lost heir, and I assure you I haven't come to claim a birthright. But I would be proud and honoured to make the acquaintance of the main branch of the family.'

Sibella said, 'Won't you come in and take some refreshment with us? My husband is occupied with business this morning, but as soon as he's at leisure I'm sure he'll be delighted to meet you.'

'I'd like that very much, ma'am, if you're sure I'm not imposing? It's mighty good of you, seeing I'm a stranger to you.'

'Not at all. We may not have met before, but family is family.'

Now she had said the right words for him. The wide

19

smile widened into a positive grin. 'You never said a truer word, ma'am. That's what we always say back home. Family is kind of sacred with us. We'd reckon it shameful to turn family away – but I wasn't sure you'd feel the same way over here.'

'This,' said Fenwick Morland in awed tones as he gazed about the Great Hall, 'is the most magnificent, the most splendid—'

'Oh, do wait until you've seen the chapel,' Sibella begged, 'or you will run out of superlatives. And there's still the Exceptional Cantilevered Staircase to come, you know.' Mary gave her a reproving look. 'But I know just how you feel,' Sibella added hastily. 'I'm new to all this myself. I've only been a Morland for three years, and I didn't even come from an old family. My father's was new money, I have to confess. But perhaps you don't suffer from that sort of thing in America?'

'I'm afraid we do, ma'am, especially in cities like Charleston where there are lots of old families. My family's new money too. It's harder for girls, of course. I have two sisters, and they'll find out what's what when they get to courting age.' He shook his head slightly. 'A man is always accepted amongst men if he rides well and shoots straight and holds his liquor like a gentleman. But women can be cruel to each other.'

'Do you live in the city – in Charleston?' Mary asked.

'Twelvetrees is about forty miles from Charleston.'

'Is Twelvetrees a farm?'

'A plantation,' he corrected.

'What's the difference?' Sibella asked.

'Well, ma'am, I guess to an outsider it's mostly the size. A farm is what we call a little bitty piece of land that just grows enough to feed the family that lives on it; a plantation is a big place, hundreds of acres, which grows a crop to sell for cash. But to a Southerner a planter is a different kind of person from a farmer. He is – or at least he's meant to be – a gentleman.'

'I suppose it is rather like the difference here between a smallholding and an estate,' Sibella said.

'I guess it could be,' he said, not knowing what these terms implied. 'But we haven't anything like this,' he went on, resuming his contemplation of the hall. 'This is just pure history. You've got to go to Europe to see real old buildings – and to England to see places like this.'

'There are no places like this,' Benedict said, coming into the hall at that moment. He looked a little cross at having been disturbed, and in finding a stranger in possession of his house.

Fenwick Morland turned round, and bowed. 'I agree with you, sir. I didn't mean any disrespect.'

'My dear,' Sibella said, 'allow me to present a long-lost cousin from America, Mr Fenwick Morland. His ancestor was born in this house, it seems. He's come all this way just to visit us.'

'Well, sir,' Fenwick corrected, anxious to be strictly accurate, 'I came to England on business for my father, concerned with the Great Exhibition in London; but I couldn't have gone back home without coming to see the ancestral family seat, not for the world.'

'You came for the Exhibition?' Benedict said, his smile warming.

'I did, sir, but I take leave to tell you that there's nothing in the whole darned Crystal Palace that can hold a candle to just standing here in this wonderful place.'

'And what is your father's business, sir?'

'Cotton, sir. We grow cotton, but we also have one of the very few mills in the South. I'm here in the hope of finding out how to make it run more efficiently, because there's no doubt it's a hard business to make a go of back home.'

'We have cousins in Manchester who have cotton mills,' Benedict said. 'You must find time to visit them. I'll give you a letter of introduction.'

'You are very kind, sir.'

'But you won't be leaving us immediately,' Sibella said. 'You'll stay for luncheon?'

Benedict capped her. 'Longer than that, I hope. I want to hear how we are related. I've often wondered what happened to the American branch of the family. You have your things with you?'

'My things?'

'Your traps. Your bags, luggage.'

'Oh, they're at the hotel, sir. The Black Swan, in York.'

'Malton, have someone fetch Mr Morland's things. And have a room prepared – the North Bedroom.'

'Yes, sir.'

'And now,' Benedict said, with an air of wishing to lay an arm across Fenwick's shoulders, had Fenwick not been two inches taller than him, 'you must let me show you round the house. And tomorrow we'll take a ride around the estate. You do ride, I take it?'

'Indeed I do, sir. Back home we raise the finest horses in the Carolinas. Horses are a passion with me.'

'Then you'll like to see our stud. We breed racehorses as well as riding and driving horses.'

'You'll stay for the birthday ball, won't you?' Mary asked eagerly.

Fenwick turned to her. 'Is it your birthday, Miss Morland?'

'Yes, on the thirtieth.' She turned to Sibella. 'He may, mayn't he?'

'My love, Mr Morland may not wish to stay so long.'

'I would like it more than anything, ma'am,' the young man said fervently. He was speaking to Sibella, but somehow managed to be looking at Mary.

CHAPTER TWO

'Yes, here it is, look,' Mary said, bending over the family record book, brushing her long side curls impatiently away as they fell over the page. 'James Matthias Morland married India Neville and had six sons – goodness! – and the youngest one, born in 1708, is Charles.'

'And he,' said Fenwick Morland with large satisfaction, 'was my great-great grandfather.'

'We're descended from the eldest son, James Edward,' Mary went on. 'It goes on over the page, look. James Edward had two sons and a daughter. The sons both died young – how sad! – so everything passed to his daughter Jemima.'

'The estate passed to a girl?'

'Morland Place never has been entailed. *That's* one of our strengths.' Mary said, running her finger down the page. 'Jemima's third son was James, and he was my grandfather. I never knew him: he died long before I was born.'

'So James Matthias Morland and this lady, India Neville, were our common ancestors,' said Fenwick, tapping the page with a forefinger. 'It kind of makes it seem more real, seeing it written down in black and white like that.'

'I remember why I know the name of India Neville!' Mary exclaimed. 'She's one of the Morland Place ghosts. She came to a horrid end – hanged herself in the great bedchamber.'

24

He was gratifyingly interested. 'No! Don't tell me!'

'It's quite true. I had it from Father Moineau, who knows all the family stories. There used to be a hook in the ceiling of the great bedchamber for hanging lamps, and she hanged herself from it with a scarf or some such thing. The hook's gone now, but people have seen her hanging there sometimes – her ghost, I mean.'

'Do you believe in ghosts?'

'I've never seen one myself, but lots of people have in this house, so I suppose I must.'

'It isn't a very Christian notion, is it?'

'But you have to keep an open mind. Science demands it,' Mary said firmly. 'And Father Moineau says God wouldn't have given us enquiring minds if he hadn't meant us to use them.'

'That's a dangerous argument,' Fenwick said. 'There's lots of parts of our nature that God means us to resist. Goodness, if a man did whatever was in his nature, he'd—' He stopped abruptly, colouring as he realised where the sentence might lead. 'Well, he'd be a pretty bad kind of person.' He was glad to note that Mary was unembarrassed, having failed – as a young lady ought – to take his meaning.

'Oh goodness, I know all that,' she said dismissively. 'Of course we aren't meant to steal and kill and all that sort of thing. But there isn't a Commandment that says "Thou shalt not think". And if we hadn't thought and enquired we'd never have found out the true nature of God, would we? We'd still be worshipping rocks and trees, like savages.'

'Well, put like that—' Fenwick said, feeling he'd been out-thought, a sensation he was unused to, particularly with such a young girl. He reverted to the family tree for relief. 'Does the legend say why she killed herself?'

'No, but it was a great scandal at the time, and her

25

husband – James Matthias – went queer in his head afterwards and lived like a recluse and refused even to talk to his children. And,' she added beguilingly, lifting her head, 'I know where their portraits are! Come, I'll show you.'

She seized his hand unselfconsciously and dragged him out of the school-room and at a quick trot along the corridor to the Red Room, a rather dark bedroom which had been made out of the inside half of the East Bedroom and consequently had no windows, only deadlights giving onto the corridor. It was hardly ever used, and had an air of neglect, the hangings and wallpaper faded and the carpet needing repair. In her scheme of refurbishing the whole house – considerably neglected by its previous owner, Benedict's mad brother – Sibella had not got around to the Red Room yet.

'Why is it called the Red Room?' Fenwick asked, looking round at the predominantly yellow fabrics.

'I don't know. I expect everything used to be red, once.' Mary was not interested in this. She led him up to the pair of oil paintings in the corner. 'Here they are, exiled to the gloomiest spot in the house, poor things. Now we've met you they ought to be restored to a place of honour. This is India Neville, by Kneller. She looks very young, doesn't she? Kneller was a court painter, so it ought to be a good painting.'

Fenwick stared at a woman in black with silver braid, one of those wide-brimmed hats the Cavaliers wore, with curled white plumes, and huge black gauntlets. She was sitting sidesaddle on a black horse with silver decorations on its harness. The skirt of the woman's riding-dress reached the ground, and she seemed to be holding the horse on a very tight rein, for its neck was arched and its nostrils flared, and it pranced showily off its hind legs.

'I guess she must have been a good rider – the horse looks quite wild.'

'She seems to have chosen her habit to match the horse,' Mary said scornfully. 'Awfully impractical – velvet marks so easily! And that long skirt must have been dangerous – suppose the horse trod on it?'

He laughed. 'You do think of the darndest things! Well, so she's my great-great-great-grandma. It gives me an awfully queer feeling to be standing here looking at her, practically in the flesh.'

'And here's her husband, James Matthias – not such a fine picture. It isn't by Kneller. Some local painter, I suppose.'

A man in long coat open over a red waistcoat, with lace cravat and lace at the wrists; melancholy eyes, and long dark curls flowing over his shoulders.

'It's a pity men don't wear their hair like that any more,' Mary said. 'It's very romantic.'

'But awfully impractical,' Fenwick mimicked solemnly. 'Suppose the horse trod on it?'

She turned to look at him, and then laughed. 'You are a dreadful tease, Mr Morland.'

'Oh please,' he said, having been waiting for just such an opening, 'won't you call me Cousin Fenwick?'

'I suppose we are real cousins?' she said consideringly.

'As real as can be!'

'Well then, as long as Papa and Mama think it's proper, I will. And you may call me Cousin Mary.'

He bowed and took her hand to kiss it. 'Your servant, Cousin Mary,' he said. The gesture was one of mock formality, but his voice was perfectly sincere.

It was Fenwick's great-grandmother who had told him the family history, which he had related to his hosts over luncheon that first day of his visit.

27

'She was a very wonderful old lady, and tough as nails – I guess she had to be, with all she went through. She died when I was nine years old, but I remember her as clearly as if it was yesterday. Straight as a wand, she was, though she was eighty-four when she passed away. And ever since I was knee-high to a cricket, she'd been filling my head with stories about the Morlands of Morland Place in the County of Yorkshire – which I guess she must have gotten from Great-Grandpa, because she'd never been to England.'

The Charles Morland who was the sixth son of James Matthias and was born at Morland Place in 1708 had grown up to be a botanist, and travelled the world collecting rare plants.

'Eventually he married – a Scotch lady, I believe – and my great-grandfather was born in Glasgow in 1751. He was called Charles too. I wish I knew what date in 1751, because it's the centenary of his birth this year. It would have been real nice to be able to be here on his birthday.'

'But you said he wasn't born here,' Sibella pointed out.

'That's right, ma'am. But on account of his mother dying when he was young and his father being away from home so much, he spent a lot of his time here at Morland Place. It was a second home to him. Well, he followed in his father's profession, and became a botanist. Great-Grandma said there was a part of the pleasure-grounds here where he planted the rare specimens he brought back from America.'

'That must be the American Garden!' Benedict said. 'To think of its being your great-grandfather who created it! We must take you to see it.'

Fenwick's eyes lit. 'I sure would like to tell my pa I'd stood there, maybe under one of the very trees my great-grandfather planted!'

He continued. On an expedition to Maryland in the 1770s this Charles Morland had met the daughter and heiress of a wealthy planter and fallen in love. Her name was Eugenie de Courcey. 'That was Great-Grandma, of course.'

'She was a French lady?' Sibella asked in surprise.

'Creole, ma'am. From the West Indies. She was very much a fine lady, and very beautiful, but there was pirate blood in her family too. I guess that's what made her so tough when the bad times came.'

The bad times were not long in coming. Charles and Eugenie married and settled down on her father's plantation on the Chesapeake Bay, and everything seemed set fair, until the intervention of the War of Independence.

'I guess Great-Grandpa couldn't forget he was English. Anyway, he backed the wrong side, and when the Americans won, they confiscated the plantation – house, land, stock, everything. He and Great-Grandma and their children were thrown out with nothing but what they could carry.'

'How shocking,' Sibella said.

Fenwick shrugged. 'Anyone who sided with the English got short shrift. Great-Grandma told me they were lucky not to have been killed.'

'But what happened to them? Where did they go?' Mary asked.

'They went north,' said Fenwick, and there was something in his voice that suggested the direction was in itself a punishment.

They sailed up the coast and eventually reached New York, where there was an agency set up to help refugees who had been loyal to England. Charles was given a grant of land in Canada. There they settled and tried to farm, but on virgin land, and in a harsh climate, the struggle had been great, and it had taken its toll. Two of their three children died young, and Charles aged before his time. Finally, in 1799, at the age of forty-seven, he died, worn out by work and worry. His surviving son, Philip, was then nineteen years old.

'Great-Grandma didn't wait to see her son go the same way. "Feeleep," she said – she always pronounced it like that, the French way – "Feeleep, we must go south!"' Mary laughed at his imitation, and he turned to her. 'That was all that mattered to Great-Grandma. "We must go south!" The North was like Hades itself to her – a pretty cool sort of Hades, I guess,' he added, 'but she liked it hot, the hotter the better. Anyway, she was the boss in that household, so they sold up and moved south.'

'To Maryland?'

'No, ma'am, they only got as far as New England that time.'

New England at the turn of the century had been an exciting place, with new industries and new processes transforming the old way of life. New England had fine, fast waterways, an abundance of timber, and a large population. The conditions were ideal for the development of manufactories. Philip was of an age to be fired with enthusiasm for new ideas, and he convinced his mother that he could make their fortune. So they bought some land on a good river and built a mill.

'Grandpa Philip was a good businessman, and it was hard for anyone with a mill not to make money in those days. They did pretty well; and then he married the daughter of another mill-owner and that helped things along. They had three children: my father, another Charles, who was born in 1809, and my aunts Louisa and Isabella. Everything went along just fine and dandy until Grandpa Philip died quite suddenly of a stroke in 1829.'

'Dear me!' Sibella said. 'You don't seem to be a long-lived family, do you?'

'Grandpa Philip was only fifty, it's true, ma'am – but he'd had a hard life in Canada, same as Great Grandpa. I guess it was a wonder he lived so long. Anyway, straight off Great Grandma started to get restless. She kept talking about wanting to go south again. Pa stuck it out for a bit, but he'd never been so keen on the mills as Grandpa. It was land he hungered for, and for land, said Great Grandma, you had to go south. So he sold up, lock, stock and barrel, packed the furniture, my aunts and Great Grandma onto the first ship he could find going in the right direction, and ended up in Charleston.'

'Did they really go, just like that?' Sibella asked, fascinated.

'That's the way folks do things in America, ma'am. We're a restless people, I guess,' he said seriously.

'Is Charleston a pretty place?' Mary asked.

'Just the prettiest city in the whole of America,' Fenwick said. 'We have grand houses and lovely gardens, and fine public buildings, and theatres and hotels and the best shops in the South. And it's by the sea, and there's a splendid promenade – the Battery, it's called – along the sea-front; and we've just recently finished laying the White Point Gardens, which is another promenading place just around the point, with paths and shrubs and fountains and everything fine about it. And in the season we have plays and balls and concerts and meetings and more ways to entertain yourself than I guess you'd find anywhere outside Europe.'

Benedict said, 'But I understood you to say you did not live in the city?'

'My real home is at Twelvetrees, I guess; but we have a house in Charleston too. I'd better finish the story, then you'll understand.'

On arrival in South Carolina, Charles Morland intended immediately to look about for land to buy; but he was seduced by Charleston's famed social life, which his grandmother and sisters were keen to enjoy. Also the girls were of an age to be needing husbands, so he decided to spend a few months in the city first. Many planters lived there permanently, leaving their estates to be run by overseers; others came into the city for the season; so he hoped to get his sisters eligibly settled.

He quickly found that ready money, such as he had from the sale of the mills, was in short supply in the South; that most gentlemen ran their ventures on a mixture of credit, debt, and a complicated system of bill discounting and mortgages. He also discovered that the two great vices amongst planters were drinking and gambling. Charles Morland had a businessman's shrewdness, a hard head, and an instinct for money. He had been meaning to rent something modest for his stay in Charleston, but opportunity presented itself and he ended by owning a fine mansion on East Bay. He bought it from a man whose finances were in terminal decline, for a small amount of cash, by offering to take over his major creditors. Investigation proved the creditors' affairs equally involved, and Charles found it possible to lay off, discount, remortgage, and otherwise sequester the debts to the extent that it was most unlikely they would ever raise their heads and demand anything so vulgar as cash to satisfy them.

The house on East Bay, though delapidated, was in the neighbourhood occupied by the grandest people and the oldest families in Charleston. The new neighbours naturally called to see what the Morlands were were like. They found Charles, though a northerner by birth, a thorough gentleman, with a proper sense of the importance of blood-lines and family history. The old lady was as high-nosed and intolerant as a grand southern dame should be, and the girls were well-mannered, and pretty without being too pretty. Cards were exchanged, and the Morlands were accepted into the best social circles. And very soon Charles, who had hoped only to find good husbands for his sisters, fell unexpectedly and completely in love himself.

She was fifteen, the daughter of one of the oldest families, and while not exactly beautiful had a vivacity and charm that did just as well. The Fenwicks, having a large number of other children with prior claims, were happy enough to part with Emily, especially since her vivacity threatened to prove troublesome if she remained unwed, and since Charles was enough in love not to be asking for cash with his bride. Within three months he had married her, and her dowry of furniture, china and slaves was very welcome in the rather bare house on East Bay.

Charles quickly found a match for Louisa. Joseph Flint was a shy and wealthy widower who, being in the building trade, was glad to carry out the more serious repairs needed on the house, for which etiquette then forbade him to send his brother-in-law a bill. Flint had the further courtesy to die after only five years of marriage, leaving his widow all his considerable fortune. She took her little boy and moved back into the house on East Bay with her grandmother and unmarried sister. Isabella had missed her chance, for Charles had left it to his grandmother to find her a husband, and Eugenie had no intention of parting with such a useful person as a daughter-at-home.

For by then, Charles and his wife had gone to live at Twelvetrees.

'And how,' Benedict asked, 'did he come to buy Twelvetrees?'

'To say truth, sir, he didn't exactly buy it. He won it.'

'Won it?'

'At cards. Piquet, to be exact.'

33

Smithson, who owned the place, was a bachelor, a heavy drinker, and a dedicated gambler. He hardly ever went near the plantation, leaving it to the care of an overseer while he pursued the pleasures of the flesh in Charleston. Charles met him at the Jockey Club, the most exclusive of the gentlemen's clubs.

It happened in the February two months after Charles had married. Every February Charleston held its race week, the most lively and exciting social period in the calendar, similar to the Mardi Gras of New Orleans: a time of balls, parties and unlicensed merry-making; and a time when most gentlemen were drunk for a week together, and huge amounts of money were won and lost. Smithson had been losing regularly and heavily to Charles for some time, and though no-one knew it, he was getting to the end of his tether. He began playing Charles at piquet on the second day of race-week. Piquet is a game in which skill and a level head can largely overcome the element of chance, and since Charles had both and Smithson neither, the points soon added up on Charles's side of the line. Smithson, knowing he could not pay, kept playing on, upping the stakes and sliding deeper and deeper into the pit. They played through the night, gathering more and more spectators around them: the game passed into history. Charles had a shrewd idea that Smithson had got beyond his means, but kept playing largely out of curiosity, to see how far the man would go. At nine o'clock in the morning Smithson could stand it no longer. Red-eyed, slurred of speech, he threw his hand on the table and declared himself not only beat, but broke.

'It's a debt of honour, Smithson,' Charles said mildly. 'Play and pay, you know.' There was a murmur of agreement from around the table.

'I can't pay, damn you! I'm ruined.' Smithson said.

'Why did you go on taking my vowels? You knew I was done up!'

'You're over twenty-one. And no-one was forcing you to play,' Charles said. But he felt a little uncomfortable, because though he hadn't known Smithson's situation for sure, he ought indeed to have called a halt long before.

'What about that place of yours, Jack?' a bystander said helpfully. 'It ain't up to much, but land is land.'

Land! Charles held down his excitement, tried to look cool and unmoved. 'What is your place, Smithson?' he asked.

'Five hundred acres up near Dorchester. But only a hundred of it's under cultivation. I never had the slaves to work it,' Smithson said. 'If you want it, it's yours. God knows it's no more use to me. Thanks to you I can never hold up my head in this town again. I shall have to go abroad.'

Charles managed to shrug. 'Very well, I'll take it,' he said, 'and you shall have back all your vowels.'

Smithson rose unsteadily to his feet. 'I'll send the deeds round to you this morning,' he said, and watched with curious pity by his former colleagues, made his way out and went up to his bedroom in the club.

The deeds duly arrived by a messenger, to whom Charles gave an envelope containing all Smithson's vowels, and a note to the effect that he did not wish Smithson to feel ill-done by, and that once he had inspected the property he would make a further payment in cash, on top of the cancellation of the vowels. The messenger was soon back, the envelope undelivered. Before he got to the club, Smithson had blown his brains out with a revolver.

Charles, who was a kindly soul, was very sorry about this; but the end of it was that he found himself owner of five hundred acres and twenty negro slaves, and a month later he packed his bags and with his pregnant wife left Charleston for what was to become Twelvetrees.

'And that's how I came to be born on Twelvetrees. It was hard for Mother at first, because she'd been used to every luxury and being waited on hand and foot, and her new house was nothing but a wooden cabin with a porch, three rooms downstairs and three up, and wind whistling through the cracks. But Pa having got the place for nothing, so to speak, he still had most of the money he got for selling the mills in hand. So as well as getting the land into shape, he was able to start building her a proper house right away. It was in the new house my brother Eugene was born, and my sisters May and Ruthie. And of course we often went to stay with Great-Grandma in Charleston, and after she died with Aunt Lou and Aunt Belle. So Charleston's our second home, and we know it quite as well as Twelvetrees.'

'It sounds an ideal life,' Sibella said. 'A country estate and a town house – the best of both worlds.'

'Yes, ma'am, that's what I have. I'm the luckiest man alive, I guess,' Fenwick said; and then he looked at Mary, and his expression grew wistful.

Benedict went in person to the railway station to meet the train from Scarborough which was bringing Aglaea and Jemima for the birthday celebrations. They had always come to Morland Place in August for a visit of some weeks, but the opening of the railway between Scarborough and York had made travel so easy and quick that they could now be persuaded to come at other times too. A visit of a few days was worth-while when the travelling took up only a few hours.

Aglaea had been Aglaea Anstey before she married – she was Harry Anstey's youngest sister. It had seemed a natural and happy conclusion for her to marry Benedict's brother Nicholas, for they had all played together as children. But no-one had realised the extent of Nicky's madness, and what she had suffered during the years of her marriage could only be guessed at. After Nicky's death, Benedict offered her a home, but she preferred to live in Scarborough, where she had once been happy. Benedict provided her with a pension, and she set up home with Nicky's ward, Jemima Skelwith. Benedict had taken over charge of Jemima's affairs, and through his agent ran the building business which Jemima had inherited from her father.

'The business is thriving, you'll be glad to know,' he told Jemima as the carriage took them homewards. 'The railway has brought so many new people and so much new trade to York, everyone is building again. We've taken on a dozen orders for new villas in the Mount area, and a whole street of cottages for the railway workers. And I'm pretty sure we will get the contract for the new Railway Hotel. That will be a great advertisement!'

Jemima turned to him, smiling. She had just passed her thirtieth birthday, a milestone which gave most unmarried women some anguish; but Jemima seemed to grow more serene as she grew older. Her brown eyes were friendly and calm, her hands in their grey kid gloves were folded quietly in the lap of her plain merino travelling-mantle. 'Who better than you to build the Railway Hotel? Everyone knows you as the father of the railways here.'

'Father? No! Not more than a very minor midwife,' Benedict protested. 'Our old friend George Hudson takes that title.'

'Do you still call him friend, after all the scandal?' Jemima said. 'I hear he dares not show his face in York these days, and that they've even changed the name of Hudson Street to Railway Street.'

'I think it's a damned shame!' Benedict said. 'I never

believed him to be corrupt, you know, only careless and impatient—'

'And arrogant,' Jemima put in. 'And bombastic.'

'All admirable qualities for a railway pioneer. He's not the man I'd want to spend a social evening at home with, but for getting things done—! You won't remember, of course, how difficult it was ten or fifteen years ago to persuade anyone to take the railways seriously.'

'But what about all the people who've lost their money? Don't you blame him for that?'

'It always was a speculation,' Benedict said reasonably. 'When you buy shares in a new venture, you must be prepared to lose your money; but no-one ever is. Those who put money into the railway expected to make a fortune, and when they didn't, they turned on Hudson and called him thief. I've lost money on railway shares myself, and I don't pretend to be glad about it, but the benefits the railways have brought far outweigh that.'

'But do you say he *didn't* mismanage the railway companies?' Jemima asked incredulously.

'It's hard to understand if you don't know him personally,' Benedict said. 'Yes, his accounting methods were haphazard, at best; yes, there *was* mismanagement; but I don't believe he was dishonest in the sense of meaning to cheat anyone. He was too sanguine in his promises of profit, which led to disappointment. And he was impatient for results and took short cuts which nowadays we couldn't condone. But without him it's very sure the railway system would not be what it is today. He was the right man for his time, that's all.'

Jemima said, 'I should have known you'd defend him, Uncle. He doesn't deserve such loyal friends.'

Benedict laughed. 'I haven't made any impression on your opinion, have I? Well, never mind, just accept that *your* accounts are kept more strictly, and your business affairs are flourishing. In fact, I've been meaning to ask you if you wouldn't like an increase in your allowance. It could easily be doubled without touching the capital.'

'No, what should I want more money for?' Jemima said. 'We are perfectly comfortable, aren't we, Aunt? We don't want for anything.'

Aglaea, who had been looking out of the carriage window as if uninterested in the conversation, turned at once and said, 'No, nothing. In fact, we hardly manage to spend what we have now.' She was like a sparrow, Benedict thought, small and plain and unremarkable, and dressed in sparrow-brown, too, with an old-fashioned deep bonnet over which, when she went walking along the front at Scarborough, she still wore an ugly, the further to shelter her face. She was forty-one, but seemed ageless, neither old nor young, her face strangely unlined, as though she had stepped out of the stream of time. Benedict had never really understood her. She had been the quiet youngest daughter at Anstey House, never asked for or giving her opinion; and when Nicky died she had wanted only to be allowed to live near the sea. She had seen it for the first time on her honeymoon, and conceived for it a passion which made her unwilling ever to leave it. It was only her over-developed sense of duty, Benedict thought, which brought her on these visits to Morland Place, for no pleasures he could offer her could ever compete with the magic of the sea.

'She won't tell you, Uncle Ben, but she sold one of her pictures last week for fifty guineas,' said Jemima. 'We're always having visitors knocking at the door asking to see her work. In fact, I've had to tell Susan not to admit anyone except between twelve and three on Mondays and Thursdays, or we'd have no peace at all.'

Benedict nodded. 'Everyone admires that picture you

gave me,' he said to Aglaea. 'The sea is so natural-looking you can almost taste the spray.'

Aglaea only smiled, but Jemima took up the subject eagerly. 'Oh, but that was a long time ago, and her style is quite changed now. She's brought you one as a present, so you'll see. And a man came from London to ask if she would exhibit at some gallery or other. I wish she would agree, because there are so many people in London this year for the Great Exhibition, he promised it would make her tremendously famous.'

'I don't want to be tremendously famous,' Aglaea said equably. 'It's bad enough as it is. You can't imagine the fuss, brother, whenever I go out to set up my easel somewhere. I used to take Stephen along just to carry my traps for me, but now I have to have him to hold off the nuisances, who *will* try to talk to me while I'm painting. I don't mind if they just look on quietly: to say truth I never really notice them once I'm absorbed. But Miss here positively encourages them, with their chatter and their idiotic questions.'

'Indeed I don't,' Jemima said indignantly. 'But what am I to do, Uncle Ben, when people come up and speak to me? It would be awfully rude to ignore them.'

'Well, my dear, but you needn't invite them all back to our house,' Aglaea said.

Jemima said to Benedict, 'It isn't everyone, it's just one gentleman, a very pleasant and respectable widower who loves painting and admires Aunt's work tremendously.'

'He was always underfoot,' Aglaea said. 'And then she needs must ask him to dinner!'

'Did you, indeed?' Benedict exclaimed. 'You forward hussy!'

'*With* his sister,' Jemima said, 'and he couldn't have been more charming. Now they take us in on their walk most days. The truth is,' she added, pretending to lower

40

her voice, 'that Mr Underwood is mad in love with Aunt, and she pretends indifference to fuel the flames.'

Aglaea laughed. 'What a romancer you are! In fact, brother, I'm tempted to agree to the exhibition in London, if only to get away from them both.'

'Well, do then,' Jemima urged. 'I don't mind what your reason, if only we can go. Oh, Uncle Ben, I *so* long to see the Great Exhibition! Is it very wonderful?'

'Very,' Benedict assured her solemnly. 'I wouldn't by any means miss it if I were you. And what's to stop you going up to London together? It's quite respectable these days; everyone's doing it. A first class ticket on the train and rooms in one of the best hotels, and there you are!'

'Two women alone in London?' Aglaea said. 'I don't think I'd care to go without a man to look after us.'

'Well, if that's all your difficulty, I can take you myself,' Benedict said. 'Sibella wants to go, so we can make up a party, if you'd care for it.'

The idea of a party to go up to London seemed to please everyone. Fenwick was anxious that it should take place before he left England. 'I long to show you around the American Court,' he said, largely to Mary. 'Although I don't think it does us justice, still there are some magnificent objects in it. And,' to Benedict, 'I'd like your opinion of some of the things in the Machinery Court. Pa only paid for this trip for me so that I can go home with the solution to our problems at the mill.'

'I think a visit to Manchester will help you more than the Exhibition,' Benedict said. 'If your time is short, I suggest you don't delay in taking that in.'

'I don't want to cut my visit here short,' Fenwick said, pondering the problem. 'But I guess you're right. Pa'd think me a noddy if I didn't get to see the mills. But then, when did you mean to visit the Exhibition?'

'Oh, that can be any time that suits you,' Sibella said

kindly. 'The Exhibition is on all summer. Why don't you go to Manchester next week, after Mary's birthday, and when you come back we can arrange the London trip.'

The words 'when you come back' seemed to please Fenwick. 'I'd like that, ma'am,' he said. 'Thank you.'

Aglaea's painting, when it was unwrapped, caused a silence. It was a seascape, but quite unlike the previous one she had given Benedict. It was much more in the style of the later works of J.M. Turner: streaks and washes of colour, and everything indistinct as if seen through a veil.

'I like it,' Sibella said at last. 'It isn't quite what one expects at first, but it really gives one the sense of a stormy day. When you've looked at it for a while—'

'It's wonderful, Aunt,' Mary said firmly.

'Very fine indeed,' Fenwick echoed her. 'Very – um – moving.'

'It only seems a pity,' Benedict said cautiously, 'when you can do such lovely, lifelike boats and seabirds and people—'

Aglaea seemed quite unmoved by the comments, both positive and negative. She looked calmly at her own work and said, 'There comes a point when you have to stop looking at things, and try to look through and beyond them. The difficulty always is, of course, expressing what you see so that anyone else can understand it. Perhaps the attempt is always doomed to failure.'

'I don't think so,' Jemima said loyally. 'I understand what you see.'

Aglaea turned her serene gaze on her. 'Ah, but how do you know you do?'

Later that afternoon Benedict accompanied Jemima up to the nursery to see the babies. 'George is getting much too excited about his birthday,' he said. 'Of course, it's the first one he remembers, so he thinks it's something just now invented for his particular benefit. *Please* don't mention the word "present" in front of him.'

'I shan't,' Jemima promised, 'but I've brought a rather splendid one for him anyway. I found it in a toy-shop in Scarborough. There are two blacksmiths with an anvil between them, and when you push the handle back and forth they strike it with their hammers, first one then the other. It makes a splendid noise—'

'Oh good!'

'—and the faster you go, the faster they hammer. It's impossible to believe they won't catch up with each other and have a terrible accident.'

Benedict grinned. 'Just the thing to delight his destructive heart. You'd make a perfect aunt – you know just what boys like.'

'I'd have liked to be an aunt,' she said, 'had the cholera not dictated otherwise.'

Benedict cursed his tactlessness. All her siblings – and her parents – had died in the epidemic of '32, when she alone had been away from home visiting Morland Place. 'I take it back. You would be wasted as an aunt. You would, and will, make a wonderful mother.'

'I'm thirty years old, Uncle,' she said calmly. 'It's much too late for that. In fact, one of the things I wanted to talk to you about was making my Will. With the business doing so well, I suppose I have a considerable fortune to leave, and I would like to leave it to Georgie and Teddy.'

'My dear, there's no need for this,' he began, feeling awkward.

'Oh, but one ought to be prepared: an accident can happen at any time. And it's only fair, since you've had all the trouble of looking after the business, that your sons should benefit.'

He stopped and took her hands, turning her to face

43

him. 'I honour your kind intentions. But really it's much to soon to be thinking like that. You are an attractive woman, and you will very likely marry and have children of your own.'

She shook her head, but smiled, unperturbed. 'Well, if I do, I can change my Will again, can't I? Let me do this, Uncle Ben. You wouldn't want the whole fortune swallowed up by Chancery if I died intestate, would you?'

Benedict looked at her helplessly. Her life, he felt, had been blighted so many times, and yet she carried on growing with the unthinking courage of nature, like a tree that is lopped and sprouts again. 'If it's what you want,' he said. 'But I think fate will surprise you. I think you will marry.'

'I'm perfectly happy as I am,' she said.

The family gathered by the fireplace in the Great Hall to greet the guests as they arrived for the birthday ball. Mary stood between Sibella and Benedict, and Sibella, looking her over anxiously, decided that no-one would be able to fault her. Mary's gown had been a worry, for her figure was fully formed and it was impossible to dress her as a child; but evening gowns were deeply décolleté and worn off the shoulder, and she was still only fourteen after all. Sibella had sought compromise with a neckline rather more rounded than dipped, and a deep lace bertha so that not too much flesh was left bare. The gown itself was very simple, of white muslin embroidered with white flowers and leaves; the bodice close-fitting, and the skirt very full, in four flounced tiers from the tiny waist. Mary's golden hair was dressed with the long side curls and the back hair turned up in a chignon decorated with fresh pink rosebuds; and she carried pink roses in her silver holder, and a new fan which Benedict had given her, of frosted lace on ivory sticks. Yes, Sibella thought, she

44

looked just right: very beautiful, womanly, but utterly innocent.

Arthur Anstey, arriving early with his parents, evidently approved. He was a tall youth whom his mother's fairness had given a rather bloodless look; and the sudden spurt of growth he had put on this last year had made him appear weedy, too. But he had a pleasant face and a nice smile, and he approached Mary with the openness of old friendship. 'I say, you look absolutely splendid! I do like the way you've done your hair.'

'Aunt Celia showed me on my last visit, don't you remember?'

'Oh yes, but I like the little flowery things in it,' Arthur said with a general wave of the hand. 'I say, Mary, I hope you've kept the first dance for me. I meant to ask when you were at our house but I forgot, but we ought to lead off together.'

Mary did not notice the anxiety under the apparent confidence. 'Well I think you might have remembered, if it was so important to you,' she said. 'Anyway, it's too late now, because I have promised Cousin Fenwick I'll lead off with him. But I'll dance the next with you, if you like.'

Arthur was extremely put out, especially when, being introduced a moment later, he found that Cousin Fenwick was taller than him, with wide shoulders and strong hands which almost crushed his when they shook. He could only comfort himself that Fenwick was shockingly brown and that girls didn't care for that sort of thing, but it was a poor delusion: with all the novels girls read nowadays about Corsairs and Gypsy Princes, a brown face was hardly a disadvantage any more.

Arthur's parents were eager to meet Fenwick – in fact, the whole neighbourhood was dying of excitement about the Long-Lost Cousin. Quite apart from the sheer romance of his sudden arrival, word had gone round that, like all Americans, he was immensely rich, and every mother was determined her daughter should dance with him. When Fenwick led Mary out for the first dance, no-one was surprised, for he was the honoured guest of the house; but when they saw how Fenwick gazed at his little partner, there were sighs, and a certain amount of muttering that naturally Benedict Morland had thrown them together, not wanting so rich a prize to slip from his grasp.

Jemima, who was standing well back watching the spectacle, was startled from her reverie by being asked to dance.

'Oh! Childie, I didn't notice you there,' she said.

'I noticed you, though,' said John Anstey. He wrinkled his nose. 'But no-one calls me Childie any more. Good God, Jemima, I'm almost thirty years old!'

'And I'm eight months older than you, remember,' Jemima said. 'Much too old to dance – though I do thank you. How are you, John?'

John Anstey, nephew of Aglaea and Henry, heir apparent to the Anstey title and fortune, had been a playmate of Jemima's in childhood, when he had been known as Childie to distinguish him from all the other Johns in the family. He had married one of the Micklethwaite girls, Polly, in 1845, but had tragically lost her in childbirth only three years later.

'I'm very well, thank you, but I haven't come to talk about me. What's all this nonsense about being too old to dance? You aren't wearing a cap, I notice.'

'Oh, caps are going out of fashion,' she said lightly; she felt a little awkward under his interested gaze.

'I'm glad to hear it. And that's a very fetching gown,' John went on.

Jemima looked down at herself with a disarming candour. 'Do you like it? I did rather think it looked well, but

46

I wasn't sure.' The gown was of dove-coloured silk with a silver lace bertha and silver lace edging to the flounces.

'*I'm* sure,' John said. 'On anyone else grey might be thought dull, but your colouring sets it off perfectly.'

'My colouring, what nonsense,' she laughed. 'You used to call me carrot-top when we were children.' But she smoothed the folds of the skirt with an appreciative hand. 'The silk was wildly expensive; I don't know what came over me,' she confided. 'It was a frightful extravagance: we go out in the evenings so little now.'

'All the more reason to get some return on your investment by dancing with me now, Come on, Jemmy, do! If a staid widower like me isn't too old to dance, how can you be? And I want to boast of having gone round with the prettiest girl in the room.'

'Girl, indeed! But if you really want me to, I will – only don't blame me if I tread on your toes, for I'm frightfully out of practice.' He led her onto the floor, and she was aware of people noticing and whispering. 'There, you've persuaded me to make a figure of myself.'

'They're just envying me,' he said, guiding her serenely through the steps.

'Really, John, you never used to say all these—'

'These what?'

'Well – such things,' she modified. 'We used to scramble about and scrape our knees together—'

'You were such a wild creature, you led me astray. The whippings I had on your account!'

'Nonsense, it was you who was wild. Aunt Aglaea says your father always thought you would be hanged. He used to call you Young Hempseed.'

'And then suddenly I was forbidden by your guardian to see you any more,' he said. 'When I think of all the years of your company I've missed, I feel quite indignant.'

She smiled despite herself. 'Idiotic!'

47

'Perhaps,' he said, smiling too. 'Is Aunt Aglaea coming to Anstey House next week?'

'Of course.'

'Come with her,' he said. 'Come and see how my children have grown; and we can walk in the garden and have a long talk about the old days.'

She glanced up at him, and then found herself blushing. It was a most peculiar feeling.

CHAPTER THREE

Benedict was accustomed, when he went to London, to staying at Shotts' Hotel, where the same rooms were always available to him at however short notice. Logic ought to have forewarned him that the Great Exhibition would have made a difference, but it still came as a shock to be told that not only could Shotts' not accommodate his party, but that every other hotel in London was packed to the attics, and there was not a bed to be had anywhere for weeks ahead, even for a single gentleman, let alone a group of six.

Unwilling to disappoint everyone, he turned his mind to his relatives. His aunt Lucy, Lady Theakston, was in her seventies, and he did not feel he could even suggest descending on her. His cousin Rosamund, Lady Batchworth, was not in Town that summer, and had lent her house to her brother Lord Aylesbury and his large family for the same purpose as Benedict's; and Rosamund's daughter Charlotte, Duchess of Southport, was heavily pregnant and thus out of circulation. That left Aunt Lucy's youngest son, cousin Tom Weston, who lived with his recently acquired wife Emily in a small house in Brook Street.

Tom had always been the cousin with whom Benedict had shared the closest relationship, and they had seen quite a lot of each other in the past year, during Benedict's visits to London. Emily, who had been a tradesman's daughter, could never think their small house other than grand and spacious, so there was never any doubt in her mind that they would manage easily to fit in another six people, to say nothing of their servants, for as long as they wanted to stay – even though the house in Brook Street boasted only three bedrooms.

'I hope we shall contrive to make you comfortable,' Emily said serenely when they arrived, 'which I think we can as long as you are not expecting to be luxurious.' She vacated the room she normally shared with her husband to Jemima and Mary, with Aglaea taking the narrow bed in the adjoining dressing-room. In the larger spare room she had put the three men, Benedict and Tom sharing the bed, with a truckle, borrowed from a neighbour, for Fenwick; while she and Sibella were to share the smaller spare room.

'And so we shall all be very snug,' Emily concluded, 'and have a great deal of fun.'

If anyone doubted it, they kept their doubts to themselves. But in the event, Emily proved right. The Morland Place people were easy-going, and though Fenwick was accustomed to a degree of being waited on which the others could not guess at, he had a pioneering spirit and a great deal of good humour. When the excitements of the day were over, the evenings were full of happy amusement, singing glees around the piano, playing foolish games around the table, or simply enjoying the lively chat of eight people with plenty to say for themselves.

The Great Exhibition was everything that had been promised, and more. None of them had been able to come close to imagining the reality. To begin with, the building itself was unlike anything that had ever been seen before: as vast as a cathedral, and yet all made of glass, rising sparkling and airy and delicate out of the green canopy of the park. There was so much greenery inside – including the full-grown elm trees which had been on the site already and which now rose majestically into the curved roof of the transept – that the glass walls hardly seemed a barrier at all, and it was hard to know what was outside and what was in. It seemed sometimes as if the Exhibition were contained in nothing more than a bubble of marvellously warm and refulgent air. The refraction of light and the soft confusion of image made it curiously hard to judge distances, so that it seemed as if the gently hazy light were expanding on and on into infinity.

Aglaea wandered like a drunken bee during the first visit, unable to take in any of the exhibits, intoxicated simply by the colours and shapes and the extraordinary *trompe l'oeil* of the Crystal Palace itself. She wanted to paint it, and knew she could never do it justice; though her newer style of painting would have brought her closer than any attempt to represent every detail with exactness. There were, of course, plenty of artists attempting that impossible: Joseph Nash, with perhaps the most daunting task, was preparing a series of official lithographs for posterity; there were illustrators from the *Illustrated London News* and *Punch* and the *Art Journal* and many other periodicals, from the provincial to the international; and unofficial sketchers galore frantically drew and rubbed out, trying to disentangle the multi-foliate images and pin them to the paper. Aglaea only wandered and looked. If she were to attempt it at all, it would have to be from memory, and then only the *impression* on her mind and spirit of what she saw, rather than the representation of it.

When Aglaea was sufficiently hardened to the wonder to begin to look at the exhibits, Jemima, who had faithfully kept at her side and restrained her own eagerness, guided her first to the French Court, where there were plenty of paintings amongst the wonderful furniture and fabrics and *objets d'art*. It was there, at the end of the first week

51

of their visit, that they were accosted by Mr Underwood and his sister, Mrs Pownall.

'How very remarkable to meet you here, Mrs Morland, Miss Skelwith!' he said. The ladies curtseyed to each other, and Jemima thought Mrs Pownall looked a little conscious, as if it were not quite such a surprise after all. 'They say all the world is coming to London this summer, but somehow I did not expect to see anyone I knew here. I am delighted to be proved wrong.'

'Have you been in London long?' Aglaea asked, for something to say.

'A little more than a week,' Mr Underwood said. 'And you?'

'A little less than a week.'

'Ah, then you did not come here directly from Scarborough?'

'We have been staying at my brother's, at Morland Place. We came from there.'

Underwood bowed. 'Clara noticed that the knocker was off your door when we passed a fortnight ago – didn't you, Clara?'

Mrs Pownall responded to the prod. 'Indeed – I meant to call and leave my card, to say that we would be going away. I did not guess we should be happy enough to meet with you here. Do you stay in an hotel?'

'No,' Jemima answered, 'with our cousins in Brook Street. We found all the hotels full.'

'Brook Street,' Mrs Pownall said with a touch of envy. 'You are very well placed, then – I am glad for you. We were obliged to take rooms quite out at Primrose Hill.'

'Very pleasant rooms, but out of the way,' Underwood said. 'However, we spend so much time here that it hardly matters. Pray, have you seen the Koh-i-noor diamond yet?'

Conversation followed on the various wonders of the

Exhibition, at the end of which Mr Underwood offered himself as a guide to the Morland ladies, who, it seemed, had not managed to see much beyond the French Court. Aglaea after a brief hesitation accepted his offer, and so the parties spent the rest of the day together, taking luncheon in one of the refreshment halls, and engaging to meet again the next day. Jemima found Underwood and his sister rather formal company, and would sooner have gone round with Aglaea alone, or have joined Benedict or Sibella; but she thought of Aglaea's pleasure and pretended enthusiasm for her sake.

Fenwick had researches to perform, and duties involving the American Court, and when he was not occupied in either of them, Benedict and Tom seemed always wanting to take him off to look at things that 'wouldn't interest the ladies'. So determined did they seem to split the party along the lines of gender that it took all Fenwick's ingenuity to reunite the halves, or at least to slip Benedict's leash and find his way back to Mary's side.

'It's like watching a pin slip-sliding along a table top towards a powerful magnet,' Sibella said to Emily one day, as they dawdled along behind Mary and Fenwick, who were deep in conversation about the applications of electricity. 'Start him off where you like, he will be with Mary before the day ends.'

Emily looked at her appraisingly. 'Do you mind it?'

'It isn't for me to mind. She's not my daughter.'

'All the same—'

Sibella shrugged. 'I don't think there's any harm in it. He's a well-brought-up young man – his manners are perhaps more formal than an Englishman's. I don't believe he would go beyond the line. In fact, it's rather amusing in some ways, because there is nothing of the coquette about Mary, and I'm sure she is perfectly unaware that Fenwick is falling in love with her. If he should ever try to get spoony, he'll get very short shrift from her – she thinks all that sort of thing silly.'

'So – what then? Something is what you don't like.'

'I just hope Benedict doesn't notice and take offence,' Sibella said with a faint sigh. 'He's very protective of Mary. If he should think anything in the slightest way improper was going on – well, I shouldn't like to be in Fenwick's shoes.'

Emily nodded. 'But he's going back to America soon, and that should be an end of it.'

'Yes, I imagine a pleasant, good-looking young man like him – heir to what sounds like a large estate – is much in demand back in Charleston. And he's of an age to want to be married. Some pretty Carolina girl will have him before the year's out. He won't think of Mary again once he's home.'

Benedict had early done his duty by taking Fenwick to be introduced to Aunt Lucy. The attention was proper, since Lucy was the last of her generation and regarded herself as head of the family in all but name; and Fenwick was eager for the presentation. It went better than Benedict hoped. Fenwick's formal manners recommended him to Lucy, and she was interested in the history of his branch of the family; and when she remembered that the botanising Charles Morland who had planted the American Garden at Morland Place had been 'like a brother' to her own father, their interest in each other became intense.

'In fact, it was my father first sent your great-grandfather to America,' Lucy remembered. 'Papa was a member of the Royal Society, and the expedition was under its aegis. They went to investigate the cultivation of potatoes, to find new varieties and study the diseases they were prone to, and so on. I remember hearing my parents talk about it when I was very little. Potatoes were rather a joke between them – they were a great passion of my father's, but in

54

those days no-one but him thought them fit to eat. And then of course the war came, and I believe they lost contact with him.'

She listened with close interest to everything Fenwick had to say about his great-grandfather and great-grandmother, and afterwards pronounced him an interesting young man, very nicely behaved, and fit to have a family dinner-party given in his honour.

'It's a pity my granddaughter the Duchess of Southport won't be able to attend,' Lucy concluded, 'but her condition would forbid it. I would wait until she could join us, but you will be gone from these shores by then: she does not expect to be confined until the end of July. We shall have to do without her, but she will be sorry to have missed meeting you.'

Fenwick, though embarrassed by such open talk of the Duchess's condition, expressed himself disappointed too. It was not mere form: to discover so many of his distant cousins were titled was wonderful, and to have gone back with a full duchess in his pocket would have been a crowning achievement. It was not for himself that he cared, but titles were held in high regard in Charleston society, and his aunts and sisters would have been very glad of the connection, to counterbalance the stain of being 'new money'.

Charlotte was reclining on a daybed in the Chinese saloon when the butler entered to announce 'Lord Theakston is here, your grace. Shall I admit him?'

'Of course.' It was not very easy to get to her feet, but Charlotte managed it for her step-grandfather. Lord Theakston, elegant and dapper and very upright for his seventy-three years, hugged her with enthusiastic caution, and then stepped back to examine her solemnly through his eye-glass.

'Lookin' well, m'dear,' he observed. 'Positively bloomin'. Heard a rumour you was increasin', but obviously there's nothin' in it. Just a hum, I can see.'

'Don't tease, Papa Danby. I'm very uncomfortable. And it's dreadful not to be able to go out or see anyone. Why is the world so foolish about these things? Why must a woman hide herself away as if she's ashamed of being pregnant?'

'Stumped me there,' Theakston said with a shake of his head. 'There's so much foolishness about, it has to come out somewhere, I suppose. But you're not exactly in purdah. Didn't I see Ashley leavin' the other day? Shaftesbury, I suppose I must call him, now his father's died. Takes some gettin' used to. Sent him a note of condolence, of course. Not that the old Earl was a loss to anyone. Most unpleasant kind of cove, I always thought. Left Shaftesbury a mountain of debts.'

'Yes, and he couldn't have died at a worse time,' Charlotte said. 'Now that Ashley's had to go up to the Lords, the Board of Health has no representative in the Lower House – except for Seymour, and we all know he's hostile to everything the Board stands for.'

'Standin' seems to be all the Board does,' Lord Theakston commented. 'Can't see it's achieved much in three years.'

'It's not for want of trying,' Charlotte said. The Interments Act, a much needed measure to close all over-crowded burial grounds in London and create new ones on the outskirts of the city, had been passed after intense struggle, only to founder on the rock of Treasury disapproval. The Metropolitan Water Supply Bill had been defeated, so Londoners would continue to drink stinking, contaminated Thames water instead of clean water piped in from the country. 'There's such hostility to everything that's for the public good. And who's going to pilot the

Lodging House Bill through the Commons, now Ashley's gone to a better place?'

'Steady on,' Theakston blinked. 'He ain't dead. Very much alive, comin' out of your house the other day – and not lookin' too miserable, either.'

'He'd come to agree the final plan for sending the Ragged School children to visit the Great Exhibition. At least there we managed to achieve something practical and solid – but only because we did it ourselves. Why is it so hard to get people to interest themselves in what clearly must be done?'

'You keep askin' them for money,' Theakston explained simply.

'They part with it for other good works,' Charlotte argued. 'Look how much the missionary societies collect every year.'

'For Bibles and convertin' African natives,' Theakston said. 'Nice *clean* causes. You keep talkin' to 'em about drains and dung-heaps, and then wonder why they grow peevish.'

Charlotte smiled unwillingly. 'At least that sort of talk keeps my mother-in-law at bay.'

Theakston sniffed with distaste. 'More likely the smell of paint. Are you ever goin' to finish your modernisations?'

'The house was very neglected, you know,' Charlotte said.

'Would be. The Fleetwoods were penniless until you married 'em,' Theakston agreed.

'Yes, and on that head, one of the things that annoys me about Lady Turnhouse—'

'Only one?' Theakston enquired ironically. He knew how ill Charlotte got on with her mother-in-law.

'—is that she expects to be the one to decide how the refurbishment is done. I wanted the kitchens and offices to be modernised first, which is logical to me. She thinks it nonsensical to spend money on what's never seen except by the servants, and wants the state rooms attended to. Such nonsense!'

'Are you expectin' a state visit?'

'In this condition, I'm not expecting any visit,' Charlotte smiled. 'But you know, in a way, it's the same problem I meet with all the time. People are quite willing to live in the same city with filthy backslums and poverty and disease, while they give money freely to Bible classes and Mission Houses. All they care about is the surface appearance of things. I can't get them to see that it's no use exhorting a poor man to be a Christian when he's living in conditions no Christian would keep his dog in.'

Theakston said, 'You don't understand their reasonin'. Vice and poverty always go together, so one must be caused by the other. If only the poor would be virtuous, they'd stop bein' poor.'

'I thought,' Charlotte mused, 'that being a duchess would give me more influence, but it doesn't really. People have to be polite to me, they can't actually cut me, but they still disapprove of what I do.'

'What about Southport?'

'Oh, Oliver never minds what other people think. He does what he wants, and encourages me to do what I want. It only amuses him that I shock people.'

'Then perhaps you should take a leaf out of his book.' Theakston eyed her with sympathy. 'Tell you what – you're feelin' low because you've been confined too much. Your grandmama was always the same when she was increasin' and couldn't get out of the house – only with her it was horses she missed, not drains.'

'How is Grandmama?' Charlotte asked, glad to change the subject. He was right, of course: usually she was much more cheerful and sanguine, even in the face of resistance.

'Well enough in herself,' Theakston said, 'but she's still worryin' about Parslow.'

'Is he no better?'

Theakston shook his head, staring reflectively at the carpet. 'She's convinced if only she can get him to leave the mews and take a room in the house, she'll be able to nurse him back to health. But dash it all, the feller's our age and more, and he's had a harder life!' He shook his head again. 'Hate to think how she'll take it when—' He left the inevitable unspoken.

Charlotte looked politely sympathetic. To her Parslow was just Grandmama's groom, who had entered her service when she was fifteen and had been with her ever since. Charlotte had been taught to ride by him, and honoured him for a fine, wise old man and 'a bit of a legend' as her brother Cavendish said; but that was all. Theakston could almost hear the unspoken thought: *Parslow's only a servant.* Sometimes Theakston told himself that, with irritation or with bewilderment. Even he did not understand what the man meant to Lucy. He *knew*, but he did not understand.

The door opened at that moment to admit the Duke of Southport. When the greetings had been exchanged, Theakston said to Oliver, 'Glad you've come in. Wantin' to ask you what you think of this business in France – what Boney's dashed nephew is up to. Just been talkin' to Palmerston at the Club, and he's noddin' and winkin' like a man with a cinder in his eye.'

'All I've heard is that Louis Napoleon is campaigning to change the constitution,' Oliver said, 'so that he can be re-elected President for another term. Whether there's anything about that to worry us I don't know. What was Palmerston hinting at?'

59

'That Napoleon means to be more than President,' Theakston said. 'Wouldn't put it past him – bein' Emperor runs in the blood. But Pam says he's a good chap, cleans his teeth and says his prayers and all that sort of thing. Devoted to democracy and wants to restore the universal franchise.'

'Which he can only do by undemocratic means, I suppose?' Oliver said. 'Well, I haven't heard anything more than I've said, but if he wants to be Emperor, does it matter? The French change their government like the English change their linen, and one more *coup d'état* is neither here nor there. It needn't affect us – we saw that in 'forty-eight.'

'Wonder,' Theakston said doubtfully. 'Damned frightenin' havin' another Emperor Bonaparte on the loose in Europe. Had enough trouble the last time. Next thing you know, he'll want to start a war. Mean to say, what else are Emperors for?'

'But Louis Napoleon is rather different, isn't he?' Charlotte put in. 'After all, he has lived over here, and he speaks English. He's a gentleman.' Theakston raised his eyebrows at the idea of a Frenchman being a gentleman, a proposition difficult for his generation to swallow. Charlotte went on, 'You remember Cav met him when he was a Special Constable, when the Chartists' meeting caused all that fuss in forty-eight. He said he was a good egg.'

'Oh, well,' Oliver laughed, 'that makes it quite all right, then.'

'Talkin' of Cavendish,' Theakston said, 'are you goin' to the Regimental Dinner tomorrow, Southport?'

'Yes, I am, but don't ask me to look after Cavendish for you. He has fifteen years on me and a head to match. The young entry like to drink deep at these affairs.'

'No, no, nothin' like that, but I wondered in that case

if I could borrow Charlotte. Come to dinner, m'dear, and cheer up your grandmama. It'd be a kindness.'

'Of course I will, Papa Danby – as long as there are no other guests. It isn't that *I* mind, but they always do, and their embarrassment embarrasses me.'

Crowded though the house at Brook Street was, it always seemed able to find another place at the table, or squeeze another chair into the drawing-room. There were always friends calling, and the visits were hardly ever short ones. Emily seemed positively to enjoy collecting as many people as she could in her house, and her cook had learned always to prepare dinner for twice as many as ordered.

Early in the second week of the Morland party's stay, John Anstey presented his card with some diffidence, but was received by Emily with her usual kindness.

'I know that, as we are not acquainted, I ought to have waited to be presented to you, Mrs Weston,' John began, 'but I understand my aunt Aglaea is staying with you, and I hoped perhaps that might be enough to excuse my calling in this way. I wouldn't wish to be deficient in any attention—'

'Make yourself easy, Mr Anstey,' Emily said as soon as she could interrupt him. 'I'm very glad you've called, and I'm sure you don't need any introduction in my house. I've been married to Tom long enough to know about the connection between the Morlands and the Ansteys, so I take you quite as one of the family.'

'It's very kind of you to say so,' John said.

'Not at all; and I hope you will make yourself free of my house. Come to dinner tonight, if you're not already engaged. I'm sure everyone will be glad to see you – for I have to tell you that you find me here alone. Everyone else is gone out to the Exhibition, and won't be back before five o'clock.'

61

'Ah, yes, the Exhibition. That's what I've come to London for, of course.'

'And have you got good lodgings? They're hard to come by, I know. We're a little crowded here, but I expect we could find somewhere to put a mattress down if you were in difficulties.'

'Thank you, but I'm very well placed. I'm staying with my mother's brother, Mr Robert Somers. He's a solicitor and has a house in Dean Street.'

'That's probably just as well,' Emily said frankly, 'for you might not be very comfortable sleeping here, though you'd be very welcome. But you must come and spend as much of your time as you can with us. I hope you will dine with us every day, if your uncle can spare you. We have very merry evenings, I promise you.'

John accepted the invitation gratefully, chatted a little longer, extracting from Emily the information as to which section of the Exhibition everyone was visiting today, and took his leave. Thus he was able quite casually and accidentally to meet Jemima and Aglaea as they strolled through the Mediaeval Court in the company of Mr Underwood and Mrs Pownall. He was very flattered by the way Jemima's face brightened when she saw him, and the eagerness with which she introduced him to her companions. Bows were exchanged, explanations given, and the group moved off again. Because of the crowds, it was not possible for all five of them to walk together. John made sure he walked ahead with Jemima, and in a very few moments they were separated from the others and as private as was possible in a public place.

'Lord, I'm glad to see you!' Jemima exclaimed. 'I have been bored to death for the last two days. Mr Underwood is a very good sort, I'm sure, but he is so very dull! And his sister simply agrees with everything he says. And they walk so slow – I could have got round in half the time and seen twice as much, for they've no powers of observation between them. They're like a pair of horses in blinkers.'

John shook his head, amused and puzzled. 'But then why go round with them? Surely you can't want an escort so very much? I see other pairs of ladies alone together, and there doesn't seem to be any danger of indecency in this place. In fact, everyone is very well-behaved – even on shilling days, I hear.'

'Of course we don't need an escort – and if we did, we've Uncle Ben and Cousin Tom and Fenwick all on hand. But the fact is that Mr Underwood is in love with Aunt Aglaea—'

'No, really?'

'Yes, really, and you needn't sound so surprised. She's a very lovable person, and quite young enough still. She has been widowed a long time, and there's nothing improper about second attachments.'

'I should think not, indeed,' John said fervently, but Jemima didn't pick up the reference.

'You were eager enough to tell me I'm not too old to dance, and she's only ten years older than me, and looks much younger.'

'My dear Jemima, I have neither the right nor the wish to object to Aunt Aggie's falling in love again. In fact I think she's setting a splendid example.' Again Jemima did not seem to catch his meaning. 'I only meant,' he went on, 'that if this Mr Underwood is so dull, can she really be in love with him?'

'Well, I think she must be, because she encourages him to join us all the time, and asks his opinion and listens to him with great attention. And if she didn't like him, she could quite well get rid of him, because I've seen her do it with other people. She's quite ruthless when she wants to be. So I have to put up with him and pretend to like him for her sake – but really, you know, I'm in desperate need of rescue.'

'Then I shall rescue you with the greatest of pleasure. Would you care to accompany me tomorrow?'

'Where?'

'It had better be far away from the Crystal Palace, or we may meet the dragon of dullness by accident. Should you like to go to the National Gallery, or the British Museum?'

'No more pictures and exhibits, if you please. I've had enough of them.'

'Astley's, then? Batty's Hippodrome? But they might be rather noisy, and I have a fancy for a quiet chat with you. No, I have it: could you like a visit to Syon House? It's open to the public all summer, and we could take a boat up the river to Brentford. They go from Westminster Pier, I think, right to the landing place. A pleasant sail up the river, and perhaps a picnic luncheon in his grace's grounds: what do you say?'

'I should like it *very* much. And it will give Aunt a chance to be alone with her beau, if she can shake off the sister.'

'Good. Then I shall find out what time the boats leave, and let you know tonight when I will call for you with a cab.'

'Tonight?'

'Oh, yes, didn't I mention? I took the precaution of calling at Brook Street and presenting myself to Mrs Weston, so I'm invited to dinner.'

Jemima narrowed her eyes. 'I begin to think you have a streak of cunning in you, Childie Anstey. I begin to wonder if our meeting was quite accidental after all.'

'Wonder if you like – I shan't tell you. It would spoil my romantic air of mystery.'

Jemima laughed at the idea, and John couldn't tell if

it was a good sign or not. After they had wandered for some time around the exhibits, chatting amicably, it was evident that they were not going to find Aglaea and her attendants again without a more dedicated search than either wanted to perform, so they left the Crystal Palace and walked across the park and back to Brook Street, where John left her at the door with a cordial shake of the hand. Jemima ran up to the room she shared, and found Aglaea already there, having come home rather more directly in a cab.

'What happened to you?' Aglaea asked. 'We looked for you, but I said there was no use searching in such a crowd, and so we left. I knew you'd be safe enough with John. He brought you home, I suppose?'

'Yes, and he's invited to dinner tonight.' Jemima explained the circumstances to Aglaea, and told her about his invitation for the next day. 'I know you won't mind if I go with him,' she concluded. 'I very much want to see Syon House.'

'*Do* you? I didn't know you knew such a place existed,' Aglaea said in surprise.

'Well, but a sail on the river, and a picnic, you know! I couldn't resist. The Exhibition is wonderful, but I do miss the fresh air.'

'I've engaged for us to meet Mr Underwood and Mrs Pownall tomorrow,' Aglaea said. 'But I can send them a note cancelling the arrangement.'

'Oh, but you could still go yourself, without me,' Jemima said.

'I shall spend the day sketching in the park,' Aglaea said firmly. 'And if you want to make plans for the following day, do so. I want to go the National Gallery, and I'd prefer to go alone, so that I can stay as long as I please with each picture.'

Jemima was happy with the arrangement for her own

sake, and was only afraid that she had spoiled Aglaea's day. She must rather have been with Mr Underwood but was evidently too delicate to meet him without Jemima's presence as well as that of Mrs Pownall. Jemima thought Mrs Pownall was a perfectly adequate chaperone, even supposing one to be needed by such people in such a place; but perhaps Aglaea thought it would look too particular to meet the Underwoods alone. As they never discussed their feelings together, Aglaea's were a closed book to Jemima.

Charlotte would have preferred the cover of darkness for her journey to her grandmother's house in Upper Grosvenor Street, but in mid-summer that was out of the question; she had to make do with a closed carriage and a voluminous cloak. Her attending doctor, Abernethy, whose views were either very old-fashioned or far ahead of his time, insisted that she must not wear stays now that she was large with child. It was a great relief – the compressure of stays gave her dreadful heartburn – but it presented a dressmaking problem, given the current fashion for tight bodices and tiny waists. It was fortunate, she thought, that her maid Norton was a skilled seamstress, because the gown of one week did not fit her the next. The one advantage was that she needed fewer petticoats to hold her skirts out: the child did that for her.

The carriage pulled up before the steps of the house, and at once the door opened and her grandmother's butler stood in the doorway to receive her. She thought of the first time she had come here, and how afraid she had been; how witheringly Denton had looked at her shabby mantle and badly dyed dress, and how she had shrunk under his gaze like a salted snail. Now she walked boldly up the steps and smiled at him.

'Good evening, Denton.'

'Good evening, your grace.' Denton did not quite go so far as to smile – it was rumoured he had smiled once, in the June of 1815, but few people believed that story – but his face assumed its softest aspect and he gave the lowest bow in his vocabulary as a sign of his approval. When the door was safely shut on the outside world, she asked, 'How is your knee?'

'Much better, I thank your grace,' Denton said, removing her mantle with a delicate flick of the wrists; and unbent enough to add, 'This dry weather is very grateful to the rheumatic aspect of the complaint.'

'You must rest it as much as possible,' Charlotte said, shaking out the folds of her skirt. 'You need not come upstairs to announce me.'

Condescension could only go so far, 'Your grace is most gracious,' Denton said firmly, bowing again, 'but I will escort your grace up to the drawing-room. Her ladyship would expect it, your grace.'

Smiling to herself, her grace fell in behind. She had not expected to get away with it. At least Denton's stately pace was welcome to her now, where in slimmer days it had irked her.

Her grandmother rose to meet her, small, slender and straight-backed as always, in an exquisite gown of emerald silk and black lace, with a mere spider's-web of black lace over her cropped grey curls instead of the usual matron's cap – for she had never entirely abandoned the fashions of her youth. She took Charlotte's hands and leaned forward to be kissed, and it was only at the touch of her lips on the cheek that Charlotte realised how thin Grandmama was. The gown, now she stepped back to look, had been carefully cut to disguise it; but the hands were thinner, and the rings were loose on her fingers.

'You look very well, my dear,' Lucy said, getting her word in first. 'The end of July, you said? I think you won't go so long. Are you feeling well? No more digestive upsets? No pains?'

'I'm feeling very well, no pains of any sort,' Charlotte said firmly, 'but what about you, Grandmama? I'm sure you have lost weight.'

'Nonsense. I'm just as I always was – strong as a horse. Come and sit down. Danby is still dressing. I could dress for a Court presentation in the time it takes him to put on his shirt. Men are such peacocks, aren't they? Does Southport take for ever to dress?'

Charlotte sat, aware she was being distracted. 'No, Oliver's usually very punctual, but he's a plain man, nothing of a dandy. Grandmama, are you well? Remember who is asking.'

Lucy tilted her head a little at her granddaughter. They shared a passionate interest in medicine and a taste for frankness. 'I am perfectly well,' she said at last. 'I might perhaps have lost a little weight, but now that I don't ride every day, I find it hard to have any appetite. Walking does not exercise me in the same way – and one is at the mercy of bores, on foot.'

'And how is Parslow?'

'Not well. The least exertion makes him breathless, and he has no appetite. He frets after his horses, of course, and he worries that I am not getting my exercise. I wish he would let me nurse him, but he won't leave his apartment.'

'Can't you insist?' Charlotte said. The idea of her grandmother's being crossed in anything was strange to her.

'It would not be fair to,' Lucy said. 'From his apartment he can just get himself down to the stable and back, if he goes slowly. From here it would be impossible.'

'But plainly it worries you. Are you not more important to him than his horses – *your* horses, actually.'

Lucy paused for a moment, but found no way to explain to her granddaughter the delicate balance of power that existed between master and servant after so very many years. And it was impossible to explain to such a young woman how alone one felt, stranded on the beach of survival when so many others had gone out with the tide. All her brothers and sisters, her first husband, her lover Thomas Weston, one child and three grandchildren, so many of her friends. To be long-lived was to see your own generation die. There was still Danby, of course, and he was most important. But Parslow had been there before Danby. Parslow her groom and Docwra her maid had been there from the very beginning, when she first left her parents' home and hired servants of her own. Docwra had been dead these ten years and more; Parslow was her last link with the past, with youth.

'Well, perhaps I will,' she said at last. 'Now tell me, how are things going with your hospital?'

Charlotte allowed herself to be turned. 'The building is going up quite quickly now – according to Oliver, that is, for I haven't seen it recently. But he always said once the foundations were in, it would all go on much more rapidly. The problem is that I still can't raise any enthusiasm for it. Polite smiles and concealed yawns are all the patronage I get. The top people seem to think a clean, modern hospital for the poor is an unnecessary indulgence. They won't give me money for it.'

'Does Southport object to your spending your fortune?'

'Oh, no! Oliver lets me do just as I please. His mother disapproves, of course.'

'That is a cross you will have to learn to bear.'

Charlotte smiled. 'I think she will like me much better if this baby turns out to be a boy. She was bitterly disappointed when Venetia was born. I'm sure she thought I did it on purpose to annoy her. But if I give Oliver a son, she will overlook all my other failings; and Abernethy says it is sure to be a boy.'

'Doctors always say that,' Lucy said. 'After all, they have a fifty per cent chance of being right. But go on about the hospital.'

'Ah, yes. Well, of course, I have founded it out of my own fortune, but I can't continue to pay all the bills for ever. Nor can I run it single-handed. It must be properly endowed and have a board of governors, and if respectable people won't help me, what am I to do, Grandmama?'

Lucy thought for a moment. 'You mean to have an operating theatre, I suppose?'

'Oh yes.' Charlotte's eyes lit with enthusiasm. 'A large one on the top floor, in the centre under a glass dome so as to get the best light. It will have observation terraces for teaching, of course, and all the newest equipment and contrivances. Everything of the best.'

Lucy nodded. 'That is your way forward. I'm mistaken if surgery is not the coming thing. Once anaesthesia is widely accepted, more and more surgical operations will be attempted. You should look to making your hospital a focus for the new knowledge and skills.'

'But to do that I must have patrons, endowments, and a board of governors, so we are back where we started,' Charlotte said. 'How am I to get the top people to support me? *They* aren't interested in surgery – they still think of surgeons as uncouth butchers.'

'Oh, quite. A physician is what you need, a fashionable, eminent physician on your roll of honour to give you tone,' Lucy said. 'A Sir Somebody Something to make speeches and praise you in the drawing-rooms of the wealthy.'

'But the Sir Somebody Somethings of this world won't care to treat paupers.'

'You don't want him to treat the paupers, child, only to tell the great hostesses how well it will be done in your hospital. You can get some poor, clever man to do the actual work – a young doctor with more enthusiasm than money. Your Doctor Snow will find you one, I dare say. If the poor are cured, the great man will have the credit, and the wealthy patrons will feel virtuous.'

Charlotte looked mulish. 'Why should anyone gain the credit if they won't do the work?'

'That is an attitude that will get you nowhere,' Lucy said. 'God knows, I'm the last person to preach patience and tact, never having had either. But the burglar knows all the ways in to the house.'

Charlotte shifted ground. 'But what could I tempt such a great man with?'

'The use of your operating facilities, of course, for his own patients, provided he puts his name to your letter-paper.

'But Grandmama, members of the Royal College of Physicians are not allowed to perform surgery.'

'What of it? There are a great many fashionable physicians who are not members of the Royal College. Indeed, I think I know who might serve you: Holder has a large practice amongst the *ton*, and I believe he's very well thought of. And he likes to be first with any new fad.'

'Sir Foulke Holder? But he's the most dreadful snob and toady!' Charlotte cried.

'Well, that need not trouble you, my dear. All you need to consider is how well it will sound: *Holder of Southport's*. Get the great hostesses talking about Holder of Southport's, and their purses will open to you. Think about it: you'll find I'm right. Ah, here's Theakston at last.'

'Evenin', Charlotte. No, don't get up! I may be doddery, but I ain't so stiff I can't bend enough to kiss you where you sit. So glad you came, m'dear. Not much compensation, I know, to have dinner with two old fogies, but the best we could do.'

'Compensation?' Charlotte asked, puzzled. 'What have I to be compensated for?'

'I haven't told her yet, Danby,' Lucy said. She turned to her granddaughter. 'I wanted to explain to you in person that I am giving a special dinner-party in honour of our young cousin Fenwick Morland, and to say how sorry I am that you won't be able to be there. But I can't put it off because he returns to America soon.'

'You didn't need to explain it to me specially, Grandmama. I understand,' Charlotte said.

'But you will be sorry to miss it,' Lucy said.

'Yes, of course. I shall be the only one who hasn't met him. Is he nice?'

'Very nice,' Lord Theakston said with a twinkle. 'Bathes every mornin', clean linen twice a day, boots polished to a sparkle.'

Charlotte laughed. 'You know I didn't mean that. Did you like him, Grandmama?'

'I wouldn't be giving a dinner for him otherwise. It was very interesting to hear his story, especially as I remember my father talking about our common ancestor.'

She went on to relate Fenwick's family history, but after a while she realised that Charlotte did not appear to be listening. Her expression was of intense preoccupation; and then suddenly she gave a cry, of alarm rather than pain, which was instantly cut off.

'What is it?' Lucy asked, as Theakston started to his feet in alarm. Charlotte met her grandmother's eyes with agonised entreaty. She might boast of being unembarrassed by her condition, but she was quite unable to say in front of his lordship that her waters had just broken.

'Is it the baby?' Lucy asked.

'Yes,' Charlotte said, and gasped as a pain gripped her. 'I think – oh Grandmama—!'

Lucy got up and crossed the room to her in a couple of quick steps. A whispered question and a nod from Charlotte, and Lucy said decidedly, 'We must get you upstairs. Danby, I want two strong footmen to carry Charlotte. The yellow bedroom will be best – tell Denton to tell Mrs Weaver to prepare it as quickly as possible.'

'Can't I go home?' Charlotte asked, unwilling to cause so much trouble.

'It's too late for that, child,' Lucy said. 'Danby, I must have Weedon at once – she knows what to do. And a message must be sent to Charlotte's woman – what's her name? – Norton; and to Doctor Abernethy. God knows where he might be.'

'Very well, m'dear,' Theakston said. He flung a glance at Charlotte, and, knowing he would only be a hindrance, hurried to the door. 'I'll send word to Southport, too,' he said over his shoulder. At least he knew where *he* was.

'Come, Charlotte, take deep breaths,' Lucy was saying, 'it will help the pains. No, never mind the chair, what on earth are servants for?'

Theakston fled.

Charlotte lay propped on the pillows while Lucy's maid, Weedon, sponged her face. She felt most peculiar. Her first child, Venetia, had been born after a long and effortful – though uncomplicated – labour; this one had shot into the world, entirely, it seemed, by its own efforts, leaving Charlotte nothing to do, and with barely a pain worth speaking of. She had been braced for this so long, she felt rather as if she had gone up a step that wasn't there. Abernethy had not had time to arrive – even Norton was still in transit. One moment she had been vastly, uncomfortably pregnant, and the next she was a deflated balloon, and mother of two.

'Is it always like this with a second child?' she asked her grandmother.

'Every delivery is different. Usually the second is quicker than the first, but I've never seen one as easy as this,' Lucy said.

She had been wrapping the baby in a towel, since the prepared clothes were still on their way with Norton, and now approached the bed with the small bundle in her arms. Her smile was transfiguring, and Charlotte felt almost afraid of so much joy and wonder. Her grandmother's face seemed almost transparent, as though an infinite light were shining through it from somewhere else. Lucy looked down at the new life she held in her arms, and addressed it with enormous satisfaction. 'I delivered your mother,' she said, 'and now I've delivered you.'

Rosamund, Charlotte, and now this little one: three generations of baby girls she had held in her arms in their first moments on earth. It was as if the fabric of time had been drawn up and pleated, pinned together with this damp new breathing life: her daughter, granddaughter and great-granddaughter were somehow all one; and beyond that, there was herself as a newborn baby, held in her mother's arms, and her mother in *her* mother's. At this moment she felt the great, irresistible current of life flowing through her, strong and sweet, and at seventy-three that was something to feel.

A little later Oliver arrived, coming up the stairs at a run, breathless with haste, pale with anxiety, smelling a little of fine regimental wines and cigars, damp with the fine summer rain that had just started. His feelings had been in turmoil ever since the message was brought to him at the dinner table, and he had rushed to Upper Grosvenor Street with all sorts of terrors fighting for

74

space in his mind, every step agonisingly leaden with the fear of being too late. He found a scene of utter tranquillity, his wife sitting up in bed, her hair brushed to a golden cloud about her shoulders, her serene face bent over the tiny white bundle in her arms. No blood, death and horror, just the most enduring image of joy in man's vocabulary.

She looked up as he came in, and gave him a smile that he knew he would never forget, of joy, love, and triumphant accomplishment.

'Your mother will never forgive me,' she said.

CHAPTER FOUR

Until his present illness, Lucy had never been in Parslow's living quarters; and he had been only once in hers – when Captain Weston had died, and he had sat up all night with her in a kind of vigil. Parslow had rooms over the stables in the mews where her horses were kept. Unlike most grand ladies, she was not a stranger to the mews: she liked to drop in to talk to her favourites, and discuss their welfare with her grooms. So her appearance, with Weedon at her heels carrying a basket, caused no surprise. She was greeted with civil nods and, after she had passed, a knowing look or two, and a shake of the head.

She saw one of her own boys, and beckoned him to her. 'Is Mr Parslow in his room?'

'Oh, yes m'lady. He hasn't been out today.'

'Run up to him, then, and tell him I am coming to see him.' It would be unkind to surprise him. When the boy appeared again at the bottom of the stairs, she took the basket from Weedon and said, 'You may wait here,' and went up alone.

The stairs opened onto a living room, with a tiny bedroom beyond. The living room reminded Lucy of a stable, with its tongue-and-groove panelled walls. There were bare wooden floorboards, and the wooden rafters reached into the roof space: she almost expected swallows to be nesting there. Everything was spare and clean. There was a scrubbed table with two plain chairs pulled up to it; a marble-topped stand bearing a tin basin and ewer; a tall cupboard in the chimney corner. The chimney was of bare brick, with a small cast-iron stove, and a plain jute hearth rug which had once been a horse-blanket. The only decorations were some horse brasses on the chimney breast, which had been polished so much they were almost featureless, and on the mantelpiece a tea caddy, depicting in brilliant colours the coronation of King William IV. In place of pictures on the walls, there were bridle racks, on which there always hung some piece of harness brought up for repair in the quiet hours. It was a room, Lucy thought, simply for waiting in, until it was time to be with the horses again.

Parslow was sitting by the chimney in a wing-backed armchair upholstered in worn red plush. He was neatly dressed in shirt and waistcoat, corded breeches and leather gaiters, as if he was just about to go down and start the morning's quartering. He pushed himself to his feet the moment he saw her, and she noted with distress how even that made him pull his breath.

'Sit,' she said.

'You must have this chair, my lady. I'll get another.'

'Sit, I said. I'm perfectly capable of drawing a chair out from the table.' He defied her for a moment, but then sat, rather more suddenly than she thought he had meant to. She put the basket on the table, pulled out a wooden chair, and sat down facing him. He bore her inspection stoically. His face was pale; there was an ominously blue tinge to his lips, and that look of tense preoccupation in his eyes which, in a horse, would have been an indication of suffering. How lined he was, she thought suddenly, how grey, how old. She had no idea of his age. He had been older than her when he first came to her, but by how many years? Three, five, ten? It was so hard to tell with a man who had worked out of doors all his life.

He was watching her watch him, and she dropped her

eyes, suddenly embarrassed. His hands rested on his knees, large, chalky-knuckled, with an old man's ridged nails; but still strong – hands you would trust. How often had they supported her, lifted her, soothed her? She knew his hands better than any other part of him. She shivered suddenly.

'I'm sorry if it's cold, my lady. It seemed too warm this morning to light the stove,' he said.

'I'm not cold. How are you, Parslow?'

'Main well, my lady. If only I could shift this bit of a cold, I could get back to work.' His eyes defied her to contradict him, but speaking had made him cough, and he had to turn his head away and fumble out a handkerchief from the pocket of his corded breeches. She could hear the breath dragging harshly in his chest; but it was not a cold, or bronchitis. It was not the lungs at all, as she well knew, but the heart, wearing out at last; and what could anyone do about that?

'I've brought you some things,' she said. Useless things, but she needed to do something. 'Some excellent pork jelly – very nourishing – and one of Fabrice's pies. He baked it especially for you, so you must eat it, or he'll be offended and leave me for Lady Tonbridge.' He smiled only dutifully at her jest. 'And some of the preserved oranges you like. And,' drawing out a bottle, 'his lordship wants you to have this, with his warmest wishes.'

Parslow took the bottle. He looked up at her in amazement. 'The '05, my lady?'

'Liberated from Napoleon's own cellar in the Tuileries Palace after Waterloo. But none the worse for that, for I believe the Emperor didn't choose his own wines. Lord Melbourne told me Boney never had time for the refinements of dining – too busy conquering the world! Never trust a man who doesn't respect his stomach, that's what Melbourne used to say.'

'It's too good for me, my lady,' Parslow said. He seemed almost distressed by the gift, which was not what she had intended.

'It isn't just to get you well,' she said quickly. 'It's for a celebration.'

He caught her meaning at once. 'Her grace has had her baby?'

'Last night – quite unexpectedly – and in my house. It was so quick, I had to deliver it myself.'

'None the worse for that, my lady. And is her grace well?'

'Both of them thriving and eating like horses.'

'I'm so very glad. If you please, would you convey my respectful congratulations to her grace?'

'I will. But don't you want to know if it was a boy or a girl?'

He shook his head. 'It was a girl,' he said.

'How did you know? Someone has told you the news already!'

'No, indeed, my lady. I didn't need to be told. I knew all along it was a girl.' He smiled reflectively. 'Two generations I've taught to ride. I wish I might teach her new little ladyship too.'

'Impatient! It must be two years at least before you can get her on a horse – though I wouldn't put it past you to try.'

He didn't answer that. 'Have they decided on a name, my lady?'

'Olivia. After her father.' Lucy shrugged. 'I can hardly object, having called one of my own Flaminia, poor little brute. I suppose Olivia isn't so bad – not as bad as Venetia, anyway.'

'Both very pretty names, my lady. Has his grace seen the new baby?'

'Oh yes, and pronounced himself very satisfied. Says

he would rather have a girl, which may not be true, but is tactful. I like that young man!'

'Any man would want a daughter, my lady,' Parslow said. Suddenly their eyes met in one of those unintended moments, too nakedly for disguise.

'Did you never want to marry, Parslow? And have a family?'

'It was not possible in my position, my lady,' he said. She started to refute this, and then became unsure of what he meant, and had to look down, feeling strangely disturbed. He went on, 'Besides, I had all the family a man could want. Lord Aylesbury and their ladyships and Mr Thomas: I watched them grow up. I taught them to ride, and I've taught all their children too. A man couldn't want more.'

She looked around the bare room, and felt a weight of sadness. A man ought to want a great deal more than this, she thought. But she did not say it, of course; and now he had begun to cough again; and when he stopped coughing, he was struggling for breath. Fear made her speak sharply.

'Why won't you let me get a doctor to you?'

'There's no need for a doctor. It's nothing but a summer cold.'

'It's not a summer cold! Good God, I'm the last one to fuss about such things, but it's ridiculous to go on in this way.'

'If your ladyship would be so kind as to let one of the other grooms take you out, just for a day or two—'

'I won't ride with anyone else. For God's sake, man, you know that's not what I mean. I want you to be well!' She bit her lip angrily. 'There's only you left!' she burst out impulsively.

'Oh, no, my lady,' he protested softly. Their eyes met again, and anything she might have said died on her lips. Words between them must always be circumscribed, drawn from a limited code-book of frequently used signals; but in his look there was communication on another level, and it took away her anger.

'You're right, of course,' he said at last, and his voice was quite different, even the lines of his face looked different. He had stepped aside from his faithful servant persona, removed the mask he kept always raised between them. She was looking at the real Parslow, the man rather than the legend, whose powerful self, felt but rarely seen, had bound her to her groom with bonds lighter than silk and stronger than steel. 'It isn't a cold.'

'What is it then?'

His eyes teased. 'It's brokken wind,' he said in the accent of her childhood. 'If I were a 'oss, tha'd shoot me.'

She tried to play, though she felt leaden with apprehension. 'I never shot a horse with broken wind in my life.'

'Depends how bad they are. Some only roar when you run 'em, but when they struggle for breath just standing still—'

'Is it like that with you?' she said, very quietly. He nodded slowly. Pain seized her throat. She was not ready to let him go. 'I can't do without you,' she said at last. 'Try to get well. You must try.'

'I'll try,' he said; and very softly, 'I don't want to leave you.'

'Think of baby Olivia. Who will teach her to ride? Try for her sake.'

He smiled, but the smile was not on his blue lips but in his dark eyes. 'No,' he said, 'but I'd do it for thee.'

'Good God, so this is my new niece, is it?' Lord Blithfield said in mock alarm as the nursery-maid proffered the wailing bundle for his inspection. 'What did you say her name was? Pluvia?'

'Don't be so horrid, it's Olivia. Poor thing, I think she has the colic,' Charlotte said. 'She's usually such a contented baby.'

'Don't she make a racket!'

'I'm sure you made just as much noise at that age.'

'Not I,' he said promptly. 'Mama would have been glad if I did. I was horrid sickly.'

'Well, anyhow, you must admit she's the prettiest baby you ever saw.'

'Oh yes, certainly, anything you say. Is Southport pleased?'

'Of course. Why shouldn't he be?'

'No reason. Of course he is. Don't be so prickly, Charley. Fact is, hard to know what to say about a new baby. I'm sure she's a jolly good one, as they go, but they all look the same to me.'

'Oliver said she was like a washed pearl, pale and pretty and complete. Venetia was very red and blotchy, you know, but Olivia was perfect from the beginning.'

Cavendish nodded, a little out of his depth. 'I'm dashed glad to see you lookin' so well, anyhow,' he said. 'Grandmother's like a dog with two tails – calls it *her* baby. You'd think you had nothing to do with it.'

'I'm glad she'll have one doting grandmother. Lady Turnhouse made quite sure I understood how much I've disappointed everyone. I was supposed to give the dukedom an heir, not burden it with another useless girl.'

'Good God, did she? The old witch! But what did Southport say?'

'That he likes girls best. He said that's why he married one.'

Cavendish smiled. 'He's a great gun! So, it doesn't matter what the old lady thinks, then, does it?'

'I suppose I shouldn't be so easily upset,' she said, and nodded to the maid to take Olivia back to the nursery.

'You shouldn't,' Cavendish said, sitting and stretching out his shiny-booted legs at ease. The sunshine streaming through the window lit his golden hair into dazzle. He was every inch a cavalry officer, with his artfully ruffled hair, splendid whiskers, wasp-waisted jacket, and skin-tight overalls displaying the glorious muscles of his thighs. He had recently grown side-whiskers to join up with his moustache, in the hope that it would make him look older; but to Charlotte's affectionate gaze he still looked like a little boy dressing up for a masquerade.

'Truth to tell,' he said, looking around, 'I looked in for a little peace and quiet. Town's crowded with the queerest-looking customers – even the clubs are full of 'em. Yours is the only civilised place left, with room to stretch one's legs.'

'I hardly know how I've escaped,' Charlotte said. 'It must be the consequence of my shocking behaviour. No-one wants to know me.'

'Everyone knows you've been increasin',' Cavendish said kindly. 'Be glad you're not Uncle Tom! I dropped in to Brook Street the other day to meet the new cousin, and you've never seen so many people under one roof. But I must say they all looked very jolly, crowded round the dining table and playing some ridiculous game Aunt Emily made up. They wanted me to join in, but I had to get back to the mess.'

Charlotte remembered the happy times she had had in Mrs Welland's lodgings in Lamb's Conduit Street when she first came to London, crowded round a table playing games. It had been the first time in her life she had known companionship and noisy family fun. She looked around the Chinese saloon, at the high ceiling, the wide areas of polished boards, the few pieces of elegant, lacquered

83

furniture thoughtfully placed around thick pale carpets; and just for a moment it looked like an emptiness rather than an agreeably spacious sitting-room. But that was just a momentary – and absurd – nostalgia.

'What's the long-lost cousin like?' she asked.

'He seems a nice enough chap.'

Charlotte smiled. 'You say that about everyone. Can't you give me more detail?'

Cavendish made an effort. 'Wonderfully polite. Clever cove, too, I shouldn't wonder.' He thought for a moment. 'Seems to have gone spoony on Mary,' he added.

'Mary? But she's only a child!'

'Well,' Cavendish said doubtfully, 'fact is, she's so dashed clever and bookish herself, she doesn't seem like one. She's turning into a diamond of the first water: pretty as you like, and full of fun, but so unaffected. I'm not surprised Fenwick's fallen over head and ears for her.'

'You sound as though you're in danger yourself,' Charlotte said, amused.

'Oh, I'm safe enough,' Cavendish said firmly.

'What's this? Have you got a new torch? What's her name?'

Cavendish looked conscious. 'It's Lady Caroline Gosling. Daughter of Lord Padstowe – d'you know him?'

'I know Lady Padstowe – nodding acquaintance. Doesn't she have quite a large family?'

'Any number of 'em. Caroline's the fourth daughter, and there are more in the schoolroom. This is her first season – she came out in April. I met her at Grosvenor House last week. She's the most beautiful girl I ever saw in my life.'

Charlotte nodded sympathetically. Cavendish at nineteen fell in love every couple of weeks, and each one was the most beautiful girl he had ever seen – until the next Congreve rocket exploded over his horizon.

84

'The first moment I saw her, I knew,' Cavendish went on. 'She was all in white, like an angel; and when I danced with her, she was like a feather. I could hardly feel her on my arm.'

'And have you seen her since?'

'Walkin' in the Park with her mother and a sister. I stopped and spoke to her for a minute. Lady Padstowe was dashed civil, I must say – invited me to a card-party tomorrow night.'

Charlotte smiled at his modesty. The charming Captain Lord Blithfield, the most handsome young officer in the 11th Hussars and heir to the Earl of Batchworth's title and wealth, was a prize in any drawing-room, particularly when there were unmarried daughters in the house.

'I'll wager she was civil! You're a great catch, don't you know that?' Charlotte said. 'And you'd be a better match than the Padstowes can really ever have hoped for, for one of their younger daughters.'

Cavendish flushed a little. 'I never thought to hear you talk like that. Grandmama's been jawing me about matches and catches and the Padstowes being thrusters and so on till I'm fit to burst, but I thought you'd be on my side.'

Charlotte was instantly contrite. It was an attitude she had run away from herself, when she had first been presented to Society. 'Darling Cav, of course I'm on your side!' But all the same, she thought, her brother was much younger at nineteen than she had been, and more inclined to trust everyone. And Grandmama was not mercenary, and very sharp about people. 'I'm sure Lady Caroline is a very nice girl,' she went on. 'It's only that – to be fair, you must admit that you fall in and out of love in ten minutes.'

'Well, I may have done when I was younger,' he admitted generously, 'but that's done with. I've met

85

the one true love of my life now. I shall love Caroline until I die, and I mean to marry her, that's all.'

It was on Charlotte's lips to say, 'That's what you said the last time,' but she bit the words back. There was no point in upsetting him, especially as the situation was bound to resolve itself within a week or so, when a new beauty appeared in his sights.

The folding doors between the two drawing-rooms at Upper Grosvenor Street had been thrown back for the party when it came up from the dining-room. The two chandeliers were brilliant with candles, for Lucy disliked gaslight, which she said made women's complexions dull and their diamonds duller; and the fireplaces were filled with arrangements of flowers – pink roses and white lilies – which filled the air with a fragrance that almost drowned the women's perfume.

All of Benedict's party was there, plus Tom and Emily and Lucy's elder son Aylesbury and his wife. Oliver had walked up after dinner to take tea and do the polite; and when she learned that he was in Town, Lucy had included John Anstey in the invitation. He was surprised and grateful, but Lucy had dismissed his humility.

'I know your uncle Jack very well – in fact, it was I who furthered his naval career; and it was always me he came to for advice. I should count myself failing in friendship if I did not take an interest in his heir. You might have had your invitation earlier if you had left your card with me when you first arrived in Town.'

John thanked her again, and settled down to a delightful evening of being licensed to talk to Jemima all he liked.

Lord Aylesbury had brought his wife and children to London to see the Exhibition, and if his mother had not invited him to a family dinner, he would have hosted one himself, for his manners were rather formal and, as an

Evangelical, he counted duty to family next to duty to God. He was in his fifties, a grey and stooping man, with an increasingly harassed expression on his kindly face. His wife's second miscarriage last year had left her sickly and fretful; his eldest son, Lord Calder, was turning out expensive, and had had to be sent abroad for a year or two where he could be expensive more cheaply; his eldest daughter's marriage, to a leading light of the Evangelical movement, seemed not to be going smoothly, if her frequent appearances in tears in his drawing-room were anything to judge by; and his second son Titus was doing at Oxford what young men had done there from time immemorial – drinking, gambling and consorting with loose women. It was all enough to try the patience of a Job, and he was not comforted by his mother's frequently telling him that it was precisely the Jobs of this world who always were plagued with constant misfortune, because God liked nothing better than a good joke at some hapless human's expense.

He walked over to his step-father Lord Theakston with a heavy limp – he had caught his foot in a rabbit-trap while inspecting his coverts a fortnight ago, and it was slow to heal – and asked after his health with a hesitant formality which did not disguise his real affection. Then he asked, 'Is our good friend Shaftesbury still in Town? He sent me a note thanking me for my letter of condolence, and said he was going down to Dorset to see about the estate, but he didn't say when. I thought I'd call on him if he's still up.'

'I don't think he's goin' down until recess,' Theakston said. 'He was at Charlotte's last week, arrangin' visits to the Crystal Palace for charity boys.'

'Yes, that's like him – not to forget the poor, even in the midst of his own troubles!'

'I gather the family estate is heavily encumbered?'

'The last time I was there the house was all but falling down, the farms were neglected, the people ignorant and the overseers corrupt. A huge amount needs to be spent, but all he has is debts, poor Shaftesbury,' Aylesbury sighed. They had been friends since their university days.

'But he's a welcome addition to the Upper House. Everyone expects him to stir the Lords to activity.'

'I don't suppose Russell will care for an active House of Lords,' Aylesbury said. 'He'd sooner we all went away to our estates and stayed there.'

'Shaftesbury's got ideas on constitutional reform that'll put a cockle-burr under Russell's tail,' Theakston chuckled.

'Has he brought them up again? About giving peerages to tradesmen, and the franchise to annuitants as well as land-owners?'

'That's the ticket,' Theakston said. 'You must come in more often, see the fun. Johnnie Russell would eat his own foot with mustard before he agreed to any of that!'

'But I don't think there's much harm in it, do you?' Aylesbury said. 'After all, there's many a peer's fortune started in trade; and there's many a peer's son has to take a job of work. I sometimes wish mine would,' he added with a sigh.

'Damned republican of you, m'boy,' Theakston said. 'Don't let your mother hear you say that.'

'But that's what gives our system its strength – new blood all the time. I'm no republican, you know that.'

'And what about the franchise? What are your thoughts on that?'

'I see nothing wrong with my pensioners having the vote – as long as they vote the way I tell them,' Aylesbury said reasonably.

'What about women? Would you give them the vote?'

'Steady on, sir!' Aylesbury said, blinking; and then

realising he was being teased, broke into a chuckle, and limped off to see that his wife was happily occupied. Thalia was sitting on a sofa at right angles to her mother-in-law, who was talking to her urgently. Aylesbury saw his wife's pale, lined face set in an expression of disapproval, and his heart sank. Her temper was growing more unreliable month by month, and he did everything he could not to annoy her; but his mother hadn't an ounce of tact.

Lucy saw him approach, and patted the sofa beside her. 'Sit here, Aylesbury, and tell your wife I am right, that she must not think of having another child.'

Thalia snapped, 'Thank you, but that is a matter between me and my husband, and if I discuss it with any other person, it will be my doctor.'

'Don't be a fool, Thalia. I know more about childbirth than most doctors, and I've seen the result of this sort of activity time and again. You're forty-eight years old and you've had ten pregnancies. Enough is enough! Back me up, Aylesbury! Do you want your wife to die?'

'Mother!' Aylesbury protested. 'I don't think that sort of talk—'

'There should be moderation in all things,' Lucy overrode him. 'Reason in all things.'

'*Whose* reason, *whose* moderation?' Thalia exclaimed, her annoyance overcoming her resolve not to discuss it. 'Always yours, mother-in-law, never God's! It is for our Divine Father to decide such matters, and for us to accept His will. Until we submit ourselves to Him, we will never create His kingdom here on earth. The sacred institution of marriage was ordained—'

'Oh, pooh!' Lucy said. 'What has come over you, Thalia? You weren't thinking of sacred institutions when you married my son. A title and a good establishment were uppermost in your mind. You had more sense then than you're showing now.'

'My choice was guided by Divine Providence,' Thalia said with icy dignity. 'Aylesbury and I were intended to marry, as part of God's plan.'

Lucy shook her head sadly. 'When I remember the wild-haired little thing you used to be – full of fun and the most shocking flirt of the Season. When I remember your mother, in fact—'

'Don't speak to me, please, of my mother. I loved and honoured her, as is my duty, but her life was shockingly irregular! I thank God I have been able to be a better example to my children, and to teach them a stronger sense of duty—'

'Duty, always duty,' Lucy interrupted. 'What about your duty to use the intelligence God gave you – such as it is? You can't leave God to decide every smallest detail of your life—'

Aylesbury crept away. There could hardly be two people further apart in their religious views than his wife and his mother, and whatever subject they began on, they usually ended with the same argument. When he saw how ill Thalia was looking, his heart agreed with his mother; but his intellect had to follow his religious beliefs. Of course, he would willingly have foregone the pleasures of the bed for Thalia's sake, but she did not want to be spared, and insisted on a regular exercise of connubiality with what struck him sometimes as a grim determination rather than an overflowing heart. The result was that the argument she was at present having with her mother-in-law was no more than academic: Thalia was already – though she hadn't told anyone but him yet – pregnant again. It was the largest and heaviest of the worries that was bowing his shoulders.

On the other side of the room, Tom was talking to Oliver with great enthusiasm.

'You must let me lend you Archer's book. You'll

find it fascinating. Though in fact, I'd say the most important thing about the collodian process is not that it's an improvement on all the others – which it is – but that it's blessedly free from patents! Not even Fox Talbot could claim that it bears any similarity to the calotype. Fenton says Talbot is the main cause of our isolation, and I'd say the exhibits at the Crystal Palace are ample proof of that. The Americans and the French are years in front of us.'

'And you think that's because of the lack of patents?' Oliver asked.

'Precisely because of that. Every time something new comes out, Talbot claims it comes under his patent and demands that anyone who wants to try it takes out a licence from him. Of course that holds people back. It's only by free co-operation and exchanging ideas that advances are made. The Great Exhibition proves that.'

'Well, I've always been a supporter of free trade,' Oliver said. 'But I didn't know that you were interested in calotypes.'

'How could one not be interested?' Tom said. 'It is the painting of the future! Sir William Newton showed me a print of his the other day, of a still life of fruit and so on, which is so beautiful – well, it's better than anything any artist could paint. It's perfect, which a painting can never be.'

'Oh, I admit the fascination,' Oliver said, 'though I'm not sure I agree with you about its replacing painting. But how did you fall into it in the first place?'

'It was my fault, I'm afraid,' Benedict said. 'I introduced Tom to Charles Vignoles – the engineer, you know – when I was up in Town helping to plan the Exhibition.'

'And then I met him again – Vignoles, I mean – at the Royal Academy with Roger Fenton, a solicitor-friend of his who was exhibiting a picture at the summer exhibition. I said something agreeable, you know, about Fenton's painting, and Fenton gave me a grin and said, 'I suppose painting's well enough, but Charles and I know a trick worth two of that.' So they invited me along to their Photographic Club.'

'Where he fell sick of the calotype fever,' said Emily, who joined them just then. 'Fortunately one of the members is the superintendent of a lunatic asylum, which will come in very handy one of these days.'

Tom put his arm round her. 'My wife likes to abuse me to all my relatives: it amuses her.'

'You will soon know everything there is to know about the waxed-paper method and the albumen method and all the other methods,' Emily said to Oliver. 'Tom needs only the slightest encouragement to expound. It's his age, of course,' she added solemnly. 'Gentlemen at his time of life always develop some seething interest or other. Some become very interested in opera dancers, others—'

'Emily!' Tom said, pretending to be shocked. 'What can you know about opera dancers?'

She chuckled. 'Well, my dear, not as much as you, it's to be hoped.'

'But think of it, Southport,' Tom reverted to his subject, 'the new portraiture! It takes hours instead of weeks, and the likeness is perfect every time. And once we can winkle the process out of Talbot's grasp, it will be within everyone's reach, not just the rich. Your ordinary, decent working man will be able to have his and his wife's and children's portraits taken, just as if he were—'

'The Duke of Southport himself,' Emily concluded.

The others laughed, but Tom seemed struck by the idea. 'Now that's a thing! Southport, you must persuade Charlotte to have her calotype taken, with the new baby. If it were known you were interested in photography, you could be very useful in putting leverage on Fox Talbot.'

'Whatever makes you think I want to be useful?' Oliver asked, his eyebrows climbing.

'But shouldn't you like a portrait of your wife and child?'

'In conventional oils, perhaps.'

'No, no, you must be modern! Painting is dead!' Tom laughed. 'I tell you what – we must pose her with Mama, as well! I see it now – three generations! It will make a splendid subject, and mark the occasion of Olivia's birth as nothing else could.'

'It wouldn't hurt the baby, would it?' Emily put in.

'Of course not. How could it?' He turned to Oliver again. 'And you'll come along to the club?'

'Do you know, I think I will.'

'I knew you'd be infected if you talked to Tom for long,' Emily said.

Fenwick and Mary were standing together, a little apart from the company, turning over the pages of a book laid on the table by the window. It was a book of birds, and they were trying to identify which species were common to both England and America, and how the names differed.

'We have a bird a little like this, but its feathers shine bright blue in the sun,' he was saying.

'Oh, I should like to see that! From what you say our birds are very dull by comparison with yours.'

'Oh, no, I wouldn't say so. But I wish you could come to Carolina – I should love to show you all our wonders.'

'I would like to go very much,' Mary said. 'I think about it a great deal. I imagine walking along The Battery and seeing all the fine wooden houses painted bright colours. And I imagine riding one of your fine horses around the fields of Twelvetrees. Only—' She paused, with a troubled look.

93

'Only what?' he prompted.

'Well, I do wonder about the slaves. Isn't slavery very wrong? It was banned in this country long ago.'

'I don't know about that,' Fenwick said carefully. 'The fact is that the South couldn't exist without the slaves – there aren't enough people to tend the fields without them. And they aren't like us, you know. Mentally they're like children, quite helpless without the white folks to look after them. If they didn't have us to tell them what to do, and keep them at work, and feed them and take care of their ailments – why, they'd just sit under a tree all day and do nothing, and starve.'

'But surely it's against God's law for one man to *own* another?' Mary asked, troubled.

'Perhaps amongst white folks it would be,' he said. 'But why would God have made darkies so different if He didn't mean us to own them?'

Mary was puzzled to answer this, not having expected God to come out on the side of slavery, and while she was coming to terms with the argument, Fenwick changed the subject.

'I like your gown very much,' he said. 'You look so very pretty in pink. I hope you don't mind if I say you are pretty?'

'Not at all – why should I mind?' she said, but she dropped her eyes and looked a little shy. She didn't like 'boys' being 'silly', but Cousin Fenwick was far from being a boy, and such things didn't seem silly taken in the context of his tall figure and broad shoulders and his marvellously musical voice.

'Do you think you might like to come to America one day?' he went on. 'I know it could not be for a few years, but then if I was to ask you – if I was to come and fetch you—?'

'I should like to come, if I was allowed,' she said; and

suddenly looked up, very serious and searching, as if she might find the answer to a problematical question somewhere in his face. 'I like *you*, cousin.'

His heart jumped at the artless confession, and it took all his self-control to remember that she was still a child. 'I'm very glad,' he said seriously. 'I like you very much, too. And I will miss you when I go back to America. We have been good friends, have we not?'

Mary seemed to be put at ease by the word. 'Yes, we have been friends.'

He put his hand in his pocket. 'I have bought a little token of our friendship, which I hope you will feel able to accept. It comes from the American Court – a little piece of America for you to keep, and remember me by.'

He put into her hand a small gold locket on a chain; egg-shaped, smooth, and with a curly, flourishing 'M' engraved in the centre of the lid. Mary opened it, and there was a second lid inside, flat this time. Fenwick reached over with a 'Permit me? There's a trick to it,' to show her how to spring the catch. The lid lifted, and inside the hollow of the compartment so revealed was a small curl of hair. Mary looked at it for a moment, and then up at Fenwick's face, with that same slightly puzzled, searching look.

'Is it yours?' she asked.

He nodded. 'There's an Indian custom I heard from my great-grandmother when I was a little child – that when someone is going far away on a long journey, you give them a piece of your hair as a talisman, and it protects them from danger.'

'But it's you that's going away,' Mary said.

He smiled. 'I'll make my own luck. And when I'm in America, you'll be far away from me, so it will come to the same thing.'

She closed the locket up again and folded it in her hand.

'It's very beautiful,' she said. 'Thank you. May I show it to Mama and Papa?'

'I think you had better,' Fenwick said. 'And I think I had better come with you.'

For Mary's sake, and because they were in company, Benedict had said very little when she showed him the locket.

'Isn't it fine?' she had said artlessly. 'I may keep it, mayn't I, Papa?'

'Let me see, chick,' he said, and took it from her. Sibella looked over his shoulder, and seemed relieved when he opened it and found nothing but a smoothness inside. Fenwick did not mention the second compartment, or offer to show Benedict how to open it, and some instinct in Mary made her hold her tongue about that too.

'I suppose this is for further engraving,' Benedict said, rubbing the flat lid with his forefinger. If it were a lover's gift, there would be a second initial here, or perhaps a true-lovers'-knot. He was glad it had been left blank. All the same – 'I'm not sure it is appropriate for you to be giving my daughter such a personal gift,' he said.

'Oh Papa, please let me keep it,' Mary said anxiously. 'It's so pretty, and Cousin Fenwick says it's from America.'

'American workmanship. It's a gift of friendship, sir,' Fenwick said. He met Benedict's eyes steadily. 'From one cousin to another.'

'I think you had better come and see me tomorrow morning,' Benedict said. He felt a little annoyed. Fenwick should not have given Mary the locket without asking his permission, and to give it at Aunt Lucy's party, where if he objected he could not express himself freely, made him feel he was being manipulated. By the following morning he had come to the conclusion that he *had* been manipulated, quite deliberately, and by someone rather skilful. If Fenwick had asked permission to give Mary the locket, Benedict believed he would have refused; now he could not take it away from her without giving her pain, and marring what was perhaps an innocent pleasure, thus putting ideas into her head he was at pains to keep out.

So he was ready to damn Fenwick's eyes as he waited for him in the drawing-room at Brook Street. The whole situation was awkward, for in that tiny house it was necessary, in order to secure privacy, to ask for it; so everyone now knew he was having a confidential interview with Fenwick and was free to guess the reason.

But when Fenwick came into the room, an expression of half-rueful supplication on his attractive face, Benedict's anger seeped inexorably away, though he tried hard to keep hold of it.

'Sir, I want to apologise sincerely for putting you in an awkward position last night,' Fenwick said at once, so stealing Benedict's first arrow. 'I realise I shouldn't have given Mary the locket in such a way that you could hardly object to it. I assure you I didn't mean to. I had meant to ask your permission first, but I had it in my pocket, and we were talking about my going away, and, well – it was the impulse of the moment just to give it to her then. All I can say is that she accepted it purely as the gift of friendship – as it was meant.'

'Was it, indeed? And do you frequently give valuable jewellery to fourteen-year-old girls for whom you feel – *friendship*?'

'No, sir – never before, and I guess never again.' He spread out his hands in a gesture of offering himself. 'I'm sure, being a father, you must have noticed what a deep

97

impression Mary's made on me. She is just enchanting! Her sweetness, her beauty, that childlike simplicity combined with a woman's intellect—'

'I don't need you to describe my daughter's qualities to me,' Benedict said.

'Sir, you've been so kind to me, you and Mrs Morland, that I shall take home with me the warmest memories and the strongest feelings of gratitude and affection towards you. Would I willingly do anything to offend you, or to hurt any member of your family? I love Mary sincerely, and I'm ready to wait many years in the hope that one day I might marry her. But I have not and would not express myself to her in those terms. To her I've spoken only of friendship.'

Benedict felt he was losing any right to object to something that he wanted to object to quite violently. Fenwick had expressed himself very properly, leaving Benedict no excuse at all to knock him down, horsewhip him, or dismiss him instantly and for ever from the house. Benedict felt, indeed, almost like crying.

'What is it you want?' he asked. 'There can be no question of an engagement or any kind of understanding. Mary is far too young.'

'I know. I wouldn't expect it,' Fenwick said.

'Then what *do* you want?'

'Only to make my wishes clear to you, sir. I'll wait as long as you like, without any kind of obligation on your part. But since I'll be many thousands of miles away, I wanted to give you the opportunity now to ask me any questions about my situation that might occur to you, while you've got me here face to face. Words on paper are all very well, but when you've got a man in your sights, you can tell much better what his character is, and whether he's telling the truth.'

'I am sure you are telling the truth,' Benedict said

unwillingly. 'I do you the justice to believe you mean my daughter no harm.'

'Harm? Why, I swear to God, sir, if anyone was so much as to—'

'Yes, yes, take that as read,' Benedict stopped him. 'And I've nothing to ask you. I cannot permit Mary to marry until she's seventeen at least, and in three years your situation may change so much as to make anything you tell me now irrelevant. Besides that, your feelings may change – no, don't tell me, I know you think them immutable.'

'But if they don't change – and I know they won't – you will let me come back and ask Mary to marry me?'

'Understand, I would never give her to a man she doesn't love. Mary is already the prettiest, liveliest girl in the Riding, and in three years' time she will be the belle of all Yorkshire. There will be hundreds of young men anxious to marry her. And her feelings at present must be considered as quite unfixed. If you come back, you must take your chance with the others.'

'Thank you, sir,' Fenwick said with dignity. 'That's all I ask.'

CHAPTER FIVE

As soon as Charlotte was well enough to travel, Oliver took her out of London. He had a country seat in Northamptonshire, but his mother was there, and he did not want to expose Charlotte to any more unpleasantness. Besides, he reasoned that a woman who has just had a baby must want her own mother. So they took the train north to Lancashire, and Grasscroft, the Earl of Batchworth's country seat. Batchworth was Charlotte's mother's second husband, and father of Cavendish; Grasscroft was on the edge of the moors some miles outside Manchester.

And Manchester was the home of Charlotte's cousin Fanny, who had been her particular friend when she first came to London, and had shown her how to enjoy the frivolities of coming out. Fanny had inherited from her mother three cotton mills, a large house, and a good deal of rented property in Manchester; so when she had married Doctor Philip Anthony – just a month before Charlotte had married Oliver – the Anthonys had decided to settle in Manchester rather than London. Doctor Anthony felt his services would be just as much needed amongst the Manchester poor; and in any case, until his father died and left him the small estate in north Norfolk, he had no house of his own. Fanny's step-papa, Henry Droylsden, who ran the mills for her, moved out of Hobsbawn House and settled in one of the new suburbs with his new wife, and Mr and Mrs Philip Anthony moved in.

Hobsbawn House was an old house right in the centre of the city, close to the mills, factories and crowded lanes; and since Manchester in August was even less salubrious than London in August, Charlotte had expected to find Fanny already installed at Grasscroft when she and Oliver arrived. It was her first enquiry when released from her mother's embrace as they stood in the hall.

'They'll be coming next week,' Rosamund answered her. 'It seems there's a public meeting they must attend.'

'In August?' Charlotte said. 'No-one holds public meetings in August.'

'I understand it's something of an emergency – a public health matter. Anthony must be there, and Fanny won't leave without him.'

'Oh. So they're still very much in love?' Charlotte said.

'Why should they not be?' Rosamund asked, less interested just then in Fanny than in the arrival of the nurses with the babies. 'Is that my new granddaughter? Oh, let me hold her! She's beautiful! Isn't she, Jes? I think she'll be the beauty of the family: Venetia looks too much like me.'

'She's very handsome,' Batchworth agreed, 'thought I don't accept the rest of your reasoning.'

'I must tell you,' Rosamund went on to her daughter, 'how much I'm enjoying being a grandmother. I never thought I would. I didn't care much for babies when I was your age, but these two I am prepared to dote on in the most foolish way. It must be encroaching age.'

'Yes, look how grey and bent she's getting,' Batchworth observed laughingly. Rosamund was as straight as a wand, and wore her foxy hair like a crown.

'Perhaps not bent, yet, but grey, certainly,' she said. 'My maid dresses the badger streaks underneath, but it takes longer and longer every morning.'

'And how is Cavendish?' Batchworth asked. 'Have you seen him recently?'

'He is coming up, isn't he?' Rosamund added.

'If he can tear himself away from his latest fancy,' Charlotte said, allowing herself to be diverted. 'Lady Caroline Gosling. She's the most beautiful girl he has ever seen in his life.'

'Another one?' Batchworth said, raising his eyebrows.

'This one may be more serious – she has a hungry mother. You may find yourself a grandmother again sooner than you looked for, Mama.'

'He's not of age yet,' Rosamund said, unperturbed. 'He can't offer without our permission.'

'It's only another few weeks,' Batchworth reminded her.

'Good God, is it?' Rosamund was startled. 'Yes, so it is. How time runs away! I was thinking he was still nineteen. Well, but Caroline Gosling is one of the Padstowe girls, isn't she? I suppose he's got to marry someone, sooner or later, and the Padstowes are perfectly respectable.'

'No money,' Batchworth reminded her.

'He'll have enough of his own,' Rosamund said easily. 'Anyway, I'm sure nothing will make him miss the start of the shooting, and at his age, out of sight is usually out of mind.'

'Talking of the twelfth,' Jes said, turning to Oliver, 'you must come to the gun-room some time and let me show you my new pair. In fact, why not stroll over there now? If our wives are going to talk marriage and babies, they won't need us.'

Rosamund hastily handed the baby back to the nurse and slipped her arm through Charlotte's. 'Nonsense. Charlotte and I are going straight to the stables – aren't we, love? First things first. We must decide what you're going to ride while you're here.'

'Nothing at all for the next few weeks,' Charlotte said. 'You forget how recently I was delivered. Doctor Abernethy forbids me horseback exercise until next month at the earliest.'

'Pho! What does he know? He's just a man and a doctor!'

'You sounded just like Grandmama then,' Charlotte laughed.

It was wonderful to be in the country, wonderful to be with her mother again, and the next few days flew by. Charlotte walked about the gardens, drove out in an ancient pony-phaeton which had belonged to Batchworth's mother, picnicked on the moors, played with her daughters, ate heartily, and every night slept the profound sleep that follows exercise in the fresh air.

But when the carriage arrived from Manchester the following week, and Fanny stepped out of it, Charlotte felt how much she had missed her since they both married. Fanny was the only friend of her own age and sex she had ever had. They had promised to correspond, but a few letters were all they had managed to exchange in two years. Somehow there was always so much to do. And this was the first time Charlotte had been north since her wedding, while Fanny had not been in London at all.

They hugged each other, laughed, looked, and hugged again. 'Oh Fanny! I've missed you! It's been so long!'

'Yes, but having babies takes up so much time, doesn't it? Dear Charley! I can't believe I'm really seeing you again! I was so afraid something would happen to stop you coming!'

'But let me look at you – you look so smart!' Charlotte cried. Fanny was the pinnacle of fashion, in a dress of spring green *gros d'orient*, the tight bodice banded with narrow velvet ribbon, the three-quarter sleeves finished with four rows of festoons in a darker green. The same festoons *en tablier* trimmed the three deep flounces of the skirt, and the cambric chemisette had delicate embroidery on the fullness of the sleeves, and lace edging the collar and cuffs. Her bonnet was of pink *gros de Tours* edged round the brim with white figured ribbon, while the inside was trimmed with pink and white silk flowers; and over her shoulders she wore a long Barège cashmere shawl, in one of the new Parisian designs, whose point almost reached the ground behind.

'I see you have your figure back,' Charlotte said. 'I hope I shall do as well. You look positively girlish.' But as she said it, her voice faltered a little, for Fanny's face looked thin, and when she stopped smiling for a moment, her expression was pinched and discontented. 'You are well?' she asked quickly.

The smile returned. 'Of course! When did I ever ail a thing?'

A sour-faced maid was descending from the other side of the carriage, and Charlotte looked at her in surprise. 'Is that your maid, Fanny?'

'Yes. Her name's Muntle.' She thrust her arm through Charlotte's and tugged her determinedly towards the house. 'I'm longing for a comfortable chat with you.

'But isn't your husband here?'

'He's coming later.'

A second carriage had just appeared, and Charlotte hung back. 'Oh yes, here he is.'

'No, that's just the nurse with the baby. Come on, Charley, don't dawdle.'

'Oh, do wait a moment, I long to see your baby!'

'You can see it later,' Fanny said carelessly. 'In any case, it's awfully plain. Kinder not to look at it, really.'

'Fanny, you can't call your baby "it"!'

'Well, he is rather an it, as it happens. You'll see. Besides, Philip called it "Lionel" – after his father, you know. Poor little thing! How could anyone call a helpless little baby "Lionel"? I suppose your babies are horrid pretty?'

'Very pretty and not at all horrid. You'll see later,' Charlotte said. 'I'll show you to your room first. Mama and Jes and Oliver are out riding until luncheon. They thought we might like to be alone at first.'

'Well, they were right. But let's go to your room – Muntle will want to be unpacking and we'll be in her way.' She was hurrying Charlotte into the house, and added *sotto voce*, 'Disagreeable creature. She disapproves of everything I do.'

'But what happened to Tibbet? Surely you didn't dismiss her?' Tibbet had been with Fanny ever since she came out.

Fanny made an equivocal face, and said in a lowered voice, 'She and Philip had a quarrel, so I had to send her away.'

'Your *maid* had a quarrel with your *husband*?' Charlotte said in disbelief.

'Oh, well, not a quarrel really, I suppose. But Philip didn't care for her. He said she was impertinent. So he chose Muntle for me instead. I'll tell you all about it later.'

Mystified, Charlotte led the way to her room. She and Oliver had a suite on the garden front, a large bedroom and two sitting-rooms, and to her own sitting-room she took her cousin, who, as soon as the door was closed, tore off her bonnet and threw it on a chair, stretched her arms out wide, and said, 'Oh, heaven, free at last! I want to run about like a mad thing and take the pins out of my hair and dance a jig. I can't do anything in front of Muntle, she's absolutely Philip's creature, and tells on me if I do the slightest thing he doesn't like!'

Charlotte sat on the windowseat, shaking her head in

wonder. 'Fanny, I can't believe you let your husband choose your maid for you – and a woman you don't like into the bargain.'

'Can't you? Then you must have a very different notion of marriage from most women, that's all I can say. What is a husband but to tyrannise over his wife? And what is a wife but to be slave to her husband's wishes?'

Charlotte almost smiled. 'I can't believe you mean that.'

Fanny, her face a little flushed, looked at her cousin with desperate eyes. 'Don't say that – that you can't believe me. I depended on you. You were my friend.'

'I still am, I hope.'

'I hope so too, for if I can't tell you, what is there left for me? It's all inside me like a boiling cauldron, and if I can't let out I shall go mad, or – or—'

'Fanny, darling, you can tell me anything, I promise you,' Charlotte said, alarmed. 'Come and sit down, and I'll listen as long as you like.'

But Fanny began walking impulsively up and down. 'I can't sit down, I must move. Oh Charley, I'm so miserable! I wish I'd never married him. I never was so taken in over anyone in my life! How is it you never told me what he was really like? You knew him before me. And you were in love with him yourself, once, weren't you?'

'I admired him,' Charlotte said, embarrassed by this turn. 'He's a very good man—'

'Oh, good!' Fanny interrupted as though the word goaded her. 'Yes, he's good! I'm told so every day, by everyone, how *good* he is and how *lucky* I am that he married me!'

'Fanny, what has happened between you? It can't be as bad as you think. You and Doctor Anthony have had a – a misunderstanding, perhaps – and—'

Fanny faced her, her expression hard. 'Will you listen to

me? Or will you shut your mind, and think like everyone else that Philip is a saint and an angel and that I must be mad and wicked not to be blissfully happy?'

'I'll listen,' Charlotte said. 'I'm sorry. What is it that's made you so unhappy?'

'Everything!' Fanny cried, and began her restless pacing again. 'Oh, I'm the luckiest of women, to be Mrs Philip Anthony – everyone tells me so! They wait after church on Sundays in the porch on purpose to tell me – all those simpering women on the committees who are half in love with him, though they'd never admit it to themselves. His seraglio, I call them. Oh, only in my own mind, of course. And doesn't he love it, having them all fawning on him, like dogs waiting for a biscuit, just hoping he will look at them, or smile. Nothing more than that, of course – naturally he's too high-minded, and so are they. That's part of the thrill, his icy propriety. How it makes them wriggle! And how they'd long to be in my place – the chosen one! How *lucky* you are, Mrs Anthony, they say to me, looking daggers because they think I'm not really worthy of him. It never occurs to anyone that he ought to feel lucky that I married *him*, and gave him my money to spend.' She turned abruptly to Charlotte. 'Doesn't it drive you wild that when you marry, all your money becomes your husband's, to do just as he likes with?'

'Oliver and I have a rather different arrangement,' Charlotte said. 'But you knew the law before you married, Fanny dear. And you don't look as though he keeps you short of money. That's a lovely gown, and it looks new.'

'He pays my mantuamaker's bills. He likes me to look smart.'

'Is that so bad?'

'Does Oliver choose your clothes?'

'Well, no, but—'

'Philip chooses mine. He chooses *everything*. If we

have a dinner-party, he decides the date, the guests, the seating plan, the menu – what I shall wear, what topics of conversation I may introduce. He decides which invitations we accept or refuse, whom I may visit and when. *He* decides; and he pays for everything. If want any money, I have to ask him, and tell him what I want it for, and if he doesn't approve, I can't have it.'

Charlotte felt awkward. 'It must be very hard for you, but I believe it is quite a usual arrangement for married women. But you have your pin money, I suppose—'

'Why suppose that?' Fanny said harshly. Charlotte was silent. 'No, if I had money in my pocket, you see, it might give me a little freedom, and that's the last thing he wants. Without money of my own I can't go anywhere or do anything. I'm a prisoner in my own house. I could climb out of the window and escape that way, but I'd have to come back eventually, wouldn't I, if I had no money? And then—'

A new thought struck Charlotte. 'Fanny – he doesn't – he doesn't hit you?'

'No,' Fanny said in a hard voice, 'not that. But there are other ways a man can punish you.' She made a small, despairing gesture. 'He's so cold, Charley; so cold!'

Charlotte didn't know what to say. She was half sure Fanny was exaggerating; but on the other hand, what did she really know about Anthony, except that he had disapproved of her, Charlotte, for being 'too mannish'? He had wanted to stop her from visiting the hospital or the slums, saying it was not proper for a lady – even though he had no right to object to anything she might wish to do. Was it not possible that marriage had given that managing strain in his nature the room to flourish to its full potential? But she could not yet quite believe in the monster that Fanny had described.

She said, 'When I think how self-willed you always

108

were, Fanny – you even used to get your way with Grandmama! I can't believe you don't have some of your own way now. Are you sure you're not exaggerating?'

'I haven't told you the half of it,' Fanny said, and suddenly she sat down beside Charlotte, and went on in a quiet voice which was much more affecting than her previous wildness. 'If you have a husband who indulges you, you can't think what it is like to be forbidden the slightest expression of your own self. A husband has absolute authority over his wife, and the law upholds it. That's the truth of the matter.' She looked at her cousin. 'Let me tell you about our lives together. Picture an evening of domestic happiness. He sits at the table reading and writing, and I sit by the fireside. I am permitted to read improving books – not novels, of course – or to sew. No singing, no music, because they disturb his study. Certainly no laughter, because that suggests improper thoughts are being entertained. No conversation, unless he wants it. No visitors, unless he invites them. I mayn't go out – ladies do no go out in the evenings without their husbands. If I get up to leave the room he says, "Where are you going, Fanny?" So there I sit; and tea comes in; and at a precise time he closes his book and says, "We will go to bed". You see? I mayn't even choose my own bed-time. I come and go by his clock, like a mill-hand.' She made a strange face. 'Do you know, that baby of his never cried. Imagine, a baby that doesn't cry! *He* forbade it.'

'But – during the day, when he's busy – don't you visit your friends?'

'I have a visiting-list. The wives of colleagues of his, mostly, or people he thinks will be useful to him. He knows who I visit, of course, because the coachman tells him. I can't go in a cab, because I haven't any money. And I can't go on foot, because I'm not allowed to walk unattended – Muntle or a footman or both must attend me – and *they* tell him.'

'Oh, poor Fanny!'

'The same people I visit, visit us – a sort of deadly rotation, like machinery wheels going round, grinding all the life out of it. And for lively entertainment we go to meetings together, and to church, of course – three times on Sundays—'

'Three?' Charlotte said. 'That does seem excessive.'

'That's what poor Tibbet said. Oh, not to Philip,' she added, seeing the question on Charlotte's lips, 'but to one of the other servants, who reported her to Philip. Philip called her up before him to rebuke her for her blasphemous talk, and she told him that too much religion was unhealthy and that what her mistress needed was a little fun now and then, and a great deal less preaching. So he dismissed her without a character.'

'Oh, Fanny!'

'My poor darling Tibbet, who'd been with me all those years! And I couldn't even give her any money to tide her over, because I haven't any.' Fanny's eyes were dangerously bright. 'The only thing that makes it tolerable, Charley, is that he's so busy, I see very little of him. He is out visiting his patients, and attending at the hospital, and going to medical board meetings; he's on a great many boards, you know. Everyone thinks him so very, very wonderful, and they think I must be the luckiest woman alive, to be married to such a clever, handsome, *good* man. "You are so very fortunate, Mrs Anthony," they say, and I have to smile as though I agreed.' She demonstrated a smile which looked more like a snarl.

Charlotte pressed her hand in helpless sympathy. Oliver had told her once that she had had a narrow escape in not marrying Anthony herself, but she had taken it as a joke – and a little male pique on his part that she had, for however brief a time, loved anyone but him. She thought of her life with Oliver, her freedom to do what she wanted which was only heightened by his support and protection. She could not imagine what it was to be in Fanny's predicament, but she could guess how hard it was. Fanny had had a childhood and young adulthood of great indulgence, had been a sought-after heiress and financially independent. It must be almost unendurable.

'But you're here now,' she said, hoping to offer a crumb of comfort. 'How is it that he has let you come here alone?'

'I might have been here two weeks ago,' Fanny said. 'Oh, that was the last straw! I'd been so looking forward to this, to spending the whole summer with Aunt Rosamund and Uncle Jes, and seeing you, and darling Cav, and riding on the moors and – oh, the freedom! I didn't think he'd be able to stop me doing things here, not in Uncle's house.' She shrugged. 'I suppose he knew that too – that's why he stopped me coming.'

'How did he stop you?'

'He said he had to stay in Manchester, and that it was not proper for me to come here without him. "Ladies do not go on house visits without their husbands." So I said that this was practically my home, and Aunt Rosamund was like a mother to me. And he said, "Yet she is not, in fact, your mother." And that was that. He made one excuse and then another for staying – I think he meant to steal the whole summer from me, bit by bit. But then, glory be, there was an outbreak of cholera in Jackson's Row, which started to spread towards us, and Sir George Hanbury said – actually in front of me – that Philip ought to send me and the baby out of town. Philip likes to keep in with Sir George because he's his senior at the hospital – so here I am! I never thought I would be so glad that we never moved away to the suburbs like everyone else. I like Hobsbawn House because it's where I was born, and Philip liked it because it was close to the centre so he could walk everywhere – and now I swear I shall never move if I can help it. If it weren't for the cholera, I wouldn't be here at all! He doesn't want me to see you. He disapproves of you, because of the things you wrote to me in your letters. He thinks you are a bad influence. Oh yes,' in response to Charlotte's enquiring look, 'he reads my letters – incoming and outgoing. Why do you think I stopped writing to you?'

'Have you told anyone else how things are with you? Surely Henry could do something? I know he's only your step-father, but he loves you so—'

'I can't tell him. It would break his heart. He's so happy with his new wife, and he thinks I'm happy too. How could I spoil that for him, when there's nothing he could do anyway?'

'But surely—'

'No! You must promise me not to tell anyone, Charley, not anyone at all. What would you tell them, after all? Philip doesn't beat me, or starve me, he doesn't get drunk, or gamble, or run about with loose women. All he does is keep control of his wife, and there's not a man in ten thousand would see anything wrong with that. And if you did persuade anyone to complain to Philip on my behalf, what do you think he would say? Do you think it would make things better, or worse?'

'Oh Fanny! I'm so sorry,' Charlotte said helplessly.

Fanny tried to smile. 'We had so much freedom, you and I, living together in that dear little house in Berkeley Street – do you remember, Charley, what fun we had? Oh, why did we ever want to change anything? But—' she shrugged, 'life is not like that, not for most women. Philip deeply disapproved of our living in Berkeley Street

112

together, you know. I see why, now – he thought it gave us dangerous ideas.'

There was a silence. Outside a crow glided down to settle in the top of the great black cedar on the lawn, folded its wings with deliberation, and gazed out over its wide territory. The sky was a hazy blue, and away to the left the moors were a purple smudge leading to the horizon.

In the end it was Fanny who spoke, with a little laugh. 'Well, now I have had my moan, and I feel a great deal better for it, I assure you. I shall now be cheerful and gay for the rest of my stay.'

Charlotte made one last effort, though it seemed hopeless. 'I suppose most women take comfort in their children,' she began, but Fanny's expression stopped her.

'Babies,' Fanny said witheringly. 'Are yours a comfort to you?'

'I'm very fond of them, and when they grow a little older, I'm sure I'll find great delight in them.'

'Perhaps *you* may,' Fanny said. 'Yours will grow up to be nice little girls, I dare say. Mine will just be a bigger horrible Lionel.'

'Fanny, your poor baby can't be horrible.'

'Can't he? You'll see.'

'And there'll be others—'

Fanny gave her an odd look. 'Will there?' Charlotte looked at her searchingly. 'I don't think,' Fanny said at last, 'that Philip cares very much about that sort of thing. He wanted a boy, to inherit everything – his father's estate and my mills and so on. And now he's got one – or at least, now he's got a Lionel,' she corrected herself with a curl of the lip, 'he doesn't—' She paused. 'We have separate rooms, of course,' she said lightly. 'We always have.'

Charlotte put her arms round her cousin, and Fanny leaned against her, and they were silent. Charlotte thought

113

of Fanny's radiant happiness when Philip Anthony had proposed to her, and how much in love she had been; and she thought of her own love for Oliver, and how glorious it was to be held in his arms every night, and how their passion for each other met and overlapped and combined. Had Fanny never known that bliss? She thought of Fanny's despairing cry, *he's so cold, Charley!* Probably she never had; and unless Anthony died and she married again, she never would.

Fanny said softly, 'We know so little about our husbands before we marry them. We aren't *allowed* to know anything, about the man to whom we must commit our lives, our fortunes – everything – for ever. It isn't fair.'

Charlotte had supposed, vaguely, that all babies had some charm; but little Lionel Anthony seemed to manage without. He was extraordinarily plain, especially considering his handsome father and pretty mother: his head seemed too large for his body and his features too large for his face; he was pasty and quite often spotty, his nose was a disagreeable shape, and he never smiled. He was extraordinarily inert, too, for a child of fifteen months: Venetia had walked at nine months and was talking well by a year old, but Lionel preferred to sit where he was put, mouth open, usually with a finger in his nose, and simply stare. He hardly ever spoke, though he did occasionally give vent to a shattering scream if a nurse tried to make him do something he didn't want to. Charlotte tried hard to feel sorry for him, rather than to dislike him as Fanny did, but her attempts withered when she found the child, on his feet for once, standing by Olivia's cot absorbedly spitting on her. As Fanny had said, he really was rather an "it".

Fanny evidently had no intention of having anything to do with him. She was like a child on holiday, wanting to be out of doors every minute, and playing games or making a noise every moment she was indoors. Everyone was happy to indulge her, and Charlotte could see that Rosamund and Jes were under the impression that her high spirits came from happiness, and were reassured. Charlotte was afraid that she was simply making the most of the time she had before Anthony arrived.

Oliver, inscrutable as ever, went along with the fun and expressed nothing in his face or manner; but after a few days he said to Charlotte, when they were in bed together, 'What's wrong with Fanny? She seems on the verge of hysteria.'

'She's happy to be here, that's all,' Charlotte said.

'That's not it,' Oliver said. Charlotte was in his arms, her head on his shoulder. '*This* is a happy woman,' he said, kissing her brow. He thought for a moment. 'Is Fanny ill?'

'No, why do you think so? Doesn't she look well?'

'Oh yes. But she behaves like someone with only a few months to live, determined to sup life's pleasures to the dregs while there's still time.' Charlotte was silent. 'Has she told you?'

'Yes – but it was in confidence.'

'Ah. Then you had better not tell me,' he said. She kissed him in gratitude for not pressing her. 'I'll tell you instead. I have a fair idea: she arrived here like a runaway, and never speaks of her husband, so I guess that the good Doctor Anthony is the root of the trouble. I always thought he was an insufferable prig and a monument of selfishness. Does he beat her?'

'No, indeed!'

'But there are other ways of being cruel.'

'You understand that?' Charlotte said, gratefully.

He chuckled. 'At the risk of sounding conceited, being London's most eligible bachelor for sixteen years taught

115

me a great deal about human nature.' Then he grew sober. 'Poor little Fanny. There is nothing anyone can do, of course. She had better take a lover.'

'Oh, how can you say such a thing!'

He drew her closer to him. 'I don't recommend it to you as a course of action, you understand. If you were ever even to look at a another man, I should consider it my fault and my failure.'

She lifted her mouth to his with a lovely gesture of surrender that quickened his passion. 'I'll never want anyone but you,' she said. But after a while her thoughts returned to her cousin. 'Poor Fanny. You don't seem to take her predicament seriously.'

'Oh, I do,' he assured her. 'But I'm afraid there is nothing in the world to be done about it.'

Charlotte felt very awkward when Doctor Anthony arrived at last, knowing what she knew. But he was smiling and affable, and expressed himself glad to see them all; and though Fanny instantly became quieter, she greeted her husband with a kiss, and smiled, and looked contented. There was nothing in the behaviour of either of them to jar, and the effort Charlotte made for her parents' sake became, in the face of such apparent normality, effortless. Two years of marriage had not changed Anthony: he was still handsome in that austere, almost unearthly way; though perhaps regular meals and a luxurious home had made him a little less insubstantial, and his clothes were now those of a wealthy and successful man. As the newcomer to the house he had the best right to talk, and he spoke about his work and the wider situation with sense and acuity. Oliver and Jes evidently enjoyed his conversation. Charlotte glanced at Oliver sometimes, wondering at his affability to this man. Of course he would never have betrayed Fanny's confidence by even the shadow of coolness, but one part of her wished he were not *quite* such a consummate actor.

On the second day they all went out riding together. Anthony kept no riding horses in Manchester – riding was one of the things Fanny had been obliged to give up, though her fortune could well have afforded the horses and stabling – but he enjoyed the exercise when he was at leisure, and was happy to be provided with a mount from Batchworth's stables. Rather than oblige anyone to stay behind to keep her company, Charlotte decided the time had come to defy Abernethy's orders, and at breakfast asked her mother for a horse. It was six weeks since Olivia was born, and the birth had been so easy she felt perfectly well and strong. Rosamund only said, 'You're sure?' and then nodded and talked of something else; Oliver she had acquainted with her decision already, and he had merely asked her to be careful and ride slowly. Fanny gave her a warm look and a little nod of delight that she would have the pleasure of her company.

But when they all rose from the table, Anthony manoeuvred to keep her back so that he could speak to her alone.

'I am not your physician,' he said, 'but as a medical man I must advise you *not* to ride with us today. It is much too soon, and you may harm yourself more than you know.'

Charlotte said politely, 'Well, but as you say, you are not my physician. Thank you for your advice, but I know my own state of health.'

Such a snub ought to have been enough for any normal person, but Anthony did not move out of her way. 'You may think you do,' he said calmly and firmly, 'but you have no medical training, and I'm afraid the little you have gleaned from books has given you a false idea of your understanding of these matters.' She was too astonished to interrupt him. 'Take my word for it that it would be very bad for you to take horseback exercise so soon after giving birth. I should certainly not have allowed Fanny to ride until three months after Lionel was born.'

Charlotte's control bent. 'I didn't know that Fanny ever rode now,' she said. 'I thought she had been obliged to give up riding altogether when she married.' She was immediately sorry, for to quarrel with him could not help Fanny.

A small spot of red appeared in his pale cheek. 'I'm sorry to see that your habit of saying anything that comes into your head has not modified with the years. I will ignore your last remark, and assure you that if I press you on this matter it is out of a sincere concern for your health, and nothing else.' Charlotte bit back the retort that sprang first to mind, and in her silence he went on, 'I wish I could tell you exactly what consequences to your health you risk by riding, but it would not be proper for me to use such language to you, or to mention by name parts of the body which a lady should never hear mentioned—'

'You may speak quite frankly to *me*, however,' Charlotte said tautly. 'I have heard them all before.'

He gave her a patient smile. 'No, duchess, no matter how many hospitals you may found, you are not a doctor; and though it may annoy you to know it, you never will be. I have told you many times before that to dedicate part of your fortune to relieving the poor is an admirable thing, but to involve yourself directly in their treatment—'

'Yes, you have told me, and I have always wondered by what right you presume to do so.'

'By the right – indeed, the *duty* – of any gentleman to protect a lady from what it is unseemly for her to know, or to see, or to do. God made us different for a purpose.'

'Oh, don't bring God into it!' she cried impatiently.

He raised his eyebrows. 'The violence of your language shows me that you know I'm right. Woman's part is to be gentle, innocent and meek; man's part is to protect and preserve that innocence. But we have strayed rather far from the point: I do most firmly advise and urge you not to ride on horseback with us today. It—'

'Sir,' Charlotte interrupted firmly, 'I am obliged to you for your concern, and in making up my own mind I shall give your advice the consideration it deserves.' Her choice of words gave him pause, and while he was deciding exactly what she meant by them, she added, 'Would you be so very kind as to allow me to pass?'

He stood back and let her go without another word. But he must have decided that she would take his advice, for when she came out of the house in her riding habit and a horse was led up for her, his brows drew down in an uncharacteristic frown. He said nothing more on the subject, but he treated her after that with a new coolness; and seeing Fanny look anxious, Charlotte hoped it would not rebound on her.

'What else would you do?' Oliver said when she confided the situation to him. 'Give up riding? Let the impudent puppy decide your regimen for you?'

Charlotte sighed. 'No, I suppose not. But perhaps I should have phrased myself more tactfully.'

'My observation of Philip Anthony is that he doesn't care in the least what women say; it is what they do that matters. If you had followed his orders, it wouldn't have mattered how you expressed yourself. As you have defied him, he resents you – golden words wouldn't alter that.'

'Perhaps you're right,' she said.

The following evening at dinner, the conversation came round to the cholera outbreak which had sent Fanny from

119

Manchester. 'It is not an epidemic,' Doctor Anthony said in reply to a question from Rosamund. 'It is endemic rather – the usual summer outbreak. Like the poor, we have it always with us; and I'm afraid we shall never be rid of it until we can pull down the dreadful places the poor live in, and let in some fresh air to blow away the poisonous vapours.'

'Do you still believe that cholera is caused by bad smells?' Charlotte said.

Anthony looked at her patiently. 'Are you about to expound Doctor Snow's opinions again?' he asked with a kindly smile.

'It is my opinion too,' she said, stung.

'You, however, are not a doctor. I'm afraid a lay opinion cannot be given any weight in a scientific discussion.' He looked round at the other men to gather their amusement at her womanish folly.

'There is nothing scientific about the opinion that bad smells are the cause of cholera,' Charlotte countered, copying his tone of voice.

He was unshakeable. 'That is not an opinion, that is a matter of fact.'

'Doctor Snow does not accept it as a fact.'

'Doctor Snow, however amiable, is not considered sound. *All* medical men of any repute accept the miasmic cause of disease.'

'The number of people who believe something does not guarantee that it is true,' Charlotte said. '*All* men once believed the world was flat. Some,' she added under her breath, 'still do.'

Oliver had a choking fit and had to restore himself with sips of wine.

'Do you think we shall have rain tomorrow?' Rosamund asked brightly. 'I thought the sky looked rather threatening at sunset.'

But Anthony was not ready to leave Charlotte's ignorance uncorrected. 'Leaving aside any medical argument, which it would be beyond a lay person to understand, it should be perfectly plain to mere common sense that it is the miasmas which breed cholera and typhoid and other diseases of the poor, precisely because they *are* the diseases of the poor. Those who live in wholesome environments do not commonly fall victim; and why else would these outbreaks always happen in the hottest part of the year, when the smells are at their worst?'

'But surely,' Charlotte said vehemently, 'experience shows that the measures taken to destroy the miasmas do nothing to prevent or check the disease. Burn all the tar and sulphur you like, and the poor in the back-slums still die like flies. Surely you must at least investigate other possibilities? If you do not keep an open mind, how many hundreds do you condemn to death?'

Now she had gone too far. Doctor Anthony drew a deep breath, and pressed his lips together hard, his eyes bright with unspoken retorts. At last he said, 'I think we should not continue this subject. It is not the thing for mixed company – or for the dinner-table.' He bowed in Rosamund's direction. 'My apologies, ma'am, for so far forgetting myself. You were speaking of the weather?'

Oliver gave Charlotte a speaking look, brimming over with amusement. *That puts you in your place!* Rosamund took up the cue from Anthony, and the subject turned. For the rest of the evening Anthony managed to avoid addressing Charlotte directly, and thereafter when he spoke to her it was with the grave sorrow a clergyman might use towards a felon condemned to the gallows. But he was much gentler and more tender towards Fanny, in order to point up the contrast as much as possible, and Charlotte was glad that her wickedness had had some good consequence.

For Fanny's sake, she behaved for the next few days with great circumspection, did not argue with the good doctor and tried to be as prettily feminine as she could. Her efforts were rewarded with a slight softening towards her. Charlotte was glad to observe it, for she hoped to persuade Anthony to let Fanny visit her in London; but when at last she broached the subject, she was comprehensively rebuffed. Cavendish had just arrived, and under the general liveliness and pleasure of greeting him, and the talk of London which inevitably resulted, Charlotte turned lightly to Anthony and said, 'I hope you and Fanny will come to London this winter and stay with us? There is a great deal going on in the scientific world which I'm sure would interest you, and it would give me great pleasure to be able to spend more time with Fanny. I am very much in want of female company.'

She had thought she had phrased the invitation very cunningly; that he would think Fanny's feminine influence must do her good. But he only said, 'Thank you, you are very kind, but it will be out of my power to leave my work.'

Out of the corner of her eye she saw Fanny look across at her. 'I'm very sorry to hear that. But perhaps in that case you will be able to spare me Fanny at least. If you are very much preoccupied with work, perhaps you will not mind if Fanny comes to me—'

'That will not be possible,' he said firmly. 'I could not think it proper for any wife to go so far from home without the protection and countenance of her husband. And Fanny,' he added, looking at her, 'would not wish it. Would you, my dear?'

Fanny did not answer. Her face was perfectly expressionless, and after a moment she bowed her head. Anthony might take this for consent if he pleased, but Charlotte had seen the gleam of tears in Fanny's eyes which she had lowered her head to hide.

The photographic portrait was a great success. It showed Lucy seated in a small gilt chair, with baby Olivia in her lap, the flowing baby-robes mingling with the wide skirts of Lucy's gown; Charlotte stood behind her, resting one hand on Lucy's shoulder.

'It would have been perfect if we could have had Rosamund in it too,' Tom said. 'We must try next time she and Batchworth are in London.'

Lucy was examining the picture with great attention. 'It is an excellent likeness,' she said judiciously.

'It's a *perfect* likeness,' Tom said, amused. 'It *is* you – just as the reflection in a glass is you. Haven't I explained to you?'

'Yes, yes, at great length,' Lucy said hastily. 'All the same, it is a very good likeness indeed. What do you think of it, Danby?'

'Any picture of you gives me pleasure,' he said. 'But I think I would still prefer an old-fashioned painting in all the colours of life, done by an old-fashioned human being, rather than a senseless machine.'

'Luddite!' Tom said affectionately. 'A painting is never a true likeness, though – the character of the artist always comes through and alters the image.'

'Well, but one can at least bribe an artist,' Lucy said, 'to make one look prettier and younger. Your camera is too truthful for vanity.'

'No artist, however skilled, could make you look lovelier,' Danby said firmly. There followed a brief silence as his words were analysed.

'I will take that as a compliment,' Lucy said kindly. 'Did you tell me that you can make copies of this photograph – exact copies?'

'One can print as many as one wants, very easily,' Tom said. 'That's the benefit of this method over the Daguerreotype. You see—'

'I should like another. Framed like this.'

'You shall have it,' Tom said.

Some days later Lucy went again to the mews to visit Parslow. This time a groom told her that Mr Parslow was still in his bed, but that if her ladyship would condescend to wait, or better still to come back later, he would go up and help Mr Parslow to get up and dress himself.

'On no account,' Lucy said. 'Come, fool, out of my way. I've tended more sick people than you've groomed horses. Go about your duties, and leave me to mine.'

Parslow's sitting-room had become tolerably familiar to her now, but she had never been into his bedroom. She did now, and found it spare to the point of bleakness. It was a little chamber nine feet by six, lit only by a small square skylight in the roof. Here was the same wood panelling on the walls, the same bare floorboards; a corner railed off with a curtain, behind which, presumably, clothes were hung; a narrow bed with grey blankets, and beside it a wooden stool bearing a tin cup. The only thing of luxury in the room was a saddle on a bracket on the wall opposite the bed: a fine saddle, of the best leather, lovingly polished to a dark, supple gleam; Parslow's own saddle, which Lucy had had made for him, oh, it must be twenty-five years ago. He would not leave it in the saddle-room, in case some other groom had the impudence to use it.

Parslow was lying in bed propped on two pillows, staring up at the skylight. He tried to struggle upright when Lucy appeared at the door, but he was too weak, and had to desist, gasping for breath.

'Be still, fool,' she said. 'Do you think I want you to get up?' He looked at her with stricken eyes, and she tried to

124

make a joke. 'You are more decent lying down, besides. Would you get out of bed and show me your night-gown?' He didn't smile, and to her anguish she saw a tear gather in his eye and roll over onto his gaunt cheek. 'Don't,' she said. 'Please don't. I can bear anyone's tears but yours.' She removed the tin cup from the stool and sat down. His face was the colour of putty, his lips mauvish-blue; but his dark eyes seemed to give life to his face, and where there was life, she thought, there must be hope. 'So perhaps now you will let me call a doctor to you?'

'I have seen one,' he said. Shortness of breath made him abandon the forms between them.

'Who did you see?'

'Cotton. He gave me – a potion.'

'What potion? Where is it?'

'Under the bed,' he said.

She looked, reached under, drew out the bottle, read the label. *Digitaline*. Extract of foxglove. Expensive stuff. Cotton must have known she would pay. 'Cotton is a good man,' she said gently, 'but he is not the greatest expert in this field. Will you let me call someone else – a specialist?'

Now he smiled. 'What use?' he said.

'You are not qualified to say,' she rallied him.

'If it will please you,' he said.

'Very well.' She leaned towards him encouragingly. 'I will find the best man there is, and bring him here as soon as possible, and he will soon have you on your feet.' She broke off. Parslow's hand, resting on the blanket, had moved to touch hers, on which she was leaning. She looked down for a moment, and then she took up his hand and held it. Tears were making her throat hurt, and she could not speak. While she struggled for control, he looked away, kindly; looked at his little window.

'There's a tree out there,' he said. 'I can see the leaves against the sky. It tells me the weather.'

She looked too; green and gold shifting against a background of blue. A fine day, with a little breeze. A good riding day. The horses would be lively, and the breeze would keep the flies off.

'A Richmond day,' Parslow said. He had been following her thoughts. When the weather was too good for ambling in the park, they had liked to go down to Richmond where it was possible to gallop.

'Too good for Richmond,' she said, mastering her voice. 'We should go down to the country.'

'You should be there now,' Parslow said. 'Wolvercote. You should go.'

'And leave you?' she said. She sat in silence for a while, holding his hand, her thoughts roving back over a long life in which he had always been present. Why had he given her his life like that? A man must work; but he could have been a stud groom, with a home and wife and family of his own. In a top stud a head man could make enough money to lay some by and perhaps even retire with a little place of his own. Parslow was the best man with horses she had ever known, and he could have had any position in the kingdom. But he had stayed with her, and all he had now was this bare room.

He said, 'I have been happy serving you.'

She looked at him. He had been following her thoughts again. She said abruptly, 'Why did you stay? You might have been rich.'

'And leave you?' He gave her her words back, with the gleam of a smile. And then he said, 'I love you.'

He must not say that, she must not hear it, it was not a possible thing for him to say to her. The words shocked her like electricity, penetrated too deeply, lodged like barbs too far in ever to be got out. She couldn't speak; and she couldn't withdraw her gaze from his. But his look asked nothing of her but that she be there to be looked at. Most people use those words not as a gift but as a demand, she thought; but Parslow's love was service, as it had been all his life. And in a moment he withdrew his gaze, and looked again at the window, and drew away his hand, too, releasing her. Making it easy for her. And then she knew how truly she could not do without him. It had been a form of words before; now it was reality. *Don't leave me*, she thought.

At last he said, 'What's in the basket? Not more pork jelly.'

'Calves-foot,' she heard herself say in a surprisingly steady voice. 'It's good for you. And some port wine. And this.'

She drew out the framed photograph and put it in his hands. He looked for a long time, a smile growing on his blue lips. 'It's very fine,' he said at last. 'It's a photograph, isn't it? A calotype, I think they call it.'

'It's for you. They can make copies of these things. I had this one made for you, to keep.'

'Thank you, my lady,' he said. 'I shall always treasure it.'

Always. Yes, he would get better. And *my lady*. Normality resumed its flow. Parslow, her groom, was ill, but she would get the best doctor to him – she never stinted with good servants – and he would be well again and everything would be all right. It was not possible that he had said what she thought he said. She must have imagined it. She chatted a little, about the family news and little bits of local gossip, and then at last she left, promising to come again tomorrow, with the best doctor in London.

It was very early the next morning that one of the grooms came up to the house, cap in hand, face twisting with anxiety and misery. Denton knew his duty. He sent for Weedon, and dispatched her at once to her ladyship, and sent a message at the same time to Lord Theakston. Danby in his dressing-gown arrived in Lucy's room to find her almost dressed, so rapidly had she responded.

'My dear, wait until I'm dressed. I'll go with you.'

'No, Danby. Let me go alone. Send for Cotton, will you?' She looked at his anxious face. 'I shall be all right.'

'Lucy, I'm so sorry.'

She tried to smile at him, but couldn't. 'Don't be kind to me, or I can't manage. Please, darling, let me alone for a while.'

So it was alone that she went to the mews, through the early morning sounds of waking birds and horses, of brooms on cobbles, and milk churns, and the postman's cane rapping. The cool air smelled of dying leaves, for summer was almost over, and the plane trees rustled in the early breeze. That was the tree he could see from his bed, she thought, hurrying under its flickering shadow.

She had hoped the groom was mistaken – what did he know, after all, of such things? There were two others, huddling together in Parslow's sitting-room, talking, and she drove them out with a savage tongue. In the little bedroom, in the narrow bed, Parslow lay just as she had left him, propped on the pillows, the photograph firmly gripped in his hand, his lips faintly smiling. Surely he was only sleeping? She could see the gleam of his dark eyes under his eyelids – they were not quite closed. She hurried to him and touched his hand; but it was cold.

She cried out: it seemed such an affront. One of the grooms, who had been lingering, came to the door in alarm. 'Go away! Go and get Doctor Cotton. *Go away!*'

He withdrew hastily. Lucy sat down on the stool as she had sat yesterday, and tried to recreate the scene. *Don't leave me.* But Parslow was not there. She wished she could cry, for the pain in her throat was unendurable.

CHAPTER SIX

The sky was grey but high, and the wind, though strong, was warm. Aglaea could see no reason to put off their walk.

'Perhaps the promenade won't be so crowded as it was yesterday.'

'Hm? Oh, yes, it was crowded,' Jemima replied absently. Aglaea looked at her covertly as she tied on her bonnet. Since they had come back from London, Jemima had not seemed her usual self. She had always been quiet, but her quietness seemed less serene, more thoughtful than before. Aglaea hoped the excitements of the trip hadn't made her dissatisfied with their normal routines. They had a very small circle of friends and few social engagements, and that had seemed to suit Jemima as much as it did Aglaea. But of course Aglaea had her painting, which occupied most of her energies, mental and physical. Jemima had no such all-absorbing interest. Walking with Aglaea, sewing and reading were her only activities, varied only by playing on the piano sometimes in the evening.

She wondered if she were being selfish towards her companion. It suited *her* to remain retired, but Jemima was younger, and perhaps longed for social amusement. They never discussed such things together: their talk was always impersonal, and their feelings were always kept hidden from each other as from the rest of the world. But Jemima did seem less contented since they had come back from London, and Aglaea wondered suddenly if she was thinking of Mr Underwood. They had not seen him since breaking their engagement with him that day in London; since they had come back to Scarborough, cards had been left on both sides, but there had been no meetings. Had he been offended, or discouraged by Jemima's preferring John Anstey's invitation? It was natural for Jemima to want to see her childhood friend, who was almost a brother to her, while she had the chance; but perhaps Underwood misunderstood the relationship. Since Jemima and John were not directly related by blood, he may have thought John a rival.

She ought to make an effort to be sociable, Aglaea decided; and if they did not meet Mr Underwood soon, she resolved to give a dinner party and invite him, for Jemima's sake.

They set out on their walk, and Aglaea soon turned from every other thought to contemplation of the sea. It had been whipped up by the wind into short, steep waves, which pounded on the beach with a noise like thunder, followed by a long, hollow rattle as pebbles were sucked down the backwash. Foam was blowing off the crests in white clouds like soap-suds, and the gulls were scudding about, screaming with excitement. The colours, she thought, were magnificent: grey sky and grey sea contained to a painter's eyes so many tints and subtle shades that it was like spreading a feast of delicacies before a gourmet. She could never understand those people who went abroad to Greece and Egypt and Turkey in search of strong sunlight and blue skies and exotic foliage to paint. Those bright, clear primary colours were to her as coarse as they were uninteresting. In this one stretch of the North Sea there was all the variety and richness she would ever need.

The strength of the wind had certainly deterred most

of the usual strollers, and those that had ventured out seemed more intent on getting along, managing their skirts and keeping their hats, than lingering and chatting. A few nods were all they collected until they had got the length of their walk and turned back. Then they saw a man approaching, bent into the wind with a hand on his hat-brim, but looking at them under it, obviously intending to accost them.

'Oh dear, now who is that?' Aglaea muttered.

'It's Childie!' Jemima cried, the old name startled out of her. The gentleman reached them and took off his hat, not without a certain relief, and bowed. The wind whipped his hair at once into mad disarray.

'Good day to you! I might expect to find delicate females at home on such a day, but I see you are intrepid walkers. You have the promenade almost to yourselves.'

'Good morning, Mr Anstey,' Aglaea said. 'We didn't see any reason to be put off by a perfectly warm and pleasant wind. But it *has* got stronger since we started out,' she allowed.

'Yes, and the sky is darkening,' John added. 'I'm afraid it will rain.'

'We have just turned back,' Aglaea said; but the sky had darkened more rapidly than she had realised, and it looked as though they wouldn't get home without a soaking.

'I think we'd better find shelter,' Jemima said.

'The tea-room seems to be the nearest place,' John said, looking round. 'Perhaps I may have the pleasure of escorting you there?'

Aglaea would sooner have got wet and gone home to her own parlour, but remembering her resolve to provide Jemima with more entertainment, she accepted Anstey's offer graciously.

He turned into the wind with them, struggled briefly

with his hat, and then gave up, clutching it in his hand as he offered an arm to each of them, and hurried them along towards the tea-room, even as the first fat drops of rain splattered against the paving and made dark circles on their sleeves.

Inside it was a haven of quietness after the roaring and pounding. John ushered them to a corner table by the window. There were only two other parties in the room – everyone else must have seen the worsening weather in time to hurry home or back to their hotels.

'And now,' Jemima said when they had settled themselves, 'you can explain how you came to meet us so completely unexpectedly on the promenade, Mr Anstey. It was the merest chance, of course?'

'No chance about it! I called at your house, and your maid said I would find you here. I came to Scarborough on business, but I couldn't leave without paying my respects, could I?'

'Of course not,' Jemima said. 'Well, tell us all the news from York.'

'Let me see,' John Anstey said, screwing up his face. 'The kitchen chimney of the Black Swan caught fire on Monday so they've only been able to serve cold food all week. Makepeace's have York Tan gloves on sale at half the price. Willans's wall-eyed roan kicked the dashboard out of a gig and lamed itself. And there's a *killing* bonnet in Mrs Pomfret's window, with a perfectly *sweet* feather and the most *delicious* ribbon trimming!'

'Clown!' Jemima laughed.

Aglaea said, 'You are such a humorist, John. Is all the family well, that's all we need to know?'

'Of course they are. Wouldn't I have told you straight away, Aunt, if it was otherwise?'

'Nevertheless, what did you come to Scarborough

133

for? I never knew your father or your uncle to have business here.'

'Oh, very well, you have me cornered,' John said, throwing up his hands. 'I came out of pure whim, having nothing to do at home and wanting a change of scene. I've no excuse but idleness and boredom. Father trained the business to run so well that I'm only in the way if I go into the offices; Uncle Jack runs everything else, Aunt Mary runs the house, and my children are the property of the nursery and brought to me once a day only, scrubbed and trussed and meek as sacrifices, to lisp "Good night, Papa", before they are whisked away to bed.'

'You should have a house of your own, an estate to run,' Aglaea said. 'There's no need at your age to be living at home.'

'Not without a wife,' John said. 'Who would give orders to my servants and look after my children? No, being at home is the only thing for now; but there's no doubt it saps the manly fibre to have nothing to do. Unless I go into politics, for which I've no fancy, I am doomed to wander the earth like a will-o'-the-wisp, without direction or purpose.'

'You're very substantial for a fairy,' Jemima observed.

'The best phantoms have all the appearance of solidity,' John assured her. 'That's why they frighten people. One would hardly be frightened by a little flickering dab of light, would one?'

'I'd find it hard to be frightened by you at all.'

'Ah, but wait until I start prophesying. First I hoot like an owl—'

At this point his performance was interrupted by a polite 'Ahem!' and they all looked round to see Mr Underwood and his sister standing by their table. 'I hope we don't interrupt,' Mr Underwood said wistfully.

134

'We were caught by the rain, and saw you through the window looking so cosy—'

'We meant only to shelter here until the rain passes off,' Mrs Pownall said almost simultaneously, 'but could not deny ourselves the pleasure of paying our compliments—'

Aglaea said as cordially as she could, 'Won't you please join us?'

'Oh, but we interrupt a family party,' Mrs Pownall said deprecatingly, even as she took the seat John had pulled out for her. 'As you have Mr John Anstey with you, you would perhaps prefer not to be disturbed?'

Jemima noticed that, despite having been 'caught by the rain', Mr Underwood was provided of a very large and stout umbrella, which had successfully kept them dry, except about the hems; and concluded that their arrival at the table was no more accidental than John's had been. Evidently Underwood was still in love with Aglaea, and Jemima hastened to make amends for her actions in London.

'No, indeed,' she said quickly. 'We are very glad to share John with you. He has been complaining of boredom, with only us to talk to.'

A quick glance flickered between brother and sister. 'Oh, then, perhaps I may be so bold as to beg the favour of your attendance at a small party tomorrow evening, Mrs Morland, Miss Skelwith *and* Mr John Anstey?' Mrs Pownall said. 'It is nothing but a little musical evening, with supper, and everyone holds themselves quite ready upon any day this week, if tomorrow should not happen to be convenient to you, Mrs Morland. But your skills upon the pianoforte are so valuable that we could not fix on anything of the sort, you know, until we could be sure you would be there.' She gave a little laugh. 'It would be a musical evening without music if you and dear Miss Skelwith could not be present.'

John caught Jemima's eye during this fulsome speech, and his eyebrow climbed so expressively that Jemima had difficulty in keeping her face straight. But she must do her best for Aglaea. 'I'm sure I should like it very much. What do you say, John?'

'I am very grateful for the invitation, ma'am, and will accept with pleasure. A little music is just what I need to drive away the cobwebs. What evening do you have free, Aunt Aggie?'

'Tomorrow will do very well,' Aglaea said, with an inward sigh. She had no particular wish to spend the evening in that way, but as it was evident that Underwood was still in love with Jemima, the sooner they all got together the better.

The weather was inclement the following evening, so John called for Jemima and Aglaea in a cab, and they drove the short distance to Mr Underwood's house on the upper side of town. Mrs Pownall, splendid in magenta silk and a much beribboned lace cap, greeted them effusively, and ushered them into the drawing-room, where the rest of the party was assembled. 'Just a small party – and all old friends – we know your retiring habits, dear Mrs Morland, and your preference for quiet, intimate evenings. And indeed, this is just the sort of small party of close friends that Frederick prefers, too,' she added, smiling fondly at her brother.

Including themselves, the party numbered twelve, all old acquaintances, if not to Aglaea precisely old friends. As they were the last to arrive, they were soon called in to supper, a meal of great elegance, quietly served by excellent servants. Aglaea thought what a good establishment this would be for Jemima, and set herself to being as agreeable as possible to Mr Underwood, who had been placed next to her at the table. Intrigue was not in her nature, but she thought she did very well when Mr

Underwood, looking down the table at Jemima, who had been seated next to John, remarked, 'Miss Skelwith seems on very easy terms with Mr John Anstey. He makes her laugh a great deal.'

'They played together as children.' Aglaea told him. 'Jemima regards him quite as a brother.'

'Indeed? But he is a widower in good circumstances, I understand. Perhaps such an establishment as he could offer might tempt Miss Skelwith? Of course, she would not wish to leave you without a companion—'

'I would never stand in her way if she wished to marry.'

'Indeed, I do all possible justice to your generous spirit. But she would want to know, if she did think of marrying, that you would not be the sufferer.'

'I'm sure she does not think of marriage. But if – when – she does, when the right offer is made her, my situation will not come into it. She knows I am perfectly happy alone.'

Mr Underwood did not seem as much cheered by this reassurance as she had meant him to be; but the strain of talking on such a subject was telling on Aglaea, and she lapsed into silence, watching the effect of the candlelight flowing over the faces leaning inwards towards each other over the table, and wondering if she could do it justice in a painting. It would have to be oils, of course: watercolour would never do for the density of the background darkness . . .

After supper, in the drawing-room, Aglaea was led to the pianoforte, and Mr Underwood stationed himself to turn for her. She played a sonata and everyone listened in a silence which betokened appreciation in some and eupepsia in others. Then Jemima was begged for a song: she complied with good humour, but would not play more than one, for she knew that there were others present who, if they were not better musicians than her, were at least much more eager to show off. Others took their turn, while she sat with John at the back of the room and managed some whispered conversation. Mr Underwood stationed himself at Aglaea's side, but Jemima noticed that he looked at her from time to time, and wondered if he disapproved of her whispering, and tried to do it more circumspectly.

Eventually tea was brought in, the musical part of the evening was abandoned, and conversation broke out; and soon after that, people were taking their leave. It was still raining, and John asked Mrs Pownall if she would send a servant out to look for a cab.

'Oh, there is no need for a cab, I'm sure,' Mrs Pownall said quickly. 'The Alcotts and the Cromptons both go by your part of town. They would be very glad to take you home. Pray give me a moment and I will go and ask them.'

Soon Mrs Alcott, one of Mrs Pownall's greatest bosom-bows, came over to where John and Jemima were standing. Smiling and gushing, she said, 'Dear Miss Skelwith, of course we should be delighted to take you up in our carriage. Not at all. Pray don't mention it. Not the least trouble in the world! Only too pleased. The carriage is at the door now, indeed. Do allow us to be of use.'

In all the bustle, Jemima and John found themselves at the door with the Alcotts – Mr, Mrs and Miss – but without Aglaea. The hall seemed full of people, none of them Aglaea, all kissing each other simultaneously and saying goodbye in refined shrieks in order to be heard over the hubbub. Jammed in the doorway and holding up the traffic, Jemima cried, 'Oh, but Aunt isn't here. Pray wait, Mrs Alcott. We can't go without Mrs Morland.'

'Oh dear, Miss Skelwith, pray come along, our carriage is holding up all the others. Mrs Crompton will

138

bring Mrs Morland home. Did you not understand the arrangement? Indeed, there would not be good room for her in ours, with Fanny as well. That's right. Mr Anstey, will you take a forward seat with Mr Alcott? It is only a short journey, so I don't fear to ask you. Ah, thank you! You see, Miss Skelwith, we should never have sat four across. It is cramped as it is – though Fanny is very small, and you are as slim as a fairy, I'm sure – but with these full fashions – oh dear, Fanny, pray mind my head! Sit forward, child, or you will pull my pins out! Miss Skelwith, was that your foot?'

Aglaea was not aware of the manoeuvring that went towards separating her from Jemima and John. She had been talking politely to Mrs Pownall when she realised that the room was emptying and her companions were nowhere to be seen. She said, 'I beg your pardon, I had better find Jemima. I suppose John has gone to find a cab?'

'I'll go and see,' Mrs Pownall said, and left the room. The noise from downstairs subsided, the voices thinned, and at last with a final sound of the front door closing there was silence. Mrs Pownall came back with her brother.

'Mrs Morland, I'm so sorry, there seems to have been a misunderstanding,' Mrs Pownall said, looking rather conscious. 'Mrs Alcott has taken Miss Skelwith and Mr Anstey home, and Mrs Crompton was to have made room in her carriage for you, but unfortunately in the confusion the Cromptons have gone without you. I do apologise! I would not have you inconvenienced for the world! You must allow me to have our carriage got out to take you home.'

'There's no need for that,' Aglaea said. 'A cab will do very well.'

'Oh no, I could not allow it! Besides, it rains very

heavily,' Mrs Pownall said. 'I'm sure a cab is not to be found on such a night. It is no trouble at all, I assure you, to have the horses put to. I will go and give the order. No, Frederick, I will do it. Pray stay here and talk to Mrs Morland. Do sit down and be comfortable, Mrs Morland, and I shall have the carriage brought round as quickly as possible.'

When she and John arrived home, Jemima sent the sleepy servant to bed, and went into the sitting-room to wait for Aglaea. The rain had eased, and John thought it would stop completely in a while. 'Then I can walk back to the hotel,' he said. 'No need to call a cab for that short journey.'

They chatted companionably for a few minutes, and when Aglaea did not soon arrive, they supposed she had been caught with the Cromptons in the interminable mill of goodbyes. 'It's a strange thing how people who have been together all evening and talked themselves to a stand-still suddenly come to life again when their carriage arrives,' John said. 'As soon as they are on the brink of departing, they think of a thousand things they simply *must* say.'

'And stand about uncomfortably in the hall for half an hour, when they could have been sitting comfortably in the drawing-room,' Jemima agreed.

'Half an hour! Yes, it might be, and you mustn't get chilly in that thin gown,' John added. 'Let me stir up the fire.'

He poked up the flames and added some more coal from the scuttle, and they sat down on the sofa together and went on talking. It was only when the clock struck the hour that they realised how time had passed.

'What can have happened to her?' Jemima said. 'You don't suppose there's been an accident?'

'No, I'm sure not,' John said. 'It's such a short journey, if anything had happened they'd have sent a message. They will have been talking and forgotten the time, that's all – as we have.'

'It's so comfortable talking to you, the minutes fly past. But it's very bad of Aunt not to think how we would worry about her.'

'It won't be *her* chat that's holding them up,' John said with a smile. 'But don't worry – I'll stay with you until she comes.' She looked doubtful, and he added, 'We are very old friends. I'm sure no-one would think it improper.'

She laughed. 'Oh, it wasn't that – I was only worrying about Aunt. Of course no-one would think it improper for you to stay. We are almost like brother and sister.'

'Are we?' John asked seriously. He met her eyes, and suddenly she found herself blushing again in that unexpectedly youthful way. 'I don't think of you as a sister.'

'Don't you?' she asked in a small voice.

'Not at all,' he said. 'Ever since I saw you at Morland Place in June I've been thinking about you, but not as a sister – not in the least. I went to London on purpose to see you – didn't you guess? And then I came here to see you, too, to be sure of what my feelings really are.' Jemima seemed to be holding her breath, and he said gently, 'Shall I tell you what they are?'

She was suddenly nervous. 'John—'

'I have fallen in love with you,' he said seriously. 'It was such a strange thing – knowing you so well all those years, and then suddenly seeing you so differently, as if you had been lit up by a great flash of light. You have always been dear to me, but now you are so very much more than that. I'm happy every minute I'm with you – and I have been increasingly hopeful that you feel the same.'

There seemed to be a necessity for her to answer that. 'I'm happy when I'm with you, too,' she said.

He put his head a little on one side and said, 'But?'

'What do you mean?'

'You seemed as though you were going to add some caveat.'

'I don't know what you want me to say,' she said. She felt confused, and her heart seemed to be pounding in a peculiar way, as though she had been running. But she hadn't run since she was a child – a child back at Morland Place, running about the fields and climbing trees with Childie Anstey – a wild little girl with rough hair and torn skirts. That was so long ago. Before – before the Other Things had happened.

John reached out and took her hand. His hands were warm and strong, but hers was cold, like a little cold stone he held. 'I see I must speak more plainly. I love you, and I want to marry you. I am a widower with three children, which may perhaps count against me; but I have enough income to support a wife in reasonable comfort, with enough servants to be sure the children need never be a nuisance to you.'

'I love children,' Jemima said; she sounded as if she were sleepwalking.

'I'm glad to hear it,' he smiled. 'Loving children is a good start towards loving adults. I know you're fond of me. Could you ever love me more particularly, do you think?' No answer. 'That wasn't a rhetorical question,' he said, gently teasing. 'I'm sorry, I didn't think this would come as such a complete surprise to you! I won't hurry you – of course you will want time to think about it. But can you just tell me, is there any hope for me?'

'Oh John,' she said, in a despairing sort of tone. The effect on him would have been comical, if it had been anyone else. His face fell and he began to withdraw his hand in such disappointment that she grabbed for it and took it back. 'No, please, don't look like that. I do like you very much. I – I *love* you, indeed.'

'But as a brother,' he said, his voice flat.

'No! I mean, I don't know. How can I know? I don't know anything about – about love, and – and – all that sort of thing.'

He looked at her with enormous tenderness, mingled with pain and hope. He thought of Nicholas Morland, her former guardian, and remembered the whispers and half-understood gossip that had come to him in snatches over the years. He did not know what her life had been like after she disappeared inside Morland Place in virtual imprisonment; he did not know what she might have suffered, or how it might have altered her view of men and marriage. He felt helpless, and angry. If Nicholas Morland had not been already dead, he'd have wanted to kill him; but that wouldn't have helped Jemima now.

'I'll be patient,' he said, folding her hand in his and holding it against his chest. 'Take as much time as you like. I love you dearly and I will always be kind to you, and if you feel you can't marry me – well, I'll still love you, and we'll be friends. But life can hold so much more, dear Jemmy. If you would marry me, I could make you very, very happy – happier than you have ever been or imagined being. So will you think about it?'

'Yes,' she said. Her hand was growing warmer now, and it felt good, safe, wrapped up in his. 'I will think about it. And – thank you.' He smiled, lifted her hand to his lips and kissed it, and then gave it back to her. 'John, you won't – go away?' she said, suddenly nervous.

'I've already told you, we shall always be friends, whatever happens.' And at that moment, perhaps fortunately, they heard carriage wheels outside. 'That will be Aunt Aggie at last. What a time she's been!'

* * *

Aglaea didn't know whether to be angry or distressed. She had been on the verge of insisting on a cab after all, or even walking home, rather than accept the Underwood carriage; but common sense and a lifelong habit of suppressing her feelings and wishes had prevailed. They had parted civilly; she wondered, on reflection, whether Underwood had even understood how much he had offended her. It was difficult for her to gauge the effect of her incorrigible reticence and gentleness on others.

'Call me Frederick!' he had cried. He had kissed her hand, clasped it, called her by her Christian name – he had even fallen to his knees. The memory of it made her blush.

'Mr Underwood, you forget yourself,' she had protested, adding – or at least she had meant to add – something about his being the admirer of Jemima. She always thought a great deal more than she said, and often in retrospect was unsure what she had actually said out loud and what she had only planned inside her head to say. But she had accused him – she thought she *had* managed to get the words out – of being inconstant, of switching his affections lightly from Jemima to her simply because Jemima had preferred to spend a day in London with her childhood companion. She thought of Jemima's trusting nature, and how hurt and disappointed she would be by her lover's defection, and had spoken very sharply.

But he had hardly heeded her, declaring his love, his devotion, his admiration, his longing to take her to wife. It was her, Aglaea, that he had been in love with all this time: he had never swerved or wavered since the first moment he had set eyes on her. That was his story. Had she been mistaken? Well, it hardly mattered now. He had asked her – begged her – to marry him, and babbled some nonsense about Mrs Pownall's being willing to move out of the house at any time and set up her own establishment if that should be Aglaea's wish. That was when Aglaea's thoughts had finally moved from Jemima's disappointment and Underwood's perfidy to contemplation of what was actually going on. Brother and sister had planned this, had manoeuvred the whole episode to leave her alone with Underwood so that he could make his declaration.

And what a declaration! She looked at him, and saw a not ill-favoured middle aged man in a ridiculous posture, a spot of colour in his cheek, his eyes bright, his mouth trembling. A dignified man making a fool of himself – and of her. In the end she had been forced to break away from him and pull the bell herself to convince him she wanted to leave. Then he had stumbled to his feet, breathing hard, and they had been locked in a most uncomfortable silence for some dreadful minutes until the door opened and Mrs Pownall came in. When she saw the look that passed between brother and sister, *that* was when she had wanted to walk out of the house; and she rather feared that accepting the use of the carriage had given Underwood hope. She had insisted on going home alone – she had carried her will that far – but the journey was too short for her to have composed herself by the time she walked in at her own front door.

She found Jemima and John in the sitting-room. They looked at her with concern, and Jemima hurried to her to help her take off her bonnet.

'Your hands are shaking!' Jemima discovered. 'Are you all right? What's happened? Come and sit down by the fire. John – some brandy! In the dining parlour, the cupboard by the chimney.'

'I'm all right,' Aglaea said, but faintly. 'I have had a – a surprise, that's all.'

John left the room and lingered a discreet time out of earshot. Jemima removed Aglaea's gloves and chafed her hands, looking at her with concern, waiting; and Aglaea said at last, 'Mr Underwood – he has – I was shocked! Everyone had gone – we were alone together—'

'Aunt! What did he do?'

'He – he proposed marriage to me.'

'He proposed to you?'

Aglaea squeezed the hand that was chafing hers. 'You may well be shocked. I was angry on your behalf. How the mistake was made I don't know, but I was sure he was in love with you. When I think I encouraged you to believe—'

'Good God, is that all?' Jemima exclaimed. 'Aunt, believe me, I *never* thought he fancied me! I always thought it was you he was in love with, and I couldn't be happier that he has declared himself at last. You can accept him without the least fear. I am very, very happy for you.'

Aglaea pulled her hand back. 'Accept him?'

'Have you not?' Jemima said. 'But—'

'I have refused him, very decidedly. Had I not thought he was *your* lover, I should have rebuffed him long ago.'

'I'm sorry. I thought you liked him.'

'I *like* him as much as anyone. But why should you think I would ever consider marrying again?' She spoke with a heat Jemima had not heard before. 'I am very well as I am. Marriage is no blessing to a woman, except as it provides her an establishment. I have a sufficient income, a comfortable home, and my time is at my own disposal. Why should I want to encumber myself with a husband?'

'I don't know,' Jemima said. 'I had hoped you might be able to tell me.'

'What do you mean?'

'John has proposed to me, this evening, just before you arrived.'

They looked at each other in painful silence for a moment. 'What answer did you give him?'

'I didn't give him any. He said I must want time to consider. He said he would be patient.'

Another silence fell. A moment later John came back in with the brandy and glasses on a tray, and said quietly, 'I think perhaps I am now *de trop*. If you can assure me that you are all right and there is nothing further I can do for you, I will take myself away.'

Aglaea made an effort to speak cheerfully. 'Yes, thank you, I am perfectly well. I shall go to bed in a moment.'

'Then I'll leave you.' He looked towards Jemima. 'May I call tomorrow?'

'Yes – if you wish. Yes, of course.'

He bowed to them both and left them, and they heard the front door close quietly behind him. Jemima roused herself to pour and mix two glasses of brandy and water, and they sipped in silence.

'We had better go to bed,' Aglaea said at last. 'We can talk in the morning.'

But Jemima had questions that would not wait. 'Why did you want me to be married to Mr Underwood, if marriage is so dreadful?'

Aglaea folded her hands in her lap and looked into the fire. '*Mine* was. But it is supposed to be what a woman wants. I wanted you to have your chance, at any rate.'

'But I could say the same as you: I have sufficient income, a comfortable home – why should I want a husband?'

'It's – the natural thing.'

Jemima's face changed extraordinarily. 'What have I to do with what is natural?' she cried.

Aglaea was silent. It was there between them, the half

buried, always unacknowledged memory of what had gone on at Morland Place. They had clung together like the only two survivors of a battle, but they had never, could never, talk about their experiences. Aglaea, indeed, was not even sure how much Jemima remembered. She had been only a child, and if nature had imposed a blessed amnesia, not for anything would Aglaea remind her of what was better forgotten. She would sooner forget it herself, and generally managed to do so.

'What shall I do?' Jemima said.

Aglaea looked at her. It seemed a genuine question. There was no-one, she felt, less suited to give advice than herself, but she roused herself to make an effort. 'Do you love him?' she asked.

'I don't know,' Jemima said despairingly. 'How can I know? What is love like? What does it feel like?'

'In God's name, why ask me?' Aglaea said angrily, and got abruptly to her feet. 'I'm going to bed.' And she left without another word.

When John called at the house the next morning, apprehensively, he found Jemima alone.

'Aunt was up early, and went out with her paints. She left a note that she wanted to be alone,' Jemima told him.

He looked at her keenly. 'Are you all right? You look as though you haven't slept.'

'I didn't, much.' She had gone to bed at last in the early hours, to lie staring into the darkness, remembering. 'Do you know what happened last night? I wasn't sure how much you heard from the other room. Mr Underwood proposed marriage.'

'To Aunt Aggie? Well, that doesn't surprise us, does it? And what did she say?'

'I think she refused him. She said to me, why should she want to get married?'

'I believe her first marriage wasn't a happy one,' John said carefully. 'And if she doesn't care for Mr Underwood, why indeed should she want to marry?'

'Why should I?' Jemima said in a small voice.

He saw it was a genuine question. 'Because you do care for me – don't you?'

'Yes – but—'

He laid a finger gently on her lips. '"Yes" is quite enough for now. I told you I won't press you for an answer. Now put on your bonnet and come for a walk. I think you need some fresh air. And we'll talk about ordinary things, and admire the view, and be like old friends.'

She looked at him gratefully. 'You are good to me, Childie,' she said.

He smiled affectionately. 'I might not be if you keep calling me that!'

The sea was dark and sparkling, the sky was blue and full of rushing white clouds chasing shadows across the town and up the cliffs. The gulls wheeled high, silent today. She walked with her arm through John's, and he chatted a little at first; but as she did not reply he gradually fell silent. She wished he wouldn't: it gave her mind the freedom to go and visit what she had not wished to think about for twelve years, since Nicholas Morland died. They walked and walked, and she was too deeply preoccupied to notice her tiredness. Finally they reached the lookout point up on the cliffs, where public subscription had placed a bench and a telescope for gazing out to sea at distant ships. Here they stopped by unspoken consent. It was still early for walkers, and they had the place to themselves. They sat down together on the bench. And at last she said, 'I don't think I can marry you.'

He was silent a moment. 'May one ask why?'

'I wish you wouldn't,' she said. She stole a glance sideways at him. He was looking at the sea, his profile dark against the sky, his hair ruffled by the wind, for he had taken off his hat and held it in his lap, his hands loosely clasped over it. Hands which seemed very ordinary, and familiar and dear – more so than was really justified, given how little they had seen of each other in recent years. 'Can't we just be friends?'

'Yes – if that's what you want,' he said neutrally.

She looked at the sea again. She had done things she had never wanted to think about again, things that made her unfit for marriage; she had experienced things that made her unable ever to trust herself to the power of a man. Her mind was peopled with black and confusing memories, with the knowledge of horrors which set her apart from normal people. How could she be a wife and mother? She could not take the clean wholesome thing John offered her and taint it. And she could not face being made to remember all over again, time and time again, as she had today – and that was what marrying him would do to her. She wanted to lock and bar the door, keep the bad things shut in, and forget them. She couldn't explain all that to John; she didn't need to explain it to Aglaea. That was why they were fit companions for each other, and for no-one else.

'It isn't what I want,' she said at last, 'but it's what I choose.'

'If you change your mind,' he said, 'I shall still be waiting.'

The burial was to be at Morland Place, in the crypt under the chapel. The coffin was taken up from London by train.

'Another wonder of the railway age,' Danby said. 'It seems fitting – she was a late convert to the railway, but an avid one, once she found it meant she could take her horses everywhere with her.'

Tom looked at his step-father in wonder that he could be so cheerful. He felt such a chasm of loss that he hardly knew what to do with himself. He veered between grief and anger, between bouts of sobbing that frightened him because he didn't seem to be able to control them, and a rage at his mother for dying so unnecessarily and leaving him behind. And yet Papa Danby looked perfectly normal: if it hadn't been for his black clothes, you would never have known he had been bereaved.

Danby looked at Tom as if he knew what he was thinking. 'I don't feel that she's gone,' he explained apologetically. 'Dare say it'll come home to me one day. But I keep thinkin' she's just in the next room. Keep thinkin', "Oh, must remember to tell Lucy that."' He tapped the side of his head with a forefinger. 'Head's runnin' slow. Can't say I'm sorry. Couldn't cope with all this business otherwise.' He waved a hand to indicate the funeral arrangements and the apparatus of bereavement.

'I'm sorry,' Tom said.

Danby laid a hand briefly over his. 'Don't be. Harder for you than for me in some ways.' He smiled a little shakily. 'In the natural course of things, I'll be joinin' her soon. Be a longer wait for you.'

'Don't,' Tom said. 'I don't want to lose you, too.'

Emily came in. 'Lose who?' She didn't wait for an answer. 'Another lot of condolences just arrived. I've put them in your business-room, Papa Danby. You'll have to get a secretary to answer them, I'm sure, there's so many.'

'Amazin' how many people you get to know in a long life. Did I show you the letter from the Duke, Em? Never knew Old Hookey so emotional.'

'Yes, you showed it to me,' Emily said.

'Stupid thing,' he confessed, 'I keep wantin' to show it to Lucy.'

'Yes, I know.'

'Wonder if we're doin' the right thing, private family funeral? Feel bad about the Duke and old friends like him – not givin' them the chance to pay their respects.'

'It's the right thing,' Emily said patiently. 'It's what she wanted.'

'She wanted to go home,' he explained to her, as if he hadn't said it all many times before. 'She still thought of Morland Place as home. Once a Morland always a Morland.' He shook his head. 'I was Johnny-come-lately to her. But I'm a Yorkshireman m'self, y'know. I understood.'

Emily came close and slipped her arm through his. 'There's about half an hour before the carriages come round. Why don't you sit down and rest?'

'Rest?' Danby said in astonishment. 'What should I want to rest for?'

'Then let me get you a glass of wine. I'm sure we could all do with something. It'll be a long day.'

'They're all long days now,' Danby said bleakly; but then he smiled down at her. 'You're a good girl, Little Em. My son did the right thing waitin' for you. Didn't know he was waitin' for you, of course – sheer blind luck on his part – but look how it turned out.'

'I'll take that for a compliment,' Emily said, and guided him to the sofa, where she could sit beside him.

He took her hand and patted it absently while he spoke. 'She was just a girl when I first knew her. No more figure than a boy – hair in a curly crop like a boy's – drove like the Dickens – rode across in those days, too. Wouldn't do nowadays, of course,' he shook his head, 'but things weren't so strict in those days. But across or sidesaddle, there was never a horse she couldn't handle.

Used to frighten me sometimes. But she never came to any harm. When she bought Magnus Apollo, for instance, and wanted to ride him in a point-to-point! You never saw Magnus, Em, but he was the deuce of a horse! Doubt if I could've handled him m'self. Old Parslow was even more scared than I was, for all that—'

'For God's sake!' Tom protested suddenly.

Danby looked up at him with innocent blue eyes. 'Said somethin' I shouldn't?'

Emily flashed her husband a warning look, and then said to Lord Theakston, 'I was wondering, Papa Danby, about afterwards, when we come back from Yorkshire, I mean—'

'After the funeral? Needn't mind mentionin' it on my account.'

'I think it was more on mine,' Tom said drily.

'Had you thought what you would do?' Emily went on. 'I mean, will you go on living here, or had you thought of moving into something smaller?'

'Think it's too big for me, do you?' Danby said. He looked round the drawing-room. He had lived here with Lucy for thirty-seven years, and everything was as she had chosen it and placed it. It had always been her house, first and foremost; just as it had been her life, into which he fitted for her convenience. He tried to remember the last time anything had been rearranged. Not for twenty years at least. How could he leave it? She was in every room, every piece of furniture, every picture and vase. If he went away, he wouldn't know where to find her any more. If he went away, he might forget her face and her voice and what it was like to be with her.

'I suppose I will rattle around, house this size,' he said doubtfully. 'But it's – I don't think—' He couldn't finish. Tom saw that there were tears in his step-father's eyes, and he couldn't bear it, and had to look away.

'If you don't want to leave,' Emily said sturdily, 'there's no reason why you should. But to make you more comfortable, Tom and I have a suggestion.' She looked at her husband, and seeing his adam's apple move up and down, realised he was not in a position just then to explain. So she went on in her quiet, cheerful way, 'You must say at once if you don't like the idea, and that will be that, but Tom and I wondered if you would like us to come and live with you here. I could take care of the house, so that you wouldn't have to worry about the servants and meals and such, and Tom would be company for you when you felt like it. And when you didn't – well, it's plenty big enough for us all to keep out of each other's way when we need to.'

Danby stared. 'You want to come and live here? With me?'

'Only if it's what you like. I didn't mean to be impertinent.'

He took her hand and kissed it fervently. 'I tell you what, Little Em: next to marrying you myself, having you live here with Tom is the nicest thing I can think of!'

She smiled. 'Oh good! Then that's settled,' she said, as if it had been nothing more than a menu or a table-plan.

'I suppose I really am head of the family now,' Benedict said, standing before the fireplace in the drawing-room at Morland Place. The weather was still warm, and the fireplace contained only a soot-speckled fan of folded paper, but it was a gesture of comfort, and he needed comfort. Aunt Lucy's death brought back to him that of his father – her brother; and besides, when the last of the generation above you was gone, it meant you were the next in line.

The house was full for Lucy's funeral, even though it was only a family affair. Her three surviving children,

Rosamund, Roland and Thomas, were there; her nine grandchildren; her nephew Benedict; great-nieces Mary and Fanny Anthony and great-nephews Georgie and Teddy; great-granddaughters Venetia and Olivia; and great-grandnephew Lionel. Three good generations.

In addition there were a number of Danby's relations, the Wiskes of North Yorkshire; and a few Cavendishes and Manverses, relations of Rosamund's father who could never be kept away from any family party where food and accommodation might be had for nothing. And there were Ansteys, too – Lord Anstey, who had once been Lucy's protégé and whose mother had been a Morland; his sisters Mary and Aglaea, his brother Henry and family, and his nephew and heir John. Jemima was there, of course, having accompanied Aglaea; and Danby reflected that she was by rights also a great-niece to Lucy, though the connection was of the bend sinister. Danby was probably now the only person left in the world who knew that, and when he died, the knowledge would die with him; but though marriage had obscured the fact, Jemima's father had been the illegitimate son of Lucy's brother James.

Despite the speed and convenience of the railway, it had already been a long day, and Danby was tired. He was an old man, and since Lucy had left him he felt his age every day. He did not exactly doze as he sat listening to the muted conversations around him, but his attention wandered in and out. He would discover he had missed half a sentence, or two exchanges, and have no memory of where he had been; the sun moved across the room in jerks rather than smoothly and imperceptibly. The old priest, Father Whatsisname, came over and sat beside him and talked about the arrangements for the funeral tonight, and Danby nodded and agreed, but he wasn't really listening. He was thinking of Lucy being a child here, and all the times afterwards she had come back to restore her spirit.

There was something *about* Morland Place, he thought. It was right she should lie here, with her own kin. He remembered when her brother Edward had died, they had buried his dog with him, though they'd had to do it secretly after the funeral proper, in case of offending anyone's religious strictures. But perhaps if Edward had his dog, they wouldn't mind in that case burying him alongside Lucy, when his time came. Little Em came towards him with a cup of tea, and he took it with a vague smile of thanks; so vague that she sat down beside him and watched him until he had drunk it.

Rosamund was standing with Tom. Of Lucy's children, they had always been the closest to each other. 'Papa Danby looks frail,' Rosamund said. 'I hope it won't all be too much for him. Perhaps we should have waited until tomorrow for the funeral, to give him time to get over the journey.'

'Best to get it over with,' Tom said. 'He's tired now, and hardly feels the pain. Anaesthesia.' He smiled to show it was a joke, but there was no light in the smile.

'And what about you?' Rosamund asked, looking at him closely.

'I don't know. I suppose like Papa Danby I can't believe she's gone. It was so sudden. And so—' He wanted to say unnecessary, the word that kept occurring to him in that context; but to say it opened the way to speculations he didn't want to entertain. 'She wasn't ill,' he said at last. 'I suppose that's what makes it hard to bear.'

Rosamund bit her lip. 'Is it?' she said. He met her eyes reluctantly. 'Come outside,' she said abruptly.

They slipped out of the drawing-room through the crowds, watched only by Father Moineau. Rosamund led the way through the door by the chapel stairs into the inner courtyard. There was no-one there, and at this time of day the shadows were long and deep and cold, though the sky above was still the clear, frail blue of early autumn.

Rosamund stopped and turned to face him, and Tom looked at her uneasily, almost sullenly, thrusting his hands into his pockets like a defiant youth facing an unpleasant interview. 'Well?' he said. 'What is it?'

Rosamund didn't know how to go on. 'It was sudden, wasn't it? As you say, she wasn't ill.'

'Not as far as I know. What are you trying to say, Rosy?'

Rosamund met his eyes. 'You *know* what. Mother hadn't ridden for weeks, and then suddenly she had herself driven down to Richmond to ride in the park. Why did she suddenly decide to go riding? And why did she fall? She could ride any horse that ever lived.'

'You said yourself she hadn't ridden for weeks. She was out of practice.'

'One doesn't forget, not after a lifetime.'

'And the horse was fresh – he'd only had led exercise.'

'When did that ever make any difference?'

'Ros, she was an old woman,' Tom said desperately. 'Old and getting frail, and she hadn't been on a horse for weeks, and the horse was fresh, it carted her, and she fell off. That's all.' Rosamund looked at him in silence, not accepting. 'What do you want me to say?' he asked angrily. 'That she wanted to die?'

Rosamund made a sound like a dry sob. 'It's true, isn't it? I've thought and thought about it, and I can't make it come out any other way. I don't want it to be true, but I think it is.'

'And why,' Tom asked in a quiet, deadly voice, 'would she want to die?'

'You know that too,' Rosamund said.

The reason was not mentioned between them, could not be – did not need to be. 'That's nonsense,' Tom said. But Rosamund read the same knowledge in his eyes.

Something had died in Lucy the day that Parslow died. Some bond between them, unlike anything else in life, had been ruptured, and Lucy had not been able to face a future so exposed, so lonely. Rosamund knew it, Tom knew it. It was what made Tom so angry with his mother, that Parslow in the end had meant more to her than her own kin, than her own children – more than Danby, more than Tom himself. But it was not as easy as that. The bond between her and her groom had been beyond words like love and duty; just something that existed, like an animal instinct. They had recognised each other as an animal knows where north is, that was all.

'So what do you want to do?' Tom asked at last.

Rosamund pulled out a handkerchief and blew her nose, briskly, like a boy. 'Nothing,' she said. 'I just needed to know.'

'You won't say anything to Papa Danby?'

'Of course not,' Rosamund said, almost scornfully. 'But he knows.'

'Do you think so?' Tom said. But of course he knew. He drew a great, uneven sigh. 'Go back in,' he said. 'I'm going for a walk.'

'Don't go far, will you? I need you to be there.'

'No, just round the moat. I want to be alone. I won't be long.'

She watched him walk across the courtyard and disappear under the arch which led to the door by the nursery stairs. She stood for a few moments after he had gone, her shoulders heavy, her heart doubting; and when she turned, Father Moineau was there just behind her.

'Oh! You startled me, Father!'

'I didn't mean to,' he said. 'I saw you come out. Where is your brother?'

'He's just gone for a walk. He needs to get a breath of air. He'll be back soon.'

'And what do you need, my child?' The dark eyes were wise and tender, and knew everything about her – like Parslow's had been on so many occasions in her wild life, when she had been hurting everyone, and herself most of all. But she mustn't think about Parslow. She came closest to understanding because he had been to her for a while what she thought he had been to her mother; but even that was a shadow.

'I need – I need forgiveness,' Rosamund said. She hadn't known she was going to say it until it was out.

'We all need that.'

'Not for me. I mean – not only for me.'

'God's mercy is infinite. Trust Him,' said Moineau.

Just like that, in a few words? It seemed too simple. She shook her head.

'Don't you believe me?' Moineau said. 'Don't you believe He can understand anything we poor mortals can think up? We are all His creatures.'

'My mother—' she began, but she could not finish the sentence.

'I know.' Moineau nodded, and his voice became soft, a gentle, soothing breeze, a cradling of warm, moving water. 'It was an accident, child, and if it was no accident, still it was by God's design. She wanted to go home, and where the soul is eager for Him, He won't refuse to receive it. Be at peace, as she is, now.'

Rosamund felt an extraordinary, hollow feeling, as though she had thrown all her weight against a door only to find it was open all along. 'You know all about it?' she said blankly.

'I know all about it.'

'How do you know? Who told you?'

Moineau smiled, and it was at once the smile of one of

the more ecstatic kind of saints, and of a man of earth and flesh and human pleasures. 'Your daughter told me,' he said. 'You are very alike, you know. Cut of the one cloth, you and she – and your mother too. Nothing is ever lost, you see. You're a grandmother yourself now – you must know that.'

And he reached out and made the sign of the cross on her forehead, and murmured, '*Benedicat te omnipotens Deus, Pater et Filius et Spiritus Sanctus,*' and then he went away.

Rosamund felt exhausted and empty, but it was with a clean emptiness, like a scoured vessel that is ready to be filled. The loss and the anger and the doubt were rubbed away. When the sun went down, they would bury the coffin in the crypt, and in the morning they would go about their lives again. The world revolves, she thought, and the great hungry earth sighs and turns and sleeps again. We are all His creatures, and safe in His hands. Nothing is ever lost.

CHAPTER SEVEN

Charlotte and Tom strolled in the garden of Southport House in June 1852. London seemed strangely quiet that summer, after the excitements of the Exhibition, and Hyde Park looked strangely empty without its fabulous ice palace. The building had won such a place of affection in the hearts of Londoners that when under the terms of the original licence it was to be pulled down and removed, a motion was introduced to retain it for the nation, and after long debate it had been purchased for £70,000 and removed to Sydenham where it was to be re-erected as a winter garden.

Now the only extraneous sound that struck the ear was the hammering of workmen repairing the roof, which was what had driven them into the garden in the first place.

'How much has changed since last year,' Charlotte said after a long silence.

'Yes, you seem to be getting it in order,' Tom said absently. 'It was quite a jungle when I first saw it.'

'I didn't mean the garden, foolish!'

'Eh? Oh, sorry.'

'No, I meant – oh, Grandmama dying, for one thing. I still can't believe she's gone. I keep thinking of her as still being at home in Upper Grosvenor Street, and wanting to go and ask her things.'

'It's even more difficult for us, living there,' Tom said. They were silent a moment. Charlotte thought again of the conversation she had had with Papa Danby almost exactly a year ago, when he had talked about Parslow's illness and Grandmama's concern. 'I hate to think how she'll take it when—' he had said; as if he had known what would happen. Grandmama's death was so very *odd*. Perhaps that was why those of them who had been closest to her could not come to terms with it. It was as though she had taken French leave, and they were waiting for her to come back and say goodbye properly.

'And then poor Thalia,' Tom went on. Thalia had died in December, during another miscarriage. It had plunged Aylesbury into a torment of guilt, even though it had been Thalia herself who had insisted on having the baby. But of course, as he had confided to Tom, he could have prevented it, by denying himself her bed; which would not, he felt, have been going against God's will, any more than, for instance, not drinking port if you were of a gouty disposition. But Thalia had not seen it that way, reasoning that while she was physically of childbearing age, she ought to bear children, her age and general health not withstanding; and that if she died of it, that was God's wish for her. Aylesbury had stopped himself saying it was not *his* wish for her, knowing where that argument would lead; but it was difficult to refrain from making love to someone whom you did, in fact, love, when they insisted on it. Thalia had been ill for most of the pregnancy, but had never complained, almost exulting in every pain or bout of sickness. It was, Aylesbury had said reluctantly to his brother, as though she enjoyed punishing the flesh, like the monks of old wearing hair shirts or beating themselves with twigs. Their mother, Aylesbury said to Tom, did not think such an attitude to religion healthy, and it was a good thing in a way that she had not lived to see her prophecies fulfilled. Theoretically, Tom thought so too – though in reality he could not be glad about his mother's death on any

162

level. But since losing Thalia, Aylesbury had become very gloomy and even more religious, shutting himself up, refusing all entertainment, and reading nothing but devotional works. The atmosphere at Wolvercote was now more suitable to a mausoleum than a gentleman's residence, and Tom had to force himself to go down there to see his brother – for Aylesbury would not come up to Town any more. It struck him that Lucy would not have enjoyed spending the summer there, as had always been her habit, and that she would inevitably have hurt and offended Aylesbury by telling him so. For that reason – again theoretically – it was a good thing she had not lived to see it.

But to look at changes on a wider front, December had marked the increasingly expected *coup d'état* by Louis Bonaparte, who had seized power in what Papa Danby described with grudging approval as a 'deuced neat operation' and made himself emperor in all but name. The public fear was that France would once again try to invade England, a fear enhanced by rumours that the French navy was putting all its resources into building steamships in order to annihilate the largely sail-powered British Navy. The newspapers and drawing-rooms seethed with Francophobia, and some leading restaurants took the precaution of re-writing their menus in English. In official circles there was division on how England should view the matter. Lord Palmerston, the Foreign Secretary, had warmly congratualated the French Ambassador in London, Count Walewski, and assured him of his support for Louis Bonaparte, while the rest of the Government was still deciding whether or not even to recognise the new regime; and Russell, to whom Palmerston had long been a thorn in the side, demanded his resignation. Russell's government did not long survive his departure. It went out in February over the Militia Bill, and Lord Derby came in to form a Tory administration, with Malmesbury at the Foreign Office.

Malmesbury was a 'dashed good fellow' according to Lord Theakston, but he had never held office before, and he was grateful when Palmerston offered to advise him on the main principles of English foreign policy.

'Naturally Pam told him to keep in with France,' Oliver had told Charlotte with amusement, 'and that suited Malmesbury down to the ground, because of course he's a personal friend of Louis Bonaparte – met him on his Grand Tour, and been on terms ever since.'

Malmesbury was also a personal friend of Oliver's, and his arrival at the Foreign Office had prompted an increasing number of messages between Whitehall and Southport House and increasingly frequent summonses to Oliver to attend and confer. Malmesbury, wisely knowing his limitations, was willing to call on any of his friends with expertise to help him out, and Palmerston, hovering in the background and frustrated by his lack of office, was willing to use any of *his* friends to extend his influence.

Oliver was at the Foreign Office at this moment, while Charlotte walked in the garden with Tom.

'He's been gone a long time,' she said as a distant clock struck. 'I wonder what they want him for?'

'What they always want him for – to pick his brains.'

'What a vulgar expression!'

Tom grinned. 'You can always tell when your brother has been visiting us. My vocabulary takes a very strange turn.'

'Oh, when was Cavendish with you?'

'Last night – he just looked in on his way back to Windsor.'

'Oh yes, he's on Palace duty, isn't he? What did he have to say for himself?'

'Nothing much. In fact, he struck me as rather evasive.'

'Oh dear, I hope it isn't a female,' Charlotte said.

'When is it not a female, with Cavendish?' Tom said.

'But he hasn't been in love for ages,' Charlotte said loyally. 'I think he's settling down at last.'

'He hasn't *told* you he's in love,' Tom corrected. 'It's my belief there's some kind of intrigue going on that he doesn't want to tell anyone about.'

'But why should he be so concealing?' Charlotte frowned. 'He's over twenty-one now – and since Grandmama died, there's no-one to tell him who he can and can't marry. Certainly Mama has no influence over that side of him, and Jes doesn't really mind.'

'Perhaps marriage isn't what's at stake,' Tom suggested.

Charlotte's eyes widened. 'Oh no! What can you mean? No, Tom, Cavendish wouldn't take a – a *mistress*. He's too good.'

Tom shook his head, laughing. 'How can you be so innocent, after all this time in London?'

She flushed a little. 'But Cav's too young – that sort of thing is for older men, or men who've been disappointed, or—'

Tom laughed at her, but ruefully. Until he met his lovely Emily, he had relied entirely on the kindness of mistresses; and Charlotte's own husband had had mistresses until his marriage. Older, disappointed men. He understood her reasoning, but it was not flattering. 'Well, never mind, if Cav is in love again, I dare say we'll soon know all about it.'

'I hope so. I hate to think of his acting secretly.'

'Not everyone shares your hatred of intrigue,' Tom said as they reached the end of the walk and sat down on the iron bench there. 'Cavendish was telling us yesterday with a certain amount of relish how Palmerston's downfall was royal doing.'

'I know that the Queen and the Prince don't like him,' Charlotte said. 'Shaftesbury says they've been scheming to be rid of him for years, but I never really thought that was true. Being Palmerston's son-in-law, he'd likely have a heated view of it.'

'Ah, but did you know that Normanby, our Ambassador in Paris, is brother to Prince Albert's private secretary, Colonel Phipps? Normanby apparently heard from Count Walewski that Palmerston had warmly endorsed the *coup d'état*, and wrote to his brother to say how astonished he was, since *he* had been told to remain strictly impartial about it. Phipps of course showed the letter to the Prince, who showed it to the Queen, who summoned Russell to demand an explanation and dispense retribution. And so – out went he.'

Charlotte was bemused. 'And Cavendish told you all this?'

'With, as I said, some relish.'

'I can't believe he'd even remember it in order,' she said. 'Animals are all he's ever cared for.'

'All who has ever cared for?' Oliver asked, appearing through the trees at that moment. Charlotte's face lit up and she held her hands out to him.

'My brother,' she said. 'How long you have been! Is everything all right?'

Oliver stooped and kissed her. 'That depends upon your point of view.' He shook hands with Tom. 'Well, and how are things in the Lower House?'

'Peaceful,' Tom said. 'One thing about the Tories, they don't rush about stirring things up like the Whigs; and besides, nobody in Derby's cabinet has the least idea what to do in Government, so they play safe by doing nothing. One can be sure of a few hours' sleep on the back benches these days.' Charlotte laughed at the idea, and he protested, 'No, I promise you! If one can keep out of the way of the Abolitionist committee, pressing one to read *Uncle Tom's Cabin* – and what slavery in America has to do with us they never can explain – and the man who wants a rest home for old cab horses, and the old fellow with the squint who hangs about the lobby muttering that the Government has personally poisoned his well and put his hens off lay, one can pass a very agreeable day within the hallowed portals.'

'Well, never mind all that – how are things in the Foreign Department?' Charlotte asked Oliver.

He held out his hand to her. 'Come walk a little, and I'll tell you. I've been sitting too long. Come with us, Tom, won't you? I need your advice too. I've been asked,' he went on as they walked, 'if I will take a trip next month to Russia.'

'Russia?' Charlotte exclaimed.

'This Balkan business, I suppose,' Tom said. 'Though why they talk about the Eastern Question, as if they know what it is—'

'The question is, what is the question?' Oliver agreed. 'Derby, through Malmesbury, with urgings from the Prince, wants me to go to St Petersburg and find out.'

'But why you?' Charlotte said. 'Surely we have an ambassador there?'

'The situation's rather delicate,' Oliver said, 'and it can't be resolved through official channels. We know that Russia has long had ambitions in the Balkans, and it rather looks as though France may be developing them. Louis Bonaparte needs to win popularity as quickly as he can, especially if he means to take the title of Emperor, which private sources assure us he does. Military action would be a way of winning popularity, especially with the army, and the Balkans would be a safer place to do it than Europe proper. We're officially friends with France, but Russia hasn't recognised the new régime yet, and if

France becomes active in Turkey, it may come to war. We don't want to go to war with Russia, of course; but we don't want to lose our friendship with France; and we certainly can't let Russia take Constantinople.'

'Or France either, for that matter,' Tom said.

'Quite. Turkey may be a bad master, but while Stratford is Ambassador in Constantinople, the Sublime Porte is virtually an extension of the Court of St James's.'

'But Oliver, you still haven't answered my question,' Charlotte urged. 'Why should they want you to go?'

'Because I know Petersburg and I know the Tsar. My father went there as Ambassador in 'thirty-three, when the Tsar refused to accept Stratford. I was seventeen then, and Papa though it would be a good education for me, so I went to live there with him for a year, and after that I was in Petersburg for part of every year until 1840 when Papa died. I learned to speak Russian, which is an advantage; but more importantly I learned my way around the Court.'

'I knew your father was Ambassador,' Charlotte said, 'but you never told me you spent so much time there.'

'Didn't I? But we've always had so much else to talk about,' Oliver said, with a particular smile that made her skin run hot. 'I expect there's lots about my past you don't know.'

'If you spent your young manhood in the Russian Court,' Tom said mischievously, 'I should think there's a lot you wouldn't want her to know. Russian women are very passionate, I understand.'

'What did your mother think about living there?' Charlotte asked, ignoring Tom loftily.

'Mama never set foot in Russia. She and Papa never really got on, and the idea of living in such a barbaric place was anathema to her. She wouldn't leave England. I think that was another reason why Papa wanted me to go with him – to score over Mama. She hates Russia even more now, because she blames it for my father's death – says the unhealthy climate in Petersburg undermined his constitution. She may be right for all I know. But it's my duty to go. I have knowledge of the situation that makes me peculiarly suited to the task.'

'What knowledge?' Tom asked.

'Knowledge – as far as anyone has it – of the way the Tsar's mind works. Do you remember in 'forty-four how he suddenly came to England, without even being invited?'

'I should think I do!' Tom said with a grin. 'The fuss it caused – urgent meetings about security – people rushing about corridors tearing their hair and muttering "protocol" at each other—!'

'Quite. Well, Nicholas was worried at the time about the increasing friendship between the Queen and Louis-Philippe of France – if you remember, she visited him in 'forty-three and a return visit was in plan – and Nicholas was afraid that if Turkey suddenly collapsed – which looked imminent then – France and England would carve the territory up between them and leave Russia out. So he came helter-skelter to Windsor to tell the Queen his views. And I was summoned to Windsor by Aberdeen – who was Prime Minister then, of course – to help ease the conversation along and explain each to the other.'

'I don't remember that,' Charlotte said with a frown.

Oliver smiled. 'I should think you would not, my love! You, if you remember, had just jilted me good and hard and fled from London to live in a Norfolk bog with a Scottish doctor and think on me never more.'

Charlotte said, 'How ungallant of you to remind me of my folly! But I seem to remember being told that as soon as I left Town, you went down to Ravendene with a broken heart.'

'I did,' Oliver said. 'I hurried down to Ravendene because my grandfather was ill. However, he rallied, and when the summons came from Windsor, I was able to obey it, and take my mind off my troubles with some diplomatic work. Very therapeutic. It's hard to think about a broken heart when you are trying to inch your way through a fractured mind! But very few people knew about it, so I'm not surprised no-one ever told you.'

'What did you think of Nicholas?' Tom asked. 'I remember Mama telling me the Queen though him completely mad.'

'Of course he is. How could an autocrat ruling one sixth of the earth's surface be anything *but* insane? But he's an interesting man – and clever, which doesn't always follow. And subtle – too subtle for his own good perhaps, but when you consider how many Tsars are murdered rather than die peacefully in their own beds, it's hard to blame him for not being open and trusting. But he can be surprisingly kind. My birthday fell while I was at Windsor, and as I happened to mention it – I can't remember how it came into conversation, but it was the most casual of mentions – he gave me the most beautiful jewelled enamel box as a birthday gift, with his portrait on the lid set round with diamonds. I have it still – it's in one of the cabinets at Ravendene. I'll show it to you one day,' he added to Charlotte.

'Perhaps you'd better show it to me before we go, so that I'll recognise him,' she said.

'Ah,' said Oliver. 'The thing is, my darling, that I have to go alone.'

'Oh, indeed?' Charlotte said, raising a frosty eyebrow.

Tom laughed. 'I'd better leave. Storm clouds approaching.'

'No, no, I need your advice,' Oliver said. 'It isn't an official visit, you see, and I can't just appear without an excuse or an invitation. No-one must know I'm gathering information or studying attitudes—'

'You mean – you're going as a *spy*?' Charlotte said, horrified. 'Oh Oliver, you *can't*!'

'Steady on, Charley, no need to insult the man,' Tom murmured.

'It's not spying,' Oliver said quickly.

'What else would you call it, pretending to be what you're not, deceiving people, asking questions designed to get information that people wouldn't give you if they knew? I'd call that spying; and it's not something I thought any gentleman would ever do.'

'My love, this is too strong. I shan't pretend to be anyone other than myself, and I shan't tell lies or deceive anyone. I shall just listen to what people tell me and make a judgement on their attitude, that's all.'

'Then let the Ambassador do it, if that's all.'

'People wouldn't talk to him as they'd talk to me. And if the Ambassador did it, it would be official business, and there would be repercussions.'

'Then it's spying,' Charlotte said, her mouth set hard. 'Tom, you agree with me, don't you?'

'Well—' Tom hesitated.

She gave him a reproachful look and detached herself from the group. 'You two obviously have a great deal to talk about. I shall go in and leave you in peace.'

'Charlotte—!'

'I should leave her go,' Tom said quietly. 'Later, when she's calmer, you can win her over.' Oliver watched his wife's retreat doubtfully, and Tom prompted, 'What was it you wanted to ask me? What sort of disguise to adopt?'

'Don't you start talking about disguises—!'

'Pax,' said Tom, lifting his hands. '*I'm* not the enemy.'

Oliver took a deep breath. 'You're right, of course. Very well: I understand your friend Vignoles is in Russia?'

'He's building a bridge for the Tsar, but it's in Kiev, not St Petersburg.'

'I can go via Kiev, that's not a difficulty. In fact, it might seem less pointed if I do. But I wondered if I couldn't make some sort of connection with him through the Photographic Club. That would give me a perfect excuse for pushing round the palaces and public offices; and I've noticed that people become very chatty when you face them with a camera apparatus and ask to take their portrait. They seem to think it's a compliment, and open their hearts to you. And somehow, I don't know quite why, it's impossible to suspect a calotypist of sinister purposes.'

Tom laughed. 'Is that how you see us? I don't think Emily would agree with you! But I should think nothing would be easier than to work your disguise. Charles would be bound to want some photographs of his bridge, wouldn't you say, and be too busy to take them himself? Naturally he would write and ask one of his fellow members of the club to come and take them for him. The only snag is that you are not – forgive me – a very experienced photographer yet, and it would be more natural for him to ask Roger Fenton or even me.'

'True. But it would not be strange if an enthusiastic beginner like myself, hearing of it from you or Fenton, should want to go along as well. Especially as I have the means to make the journey comfortable for all concerned.'

Tom grinned. 'Now there, I think, you should endear yourself to Roger! He dearly loves luxury, and never quite has enough of it, his income not being equal to his really rather ducal tastes. Offer to pay for everything on a lavish scale, and he'll be down at the harbour packed and ready before you can say "knife".'

'You think it should be Fenton, do you? Not yourself?'

'He is the president of the club,' Tom pointed out. 'And besides, I don't want to go. I wouldn't want to leave Emily.'

'I don't want to leave Charlotte,' Oliver said, stung by the implication.

'Ah, but you are stirred by the proddings of duty. Being thoroughly selfish, I've never been susceptible to that sort of inconvenient notion,' Tom said.

Oliver found his wife in her private sitting-room, a pleasant little chamber adjoining the bedroom, all decorated in green and gold. Here she had her writing desk and the books she read for pleasure; and the window looked over the garden. She was standing by the window with her back to the door when he came in. He walked across to her. 'Charlotte?'

She spoke without turning round. 'I hate lying and subterfuge and deceit. *Hate* it!'

'My love,' he said reasonably, 'you have it out of proportion.'

Now she turned, scanning his face. '*Have* I?'

'I think so.'

'Secrets are terrible things. They destroy everything – trust, honour, morality. They grow in the dark and spread out and branch until the whole fabric of life is undermined and rotten and ready to cave in.'

'I agree with you,' he said. 'I would never have any secrets from you, nor deceive you. My dear, can't you trust me?'

'I do trust you.'

'It seems not. I've been asked to do something which I am uniquely qualified to do, and which I think should be done. It will be unpleasant to me, but one can't avoid duty because it's unpleasant.'

'But to spy is dishonourable!' she cried.

173

'Perhaps.'

'Then let someone else do it!'

'As you let someone else do your work in the slums?'

'That's different,' she said flatly.

'Is it? Perhaps you should tell me how.' She was silent, angry and seeking for words. 'Life is not as simple now as it was once. You know that the influx of poor people into the towns has given rise to new and complicated problems. Once it was possible to let each land-owner look after his own poor and sick, but now there are thousands who belong to nobody. The problem is not capable of a simple solution. What you do may once have been wrong for a lady in your position, but you know that it now can't be judged by the old rules. Similarly, war is no longer a matter of two kings facing each other across a flat field with five hundred men apiece and fighting it out. In those days, when the issues were clear and simple, spying was a dreadful dishonour. It's much more complicated now. New conditions create new rules.'

'That sounds like a justification for immorality.'

He smiled ruefully. 'You are so very hard on me, Charlotte. Won't you give me the freedom of my conscience, as I give you yours? I wouldn't try to prevent you from doing what you thought must be done, though society condemned it – or, more importantly, though my mother condemned you!'

She began reluctantly to smile. She never could resist his teasing. 'Your mother will hate your going to Russia.'

'Oh, I do hope so!'

'But Oliver, I can't like it.'

'Then don't. I didn't like your dressing the ulcerated legs of drunken prostitutes, but I suffer from a queer sort of love that wishes to see you follow your own conscience.'

174

'Oh, don't! You make me ashamed, that my love is not so generous as yours.'

He gathered her in his arms. 'That's an easy flaw to mend. Kiss me, and let me go.' He touched her lips lightly with his. 'Come, am I forgiven?'

'There was never anything to forgive,' she said. 'I didn't blame you.'

'Oh? It felt like blame.'

'I was frightened, I suppose.' She slipped her arms round his neck, so that her body was pressed against his. 'I don't want you to go away.'

'I don't want to go away either.' He kissed her ear and her neck. 'On the subject of which,' he went on, kissing the delicate hollows of her collarbone, 'since I will be away for such a long time—' letting his lips drift further down, '—several weeks at least—'

'Oliver!' she gasped, but it was nothing to do with his words.

'—I did rather wonder,' he continued imperturbably, 'whether you might spare me half an hour of your valuable time?'

'Now?'

'Right now, if it's convenient to you.'

'I'm sure that can be arranged,' she said. 'Would you care to come to my bedroom?'

He swept his arm down behind her knees and picked her up with a fine display of muscular strength – for she was no featherweight. 'An outrageous suggestion, duchess,' he said.

'I'm so glad you think so,' she murmured, allowing herself to be carried away – in all senses.

A small, pale-faced, balding man in his late thirties, with a brisk air and a flat Yorkshire accent, presented himself at the door of Southport House one day in July. His clothes were neat but not out-of-the-way, and he had come on foot, and well before the usual polite hour of calling; but the staff knew that this particular visitor had privileged access to her grace, whether they liked it or not. The butler himself showed the visitor up: not to flatter the visitor, but for the opportunity to express by his icy demeanour his disapproval of the duchess's lack of state – for a servant's status depended on that of his mistress, and a lack of ceremony touched a butler's pride.

'Doctor Snow is here, your grace,' said Ungar in the tone of voice that suggested it would be better for Doctor Snow to be almost anywhere else.

Charlotte, who had often felt out of place in the rank to which she had been called, was nevertheless not prepared to be bullied by her own servants. 'Yes, show him in, Ungar,' she said with a touch of impatience. Ungar removed his bulk sideways just sufficiently to admit the visitor, and paused for an unnecessary and significant heartbeat before withdrawing, to imply that if he were her grace, he would count the silver.

'Well, your grace,' Snow said, taking the chair Charlotte offered and placing his hands flat on his knees with a businesslike gesture, 'I think I have the answer to your problems.'

'You are going to be the attending physician at my hospital,' she said, smiling.

'Now, ma'am, don't let's have that argument again. You know very well I'm not what you want. I haven't the time to do the work, and I'm not eminent enough to be your figurehead – besides not being considered *sound*.' He made an equivocal face as he spoke the word.

'I think you very sound,' Charlotte said stoutly.

'Aye, but then most people think you as mad as me, don't they?' he said frankly.

'Well, not *quite* so mad,' Charlotte murmured, and he

laughed. Doctor Snow had published a pamphlet in 1849 suggesting that cholera was not contracted from the foul air which hung around slums, as everyone else believed, but ingested in water or food contaminated by the faeces of those already infected. It was, the medical profession agreed, a ludicrous and reactionary suggestion. Added to that, Snow was an enthusiast for this newfangled notion of anaesthetising patients by administering ether and chloroform, a practice which was set to sap the moral strength of the nation and call down the wrath of God – if it did not kill every patient in the land first. Further, Snow was a vegetarian and a teetotaler, and addressed everyone of whatever rank frankly and without excess of deference. The man was quite clearly an outsider of the worst sort.

'I shall be very glad to use your facilities for my researches,' Snow went on, 'and I'll help you in any way I can. But what you need to walk your wards is a young man fresh out of medical school, full of enthusiasm and with nothing in his pockets; someone you can make your own. And I think I have the very man for you. His name is Reynolds. He comes from Glasgow, but he studied at Edinburgh under Simpson, so he's well grounded, and absolutely sound.'

'Which means, I take it, that he agrees with all your theories?'

'I'd hardly recommend him otherwise, would I?' Snow said. Snow and Simpson, Charlotte's man Abernethy, and the Queen's physician Sir James Clark, had all studied together at Edinburgh, where Simpson was now Professor of Obstetrics. Simpson was a pioneer of anaesthetism: he had been administering chloroform to women in labour for four or five years already. 'Simpson thinks him brilliant,' Snow went on. 'He sent Reynolds to me with a letter of recommendation, asking me to find a place for him.'

Charlotte frowned. 'Why doesn't Professor Simpson want to keep him? Surely a brilliant assistant is not to be parted with lightly?'

'There's no getting past you, is there?' Snow said. 'The fact is he's young and fiery and puts a lot of noses out of joint. You know what your great men in hospitals are like: demigods who don't take kindly to being contradicted. Reynolds is too outspoken. When he thinks something is wrong, he says so. And he doesn't suffer fools gladly, which makes him unsuited for private practice – where most of your patients are fools and pay good money for the privilege of being so.'

'And this is the firebrand you offer me? You quite alarm me.'

'You needn't worry. He'll be wax in your hands, I promise you. He's as soft in the heart as he is hard in the head. And he's right for your purposes. True enough, he hasn't an ounce of tact and says just what he thinks, but that's an advantage when dealing with poor folk. And he'll be grateful to you, which will always give *you* the upper hand. Now what do you say, your grace? Shall I bring him to see you?'

'Ineeed you shall, and the sooner the better. The building is all but finished, and I'd like to begin treating the poor as soon as the fitting out is completed.'

'Tomorrow, then? Will that suit you?'

'Yes, if you come early – at about this time?' Snow nodded. 'And if you're really sure you won't be my figurehead—' Charlotte began.

'No, no, I'd do you more harm than good, believe me.'

'Then – what do you think of Sir Foulke Holder?'

'He's an eminent man,' Snow said. 'He has some of the richest patients in Town. I don't think there's much harm in him.'

'That sounds less than enthusiastic. Come, speak your mind. Tell me what you really think of him.'

'He's too afraid of upsetting his patients. He follows fashion and plays safe, never thinks unless he's forced to, fawns on the rich and powerful, and treats ailments that don't exist rather than refuse the fee.'

'Is that all?' Charlotte said, amused.

'He would rather flatter a rich woman that she has an obscure and interesting condition, than tell her to eat less and go for a long walk, or do a good, hard day's work and stop fancying herself sick.'

'In fact, he's just like every other doctor in Town, except you. You would always tell your patients the unvarnished truth, of course?'

He smiled guiltily. 'Perhaps not quite always. I have to live, too. But the difference is, I mind about it. But how do you mean to tempt Sir Foulke?'

'With the use of my facilities. My grandmother thought surgical operations were the coming thing, and that a man so determined to be fashionable as Sir Foulke would be glad to be in the forefront.'

Snow looked doubtful. 'I have always seen him as a follower rather than a pioneer of fashion.'

'But if the opportunity is offered him, with no effort on his part? And the facilities will be quite different from anything ever seen before. You see, the building is a rectangle, and on the short side there will be a fine courtyard with a sweep for carriages, a porch with doric pillars and wide steps, and an entrance hall with carpets and chandeliers and everything splendid about it. There will be a suite of consulting rooms on the first floor, fitted out in the first style, two rooms on the second for preparation and recovery, and private stairs from there to a small operating theatre. All this will be for the use of the wealthy patients only. The main entrance

179

will be on the long side of the rectangle, and there will be no communication between the general hospital and the private suites, so the rich need never know of the existence of the poor.'

'Ingenious,' Snow said. 'Well, I hope your plan succeeds. By the by, what do you mean to do about nurses? I know what you think of the usual sort.'

Charlotte said, 'I have a plan for that; but I shall keep it to myself for now, until I'm sure it will work.'

'I say, Charley, who was that I saw leaving your house as I was walking up?' Cavendish said when he was shown into her presence the next day. 'That dark-haired fellow in the country suit?'

'That was my new doctor,' Charlotte said.

'What? Surely you ain't cashiered Abernethy, for a fellow who can't afford Town clothes?'

'Oh Cav, what does it matter what he wears?'

'A man *is* what he wears. Besides, he can't be much good as a doctor if he don't make enough money to dress himself,' Cavendish pointed out.

'Well, in any case, I didn't mean he was my doctor. I mean he's the doctor who is to attend the poor at my hospital.'

'Oh, I see. Good-looking chap,' Cavendish said thoughtfully.

'Is he?'

'Didn't you notice?'

'No, I was blinded by his suit. I couldn't look at anything else.'

Cavendish laughed. 'All right, truce! What's he like?'

'Interesting. Full of enthusiasm and ideas. He agrees with Doctor Snow about the passing of cholera in food and water, of course—'

'Of course.'

'And he has other theories just as radical, which he's burning to try out in my hospital. He believes that there are poisonous principles – seeds of infection, he calls them – for all sorts of conditions. For instance, in obstetrics—'

'Obs – what?'

'Childbirth,' she explained kindly. 'He believes that the seeds of puerperal fever are carried from one woman to another by the attending physicians. He's been corresponding with a man in Vienna who has had some remarkable results just by making the doctors wash their hands.'

Cavendish burst out laughing. 'Wash their hands? I thought you were going to produce some miraculous nostrum made out of powdered unicorn horns!'

'I don't know why you think it's so funny,' Charlotte said.

Cavendish sobered a little. 'Seriously, Charley, it ain't the thing for you to be talking about that sort of stuff with strangers.'

'Strangers?'

'People outside the family. It's bad enough mentionin' it to me, but to encourage a man you hardly know to talk about childbirth in front of you – well, you never know where it may lead.'

'What *can* you mean?'

Cavendish looked awkward. 'Well, if a chap finds he can talk about that sort of thing to a female, he don't respect her quite so much, quite aside from coarse ideas inflaming his – you know – his animal nature; and the next thing you know—'

'I am palpitating with horror,' Charlotte laughed. 'Pray don't stop there! What must I expect?'

'You can laugh all you like,' Cavendish said stubbornly, 'but I saw him. A young man, handsome, dashing – a bit of a corsair even, by his looks. And you're not

181

so very old yourself, Charley, and quite pretty in your way—'

'A thousand thanks.'

'Well you are! A chap could go a long way to find a better-looking woman, when you smile and make the effort to look your best. And I dare say you saw him alone, too – and with Southport out of the house – out of the country, even – well, don't blame me if this doctor of yours gets out of hand, that's all, and says something you don't like. He might even,' he added with muted horror, 'try to kiss you.'

'Oh Cavendish!' Charlotte said with affection and amusement. 'Doctor Reynolds is not going to take liberties with me. His mind is on higher things.'

'No man's mind goes that high,' Cavendish said darkly.

'Anyway, what did you come to see me about? Or were you just passing?'

'Oh! No, as a matter of fact, I have some news to tell you. Fairly tremendous news. Are you sitting comfortably?'

'You alarm me. What is it I need to be sitting down for?'

'Oh, it's good news! In fact,' he looked a little bashful, 'well, the truth of the matter is, I'm engaged to be married.'

Charlotte stared, wordless for a moment. 'But – but I didn't even think you were in love with anyone at the moment. The last I heard about was Miss Vansittart, but I thought you'd got tired of her.'

'No, nonsense,' Cavendish said, 'what are you thinking of? That was years ago.'

'Six weeks ago, by my reckoning.'

'Well, a deuced long time. Two months at least. This is someone quite new. Though when I say new, I've known her for ever, but it's not Miss Vansittart at all, it's Miss Phipps.'

'Miss Phipps? You haven't said a word to me about Miss Phipps. Who is she?'

'She's the most beautiful girl in the world,' Cavendish said fervently. 'Yes, I see you smile – *that's* why I didn't tell you anything about her. You're always making fun of me, so I thought I'd keep Alice to myself.'

'Alice?'

'I told you, we're engaged to be married. I can call my own fiancée by her Christian name, can't I?'

Charlotte patted the sofa beside her. 'Put your hackles down, darling, and sit here and tell me all about her. I shan't laugh or tease. Where did you meet her?'

Cavendish sat. 'Well, strangely enough, it was at the Great Exhibition. She and her Mama had come up with a party from Northamptonshire, and I was attending Lord Cardigan that day, and so we met. Well, I think it was Mrs Phipps who accosted the Lord, but they're neighbours, you know, and so he had to introduce everybody all round. Mrs Phipps was very charming to me, but oddly enough I hardly noticed Alice then, though I know she was there and I must have spoken to her, but for the life of me I can't remember thinking she was wonderful or anything of the sort, which is villainous of me. But I seem to remember she was dressed very modest, like a schoolgirl, and it ain't done to notice girls not out very much, so maybe that was it.'

'And was Mr Phipps there?'

'Oh no, he's dead. But he was the rector at Deene. It was Lord Cardigan got the fellow the preferment in the first place.'

'Ah, so Lord Cardigan knew the family well?'

'No, I'll tell you how it was. You know how Lord Cardigan is so friendly with Prince Albert? Well, this

Mr Phipps – Alice's father – was a distant cousin to Colonel Phipps who is the Prince's secretary, and he – Alice's father – he asked the Colonel if he could use his influence to get him a better living. So the Colonel mentioned it to the Prince and the Prince mentioned it to Lord Cardigan and the Lord did the deed. Only the poor chap didn't last long, and when he died he left Mrs Phipps and Alice in very poor fettle, because of course the income died with him, and Mrs Phipps had only a very small fortune of her own, and Phipps had never been able to put anything away. So they've been having a hard time of it, poor things, living in a tiny cottage in the village where the damp was affecting Mrs Phipps's rheumatism.'

Charlotte was more and more alarmed by what she was hearing. A clergyman was respectable enough, of course, and the connection with Colonel Phipps and Lord Cardigan was good; but if they were so necessitous, what was more likely than that the mother had fastened onto the lucky introduction to the heir to an earldom – who was, moreover, young and naïve – and manoeuvred him somehow into an engagement?

'So that was last summer? And how did you come to meet them again?'

'Down at Deene, when Lord Cardigan invited me just before Easter. I went to church on the Sunday, and there they were! It was the most wonderful chance.'

'Yes, I'm sure it was.'

'And that's when I first really noticed Alice. She had on a new bonnet, very fetching, and a very pretty mantle, and as soon as she saw me, Mrs Phipps came over and claimed the acquaintance and was very civil and friendly.'

'And is that when you fell in love with her?'

'Well, no, not quite. I thought she was dashed pretty, but you know Northampton is such a distance, and with

184

my duties – I didn't see how I would see her again. But when I went down to Windsor to do my turn there, to my absolute amazement I found they had moved there too!'

'Yes, that must have been a surprise,' Charlotte said thoughtfully. 'How did that come about?'

'Oh, through Colonel Phipps, of course. Mrs Phipps had written to him asking for his help, for the sake of her dead husband, and the Colonel is such a good fellow – well, he talked to the Prince, and the upshot was that they found a snug little house on the Royal Estate that was vacant, and let Mrs Phipps have it for a peppercorn, which meant they could live much better on Mrs Phipps's income, and have a man as well as a maid, where in Deene they only had one girl, which made Mrs Phipps feel very uncomfortable.'

'I'm sure it did. And how did you come to be engaged?'

'It all happened rather suddenly,' Cavendish said. 'In fact, I hardly know, really, how it came about. But I was sent over one day with a message for Mrs Phipps from the Colonel – a reply to something she'd asked him, I believe – and he sent me because he knew I knew them. So Mrs Phipps took the letter away to open it in another room – where she had paper for replying, or something of the sort – and I was left alone with Miss Phipps.'

Charlotte could imagine it. She could not think Mrs Phipps had inveigled herself to Windsor in the hope of meeting Cavendish again, but having discovered him so fortuitously on her doorstep, she would hardly have wanted to waste such an opportunity.

'And what happened then?'

Cavendish looked a little conscious. 'Well, it was very odd, really. The window was open onto the garden and a bee – or it may have been a wasp, I didn't really see – came in and Alice was very much frightened, so I went to deal with it, and she was crying like the deuce, and

185

the next thing I knew—' He paused, frowning as he tried to remember the exact sequence. 'Well, the next thing I knew she was in my arms, sobbing against my chest, you know, and I was thinking it didn't feel half bad. But then Mrs Phipps came back in in a hurry and looked very sharp indeed and so I – I asked for Alice's hand.'

Charlotte looked at him gravely. 'Oh Cav!'

He flushed. 'I wish you wouldn't say "Oh Cav" in that way! Alice is a perfectly lovely girl, and I'd have asked for her hand anyway.'

'You don't think you were manoeuvred into it?'

'Not a bit. Oh, I knew you'd take that attitude, just because they don't have any money,' he said angrily. 'I shouldn't have told you. If she was a duke's daughter, you'd think it was just the thing.'

'It isn't rank or money. You ought to know me better than that. I only wanted to be sure you had a free choice in this; that out of all the females in the world, this is the one you want.'

'I love Alice with all my heart,' he said, meeting his sister's eyes defiantly, 'and I wouldn't give her up even if—'

'Even if?'

His eyes slid away. 'Mrs Phipps has sent the notice in to the papers, so I couldn't get out of it even if I wanted to. But I don't want to, not a bit. Oh Charley, I wish you'd be nice about it! Alice is a splendid girl and I'm sure you'll love her as much as I do.'

'And Mrs Phipps?'

'You don't love your mother-in-law.'

'True.'

'And she needn't bother us when we're married – except that Alice is very fond of her so we'll have to have her with us at first. But after a bit I can find her a house of her own. She's already said that she doesn't approve of interfering between young couples, and that children shouldn't live with their parents when they marry; so you see she has the right ideas.'

'I'm glad to hear it,' Charlotte said, and made an effort for her brother. She smiled and took his hand and said, 'I am very pleased for you, darling, and I hope you'll be very happy. When can I meet her?'

A look of great relief passed across his face. He had evidently expected a worse reaction than he got, which made Charlotte suspect that the situation was as bad as she feared. 'Next week. They are coming up to Town on Monday so that Mrs Phipps can start ordering Alice's wedding-clothes. They're dying to meet you, and I dare say when you have had them here, Mrs Phipps will want to invite you to dine.'

'Oh, have they a house in Town? I thought from what you said—'

'No, they're going to stay in our house in St James's Square. Well, I don't like to think of them in an hotel, and besides, they can't afford it.'

'You've asked Mama if they can live at St James's Square?'

'Not yet, but I'm sure she won't mind. It was Mrs Phipps's idea,' Cavendish said innocently. 'She said how nice it would be for Alice to be married from there, and I said I'm sure Mama and Papa would be delighted, and she said if they didn't care to come to Town much, she could get it all in order and have it ready for them when they came up for the wedding. It seemed to me a very practical idea. I suppose she's had to learn to manage.'

Managing, Charlotte thought when Cavendish had finally gone away, seemed to be what Mrs Phipps did best. It was hard to blame her: left penurious and with a daughter on her hands, what could she do but try to secure the best match possible? Luck had gone her way, placing

187

the young viscount in her way three times – though it was not entirely random, given the connection through Lord Cardigan and Colonel Phipps. But his arrival at the cottage with a message could hardly have been anticipated – unless, indeed, she had written something to Colonel Phipps that demanded an answer with the very hope that it would be Blithfield who was sent. Once he was at the cottage, Mrs Phipps evidently lost not time in leaving them together. Charlotte acquitted Mrs Phipps of crouching outside the window and releasing a wasp into the room, but the wasp was certainly fortuitous. If it existed. She wondered, suddenly, whether Cavendish had seen it at all, or whether Miss Alice was as managing as her mother, and a good actress into the bargain. At all events, Mrs Phipps reappeared at just the right moment to catch Blithfield embracing her daughter, and Cav's innocence and honour did the rest.

It did not sound like a very promising start to a marriage, and Charlotte's hope was that she had read too much into the story, and that Cavendish really was in love with Alice, and the rest had been the blind workings of fate. She determined to suspend her judgement until she met the Phippses; but it was lucky Grandmama was not still alive, or there would have been terrible storms. Mrs Phipps might not have been a match for Lady Theakston, but if there had been a pitched battle, Cavendish would have been the one really to get hurt.

BOOK TWO

Breaking Free

Who knows what's fit for us? Had fate
Proposed bliss here should sublimate
My being – had I sign'd the bond –
Still one must lead some life beyond,
Have a bliss to die with, dim-descried.

Robert Browning:
The Last Ride Together

CHAPTER EIGHT

If Charlotte had hoped that Mrs Phipps was indifferent to rank and harboured a purely disinterested desire to become acquainted with the sister of her daughter's lover, the hope did not last beyond the first moments of the first meeting. Ungar, looking strangely bemused, announced Mrs Phipps and Miss Phipps, and a whirlwind passed him with both hands outstretched crying, 'My dear, dear, *dear* duchess! What infinite, *infinite* joy to meet you! When our dear Lord Blithfield told us that you wished to make our acquaintance on the earliest possible day, I said to Alice, Alice, my dear, that is true breeding. I did! You may laugh at me, but so it was! For, I said to her, your true noblewoman is always affable and condescending, and those who think rank entitles them to be arrogant and proud quite mistake the matter. But our dear Lord Blithfield is so remarkably free from anything of that sort that I knew how it would be. He could not be so modest and charming himself if his family was not equally delightful, and he *is* charming, I take leave to assure your grace, and I thought so from the first moment I met him, before there was any question of his falling in love with this chit of mine! At the Crystal Palace where we first met I said to Lord Cardigan – a dear friend of the family, as I suppose you know, and quite ridiculously devoted to me! – what a charming young man that was, and such a credit to his regiment, and his lordship said something affable – I forget what – but,' with a little laugh, 'it was outrageously complimentary so it is best if I *do* forget it, perhaps! But it is a great thing to find such easy manners in a boy brought up to the purple, if I might put it that way, for I assure you we know a great many people of rank – through our connections at Court, you know – and they are not all so affable as Lord Blithfield by any means. But his manners are everything one would expect of a gentleman, and so I said to Alice – didn't I, Alice, my dear? Pray make your curtsey to her grace. You must forgive this silly girl of mine, your grace, I fear she is quite overcome! She has lived so sheltered, you know. Mr Phipps was perhaps nicer in his ideas than is generally the case these days, and Alice was brought up as strict as anyone in the country, I believe.'

Charlotte managed to retrieve her hands and say something civil, and when Mrs Phipps drew a long enough breath she asked them to sit down, and nodded to Ungar to bring refreshments. Then she was at liberty to study her visitors. Mrs Phipps she guessed to be about forty, plump but well-corseted, and with small features which must have been pretty when she was young, but were now were too small for her face and gave her the look of a ruined and petulant baby. Her rosebud lips were remarkably red and the cheeks youthfully pink, her curls an extraordinarily bright gold. The curls peeped out from a bonnet of black glazed straw trimmed with tartan ribbon, which looked new, as did the gown of tartan silk, richly patterned in green, purple, red, black, white and blue, very full-skirted, trimmed with black silk fringe and jet buttons. The lady wore jet earrings and a handsome cameo brooch, and carried a black silk umbrella with an ivory handle. Charlotte concluded that the touches of black were to do with fashion rather than a statement of widowhood, for Mrs Phipps did not present the appearance of a woman who had renounced the pleasures of this world.

Miss Phipps was very different: a tall girl, very slender – almost too slender – and with hair so fair it was almost white, and a delicate skin whose pallor looked more unnatural than unhealthy, as though she had come from another world, or been reared in the dark. The effect was saved from insipidity by pretty features and very bright blue eyes – Charlotte could see how a susceptible man might be overcome. Miss Phipps seemed very timid and shy, and had not spoken a word since she entered. She too was dressed in a new gown – evidently Mrs Phipps had felt secure enough to be spending money – of sky blue embroidered muslin which may have been suitable to her age and degree but did nothing for her colouring, and a white silk bonnet covered in blue lace. Despite the warmth of the day, she wore a cashmere shawl which she continually drew round her shoulders. Charlotte thought it was a nervous gesture, but seeing that her thin hands were mottled and blue, concluded rather that she felt the cold.

Charlotte was free to make as lengthy an observation as she wanted, because Mrs Phipps talked seamlessly, requiring no answer, though she punctuated her flow with questions. And while she talked, her busy bailiff eyes were everywhere, assessing and memorising. Miss Phipps drooped more the longer they stayed, but the surroundings seemed to invigorate Mrs Phipps, who grew brighter and more cheerful with every inventoried ornament. Charlotte herself was comprehensively surveyed, a little at a time. She felt she would rather have got it over with in one good long stare, had Mrs Phipps not been too genteel to do such a thing, for the little tugging glances were like being torn by a sharp beak: peck, peck – away went her coiffure, with the plaits and the hair ornaments; peck, peck – her earrings; peck – her necklace; peck, peck – her gown. It made her nervous. If Mrs Phipps stayed too long, she would be quite naked.

But the lady's garrulousness was a good thing in one way: Charlotte learned a good deal in a short time about these future additions to the family. Mrs Phipps had been a Miss Trewint, daughter of a clergyman herself, genteel but poor. The Trewints were a Somersetshire family with land; Trewint père, however, was a younger son with no claim on the estate but the family living. It was a good living, but as he had unfortunately married for love rather than money, and as the marriage was blessed with seven children, it had had to be stretched rather too thin around so many. Miss Trewint had been lucky to have two thousand pounds to catch a husband with: her younger sisters had to manage on less.

It was natural as a clergyman's daughter that she should have been courted by clergymen, and she had selected Mr Phipps from amongst them for his good looks and dashing air, and his talk of eminent relatives. It proved a poor choice, however, for Mr Phipps was amiable and lazy, lacking the driving ambition which alone could make a fortune in his profession. His living was a poor one with a bad house, but he seemed not to want more. Charlotte gathered it was Mrs Phipps who had spurred her husband to apply to his distant cousin at Court for preferment; and having got the living at Deene, he would not try to improve their situation by ingratiating himself with the rich and powerful. Instead he interested himself in his books and his cellar, taking long, elaborate dinners, and long, solitary walks. Mrs Phipps thought this love of nature unnatural, but Charlotte could see the attraction of being alone with a tree after only half an hour in Mrs Phipps's company. Eventually Mr Phipps caught a cold while lingering too long in the dews of dusk, and the cold turned to an influenza which carried him off. Mrs Phipps seemed inclined to blame him for dying, when a little effort might have pulled him round. He had certainly left her in a dreadful position, with nothing saved, and no son to provide for her, though fortunately only one daughter to support.

Much as she already disliked her, Charlotte could not but feel some sympathy with Mrs Phipps. She received a very graphic picture – probably more than Mrs Phipps meant to impart – of a lifetime of dreary struggle to maintain a certain degree of gentility; of mended stockings, borrowed gloves and made-over gowns; of missed meals and determined smiles, of making do and contriving and pretending. Charlotte did not underestimate her plight: to marry well was all Mrs Phipps could have done to save herself, and all that could be done to save her daughter. It was to her credit, perhaps, that she had not let her misfortunes cow her; but she had let them harden her. She was plainly a toady and a schemer.

How much scheming had gone into the catching of Cavendish was one thing that Charlotte was anxious to know, but it was difficult to discover from Mrs Phipps's conversation. She was pretty sure Cavendish had been bounced into the actual proposal, and guessed that Mrs Phipps had been listening outside the door for the right moment to surprise the young people. She seemed then to have hastened to make sure of her quarry by immediately sending notices to the papers. The rest was impossible to be sure of; and the wasp was the greatest mystery of all. Miss Phipps seemed too languid, pale, timid and shy to have done anything so full-blooded as to trap Cavendish by pretending fear of being stung; yet could any insect in the history of mankind have entered the scene more opportunely? Bruce's spider was nothing to it.

When the guests rose at last to go, Charlotte was none the wiser. Miss Phipps, her eyes wedded to the floor, whispered a soundless goodbye and thank you as she curtseyed, Mrs Phipps said a great deal she had said before, looked forward to meeting dear Lord and Lady Batchworth in the near future, and promised the dear, dear duchess that they would meet again *very* soon; and then they were gone.

Charlotte went up to her sitting-room, and was about to ring for Norton, when Norton appeared with a bottle of lavender water. 'I guessed you'd have the headache,' she said. 'Lie back and close your eyes and I'll bathe your temples.'

Charlotte and Norton had been through a great deal together, and when they were alone, they did not keep ceremony. Norton was more a friend than a servant, Charlotte often thought, and there was almost nothing she did not tell her.

'Oh, Norton! I've been talked to death. That dreadful woman!' she said now, putting her feet up on the footstool Norton placed for her.

'Trapped his lordship good and hard, I suppose?'

'I don't know. I rather think he may have trapped himself. The girl seems innocent of anything, however – except being rather insipid.'

'Pretty, though,' Norton said. 'I got a glimpse over the banister. But I suppose her ma chose the dress for her – *just* the wrong colour with that sallow skin. You need to be a pink-faced, golden blonde to wear that shade of blue. They've no money, I suppose?'

'None – but what made you think so?'

'You can tell,' Norton said cryptically. 'And a warren of poor relatives, I make no doubt, ready to descend on you and eat you out of house and home.'

'I don't know about that. Mrs Phipps was one of seven, but Mr Phipps is dead and Miss Phipps is their only child, so at least we're saved the spectre of the gamester father

196

and the brother wanting his colours in an expensive regiment.'

'Poor Lord Blithfield,' Norton said. 'Such a good, gentle boy, so warm-hearted. He ought to have a proper wife who will love him.'

'Perhaps Miss Phipps does love him. We mustn't judge too soon. Poor people do fall in love, you know.'

'Funny how often they will fall in love with rich people, though,' Norton said cynically. 'There now, does that feel better?'

'Much. Thank you,' Charlotte said, her eyes closed.

'Well you stay there, and have a rest. It's early days yet, but it'll do no harm to keep your feet up.'

'Early days for what?' Charlotte murmured.

'Well, now, I thought you would have been able to tell me that.' Charlotte opened her eyes and saw Norton smiling significantly down at her. 'It seems to me that something which ought to've turned up hasn't.'

Charlotte thought, and frowned, and said, 'D'you know, I can't remember. With his grace away I suppose I don't think about it. Are you sure?'

'I know the dates, and I'm sure you're late. And with you being as regular as clockwork as a rule, it seems to me—'

A slow smile spread over Charlotte's face. She remembered the day Oliver had told her he was going away, and had carried her into the bedroom. She wouldn't be at all surprised if that hadn't done the trick. It certainly ought to have, at any rate, if emotions had power. 'He'll be so pleased,' she said. 'I won't say anything in my letters. I'll wait until he comes home to tell him.'

'You'd better concentrate your mind on having a boy this time, my lady,' Norton said with mock severity. 'There's a limit to how patient even a loving husband will be.'

*   *   *

The negative aspect to suspecting that she was pregnant again was that it meant very soon she would be forced to retire for a wearisome six months, which would interrupt her work dreadfully. She had better hurry to put it on a firm footing, she thought, and made an appointment to go round and see Sir Foulke Holder at his house on the corner of Devonshire Street and Harley Street.

Sir Foulke – a tall and bulky man with a florid face and a head of tightly curly hair, which he carried very high, like a horse on a bearing-rein – greeted her with large affability, through which curiosity shone with a transparency Charlotte found rather reassuring.

'Welcome, your grace! What a pleasure to welcome you to my humble establishment! But indeed, there was no need for your grace to take the trouble to come here. I should have been more than happy to wait upon you at Southport House at any time. You should not have given yourself the trouble, indeed you should not, especially if – that is, I suppose – I trust your grace is in good health? Allow me to set you a chair. Please tell me how I may be of service to you. I assure you, you may speak with perfect frankness. Not, of course, that your grace is likely to wish – but I can assure you that while Doctor Abernethy is a good friend, nothing confided by a patient is ever divulged to anyone else, not even a close colleague, without permission.'

Charlotte sat, and came directly to the point. 'I have not come to you as a patient, Sir Foulke. Excellent as your reputation is, I am quite happy with Doctor Abernethy. No, it is a business proposition I have for you.'

'Ah,' said Holder, and his face seemed to sharpen. 'A business proposition, is it? Pray continue; I am all attention.'

Charlotte explained the matter to him briskly. 'All I am

asking from you is for your name to be associated with the hospital; to be placed at the head of notepaper and subscription lists; and for you to mention the hospital in glowing terms when the opportunity arises. I need trustees, patrons from the ranks of society: you can deliver me those. In return, the facilities are yours to use whenever you like – and they will be of the most superior sort, I assure you. Operating rooms, laboratories – everything. The treatment of paupers will be an entirely separate activity, and you need know nothing about it. You may wish occasionally to interest yourself in an unusual case, but that will be as you choose. There will be no obligation to do so.'

'Who attends to the paupers?'

'I have another doctor – young, brilliant, and penniless.'

'May I know his name?'

'Reynolds. He studied under Simpson in Edinburgh.'

'No, I don't know him. Well, your grace, I cannot decide all at once, and I am sure you would not want me to. It interests me, certainly; but to be frank, I do not think you will receive the benefit you hope for. The best people, the cream of the *ton*, if I may put it so, will not go to a hospital, no matter how luxuriously you appoint it. They will wish to be treated at home, as they have always been.'

'Even for surgical operations? Surely they must see the benefit of having a specially designed environment in such a case?'

'Surgical operations are, by their nature, hideous and dangerous enterprises, where the refinement of the surroundings makes little difference. The amputation of a limb, if such a dreadful thing became necessary, they would think better done in the comfort and privacy of their own home.'

'But what about more complicated procedures under anaesthesia?'

He shook his head. 'Certainly the rendering of the patient insensible might make it possible to carry out more lengthy and complicated operations in the future. But for the moment, it remains a matter for experimentation upon the lower orders. One could not recommend it to one's patients. For one thing, the risk of death from shock and infection is still very high; and for another, anaesthesia is by no means approved of. You don't need me, your grace, to tell you that.'

'But you, Sir Foulke, you approve of it, do you not?'

'My dear ma'am, it is not my business to approve of anything my patients do not approve of. If it became fashionable – if it became acceptable – but that is another matter. Unless a miracle happens, I cannot believe that people of rank will submit themselves to something which is regarded as ungodly.'

'But if it became fashionable, you would use it?'

'If a patient requested it, I would defer to their request. For the time being, however, I think it would only be the middle orders who would request it. A prosperous tradesman – a merchant at best.'

'Do you have such patients?'

'Certainly. It would be impossible to support a practice without them.' A glimmer of humour came into his face. 'The best people, if you will forgive me, and excluding present company of course, are not always the best payers. Certain of my patients seem to believe that the honour of attending them ought to be payment enough.'

Charlotte laughed. 'You are educating me, Sir Foulke. I had no idea I was being so *gauche* in settling my bills promptly. Well, then, accepting all your caveats, I shall leave you to think over my proposal. Even if you only use my facilities for your paying customers, your name would be useful to me. And who knows how things may change?'

Lord and Lady Batchworth did not put Mrs and Miss Phipps to the trouble of travelling to Lancashire: Cavendish's letter brought them hurrying to London, to arrive on Charlotte's doorstep in a state of bemusement.

'Charlotte, what is going on? Is it really true? Who is this female?' Rosamund asked as soon as the servants had withdrawn.

'I'm afraid it is true,' Charlotte began, and stopped as her mother sank into a chair and put her hand to her head.

'Afraid? Then it's bad, is it? Tell me the worst: vulgar, penniless, what?'

Jes put his hand on his wife's shoulder. 'Don't jump the gun, my love. She's been fretting all the way down in the train, but I told her Cavendish isn't a complete fool. He wouldn't offer for someone hopelessly unsuitable.'

'He's so innocent, he probably wouldn't know a suitable girl from the other sort,' Rosamund said. 'I've been having images of some hard-faced adventuress ten years his senior calling me Mama.'

Charlotte laughed, relieving the tension. 'No, no, it's not like that. She's a girl of seventeen or eighteen, daughter of a clergyman, perfectly respectable; rather pretty but very shy. She's quite well-connected: her mother's family have land in Somerset, and her father was a cousin of Colonel Sir Charles Phipps, Prince Albert's secretary.'

Rosamund narrowed her eyes in suspicion. 'Then if she's so irreproachable, why all the hurry? There must be something wrong with her.'

'No money,' Charlotte said.

'I guessed that,' Jes said. 'How bad is it?'

'The father died and left nothing, and the mother had only two thousand pounds.'

'Two thousand a year?' Rosamund said, with a return of hope.

'No, Mama, two thousand pounds. A hundred pounds a year to live on for both of them.'

'Debts?' Jes asked.

'I don't think so. You see, it could be much worse. The drawback is—' She hesitated.

'Don't torment your mother,' Jes said severely.

'You don't take this seriously at all, do you?' Rosamund complained.

'My love, Cavendish is over twenty-one. He must take charge of his own life.'

She looked at Charlotte. 'What is it, then?'

'Nothing, really – just that Mrs Phipps is rather pushing, and Miss Phipps is rather milk-and-water, and I couldn't help wondering if Cavendish had made a completely free choice. Not,' she went on hastily, 'that I've any reason to suppose he hasn't—'

'If he hasn't, he'll have to abide by it,' Jes said.

'Well, yes. It's been in the papers now. And Cav wouldn't jilt Miss Phipps even if he wanted to.'

'It all sounds perfectly grim,' Rosamund said. 'When he could have had any girl in the world, why did he have to choose that one? If only Mother had been alive, she would have stopped him. I suppose this ghastly woman will have hordes of penniless relations who'll overrun us like rabbits, too.'

'You don't have to accept the rabbits, my dear,' Jes said, 'but for the rest – you'll just have to make the best of it. The girl may be perfectly sweet, and if Cavendish does love her, everything will come out in the end. And now, if you'll forgive us, Charlotte my dear, I think we'll go home. It's been a long journey, and I think your mother needs time to prepare herself to meet the dragon, which I suppose will happen tomorrow.'

'Oh dear,' Charlotte said. 'Didn't Cav tell you? He is an idiot.'

'Tell us what?'

'You may be going to meet the dragon rather sooner than you bargained for. She and her daughter are living in St James's Square.'

'It's a big enough square not to meet her tonight, surely,' Rosamund said.

'No, my dear,' Jes said with a humorous look, 'I rather think Charlotte means she's living in *our house* in St James's Square. Am I right, Charlotte?'

To which Charlotte could only nod meekly.

Both for Cavendish's sake, and at Rosamund's request, Charlotte took some pains to try to get to know Miss Phipps better. Rosamund nobly endured the mother so that Charlotte could abstract the daughter alone to ride in her carriage and visit the shops. Charlotte found it hard work. Perhaps understandably, given her background, she had no opinions, and seemed to find the idea odd that she might have them, rather than have them provided by her mother – or her grace – or, in the future, Lord Blithfield. But as she grew more comfortable with Charlotte, and talked a little more, it became clear that she had very little on which to base opinions. She was very ignorant. She had never had a governess or been to school, and her education had been such as her parents had seen fit, or had the inclination, to give her. She knew nothing of public affairs. She had hardly read a book in her life, and the major figures of literature and poetry were unknown to her. History was a few romantic stories – Alfred and the Cakes, the Little Princes in the Tower – which happened 'in the olden days'. The Napoleonic Wars were 'in the olden days': when pressed, she supposed that Bonaparte was coæval with Julius Caesar, and was astonished, but not mightily interested, to learn that the Duke of Wellington had been at Charlotte's wedding, and was still alive. Geography was the geography of Northamptonshire; beyond that was England, and then Abroad – where many of the Olden Days things happened. She had heard of France and Italy, but thought that Paris was a separate country.

Her tastes were both childish and sentimental. She liked tinselly things, baby pinks and blues, pictures of dying animals and crying children. Her abilities were confined to needlework, sketching, and playing the pianoforte, which she confessed she had been obliged by Mama to learn but did not much like. Then what did she like? She thought long and hard about that. She liked being pleasant – sitting nicely dressed with nice people, having tea, and not being scolded by Mama. She liked little children, if they were pretty and pleasant and not rough. She had once had a bird in a cage which she loved very much. She would like very much one day to have a little dog, a spaniel perhaps. She didn't like big dogs, because they frightened her and muddied her gowns.

On the positive side, there was no vice or guile in her. She disliked nobody, held no grudges, wished everyone to be happy. And Charlotte absolved her of any plot to trap Cavendish. She had no understanding of how it all came about: it was like one of those stories in her history book. She really loved Cavendish, and the emotion was as strong and positive as was possible in someone so woolly-minded. She seemed – another point in her favour – indifferent to his rank; in fact, Charlotte believed she had only a very hazy idea of what it was, and was sure she did not differentiate, for instance, between an earl and a duke. It would be nice to have a title – to be Lady Blithfield – because then people would be nice to her, but that was all. She liked Cavendish because he was handsome and kind. He spoke gently to her, and was never cross, and it would be lovely to be with him all the time and be pleasant always. Charlotte did not despair of her improving under Cavendish's influence, once she was got away from her mother. She had no conceit of herself that would resist correction. On the other hand, she was mentally lazy, and when Charlotte tried to tell her things, her attention would drift after a minute or two, and she would be exclaiming about a sweet bonnet in a shop window in the middle of Charlotte's explanation of how the Queen and Prince Albert were related. But perhaps, she thought generously, she might find Cavendish better worth listening to. Cavendish was a hero to her: the bravest, cleverest, handsomest man in the world.

Mrs Phipps did not improve on acquaintance. She remained what she had seemed at first, vulgar and grasping. She was not without a certain native cleverness, but she had never done anything to improve it, and her value for mental attainments was demonstrated by the way she had brought up her daughter, and her ambitions for her. She wanted wealth and rank for Alice, and to that end would have married her to a vicious reprobate or a dribbling idiot if necessary. Installed in the Batchworths' house in St James's Square, she was driving Rosamund to distraction. Jes was able to escape her all day, and could have absented himself most evenings, too, had he not felt it would be unfair to his wife. But Rosamund was at Mrs Phipps's mercy, and after a very short exposure to her was willing to push for as early a wedding as possible.

'Anything to get away from her!' she said to Charlotte. 'She follows me everywhere, and dear-Lady-Batchworths me to death. The only thing worse than the way she fawns over me is the way she fawns over you. I only merit one "dear"; you always get two, if not a "dearest".'

'Poor Cavendish!' Charlotte sighed. 'What a life he will lead.'

'If only he would – but no,' Rosamund checked herself. 'We wouldn't want him to be the kind of man who could jilt a helpless girl, however horrible her mother. We must just hope that he really loves her. And I doubt,' she added, 'whether he will be patient with Mrs Phipps for ever. There's a core of steel in Cavendish which hasn't shown itself so far. She hasn't fatally annoyed or upset him yet, and he's very easy-going. But when she does—'

So the wedding was set for the middle of August, the earliest date that would not give rise to gossip about unseemly haste. When the date had been announced, Cavendish came to see Charlotte.

'I wonder if I could ask you a favour?'

'Of course, love. What is it?'

'Would you help Alice with her clothes? Mrs Phipps chooses them for her, and somehow or other she always looks wrong. I suppose she doesn't have any taste – Mrs Phipps, I mean, although she always looks smart enough herself, in her own way; but Alice—' He hesitated, puzzled.

'Norton says it's because of Alice's unusual colouring. Mrs Phipps sees her simply as a blonde, and chooses blue; but Norton says with her skin she should never wear blue, or at least not those bright shades of it.'

'Yes,' Cavendish said eagerly, 'Norton always knows about that sort of thing. Won't you help her, and get Norton to choose things for her? I want her to look her best.'

'Of course I'd be delighted to help,' Charlotte said, 'but won't Mrs Phipps object? Mothers always want to dress their daughters for their weddings.'

'You can leave Mrs Phipps to me. She won't object.'

'Dearest, how grim you sound! Have you had a falling out?'

Cavendish looked uncomfortable. 'Not at all. No. Well,' he admitted, 'you may as well know, but don't tell anyone else, if you please – and especially not Alice. But Mrs Phipps has been running up bills all over Town which she expects me to pay. Clothes for herself, clothes for Alice – of course I want them to look well, but she should have asked me first, not left me to find out when the accounts reached me. And there are other things too – jewels and plate and clocks and things like that – that I've never seen.' He stopped and bit his lip.

'Oh Cav, no!'

'I suppose she is salting things away, in case something goes wrong.'

'But that's tantamount to theft!'

'I don't think she sees it that way. She doesn't understand that I would never let Alice down like that. She's just making sure that if I prove a cad and jilt her, she has a little something put aside to keep them both. Given how poor she's always been—'

'But that's no excuse. It's horrid!'

'Yes. Well, not a word to anyone – you promise. And don't worry, I've had a word with her. She didn't like it a bit, but it gives me a handle with her. If she objects to your choosing Alice's clothes, I shall threaten to cut off her credit.'

'Oh darling, what a mother-in-law you're going to have.' Charlotte's sympathy for her brother drove her to an indelicate question. 'Cav, you do love Alice, don't you?'

His gentle, boyish mouth hardened. 'And if I didn't, what would you have me do about it?' Charlotte could not answer. 'Exactly,' he said. 'Don't ask me such a thing again, Charley. Not even you have the right to ask me that.'

Charlotte had hoped that Oliver would be back well before the wedding, but as August opened, a letter came from him to say that he would be staying at least another month. It was well, Charlotte thought glumly, that she had plenty to occupy her. Choosing Alice's wedding-clothes proved a less arduous task than she had expected, for if Alice had no natural taste, she was at least entirely biddable; and once she saw herself in the first of the new things, a day-dress in creamy-yellow silk, she agreed with obvious sincerity that it suited her better.

'Indeed, your grace, indeed, you make me look almost pretty,' she said with the first enthusiasm Charlotte had ever known her display.

'You are pretty, Alice,' Charlotte said.

'Oh no!' Alice said, surprised into contradiction. 'I'm too tall and too thin and too pale, Mama says, and my hair ought to be a proper gold like hers, not this moony colour.'

'I would not wish to contradict your mama,' Charlotte said, 'but though you are perhaps a little too thin, you are not a bit too tall, and your colouring is a great deal more interesting than the conventional. You should cherish your uniqueness, and make the most of it. That is what Cavendish would want you to do.'

'Do you think so?' she asked, humbly pleased.

'Of course. It is you he fell in love with, isn't it? Not someone else – so why should you wish to resemble someone else?'

Such a rhetorical question was too difficult for Miss Phipps, but she gathered she was being praised, and that was enough for her. And what Cavendish would like was her guiding principle. 'He is wonderful, isn't he, your grace? And so very handsome – such lovely whiskers.'

'Yes, he is handsome,' Charlotte said absently. 'You should have very pretty children.'

Miss Phipps was so shocked at the mention of such a thing, she came very close to blushing, and would not look at anything but the floor for the next ten minutes.

But all of Charlotte's time was not given to Cavendish's affairs. She was busy recruiting nurses for her hospital, according to a scheme which she had worked out with Norton. The idea first came from a prostitute whom Charlotte had helped, who told her that, if she found it hard to find women willing to be nurses, she should recruit prostitutes, since they would not be squeamish, there being little they had not seen, while most of them would do anything for a roof over their heads and three meals a day.

Charlotte had had experience of hospital nurses, and was determined that her hospital would do better. Since attending the sick was considered work fit only for the lowest, nurses were generally ignorant, dirty and careless at best, thoroughly vicious at worst. As they were obliged to live on the wards, without privacy or protection, the degradation of their situation usually drove them to drink (if it was not the drink which brought them low enough to be nurses in the first place), and scenes of drunken promiscuity were commonplace.

Charlotte did not quite consider that lifelong prostitutes would be the best recruits for her hospital, but she knew from Norton's experiences before she went into service that there were many women who wanted to be decent, but who were driven to prostitution because it was the only way to support themselves. Seamstresses, for instance, were paid such pitiful piece-rates that working until their fingers bled could not earn them enough to feed and clothe themselves; and women left alone with a child to bring up had double the problem. Good-hearted women brought low through no fault of their own was what she was looking for: grateful enough to do the work, decent enough to want to regain their self-respect through honest labour and clean living.

Norton, with the help of Charlotte's agents, scoured the poorest parts of the city for women in dire straits who longed for a chance to leave the dirt and degradation. If they displayed interest in being redeemed, the next stage was for them to be interviewed by Charlotte, who was determined not to have any woman in her nursing *corps* whom she had not personally approved. Whether they were accepted or rejected, she gave each interviewee five shillings for her trouble, the news of which quickly got round, so that soon the candidates were seeking out Norton, rather than vice versa.

The room in which Charlotte interviewed was a small corner room on the first floor which had been specially furnished – or perhaps, rather, unfurnished, for it was not her wish either to frighten the women or to give them false expectations. It contained two plain chairs and a table, the oldest and dullest piece of carpet, and only a fearfully dark and ugly painting of a long-dead Fleetwood over the chimney to break the monotony of the walls. To this room the women were conducted by way of the kitchen corridor and the backstairs. Even with these precautions, some of the candidates were pathetically over-awed, and could hardly bring themselves to sit down when told.

Mrs Webster's story was typical. She was a country girl, born in Essex, but had come to London when she was twelve to go into service, since there was no work to be had in her village. She had worked as an under-housemaid for four years, and had done most of the things which would fall to the basic duty of a

210

nurse: making beds, laying fires, washing floors, emptying chambers, mending sheets, cleaning and fetching and carrying. Then when she was sixteen she had fallen in love with a footman. Marriages amongst servants were forbidden in her household, but she had been persuaded by him to a secret marriage. They had hoped eventually to be able to find another place together as a couple, but before that could happen she had become pregnant, and they were both dismissed without a character. Their situation was desperate.

'Webster did his best by me, ma'am, but he didn't know anything but being a footman, and no-one would give him a place with me with a baby on the way.' He had done casual jobs at first – finding cigar-ends, holding horses, running errands, anything he could get to earn a few coppers – but then at last he had seemed to strike lucky: he had got work as a market-porter, a well-paid job which allowed them to eat properly and rent a room to themselves. But he hadn't the physique for the work. He was always injuring himself, and finally suffered a rupture which laid him off for good. Mrs Webster had taken in needlework, while Webster whittled matches at home, but between them they could never quite earn enough. Gradually they starved, and when winter came Webster had fallen a victim to the 'old man's friend', pneumonia, and died. Left alone, Mrs Webster had struggled to support the baby on her pitiful income, but had eventually to follow the advice and example of most of the women she knew, and take to part-time prostitution.

'But I never liked it, ma'am, and that's the truth. I wasn't brought up that way, and it was terrible shame to me to go the bad way to live. So when Mrs Norton said she might have work for me, I said, begging your pardon, ma'am, I was ready to do anything decent that would

211

support me and the child, and keep me from having to do that dreadful thing.'

'The work I offer you is not pleasant, Mrs Webster,' Charlotte warned. 'But it is good, useful work – Christian work. And I hope my women will set an example and redeem the name of hospital nursing, so that it becomes an honourable profession any woman would be proud to follow.'

'What work would I have to do, ma'am, if you don't mind?'

'Prepare and strip the beds, wash the patients, bring their food, feed them if they cannot feed themselves, bring and empty bedpans. Keep the ward clean, wash floors, scour vessels, roll bandages, repair sheets and nightshirts. In addition you would learn how to perform some medical duties – to clean wounds, for instance, and put on dressings and bandages. Should you find that disgusting?'

'Well, ma'am, I can't be sure until I've tried; but like you say, it's good work, and I think I should not mind it too much. I've done unpleasant things aplenty which wasn't no use to anyone.'

Charlotte nodded. 'As to general conditions: my nurses will live in the hospital, but in a dormitory quite separate from the patients. Each nurse will have her own bed, and a locker or cupboard in which to keep her clothes. She will wash every day and bathe once a week. Each nurse will have two cotton gowns of a uniform design, one pair of shoes, and two clean aprons and caps a week. Laundry will be done in the hospital basement – I expect my nurses to appear spotless at all times. In addition to her laundry, clothing, bed and three meals every day, she will receive wages of two shillings and sixpence a week. As to behaviour: my nurses must be a model of decency and modesty. There is to be no swearing, no spitting, no profanity. There will be no visitors to the dormitory at any time. Any nurse who is familiar with a patient will be dismissed instantly.'

'Oh ma'am, if I was never to have to do that thing again, I should count myself lucky,' Mrs Webster said with emphasis.

'Absolutely no lush,' Charlotte went on. 'Any nurse found drinking, inside or outside the hospital, will be dismissed instantly.'

'I never had that habit, ma'am, thanks be to God.'

'Any nurse who steals from a patient or procures him drink will be dismissed instantly. Any nurse who quarrels with another will be dismissed. My nurses will attend a service in the hospital chapel at least once every Sunday. Hours of work will be twelve hours in twenty-four, divided into watches. Nurses on the ward at night will always work in pairs for protection. There will be one whole day off a month, and three extra days a year for good behaviour. Nurses will behave decently and modestly at all times, whether in the hospital or outside. I have long ears, Mrs Webster, and I hear everything.'

'Yes, ma'am.'

'Do you have any questions?'

'Yes, ma'am – about my little boy?'

'We cannot have children in the hospital, of course; but I have experience of placing children in good, Christian homes where they will be well cared for and decently brought up. I should find such a place for your child, at a charge to be deducted from your wages. Eighteen pence is the usual amount. I should make sure it was near enough for you to visit him on your days off. Eventually I shall arrange for him to be put to a trade, so that he can earn his own living.'

Mrs Webster's eyes filled with tears. 'Oh ma'am – oh ma'am.' She was overcome, and had to wipe her eyes and nose on her sleeve before she could go on. 'For the chance of that, ma'am, for the chance of my boy growing up to a proper trade, I'd work day and night for no wages, I swear to God I would!'

'There's no need for that, Mrs Webster,' Charlotte said, smiling. 'Do I take it you would like to be considered for the work?'

'Oh *yes* ma'am – if you please!'

Most of those who came as far as Charlotte's interview were eager to be taken on, as Mrs Webster was. Norton's filtering was rigorous, but some disliked the nature of the work and refused; and some Charlotte rejected as too stupid or too debilitated, or because she doubted their sincerity or their ability to stay sober. But there were enough candidates for Charlotte to be choosey.

It was much harder to find a suitable superintendent of nurses. Those who had done something like it before would not work with what they thought of as low women, even despite the almost conventual rules by which they would live; and those who were willing to take the position were either incapable of fulfilling the duties, or had previously been dismissed for drunkenness or indecency or theft.

It seemed hopeless. 'We are getting nowhere,' she said to Norton. 'Our advertisement is attracting the wrong people. Where else can we look? Where can we find a woman who would be glad of the job, who isn't somehow disqualified from it? An educated woman, into the bargain?'

Norton shook her head. 'I don't know. She needs to be able to keep discipline, too.' They looked at each other, and the same thought dawned on them simultaneously.

'Poverty, education, and gentility; humility, desperation and consequent gratitude.' Charlotte asked, beginning to smile. 'Who am I describing, Norton?'

'A governess, my lady,' Norton said.

'It ought to have been obvious from the start,' Charlotte chided herself. She had been in the situation herself, and had faced the idea of being a governess with despair. If at that time she had been offered the alternative of nursing superintendent, she would have jumped at it. Enquiry and patience led eventually to Miss Barthorp, a lady of thirty with smooth dark hair and a plain, sensible face, who had been obliged through poverty to become a governess. Nine years of varying degrees of misery and humiliation in private families had sent her applying for positions in girls' schools, but Charlotte's suggestion intrigued her much more.

'I know nothing of nursing, your grace, but I have kept my pupils in tolerable order, without any help from higher authority: their parents generally liked nothing better than to countermand my orders and encourage their offspring to defy me. I don't think grown women could be much more difficult, especially if I know – and they know – that I have your support. And it will be useful work, too. I can't tell your grace how I have longed to be useful! Teaching spoiled girls how to catch husbands is not my idea of making a contribution to the general weal.'

Charlotte liked her. She herself had longed to be useful – it was what had led her to her present preoccupations – and if Miss Barthorp were sincere, she would be only too glad to give her the opportunity.

So the weeks passed. The hospital was largely finished, and Doctor Reynolds was already at work in the dispensary, which had been completed first, seeing patients who did not require beds. Charlotte had the nurses' dormitory fitted out next, so that the first of them could be installed and help with the preparation of the wards. Miss Barthorp's rooms – a bedroom, a sitting-room, and a small office – were furnished after consultation with

215

her, a consultation which left her almost in tears at the idea that she might choose the colour of her drapes or the style of her settee, and she moved in to learn the ways of her new charges. There were to be twenty nurses, and six of them had children to be settled, which meant a great deal of work and some expense, for though their mothers were to pay their weekly board, Charlotte always settled a lump sum on the foster parents to allow them to make suitable modifications to their homes and ways. Then when ten of the nurses had been installed, the tenth brought chicken pox with her and gave it to five of the others, so Miss Barthorp and her band had their first experience of nursing before the hospital had even opened its doors.

London, of course, was emptying of high society all this while, which was a good thing from Charlotte's point of view, leaving her freer to do what she must. It didn't much please Mrs Phipps, who wanted as many people as possible to see her daughter carried off in triumph. A society wedding in August seemed to her almost a contradiction in terms. The weather was so humid that Charlotte began to agree with her, and was thinking of trying to persuade her mother to put it off. Then the bride-to-be decided matters for herself by contracting the prevailing chicken pox.

Mrs Phipps was beside herself – what if her child should be marked? Cavendish was touchingly worried, and his applications to Charlotte for information and reassurance went a long way to convincing her that he really cared for Miss Phipps. There was nothing for it after all but to postpone the wedding, and take Miss Phipps away into the country. Mrs Phipps was eager for Grasscroft – probably, Charlotte thought, to inventory her daughter's future inheritance – but Cavendish vetoed this (to his parents' unspoken relief) as being too long a journey.

Instead he suggested he should escort Alice himself down to Wolvercote, where as the children still at home had all had the chicken pox last year, she would be a danger to no-one, and there would be plenty of room indoors and out for her recovery. Mrs Phipps was reconciled by the idea of seeing the avuncular seat, and adding another earl to her collection, and bought five new pairs of gloves and a dozen of stockings in anticipation of lively country-house entertainments. Charlotte imagined Mrs Phipps enveloped in the religious gloom of Wolvercote, and felt a secret, reprehensible satisfaction. But it was obvious there had been no sense of irony in Cavendish's choice. He loved his uncle, gloomy or not, and enjoyed his cousins' company, and his choice had been dictated by nothing but Alice's comfort.

Rosamund and Jes went back to Lancashire with great relief, begging Charlotte to come with them; but she had too much to do at her hospital. The August weather had brought typhoid and dysentery to the back-slums, and it was important to get the fever ward finished and the most able of her women ready for duty. Besides, she hoped that Oliver would soon be home, and wanted to be in London to meet him. But September brought another letter putting off his return; and by the same post came a letter which shocked her like a sudden dousing of cold water.

Your Grace,

My Compliments to your grace. Word has reached my ears concerning the Nature of the Females your grace has recruited to work as nurses in your grace's Hospital Wards. While it is not my purpose to Criticise your grace's Dispositions, it falls to my unhappy duty to point out the Unsuitability of such an arrangement in every way. Nothing could be more Detrimental to the Reputation of the Hospital, and of those associated with it. Indeed, to give employment to females of that order may rightly be viewed as Encouraging them in their disgraceful immorality. I believe and pray it cannot be your grace's intention to turn the Hospital into a House of Ill Repute, but such must be the inevitable consequence of giving rein to the Proclivities of the Weak and Vicious. However, I must consider my own position and credit. As medical attendant to persons of the Highest Respectability, I must have their reputation at heart as well as my own, and I must therefore, with all respect, decline to have Anything further to do with the Hospital in Any Capacity. I must further ask your grace not to mention at any time that your grace has approached me in regard to this Matter.

With my humble duty and respect to your grace,
I am your obedient servant,
Sir Foulke Holder, Bart.

'What is it, my lady?' Norton asked anxiously, discovering her mistress in tears over a letter. 'Not bad news, I hope?'

'I've been snubbed, Norton – snubbed by a wretched, pompous, puffed-up old booby!' She took the handkerchief Norton proffered and blew her nose. 'It must be my condition, I suppose. I don't know why I should let him upset me so,' she went on as Norton read the offending letter. 'But with all his respects and your graces, he is saying that his credit cannot stand to be associated with me! And to call my poor nurses wicked and vicious! I'd like to see what he would have done in their position. I'd like to see him stripped of everything and trying to survive in the gutter with every hand turned against him. I don't suppose he would come off with much credit.'

'No, miss,' Norton said absently, still reading thoughtfully.

'The worst of it is, I know he will tell everyone, just to distance himself from me, and I will never get another physician to sponsor me. Oh, that hateful, smug, sanctimonious beast! I could kill him!'

'Don't take on so, my lady,' Norton said, still thoughtfully. 'I think I know a way we can scotch him.'

'What way?' Charlotte asked eagerly, hope beginning in her wet eyes.

'I can't tell you yet,' Norton said. 'I must find out a few things first. But give me a day or two, and see if I don't give you a rod to beat him with!' She nodded encouragingly, and found another handkerchief. No-one was to upset her lady, and get away with it, not if Norton could help it.

CHAPTER NINE

'One has a certain sympathy with him,' Doctor Snow said. 'After all, he's got his living to earn, and his patients are bound to take the moral view of prostitution.'

'But they're not prostitutes,' Charlotte said crossly. 'I've met plenty of prostitutes in my life—'

'I wouldn't go telling everyone.'

'Well, I won't. But I know I can speak frankly to you. My poor nurses are not prostitutes, they're simply unfortunates who have had to survive, and some of them, not all by any means, did so by selling their bodies.'

Snow shrugged. 'They're fallen women, and no-one in the *ton* is going to care about the difference.'

'Fallen women! Good God, there's a society dedicated to the rehabilitation of criminals who've served their sentence. These women, who have committed no crime, are condemned without trial and for the whole of their lives.'

'You can't change society in a day.' His eyes twinkled. 'But don't let that consideration stop you trying. I know how you feel.'

'Yes, you do,' she said gratefully. 'You have the same thankless task, to persuade people of the truth about the causes of cholera, when they prefer their ignorance against all reason.'

'Just so. And on that subject, I can give you the happy news that the fever in Barker's Court is not cholera after all, thank God.'

'Thank God indeed! And as the weather's cooling now, we may perhaps miss it altogether this year.'

'I wouldn't be too sanguine,' Snow said. 'The first two major epidemics both began in October. But we can hope. What is life without hope?'

What indeed, thought Charlotte. She had been busy at the hospital, helping to nurse the influx of sick and simultaneously train her nurses in their new and alien duties. She had quickly learned which were clumsy and which dextrous, which could be trusted to get on alone, which had to be supervised the whole time. One or two had shown reluctance to perform the unpleasant tasks, and had shrunk back from vomiting and voiding patients: if they did not get over their squeamishness they would have to go. Mrs Webster was the best of them so far, she thought: handy and sympathetic, willing and obedient. She had the knack of always being in the right place at the right time. One girl, the youngest of her recruits, over whom Norton had expressed doubts, had been very enthusiastic about the dormitory and the bathing facilities, the uniform dress and the food, but when on the ward always managed to be somewhere else when there was something to be done that might dirty her hands or her apron. Mrs Mitchell would bear watching, Charlotte thought; but a glance in Miss Barthorp's direction told her she did not need to warn her of that. Miss Barthorp was quick and observant, and had already won the respect of the nurses. It was Miss Barthorp's suggestion that all the nurses, whatever their marital status, should be addressed as Mrs. Decent females were not yet what patients expected to find on the wards, and addressing them all as married women might give more confidence on both sides, she thought.

There was so much to do that she had, blessedly,

forgotten Holder and his snub, until Norton brought up the subject.

'About Sir Foulke, my lady,' she began.

'Oh, that wretched man! I'd rather forget him,' Charlotte said.

'If he lets you,' Norton said. 'He might spread poison about you, don't forget. After all, who is to know what the nurses were before, unless someone tells? It isn't branded on their foreheads.'

'That's true.'

'I told you I could give you a rod to beat him with, didn't I? Well, you see, I had heard something about him when we were in Devil's Acre one time.'

'Something to his discredit?'

'Oh yes,' Norton said with a smile. 'I didn't want to mention it to you until I had all the facts, but I've seen the woman now, and she's willing – eager, even – to speak up. So you can go and front him, my lady, and make him squirm. This is the way of it.'

Charlotte listened to the story with growing anger. Norton was against Sir Foulke because he had upset her mistress; but Charlotte was filled with a purely disinterested fury at the man's hypocrisy.

'You're sure of this, Norton?' she asked at the end.

'Not a doubt in the world. I can fetch the woman here if you want, and she'll tell you herself.'

'Yes, do that,' Charlotte said. Her fury was well contained now, and she looked grim. 'Bring her here, and I'll go and see Sir Foulke, and have a word with him.'

Sir Foulke Holder's house was brightly lit, and when the door was opened there were sounds of many voices within. The butler, a scrawny man with a prominent adam's apple, seem inclined to deny Charlotte entry.

'Sir Foulke is hentertaining,' he said.

'Do you know who I am?' Charlotte enquired.

The man blinked. 'Yes, your grace,' he admitted at last, as though he knew it weakened his case.

'Very well. Sir Foulke will see me.' The adam's apple went up and down the throat as the man considered his options. 'It is a matter of the greatest urgency,' Charlotte said beguilingly. 'Pray show me to some quiet room, and ask Sir Foulke to be so good as to give me a moment of his time at once.'

This was, after all, a duchess, the butler considered. It didn't do to upset duchesses. He bowed very low indeed, to make up for his former hesitation, showed her across the hall to a darkly furnished, manly sort of room with a great many books in it, and left her alone. She hadn't long to wait. Sir Foulke came so quickly she could imagine the scene in the drawing-room as the butler approached and whispered in his master's ear. Consternation at the very least must have crossed that florid face. A quick, heavy tread preceded the opening of the door, and Sir Foulke came in in full evening dress, ribbon and star, with a number of emotions struggling for supremacy in his face.

'Your grace,' he said, bowing. 'I am at a loss to understand to what I am to owe this—'

'You shall not wonder for long,' Charlotte interrupted him pleasantly. 'I am sorry to have called you from your guests, but what I have to say could not wait, and is soon said.'

'Indeed, ma'am,' he said, scanning her face, not knowing whether to be haughty or conciliatory. Had she come to quarrel or plead? This was a duchess after all – and a rich one – and Southport was 'in' with the Government and at Court. 'Won't you sit down?' he conceded at last.

'I would sooner stand, thank you,' she said. 'I received from you a letter, accusing my nurses of immorality, and

223

myself of – I know not what – running a brothel in my hospital, perhaps.'

'Good God! Your grace—!' Holder paled at hearing such a word from a lady's lips.

'Don't worry, I haven't come here to quarrel with you over the letter, ill-advised and impertinent though it was—'

The use of the word stung him. 'Ill-advised it may have been, only time will tell that, but if it is impertinent to tell the truth, and to stand firm against sin, vice, and immorality – then, yes, I stand convicted, and proudly!' He was rather pleased with the way that speech came out, and the duchess nodded and looked impressed.

'I am so glad you have put it that way, Sir Foulke, because I have come here in that very cause – to tell the truth, and stand firm against – what was it? – sin and vice? Oh yes, and immorality. How well you put it! If the world of medicine could only spare you, you would be an ornament to Parliament.'

Holder was silent, suspecting irony and wondering what was coming next. She looked at him appraisingly. 'Does the name Margaret Stone mean anything to you? Or perhaps you know her better as Daisy? A charming diminutive, is it not?'

His face darkened alarmingly, and he had difficulty speaking. 'What – what—' he spluttered.

'You do know her, then?' Charlotte asked sweetly.

A speck of white appeared at the corner of his mouth. 'No!' he managed to jerk out.

'We are both warriors in the cause of truth, don't forget, Sir Foulke. Daisy Stone has told me her story, and a very sad one it is. How she was the daughter of a respectable tradesman before you seduced and debauched her. How when she became pregnant you cast her off. Her father wouldn't have her back then, because you had ruined her – that's what he called it. Alone, outcast, penniless, and with a baby to support. I wonder what you would have done in the circumstances, Sir Foulke? How would you have managed? Creditably? In desperation she even came to your house, which I must say showed either great courage or enormous optimism, but you refused even to see her. She is bringing up your son without your help, Sir Foulke, but it is a great struggle. I wonder you have never wanted to see him. Most men want a son, to follow in their footsteps. Would your son look up to you, do you think? Would you teach him honour and morality?'

Holder's face had gone through changes while she spoke. At the beginning it had become so suffused she wondered for a delirious moment whether he might have a stroke right there in front of her. But as she went on he grew calmer, and now as she paused he said, 'The woman is lying. I have never heard of her in my life. You have been taken in, duchess.'

'Oh, I think not,' Charlotte said, raising her eyebrows. 'But it is easily tested. She is in my carriage outside. I'll bring her in and see if she recognises you. The child too – and I must say, Sir Foulke, he has quite a look of you. He would be a handsome boy, if he had ever had enough to eat in his life.'

'If this is some clumsy attempt to blackmail me—' he began haughtily.

Charlotte lost her temper. 'How dare you! Who do you think you are talking to? I have come here to confront you with your own disgusting hypocrisy. You write to me of "Women of that order": what order of man are you, Sir Foulke Holder?'

'If you choose to believe the lies of a woman of that stamp, instead of the word of a gentleman—'

'If you were a gentleman, I might believe you,' she said. He paled at the insult and drew himself up, but before he could speak she went on, 'But as to what stamp of woman Daisy is, she was a decent girl from a respectable home before you seduced her.'

'If she had been a decent girl, as you put it, she would not have succumbed.'

'She didn't, at first, did she? But you wanted her so badly, you promised her marriage, and she was dazzled, poor creature, and naïve enough to believe you.' She saw him open his mouth to deny, and pressed on angrily. 'Yet all that is beside the point. If she succumbed, whatever the reason, it was to the same act that you were so eager to perform with her. If she sinned, your sin was the greater. You were older, wiser, a man of the world. She knew nothing beyond the confines of her father's house. Which is the monster, Sir Foulke, the seducer or the seduced? Which got the greater pleasure from the act? And which pays the price? Which lives in opulent luxury, and which struggles against starvation in a single draughty room?'

Now Sir Foulke would be heard. 'I am at a loss to understand your grace's argument. If you wish to believe every word told you by some low slut you have picked up out of the gutter—'

'Who put her in the gutter?'

'She put herself there. She and all those women you are so busy filling your hospital with. Vice brings its own punishment in this world. If they had kept their virtue, they would not be reviled; but when they part with it so lightly, the whole world knows what they are.'

Charlotte was trembling with rage, but she kept her voice low and even. 'Every woman in Daisy Stone's position is there because a man committed that same act for which you blame them. You are one of those men, Sir Foulke. The vice, the immorality, the blame are all yours.'

He shook his head pityingly. 'Oh duchess, how little

you understand the world! If you argued such a thing publicly you would be laughed to scorn. What I do and what the likes of Daisy Stone do are matters so far separated they might exist in different universes! There are different rules governing the conduct of men and of women, as everyone knows – everyone except yourself, it seems. And if you will take my advice, you will learn it quickly, before you make yourself an outcast from decent society. And now,' bowing, 'if you will excuse me, I must return to my guests.'

Charlotte stopped him. 'What do you propose to do about your son, Sir Foulke?'

'I have no son, ma'am,' he said. 'I have no wife. It has been a matter of regret to me sometimes, but my work has always come first with me.'

'What if I tell the world Daisy Stone's story?'

'What if you do? No-one would believe you.'

But she had seen his eye flicker. 'Are you sure about that? If your reputation could not bear the taint of being associated with my hospital, could it survive the speculation that would follow my revelations? After all, society would wonder why I put up such a story if it were so easy to knock down.'

His eyes narrowed. 'What do you want?'

And she laughed, shocking him. 'Oh, do not fear I have come to *blackmail* you!' she said, throwing his word back at him contemptuously. 'I am too far above you in every way to covet anything you have. All I want is your silence. I do not know who told you that my nurses were "fallen women", as I suppose you would say, but there is no need for anyone else to know. I want your word that you will say nothing to anyone to harm the reputation of my hospital or my nurses, that's all.'

He went through a silent struggle. 'You have my word,' he said at last.

'Thank you.' She contemplated him a moment longer. 'It is not quite true that that was all I wanted. I had hoped to bring you to an acknowledgement of your sin, but clearly that is impossible. But be assured, I shall take care of Daisy Stone and her child – *your* child. Not for your sake, you understand, but for theirs. Remember, if ever you feel inclined to abuse me, that they are my pensioners.' And with that she walked past him and out of the room, not even waiting for him to open the door for her. The butler, lingering in the hall, had to race her for the front door.

In the carriage she found herself still trembling. Daisy Stone, with her boy asleep on her lap, spoke out of the darkness. 'He didn't want to see me, then, ma'am?'

'I didn't want you to see him,' Charlotte said. 'Don't be afraid, Daisy, I will take care of you both. You shall not want.'

'No, ma'am. Thank you very kindly, ma'am,' Daisy said. But her voice was sad. Charlotte might be more reliable, but she was not the man who had won Daisy's heart. Charlotte knew that her new pensioner would much have preferred a more uncertain future with acknowledgement, and the chance of seeing Sir Foulke again. Women, she thought, are their own worst enemies.

Three days later, Ungar brought a card to Charlotte as she sat writing letters.

'A gentleman wishes to see you, your grace.' She could always tell from Ungar's voice when he approved of the gentleman. She took up the card. Sir Frederick Friedman. She knew the name very well: he was a surgeon at St George's, and a 'specialist', as the term was, in the field of nerves.

'Show him up.' She couldn't imagine what he might want. She had no connections with anyone at St George's.

He was a distinguished-looking man in his early fifties,

with fine, waving silver hair which contrasted oddly with
his eyebrows and whiskers, which were still black; firm
features and quick eyes proclaimed his intelligence, as his
fine clothing proclaimed his wealth and success. Charlotte
could see why Ungar approved.

'Forgive me for imposing on your time, your grace,'
he said, advancing confidently with the air of one who
usually found himself welcome wherever he went. 'I hope
you will forgive the liberty. I have not been presented to
your grace, but I hoped my reputation might have gone
before me.'

'Your reputation is introduction enough, Sir Frederick,'
Charlotte said, interested. 'Please sit down and tell me
how I can help you.'

'I hope we may be able to help each other,' he said,
smiling. He sat, looking completely at ease, and it made
Charlotte feel comfortable too. 'I understand that your
hospital is on the verge of opening, and that you have
not yet appointed your medical staff.'

'You understand almost correctly. The hospital is
already functioning, but not fully. We were obliged to
open a fever ward to deal with the outbreak of typhoid.
The rest should be ready in a matter of a week or so. And
I have a physician in residence, but not a surgeon.'

Friedman nodded. 'You also, I understand, have a
body of nurses in training.'

Charlotte stiffened. 'I have. Ten are at work already,
under a lady supervisor. Another ten will eventually
join them.'

He smiled. 'I am delighted to hear it, ma'am. I am very
much an advocate for the better training of nurses. Doctors
cannot do their work without skilled and dedicated help,
and good nursing can make a vast difference in the survival
of the patient.' Charlotte blinked in this unexpected
sunshine. 'You perhaps will not know, ma'am, that I

229

am well acquainted with the work of Pastor Fliedner in Kaiserwerth, although I do not entirely agree with his methods. To my mind nurses ought to be doing a great deal more than washing the floors and making up the fires.'

'Yes, yes, you are right! Much of the simpler medical treatment can be delegated to nurses, leaving the doctors more time for the skilled work.'

'Exactly my own feeling, ma'am!' His eyes crinkled engagingly. 'Females are every bit as capable of being trained as men, and their natural sympathies make them by far the more likely sex to make good ward attendants. I have followed the fortunes of Mrs Fry's Nursing Sisters at Guy's, and the St John's House nurses; but your scheme, from what I hear, will be a great deal more radical.'

'I do hope so. I intend to be rigorous, and to have the women properly trained, not just to hold hands and proselytise, but to do real work. They will, of course,' she added hastily, 'be strictly supervised to ensure both their good behaviour and their protection—'

'Quite, quite. In the present climate of hostility one must make one's bow in that direction, but the weakness of Kaiserwerth and many of the other nursing societies has always seemed to me that they put religion before medicine. No use praying at a man while he bleeds to death. Bandage first, catechism afterwards – that's my view!'

Charlotte laughed. 'I must tell you, Sir Frederick, what a breath of fresh air you are to me, after all the stuffy resistance I've met!'

'Oh, we are not all crusty old fossils in the medical profession! Most, I grant you, but not all.'

'I'm glad to hear it. But now, what is it that I can do for you?'

'Well, ma'am, I understand that you have not yet

appointed a surgeon, and I am here in the bold hope that you may consider me. My qualifications I may set out as my reputation, which I hope speaks for itself, and my ability to attract medical students, who you will need to walk your wards. In addition, I am entirely on your side with regard to training nurses, and would be glad to take an active part in your campaign of war. For my part, the facilities you have installed beckon me with a siren call. It would advance my research enormously to have the benefit of your operating theatres and laboratories – to say nothing of a steady supply of pauper cadavers. My speciality depends greatly on dissection, as you can understand, and I can never get hold of enough bodies for my needs.'

She liked him the better for knowing that he could mention such subjects as cadavers without shocking her. He seemed, in fact, in every way desirable – the reputation she needed for respectability, together with the right attitude of mind. She felt as though she had been pushing a boulder up a hill, and had suddenly come to the top. 'I am sure you would suit me perfectly, Sir Frederick,' she said.

He lifted a hand. 'I don't expect an answer immediately, ma'am. You will need to consult your medical advisers. But if there is anything you wish to ask me before that, I am at your command.'

'I am sure my advisers will think as I do, Sir Frederick,' she said. They talked a little more about the arrangements, and all his suggestions seemed sensible to her. Then he rose to take his leave, and she said, 'By the way, Sir Frederick, what was it prompted you to approach me?'

'I was given the hint from a most unexpected source. Sir Foulke Holder told me that you were hoping to appoint a surgeon of reputation, and that he thought I would suit.'

Charlotte frowned. 'Sir Foulke Holder? What did he tell you about my hospital?'

'Oh, nothing that I did not know already – that you had fine facilities and nurses in training. To tell you the truth,' he smiled, 'I think he was hoping to get rid of me. He is on the board at St George's, where my views on nursing are well known, but not equally well liked. Probably I would have come to you on my own initiative, once I knew you had not yet appointed a surgeon, but he put the spur to my side, that's all.'

Damn Holder, Charlotte thought when Friedman had gone. He had sent her the perfect surgeon, presumably as a bribe for her silence, or perhaps a peace offering. She was glad to have Friedman, but the last thing in the world she wanted was to feel any kind of gratitude towards Holder.

The Duke of Wellington died. 'He was eighty-three, I know, but somehow one didn't expect it,' Lord Theakston said to Charlotte when she came to share her sadness with him. 'Thought he was immortal. Silly, really.'

'I know what you mean, though,' Charlotte said. 'He seemed to exist outside the normal flow of time.'

'He was a great man,' Danby said.

'I'm so glad I knew him. Strange to think that he was at my come-out, and at my mother's. He was so kind and pleasant to me, putting me at my ease.'

'People thought of him as a cold man, but I'll never forget how he cried after Waterloo when he looked at the casualty lists. Hated war. Funny thing for a general. But he beat old Boney hollow. Never be another like him.'

He lapsed into silence, and Charlotte sat quietly, looking at him. Since Grandmama had died, he seemed to have grown frailer day by day. At first he had seemed as vigorous as ever, walking down to his club every day,

232

attending debates in the Upper House, visiting army friends and discussing politics, soldiering and wine. But little by little his activities dropped off; little by little he did less, until now, only a year after Grandmama's death, he hardly stirred from the house any more, sitting for long hours in a chair in a patch of sunshine, watching the shadows on the wall. Nothing could make him less neat and particular in his appearance, but within his exquisitely cut coat and trousers, under his snowy linen, he was as thin as a bird, fragile bones and suddenly visible veins, looking as if a puff of wind might blow him away. Charlotte was reminded of a twig which had burned to ash in the fire, still holding its shape in ghostly grey, until one touched it and it fell into dust. He was Papa Danby still, but he was growing transparent, and soon he would be gone completely. She looked at his serene face, and knew that she must not mourn, except for her own sake. He had never wanted anything but to be with Lucy, and without her, this world had become the insubstantial dream, and where she was the solid reality. That was what a ghost was, Charlotte thought: a person out of his proper world. As she, full of the juice of life, would be a ghost if she could somehow appear in the next world, so Papa Danby, who belonged there, seemed a ghost in this one.

'But you'll stay for the wedding, won't you?' she asked anxiously. His eyes came back to her, and he smiled. He did not seem to think it a non-sequitur, or wonder at her choice of words.

'Oh yes,' he said. 'I must be here for that.'

'Talking about the wedding, are you?' Emily bustled in with something on a tray. She couldn't get out of the habit of doing things herself, which had thoroughly disconcerted Lucy's well-trained servants at first. But they were too polite even to hint at disapproval when she appeared in the kitchen or called down the hall instead of ringing a bell; and now they had grown used to her. 'Here's your beef tea, Papa Danby. And don't tell me you don't want it! You know perfectly well it's for my benefit, not yours. I have to see someone eat every few hours, or I get restless, and you're the one I can bully most easily.'

Theakston took the cup obediently, but looked at Charlotte with a twinkling eye. 'She does, you know. Bullies me horrid.'

Charlotte laughed. 'I can see how miserable it makes you.'

Emily bent and kissed the top of Theakston's head – but carefully, so as not to disarrange his hair. 'It's guilty conscience, too,' she said. 'I wish I could have given you a grandchild; but God willed otherwise.'

She knows, Charlotte thought; and it seemed a very good and strong thing that there was no pretence between her and Papa Danby. They had loved each other from the first moment, and recognised an honesty in each other.

Theakston reached up a hand and covered Emily's, which was resting on his shoulder. 'Still time,' he said. 'Only been married three years.'

'Nearly four,' Emily said. She wanted a child so much that Charlotte felt almost guilty for conceiving so easily. She was three months pregnant now, and beginning to show. If she did not tell the news soon, it would be discovered anyway, but she held off because she wanted Oliver to be the first to know. But looking at Emily and Papa Danby, she thought suddenly that it would be dreadful if she delayed too long, and he died without knowing. He had said he would wait for the wedding, but the sunlight seemed to pass through him without hindrance as he sat smiling at her.

So on an impulse she said, 'I know it isn't quite the same, not quite as good as if Emily were to say the same thing, but I'm going to have another child.'

234

He didn't say anything, but a slow, lovely smile spread across Papa Danby's face. Emily, however, stared for a moment, her mouth trembling, and then burst into tears.

Charlotte hurried to her in distress. 'Oh Emily, I'm sorry! Please don't cry! I didn't mean to make you cry. I only thought – I hoped perhaps it might help. I'm so sorry!'

Emily clutched her, shaking her head and trying to speak through her tears. 'No, no,' she managed to say at last, 'don't be sorry. Never be sorry about that! I'm happy for you. I'm glad you told me. All babies are welcome, even if they're not mine.' Charlotte took her into her arms, and she laughed and cried all at once on Charlotte's shoulder, while Papa Danby looked on, smiling serenely. What a lot he'd have to tell Lucy, he thought, when they finally met again.

Mrs and Miss Phipps were back in London. Rosamund and Jes had come back first to open up the house in St James's Square, and the Phippses were now re-installed there and the wedding preparations were well under way. Alice had recovered fully from her chicken pox, and thanks to Mrs Phipps's endless vigilance in preventing her daughter from scratching, not the least pock disfigured her pale face. The wedding-clothes were finished, the invitations sent and answered, the Archbishop and the Abbey standing by. The bride was to be married from her future mother-in-law's house, and Lord Batchworth was to give her away. Everybody, as Mrs Phipps reminded herself rapturously, who was anybody would be there. They would even have had the Duke of Wellington if he could have hung on a few weeks longer.

Cavendish was to stay at Southport House and leave for the Abbey from there, with his cousin Viscount Calder as groomsman, and the wedding-feast was to be held at Southport House afterwards – nowhere else was big enough to accommodate the numbers. Charlotte was also to accommodate the Aylesbury family, and the Morland party from Morland Place, and when Norton told her disapprovingly it was too much trouble for her in her delicate condition, she said that it wouldn't be the least trouble at all. 'I have a house full of servants. I shan't be making the beds and serving the meals myself, you know.'

'I know that, my lady, but—'

'But you don't like Mrs Phipps, and you still wish Lord Blithfield was marrying someone else.'

'It isn't my place to wish anything of the sort,' Norton said stiffly.

Charlotte laughed, and patted her hand. 'I'm not doing it for Mrs Phipps, nor yet for Miss Phipps, so you can take that look from your face. And don't worry about the baby. I'm feeling very well.'

She was, having gone through the awkward three-month adjustment; though she was growing large at such a rate she was beginning to wonder if they had the dates right. She was going to have to have Norton let the seams out of the new gown she had had made for the wedding.

'And Lady Turnhouse coming to stay as well,' Norton concluded, 'when you should be having nothing to upset you.'

Charlotte's mother-in-law could not resist an invitation to a tonnish wedding attended by all her lifelong friends, even if the bride was as suspect as could be.

'Lady Turnhouse will be so pleased I'm with child, she'll be as nice as pie to me, you'll see,' Charlotte said.

'Yes, and she'll make the visit last a twelvemonth on the strength of it,' Norton said.

Everyone would be coming to London for Cavendish's

wedding, everyone except poor Fanny Anthony. But almost at the last minute, a letter arrived from Fanny to say that she and Doctor Anthony would be coming after all. 'Philip wants to attend a symposium on the treatment of typhoid fever at Guy's, so I shall be allowed to attend the wedding as a by-the-way. Dearest Charley, I so long to see you! We shall talk and talk and talk. Thank you for asking us to stay. I hope it won't be awkward for you, but in such a crowd perhaps we will pass unnoticed. I hope Philip may find so much fever to discuss that we shall stay a month, but I do not hold out too much hope.' Evidently, Charlotte thought, he had been too busy to censor that letter.

They arrived on the day before the wedding. Philip Anthony greeted Charlotte with the same cool courtesy as always, expressed himself grateful for the invitation, and asked after Oliver. Fanny waited only for the formalities to be exchanged before flinging herself into Charlotte's arms to hug and kiss her, and shed a few tears of happiness. Charlotte returned her embraces, feeling with concern how thin Fanny was grown, and when she could finally look at her, she saw that despite the high fashion of her clothes and hair, her face was worn and unhappy, and her youthful prettiness gone. She met Charlotte's eyes with a speaking glance, but any real conversation had to wait until they could be alone.

'I see you have not brought little Lionel with you,' Charlotte said, with a plan in mind.

Anthony raised his eyebrows. 'To what purpose? He is too young to gain any advantage from the journey or the occasion. Far better he should remain where he is and continue his normal regime.'

'How wise you are,' Charlotte said. 'But you must miss him so, Fanny. As soon as you have rested from your journey, you must let me take you to the nursery and comfort yourself with my little ones.'

This sentiment seemed to find approval with Anthony, and as soon as she had taken off her bonnet and tidied her hair, Fanny was ready to be rescued.

'Oh darling, Charley, what a relief this is,' she exclaimed, squeezing Charlotte's hand as they went upstairs. 'I thought I would never see you again! But to be here, and see all my family again – and I was sure he would not let me come! And to be without Lionel, too, the little beast! He is going to be the exact copy of his father, you know. But how could Oliver leave you so long alone? And how are things with your hospital? And who is this creature Cav is marrying? Tell me everything, quick!'

They reached the top of the stairs, and Charlotte had to pause to catch her breath. Fanny looked at her in surprise and then her gaze became intent. 'No! Don't tell me! Charley, you aren't – are you?'

'Three months,' she said. 'Just before Oliver went away – he doesn't know yet. I wanted to tell him face to face, and he was to be the first to know, but he's been gone so long and I've got so big it was no use trying to hide it any longer.'

To Charlotte's dismay, Fanny burst into tears. Charlotte took her in her arms and let her cry on her shoulder, reflecting that if this was the effect she was to have on people, the new baby would have a watery start. Fanny soon recovered herself and said, 'I'm sorry, Charley. I'm overwrought, that's all. But for you and Oliver to have a baby is such a lovely thing, and so different from me with horrible Lionel – there now, I've had my cry, and I shan't any more. I'm here to enjoy myself, before I'm locked up again.'

'Oh Fanny! It's no better, then?'

'No,' she said. 'I don't see how it can ever get better.

238

Sometimes – sometimes I think I must do something, anything to change things. But what can I do? I can't tell you, Charley, how desperate I feel sometimes.' Charlotte was silent, not knowing what to say. And then Fanny straightened her shoulders and said, 'And that's all I'm going to say about that! Come, now, show me these babies of yours.' They went into the nursery. 'Oh, goodness, how they've grown! Good afternoon, nurse. Little Olivia is such heaven! The prettiest thing in the world. And Venetia, you're the image of your Mama. Yes, come and kiss me, you angel! Do you remember me? I am your Aunt Fanny. I may be an aunt, mayn't I, Charley?'

'Whatever you please,' Charlotte laughed. Venetia scrambled down at once from her chair and submitted to being kissed with reasonably good grace, and then inspected Fanny solemnly.

Well,' Fanny said, 'you have stared hard enough. What do you make of me?'

'You have a very pretty gown,' Venetia said judiciously.

'And is that all?'

'And you smell very nice.'

'That is otto of roses. I have a little bottle in my reticule. If Mama permits, perhaps you shall have a little on your handkerchief.'

'Do you have it on your handkerchief?'

'No, I wear it on my skin, but little girls mayn't do that.'

'I'm not a *very* little girl. I'm greater than 'Livia.'

'But you're not as great as me and Mama.'

'When I are, can I have otters on my skin too?'

Fanny laughed. 'If Mama says so.'

'May I, Mama-duchess?'

Charlotte assented, and Venetia took Fanny firmly by the hand and led her to a seat where the contents of her reticule were comprehensively examined. Olivia, wanting her share of the treat, came over and tugged Fanny's sleeve, and was taken up at once onto her lap. Charlotte watched, torn between amusement and sadness. Fanny seemed so happy, and chatted with the children so naturally, it was plain she had a bent for motherhood. What a dreadful shame and waste that she should be denied more children, and should have so little affection for Lionel.

The wedding was a triumph. Rosamund and Jes had spent lavishly enough to satisfy even Mrs Phipps, for they were anxious that no hint of compromise should overshadow their son's future. No-one must have any reason to suppose that they were less than delighted with his choice. Cavendish looked happy, and so handsome in his dress uniform that every unmarried woman in the congregation sighed wistfully – and some of the married ones, too. He stood waiting by the steps, chatting to his groomsman, Aylesbury's eldest son, Viscount Calder. Calder was a stocky young man with curly brown hair and a pleasant face, marked with very fine, arched eyebrows. Charlotte, examining him idly as she waited with everyone else for the bride to arrive, remarked how much he looked like his uncle, Tom Weston, who had just those same eyebrows, and the same build. But her vague wonderings were interrupted by the fanfare which marked the arrival of the bride. Drifting down the nave on Lord Batchworth's arm, Alice looked perfectly unearthly. Her gown of ivory satin was swathed in a mist of gauze, her pale hair dressed with white roses, her long veil so fine that it floated behind her as though she had just descended from a cloud, and a little of it was still clinging to her. Her skin was so white it seemed to glow in the dimness inside the Abbey, and the only colour about her was the blue of her eyes, intensified by the lack of competition. Even Mrs

Phipps drew in her breath and held it at her daughter's extraordinary loveliness; and Cavendish, as he turned to look at her, was dumbstruck. An approving whisper ran round the congregation: plainly it was a love-match – look at his expression – how charming – how good of the Batchworths to accept her so completely. And then the service began.

The preamble had just finished and the Archbishop was just beginning the recital of the vows when there was a little commotion behind the choir seats, in which the close family was sitting. A latecomer, Charlotte thought; but why didn't they stay quietly at the back, instead of making a fuss? When the ripple of movement reached the front row in which she sat, and she heard whisperings of comment from around the Abbey, and even the Archbishop glanced across and faltered a moment in his recitation, she felt cross on Cavendish's behalf, and refused to crane and gawp like everyone else. She kept her eyes forward, frowning disapprovingly to show that she did not care for such selfish behaviour. And then the intruder actually pushed along the line and arrived next to her, and before she could turn to scowl, her hand, resting on the stall in front, was taken up by a large, strong, male one that she knew very well. Her head whipped round, and there was Oliver, smiling down at her – very brown from his journeyings and rather travel-stained and rumpled, but undeniably Oliver. Her face broke into an irresistible smile, as he lifted her hand to his lips and kissed it. But a note of disapproval had entered the Archbishop's voice, and she hastily rearranged her expression and faced forward, not to spoil Cavendish's moment for him.

There was just time after the return from the Abbey and before the wedding-breakfast for Oliver to run up to his room to wash and put on clean linen at least. Charlotte went up with him, and Oliver's man, Dinsdale, loitered tactfully on the stairs to give them a few moments together.

They spent the first of them in breathless silence, locked in an embrace which neither of them wanted to break.

'How did you suddenly appear like that?' were Charlotte's first words when their lips parted at last. 'Why didn't you tell me you were coming?'

'My business was finished and I had the chance of a quick passage from Kronstadt. There wasn't time to let you know if I was to make the ship. And when I landed I realised there was just time to reach the Abbey if I came in my travel-dirt.'

'I'm glad you did,' she said, kissing him again. 'What do you think of Cavendish's bride?'

'Nothing at all,' Oliver said sternly. 'I have far more important things on my mind – for instance, how come you didn't tell me you were pregnant?'

'How did you know?'

'I've just had my arms around you, idiot, and found someone had come between us! Why didn't you tell me?'

'I wanted to tell you face to face, not in a letter, and of course I didn't expect you to be gone so long that it would have become obvious.'

'I see. So it's my fault?'

'Indubitably. If you'd come home when you were meant to, you'd have been the first to know. But I wanted to see your expression when I told you.'

He kissed her brow, and then hugged her again briefly, with a little tremulous sigh. 'Tell me now, then, and you shall see as much of my expression as you please.'

'Very well.' She looked up at him solemnly. 'When you went away, you left me a parting gift. I am with child, my dear love.' He didn't say anything, but what she saw in his face was almost too much to bear.

* * *

Cavendish and the new Lady Blithfield went to Grasscroft for their honeymoon, and Rosamund and Jes remained in London to keep Mrs Phipps from following them. Doctor Anthony went out every day to meet his medical friends, having left strict instructions that Fanny was not to leave the house unaccompanied. Since Charlotte was very preoccupied with her suddenly returned husband, Emily stepped in to rescue Fanny and accompany her wherever she wanted to go; and the two of them frequently called in at St James's Square and rescued Rosamund from Mrs Phipps.

Anthony's presence made some discussion of medical, and more specifically hospital, matters inevitable. He visited Charlotte's hospital, and pronounced himself impressed with the arrangements, a generous praise which would have embarrassed her had he not spoiled it by immediately condemning the whole notion of female nurses.

'I am sure you must agree with me, duke,' he said. 'It is not something one would wish to see decent females do, even those of the lower orders. However well regulated the surroundings, it is the nature of attending the sick and injured to be disgusting, and more than the female spirit can bear.'

Charlotte thought despairingly that between Anthony, to whom all women were delicate flowers, and Holder, to whom they were corrupt and corrupting, there must be someone who thought that they were human beings, with minds of their own and the same right to make them up as men. Before Oliver was obliged to reply, Charlotte said quickly, 'Well, you see, Doctor Anthony, that there are other medical men who do not agree with you. Sir Frederick Friedman is wholeheartedly for the training of nurses.'

'Yes, Friedman may be,' Anthony conceded generously, 'but of course *he* studied in Vienna.'

243

Charlotte saw Oliver's mouth begin to twitch, and felt it was time to be tactful. 'We shall never agree on that subject, so let us agree to disagree. I am glad you find something to approve of in my hospital, and I hope in time my nurses will prove their worth to you and to the world. Let us change the subject. Won't you tell us about your symposium?'

Anthony gave a summary of the day's talk, and expounded his own views about typhoid and its treatment, and Charlotte determinedly held her tongue. Then the talk turned to Russia and Oliver's trip, and photography in general. 'The Photographic Club is talking of holding an exhibition this winter,' Oliver said. 'It will be the first thing of its kind, of course, and they mean to bring together as many examples of the various branches of the art as possible. I hope some of my own views of Petersburg will be thought good enough to display. If we can persuade the Queen the the Prince to attend, it will be a great thing for the Club. They are already very interested in photography, or at least the Prince is. I hope you will honour us with a visit when the exhibition opens? Do come to Town, and stay with us, and let me be your guide to the magic pictures.'

Charlotte flashed him a look of gratitude; but it was premature. Anthony frowned a little, and said, 'I am most honoured by your invitation, but I'm afraid it is rarely possible for me to leave my work.'

Oliver tried, for Fanny's sake. 'All work and no play, you know, Anthony! A break will leave you refreshed and in better frame for your labours. And I'm sure you could not bring yourself to miss such a feast of photographic art as I promise you will be on display.'

'I know nothing of photography,' Anthony said in a voice of utter indifference. 'However, if I find my work in such a state as to permit my absence, I will be happy to avail myself of your hospitality.' And he bowed to them both.

Afterwards, in their bedroom, Oliver said, 'Did he always talk like that? How could you ever have fancied him, Charlotte?'

'No, he was always solemn, but not so pompous. But as people get older, they get more themselves, don't they?'

'Poor Fanny,' he said.

'Yes, to have more and more of Anthony year by year is grim indeed,' Charlotte said. He caught her hand as she passed him and pulled her hard against him. 'And you get more and more autocratic,' she said, leaning comfortably in his arms. 'Born to be a duke, Oliver Fleetwood.'

'And you,' he said, nuzzling her neck, 'get more and more delightful. Almost edible, I might say, my delicious – little – duchess—'

Which was all the talk there was for then.

CHAPTER TEN

One morning in March 1853, Charlotte was walking downstairs to breakfast when, two steps up from the landing, she slipped. She clutched the banisters and managed not to fall, but came down heavily on her leading foot, having effectively taken two steps as one. She wasn't hurt, but her heart was pounding: she had given herself a fright as well as a jolt. When she had her breath back, she went on towards the breakfast-room, but as she came in through the door a pain doubled her up.

Oliver, already seated and reading the paper, jumped up and ran to her.

'What is it, my love? Is the baby coming?'

'I think so,' she said, and told him what had happened. 'I'd better get back to my room while I can,' she said. 'What a pity – the bacon smells delicious.'

'Yes, and there are some rather fine kidneys too,' Oliver said, passing his arm round her waist to support her back towards the door. 'You really must time the next baby better.'

She made a strange sound, a cross between a snort and a wail. 'Don't make me laugh, please! Remember what happened last time.'

'I hope you can walk upstairs,' Oliver said, guiding her towards the flight. 'I doubt whether even two footmen could lift you. If it's not a boy, it will be an Amazon, and we may have to – ah, Ungar! Send for Doctor Abernethy at once, will you, and fetch a footman to support her grace from the other side. And send Mrs Norton to her grace's bedchamber.'

Abernethy and the midwife arrived, and the door of the confinement chamber closed on the world. The morning wore on. Oliver went to his business-room and pretended to work. When Ungar came in to announce luncheon, he was surprised and a little indignant.

'Your grace had no breakfast,' Ungar reminded him.

'There's no news?'

'No, your grace.' With surprising kindness Ungar did not point out how unnecessary the question was. 'The cook has prepared a very light meal, your grace,' he coaxed, 'and it would help to pass the time.'

'Very well,' Oliver said. He followed Ungar to the small dining-room, where a place had been set with all the usual elaboration and two footmen waited to serve him with the usual ceremony. The cook had prepared a delicate clear bouillon, a fried sole, a breast of chicken with a lemon sauce, and some apple fritters. Oliver ate boiled water, fried carboard, papier-mâché, and leather; but it did at least, as Ungar said, pass the time. He spent the early part of the afternoon walking up and down the library, and despite the fact that it was what he was waiting for, he almost jumped out of his skin when the door opened and Doctor Abernethy came in.

'If it please your grace, I would like to call in a second opinion,' Abernethy said.

Oliver felt himself go white. 'What is it? What's wrong? Tell me, for God's sake!'

'Pray, calm yourself, sir. Her grace has been labouring without result for some time now, and I feel that it would be wise, merely as a precaution, to have a second opinion. It is not at all unusual for the first stage of labour to last this long, even though it is not a first child. Her grace's last delivery perhaps gave us false expectations.'

Oliver drew a long breath. 'By all means, call someone. Who have you in mind?'

'If it pleases your grace, Doctor Snow,' said Abernethy. 'He and I know each other's work, and he was one of Professor Simpson's best pupils. There is no better man for a case of this sort.'

'A case of which sort?' Oliver asked suspiciously.

Abernethy tried to say it as matter-of-factly as possible. 'I have a suspicion that the child may be laid wrong.'

Oliver swallowed. 'Yes, fetch Snow,' he said when he had his voice under control. 'She knows him and likes him. Meanwhile – can I see her?'

Charlotte was drenched with sweat, her hair plastered down and dark with it, but otherwise she did not seem unduly distressed. 'I'm sorry to be taking so long,' she said. 'I must be keeping you from your luncheon.'

'You must imagine I've been worrying about you! I had it an hour since.'

'What did you have?' she asked suspiciously, and he looked blank. 'Just as I thought! I—' She broke off with a grimace, and fumbled for his hand. Her grip was amazingly hard, and he didn't know whether to be comforted by her strength, or worried by the pain it must reflect. After a little she relaxed and opened her eyes. 'I'm sure it's a boy,' she said. 'None but a boy would be so stubborn.'

'Abernethy's calling for Doctor Snow.'

'Yes, I know. He's a good man. And he has very small hands.'

Oliver didn't quite understand this remark, and a separate part of his brain told him he didn't want to. When Abernethy came back in a moment later, Charlotte released Oliver's hand and said, 'Go on, now, go and amuse yourself. There's no need for both of us to stay.'

'In that case, it had better be you,' he said. He stooped

to kiss her salty brow, and went away to pace some more.

Snow arrived and was shown upstairs. Time wore on. Abernethy came down again, looking a little less composed than before. 'The child is laid wrongly,' he told Oliver. 'Snow is trying to turn it, but it is proving difficult.'

Oliver had to ask, though he did not want to give voice to the words. 'Is she in danger?'

Abernethy hesitated just a moth's wing before replying, 'I don't think so. The labour hasn't severely taxed her grace yet. But I should be glad if it did not go on much longer.'

'So should I,' Oliver said politely.

It grew dark, and Oliver lapsed into a state of unreality. He paced and paced, and knew by the aching of his legs how far he must have walked. He kept having to touch things to assure himself he wasn't asleep and dreaming; and what he touched felt unreal and too distant, as though he was dreaming. The next time, it was Doctor Snow who came downstairs. His coat was off, his shirtsleeves rolled up, his brow and the balding front of his head beaded with sweat.

'Snow, you will tell me the truth,' Oliver said. 'Is she in danger?'

Doctor Snow surveyed him consideringly, as if gauging whether he could take it. 'If I cannot deliver the child soon, it may die. Then I would have to deliver it by cutting it up, which would be distressing for the mother, but necessary to save her life.'

'Oh God,' Oliver said.

'But I hope it won't come to that. With your permission I wish to administer chloroform to the mother while I try to repel the child back into the womb and turn it.'

'Good God, can you do such a thing?'

'I could not have done so at the beginning when the contractions were strong. Now they are weaker I may be able to.'

'Weaker? You mean, *she* is weaker?'

'That too,' Snow said. 'But this is wasting time. Have I your permission?'

Oliver made a helpless gesture. 'What does she say?'

He shrugged. 'She trusts me. But it's your permission I need.'

'Is there danger in it?'

'There's always danger. But it's better this way.'

'Do what you must,' Oliver said. Afterwards, when Snow had gone, he wondered if the little Yorkshireman was experimenting on Charlotte – eager to use his damned witches' brew, taking advantage of the situation and Charlotte's trust. He remembered Philip Anthony saying that Snow was not sound. Had he delivered his wife to an executioner? Better the child should die than – God, no, he couldn't even think of it! He paced and paced. The clock on the mantelpiece started to strike six; clocks all over the house joined in like a clamour of accusing voices. Suddenly he could wait no longer. He flung out of the room and ran up the stairs, hardly knowing what he meant to do; paused only an instant at the door of the room, and then burst in. The wail of a baby greeted him. The midwife gasped with horror at the sight of Oliver and flung herself between him and anything forbidden he might see; and Snow, who had been bending at the end of the bed, straightened up with something small and blood-smeared in his hands.

The thing Oliver noticed, besides how very small the small thing was, was that Doctor Snow was smiling.

'A boy,' he said. 'All is now clear. This one had his arm back, and the arm we were trying to deliver belonged to the other.'

'Other?' Oliver said, dazed. Snow turned away and Abernethy did something to the baby and then Norton hurried forward with a towel. The wailing had now developed a trembling note, like a sob, which was affecting Oliver deeply. It sounded so broken-hearted, it made him want to weep too.

'Yes, show it to him,' Snow murmured to Norton.

'Other?' Oliver said again, through his rising tears.

'Twins,' Snow said across Norton's approaching shoulder. 'There were two of them. The second will be along soon. I recommend you go and wait in another room.'

And Norton, her face awash with tears, held up the baby to show him. Nothing to see but a tiny smeary face, a little trembling mouth giving vent to those sounds of bitter loss. He hadn't wanted to leave her. I don't blame you, Oliver addressed his son silently. But there were no tears from the baby; they were all his and Norton's.

'A son, your grace,' Norton said, her voice hitching with ridiculous sobs. He nodded dumbly. She managed to smile, a little waveringly. 'Go on now,' she said. 'She's going to be all right.'

He went, but got no further than the first chair he came to, in the corridor a few feet away, where he sat down hard. Shortly he heard the wailing of the second baby. Thank God! He tried to thank God, but his brain refused to function. He could only sit, numb and helpless, like the survivor of an earthquake.

A very long time afterwards, it seemed, Norton came out to fetch him in to see Charlotte. She looked exhausted, and plainly could hardly summon the strength to whisper, but her eyes were full of triumph and a soft, shining love that made his knees feel weak.

'Two boys,' she said. 'That will be nuts for your mother.'

251

'Extravagant,' he said. He took her hand and held it against his cheek a long time.

'I don't like to do things by halves,' she said.

'Never again,' he pledged. 'Four children is enough.'

'We'll see,' she said drowsily. 'Oliver—?'

'Yes, my darling?'

'When I had the chloroform – I thought Grandmama was here. At the end of the bed. It was nice.'

He had nothing to say to that; and a moment later she was asleep.

The next morning Charlotte was sitting up in bed and eating breakfast when Oliver came in to see her.

'How are you feeling?' he asked.

She smiled. Her eyes looked shadowed, but otherwise she seemed quite normal. 'Tired,' she said. 'As though I spent the whole of yesterday digging potatoes. And hungry.'

'So I see,' Oliver said, eyeing her tray with fascination. 'Buttered eggs, sausages, bacon, kidneys—'

'I missed them yesterday.'

'And what's in this bowl? Good God, kedgeree as well?'

'I can't tell you how hollow I feel,' she said apologetically.

'You've a right to,' he said, sitting on the edge of the bed. 'But really, my love, *two* boys! Couldn't you show a little restraint?'

'I suppose I love you too much. Have you seen them? They're rather nice, aren't they?'

'Very nice.' He smiled at the word, and at the memory that came into his mind of the little broken-hearted one.

'And wasn't Doctor Snow a marvel?'

'Do you remember anything about it?'

'Everything,' she said. 'I was never insensible, you

know. He gave me just enough chloroform to take away the pain. It was a lovely, warm, drifting sort of feeling.' He wondered if she remembered saying that she had seen her grandmother, but thought better of asking her, in case she didn't.

'What do you think we should call them?' he asked instead. 'I suppose the elder of the two ought to be Henry. It's the family name, and my mother will expect it. I was only called Oliver because Grandfather was still alive and Papa thought three generations of Henrys at one time would cause confusion.'

'Henry, if you like,' she agreed, buttering toast as though she were mortaring a brick. 'Can he be Henry Oliver, after my favourite husband?'

'If you insist. And would you like to name the second-comer after your father?'

She put down to toast. 'Do you really mean it?'

'Of course, if it will please you.' She nodded, overcome, and he hastened to lighten the moment. 'Marcus Charles, then, after my favourite wife.'

'Marcus Charles,' she repeated. 'It sounds rather well.'

'Poor little mite,' Oliver said, smiling broadly. 'Fancy losing the very first race of your life like that! What kind of precedent is that to set?'

'He only lost it by a head,' Charlotte said, and then realised what she had said and clapped her hand to her mouth, and they both began laughing.

When he left Charlotte, Oliver went to his business-room and began to write the letters, to his mother first of all, at Ravendene, and the Batchworths at Grasscroft; then two notes to be taken round by hand, one to Cavendish, still living in St James's Square, and one to Tom at Upper Grosvenor Street. When he had finished these he paused a moment and let the pleasure sink in.

Not just a son-and-heir, but two sons! Two fine boys –
Abernethy said they were in perfect health, despite their
long ordeal, and small only because there were two of
them. They must have been lying wrapped in each other's
arms for Abernethy not to have heard two heartbeats
when he listened with the stethoscope. And then they
had even tried to be born simultaneously instead of in
tandem, and nearly killed their mother in the process.
The sound of that grief-stricken wailing haunted Oliver's
thoughts as though it had come from him. If he had lost
her—! She would never go through that again, he was
determined. Two daughters and two sons – a man could
not want more.

Two sons. The first-comer, Henry Oliver, was now
Viscount Turnhouse, a title Oliver had never borne
because his grandfather was still alive when his father
died. And the runner-up, who had thrust his arm out
as if he wanted to keep hold of his brother, and thus
caused all the confusion – the latecomer was Lord Marcus
Fleetwood. Venetia and Olivia had been taken to see the
new babies early this morning. Venetia had looked at
them rather dubiously, but Olivia had been charmed,
and hung over the cots burbling at them. Then Venetia
had decided she must stake her claim, pushed Olivia
aside and said firmly that they were *her* baby brothers,
not 'Livia's.

'Mine too,' Olivia pleaded, her face buckling with
disappointment, 'Oh please, 'Netia, mine too!'

'Well, you can share,' Venetia conceded, graciously.
'But that one's mine. You can have the little one.' It
happened that Lord Marcus Fleetwood was larger than
Viscount Turnhouse, so Venetia had laid claim to the
younger brother. Oliver wondered how long the arrangement would last after she found out the truth of it.

He returned to his writing. His aunt Lady Preston in

Berkeley Square. The Aylesburys at Wolvercote. The Morlands at Morland Place.

Ungar came in. 'Mr Weston is here to see you, your grace. I have shown him into the library.'

'Very well.' Oliver flung down his pen. That was quick: the message could only just have reached Upper Grosvenor Street. In the library Tom seized his hand in both of his. 'Congratulations! Ungar just "took the liberty of informing me" that you are the father of twin boys! He said you had sent a note round – it must have passed me on the way. Charlotte – is she—?'

'She's perfectly all right. Sitting up and eating like a horse, despite the fact that – well, it was touch and go at times, but Doctor Snow pulled her through. He's a magician! I've told her she's never to frighten me like that again – and all for the sake of two sons, when one would have done! But I suppose it's always useful to have a spare.' Oliver came to the realisation that Weston was not rejoicing on the same plane as himself. 'What is it, old fellow? Not bad news?'

'I'm afraid so,' Tom said. 'I came in person to make sure of seeing you first, so that you could break it to Charlotte at the right moment.'

Break it to her? Oliver's feet settled back down onto the carpet. 'Lord Theakston?'

Tom nodded. 'It was to be expected, of course, but even so—' He had to stop for a moment, and then cleared his throat and continued. 'He was dozing in his chair all yesterday afternoon. Emily went in to look at him every now and then – she took him tea at five, but though he woke and smiled at her, he wouldn't take it. She thought it best just to let him sleep. But when she went in just after six to see if he wanted to be dressed for dinner, he'd slipped over in his chair, and as soon as she touched him she knew he'd gone.' Tom swallowed a few times, and went on, 'It was very easy. Every man must hope for such an easy death. But I – I shall miss him.'

Oliver laid a hand on his shoulder, and they were silent a moment.

'Will you find the right moment to tell Charlotte? I'm sorry to put a damper on your happy day.'

'I'll tell her. I'm so sorry, Tom. He was a fine man. But as you say, it was to be expected.'

Tom smiled ruefully. 'Funny how you never expect the expected, though.'

Oliver expected Charlotte to cry, but though her eyes grew shiny, the tears did not spill over. 'It was his time,' she said. 'One can't wish him back – he wanted to be with Grandmama, and now he is.'

'That's the best way to think of it,' he said.

'I loved him very much,' she said after a moment.

'And he loved you. You gave him great pleasure in his last years. I just wish he'd known about our boys.'

It was just before six when Snow had administered the chloroform, and Charlotte had seen Grandmama standing at the foot of the bed. And there had been another hazy outline beside and behind Grandmama. She had thought she was seeing double, but she understood now. Grandmama had come for Papa Danby, and on the way they had paused to see the outcome of Charlotte's labour. That was why she couldn't cry: he had gone away to be happy, and had seen her boys before he went.

'He knew,' she said.

Charlotte was still in confinement when Lord Theakston's Will was read, but Cavendish came round to see her afterwards and told her about it.

'It didn't take long,' he said. 'The lawyer tried to spin it out with whatsoevers and howsoevers, but the upshot of it was that he left everything to Uncle Tom – said Mama and Uncle Aylesbury were provided for and didn't need any more. And there was a deuce of a lot to leave, too! You see, Grandmama left her fortune to Papa Danby to do as he liked with. Well, even though they'd always lived very comfortable, she never spent all her income, so it had mounted up. So Uncle Tom inherits her fortune and Papa Danby's. It was a queer thing, though,' he added, frowning, 'how it took Aunt Emily. When she heard it, she burst into tears.'

'Not so very surprising, perhaps,' Charlotte said.

'Yes, but it wasn't happy crying. She seemed to be trying to laugh at the same time, and it wasn't happy laughing either. Uncle Tom went over to try and quiet her, and she sort of clutched him and cried out, "But I don't want *money*! We've got enough *money*!" And then she said something about you, I didn't catch what, and Uncle Tom looked a bit embarrassed. What d'you suppose she meant?'

'Aunt Emily would dearly like to have a baby,' Charlotte said. 'I think perhaps—'

'Oh, I see. Sorry,' Cavendish said, and lapsed into thought. Then he looked up at Charlotte under his fair brows. 'I suppose it ain't the thing to say much yet, but – well, Alice thinks she might be – not absolutely sure yet, but—'

'Cav, really? I'm so pleased for you! How clever you are!'

He smirked self-consciously. 'No cleverness in it. But I am pleased. Don't know what sort of crack at being a father I shall make, but – oh, I say, not a word to anyone, by the way.'

'Of course not. Not until you say.'

'Only we don't want Mrs Phipps to know until she has

to.' He never called his mother-in-law anything but Mrs Phipps. 'How did yours take it – the twins, I mean?'

'Lady Turnhouse was almost beside herself with joy. And it has quite reconciled her to me,' Charlotte said. 'If I'd had one boy, she would still have blamed me for keeping Oliver waiting so long, but producing two at once has redeemed my character. She calls me "my dear" and beams on me – it's most disconcerting. I have to stop myself looking over my shoulder to see if there's someone behind me.'

Cavendish grinned. 'It was rather going it, wasn't it, Charley – twins?'

'Oliver hasn't dared to tell her that I was given chloroform, so don't you mention it to anyone either.'

'How could I? It ain't the sort of thing one talks about in the mess – one's sister's labour.'

'No, quite – but poor Doctor Snow was hoping that he might use me as an advertisement. If the leaders of society – that's me, by the way, in case you didn't recognize me – will only endorse its use, all the poor suffering women who are denied it because it's frowned upon by their husbands and physicians will be able to follow the fashion and enjoy the benefits. But I had to forbid him to tell anyone, for if Lady Turnhouse finds out, I'll be back in her black books; and it is nice to live in harmony at long last with one's in-laws.'

Cavendish looked moody. 'Wish I could say the same. She's got to go, Charley. It ain't so much that she bothers me – I just let it run off my feathers – but she's always tugging Alice's ear, putting her in a frazzle, making her cry, making her fancy herself nervous. And when she finds out about the baby – if there is one – it will be ten times worse.'

'I'm only surprised you've let her live with you so long,' Charlotte said.

'Oh well, she works on Alice to make her think she can't manage without her. And the fact is,' Cavendish confessed, 'I'm not so plump in the pocket I can afford to set her up in a house of her own. Papa settled on me very generously when I married, and of course I live rent-free; but I have to pay all the running costs, and it isn't a cheap house to run. And then there's Alice's clothes, and the horses, and my mess-bills – and it don't do to be paltry when one's an officer in the 11th. The Old Man expects certain standards, you know.'

'I know.'

Cavendish sighed. 'I don't want to get into debt, and I don't want to have to ask Papa for more, but I can't see but what this baby is going to strain matters even more.'

'Babies do seem to eat money. You can always come to me,' Charlotte said.

Cavendish blushed. 'Thanks, Charley – that's dashed decent of you. But I ain't sunk so low as to be cozening my own sister yet.'

In the event, John Snow did not need Charlotte's endorsement of the chloroform, for less than a month later he was provided with a far more important sponsor. Doctor Abernethy spoke to Sir James Clark, the Queen's medical attendant, about the Duchess of Southport's experience, and Clark, knowing how much his royal patient feared and dreaded the pains of childbirth, recommended to her and the Prince that they too should call in Doctor Snow. The Queen was brought to bed of a son on April the seventh, 1853, and during the last stages of labour, Snow administered to the Queen, as he had to Charlotte, just enough chloroform to ease the pain without inducing insensibility.

The Queen was delighted with the experience – 'soothing and quieting', she called it; and 'that blessed chloroform'. Within days a debate was raging in the popular press. Many commentators were horrified that the Queen had been 'experimented' upon and placed in such terrible danger, and some hinted that it was tantamount to treason so to threaten the Royal person; the *Lancet* was eloquent about the dangers of any form of anaesthesia, and argued that even when it did not cause death by first intention, it must delay the healing process, perhaps with fatal results. The clergy were outraged that anyone should attempt to circumvent the pains of childbirth, which were ordained by God as a woman's lot, the punishment for Eve's wickedness in the Garden. 'In sorrow shalt thou bring forth children', it said in the Bible; to remove that 'sorrow' was a blasphemous act and would call down the wrath of God on the nation.

But Society, and particularly the female part of it, having heard all the arguments, knew where its loyalty lay. The Queen had *asked* for anaesthesia, and having been given it, had praised and approved it. Snow, Clark and Abernethy made sure those facts were as widely known as possible. The Queen was at the pinnacle of society, and the Court was the fount of etiquette. If the *ton* had to choose between being blasphemous and being unfashionable, there was no question which was the unthinkable alternative. At first there was a trickle, and soon a steady stream, of requests for chloroform; and not only for childbirth-pains, but for minor operations too. Word soon circulated about the special suite of rooms, including a well-appointed operating theatre, which existed in the newly opened Southport's hospital; and more words followed the first, that the dear Duchess of Southport had herself had the chloroform for the birth of her delightful twin sons – indeed, she might have died without it! Soon Charlotte had the pleasure of knowing that the private and luxurious part of her hospital was constantly in demand; and the rather more dubious pleasure of knowing that she herself was on the way to becoming not only acceptable to Society, but even popular.

That year, Benedict decided to revive the tradition of the mid-summer fair at Morland Place. It was part of his most treasured childhood memories, and he wanted his sons to have the same. The fair had always been held after hay-harvest as a thanksgiving and a reward to the Morland tenants and employees for their hard work throughout the year. It had last been held in 1829: the following year his father's death had caused it to be cancelled, and his mother had never revived it; and Nicholas had always preferred the privileges of being Master of Morland Place to its obligations.

But now the estate was getting back into order after Nicky's neglect; the family fortunes were prospering; Benedict's sons were growing into fine, sturdy little boys; and Sibella was with child again. These all seemed excellent reasons to him to give the estate workers, tenants and villagers back their great celebration.

'Teddy might perhaps be a little young to understand it all,' he said, 'but Georgie will relish every moment.'

'I think it's a wonderful idea, Papa,' Mary said. 'We shouldn't let our great traditions die. Parts of the mid-summer celebrations have their roots in the pagan rituals of ancient history, you know. Father Moineau was talking about it only the other day.'

'Ah well, if a Catholic priest can't tell you about pagan rituals, who can?' Benedict said lightly, and Mary laughed. He looked at her with the love and pride which increasingly had a wistful tinge to it. Her sixteenth birthday would fall on the thirtieth of June: she was most

261

thoroughly a woman now, and the most beautiful woman Benedict thought he had ever known. Her mother had been pretty, but Mary outshone her like the sun to a candle. She was beautiful and clever and good and loving; and the lovelier she grew, the more it hurt him that she was not his.

The local lads were all in love with her, but her intellect was so far ahead of theirs, in most cases it remained a distant and hopeless adoration. They paid their dues at Mary's shrine, but set their sights lower, on girls more like themselves. It worried Benedict a little from time to time. When she was a child, he had been pleased to think no-one would be good enough to marry his treasure; now he thought the boast was in danger of becoming reality. She did have two very constant admirers, however: one was Arthur Anstey, who at nineteen had filled out from the rather weedy boy into a good-looking and sensible young man, already following in his father's footsteps and showing great promise. The other was Arthur's cousin, Evelyn Laxton – usually known as Edye. His father, Sir Cedric Laxton of Heslington Grange, was brother to Arthur's mother. Edye had some advantages over Arthur. At twenty-three he was a man of the world – important when dealing with a very clever young woman. He was also a man of leisure: he would one day inherit his father's baronetcy and estate, so he had no need of a profession. Arthur, on the other hand, had to study, and was away for a good part of the year at university, leaving the field clear for his rival.

Both, however, would be present for the mid-summer fair. The day dawned grey and rather chilly, and at breakfast everyone was getting up every few minutes to go and peer anxiously out of the window. The men were at work early putting up tents and laying out trestles, and the flags on the tent-tops hung limp against a blank sky.

But by the time breakfast ended they had begun to flutter, and soon a little wind got up which gradually rolled the grey away, and a bright, blue and breezy day set in.

All the traditional elements of a mid-summer fair were to be there: Mary and Father Moineau had pored together over old books, and particularly over the Morland Place household accounts, to be sure that nothing was missed out. Food was most important, of course. A cook-pit had been dug, in which a whole ox would be roasted, to augment the hams, pies, pasties and sausages, the fruit and cakes and bread and wonderful multi-coloured jellies with which the neighbourhood would be regaled. Morland Place cider and beer would ensure a certain jollity prevailed; with lemonade and soda-water for those who preferred to keep a clear head.

For entertainment there would be the various booths; skittles, a coco-nut shy, a Punch-and-Judy; wandering acrobats, jugglers and morrissers; and plenty of music from half a dozen bands. The traditional tests of skill would be held: archery, wrestling, jumping, and foot races, with prizes for the winners. And for those who didn't mind making fools of themselves, there would be the slippery pole, apple-bobbing, blindfold pillow-fights, and that old favourite, the pig-alley, which had been made good and muddy by a couple of dozen buckets of water. Benedict had lined up half a dozen very energetic and muscular young pigs who would be certain strenuously to resist being grabbed hold of.

And when it grew dark, there would be dancing on a specially laid floor in the open air under coloured lanterns; and the evening would finish off with a fireworks display. The whole neighbourhood had been talking of nothing else for weeks: it would be the greatest thing of its kind in memory, and speculation was rife about how much it was to cost. Benedict himself had had a moment's unease as the bills mounted up, but had dismissed it when he saw how enthralled Mary was in the preparations. He begrudged her nothing; and while the public understanding was that the fair was to be a celebration of Morland Place and its returning prosperity, everyone in the house knew that it was all being done for her.

The fair was officially to open at twelve, but by eleven the crowds were already so dense that when Benedict got up on the dais to make his speech, with Sibella, Mary and the little boys beside him, only the front ranks could hear what he said. Everyone cheered lustily, however, whether they heard or not; having declared the fair open, Benedict raised his hand, and the brass band behind him struck up with such good will that several people ducked.

As the family stepped down from the dais, Edye Laxton and Arthur Anstey both presented themselves, and simultaneously asked Mary if she would care to accompany them round the booths. Arthur glared at Edye, and Edye tried to gain an edge by smiling in a superior way which suggested that he was above such childish rivalry. 'I'd love to,' Mary said, stepped between them, took an arm of each, and guided them away towards the coco-nut shy.

Father Moineau watched with a smile, and said to Benedict, 'I don't know if you realise it, but your daughter is a diplomat. Young Arthur is far better at shying balls than Edye Laxton – he bowls for his university cricket team – but Edye is the better shot, so she will let him excel at archery afterwards. She will keep the peace between them, and each will go away thinking she favours him above the other.'

'But which does she really favour?'

Father Moineau only smiled. 'I think I shall go and watch the punchinello,' he said. 'I like to hear the children laugh.'

Jemima and Aglaea had of course been invited to stay

for the occasion. Having seen Aglaea happily settled for a comfortable chat with Henry and Celia, Jemima walked off on her own to look at the booths. She was standing watching the Indian toffee man pulling out his strange ropes of candy when a voice behind her said, '*We're* all far too old for taffy, of course, but perhaps we should buy this lady a pennyworth?'

She turned. John Anstey held the hands of his younger children – Polly, who was six, and Freddie, five – while his elder boy Jackie, seven, stood beside him, torn between the desire to look dignified and the torturing smell of hot sugar.

'But I couldn't possibly be the only one to eat it,' she said. 'Think how foolish I would look. You must all have some too, just to save my face.'

'What do you think, children? Should we sacrifice our dignity?'

Polly and Fred had no idea what he was talking about, but they said yes on general principle, and Jackie nodded silently, pulling his lower lip in under his teeth in a self-conscious smirk.

'I'm so glad you came,' John said as they walked on with their papers of toffee hot in their hands. 'When I last spoke to Benedict, he didn't seem sure that you would.'

'Aunt had a bad cold which she couldn't shake off, and it kept her from painting for so long that all she wanted to do was get back to it. So it seemed that she wouldn't want to leave Scarborough, even for the sake of seeing her family.'

'And you, of course, wouldn't leave her?'

'How could I?'

'Despite the fact that when she's working she doesn't know there's anyone else on the planet, let alone in the house with her?'

Jemima frowned. 'But when she stops work at the end of the day she's glad of the company. And besides, someone has to look after her. I'm sure she wouldn't eat properly if I weren't there.'

'Well, you're here now, and I'm very glad to see you. Why did Aunt Aggie change her mind?'

'I don't know. She said to me quite suddenly one evening, did I want to go to Morland Place, and I said yes, quite, if *she* wanted to, and that was that.'

'Daddy, Daddy, look!' They had reached a small crowd gathered round a man with two dancing dogs. He sawed away on a fiddle, and the dogs, wearing frills round their necks and middles, pranced and pirouetted on their hind legs. 'Can we watch – oh Daddy!'

'Go on, then,' John said, and the three children wriggled through to the front of the crowd. John and Jemima watched absently. At last John said, 'Jemmy, has it ever occurred to you that it isn't your responsibility to look after Aunt Aglaea?'

She turned to him so quickly that it was plain she had been thinking along the same lines. 'But she has been so kind to me! I owe her everything.'

'Not so. I'm sure *she* wouldn't say so if you were to ask her.'

'I wish you wouldn't say such things.'

'I have to. I know I said I would wait for as long as you liked, but it's been two years now.'

'John, don't!'

'I must. Jemmy, you don't have to spend your life repaying a debt that was never yours.'

'Perhaps I do,' she said, interrupting him. Her face was turned half away from him, her expression so dark that it made him feel desperately sad. 'You don't understand, Childie. You don't know—'

'Know what?' But she only shook her head. 'Well, then,

if you really feel so dead set against me, oughtn't you to tell me?' She looked at him apprehensively. 'Tell me to go away, and I will go away. Tell me you don't love me and don't want to marry me, and that will be the end of it. You can't think I would go on bothering you in the face of a determined refusal.' She was silent. 'Well? Give me an answer.'

'I can't,' she said, and it was almost a wail. 'I don't – oh, I don't *know*!'

'Yes you do. At heart, you *do*.'

She stared at him, her face working. 'Even if it were possible to marry you,' she said at last, 'how could I leave Aunt? She can't manage alone, with nothing but servants. It's unthinkable. And she'd never leave Scarborough – and *you* can't leave York.'

'It's nothing to do with Aunt Aggie,' he said sternly. 'You're using her as an excuse to avoid the issue. That isn't fair to me or yourself.'

She looked at him with anguish for a moment, and then abruptly turned away, hurrying through the crowds with her head bent in a way that made him think she was crying. He sighed, feeling puzzled and sore and guilty, and stared with unseeing eyes at the dancing dogs, his mind very much elsewhere.

Arthur had got Mary to himself for a moment, since Edye Laxton was at the butts, displaying his noble profile as he took part in the archery contest.

'Mary, you will dance with me this evening, won't you?' Arthur said, loath to lose the opportunity, even though Mary was not looking at him.

'Of course,' she said absently.

'But I mean the first dance – you will give me the first dance?'

She looked at him then. 'I don't know. Perhaps.'

He couldn't help himself. 'You won't give it to *him*, will you? Promise me that, at least.'

'Oh Arthur!'

'I can't help it! I can't bear it when you smile at him. He's so – so false! Everything about him! He's all show and swagger and – and—'

'He's your cousin. How can you talk like that?'

'Because I love you!' Arthur burst out. 'You know I do. I've loved you for years and years, and now he appears on the scene with his silly smile and his airs and his fancy talk and takes you away from me! I can't bear it!'

'Arthur, you mustn't talk like that. It's silly.'

'Don't call me silly! I mean – I'm sorry, I didn't mean to speak so to you, but you never used to think me silly before *he* started setting his cap at you.'

'I don't think you silly now, Arthur dear – I only said that was silly talk. To speak of someone "taking me away" from you, when you never owned me in the first place – and as if I had no say in the matter. I'm not a toy or an ornament, you know. I am a human being with free will, and I will choose what I do, and who I love, and eventually who I will marry.'

He was a little mollified – she hadn't said she preferred Edye. 'You don't think your papa will have something to say in the matter?'

'Of course he will have a say, but he'd never make me marry anyone I didn't want. And I don't think,' she added, with less confidence, 'he would really prevent me from marrying someone I did want.'

Arthur saw the slight shadow in her eyes as she said it, and it chilled him. 'Do you want to marry someone then?' he asked. She didn't answer at first, and he was almost glad – somehow he thought he might not like the answer.

Then at last she said, quite neutrally, 'I have seen the man I want to marry.' Her hand was resting over the pocket in which she carried the gold locket. Benedict would not allow her to wear it, but she always had it with her.

'Who is it?' he asked in a very small voice.

She turned her head and smiled at him, and it struck him to the heart, because she was so very beautiful, and her smiles were like glorious sunshine when they were directed at one; but this was a smile of which the main constituent was kindness. It was not the smile of a girl looking at the man she loved. 'I can't tell you that,' she said. 'It is a secret.'

'But it isn't Edye?' he pressed her, and she laughed. He felt comforted. It wasn't so bad if she loved someone else, as long as it wasn't Edye. And he didn't quite give up hope. She had seemed doubtful about this secret person, so perhaps it was someone unsuitable; and whatever she said, her father wouldn't give her away to anyone unsuitable. In fact, Arthur himself was the most suitable match for her in every way, and he expected that to tell in the long run. That and the fact that he had loved her longest. She wouldn't favour Edye over him, he was sure of it – well, almost. Edye might be sophisticated and know about fashionable things, and he would have the title one day, but Arthur was far cleverer and better educated, and Mary cared about such things. And she enjoyed discussing legal matters with him. It occurred to him suddenly that he was being foolish trying to compete with Edye on worldly terms. His strengths lay elsewhere. With this in mind he started to tell her about the latest phase in his studies at university, and was vindicated a few minutes later when she was so intent on what he was telling her that she missed Edye's winning shot at the bull.

* * *

Aglaea and her brother, having left Celia, who was not a great walker, went for a stroll round the periphery of the jollifications, chatting about family matters and York news. It was Aglaea who saw Jemima first: she was sitting some distance away on the bottom step of a stile, her head bowed in an attitude which did not speak happiness. Aglaea was debating whether it would be kind or cruel to draw Harry's attention to her when Harry noticed her himself. 'Hullo! There's Jemima. Why is she sitting there all alone? Is she unwell, do you think?' Aglaea didn't immediately answer, and Harry went on thoughtfully, 'I think she's crying. I do wish she would make up her mind to marry John and be done with it. This hesitation does no-one any good.'

'Do you think she wants to?' Aglaea asked, surprised that he knew about it.

'John says so, and he's a sensible man, not given to self-delusion. Of course, he doesn't fully understand why she hesitates, but you and I, Ag, who know what Nicky was really like – we can make a good guess.'

'Do you think that is why she refused him?'

'Don't you? I can't think of any other reason. What she witnessed at Morland Place might have put her off the idea of marriage for ever, leaving aside—' He paused a moment. It was a delicate area. He didn't know exactly what went on here when Jemima was a girl, but there had always been rumours. 'If she thinks all men are like Nicky underneath, poor John will have a mountain to climb.' Aglaea was silent in thought. 'It really needs a woman to talk to her,' Harry hinted. 'I suppose you couldn't—?'

Aglaea looked at the distant figure and felt she had been immersed in a dream and had suddenly woken up. She had thought Jemima didn't want to marry John. Selfishly, perhaps – because she didn't want to lose her – she had believed what was convenient to her.

'I'll speak to her,' she said abruptly. 'Go back, Harry. It must be me alone.'

Harry squeezed her arm in silent gratitude, and walked away. Aglaea went on towards Jemima. Jemima looked up; fumbled for her handkerchief and wiped her cheeks; sat up straighter and tried to smile. Aglaea fixed a serene look on her face, as if she hadn't noticed anything.

'I wondered where you were,' she said when she was near enough to be heard. 'You had enough of the noise, I suppose? I don't blame you. May I sit with you?'

'Of course,' Jemima said, making room.

Aglaea sat, and they looked at the view in silence for a while. 'Have you seen Childie yet?' she asked after a moment.

'Yes – he's here with the children. We walked about a bit, and then – well, I went off on my own.'

'I suppose he asked you to marry him again?'

'Yes,' Jemima said. Just that. Aglaea looked sidelong at her, trying to gauge her feelings.

'You and he get on so well. Would you dislike it so very much?'

'Oh, no!' Jemima said with an extraordinary, leaping eagerness in her voice, which told Aglaea almost everything she needed to know. 'At least – I don't think so. I mean – I do like him very much. But—' By degrees her voice had become flat again, toneless. 'It isn't possible.'

'Why not?'

A pause. 'Well, for one thing, I couldn't leave you all alone.'

Sometimes a person will go on walking with a stick long after they cease to need it, because they are afraid to put it aside. Then it needs someone to take it away and snap it in two. 'Well, it's strange that you should bring that up,' Aglaea said, her eyes fixed dreamily on the horizon, 'because I was looking for you to tell you that I have decided to marry Mr Underwood.'

'*What?*'

'Oh yes. He has asked me again, and I would like to accept him. But the difficulty for me would be what to do with you, if you did not marry John. You could live with us, I suppose, but I rather fancy Mrs Pownall would be jealous of her housekeeping duties, which would leave you nothing to do.'

'But – but I thought you hated marriage?'

'Hate it? No, why should you think that? With the right person, it is the best and most comfortable thing for a woman. I think Mr Underwood and I would suit very well; but if you are determined not to have John, perhaps I had better refuse him after all, and we can go on as we are.'

Jemima looked at her doubtfully. 'You aren't saying this just to—?' Aglaea looked at her enquiringly, pretending not to understand. 'No, of course you wouldn't. That would be ridiculous.' She bit her lip. 'Perhaps, if you really do want to marry Mr Underwood, I should say yes to John.'

'My dear Jemima, you can't marry John just to suit me!'

'No! No, it isn't that. I – I do want to marry him.'

'Ah well, then it's decided. Excellent.' She stood up, not to allow Jemima time to change her mind. 'I must go back and find Celia – she was feeling the heat rather. Shall you walk with me?'

'No, I'll follow in a little while.'

Aglaea nodded and walked away. Marriage to Mr Underwood, she thought, was not such a great price to pay to redeem Jemima. Aglaea had endured five years with Nicholas Morland: any other man must be easy in comparison. And from what she had observed, Mr Underwood would bend to her will in most things. Perhaps he might even be persuaded to agree to a long engagement – a very long engagement.

CHAPTER ELEVEN

Charlotte did not recover so quickly after the birth of the twins, but by the end of May she was up and about again and ready to resume her interest in the hospital. Miss Barthorp was handling the nurses very well. Two of them had had to be dismissed and replacements found, but now the full body of twenty was installed and working, and both Doctor Reynolds and Sir Frederick had pronounced themselves pleased with the result. Miss Barthorp had promoted Mrs Webster to First Nurse, and between them they kept order and assigned duties.

Miss Barthorp had proved inventive, and had asked for a number of alternations to the layout of the wards, stores and nurses' quarters. For instance, on her advice Charlotte had had a bell system installed so that nurses on the wards at night could call for help in an emergency. She had suggested a chute to take the soiled linen down to the laundry in the basement, to save having to carry it down. This proved a boon to the nurses; but then the wards were frequently left short of linen while clean sheets lay unused in the basement for want of a porter to carry them. At last Miss Barthorp suggested a second shaft next to the chute, with a hoist and pulley system, so that the clean laundry could be hauled up by the shortest route.

But Miss Barthorp was soon obliged to tell Charlotte that she couldn't both supervise the nurses and keep control of the physical material of the wards. Things were always going missing, and when a nurse could not find a bed-pan or a tin plate – or sometimes when she simply could not be bothered to wash them – she would take them from another ward, which would then have to scavenge from yet another.

'We need a housekeeper, your grace. It needn't be anyone with an interest in medical matters – just someone with an orderly mind, a grasp of detail, and a great deal of determination. I suggest that each ward should have its allocation, and that everything should be marked with the ward number. Then if the housekeeper finds something on the wrong ward, she can discipline the culprits. And she should have a central store of replacements, with a stout lock on it, and issue items only on proof of need – otherwise there will be no end to the supply, and a constant run on your purse.'

Finding the right housekeeper was difficult, for hospitals still had a bad name in the community at large. Eventually, however, advertisement and high wages attracted a Mrs Overmoigne, who had been housekeeper in a great house whose master had just died. The mistress was moving to a dower-house where she had no need of a housekeeper in the same style, and Mrs Overmoigne had taken a dislike to the new master's wife, and wanted a new position. Charlotte interviewed her, and found her quick-eyed and clever, with a strong liking for order, and with an overpoweringly autocratic nature, which suggested to her that the new master's wife was probably every bit as glad to get rid of Mrs Overmoigne as she was to go. She seemed to be just what was needed to bring order and discipline into the supply of goods to the wards, and Charlotte hastened to employ her.

Lady Turnhouse deeply disapproved of Charlotte's activities. She had never liked living in the country, and now that Charlotte had seen fit to fulfil her duty and give Oliver a son, she was glad of the excuse to come back to London, take up her own apartment in Southport House, and resume the social round she had missed so much. She adored the boys – though she still ignored the girls – and she would have taken Charlotte thoroughly to her heart if only Charlotte had behaved herself. But Lady Turnhouse's happy dream of leading society at Charlotte's side was exploded by Charlotte's outrageous behaviour. Lady Turnhouse was always fielding pointed questions about her daughter-in-law, and being forced into the horrid quandary of whether to defend her, or join in the condemnation. The dilemma was made worse when Charlotte and Oliver were invited to spend the day at Windsor, and bring Venetia to play with the Royal children. The Queen was eager to discuss with Charlotte her experience of childbirth under the benign influence of chloroform, and to ask her more about her work to relieve the sufferings of the poor, while the Prince wanted to discuss the Turkish situation with Oliver.

Early that year the Turkish government had sent troops into Montenegro to put down a rebellion, and Russia had objected, on the grounds that the Montenegrans were Christians and the Turks Muslims. The Tsar claimed the right to protect all Christian subjects of the Turkish empire, and sent Prince Menshikov to Constantinople to threaten the Sultan with war if he did not withdraw. Lord Stratford, the British Ambassador to the Sublime Porte, told the Sultan to stand firm; now Menshikov had departed with the threat that if the Sultan did not remove his troops from Montenegro, the Tsar would put troops into Moldavia and Wallachia. The Prince wanted Oliver's opinion on whether the Tsar meant it or not. Derby's short-lived government had gone out last December, and Lord Aberdeen was now Prime Minister, with Clarendon Foreign Secretary. Clarendon had been an attaché in Petersburg, and had the same opinion of the Tsar as Oliver – that he was mad enough to do anything; Russell thought the Tsar's intention was to break up Turkey, and Palmerston, who was now Home Secretary, thought bold action and a firm stand the best way to stop him; but Aberdeen believed his threats were bluster and would come to nothing, and with most of the Cabinet was very much against Britain's doing anything that might lead to war.

A divided Cabinet produced a half-hearted solution: the British fleet was to move up the Mediterranean to the mouth of the Dardanelles, to show support for Turkey, but was not to pass through, because that might provoke the Russians. And when in July the Russians did move their troops into the Danubian provinces, that was not regarded as necessarily an act of war, since they did have the right by Treaty to do so. The French fleet joined the British; the wheels of diplomacy began to turn; Austria tried to negotiate a settlement; and Aberdeen closed the Parliamentary session with the hope that peace would be maintained.

Oliver was doubtful. 'There's such a hatred of Russia in general in this country,' he said to Charlotte, 'that if the Tsar doesn't withdraw, I'm afraid popular opinion may push the Cabinet into it. And I don't believe the Tsar will withdraw. He wants the territory, and most of all he wants the Straits – and we can't let him have them.'

Cavendish agreed with him, though for different reasons. 'Our army hasn't had a decent campaign since 1815, nothing but a few skirmishes in India, which don't count. What's the use of having an army if you never fight anyone?'

'Oh Cavendish, you can't really mean that,' Charlotte said.

'I'm just telling you what people say.' Cavendish said. 'But if it came to war, there'd be nothing to be afraid of, you know. Our men are the best fighters in the world. The Russkies wouldn't stand up against 'em for five minutes. It'd hardly be a fight at all, really – more's the pity.'

Jemima married John Anstey on the fifteenth of July. Both had wanted a quiet, private wedding: John was a widower, and Jemima, despite her capitulation, still had many confused doubts and worries. The head of the family, Lord Anstey, who was John's uncle, was almost sixty, and though still hale, was a man of simple tastes, who would have been glad to let John marry as he wished. But his unmarried sister Mary, who ran his household, had other plans, and her sisters Louisa and Charlotte supported her. They both had children of dancing age, and they were not going to let any Anstey, let alone the heir, take a bride with so little ceremony. So Anstey House erupted into a huge family party. As well as Ansteys of three generations there were Shawes, Chubbs, Somerses, and Keatings who all regarded Anstey House as their natural home, and Micklethwaites and Applebys and Laxtons besides who were family connections. The Morland Place family was there, and Aglaea came to see her former companion off, looking unchanged though her hand was resting on the arm of Mr Underwood. Mr Underwood seemed rather more bemused than happy, but that was a natural reaction in anyone seeing the Anstey family *en fête* for the first time.

Harry Anstey was delighted that his sister was marrying, as well as Jemima. He was an old-fashioned soul who believed – despite Aglaea's life with Nicholas Morland – that women ought to be married, that they couldn't be happy otherwise. He was inclined to question Mr Underwood fairly rigorously; but Underwood himself seemed so dazed by his good fortune, and looked at Aglaea with such adoration, that Harry's questions died on his lips.

'It's the best thing for you,' he said to Aglaea when he had a moment alone with her. 'You ought to have remarried long ago, really. Like getting back on a horse when you've had a fall – you should do it right away, so that you don't lose your nerve.'

'Is that your advice?' Aglaea said with a faint smile. 'I wonder you didn't give it before, then.'

'You went off to Scarborough,' Harry said. 'But I'm glad all's well at last. This Underwood seems a very decent fellow.' Aglaea said nothing. Harry groped for the right words. He had never really understood his youngest sister. There had always been so little to get hold of. She was so quiet, not laughing and crying and quarrelling and making up like other Ansteys, never giving her opinions, never voicing her thoughts. And there was this queer business of the painting, too. She plainly had great talent, though her later pictures were strange. But she had a growing reputation, and he knew of several people who were already collecting her pictures as though she were a Constable or a Gainsborough. And now she was marrying – quite suddenly, it seemed, though she had known the fellow for years – and still she did not say that she was happy, or in love, or of any of the things women said. He laid a hand on her arm. 'Nicky was a bad lot, Aggie, but he was different from other people.'

'I know,' she said. So far, being engaged to Mr Underwood had hardly made any difference to her life. She lived in her own house as before, painted every day, and dined at the Underwood house only twice a week, and always in company, which allowed her to remain silent, for everyone else always had plenty to say for themselves. No date had yet been set for the wedding. Mr Underwood seemed very diffident and afraid of pressing her on any matter in case it disrupted her genius. He had an almost ridiculous reverence for her painting, which she could see might prove very useful in future. Only one serious conversation had been held since she had informed him, by letter, that if he still wished to marry her she was willing to oblige him. In that conversation she had told him that she would be perfectly happy to live in his present house, and that she did not by any means wish Mrs Pownall to leave. 'I do not want to disrupt your household,' Aglaea said. 'Besides, the house seems very comfortable and well-run, and I'd be very bad at anything of that sort.'

'I know Clara would be glad to stay after all, if it suited your ideas,' Underwood said with some relief. 'She regards it as her home after all these years.'

In fact, Aglaea thought, Mr Underwood's house seemed much more comfortable than her own, and the cleanliness and orderliness satisfied some need in her. It might, she thought, be better to marry at once and move in there, rather than press for a long engagement. After all, once Jemima had gone, there would be no-one to order meals and so on, and Aglaea disliked having to deal with servants. And when Mr Underwood showed her over the parts of the house she had not previously seen, she had noted that there was a large spare bedroom at the back which had a high ceiling and a perfect north light, which would make an excellent studio. Her cottage boasted nothing so comfortable. Thinking of it now she left her brother to go and find her affianced. Henry, in mid-sentence, reflected as he watched her drift away that really, Aggie was getting rather odd these days, and that it was high time she married and was brought down to earth a bit.

Finding Mr Underwood rather stranded in the middle of a group of Anstey husbands, all talking as hard as they could over the top of one other, Aglaea drew him away with a delicate hand on his arm, and said, 'Do you know, now that Jemima is leaving me, I think perhaps we ought to be married quite soon. What do you think?'

'I'm s-so glad you think so,' he said, stammering a little in his eagerness. 'I have been thinking how uncomfortable it would be for you alone in that cottage. And not – not quite proper for a lady.'

'Oh, good,' Aglaea said, a little vaguely. She was looking at the effect of the sunlight on a vase of flowers in one of the deep window-embrasures. No, the colours weren't right. When the chrysanthemums came out, that would be the thing – the bronzes and the bronze-reds against the grey stone . . . She pulled herself together. 'What do you say to next month, Mr Underwood? But a quiet affair,' she added quickly. 'Nothing like this. In fact, I think we must keep it quite secret until it is over, or my family will take us over completely.'

It was not entirely what Mr Underwood would have chosen. He would not have cared for an Anstey festival, but he would have liked to show off his bride before his Scarborough acquaintance. However, what Aglaea wanted she must have, and he was only too grateful that she was willing to have him at all.

'Just so,' he said. 'Whatever pleases you, my dear, pleases me. And indeed, Scarborough in August will be full of visitors, and much of our acquaintance will be away. Something quiet – just Clara and a few close friends—'

'Mrs Pownall and one other person for witnesses are all we need,' Aglaea said. He looked a little crestfallen, but cheered up considerably when she said, 'And for the honeymoon – if you have no objection, I should like to go to Paris.'

'Paris!' He thought that if she chose so exciting and vibrant a place, the deep vein of passion he thought he saw in her paintings must exist in more accessible form too. 'Paris, indeed – very good! It shall be just as you please,' he said happily.

Aglaea smiled. She was thinking of the light in Paris, and the famous painters she might meet there, and the studios she might visit; and of course Mrs Pownall could entertain Mr Underwood and take him sight-seeing while she painted. And she was thinking of the nice back bedroom which she would make her studio when she returned. The small room next to it would do for her bedroom, she thought, and then she would be quite out of everyone's way. Mr Underwood might not have looked forward to their marriage with such dizzy antici-pation had he known that her first husband had told her that married people of her rank always had separate bedrooms. And Aglaea might not have contemplated marriage with Mr Underwood with such complacency if she had known that the few intimacies she had ever shared with Nicholas Morland did not amount to what the rest of the world regarded as sexual congress. In her absolute innocence and ignorance, she did not know that she was still a virgin.

Benedict was talking to John Anstey. 'Jemima's accounts are all in order now, and the business is in good heart. The Station Hotel is a great advertisement for it, and the order-books are full for eighteen months ahead. You are taking on a considerable heiress, you know.'

John said, 'I'm marrying her for her money, everyone knows that.'

Benedict laughed. 'If I thought that, I'd be after you with a horsewhip. No, no, old fellow, it's plainly an affair of the heart, and I'm very glad of it. Jemima's had a difficult life, and it's time she had some happiness. But I won't deny I shall be glad to hand over the running of her affairs to you. I've enough to be doing with my own

estate. How will you combine it with your own business?'
The Anstey fortune came from coal.

'I shan't,' John said. 'I'm training my brother Hal to take over the family business; and when my boy Fred is older, he'll go into it with his uncle. I intend to be a man of leisure – so much so that I shall probably be glad of the Skelwith business to keep me from boredom.'

'Are you going to live here?' Benedict asked, looking round at the vast hall and the children running every-where and the hordes of Ansteys all talking nineteen to the dozen.

John grinned. 'Not I! No, Jemima and I are going take a neat little house in Clifton to begin with, just for ourselves and the children. I suppose in the fullness of time we shall have to come back to Anstey House – I mean, when Uncle Jack dies and I become head of the family – but we mean to have our private time together first.'

'Good for you!' Benedict said, and then added hesi-tantly, 'You will make her happy?'

'If I don't,' John said sincerely, 'I give you leave to shoot me.'

Edye Laxton, catching Mary alone for a moment, thought a wedding was a good occasion to ask her to marry him. He saw the refusal forming on her lips before he had even finished the question, and hurried on, 'Oh, do at least consider it, Mary! Come, you must marry someone, and you know you like me. Pa would like it above anything, and you could have anything you wanted – horses and – and books so on. And you'd be Lady Laxton one day when the old fellow shuffles off – which won't be for a long time, of course – but meantime we'd be very jolly, and travel and go everywhere. Wouldn't you like to see Europe?'

Mary smiled patiently. 'Thank you for asking me, but

I'm not going to marry you, and I never will, so please don't go on. I'm sorry if it pains you, and I do like you very much, but I could never marry you. It's better you should know that right away.'

Edye studied her face. 'You fancy someone else, is that it? Don't tell me it's that idiot Arthur Anstey!'

'Arthur isn't an idiot – he's a very clever boy, and very kind.'

'It is him! God, I can't bear it! I shall shoot myself!'

'Don't say such things,' Mary said sternly. 'I don't want to marry him, either. To tell you the truth, I don't think I shall ever marry.'

'Then you ain't in love with some pitiful fellow?'

Mary hesitated, but decided it was best to put him off any possible hope. 'He's not pitiful, but I don't know if I shall ever see him again. And if I don't, I shan't marry anyone. So now will you give up this nonsense and just let us be friends?'

'Oh well, if you say so,' Edye said. He was by no means discouraged. If she were only in love with someone she might never see again, he counted her still available; and he would think the worse of himself if he could not put an absentee lover from her mind, when he was here in the flesh – warm flesh, and hot blood to boot!

Jemima had been taken upstairs to change for the wedding journey by John's sister Lol, who was taking care of John's children while they were away. While Lol was helping Jemima with her hair, they were joined by John's other sister Feddy, who was also married with children of her own, and the two chatted and laughed and made sidelong remarks that Jemima didn't understand but knew she ought to, so that by the time she was allowed to come downstairs again, she was very nervous, and feeling slightly sick.

There was a rush of goodbyes, such a commotion of hugging, laughing and shrieking that Jemima hadn't a chance to think about anything. She saw everything through a confusion of movement, faces darting at her from all directions, kisses and injuctions striking her cheeks and ears like mothwing blows, as unheeded as uninvited. Aglaea appeared briefly before her, and laid her cold cheek against hers and wished her happy; and then she was out of the house and in the carriage and driving away from the laughing, waving multitude, with a gaggle of children running after them, shrieking for John to throw the pennies.

They weren't going far, just to Harrogate for the first few days; afterwards John had promised to take her to the Lakes, which she had long wanted to see. But he had said he wanted to have her to himself just to begin with, with no distractions. She thought about this as the carriage took them out of York and onto the quieter roads, and it made her more nervous still.

At last John said, 'Well, wife?'

She looked at him almost reluctantly. 'Well – what?'

He smiled. 'I was beginning to wonder if you were regretting it. You haven't looked at me or spoken to me for hours, and then when we got into the carriage I was sure you'd want to take the first opportunity to kiss me. Instead of which, you resolutely ignore me.'

She looked confused. 'Oh – no – I—' And that was as far as she got.

John thought he understood. She was thirty-two years old, but she had never known a man, never even been courted as far as he knew. He reached out and took her cold hand and drew it into his lap. 'Jemmy, dearest, we are old friends, are we not? Well then, let's be comfortable together. You can't think I would ever do anything to hurt or frighten you?'

'No. No, of course not – but—'

'You are worried about later. Tonight. About what married people do together.'

She blushed painfully. 'Your sisters said things – I didn't really understand – but they laughed, and—'

'Damn my sisters to Hades,' he said pleasantly.

'I'm afraid. I can't help it, but I am!' she admitted in a doleful wail. 'I'll do the wrong thing, and I'll disappoint you, you'll hate me! I should never have married you! You ought to have a proper woman. I'm no good to you, John!'

Half of him wanted to laugh, even while his heart turned painfully with pity. 'Hush,' he said. 'Hush. Listen to me. No, no, just be still and listen.' She quieted, but sat with her face turned slightly away from him and her hand resisting his grasp. 'Do you love me?' he asked.

'I don't know. How can I know? I don't know how people love.'

'Never mind people. We aren't other people, we're just us. And I know you, Jemima Skelwith. I know all about you. Nothing you've done or seen or suffered shocks me, except as it made you unhappy. And now it will be my pleasant task to wipe all that away and make you happy instead. Are you listening to me?'

She nodded dumbly.

'Very well. Then believe me when I tell you that everything will be all right. What you and I do together won't be like anything that's gone before, and when it comes, it will be as natural as breathing to you, and you'll forget all the horrid things anyone has ever said or hinted, and all the silly, unseemly jokes. It will be a very fine and private thing, just for us. It will be – oh, grave and reverent and comfortable and merry and wonderful!'

'All those things?'

'I promise you,' he said, kissing her hand. They travelled on in silence, and still she didn't look at him, but he could feel that she was more at ease, and her hand grew warm in his. How long a shadow evil could cast, he thought; and he swore to himself that if he achieved nothing else in this life, he would deliver Jemima from the memory of Nicholas Morland, and carry her out into the sunshine again.

Sibella was brought to bed in early September of a daughter. She had expected another boy, and when the baby was laid in her arms, she cried – not with disappointment, but with a sort of trembling fear for what the future would hold for this little, helpless girl. She understood boys, she knew how to be a mother to boys; but the life of girls seemed so much more fraught with danger. And there was Mary to consider. How would the arrival of another daughter affect Benedict? How would he take a rival to Mary into his heart? If he did not, the child was doomed; and if he did, Mary was doomed.

'Overwrought,' said the midwife, handing her a handkerchief. 'You've a fine babby, just be grateful and thank God.'

Benedict, when he came in to see her, seemed to be glad and nothing else. He thanked God for Sibella's safe delivery, admired the little, dark-headed thing, and agreed with the midwife that her hair would probably curl.

'I thought it would be a boy,' Sibella said. 'I wanted a boy.'

'Well, but you ought to have a girl,' Benedict said. 'Every mother ought to have one little girl to dress up.'

The words seemed somehow ominous to Sibella. Why had he spoken about the baby as if it was hers alone, and not theirs?

'What shall we call her?' he said.

'I don't know. What would you like?' she asked, hoping for clues.

'Well, if you have no preference – perhaps, if you wouldn't mind it, we might call her after my mother.'

'Héloïse?'

'That was a contraction. Her name was actually Henrietta Louisa,' Benedict said. 'What do you think to that?'

Sibella felt a large relief. She knew Benedict had loved his mother dearly. 'I think it sounds very well,' she said.

Mary was enchanted by the new baby. 'Only look, how perfect! Her little finger-nails!' she exclaimed, hanging over the crib. 'She's so small. Are new babies always that small? I can't remember Georgie and Teddy being so small.'

'One forgets,' Sibella said. 'I suppose they are.'

Georgie and Teddy were pretty well indifferent to the new arrival. 'Will it be a girl?' Teddy asked doubtfully.

'She already is a girl. A little sister for you,' Sibella explained.

'She's got a lot of hair,' Georgie remarked, 'but it's all black, not like Mary's. I don't think she's very pretty,' he added in a hoarse, tactful whisper.

Mary caught Sibella's eye across their heads and laughed. 'She will be,' she said. 'You must give her time. Babies are hardly ever pretty when they're as new as this.'

'Was I?' asked Teddy the self-regarding.

'Not a bit. You were horrid, like a drowned rat.'

Georgie was still staring critically at the sleeping baby. 'I think puppies are nicer,' he said at last, 'but I expect it will be all right when it gets older.'

The baby was baptised that evening by Father Moineau in the chapel. Mary carried her down, cradling her in a very natural and motherly way. Standing in a halo of candlelight with her golden head bent over the shawled bundle, Mary looked so beautiful, and so suddenly separate from him, that Benedict felt the shadow of loss on him, the beginning of age. The baby hardly stirred at the touch of the water. The boys were silent with the solemnity of the occasion, but when released from the chapel afterwards and with the promise of cake and lemonade and other good things, they grew noisy and boisterous, and inclined to take the baby's name as a joke. 'Henrietta Morland. Which Morland did she eat?' Georgie chanted the question, and whichever answer Teddy gave, it threw them both into paroxysms of giggles. Mary looked on their fun indulgently, following them out with the baby in one arm. Benedict thought, she has enough love for all of them, and for all of us, no matter how we are related in blood. It behoves all of us to be as generous.

The next day while he was working in the steward's room, Mary came to him.

'What are you doing here, chick? Shouldn't you be at your lessons?'

'Father Moineau felt a sudden need to pray,' she said. She stood before him in a patch of sunshine, making slow patterns with a fingertip on his desk. 'Can I ask you something, Papa?'

'Of course,' he said. She did not immediately speak, seeming to have difficulty with framing her question, and he put down his pen and gave her his full attention. 'What it is, love? Is something troubling you?'

She looked up and then down, a little frown between her fair brows. 'I don't quite know how to put it. You – you won't be angry?'

'How could I be angry with you? You can ask me anything, you know that.' Still she didn't speak, and he said cautiously, 'Perhaps it's something your mother could better explain to you.'

She looked up, puzzled, and then a wide smile spread

289

over her face. 'Papa,' she said indulgently, 'I'm sixteen. I've lived all my life on a farm. *And* I've studied the classics.'

She had succeeded in embarrassing him. He felt himself blush ridiculously. 'Well, then, love,' he said hastily, 'what is it?'

She gathered herself. 'It's about Morland Place,' she said. 'You see, I've been studying the family history for a long time. I know that the estate isn't entailed and that it's in the gift of the owner, and I've read some things my grandmother wrote, about each owner being the guardian and making sure that they pass it on the right person, who will be a good guardian in their turn.'

Benedict began to have an idea where this was going, and he didn't like it. 'Yes?' he said apprehensively.

'And also I've discovered that you had an older sister called Fanny, and that the estate was once all going to be hers.'

'Perhaps it may have.'

'But she died. And then it was all given to my grand-mother – not my grandfather.'

'Mary, what is it you want to know?'

The blue eyes came up and looked very directly into his. 'Papa, I have to ask you – am I to inherit Morland Place?'

He desperately didn't want to answer that, but in the face of that gaze like blue fire he had to say something. 'Why do you think you might?'

'Because I'm the eldest, and it hasn't mattered before if the eldest was a girl. I'm much older than my brothers, so I thought that perhaps you might want to make me the guardian, because I would be a good one.'

'Aren't you rather heading the fox?' he said clumsily. 'I'm not dying yet.'

She put her hands on the desk and leaned forward.

'No, of course not, you're quite young really. I'm sure you'll live a long time. In fact,' she said passionately, 'I wish you would live for ever! But the person who will be next guardian will have to be trained in their duties so that they understand everything. Isn't that right? Because even if the guardian is a woman she will have to understand all the business to make sure it is done properly.'

Benedict thought of his mother, who had not thoroughly understood the business, and so had let his father and his brother do it for her; and the results of that had been ruinous. He looked at Mary's blazing, passionate face, and knew that she would be a good guardian, in the old terms. But what was well enough for mediæval times would not pass today. It was a modern world now, and farming and business had become too complicated to talk in that old-fashioned, superstitious way. Morland Place needed more than spiritual values – it needed a good business head and skilled hands at the reins. And even as he argued with himself, he knew that Mary had those, too. He looked for something evasive to say.

'Well, there's plenty of time yet before I am in my dotage. Why are you suddenly asking this now?'

'Because I need to know,' she said. She straightened up slowly, seeing the doubt and hesitation in his face, perhaps reading there the answer she had sought. 'I need to know what I am to do with my life. I must have something to do, Papa, and I thought – if I was to be guardian – I could start learning how – how to run the estate. But if not – well—'

She stopped, like clockwork run down.

'My love, you will get married,' he said. 'You will marry and have a house of your own and children, and that will be plenty to keep you occupied.'

'You mean,' she said in a voice utterly devoid of light, 'that you don't intend me to have Morland Place.'

He opened his mouth and shut it again, and then said, 'I haven't decided.'

'You have,' she contradicted flatly. 'Why? Why not me? Just because I'm a girl?'

He tried getting angry. 'I won't be hectored like this, Mary. I've said I haven't made up my mind, and that's that.'

She ignored that. 'Then what am I to do?' she said. 'What will I do with the rest of my life?'

'What every woman does,' he said.

'I shall never marry,' she said, 'if that's what you mean.'

'You *will*,' he insisted. 'You think that because you haven't met the right man yet you never will, but you are very young – though it's easy to forget it because you're so quick and clever. But you're only sixteen, love, and there's plenty of time. You'll find you fall in love quite suddenly, and everything will change. And when the right man comes and asks for you, I'll give you a splendid dowry, don't worry about that.'

'A splendid dowry, if I marry some mutton-headed Laxton or Anstey, and turn myself into a dairy cow; but I'm not to have Morland Place, though I'm so quick and clever you forget I'm only sixteen! Just because I'm female. How is that fair?'

'That's enough, Mary. It's not for you to question my decisions. You had better go back to your studies.'

She gave him a strange look, which he could understand perfectly well – *what's the point of studying when I'm only a girl?* – and went without another word. When the door closed behind her, he put his head in his hands and felt his thoughts whirling. It was the terrible dilemma that he had always known would raise its head, and which he had never wanted to face. When he married Sibella and she gave him boys, it ought to have solved the problem, and it would have, had Mary been an ordinary girl. But she was not ordinary; and she would make an excellent mistress of Morland Place. In any other family, of course, the question would not arise, but Morland Place was different, and Mary was different, and the two so obviously belonged together – except that she was not a Morland.

When she looked at him just before she left, he had seen her father in her. Mostly she looked like her mother, but in certain of her expressions there was a ghostly look of Carlton Miniott – a mocking ghost that said *I took your wife from you, and I will take everything else if I can*.

Mary was not a Morland, and how could he leave Morland Place to her? Even if she would be the best guardian, how could he leave Morland Place to Carlton Miniott's child? He screwed the heels of his hands into his eyes and drew a sigh of weariness. He would never be free of the past; he would be haunted always by his first wife's sins. What did the Bible say about visiting the sins of the father on the sons? It was true – and as Mary said, how was that fair?

And worst of all he couldn't even tell her. He had to let her think he was denying her through simple prejudice. He knew he had lost a little of her respect, because she thought him less generous-minded, less – perceptive than her. It was bad for a child to feel superior to its parent.

But she would marry, of course she would, and then all this would be forgotten. She was so adamant that she couldn't marry, but that was just childish talk. She would meet someone one day. Perhaps not in York – she needed a larger pond to fish in. Next year, when she was seventeen, he would let her come out in London; do the thing properly, a ball, the Season, presentation – everything. She'd find a husband in London all right. She was pretty enough and clever enough for an earl or a duke.

Charlotte would help, surely? And marriage to an earl or a duke would be compensation enough, wouldn't it?

He got up wearily and went out into the hall, and then, on an impulse, went into the chapel. It felt alive, full of murmuring movement, as though all the prayers that had been spoken in it still lived there, and pattered about like ghost-mice, repeating themselves for ever. Father Moineau was just getting up from in front of the high altar – a little stiffly, hoisting himself by the altar rails – and he turned and came towards Benedict as if he had known he would be there.

'Father,' Benedict began, and paused, not knowing whether to ask or tell. Then, 'Mary's been to see me. She asked me if she would inherit Morland Place.'

'Ah,' Moineau said. 'Yes, I have foreseen that.'

'She would be the best person for it, I know. And it would mean she would never go away, and I don't want her to go away.'

'Yes, I know.'

'But I *can't*! How can I? Knowing what you know, tell me, how could I?'

'No, I see that you feel you couldn't.'

'Am I wrong?'

'It's not a matter of right or wrong. It's a matter of decision. And I don't see how you could have decided anything else.'

'But it's not fair!' Benedict cried.

'No,' Moineau agreed gravely. 'Love hardly ever is. Tell me, whose daughter is Mary?'

'You know that.'

'Do I? Whose do you think she is? That man's – or yours, who brought her up and cared for her and loved her, and whom she loves?'

Benedict saw what he was asking, saw where it might lead him. 'It's not that simple,' he said harshly.

'No-one ever said it was simple,' Moineau said.

'You think I'm wrong. You think I ought to give it to her.'

'My son, I don't think anything. The decision is yours – and the responsibility, and the pain.'

Benedict stood for a moment, his brow bent, going over and over it. 'I can't,' he said at last, defeated.

Moineau laid his hand on Benedict's shoulder. 'Then there's nothing more to be said.'

CHAPTER TWELVE

Russia and Turkey went to war in October 1853 over the occupied Principalities, but there still seemed no strong reason why England should join in. Then in November the vastly superior Russian fleet attacked the Turkish fleet in the Black Sea, at Sinope, and destroyed it. The Turkish ships were blown to matchwood, and the Russians fired grapeshot into the wreckage in the water to kill any Turkish sailors who had survived. The newspapers called it a massacre; public opinion was outraged. It was not the British way: the Royal Navy had a code of honour, which said that in naval warfare, it was the ships that were enemies, not the sailors. Any enemy sailor rescued from the sea or from a wreck was always treated with brotherly kindness by British tars, and the popular papers were violent in their condemnation of the Russians' 'barbarity'. There had always been a popular feeling in favour of going to war, and now it was whipped up into a frenzy. Foreigners in general became the objects of hatred, to the extent that it was rumoured that Prince Albert was a Russian sympathiser, if not an actual spy, and that it was he who was persuading the Government not to declare war. At one point rumour had crowds gathering at the Tower of London in the expectation of seeing the Prince taken in by Traitor's Gate to be executed.

To show support for the Turks, the English and French fleets were ordered through the Straits in January 1854. The Tsar retaliated by withdrawing his ambassadors from

London and Paris. Diplomatic notes were passed back and forth. Austria and Prussia asked Russia to withdraw from the Principalities, Britain and France demanded it. Aberdeen dragged his feet as hard as he could, saying that war was not inevitable, unless the British were determined to have it – which for all he knew might be the case. But the Tsar ignored both requests and threats, and at last it could no longer be avoided. War was declared in March, between Russia on the one side, and England, France and Turkey on the other. There were dissident voices, who said it was ridiculous to be fighting Christian Russians on behalf of Muslim Turks, and that Balkan matters were never worth rolling up the sleeves for; but most of the populace was wild with joy. Britain hadn't had a good scrap with anyone in forty years, and war fever was in the air. When the news of the declaration broke, the nation held a party to celebrate.

One day towards the end of March, Charlotte was writing letters in her sitting-room when she gradually became aware of a sound of raised voices and thumping feet somewhere nearby in the house. Putting down her pen she listened for a moment, and then rang the bell. To her surprise, it was answered by Norton, looking ruffled and flushed in the face, and with a brightness of anger in her eyes.

'Norton? What is that noise? Is someone ill?'

'Not yet, my lady, but someone soon will be, if something isn't done,' she said with unaccustomed heat.

Before Charlotte could enquire further, Ungar appeared, moving with unaccustomed speed. 'You rang, your grace?' he said, out of breath.

'What is going on?' Charlotte said.

Ungar got his word in first, with a sidelong glare

at Norton. 'The chimney sweep is here, your grace, that is all.'

The sweeping of the chimneys, like other domestic details, was not something that normally intruded on Charlotte's day. She looked at Norton for explanation.

'The sweep's boy got hooked up on something in the chimney,' Norton explained quickly. 'He couldn't go back, so he went forward, took a wrong turn, and now he's stuck.'

'I assure your grace, it is nothing that need trouble your grace,' Ungar said with a mixture of embarrassment and annoyance, looking at Norton as if she were some impudent boy who, bursting in without knocking, had caught him putting his trousers on. 'I am most distressed that your grace has been disturbed by the noise, and I will ensure that it does not happen again.'

Charlotte looked at him steadily. 'Stuck where?'

Ungar was deeply reluctant to go into it, but he could not refuse to answer a direct question. 'Somewhere in the old nursery chimney, your grace.'

The old nursery was a chilly, empty chamber with a north aspect. Charlotte's children had a rather more cheerful suite along the west front, and the old nursery was used only as a corridor, or sometimes on wet days in summer for games requiring a large empty space.

'The chimney there would be cold, you see,' Norton added for explanation. 'He'd naturally turn that way.'

Charlotte accepted the point. 'Well, he must be got out, that's all. But why was there so much shouting?'

This time Norton beat Ungar to it. While he was trying to frame some polite and circumlocutory way of not telling Charlotte what was happening, Norton said, 'Because the sweep says the only way to get the boy out is to break down the chimney wall, and Ungar won't have it.'

'Ungar?'

'The mess, your grace,' he said in anguish. 'The disruption. The damage!'

'But what do you propose then? You can't leave the boy in there.'

'It's my belief, my lady, that if the boy would make strenuous efforts, he could release himself—'

'It's his "strenuous efforts" that have got him stuck!' Norton cried angrily.

Charlotte silenced her. 'Go on,' she said to Ungar.

'I propose lighting a small fire in the old nursery fireplace so that the heat will drive the boy back up, to find another way out.'

'And if he really is stuck, the smoke will stupefy him. I don't think that is a very sensible suggestion, Ungar. We will leave aside the question of its inhumanity.' She stood up. 'Show me,' she said.

Ungar set his face in lines of stern disapproval, and the trio set off. In the old nursery an appallingly dirty man stood arguing with a footman and Mrs Collins, the housekeeper, while two housemaids hovered in the background, thrilled at the interruption to their humdrum day; and at the far door, Venetia and Olivia stood holding hands, their eyes round with excitement.

As Charlotte appeared, everyone fell silent. Mrs Collins curtseyed with an I-told-you-so look, the maids curtseyed in deep apprehension. Ungar flung the sweep a look which said he would never work in *this* house again after disturbing her grace, which the sweep returned defiantly, and the two little girls ran to her, smiling and ready to chatter.

'What are you doing here, you bad things?' Charlotte said, but with a smile. 'Where's Miss Frogmore?'

'She went to find a book, and we heard the noise and came to look,' Venetia said. A nursery-maid appeared in the doorway, evidently looking for them, and shrank back with a gasp as she saw the duchess. Charlotte beckoned her sternly forward, as Venetia went on confidentially, in a piercing whisper, 'There's a boy in the wall, Mama-duchess, and the black man says he will dead.'

'Die,' Charlotte corrected automatically. She saw Olivia's lips trembling at the idea of a dead boy in the wall, and went on hastily, 'but he's not going to die, we're going to get him out. And you must go back to your lessons.'

'Oh no *please*, we want to see!' Venetia cried, but Charlotte pushed them back gently into the grip of the nursery-maid.

'There'll be nothing to see. Take them away, Rebecca, and keep the nursery door shut. There may be a lot of dust.' She thought there might also be noises it was better for the children not to hear. 'Go on, now. I'll come later and tell you all about it, I promise.'

When the children were gone, everyone seemed inclined to speak at once, but Charlotte held up a hand and turned to the sweep, who was looking embarrassed now, turning his cap round and round in his hands, his eyes darting whitely from person to person. 'Now, Mr—?'

'Figgis, mum.'

The housekeeper hissed with outrage. 'Your grace! Say your grace!'

'Peace, Mrs Collins,' Charlotte said. 'Now, Mr Figgis, tell me what has happened here.'

'Well, mum – yer grace—' Figgis looked distracted, and decided a bow might help matters along. 'It's like this 'ere. I puts the boy in down below in the old kitchen, and up 'e goos right enough, but he must a' got isself hooked up be 'is belt. There is 'ooks in 'at 'ere chimbley, which I knows it, on account of climbin' it meself when I was a lad.'

'Yes, go on,' Charlotte said encouragingly.

'Well, mum – yer grace – I 'as a look and I can just see

'is feet, so I gets in hunder the cowl and tries a-tuggin' of 'im, but it ain't no good, so I gets me rod with the nail in the end and gives him a few jabs in 'is soles to make 'im goo uppards.'

'Couldn't he release himself?' Charlotte asked.

'No, mum, for that 'ere flue bein' so narrow, you 'as to keep yer arms out afore yer. You can't get 'em down to yer sides.'

Charlotte thought about it. 'But that's terrible!'

Figgis grew confidential under the warmth of her sympathy. 'It *his* a bad chimbley, and no mistake, mum – yer grace. Not but what it wasn't built right in the fust place – mos' of the chimbleys in this 'ouse is a pleasure to sweep, mum, but they was alterations done twenty year back, and that 'ere flue was put in to make a new lot o'rooms.' He demonstrated with a piling movement of his hands. 'Mean work it was, beggin' your pardon, mum, an' a trile to sweep it 'as made it. I don't like puttin' the boy to it, but if folks wants their chimbleys swep', what is a man to do?'

'We shall see about that later,' Charlotte said. 'But first we must get this boy of yours out. Do you know where he is?'

Figgis gestured succinctly towards the top of the chimney wall. 'In there, mum – yer grace – in the flue, atween this floor and the next. 'E won't come down, or 'e can't. And the fireplace bein' so narrow, there ain't no way to get at 'im, yer grace, uthout knocking down the chimbley breast.'

'Then let it be done,' Charlotte said calmly.

Though this was what he had been demanding, he hesitated now that the lady of the house was here. ''Twill make a tidy mess, yer grace, I can't disguise.'

'What must be done must be endured. Get on with it quickly, before the boy suffocates.'

Figgis nodded, licked his black lips with a grey tongue, and took up the sledgehammer which was lying on the floor at his feet. Ungar stepped forward. 'If your grace pleases—' he said, stretching his arm towards the door. 'There will be a great deal of soot and mortar.'

'Yes, very well, I will take myself out of the way.' She went to the door, and as he opened it for her said quietly, 'Mark me, Ungar – the boy is to be got out as quickly as possible, no matter what the damage. Give the sweep any help he needs. And as soon as the boy is out, call me. He may well need medical attention.'

'Yes, your grace,' Ungar said, suffering deeply.

Charlotte returned to her room and listened through the closed door to the thuds and rumblings as the chimney breast was demolished. A law against using climbing boys had been passed more than ten years ago, but the reality of the matter was that even where chimneys could be swept by machine – and there were many, especially in the great houses, that could not – most householders, or at least their servants, preferred the use of boys, which were thought to be cleaner, safer, more reliable and more thorough. And the sweeps themselves, having survived the horrors of climbing in their own boyhood, had a curious prejudice against seeing the practice replaced.

A thunderous noise like an earthquake made her jump, and she feared for an instant that the whole house might be going to come down; but it was followed by a silence, and a few moments later Norton, not a little sooty about the face and clothes, opened the door and said, 'We've got him.'

'Alive?'

'Only just.' Charlotte hurried to join her and they returned along the passage to the old nursery. Clouds of soot hung in the air, swaying in the draughts coming from the door and window. There was a heap of rubble,

302

mortar, soot, twigs, bones and miscellaneous bits of metal in front of the ruinous hole in the wall, and the sweep was crouched on the floor over what seemed to be a bundle of black rags.

Ungar gave one anguished cry, 'Your grace, I beg you—' as Charlotte came in, and then was forced to break off as a fit of coughing followed his inhalation of soot. Warned, Charlotte breathed shallowly as she knelt down beside the sweep to look at the boy. He was so small, and so thin, naked except for a loin cloth and a much scarred leather belt round his waist, and black from head to foot, except where his elbows and knees showed red and raw even through the blackness.

'Good God, how old is he?' she murmured to Figgis, who was shrinking back from so near a contact with the nobility. She wasn't sorry about the shrinking, on the whole – he smelled very bad indeed.

'Atween five and six, mum. I couldn't say to a month, on account of 'is mother didn't say.'

Charlotte said nothing, trying to find a pulse; but she was horrified. This child was smaller, though a year older, than her own daughter Venetia. 'He's alive,' she said at last. 'We had better get him out of all this dust.'

'I'll tek 'im away, mum – and mortal sorry I am about all thisere mess, mum, though I thank 'e kindly for agettin' of the boy out in time to save 'is life.'

The boy was stirring now. Common sense said it was best for Figgis to take him away, but Charlotte was not being moved at that moment by common sense.

'I should like to keep him here for a little while,' she said.

'Keep 'im, mum?' Figgis was utterly perplexed.

'I want to be sure he has suffered no harm. To do that I must have him washed – he may have injuries under all this dirt – and perhaps have the doctor to look at him.'

'Doctor, mum?' Figgis cried, horrified. 'Oh no, mum, don't 'e do that, beggin' your pardon, mum! Not a doctor!'

'Mr Figgis, do you know who I am?'

He seemed to shrink. 'Yer grace, I should a' said. I didn't mean no 'arm by it, yer grace—'

She hated to see him cringe. 'No, no, what I meant, Mr Figgis, was, do you know that I am the founder and patron of the Southport Hospital, which takes care of poor people who cannot afford to pay for medical treatment?'

He writhed. 'Yes, yer grace, I 'ave 'eerd tell of sich a place.'

'Then you know that I understand medical matters, and you can trust this boy to me entirely. If he has taken no harm, you may call for him this evening and take him away. Come when you have finished your day's work. Do you understand?'

Figgis assented, miserably. When the likes of him got mixed up with the likes of Charlotte, his heart told him, there was no end of the trouble to be expected; and doctors and hospitals were as terrifying as duchesses. Charlotte took pity on him.

'Don't be afraid. I won't harm the boy, and there'll be no trouble for you. Go away now, and come back this evening. Oh, by the way – what's the boy's name?'

'I call 'im 'Arry, yer grace.'

When he saw Figgis departing, the boy gave a cry of panic, thinking he was being abandoned with hostile strangers. Charlotte waved Figgis on, and said to the boy, 'Be quiet. No-one is going to harm you.' The white eyes rolled round to her. 'Your master will be back for you in a few hours. Meanwhile we are going to see if you have taken any hurt from the chimney. If you do as you are told like a good boy, you shall have something very nice to eat by and by. Do you understand?'

The child said nothing, but a few tears of desperate misery rolled out of the white eyes and made paler marks down the black cheeks. He was as much afraid as hurt, she thought. She realised that she couldn't entrust the washing of this imp to any of the servants, who would think it unnecessary and humiliating and probably take it out on the child. Even though it would drive Ungar wild, she must do it herself. And then she altered the thought to, especially as it would drive Ungar wild.

'Norton,' she said, quietly, so as not to startle the child, 'will you help me?'

'Yes, your grace.' Norton's eyes were bright with approval.

'Very well.' She prepared to lift the boy, but Norton stayed her.

'Best let me, your grace. He might be lousy.'

There was an intake of breath from Mrs Collins at the word, and Charlotte met Norton's eyes and grinned. 'Does it occur to you,' she said, 'that you and I have probably seen more lice than the whole of the rest of the household put together?'

'No probably about it,' Norton replied.

Undersized and thin though the child was, it was a two-handed job, and not an easy one, to bath him. He was terrified of the water, and cried that he would 'drownd' for sure; and he screamed and sobbed and fought against the bathing as though it were a wicked and undeserved punishment. Charlotte had expected the soot to wash off, but it seemed ingrained in the skin, and they were forced to settle for a natural grey hue, rather than flesh-colour. He was lousy, and washing his hair caused the worst panic of all; but at least all this resistance proved that there was nothing seriously wrong with the boy. Screaming made him cough, but that was hardly surprising.

305

When most of the dirt was off, it was possible to see his other injuries. The knees were so raw and bloody, it looked at first as though his kneecaps had been pulled off; the elbows and the tips of his toes were likewise painfully scraped, and his thighs were scarified, as though they had been attacked with a wire brush. There were, in addition, the marks of beatings on his back, some old and some recent. And this boy, Charlotte thought, was only five years old.

His was very thin, too; and when she could see his features, quite unprepossessingly ugly. Once out of the water he seemed to lose all his resistance. The washing on top of everything else that had happened that morning had exhausted him, and he huddled in the blanket they had wrapped round him, shivering and apathetic, staring at them helplessly like a calf staring at the butcher.

'Now, Harry, I expect you're hungry, aren't you?' Charlotte said. He didn't speak, but there was the hint of an answering flicker in his eyes. She had ordered the food prepared before they began the washing, and now sent Norton to hurry it along. She soon returned with a tray: a plate of pease pudding and mutton sausages, another of bread and butter, and a bowl of rice pudding with a spoonful of jam in the middle. Charlotte raised enquiring eyes to Norton's face. 'Is this really suitable for a child of his age?'

Norton almost shrugged. 'I'll warrant it's what he likes,' she said. She was right. He took a moment or two to believe it was for him and not a trick, and then attacked the food with both hands and such voracity Charlotte was afraid he'd choke. Even when he was obviously full he went on trying to pack the remains away, and eventually Charlotte drew the tray from his hands and said, 'You can have more later, I promise you.'

'Honest?' he said doubtfully.

'Bible oath.' He relaxed his grip, and she took the tray away. As the unusual amount of food hit his stomach, he began to grow sleepy, and Charlotte, guessing that a bed would only intimidate him, sent Norton for some more blankets, dragged a rug into a corner, and settled the child down to sleep. On the brink of drifting off, the boy suddenly opened his eyes and said, 'Fank you, miss.'

Charlotte smiled. 'Don't be afraid, you're quite safe here. Someone will be with you all the time.'

He slept so suddenly it was more like a dead faint. Charlotte watched a moment or two and then stood up. 'Now,' she said quietly to Norton, 'you and I can get out of these filthy things. But the boy mustn't be left. If he wakes up alone he might run away; and I don't trust the other servants.'

'I agree with you, my lady,' Norton said.

'If you take first watch, I'll go and have my bath, and then come and relieve you.'

After Charlotte had washed and changed, but before she could return to Norton, Oliver came in from his morning's engagements.

'What have you been up to, my love? The servants are fermenting like yeast downstairs, and Ungar has the eyes of an early Christian martyr.'

Charlotte told him, and he seemed inclined to be amused. 'Thank God my mother wasn't here. Though she will have it all from Mrs Collins when she gets back. I hope you're prepared to justify yourself, dearest.'

'What would you have me do – leave the child to suffocate?'

'Of course not. Don't fire up at me. The brute had to be got out, that's plain. But you should have let its master take it away. What good can you do keeping it here?'

'Oliver, he isn't an "it". And I had to see that he wasn't hurt.'

'Hmm.' Oliver eyed her, unconvinced. 'You aren't thinking of keeping this child, I hope?'

'No, of course not,' she said, much to his relief. 'Figgis can have him back tonight. But you know Shaftesbury is trying to get a new Bill through Parliament at the moment about climbing boys, and it occurred to me that I might be able to get some useful information from Figgis and the boy.'

'You mean to interview this sweeping fellow? You had better pay him well, if you want him to incriminate himself.'

'Oh, I shall. He has to make his living, I suppose – it's just that it seems so horrible that he has to make it by sending boys like this up the flues. Oliver, he's hardly older than Venetia! Just think what his life must be!'

Oliver nodded. 'But there are thousands of climbing boys – and thousands of children doing even worse things to earn a living. You know that. You can't change the whole world by yourself, my love.'

'I know. But one thing we will change – that narrow flue must be rebuilt. Figgis said the other chimneys were wide enough to climb without difficulty, but that that one had been altered. Well, it shall be altered back.'

'Just as you please.'

'I wish,' she added, frowning, 'we could save this little child from having to climb any flue.'

'But if you removed him from the life, he would have to do something to earn a living. And the sweep would get another boy.'

'I know,' she said, sighing. 'I know that. But I can't help minding.'

He kissed her brow. 'I'm glad you mind. It's one of the things I love about you.'

She lifted her face for more kisses. 'Only one? Tell me another.'

'Well, for instance,' he said, 'I particularly like the fact that you have soot in your ear.'

'What? Oh, I must have missed a bit! How vexatious!'

He was laughing. 'Not at all. It's most becoming. You might set a new fashion, you know.'

When Figgis returned in the late afternoon for his boy, he had obviously bathed himself, for his features, though grey, were distinguishable, and his clothing had been changed.

'Before I give you your boy, Mr Figgis, I would be obliged if you would answer a few questions,' she said. 'No, please don't be alarmed. I told you there would be no trouble, and I keep my word. But I am a friend of Lord Shaftesbury, and I would like to have some information about the life your boy and others like him lead, so that I can help his lordship finally put an end to the use of climbing boys. You see I am being quite frank with you. You seem a good sort of fellow, Mr Figgis. I am sure your heart tells you it is not right for little boys to have to go up chimneys in this way.'

Figgis looked uneasy, but he said, 'Well, mum – yer grace, I should say – it ain't that I'm nessacellary approvin' to the use o' boys, nor yet disapprovin', but folks will have 'em, and I must make my living. I was a climbing boy meself thirty year ago, and a shocking cruel thing it was, which I shudder to think of it now.'

'You were a climbing boy, were you? Tell me about it. Were you as young as Harry when you began?'

'I was five, your grace. Five or six is the usual age to begin. Younger than that they are too weak. I've knew 'em taken up as young as four and put to it, but they are too weak at that age, to my mind, and they goos off too easy.'

'What do you mean, they "go off?"'

'Well, yer grace, they like, die,' he said uneasily. 'It ain't one thing or another, they just goos off, sometimes in their sleep, sometimes even in the chimbley. I've knew 'em just curl up in the flue and go off so easy, it's like as you might fall asleep just a-settin' in your chair by the fire.'

'Why don't you take them older, then, when they are eight or nine, perhaps, and stronger?' she asked.

'Well, mum, you couldn't train 'em if they was that old and set in their ways. Which it ain't a nacherel thing, for a boy to go up a flue. They is nacherelly afeard, and even with the little 'uns, you can't be soft with 'em, you have to use vilence to learn 'em. It makes me shudder to think how I was learned myself, but it 'as to be.'

'This boy of yours – his knees and elbows are very badly injured.'

'They will 'arden, yer grace, in time. That is the cruellest thing about learning 'em, for they will tear off the skin again and again until it 'ardens. But we rubs it with brine, which we get a tub from the pork shop. Strong brine, well rubbed in before a 'ot fire, chiefly on the raw bits.'

'Good God!'

He looked upset. 'They don't like it, yer grace. You 'as to stand over 'em with a cane and give 'em a lick or two. Or sometimes you promises 'em a bit o' somethin' tasty if they will stand another rub or two. And then they goes up the next chimney and pulls it all off again. It's cruel 'ard. Some boys goos years afore they hardens proper.' He shrugged. 'But I got through it, yer grace, as you can see. And when I got too big to climb, I became a journeyman sweep, and started off a boy of my own. It ain't a bad life, yer grace, once they gets used to it. When they are seven or eight they are very nimble and strong, and they can earn a good living. Our climbing boys is the henvy o' the world, as everyone knows. They gets stole sometimes, by kidnappers, who drugs 'em and takes 'em away to France, where they sells 'em. They can get ten pund in France, so I hear tell, for a Henglish climbing boy.'

'You would not sell a child, surely?'

'No, yer grace, not me! A sweep wouldn't do it, for a well-learned boy is wuth a lot more'n ten pund to him. But we 'as to buy 'em in the beginning. Mostly it's the wust parents as wants to be rid of their little 'uns, or maybe they needs the money. I was on the parish, yer grace, that's 'ow I went into it.'

'The parish guardians sold you?'

'That's right, yer grace. Five year old, an' sold like a parcel.' He sniffed sadly. 'Like negro slavery it is, only nobody don't know about it.'

'Well, it shall be known about,' Charlotte said. 'I shall tell Lord Shaftesbury what you have told me, and something will be done.'

'Lord Shaftesbury is a fine and kind gennleman, as everybody knows, yer grace, to worrit himself about it. But there won't come no end to climbing boys until gentry folks changes their minds and will have the machinery to sweep their chimbleys, 'stead of boys.'

'I understand you. Well, Mr Figgis, your boy is fed and bathed and ready to go with you. And since you have had the trouble of being without him, and of coming back to fetch him, here is a sovereign for you.'

Figgis brightened a little at that. 'Thank 'e kindly, mum – yer grace.'

'And if I should want, or Lord Shaftesbury should want, to ask you some more questions, you will come?'

'Hany time as it suits yer grace. But chimbleys is what they is, yer grace, and it ain't no use fightin' agin it, to my mind.'

Charlotte went with him to fetch the boy. Harry looked up as Figgis came into the room, and shrank back on himself, the warmth and comfort seeming to flow out of his face like water poured out of a bowl. Charlotte felt desperately sorry for the child, and thought that perhaps she should not have interfered in the first place, for having given him a taste of paradise must make the hell of his normal life seem more bitter. But Figgis did not seem a wantonly cruel man, and had survived a climbing-boyhood himself to an apparently healthy and contented adulthood. And as Oliver said, if she took this boy away, Figgis would only get another. But the look the child threw to her as he was taken away seared her mind – a look not of reproach, but of mute and miserable acceptance that the pleasures of life were not for him.

Later that evening Cavendish walked in, with a wide grin on his face. 'We have our orders,' he said. 'Embarking on April the eighth. I hope I may depend on you to come and see me off, Charley. Dockyard Stairs, Woolwich, nine o'clock – early to be abroad, I know, but there's bound to be a band and a great deal of cheering.'

'You're going to the war?' Charlotte said.

'Don't look so blue, dear girl,' Cavendish said. 'It won't be for long. We'll thrash those Russkies in no time and be back long before Christmas.'

'I don't know how we ever got into it,' Charlotte said. 'It seems extraordinary to me that we should find ourselves defending the Turks, who are a dreadfully cruel and barbaric race, in alliance with the French, led by the nephew of the man we defeated at such cost only forty years ago.'

'Put like that,' Oliver said, 'it sounds unbelievable. But the fact of the matter is, my love, that Russia has not given up her designs on Constantinople, and she will not – or rather the Tsar will not – do so until we've shown our teeth a little.'

312

'Just so,' Cavendish agreed quickly. 'Some dogs need a licking to bring them to hand. But it won't take us long to teach him who is master. One good battle, and he'll be running with his tail between his legs.'

'One good battle *where*?' Charlotte asked. 'Russia is such a big place.'

'Palmerston is urging an attack on the Crimea,' Oliver said. 'I must say it is the only obvious target. Russia has an important naval base at Sebastopol. If we destroy that, it will have no base for its Black Sea Fleet – if the destruction is complete, indeed, it will have no Black Sea Fleet. Then Russia will be forced to come to terms.'

'But that must be a naval exercise, surely?' Charlotte said.

'It would have to be supported by land forces, if the whole base is to be reduced,' Oliver said. 'Palmerston thinks sixty thousand men could do it in six weeks.'

'It's a pity Palmerston ain't Prime Minister,' Cav remarked.

'Siege warfare?' Charlotte said. 'There'd be nothing there for you, then, Cav. Nothing for the cavalry to do.'

'Don't worry, we'll find ourselves a fight,' Cavendish said cheerfully. 'And once Sebastopol is taken, we'll press out into – what are those places called, Southport, that you were mentioning?'

'Georgia and Circassia.'

'That's the dandy – we'll rough 'em up a bit there, just to drive the lesson home.' He eyed his sister sidelong. 'You needn't look like that, Charley. The fact is we're all rarin' to tweak the bear's nose. What's the use of an army if you never go to war?'

'But you have a wife and child now,' Charlotte said. Lady Blithfield had been brought to bed of a son in November. 'How can you bear to leave Alice and little William?'

Cavendish looked sheepish. 'Oh, they'll be all right without me. To tell the truth, I'm really rather keen to—' He glanced at Oliver, who had picked up the newspaper and seemed not to be listening. Cavendish lowered his voice. 'Since Alice's confinement, I can't get rid of Mrs Phipps. And if *she* won't go, *I* may as well. I practically live at the club and in the mess now, so Alice will never miss me. I don't suppose she'd notice if I never came back.'

'*I'd* notice. Please don't talk like that.'

'Oh well – nothing will happen to me, you know. But—' He bit his lip, on the brink of a confession he obviously thought he should not make.

'What is it?' Charlotte asked quietly. 'You can tell me.'

'Nothing. No, really. I mean, there was never anything I could have done about it, was there? But if I'd had the choice – do you remember asking me, if I could choose anyone in the whole world, would I choose Alice?' He stopped, and shrugged, unable to say more. He should not have said so much, and wouldn't have to anyone but Charlotte. But seeing her so continuously happy with her husband, seeing how she and Oliver conversed together and shared their interests, how they even laughed together about his difficult mother, it made him sad and increasingly bitter that he had married a girl he could not esteem, with whom he had no conversation, and whose mother was holding more and more power in his household. Since the baby had been born, Alice had convinced herself – or had been convinced – that she was sickly and could not manage alone, without her mother. Now to send Mrs Phipps away, Cavendish would have to be cruel to his wife; and frankly, he would sooner not upset her, when he had so little desire to be left alone with her. She had done nothing to forfeit his love, except be herself. She bored him, and he felt guilty about that

314

even while it irritated him. Rather than fight with Mrs Phipps and endure Alice's tears, he would sooner leave the situation as it was, and simply remove himself from the scene. But it was no way to live, and it depressed him. The war was a godsend. He was looking forward to it more than anything in the last six months.

Charlotte understood what he had not said, and was very sorry, for all concerned. She knew how important her marriage was to her, and wished more than anything Cavendish could have such a love to strengthen his life. But as he said, there was never anything he could have done, once he had felt himself honour-bound to marry Alice, and voicing regrets would only make the situation worse.

A little while later, Tom walked in on his way back from the House. 'Everyone's talking nothing but war, war, war,' he complained. 'I don't mind the ones who are hoping to make a fortune out of selling corn and beef and horses to the Treasury, but it's the bloodthirsty patriots who wear me out. I had one old fellow bawling "We'll show 'em!" in my ear for full twenty minutes, but when I asked him what we'd show, and to whom, and why, he couldn't tell me. "Why, sir, you ain't another of these Coburgs, are you?" he said to me; and since I didn't want to follow Little Albert to the Tower, I left him to it.'

'Cavendish has got his orders,' Charlotte told him.

'For Scutari?' Tom asked.

'Some such place,' Cavendish said.

'It's all one to you, I suppose,' Tom grinned. 'Well, you shall have Lord Raglan for company pretty soon. He's been confirmed as commander-in-chief.'

'I thought he would be,' Oliver said.

'The dear old fellow looked quite dazed. "Well, my boy," he said to me, "I must try to think what the Duke

315

would have done. That will be my touchstone." And then he grew quite moist about the eyes and patted my arm and said, "What a pity it is your pa can't be here to come with me." He's only ten years younger than Papa Danby, you know. He ought to be dandling his grandchildren on his knee, not going out to Varna to fight the Russians.'

'Where the deuce is Varna?' Cavendish asked.

'On the coast of the Black Sea,' Tom explained kindly. 'In the Danubian Principalities, where you would have to be to fight the Russians, since that's where *they* are.'

'You have it wrong, surely,' Oliver said. 'I thought the attack was to be at Sebastopol? I had it from Palmerston that that's what Napoleon favours.'

'Russel says no-one knows anything about Sebastopol, the strength of the fortifications, the numbers of men, even whether it's reducible at all. And Aberdeen says that since the purpose of the war is to get the Russians out of the Principalities, that's where we have to fight them. Raglan seemed quite sure about it, anyway. I think you can take it that's where you're going.'

'How did you come to be speaking to Lord Raglan at such length?' Charlotte asked. 'Where did you meet him?'

'At the Horseguards. I was called in to give advice,' Tom said with a smirk.

'What about?'

'The Government has decided to attach a photographic staff to the army. Yes, it's true! Captain Hackett of the 77th has been put in charge of it, and he's to have two sappers under him to carry the equipment.'

'Why sappers?' Oliver asked, amused.

'In case they have to build a developing-room, I suppose. I wasn't told,' Tom shrugged. 'Don't ask me to explain the military mind. At all events, I was called in to advise them about equipment and training. I suggested they should take a civilian photographer with them – a professional – and put them in the way of someone I think might be willing to go.'

'What do they want photographers for anyway?' Cavendish asked. 'How can they help?'

'I should have thought that was obvious – to send home from the front not just dispatches but graphic images. For the first time it will be possible for the Government back in England to see exactly what the commander-in-chief sees at the front. The improvement in information will be phenomenal.'

'There have always been war artists,' Oliver said, 'but a sketch or a painting can only convey the feeling of a place, not the true detail. And they take so much longer to execute than a photograph. I think it's an excellent idea.'

Tom was about to add something more when there was a commotion outside the room, and a heavy thud against the door itself.

'What the deuce is that?' Oliver exclaimed. He strode over to the door and flung it open, and a small child tumbled in, followed by a footman with his wig awry.

'Good God, it's the sweep's boy,' Charlotte said.

'I beg your pardon, your grace,' the footman panted, 'but he got away from me, and when I grabbed him he fell against the door.' He reached down to collar the child, who whipped his head round with amazing speed and bit him. The footman forgot himself. 'Come 'ere, you little perisher!' he bellowed. But the child was scrambling across the floor on all fours in the direction of Charlotte, and having reached her, dragged himself round behind her by her skirts.

'Stand still!' Oliver commanded as the footman seemed likely to throw himself at the duchess's legs in the attempt to recapture the fugitive. The footman halted, scarlet in the face. The sweep's boy cowered behind Charlotte, clutching folds of her skirt in two small fists as though that would protect him. Cavendish and Tom were suppressing their laughter, and Oliver turned to his wife with a polite look of enquiry. 'Much as I am enjoying your scheme to enliven our domesticity, may I ask you, my dear, what this child is doing here? I thought you'd handed him back to his master.'

'I ent a-gooin back!' the child cried shrilly. 'I'm a-stoppin' 'ere.'

'I did give him back,' Charlotte said. 'I suppose he must have run away. Palmer, where did the child come from?'

'I beg your pardon, your grace, no-one knows. He must have slipped in through the side door some time this evening, your grace, and then found his way upstairs. Mr Ungar saw him creeping along the passage, and instructed me to catch him, your grace.' He glared at the child, or the small portion of it that was peeping out from Charlotte's skirt.

She craned her neck round to meet the boy's eye. 'What were you doing, my dear?' she asked mildly. 'Why did you come here?'

'Came to steal something, your grace,' Palmer said fiercely. 'Young limb!'

'Be silent,' Charlotte said, soft but deadly. And to the child again, 'Why did you come here?'

'I wanter stop 'ere,' he said. 'You was nice to me. You give me soss'jis.'

'But you don't belong here. You belong with Mr Figgis, your master. You must go back to him.'

'I ent a-gooin' back. I don't wanter,' the child wailed.

Charlotte met her her husband's eye. 'It's my fault,' she said. 'I shouldn't have interfered.'

'I'm afraid I have to agree with you,' Oliver said. 'But now you have, we shall have to take the matter in hand.

Very well, Palmer, you may go. Tell Ungar I shall let him know shortly what it to become of the boy. And send a message to Figgis that the boy is here.'

Palmer went out. At the mention of Figgis the child broke into loud sobs.

'What the Dickens is all this about?' Tom asked.

'It's the sweep's boy,' Charlotte said through the noise. 'Got stuck in a chimney this morning – had to break the wall to get him out. I kept him here to make sure he wasn't hurt – washed and fed him – and now—'

'Now he's had a taste of heaven, he doesn't want to leave,' Oliver finished for her.

'That's the sweep's boy?' Cavendish said in amazement. 'But he's so small. He can't be more than three or four.'

'Five, so I'm told,' Charlotte said. 'Won't you let go of my skirt and come out, my dear? No-one's going to hurt you.'

'I ent a-gooin' back,' the boy wailed, clinging on harder. Charlotte heard the stitches in her waistband creak.

'Leave it to me,' Tom said. He took a couple of swift steps, took hold of the child's wrists, and said firmly, 'Let go, there's a good boy. You don't want the nice lady to take against you, because you've spoiled her dress, do you? Let go now, and I promise no-one shall hurt you.'

Charlotte felt the pressure go from her skirt, and Tom led the sobbing child round from behind her. She sat down gratefully; Tom sat opposite her, still holding the boy in front of him by both wrists. Harry looked at her, half hopeful, half despairing. 'What am I going to do with you?' she asked rhetorically.

'I should think something to eat, to stop this caterwauling, would be a good idea,' Tom said. 'Now then, you young limb,' with a little shake, 'd'you see that bowl

of fruit over there?' The limb drew a shaky breath and
followed the direction of Tom's eyes. 'Would you like an
apple from that bowl?' A nod of the head, the sobbing
easing to a hiccough. 'Very well, you may go and take
one, if you promise not to make any more noise, and not
to run away.'

The child stared, considering. 'You ent coddin'? I wunt
get licked?'

'I promise you.'

'Try "Bible Oath",' Charlotte suggested drily.

'Bible oath,' Tom said obediently, 'you may have an
apple, and no-one shall lick you.' Cautiously he released
a wrist and then the other, and the child walked warily
over to the bowl on the side-table and stared at it. 'Is
them fruit?' he asked the air in quiet amazement. Then
he reached up and took an apple, paused for a moment
to see if anything was going to happen to him, and turned
back to look enquiringly at Tom.

'Good boy. Now sit down just there and eat it, and
don't make a noise.'

'You'd have done a fine job in the Garden of Eden,'
Oliver said with amusement as the child obeyed. 'Now,
what's to be done about this? I recommend we send the
brat back where it belongs and leave it to the master to
manage.'

'What if he runs away again?' Charlotte said.

'That is not your problem.'

'But it is. I've done the damage.'

'You can't send him back,' Cavendish said. 'Not a kid
that small.'

'He will grow bigger,' Oliver assured him.

'Not up chimneys,' Cavendish protested further. 'It
ain't human.'

'Then what,' Oliver asked, 'would you propse? To
adopt it? A brother for little William, perhaps?'

'Oh – well—' Cavendish was embarrassed. 'I don't mean—'

'I thought not.'

'I'm off to Scutari in a week, in any case,' Cavendish remembered with relief.

'And I hope, my dear, that you don't propose to keep it,' Oliver said to his wife.

'He's not an it,' Charlotte insisted again.

'I'm afraid he is,' Tom said. 'The most ill-favoured it I've seen for a long time, poor wretched infant. But he must have some intelligence, to have found his way back here through the streets and in the dark. And some determination and cunning to have got in. And the good taste to choose you, Charley my dear, for his protectress.'

'Thank you, Tom. Well, I suppose I must try and find a home for the poor thing,' she said. She had placed orphan and unwanted children before, and one more wouldn't make any difference. 'Figgis will have to be compensated, of course, and—'

'I'll have him,' Tom said.

Charlotte stared. 'What do you mean?'

'Just what I say. I'll take him in. Take him home with me. Feed and clothe him. Look after him.'

'But *why*?' Charlotte said in astonishment.

He met her eyes. '*You* ask me that?'

'You don't mean – for Emily? But Tom, if you wanted a child for Emily to take care of, I could have found you one long ago. There are all sorts of societies – well, Emily must know of them too. You could get a nice, pretty child, instead of—' She made a helpless gesture. 'Why this one?'

Tom looked sheepish. 'Maybe because he isn't nice, and pretty. Emily's not a fool, you know. She'll know this one needs her.'

321

'There are thousands like him, that need just as much.'

'But this one's here, don't you see? This one found us. Don't you believe in Providence?'

Charlotte shrugged. 'Far be it from me to get in the way of philanthropy. But shouldn't you ask Emily first?'

Tom grinned. 'I think the less warning she has, the better. A *fait accompli* is the safest bet.' All this conversation had been carried on in low voices, so that the child shouldn't hear. Now Tom spoke up. 'Now then, boy, how would you like to come home with me to live?'

'I wanter stay wiv the lady,' he said promptly.

'Well, you can't. But I have a wife at home who's every bit as nice and kind as this lady – even nicer, really. So what about it? Speak up!'

The child considered. 'You wunt send me back to 'im?'

'To Mr Figgis? Certainly not.'

'You wunt send me up the chimbleys no more?'

'Never again.'

'You wunt lick me?'

'Certainly I shall, if you are naughty and disobedient, but not otherwise. And you shall have good things to eat and a bed to sleep in, and learn to read and write, and one day perhaps you'll get a job as a footman, like the one that tried to catch you out there, in a wig and white breeches.'

The child wavered. 'Will there be soss'jis?'

'Any amount of 'em.'

'My eye!'

'And faggots and meat pies and sausage rolls.'

'Prime!' the boy said, his eyes lighting. 'I'll come along of you, all right, mister.'

Tom grinned at Charlotte. 'So much for disinterested love. Has the creature a name?'

'Figgis said it was Harry.'

'Very well, Harry—'

'I ent 'Arry. Ass what *'e* called me,' the child said contemptuously.

'Then what is your name?'

'Tommy – sir.' The *sir* was added as a mark of new respect for this purveyor of the cooked meats to come.

'God bless my soul,' said Tom, and turned to Charlotte. 'Well, if that's not a sign, I don't know what is.'

Charlotte laughed. 'If it had been Emile, I must have taken it for a sign. But I'm afraid you'll regret it, Tom,' she added seriously. He smiled and shrugged. 'If you do think better of it, let me know, and I'll try and find a place for him. Norton and I have placed quite a few, you know.'

'Oh, I think this will work out all right. There's something about young Tommy, ill-favoured or not.'

CHAPTER THIRTEEN

Charlotte lived from day to day expecting news of a disaster from Upper Grosvenor Street; but when she next met Tom, on the morning they saw Cavendish off to war, he was cheerful and inclined to 'tell her so'.

'Emily isn't coming this morning – she said her good-byes to Cavendish last night. She stays at home with little Tommy.'

'So he hasn't burned the house down or stolen the silver?' Charlotte enquired.

Tom pretended outrage. 'How can you suggest such things? No, he's settling in very well – enjoying a childhood he missed on the first attempt. He adores Emily, can't bear to be out of her sight. And he's eating like a coach horse. I think,' he added judiciously, 'that when he's better nourished, he won't be so ill-favoured. He will never be a handsome boy, but he will pass on a foggy day, as the saying is.'

'But Tom, what will you do with him?' Charlotte asked, half amused, half alarmed. 'When he gets bigger?'

'We'll cross the bridge when we come to it. For the moment Emily has something to nurture, and she's enjoying herself teaching the child – not just his manners, but his letters, too. Now he's not frightened, he begins to show some quickness: I think he may do well. Perhaps in a year or so we might send him off to school – and then, who knows, start again with another unlucky infant. If it makes Emily happy, I don't care. It can't do the brats anything but good.'

'Have you thought what would happen to little Tommy if Emily should have a child of her own?' Charlotte asked.

'I don't think that will happen,' Tom said, in a voice that invited no further question. Fatherless himself, he supposed he would remain childless – a small cul-de-sac off life's main thoroughfare. It seemed appropriate to his strange life; but he was sorry, especially for Emily's sake.

The scene at the Dockyard Stairs was a bright one, with the steamer *Albion* dressed overall; flags everywhere straining bravely in the stiff April breeze; crowds gathered to see the soldiers off, a bright flutter of waving scarves; and the band of the Royal Artillery playing their most stirring marches, instruments gleaming in the fitful sunshine. Carriages were drawn up behind the bulk of the crowd, and here the officers said fond farewells to their families. Alice was in floods of tears, clinging to Cavendish with limp white hands, unable to speak. Cavendish did his best to be bracing, but Charlotte reflected it was not a very cheerful sending-off for him, despite the fact that he had somehow persuaded, or commanded, his mother-in-law to stay at home. Alice's pouring grief was as violent as if Cavendish was on his way to certain death, while he was looking forward to the exciting trip and even more exciting war. He wanted to be fretting about his horses, Rowan and Bracken, thoroughbred chestnut geldings, who had never been on a ship before. He wanted to be making sure his man got all his luggage aboard, especially the tin box containing his best cap which had already been mislaid twice. Charlotte saw that it took all his patience not to snatch those white hands off his sleeves and fling them back at his wife.

'You will be somewhat of a crowd on board,' Oliver remarked. 'I hope you have a steady passage. Three weeks of other men being sick all round you would be a trial.'

'Thank you, sir, for those cheering words,' Cavendish grinned.

'What sort of sailor are you?' Tom enquired with interest.

'I really don't know. I've never done it before. But I'm sure to be a good one.'

'If it gets rough and you do feel bad, go on deck and stay there,' Tom advised. 'Take it from one who knows.'

Cavendish shook his head. 'If it gets rough, I'll be below with my horses. They must come first.'

'Ah yes, of course,' Tom said. 'Silly of me. Well, old fellow, I hope you have as jolly a time as you expect. Be brave, and kill lots of Rooshians!'

'I'll do my best.' Cavendish shook hands with Oliver and Tom, and kissed Charlotte, murmuring in her ear, 'Take care of Alice and the boy for me, Charley. Don't let that woman completely crush them.'

And then he turned to his voiceless, dripping bride for a last hasty kiss, before detaching himself and hurrying on board. The gangway was quickly run up, and the band struck up with *Cheer, Boys, Cheer* as the steamer manoeuvred out into the stream. The men on board obeyed the injunction literally, roaring themselves hoarse, answered by wild cheering from the waving families, the dockyard workers, and the crews of the other vessels moored nearby, as the *Albion* worked out into the passage and away downstream. And then she was gone.

'Do you really think they will be back soon?' Charlotte asked Oliver as they climbed back into the carriage.

'If they make a firm enough strike against the Russians in the Principalities, I think it may be enough to make them withdraw.'

'And if it isn't?'

'Then there will have to be a strike elsewhere to convince them we mean business.'

'But at all events, they should be home by Christmas?'

'It seems likely,' Oliver said.

If the purpose of the war was to drive the Russians out of the Principalities and back over the river Pruth into their own territory, then the war was over before the British and French troops had even reached the theatre. The Allies arrived in Scutari at the end of May, and there was a long administrative delay before they could be transferred to Varna. And in June the Turkish troops, who had been engaged against the Russians since October, made a determined attempt to relieve the siege of Silistra, and beat off a counter-attack by the Russians under Prince Gorchakov. The prince was wounded in the action, and the next day the Russians began to withdraw northwards towards their own border. By the end of July they had crossed the Pruth: the war was won, and the Allies had not fired a shot.

Aberdeen was delighted and would have been glad to call the British troops home; but the newspapers would not have it. The public had been clamouring for war, had prepared itself for it, was keyed up to fever pitch for bulletins of glorious battles and resounding victories, for feats of heroism, stubborn defences, brave deaths and miraculous survivals – above all, to hear the British lion roar and see the Russian bear tremble. This Grand Old Duke of York business was not the thing at all. Indignation turned itself on Lord Aberdeen. *Punch* showed him blacking the Tsar's boots; scurrilous songs were sung about him; crowds demonstrated noisily in London for a proper war with blood, glory and plenty of dead Russians.

The Emperor of France was facing similar difficulties, needing a military victory to secure his popularity, and talk was resumed between the two governments over the possibility of reducing Sebastopol. Apart from the public hysteria, there was a logical argument for it: unless the Russian naval base in the Black Sea was destroyed, Turkey could not be considered completely safe from attack, nor Constantinople completely safe from seizure.

And while the argument went on at home, the soldiers waited at Varna for orders. It was horribly hot and debilitatingly humid; the men were attacked by plagues of flies, gnats and leeches, and the inevitable dysentery ran through every regiment. There was nothing to do. The army sweated, scratched, quarrelled, and slouched listlessly thorugh its routine duties. Soon it was threatened by a more deadly enemy than the Russians. It was a cholera year: all around the Mediterranean outbreaks were being reported, as the disease was carried from country to country via the seaports. Towards the end of July a French ship out of Marseilles brought the disease to Varna. It struck the French camp first, and within days leapt like a forest fire to the English camp.

Cavendish wrote to Charlotte.

'Don't tell Alice – I would not have her alarmed – but I can say to you what I would not to anyone else. The cholera is very bad here. We moved the camp last week, but did not manage to shake it off. There are more cases every day. The 50th lost nine men yesterday. Fifteen died in one night at the hospital. The hospital is a converted a barracks at Varna. All the cases go there. Poor creatures, the only transport is a springless bullock-cart, so it is a very long and jolting journey. And when they get there – oh Charley, how we need some of *your* order! You cannot picture the miserable place the General Hospital is. Nothing but filthy mattresses on the floor, and the floor half rotten, harbouring fleas and lice, and rats living underneath, poking their heads up through the holes like cats looking for mice. Every man who has gone in with cholera has died. The men are more afraid of the hospital than the disease. They drink the local brandy, which is supposed to be a preventive, but it just makes them drunk, and then they lie where they fall, and get burnt by the sun and bitten by the insects. I would to God we could get out of this place! We cannot keep order, nor morale amongst the men. There is talk that we may go to the Crimea after all, but such is the general state of apathy, most of the fellows here do not care if we go to Sebastopol or South America or Southend, or nowhere at all.'

The cholera at Varna did at least spur the Government into making a decision about an expedition to Sebastopol. However difficult it might be to take the town (and there were those who said it was impossible) the Crimea would at least be a healthier place for the soldiers than Varna. It was thought that Sebastopol was fortified only on the seaward side; moreover, it was so far from the military heart of Russia that reinforcements took three months to march there, and it was said that two-thirds of them died on the way. So if the Allies landed sufficient men, supported by the Navy they could take Sebastopol from the unfortified landward side, reduce the defences, destroy the Russian fleet, and remove the troops before winter started.

As the Cabinet debated, the arguments were gone over thoroughly and in great detail in the newspapers, particularly *The Times*, so there was no hope of surprising the Russians. 'I suspect the Tsar has the news from London before Lord Raglan,' Oliver said gloomily.

Worried as Charlotte was about Cavendish, she was obliged to keep a cheerful face before Alice, who could be driven to paroxysms of weeping by the least thing.

Charlotte was surprised that the girl she had seen as merely dull, meek and biddable should have such a bent for hysteria; but she soon learned that it was Mrs Phipps who did the mischief, playing on her daughter's natural fears and encouraging her to tease herself until she went over the edge. It was, Charlotte came to understand, Mrs Phipps's defence against banishment. She meant to make herself so indispensable to Alice that Cavendish could not send her away. An Alice phlegmatic, easily governed, obedient to the will of the last person who spoke, presented no maternal excuse; an Alice teetering always on the brink of nervous prostration and clinging to her mother, begging not to be separated, was an irresistible justification.

Charlotte began to see why Cavendish disliked Mrs Phipps so much. Little as she enjoyed Alice's company, Charlotte made it her business to abstract her as often as she could from her mother's influence, even if it was only for half an hour; and while she had her alone, to try to talk her into a better frame of mind. After some trial and error she devised a plan which worked pretty well. She invited Alice to bring baby William to Southport House to play with – or rather be played with by – her children. Mrs Phipps was all in favour of this. Nursery friendships endure, she reasoned, and if William became a valued companion of little Viscount Turnhouse and little Lord Marcus, he would be firmly attached to the ducal house for life – which meant his grandmother would be too. She also cast covetous eyes on Lady Venetia and Lady Olivia. It would be nice for William to marry a duke's daughter, and when they were all grown up, the age difference would be nothing.

Having deposited William in the nursery, Charlotte deposited Mrs Phipps with Lady Turnhouse. Lady Turnhouse liked obsequiousness, and regarded being flattered and deferred to as simply her right, so she thought Mrs Phipps an agreeable woman with sensible ideas, and quite enjoyed talking to her. Furthermore, Lady Turnhouse had taken a violent liking to Cavendish, on whom she lavished all the affection and approval she could not bring herself to give to Charlotte; and Mrs Phipps could never hear enough of Cavendish's praises. Add to that the eternal topic of grandchildren, and there was plenty for the two dowagers to discuss; and since Lady Turnhouse was just the sort of grand dame that Mrs Phipps could genuinely admire, it was acceptable to both that Lady Turnhouse should do most of the talking while Mrs Phipps undertook the agreeing and flattering part of the business.

This left Charlotte free to concentrate on Alice, and if her conversation irked, she could always persuade her to play on the pianoforte, which soothed the nerves and did them both good.

'*Must* you turn my home into a bear-garden?' Oliver complained, finding what he called the Phipps Menagerie installed again. 'I shall go and live with Tom and Emily. They treat me with proper respect.'

But soon all other considerations were driven from Charlotte's mind, for in August the cholera reached London.

'Surely,' said Lady Turnhouse emphatically, 'there is no need for you to go in person to the hospital? Are not these *nurses* you have gone to such lengths to employ and train capable of doing their own work?' She invested the word 'nurses' with so much withering contempt that she might have been talking about the lowest of hardened criminals, rather than women who gave comfort to the sick.

'Yes, they are capable,' Charlotte replied patiently, 'but there are not enough of them. Hundreds are falling sick every day. Every willing hand is needed at a time like this. The cholera strikes hard and spreads quickly.'

Lady Turnhouse turned down her mouth in disgust. 'Amongst the poor. It is a disease of the poor. I cannot understand how you can have to do with such – such vileness.'

'No, I know you can't.'

'If you do not care for yourself or your own reputation, you might perhaps consider your husband, who has risked everything for your sake, and receives very little consideration from you in return for his generosity.'

'What, pray, has he risked?' Charlotte enquired dangerously.

It did not suit Lady Turnhouse to answer that. 'In his name I beg you will give up this unseemly behaviour. You have already shocked a great many people by your *curious* preoccupations, though I have begged you again and again to remember your station and what is expected of you. It may have been very well to do just as you pleased when you were a nobody, but a duchess has others to consider besides herself, a reputation to guard, above all a position to maintain. I would not, of course,' she added witheringly, 'expect you to understand the meaning of *noblesse oblige*—'

'I think on the whole that is wise of you,' Charlotte said gravely.

Lady Turnhouse breathed hard. 'It may amuse you to be insolent towards me, but consider, if you will, the consequences should you bring this vile disease back to the house. How can you risk the lives of your innocent children by this wanton attachment to your own will?'

'You have already pointed out, ma'am, that it is a disease of the poor; and I have told you many times that it is passed from person to person through contaminated food and drink. No-one in this house is in the least danger from my going to the hospital; but if you are afraid for yourself, you may of course retire to Ravendene until the crisis is over. And now I must ask you to excuse me further conversation. I must go where I am needed.'

She collected Norton and went out to the waiting carriage, much less calm than she had managed to appear before her mother-in-law. 'Does she think I enjoy the sights and smells? That I do it for pleasure?'

'It doesn't signify what she thinks,' Norton said calmly. 'You do very well not to lose your patience with her. It isn't worth it.'

'But it angers me all the same. Cavendish goes off to war, and she says he is nobly doing his duty, though it must be every bit as unpleasant to be on a battlefield as in a hospital. Indeed, they're much the same thing, except that in a hospital death is the enemy.'

'You can't expect her ladyship to see that.'

'Don't be so reasonable, Norton,' Charlotte said. 'It annoys me.'

'You're a female, Lord Blithfield is a man. That's it and all about it.'

'And what cannot be cured must be endured – yes, I know. Spare me your gypsy platitudes!'

Norton lapsed into a resigned silence and looked out of the window while her mistress recovered her temper.

'The worst of it,' Charlotte said after a while, in her normal tone of voice, 'is that there is so little we can do.'

The frightening thing about cholera was the suddenness with which it attacked and the speed with which it killed. It began with violent diarrhoea and vomiting, followed by agonising cramps in the belly and legs, fever, and torturing thirst. Within hours the victim would be sinking, with a dusky skin, cracking lips, sunken eyes, and that characteristic pinched looked about the features. Death might come within a few hours of the first attack, or the patient might linger twelve to twenty hours, if they were strong to begin with. But most of them did die. The mortality was frightful: most of them never got as far as the hospital. The only thing that could save a sufferer was his own individual strength, and good nursing.

The latter was what Charlotte could offer at the Southport. When the outbreak had begun, they had emptied one ward to serve as fever ward. The nurses had been very frightened, unwilling to take care of the cholera victims for fear of catching it themselves. Though Miss Barthorp had explained to them the nature of the disease, she had not managed to reassure them and begged Charlotte to intervene. Charlotte asked Friedman to add his medical weight to her authority.

'I am not convinced, as you are,' Friedman said. 'I cannot see that there is any real ground for Doctor Snow's contention. But if it will keep the nurses at their post, I will be glad to come along and agree with everything you say. A good lie in a good cause has my support.'

So Charlotte herself addressed the nurses, and they listened quietly, and were evidently impressed by the presence of Sir Frederick at the duchess's side. Charlotte explained how cholera was spread through the contaminated body fluids of the victims. 'So it is very important that the bedpans are emptied only in the latrines, and that the patients' eating and drinking vessels are kept entirely separate. For your own health you must also make sure that you eat and drink nothing while you are on the ward, and that when you come off the ward you wash your hands and faces thoroughly before eating and drinking. If you follow these simple rules, I can promise you that you will be in no danger from the disease. Sir Frederick?'

'Yes, I am here to endorse everything that her grace has said to you. Follow her rules to the letter, and all will be well.'

And he smiled on them, which probably went further to reassuring them than anything Charlotte said, for he was extremely handsome, and once they had been on the receiving end of one of his smiles, any of the nurses would have died for him.

Though they began with one fever ward, the epidemic spread so rapidly that by the end of a week they were obliged to empty the other wards and dedicate the whole effort to nursing the cholera victims. It was wearisome, disgusting and pitiful work. But at least at Southport's a few did survive. The hospital water supply was clean – that was one thing Charlotte had made very sure of – and if a patient was not too debilitated before he arrived, being separated from the source of infection, and given clean water to drink, was sometimes enough to allow him to recover by his own natural strength.

But the dead far outnumbered the living. In the worst-hit parishes there were too many for conventional burial, especially when, as so often happened, whole families succumbed, leaving no-one to attend to the obsequies. Then the poor corpses were loaded into carts and taken to communal limepits.

In the second week of the outbreak, Charlotte received an anguished message from Doctor Snow.

'I know how you must be circumstanced at the Southport, but you also know what the Middlesex is like, how different from your own establishment. I beg you to come with as many of your nurses as you can spare and restore – no, *create* – some order.'

Charlotte remembered conditions at the Middlesex Hospital during a previous cholera outbreak, and could not refuse his plea. They could not really spare anyone, but four people who knew each other's ways could make a difference at the Middlesex, she thought, so she took

Mrs Webster and Mrs Glyn, and went with Norton to see what they could do to help.

The scenes inside were appalling: filth, disorder, stench, the dead and living lying down together, equally ignored; sufferers raving with fever, or silent with the apathy of approaching death, lying where they had staggered or been deposited. There were too few nurses. Many had run away out of fear of the disease, and of those who remained, many were drunk and unwilling to touch the patients. As at Southport's, the other patients had been sent home to make room for the cholera victims. They came in all through the day and night, for the Middlesex was situated in Soho, in the heart of the worst affected area. The crowded, narrow streets and teeming courts and alleys were packed with the poor and unfortunate, and a particular haunt of prostitutes, and the cholera went through them like wildfire.

Doctor Snow greeted her with huge relief. 'Thank God you are here! I feel like Horatius.'

'I wish I could have brought you more help,' Charlotte said, 'but we are inundated too. This is a nightmare, doctor. I wish to God those who opposed the Board of Health could be brought here to see it.'

'They still wouldn't believe it was any of their business,' Snow said. 'And they wouldn't believe that proper sewerage and clean water would stop all this in a moment.'

'Have you any idea how it began this time?'

'Not how it began. But the place itself is responsible for the spread.' His own practice was based in Frith Street, and he knew the area very well. 'I have been trying to keep a record of where the victims live, to see if we can't track down any particular source of infection. I wish you will ask them as they are brought in, and keep a note.'

Charlotte agreed, and she and her women went to work. It was a task, she thought, similar to that of Hercules in the

336

Augean stables. As fast as they cleared a space or cleaned up a mess, another sufferer would stagger in, always filthy and frequently drunk and raving, to take the space and restore the mess. And when they managed to clear a corridor, they would only have to turn their backs for a minute to find someone had deposited another victim on the floor and beaten a hasty retreat.

But some of the nurses and orderlies, though ignorant, were willing, and glad to be given direction from someone with authority and understanding. She set the orderlies to removing the dead, and the Middlesex nurses to cleaning up the worst of the mess, while her own women did what little could be done for the patients, and directed the work. Everything was made more difficult by the inadequacy of the place itself, the lack of equipment, of room, of privvies, the porous nature of the floors and walls, the lack of laundry facilities. It was hospitals like this which had driven her in the first place to build Southport's, and if she had needed convincing that she had done right, this present experience would have provided it.

She soon discovered that she was not the only lady attempting the impossible at the Middlesex. In one ward she came upon a figure in a neat black gown covered with a white apron, who was directing the nurses in much the same way that Charlotte had been. The woman, about Charlotte's own age, was tall, very slender, with thick dark brown hair very neatly parted and pinned behind. Her pale, oval face was rather pretty, with delicate features and level grey eyes, but what struck Charlotte most was her serene, pensive, and rather sad expression. Everyone else she had met was either frowning, distressed, or grim with effort; this woman seemed like a visitor from another world, gazing down from a great height where nothing could touch her. Yet there was no doubt she was making a difference to the ward, even as Charlotte's women were.

Later, in a moment of comparative quiet, she was introduced to Charlotte as a Miss Nightingale, who was Lady Superintendent of a nursing home for sick governesses in Harley Street. Her solemn face was transformed by a very sweet smile when she learnt who Charlotte was. 'I am very glad to meet your grace. I have been so interested in your scheme to train female nurses. Doctor Bowman has told me about it – you know Doctor Bowman, the surgeon, of King's?'

'I have heard of him, of course, though we are not acquainted.'

'He is the surgeon appointed to the Institution where I am superintendent. I once assisted at an operation he performed, using chloroform,' said Miss Nightingale with permissible pride.

'Did you indeed? That must have been a very interesting experience.'

'Doctor Bowman was good enough to say that my skills were of the greatest assistance to him. He is very eager to set up a scheme like yours at King's, for taking in and training a body of female nurses. He has asked me to take the post of Superintendent of Nurses.'

'Should you care to?' Charlotte asked.

'Oh, I should like it of anything,' Miss Nightingale said eagerly, but then the animation drained from her face, and the pensive, remote look was back. 'But my family are very much against it. I do not know how it will end. Might I ask – did your grace meet with much opposition? How did you manage to persuade them to let you do this – this *unfeminine* thing?' She said the word with delicate irony.

'It was easy for me,' Charlotte admitted. 'My father was dead, and I was of independent means, so no-one could stop me. I do feel for you, Miss Nightingale. I should hate to be prevented from doing what I thought right.'

'Your grace's husband does not object to all this?' with a wave of the delicate fingers at the surroundings.

'He encourages me. He is the best man in the world. My mother-in-law disapproves strongly, but as long as he supports me, I am safe.'

'He must be an unusual man,' Miss Nightingale sighed. 'If he encourages you, I would say he must be unique. Most gentlemen think females are fit for nothing but sitting on a sofa and laughing at their anecdotes.'

'I had the advantage, too, that my grandmother was always fascinated by medical matters, and ran her own hospital in Brussels after the battle of Waterloo. She was a great advocate for females training to be doctors. She longed to be a surgeon herself.'

The grey eyes widened a little. 'Oh no, that would not be right. I could not agree with that. The natural place for females in medicine is as nurses, working under the complete authority of the doctors. *That* is the way to ensure order.'

They had no time for more conversation, but over the next few days Charlotte had opportunities to observe Miss Nightingale, and was struck by the strange contrasts of her character. She did not stint herself, worked harder than anyone around her, and performed the most unpleasant duties without flinching, without expressing in her serene pale face the slightest distaste. She held the hand of the dying, and her gentle, soothing voice plainly brought them great comfort; yet Charlotte came to feel that this strange young woman had no real sympathy for the patients as individuals. It was as if she had managed in her mind to separate the sickness from the sufferer. She cared deeply that the sickness should be defeated, but not because she had any warm feeling for the body it inhabited. It made her, Charlotte thought, a singularly effective nurse, because nothing ever upset her; but it did not make her very likeable.

One day Doctor Snow sought Charlotte out in a state of great excitement. '*Eureka!*' he said. 'I have it, I'm sure of it! The Broad Street pump!'

'The source of infection, you mean?'

'The pump is at the Cambridge Street end, and by far the most victims have come from Broad Street and the alleys and courts at the Cambridge Street end. I've got the figures here.' He slapped the piece of paper he was holding triumphantly. 'Six hundred dead this sennight!'

'Good God!'

'Aye, it's a leveller! And of forty-nine houses in Broad Street, only twelve without a fatality. Well, I'm going to put a stop to it, right this minute. I am going to the vestry clerk to have the pump handle removed. That'll force the people to go elsewhere for their water, and then we shall see!'

He left in a state of great excitement. Charlotte did not expect the business to take long, but he had not returned by the time she left the hospital for the night. She was unwilling to leave, when there was still so much to do, but she had not been home for three days, and was dropping with fatigue. 'You'll do the poor sufferers more good if you take the time to eat and sleep,' Norton said sternly. 'It won't help to have you taking ill yourself. Webster and Glyn had last night off.'

Charlotte frowned. 'If I go, you go too, do you understand?'

'I'll go all right, my lady,' Norton said grimly. 'I want a bath and some clean linen. I never thought,' she added, bustling Charlotte into her shawl and out of the door, 'that being a lady's maid would be such hard work. If I'd known when you asked me—'

'You'd still have said yes,' Charlotte said, with a smile. 'You must admit, your life is never boring.'

'Sometimes I think I'd settle for a bit o' boredom,' Norton retorted. 'It'd make a nice change.'

It was glorious to be back home, free from horrible smells and horrible sounds; glorious to get into a bath and wash the hospital stench from her skin and hair; glorious to sit – actually sit!—and eat without being interrupted. Oliver had not been expecting her, and was dining at his club. The kitchen had not been expecting her either, but she wanted nothing elaborate. Soft white bread, cold beef, fruit and a bottle of burgundy were an epicurean feast to the unsated palate. She told Ungar she would see no-one, and was surprised when he came in to announce a visitor; but he said, 'It is Doctor Snow, your grace, and he insisted that you would want to see him.'

'Very well,' Charlotte said. She was even more surprised by Snow's appearance when he entered a moment later. He was dishevelled, his clothes were dusty, and he was holding a large piece of rusty iron in his hand, which he waved at her, with a huge grin on his face which made him seem suddenly half his age.

'Do you know what this is?' he said as Ungar closed the door behind him.

'I can't begin to imagine.'

'This is deliverance! This is public health! This is the handle of the Broad Street pump!

Charlotte began to laugh. 'Did the parish clerk give it to you as a souvenir?'

Snow sat down, laughing too. 'No, your grace, it was not as simple as that! The clerk said he had no power to do as I asked, without authority from the Guardians. So I went to see them, but I couldn't persuade them of my case. The Broad Street pump, they said, was the only one working for many streets around, and if it were disconnected, people would have to walk half a mile or more for water. Let 'em walk, says I. Better than dying for a glass of water – which was a joke, by the by, but they are solemn people, the Guardians, and they didn't laugh.'

'So I imagine.'

'No, they said that the water had nothing to do with the infection, that it was caused by the bad air around the dung heaps as everyone knew, and that they were already setting up braziers on every street to burn sulphur to purify the air, and would be putting in hand the removal of the worst dungheaps as soon as they had the men available for the work. I argued every way I could, but I couldn't shake 'em. So I went back to the clerk and said, I haven't got permission, you must do without.'

'What did he say to that?'

'He hadn't anything to say to that, but he had an answer ready to the promise of five sovereigns and an undertaking that no-one would ever know his name,' Snow said with a grin. 'It was dark by then, which helped persuade him. The handle was rusted on,' he added, waving his piece of metal again, 'so we had to borrow a hammer and knock it off. I would have left it with my fellow conspirator, but he looked at it as if it was a viper, and said, take it with you, for God's sake! So here it is – and now we shall see.' The animation suddenly drained from his face, and Charlotte could see how mortally tired he was.

'We shall see indeed,' she said. 'If you're right, you will have done a great public service.'

'And if I'm wrong, I'll likely end up in gaol – but never mind it.'

'I'll see you don't,' Charlotte said. 'His grace has influence, and he'll use it at my request.'

'I would to God he had influence to change men's minds, and make them listen to reason!' Snow said discontentedly. 'They believe that cholera grows from

342

the smell of ordure – as well believe you could grow a rose-bush by sprinkling otto of roses on the earth.'

'Reason doesn't come into it, when it comes to disease,' Charlotte said. 'You know that. Faced with pain and death we all still believe in magic. You're tired, Doctor Snow. Let me ring for refreshments for you. I have had a simple supper on a tray – bread and meat – quite delicious when you're hungry. Let me send for something for you.'

'No, no thank you, your grace.' Snow stood up wearily, his joints cracking as he moved. 'You're very kind, but I shall go home to my bed. I shouldn't have disturbed you, but I wanted to share this—' he waved the pump handle again, 'with somebody, and I thought of you first.'

'I'm glad you did,' Charlotte said. 'And I hope you are proved right.'

At that moment the door opened and Oliver came in. 'Good evening, wife of my heart.' He eyed the two of them, and the pump handle, with curiosity. 'For a woman who enjoys robust health, you spend an extraordinary amount of time in the company of medical men! Good evening, Snow. Is that some new kind of instrument for administering anaesthetic? One sharp tap on the bean, and a man will know no more pain, I judge.'

Snow looked immeasurably weary. 'Good evening, your grace. Will you excuse me if I leave her grace to explain it to you? I was just leaving: I must snatch some sleep before I am called again.'

When Snow had gone, Charlotte rose and went to kiss her husband. He sniffed delicately, and then took her into his arms. 'You're tired,' he observed.

'Hmm,' she said, leaning comfortably against him. 'Not so tired, though, that I'd refuse if you asked me to go and look at the children with you.'

'Will you come and look at the children with me?' he

asked obediently. 'And will you tell me why Snow was here at this hour, waving a piece of rusty iron?'

'If you insist,' she said. 'I'll tell you on the way up.' A little while later they were in the nursery, gazing with satisfaction on the faces of their sleeping children – something they liked to do now and then, what Oliver called 'stock-taking'. And very soon after that they were in bed, and Charlotte, held safe in his arms, was tumbling down a long, soft, dark laundry-chute into sleep.

The result of Snow's action made itself felt in a matter of days. The spate of new victims from the Broad Street area slowed to a trickle, and in three days dried up completely. Snow was jubilant; Charlotte rejoiced with him, and returning to her own hospital, found Sir Frederick duly impressed by the experiment. 'It does not prove the thing, but it is a very strong argument,' he said. 'If his research could only isolate the cholera seed, there would be no more doubt. But even on present evidence, I am willing to be convinced.'

Reynolds, of course, was already convinced, and he too rejoiced that the argument must now be accepted. 'He will write it up, and the whole medical profession will give up the old idea, and then the Government *must* act,' he said happily.

But Friedman shook his head over that. 'I would not be too sanguine if I were you. What men, even medical men – or perhaps I should say *especially* medical men – believe doesn't depend on what is reasonable or rational or subject to proof. It depends on what they want to believe. Oh, minds will change,' he added, seeing Charlotte's passionate look, 'but not for a long time. It is a matter of balance.' He held out his hands like a pair of scales, the right one lower than the left. 'You add one mind after another to the side of new argument, and

nothing happens; the old order persists; until suddenly—'
He lowered his left hand and raised the right. 'Suddenly
there are enough minds on the new side, and opinion
changes almost overnight. And the odd thing is that once
the balance has gone over, no-one remembers that they
ever thought differently.'

'I suppose it is some comfort to think that if we
wait long enough, something will be done to save lives,'
Charlotte said with irony.

Sir Frederick smiled. '*May* be done. Sometimes you
never manage to collect enough minds to tip the balance.
And sometimes,' he added with a grin, 'the pan is screwed
down by those who have an interest in keeping it down.
You look indignant, duchess? But I have to advise you
that, though it may shock you, there are very few practi-
tioners of medicine who are as disinterested as you. There
are few who can afford to be.'

Reynolds repudiated this angrily. 'There is never sufficient excuse for a man to smother his conscience and his
intellect.'

'You are holding yourself up as an example?' Friedman
enquired smilingly.

'Yes, by God!'

'Ah, but you come in on my side, Reynolds, don't you
see? You are under the Duchess of Southport's patronage.
You are one of the lucky few who can afford to serve
the truth.'

In September the Allied Army at last, and with desperate slowness, moved from Varna, took ship and sailed
across the Black Sea towards the Crimea. In London the
cholera abated, and Charlotte was able to return to her
usual occupations. A letter arrived from Manchester, a
formal note from Fanny to say that her husband's father
had died. Anthony was the only son, and inherited the

estate – a small but pleasing demesne near Blakeney, in Norfolk. Fanny said that Anthony would have to go into Norfolk to settle affairs, but did not say whether she would be going with him. Charlotte had not even had time to begin a letter of condolence in reply when Fanny arrived at Southport House in a hackney from the station, accompanied only by a carpet-bag.

The method of her arrival and the lack of notice filled Charlotte with alarm, but in front of the servants she expressed nothing but calm pleasure at her cousin's arrival. As soon as they were alone, Fanny fell into her arms, between laughing and crying, and said, 'Oh Charley, you must take me in, or I'm undone. I've run away.'

'Good God, what do you mean? Where is Doctor Anthony?'

'I told you in my letter, he had to go into Norfolk.' She released herself and sat down on the sofa, pulling out her hat pins. 'I begged him to let me come and visit you while he was gone, but he wouldn't agree. He said he couldn't trust me to behave myself in London,' she said, throwing down her hat beside her. Charlotte noticed with a pang the grey hairs in Fanny's dark head. They were new since she had last seen her.

'I know he doesn't care for me,' Charlotte began cautiously.

'Oh, he doesn't *care* for anyone, except Philip Anthony! So then I asked him to let me go and stay with Aunt Rosamund, but he wouldn't agree to that, either. Didn't trust me not to run off from there, I suppose – which I would have, so he was quite right. He said I must stay at home like a good wife, and to make sure I did he gave the servants orders that I wasn't to leave the house until he got back.'

'Oh Fanny, no!'

'Oh Charley, yes! Have you still no idea of the kind of life I lead?' She jumped up and walked around, twisting her thin hands together. She seemed almost feverishly excited, her eyes bright and a spot of colour in each pale cheek, and Charlotte wondered whether she had caught some infection on her journey – or whether, worse thought, her mind was beginning to be disordered. But Fanny went on rationally enough, though speaking very quickly, almost breathlessly, as though she expected to be interrupted. 'I was determined I would not be left a prisoner, especially as he didn't know how long he was to be gone, but it was bound to be three or four weeks, and three or four weeks locked in that house I knew would finish me. So on the night of the day he left, when I thought the servants would be off their guard, I climbed out of the window. That's why I couldn't bring much with me, only just the one small bag, so I depend on your lending me everything I need, dear Charley. And then I walked to the station. Of course there wasn't a train until the morning, and I was terrified they would find out I'd gone and come after me. So I kept walking around. There were some very horrid people hanging about the streets, I can tell you, and every time I stood still some horrid man would come up to me and make disgusting suggestions. I suppose they took me for a prostitute.' She gave a nervous laugh.

'Oh Fanny, weren't you frightened?'

'To tell you the truth, I was too much afraid of being caught and taken back to be frightened of anything else. But at last the station opened and I bought my ticket and then I was able to go into the waiting-room where the horrid people can't come. But there was a dreadful female, an attendant of some sort, who kept staring at me, and I made sure she knew who I was and was going to call a constable! And then I thought I ought not to have

347

bought my ticket so soon, because there was ages to wait for the train, and anyone enquiring would have known where I was going. But of course,' she added, waving her hand, 'they would guess that anyway.'

'But Fanny, how did you buy the ticket? Where did you get the money?'

'It was my running-away money – I've had it hidden away for ages. You see, last Christmas Uncle Jes gave me a bracelet which happened to be identical to one I already had, so he said I should exchange it at the shop for something else. So I waited until one day when I was able to go without Philip, and in the shop I chose something much less expensive, and asked the jeweller to give me the rest in cash. Well, he looked a bit strangely at me, but I'm a very good customer there, and so is Aunt Rosamund, so he did as I asked, and I begged him not to tell anyone, and he agreed. And I hid the money in my room, under a loose floorboard under the bed. I was terrified all the time that it would be found, but it wasn't. So when the moment came, all I had to do was get it out and pack a few things in a bag and climb out of the window. Thank God Hobsbawn House is covered in little balconies and trellises and sticking-out bits, or I should never have done it!'

'You might have fallen and been killed.'

'Well I wasn't. I was rather fun, in a way – or at least, once I was on firm ground again it seemed fun. So here I am, Charley, and oh, I can't tell you the relief!'

'I'm glad to see you, dearest Fanny – but what do you mean to do?'

'Do? Be free! What else?'

'But there will be such trouble when Doctor Anthony finds out you are gone. They are bound to write and tell him, or telegraph.'

'Yes, I suppose they are – hateful, sneaking, spying

things! And he'll guess I came here, and come after me.'

'Fanny, don't you think he'd be less angry if you went back now of your own accord, rather than wait for him to take you back?'

She was suddenly still, her face pale but determined. 'I'm not going back, Charley. Not ever.'

Charlotte was aghast. 'But Fanny, you must!'

'Must I?' Fanny said, giving her a strange look. 'Well, you are a fine friend, aren't you?'

'But where would you go, what could you do? You're his wife. He could divorce you.'

Fanny laughed. 'Oh, and that would be such a punishment! To be divorced from Philip Anthony, how could I bear it?'

'Don't laugh, Fanny.' Charlotte was grave. 'He would keep all your money. He would keep your child and you would never see him again.'

'He is welcome to Lionel,' she said with contempt. 'They suit each other. As to my money—' She shrugged. 'It isn't mine now. I have no control over it. I mayn't spend it. It's his already – what have I to lose?'

'Your reputation. You would be disgraced, an outcast.'

Fanny cocked her head. 'Would *you* cast me out? Would you hate me and shun me?'

'No, of course not, but—'

'But?'

'He'd come here for you, Fanny. You know it would be the first place he'd look. He would make a fuss and take you back.'

'You could hide me.'

'And say I hadn't seen you?'

Fanny made a strange face. 'Oh, I couldn't ask you to lie for me, of course. That would be too much to ask.'

349

Charlotte bit her lip. She felt wretched. 'I didn't mean that. But, oh Fanny, you will be so unhappy! Go back, please go back! There's no other way. There will be no life for you separated from your husband.'

'There is no life for me with him. It's no use, Charley, I won't go back. With your help or without it, I'm free now, and I won't go back.'

'Free to suffer? Free to starve?'

'Perhaps that's the only freedom there is.' Fanny stared at the floor a moment, her brows drawn with thought. 'Yes, I would sooner starve in the gutter than go back. At least that would be a quick death. Hunger would be more merciful than Philip Anthony, who keeps me alive so that he can starve my soul.'

Charlotte was silent, horrified that things had come to this pass. She had always reserved a part of her mind that said Fanny must be exaggerating her ills a little. Now she felt ashamed that she had not thoroughly believed her. But if she had, what could she have done? A woman belonged to her husband, and no-one had the right, or the power, to interfere between them.

Fanny suddenly seemed desperately tired. She looked at Charlotte with a beaten air, like an animal run to bay.

'So,' she said, 'are you going to turn me out, Charley?'

'No, of course not,' Charlotte said. She put her arm round the brittle shoulders and said, 'You are welcome in my house for as long as you want to stay. I'll have a room made up for you at once, and – Fanny, when did you eat?'

'Dinner last night. I'm frightfully hungry.'

'I'll have them bring something right away.'

Fanny leaned against her a little, with relief. 'Thank you. I knew you would help me. But Charley, what will Oliver say?'

Charlotte had been wondering that. He would not

approve, of course; he would say, as Charlotte had, that Fanny ought to go back. But she thought he would not interfere. He had always regarded Philip Anthony as a joke, and he would have contempt for a man who could not keep his own wife. Besides, his chivalry would put him on Fanny's side. Charlotte was almost sure he would not interfere.

'He'll be glad to have you stay,' she said.

But she had hesitated too long. 'It's no good,' Fanny said. 'The only chance I have is to hide from Philip. If I stay here he will find me. And I don't want to come between you and Oliver.'

'You won't. Don't be silly.'

'Charley, would you give me some money?'

'Of course, dearest, anything you want.'

'How much have you about you now?'

'I have money in the drawer in my sitting-room – about fifty pounds, I think. But—'

'Will you give that to me? I can't promise ever to pay you back.'

'Fanny, you can have anything of mine, you know that. But we'll talk about it later. Rest now, eat. You're safe for the moment. Philip isn't going to arrive here today.' But even as she said it, she thought that if the servants telegraphed him first thing this morning, and he guessed where she had gone, and set off immediately, he might easily arrive at Southport House tonight. Well, if he came, she would hold him off. Whatever his legal rights, he would not bully his wife in *her* house. 'We'll think what to do, don't worry,' she said firmly. 'And you shall have all the money you want. Now let's see about some luncheon for you.'

Fanny said she wanted to rest, having had no sleep the night before, so Charlotte had the room along from her own prepared, and a tray sent up, and hot water, and left Fanny preparing to wash, eat and sleep for a few hours. Then she sat, going over and over the situation, trying out various possibilities. There would certainly be unpleasantness, she thought; there was no escaping that. But she could not believe Anthony would want Fanny back when she had proved herself so averse from him. He would divorce her, keep her money and her child, and Fanny would be free to make whatever sort of life there still was for her. She would be incapable of earning a living, of course – Fanny had never worked in her life. Well, if Anthony would not grant her a pension, Charlotte would keep her. And she would stand by her if there was criticism – as there was bound to be. Lady Turnhouse would have a fit, of course – but Charlotte was used to shocking Lady Turnhouse.

Charlotte had been meaning to go out in the afternoon, but did not dare leave the house in case Anthony arrived. So she left instructions that when Mrs Anthony woke and rang, she should be called, and went to walk in the garden to refresh her spirits a little. Later, when it was her time to go to the nursery to see the children, Fanny still had not rung; but thinking that it might cheer her cousin to see the children, and knowing the children would like very much to see Fanny, she went along to Fanny's room on her way upstairs. She tapped gently at the door, and receiving no answer, went in.

The room was empty. The wash-stand had been used, the luncheon tray had been cleared to the last crumb, and there was a pair of dirty stockings across the bed, but no Fanny and no carpet-bag. Charlotte stared for a moment, and then hurried to her sitting room. On her desk lay an envelope with her name across it in Fanny's handwriting.

'Dearest Charley, forgive me, but it is best this way. You know that he will come looking for me, and it's better that you don't know where I am, so that you can say so with conviction, and swear to it if necessary. I have taken the money – 40*l* – as you said I might, and some clean stockings and handkerchiefs, so don't think your maid has stolen them! I love you, Charley. Kiss your dear children from me, and cherish your good husband. If mine had been like yours, I might have been able to stay. But I won't go back. God help me now. Your poor, affectionate Fanny.'

Charlotte sat at her desk with the letter in her hand for a long time. She would have liked to cry, but her sadness was too profound for tears.

CHAPTER FOURTEEN

Oliver was horrified. 'Why did you let her go?'

'I didn't know. She just slipped away,' Charlotte said miserably. 'I asked her to stay, I told her—' She stopped, fighting tears. She felt so guilty: had she been more sympathetic, Fanny might not have run. She had not come down firmly enough on Fanny's side; and yet she had felt – she still felt – that a woman's place was with her husband. For a woman like Fanny, brought up in luxury and unused to fending for herself, even the coolness of a loveless marriage must be better than the unprotected fury of the world outside it. But she had not understood how utterly desperate Fanny was. 'What can we do?' she asked.

'We must try to find her. God knows what will happen to her, wandering alone in London,' Oliver said. 'Can you think of anywhere that she might go?'

Charlotte shook her head. 'She has no friends in London, apart from us – the family, I mean.'

'We'll send first to Upper Grosvenor Street and St James's Square, in case she goes there; and telegraphs to your mother, Aylesbury and Morland Place.'

'She wouldn't go to St James's Square,' Charlotte said. 'She knows Cavendish isn't there.'

'But she might if she's desperate. We can't take the chance of missing her.'

'As well tell the world as tell Mrs Phipps.'

'The world will know soon enough,' Oliver said grimly.

'But I think it most likely that she would go to your mother. I wonder she didn't go there first.'

'Too close to home,' Charlotte said absently. She was thinking of Philip Anthony now. 'I wonder if he will come here today. I dread meeting him. What will he say?'

'Nothing to you, my love. I will make sure he addresses anything he has to say to me – and I may tell him a few things in return.'

'He could arrive at any moment. It's awful, Oliver, having him hanging over us. I wish he would come and be done with it.'

'The longer he stays away, the better. It gives us more chance of finding her first.' Down below the street doorbell jangled, and Charlotte flinched. Oliver went quickly to the window. 'It's Richard Mayne.'

'The police?' Charlotte seemed to shrink with fear. 'What is it? My God, surely not already—?'

'It's all right, I sent for him. She must be searched for, and Mayne has the men and the expertise.'

Charlotte said nothing. Oliver must have sent for Mayne the moment he heard the news, and that fact convinced her as nothing else that Fanny was in danger. She had never been alone in her life; never walked anywhere alone, found her own food and lodgings, never dealt with rough people or endured the stares and coarse comments that a female alone and out of her place must attract. Just as Charlotte knew that *she* could have coped in that situation, she knew Fanny could not. But would she seek help, or would fear and hatred of Philip Anthony drive her still to run?

Mayne was kindly, sympathetic. Charlotte told him what had happened; he asked her if there was anywhere Fanny might go, anyone she might trust; he took down a detailed description of her and her clothing. And then he said, 'Don't worry, your grace. We'll find her. She'll have taken a hackney, for sure, and the drivers are intelligent, noticing men. We'll find the cabman who drove her, and he'll tell us where she is. And I'll have enquiries made at the railway stations.'

Charlotte looked at him with stricken eyes, unable to frame the question she wanted to ask. He seemed to understand. 'Ten to one but she'll be perfectly all right. There are parts of London that are rough enough, but the fact of the matter is that most people are kind at heart, even in the worst places. *You* must know that from your own experience, your grace. If she is wandering, lost, someone will take pity on her, you can be sure.'

'Thank you,' Charlotte said. She was almost convinced.

The dreaded interview with Doctor Anthony did not take place that day. When he received the news from his servants of Fanny's flight, he had assumed that she had gone to Grasscroft. There he had gone, furious at the interruption to his business and the shame his wife was bringing on him, but not alarmed. At first he would not believe that they were not concealing her somewhere, and almost got himself ordered from the house for doubting Rosamund's word; but while the altercation was still going on, the telegraph arrived from Oliver, and most of his anger was replaced with anxiety. Rosamund was horrified. Having been almost a mother to Fanny for so long, she knew how helpless she would be alone in the London streets, and it gave her an insight into how unhappy she must have been with Anthony to risk it. And yet she saw now from his stricken face that he did care for Fanny. It was not all wounded pride and fear of public exposure: he paled in contemplation of Fanny's plight, and said quietly, 'I must go at once. She must be found. God knows what may happen to her.'

Rosamund put out a hand, but did not quite touch him. 'If you find her – *when* you find her – be gentle with her.' He looked at her whitely, but she persevered. 'I don't want to pry, or interfere, but do consider how unhappy she must have been to run away.'

His expression hardened. 'Of course, I would expect you to side with her.'

'It isn't a matter of "siding" with her. If you love her, try to understand what drove her to it. I don't say it was your fault—'

Unfortunate choice of words. 'I will not discuss this with you, madam,' he said icily. 'I am capable of dealing with my own wife.'

'Anthony, please—'

'If you had set her a better example,' he said, 'she might have known her duty better.'

Batchworth saw Rosamund flinch, and a murderous rage filled him. He stepped towards Anthony. 'I should kill you for that! Good God, what kind of a monster are you? I'm not surprised Fanny ran away. I only wonder she stayed so long.'

'Jes, no – please.' Rosamund caught his arm. 'This won't help Fanny.'

Jes drew in a shaky breath. 'You had better go,' he said quietly. 'I pray you find her before it's too late.'

Anthony stared at them a moment, and then gave a curt bow, and left.

Oliver received Anthony, and patiently allowed him to pour out all his anger. Had he allowed himself, Oliver could have taken sufficient offence to call him out, or throw him out; but instead, detaching his mind from the personalities, he wondered dispassionately what had

357

made the doctor so resentful. Anthony was intelligent, handsome, educated, had come from a comfortable background, and had married an heiress who provided him with every luxury. Why was he so filled with bitterness? It seemed rooted in envy. Had he not advanced as far in his profession as he thought he should? Did he find the respect of the middling sort in Manchester insufficient for his pride? Did he resent the fact that his wealth came from Fanny and not from his own father or his own efforts? Whatever it was, a stream of criticism was directed impartially towards Charlotte, her parents, her late grandmother, and Oliver himself, for encouraging independence and loose behaviour in women. Fanny had run off because her mind had been corrupted; wealthy, titled and immoral people had done the corrupting – that was his thesis.

When he ran out of steam, Oliver said, 'Very well, you have had your say. I will not say you are wholly mistaken, because on mature consideration you will know that you are – and your reflections on your own conduct will be of little comfort to you.'

'Do you dare to suggest that—?'

Oliver lifted his hand. 'Try not to rant at me. It gets us nowhere. You, perhaps uniquely, must know why Fanny ran away. That is not my business. But if you will be quiet for a moment, I will tell you what we have done so far to try to find her.' Anthony subsided into a sulky silence, and Oliver told of their enquiries. 'If you can think of any other courses of action,' he concluded, 'I will be glad to give you any assistance you require to carry them out.'

'You, give assistance? That is laughable! Do you suppose I do not know that it was Charlotte who encouraged her to quit her home in the first place, that she is concealing her at this very minute? I know why you have kept me talking here, why Charlotte does not appear.

358

She dare not face me, because I would see the truth in her face!'

There were only two possible reactions to that. Oliver laughed. It was a laugh quickly stifled, because the outrage in Anthony's face did not entirely conceal a genuine pain, but it was better than knocking him down. 'You are a fool, Anthony. Fanny ran away from you, God knows why; but she ran away from here because Charlotte told her she must go back to you. Charlotte has been searching the back-slums for news of her; her maid is out at this very minute pursuing enquiries. But if you would care to waste your time searching this house, you are very welcome to do so. You could, on the other hand, accept the word of a gentleman that Fanny is not here, and save yourself both time and humiliation.'

Anthony's mouth turned down bitterly. 'Do you think I am not humiliated as it is?' He looked away with a weary sigh. 'Oh, what is to be done? I must get her back. Where could she have gone?'

Oliver took pity. 'If she is in London, I believe she must have taken shelter somewhere. If she were wandering the streets, I am sure something must have been heard of her by now. The police are making their own enquiries, but I would suggest employing a private agent to ask at all the hotels. It is most likely she took a room at one of them.'

'*If* she is in London?'

'She may have left London. In that case, she could be anywhere. You had better hope she has not.' Anthony's head was bowed with misery. Oliver laid a hand on his shoulder. 'She will be found. Consider, she has very little money. When that runs out, she must come to one of us.' Anthony seemed to take comfort from the thought, and Oliver had believed it himself at first; but he had seen the doubt in Charlotte's eyes when he had said the same to her. Charlotte had seen and talked to Fanny; she had an idea of the extent of Fanny's desperation.

When Fanny had left Charlotte's house, she had had no idea in her mind but to put distance between herself and possible pursuit. She had walked hurriedly, without seeing or caring where she went, but some deep animal instinct had turned her northwards. Afraid of the narrow, odiferous side-streets, she had kept to the main thoroughfares, and eventually found herself at Regent's Park. The greenness and the waving trees had soothed her, and she slowed her pace a little, feeling how tender her unaccustomed feet were growing. The trees were just beginning to turn, and now and then a yellowing leaf detached itself and planed gently downwards. Birds were hopping about in the bushes, and now and then a squirrel appeared, flirting its tail from a safe branch as she passed. She skirted the park, almost enjoying this part of the walk. But when she reached the far side she began to feel very tired, and alone, and afraid. It began to grow dusk, and the openness of Primrose Hill frightened her. She had never been alone at night without shelter or company; she had lived her whole life in cities; she turned away from nature, and walked towards houses.

So far she had attracted no attention; but now as she walked along a high road in the gathering gloom – a woman in good clothes, alone, and carrying a bag – glances began to be directed towards her. They were not very prolonged, and no-one offered to molest or even address her, but Fanny felt threatened. Moreover she was hungry and her feet hurt. She must find shelter.

She came to an inn – the Coach and Horses – an old posting-house, its trade now sadly fallen off since the railways had done away with the stage coaches. But it seemed familiar to her: she had stayed at coaching inns often in the past, and it seemed to offer safety and shelter. She went in. The landlord viewed her with some suspicion at first, as if he might have thought her a lady's maid who had stolen her mistress's garments; but her undoubted gentility and her air of being accustomed to command convinced him. He was not in the business of turning away trade, not these days, and though it was certainly odd for a female of her order to come in alone on her own feet, it was not against the law of the land. A runaway, he thought; but she was over twenty-one, so it was not his business. If her husband came a-looking for her, he would hand her over and see if there was anything in it for him. Meantime, he would see she paid in advance.

Fanny gave her name as Mrs Freeman, too weary to think of anything more original. She gave him money for the room, and then said, 'Must I pay you now for my dinner as well?'

'No, ma'am,' the landlord said, satisfied by the sight of her purse of her ability to pay. 'That will be all right. You'll want dinner in a private parlour, I dare say? The coffee-room gets a bit noisy at night.'

'Oh, yes, if you please,' Fanny said eagerly.

'What time would you like to eat, ma'am?'

'As soon as possible. I am very hungry. Give me time only to tidy myself. Will you have hot water sent up at once?'

'Yes, ma'am, assuredly,' the landlord said happily. She was certainly a lady, then, if she wanted to wash before eating. And she had paid what he asked for the room without flinching – didn't know the cost of things, that was for sure. 'Dinner in half an hour, then, ma'am? I'll send the girl to show you the way.'

'Thank you,' said Fanny absently. And as she was turning away, 'What is this place?'

'The Coach and Horses, ma'am.'

'Yes, but what town?'

'Kentish Town, ma'am,' he said, smiling inwardly. Didn't even know where she was.

'Kentish Town,' Fanny repeated dully. She had thought herself much further away than that. But who would think of looking for her here?

The room was stale and grubby with disuse, but she saw clean sheets put on the bed by the girl who brought the hot water. A little later the same girl came to escort her to the private parlour – a cramped room situated over the tap, whose reek of stale beer and stale tobacco came up through the gaps in the floorboards, together with the sound of coarse voices and harsh laughter. Fanny felt too hungry to care, and was glad that her dinner was brought in immediately, on a large tray borne by the beefy bare arms of a fat woman who eyed her with undisguised interest. 'I am Mrs Cobbling, the landlady, ma'am. Your dinner, ma'am,' she said, lowering the tray and unloading the dishes onto the table. There was some kind of fried fish, a chicken roughly disjointed and covered with a thick sauce, a dish of potatoes, another of cabbage, and a slab of pale pudding pocked with raisins. 'There, now, ma'am – and a bottle of our best burgundy. Cobbling didn't say what you'd ordered to drink, but if you've had a long journey, you will need a restorative, I dare say.' Fanny did not rise to the bait, and the woman went on, pouring out a glass, 'From the north, I think you said, ma'am? Have you come far today?'

Fanny looked at her, dazed. 'No. Yes. I don't know. Thank you, I have all I need now.'

'I'll leave you then, ma'am,' Mrs Cobbling said, disappointed. 'You'll ring if you need anything more?'

Left alone, Fanny attacked the food with almost desperate hunger; but her appetite soon sickened. She was too tired, too miserable, too much out of her place to eat more than a few mouthfuls. The fried fish did not seem fresh, the chicken was tough and stringy. She ate some potatoes, tried the pudding, drank a little of the wine and found it muddy and sour. Tears of self-pity rose up in her throat at the thought that she should come to this, at the mercy of impertinent strangers, and forced to eat such a meal. A roar of merry-making from below made her start, and she suddenly felt very afraid. Suppose the landlord mentioned that she was here, alone; suppose someone came up from below and attacked her. She thought she heard footsteps on the stairs, imagined the door-latch was moving. No! It was imagination. She wanted her bed, wanted desperately to sleep and escape the present. She got up, bravely flung open the door – an empty landing – and hurried up the stairs and back to her room as if the Furies were after her; which, indeed, they were. In the bedchamber she put a chair against the door so that she would at least have warning of anyone entering, pulled off her clothes, and climbed into bed. The stale reek of the mattress came up through the cleanness of the sheets, and she was shivering cold. A smell of fog came in through the ill-fitting window, an autumnal smell that was piercingly sad, but somehow oddly reassuring. She thought of autumn days at Grasscroft, riding over the moors with Aunt Rosamund and Cavendish; and smiling, fell deeply asleep. In her exhaustion she slept so heavily she did not hear the noise of the chair falling over. In the morning it was replaced neatly against the wall, and she thought she must have dreamed that she had put it against the door.

She felt hardly refreshed by her sleep, though she had slept long; her spirits were too much oppressed, and she had struggled all night with difficult dreams. She must move on today, she thought – but where? The impossibility of her situation struck her for the first time, and forcibly. Where could she go? She had no means of supporting herself once Charlotte's money was spent. What work was she fitted for? Who would employ her? How could she find somewhere to live? Who could she trust? Her only thought was to go north. Not to Manchester, of course, because Manchester was Philip; perhaps to Yorkshire. She thought that away from London she might find decent, kindly folk who would help her. Here she felt threatened. She had worked briefly in the slums alongside Charlotte, and London away from the centres of fashion was tainted in her memory by the association.

North, that was the thing – but not on foot. In all her wandering yesterday she had covered so little distance at such vast expense of energy. No, little money though she had, she would lay out part of it on a railway ticket. It would be worth it. And perhaps in the north she would find some nice country dame who would give her a home in return for – well, there must be something she could do for a nice country dame. Didn't people employ lady-companions? The thought of getting away from these sordid surroundings filled her with new hope. She dressed herself, packed her bag, and went downstairs.

At the foot of the stairs she encountered the landlord. 'Good morning, ma'am. I trust you slept well? You'd be ready for your breakfast, I dare say. I have some uncommon good sausages—'

'No, thank you, no breakfast,' Fanny said quickly. She imagined them, full of grit and gristle. She wanted nothing more under this roof.

'Some coffee, then,' the landlord offered.

'No, I must be leaving. I will settle with you for last night's dinner, and then—'

'Oh no, ma'am!' Cobbling said quickly. 'There's no

charge for that. That came in with the price of the room. Nothing more to pay, I assure you.'

He smiled so kindly that Fanny felt she had misjudged him and his wife. They had taken her in, after all, without knowing anything about her. And dinner had been plentiful, if it had not been to her taste.

'Thank you,' she said. 'Can you tell me, which way is the nearest railway station?'

He gave her instructions, an elaborate list of turnings and landmarks which she did her best to remember, and bidding him good morning she took up her bag and went out. It was a cool, misty, autumn-smelling day, but the hazy sunshine seemed to promise better things to come, and she felt more cheerful for her reappraisal of the landlord's character. But she must have misunderstood his instructions, for she could not find the railway station, and soon was lost in a maze of streets. Her legs, tired from yesterday, began to hurt. She couldn't find her way back or forward, and taking the courage at last to ask a woman hurrying by, she was told, with a suspicious look, that she was going in the wrong direction. The woman directed her back to the main thoroughfare; and after several more enquiries, she came at last to a railway station. She was famished now, and seeing a coffee-stall outside the station, she went there first, too hungry and weary to care what anyone might think of a female of her order eating and drinking in the street. She asked for a cup of coffee and a hot pie – the smell was making her ache with hunger.

'Tuppence, miss,' said the stall-owner, putting a cup and the pie wrapped in a piece of paper before her. Fanny took her purse out of the carpet-bag and opened it. And stared. And stared again. The notes were gone, and the large coins. All that was left was a few coppers and a sixpence.

'I've been robbed,' she said. Her voice was barely a whisper.

'How's that, miss?' the stall-owner said.

The chair had been moved in the night, she thought. Someone had come in. She must have been too sound asleep to hear. The landlord? Only he had known what she had in her purse. Was that why he didn't want her to pay for her dinner – because he didn't want her to discover the loss until later? Had he deliberately sent her the wrong way, so that she would not be able to find her way back to confront him? But if she confronted him he would deny it, and what proof did she have anyway?

'Beg pardon, miss, is summat wrong?'

She looked up at the man unseeingly. 'I've been robbed,' she repeated blankly. 'My money's gone.'

'No rhino, no wittles!' He began to take back the coffee and the pie, but she could not bear now not to have them. 'No, no, I still have tuppence. Wait!' She fumbled for the coppers, put them on the counter, and the grimy hand made sure of them, and let the vittles be. What did it matter any more? she thought hysterically. Tuppence either way could not save her, and she wanted that pie and that coffee more than she had ever wanted anything in her life. She hadn't enough now for a railway ticket. She hadn't enough for another night's lodging. She hadn't enough for more than one more meal. She was destitute.

She ate the pie slowly, and sipped the coffee. Destitute! Oddly enough, in her present state of mind, the word did not frighten her as much as it should. There was an odd sort of freedom in it. She had got to the end of the tether, and the rope had frayed and broken, and now she was a stray dog, free to go anywhere. She was no longer bound to look for a decent hotel or clean lodgings. They were as much out of her reach as a back-ken. She had no more

366

decisions to make about whether to walk or go by railway; no more decisions of any sort. She would sleep where she dropped, and if no-one fed her, she would die of hunger. When she had finished her meal, she looked for a moment at her greasy fingers, and then slowly, with a sense of breaking some last bond, wiped them on her skirt. Then she picked up her bag, and under the curious eye of the coffee-stall-owner, walked away; away from the station, and back towards London. The streets of the Great Wen were the place for a destitute woman. Let London take her to its bosom, and do what it liked with her. Let her end her days there.

The Allied army had landed at Calamita Bay in the Crimea on the 14th of September without opposition and begun to march towards Sebastopol; and now news came back of the first battle of the war, against a large Russian force at the river Alma. It was just the sort of battle the public had been wanting and waiting for, and the streets erupted with celebration. A superior Russian force, holding the better tactical position, had been dislodged and driven to flight by the sheer fury of the British attack. The Russians had been routed, and lost over five thousand men; British casualties had been less than two thousand. The French had helped a bit, of course, but the business had really been done by the pluck and steel of the British regiments, and the Guards and the Highlanders in particular had distinguished themselves through their unwavering discipline, advancing without flinching through heavy fire – and uphill!

The newspapers were full of gloating, there was singing and cheering in the streets, bonfires and fireworks and drunken celebrations all night; twenty-six new-born babies up and down the country were named Alma. Wellington's name was spoken like an incantation. The first full-scale battle between European forces since Waterloo had been an undoubted, glorious victory for the home team! The Duke would have been proud of dear old Lord Raglan.

Cavendish's letter added other detail. 'It was tremendous fighting, and when the Russians took to their legs, we could have finished them then and there if we'd been allowed to pursue. But the French commander, St Arnaud, would not move. He is very sick and old, and says no to everything, and Raglan would not move without the French, of course. He is so very polite and gentlemanly the French have their own way all the time. So the Russians went scrambling off towards Sebastopol, amazed at their luck. Worst of all was that Raglan would not let the cavalry pursue. We could at least have taken their guns, but no, he said we must be "kept in a band-box". What is the use of that? Our Old Man is furious, and so is Lucan. They both think we have been disgraced. Of course, they won't agree about it openly. They have been snipping at each other like two pairs of scissors ever since we landed at Calamita.'

The Old Man was of course Lord Cardigan. He and Lord Lucan, his brother-in-law, had been at daggers-drawn for years, and the situation had been made worse by Lucan's having been given overall command of the cavalry, which put him over Lord Cardigan, who had only been given command of the Light Brigade. Lord Cardigan felt the positions ought to have been reversed, and hated Lucan all the more for it.

Cavendish went on, 'The night after the battle was the worst I have ever spent. They never tell you in your school lessons what it is like *after* the glorious victory. We bivouacked out on the hillside amongst the dead and wounded, weary and depressed. Water was terribly short. It has been short ever since we landed, which means that the horses suffer dreadfully. The river was churned up from the battle, and in any case, Raglan would not let us go down there for fear of ambush. The wounded cried and moaned all night, from pain and thirst. The medical men can do little for them, with hardly any supplies or equipment – and none of your magic anaesthetic, needless to say. The morning after, bearer parties started taking them down to the ships, poor devils, to be transported to the hospital at Scutari. God knows how many will survive the journey. There were a good many dead of cholera, too. We have still not managed to shake it off, and men were dropping out all the time on the march here.

'Well, now it is the 22nd, and we are still here, above that accursed river, while our commanders-in-chief argue about what to do. Raglan wanted to press on at once and take Sebastopol while the Russians were still reeling, but the French would not go, and now any chance we have of surprise is lost. We are spending today burying our dead – a melancholy business. But be assured, dearest Charley, that I have not a scratch on me. I am, as our commander wishes, band-box fresh. Tell Alice so – she will believe you. And kiss the dear baby from me. This place, where I am, is so strange, that home seems like a dream.'

Lord and Lady Batchworth came to London not so much because they thought they could do anything about Fanny, but to support Charlotte's spirits, and because it was intolerable to remain so far away at such a time. With Mrs Phipps installed in St James's Square, it was desirable as well as natural for them to stay at Southport House.

Rosamund and Charlotte exchanged a long and silent embrace, and it was difficult to know which of them was comforting which. 'My poor darling,' Rosamund said at last.

'I feel so guilty,' Charlotte said. 'If only I'd assured her of my support, perhaps she wouldn't have gone.'

'People do what they have to,' Rosamund said. 'There's no benefit in blaming them or yourself.' She of all people had had to learn that. 'My poor Fanny,' she went on, 'what could have become of her? She's the last person in the world to know how to take care of herself. Where could she have gone?'

Charlotte met her mother's eyes reluctantly. 'Don't you think that must mean that something bad must have happened? If she were all right, we'd surely have heard something by now. She had very little money. She would have had to go to someone for help.'

Rosamund shook her head. 'I don't know what to think. Oh, it's like a dreadful nightmare! I feel as if I'm reliving the past, when your father disappeared with you, and we couldn't find where you had gone. But see,' she tried to draw comfort for them both, 'how well you were concealed, and no harm came to you. If Fanny really wants to hide, perhaps that's why we've heard nothing. Perhaps it just proves how resourceful she's being.'

They talked the situation over and over, treading the circle round. Oliver and Jes meanwhile discussed courses of action, agreeing that everything was being done that could be done, yet wondering what else they might do – treading a circle of their own.

The Batchworths spent several days going over the same ground, literally and figuratively, that Charlotte and Oliver had covered, and discovering themselves to be equally baffled. They half-heartedly proposed going home, but Charlotte begged them to stay until something was known either way, and they agreed gladly. Batchworth had friends to catch up with, and Rosamund wanted to consult a specialist about the arthritis that was

370

beginning to trouble her. And in London they had their grandchildren to spoil – Charlotte's four and Cavendish's little William, who spent a great deal of his life in the Southport nursery; and the war news reached them more quickly, too. But of Fanny nothing was heard, and while they tried to interpret that as good news, they saw in each other's eyes the growing fear that she was dead.

The news from the front was less happy than had been expected after the decisive victory at the Alma. Everyone had expected an early end to the campaign: that the Allies would follow up their success in the field with a quick strike at Sebastopol from the north. But the French commander, St Arnaud, a dying man, would not agree to anything so precipitate, and the senior British engineer, Sir John Burgoyne, said such an attack would be too dangerous without a siege train. But a siege from the open north side of the city would leave the Allies too exposed. The French proposed marching right round Sebastopol to attack it from the south. Here a peninsula jutted out into the sea, affording the Allies protection to the south and west; with Sebastopol itself to the north, the only direction from which counter-attack could come was from the east.

The British contingent reached the high plains to the south of Sebastopol on the 26th of September, the French arriving the following day. The peninsula had three narrow inlets which would serve for ships to land supplies, and Lord Raglan chose the harbour in the south-eastern corner, at Balaclava, leaving the two westerly inlets for the French. This left the British army with the task of protecting the whole Allied force from attack from the exposed eastern flank, as well as conducting its half of the siege.

But Cavendish wrote, 'We would all rather do more than our share than leave it to the French. Now that poor old St Arnaud is dead, they are commanded by General Canrobert, who is a very kind and pleasant fellow, from what I understand, but no more decisive than his predecessor; and besides the French are so wedded to their comfort, there's no relying on them once they have their tents up and their fires going. For our part, we still have not shaken off the cholera, and our numbers are very much depleted since leaving England, but our morale is high, and we hope soon to be in action.

'Balaclava is a pretty village at the end of a very narrow and steep-sided inlet, overlooked by the ruins of an old Genoese castle. The inlet is tiny, only about half a mile long by a quarter wide, and the harbour wharves are only 75 feet long. It will be difficult for our ships to unload here; I suppose they will have to take turns! The village was a favourite summer resort for the townsfolk from Sebastopol, and there are pretty villas with green-tiled roofs and gardens full of roses and honeysuckles, with orchards, vineyards and neat vegetable gardens behind. From the village a steep, unmade road rises up to the village of Kadikoi, then onto the plateau before Sebastopol – though when I say plateau, you are not to be imagining some nice, level Salisbury Plain! It is furrowed with deep ravines and hummocked with foothills – bad cavalry country.

'You could not conceive anyone more eager to get to grips with the enemy than the cavalry, having had no chance to win our battle honours. The Lords Lucan and Cardigan agree on that if on nothing else. No, I speak false – they agree on despising poor old General Scarlett, the commander of the Heavy Brigade, because he has two Indian officers to advise him, and if there's anything the Lords hate more than each other, it's Indian officers! All nonsense, in my view. The Indian officers are good fellows on the whole, and they have seen action, so they know

372

what they are talking about. There's a dreadful conceited fellow on the staff here called Nolan – General Airey's galloper – who thinks he knows everything about cavalry manoeuvres, despite the fact that he's seen no more action than I have. With the slightest encouragement he spouts his theories on how the cavalry can win any battle, even unsupported by infantry, as long as they ride hard, charge straight, and are commanded by gentlemen. He blames Lucan that we did not follow up at the Alma, calls him Lord Look-on, and is insufferably rude to him on every possible occasion. Of course, he despises Indian officers, but I know Lieutenant Elliott, one of Scarlett's, tolerably well, and I know which I would sooner spend an evening with! Nolan's a braying ass. Unfortunately, he really can ride, so one is forced to pay him some measure of respect.

'Lord Raglan is eager to attack Sebastopol at once, for the fortifications seem to have been very much exaggerated. A quick and decisive action now will take the Russians unprepared – General Cathcart says we can walk in with hardly the loss of a man. I hope it will not be quite so easy! But be assured we shall all be home well before Christmas.'

On the 8th of October Oliver was summoned to Horseguards, and returned at length looking grave and thoughtful.

'It seems that there is not to be a quick attack on Sebastopol,' he told his assembled family. 'The French wouldn't agree to it, and now it's clear that the Russians are improving the fortifications at an impressive rate. Raglan's intelligence officer, Calvert, says they have the German engineer Todleben inside Sebastopol, ordering the works. So there's to be a regular siege to weaken them before any full-scale attack.'

'A siege? For how long?' Batchworth asked.

'Does that mean Cavendish won't be back before Christmas?' Charlotte said almost simultaneously.

'It could be a long business,' Oliver said. 'We have thrown away our advantage. The Russians have been marching reinforcements in from Odessa – intelligence suggests they have nearly forty thousand men now, and the redoubts are being strengthened every day. They will have to be reduced by long bombardment before they can be attacked with any hope of carrying them.' He cleared his throat. 'They want me to go, to help with the intelligence-gathering.'

There was a little silence. 'When would you have to leave?' Charlotte said at last, her voice quite steady.

'Immediately. Tomorrow, or the next day. As soon as I've had time to pack.'

'You must do your duty, of course,' she said.

Later, when they had gone up to dress, Charlotte followed Oliver into his dressing-room, and Oliver sent Dinsdale away with a quick and meaningful glance.

'Yes, my darling?' he said when they were alone. 'Have you come to quarrel with me? You were very restrained when I broke the news – no accusations of spying.'

'Don't tease,' Charlotte said with a frown. 'This is quite different, and you know it.'

'Then what is it?'

'Take me with you,' she said. He looked surprised. 'It's not impossible, is it?'

'By no means,' he said. 'Lots of officers take their wives – to say nothing of the interested civilians who swarm about the edges of a war. My surprise is that you should want to go.'

'Surprised that I should want to see that my brother is well?'

'You've just had a letter from him. You know he's well. What's the real reason?'

She stepped up close. 'If you're to go, I want to be with you. You said it might be a long business. I can't be without you for so long.'

He took her in his arms. 'How very gratifying that is! But consider, it will be uncomfortable, and it may be dangerous.'

'If it's dangerous, all the more reason I should be with you. As to discomfort – I fancy I know more about that than you do.'

'So you do,' he said, smiling.

'Cavendish says there is cholera. I know a great deal about nursing cholera victims. I may be able to help.'

'And what else?'

She looked up at him. 'Since the twins were born, and you swore I would never have to suffer that again, you have shown such self-control – one might almost say, to an unnatural degree—'

'Ah, now I have you! You think going to the Crimea is just an excuse! You think I shall be unfaithful to you and cavort with camp-followers!'

She smiled. 'No, it's not that. But Oliver, since we cannot be lovers any more in – in the fullest way, it's more important to me than ever to be close to you, especially to sleep with you and be held in your arms every night. I don't think I could bear to be parted from you for – however long it will be. I don't think I could bear it.'

'You would sooner lie with me on the hard ground in a damp bivouac, than without me in your goose-feather bed at home?' he said with a gently teasing smile.

'Infinitely rather.'

'Then who am I to deny you your pleasures?' He kissed her brow lightly. 'Come with me and be my camp-follower. But, dearest, what of Fanny? Can you leave London, not knowing what has happened to her? Supposing she tries to contact you for help?'

'I've thought of that,' Charlotte said. 'I'm sure Mama would stay here, in case Fanny comes back. But I don't think she will.' She looked up at him. 'It's been three weeks now. How could she survive so long without money? I think she must be dead.'

He laid a finger on her lips. 'Don't say that. There is always hope. But if your Mama would stay, that would be a very good thing. She will be able to look to the children – or had you forgotten your four children, duchess?'

'I hadn't forgotten them,' she assured him. 'But my husband comes first.'

'A very wifely sentiment,' he said. 'Very well, you shall come with me to the Crimea. And I think, in that case, it might be better if we hired a private yacht to take us. From what I hear, it may be as well to have our own means of transport out there – and somewhere to sleep, if things get too bad on shore. I think I know where we can lay our hands on one. Lord Mauleverer has a very fine pleasure steamer; and Lord Mauleverer is over head and ears in debt.'

On the following day, *The Times* published a despatch from its correspondent in Constantinople, W.H.Russell, describing the sufferings of the wounded from the battle of the Alma. Sick and wounded British soldiers were transported by boat to the barrack hospital at Scutari – so much was common knowledge. That the hospital at Scutari was an unpleasant place would have been assumed by anyone who gave half a thought to the matter, since all hospitals were unpleasant places. But Russell, with bitter and flourishing pen, conjured up such a vivid picture of the agony and suffering of the brave soldiery, and fulminated so furiously against the inefficiency of the administration and the lack of preparation for their treatment, that his despatch whipped up in the public a wholly unprecedented indignation.

'. . . there are not sufficient surgeons . . . no dressers and nurses . . . men left to expire in agony . . . the commonest appliances of a workhouse sick ward are wanting . . . men must die through the medical staff of the British Army having forgotten that old rags are necessary for the dressing of wounds,' he thundered. The public, which normally concurred with the Duke of Wellington's opinion that soldiers were a villainous rabble and the scum of the earth, demanded to know why the noble heroes of the Alma were being neglected in this appalling, this criminal manner. It was remembered that the Secretary at War, Sidney Herbert, whose responsibility it was to provide for the sick and wounded, had a Russian mother. Was he deliberately trying to undermine the British Army? Was he in the pay of the Russians?

Charlotte, who knew Sidney Herbert as a friend of Lord Shaftesbury, hardly knew whether to laugh or cry. Herbert was a sensitive man, highly educated, deeply pious, an evangelical and a philanthropist who probably cared more about the welfare of the common soldier than the whole readership of *The Times* put together. But in the throes of packing and making her preparations to go to the Crimea, she had no time to worry about it. However, on the 11th she was visited by Lord Palmerston, who, sitting on her sofa, stretching his elegant legs and crossing them at the ankle with an air of absolute ease, said, 'This despatch about the hospital at Scutari is stirrin' up the devil of a stink. Makes you wish we had control of the press the way they do in France and Russia, damn it. Beg your pardon, duchess.'

'Please, sir, damn away. No ceremony with me,' Charlotte

smiled. '*The Times* seems resolved to discomfit the Government.'

'Yes, and never mind the cost! You'd think when we're at war we could expect a bit of loyalty. Of course this Russell fellow is the damndest blackguard – renegade Irishman, you know the sort, had trouble with 'em in the French wars. Born with a grudge and a gift for words – the sort of sneakin' dog that takes meat from your hand one minute and bites your ankles the next, damn his hide!'

'Then there's no truth in his story?'

Palmerston shrugged. 'Dare say there is. Hospitals are hellish – *you* know that, duchess – and a military hospital's always ten times worse than a civilian one. But this talk of lackin' medical stores – sent out tons of the stuff! Still sendin' it! Some of it got sent to Varna after the troops had gone – may have been some delay sendin' it back to Scutari, but it must be there by now. Whole place must be swimmin' in sheets and bandages.' He rubbed his nose thoughtfully. 'Herbert's takin' it damned hard, all this criticism. Got a bee in his attic now about female nurses.'

'Mr Herbert has?'

Palmerston nodded. 'Hospital orderlies are never up to scratch – old and invalided soldiers, usually, servin' out their time. No enthusiasm for the job, hey?' Charlotte could imagine how much of an understatement that was. 'But the Frogs have got Sisters of Mercy, and now the Opposition is asking why *we* don't have 'em. Not a Catholic country, of course; but female nurses are rather in the public eye since you started your hospital, and Guy's and King's are gettin' 'em in too.'

'Just so.' Charlotte began to see where this was going.

'Can't have females nursin' in the field, of course; but back at Scutari, no reason why not. Might even do a bit of good, clean the place up a bit. How would you feel about it, duchess? Full backing, of course, all expenses paid – recruit a body of nurses and take 'em over to Scutari. Spike the Opposition's guns. Wipe *The Times*'s eye. What do you think?'

'In the normal way I'd be glad to help you, sir,' Charlotte said, 'but I'm preparing at this very minute to go to the Crimea. Southport has been asked to join the Intelligence Department there.'

'Quite, quite,' Palmerston nodded. 'Thought you'd like the excuse to be near him. Only just across the water, Scutari,' he added beguilingly.

'I mean to be much nearer to him than the width of the Black Sea,' Charlotte said. 'I'm flattered that you thought of me, but I'm afraid I shall be otherwise engaged. And, to be frank, I've done my stint at struggling to create order from chaos. I don't really want to begin all over again.'

Palmerston looked disappointed. 'Not somethin' I'd care to do m'self, but thought you might have a fancy for it. Ah well, no harm in askin'.'

An image came into Charlotte's mind, of cool grey eyes and a hard jaw. 'There is someone – a lady – I met her at the Middlesex during the recent cholera outbreak, doing the same sort of work. She seemed to me to be a sensible sort of female – a Miss Nightingale.'

Palmerston nodded. 'Oh yes, I know her. And Herbert's already thought of her. She's quite a friend of Mrs Herbert. Wild to do nursin' work, God knows why, but her family don't approve.'

'Oh, so he's already asked her?' Charlotte said.

'Not yet. Dare say he will now, but I wanted to ask you first.'

'I'm sure she'll be very efficient.'

'Oh, I dare say. But it ain't just a matter of good intentions, you know, duchess. The medical officers won't take kindly to havin' females sent out from home – they'll take it as a criticism. Bound to. They'll be hostile. You were my first choice because they couldn't be rude to you.'

'Because I'm a duchess?' she said amused.

He nodded. 'And because of your connections. The Nightingales ain't anyone. And frankly, m'dear,' he added with a twinkle, 'because you get more formidable every year! I haven't met the man yet who'd have the gall to face up to you.'

'You haven't met Doctor Anthony,' she said, with a little sigh.

CHAPTER FIFTEEN

Mrs Welland's lodging house in Lamb's Conduit Street saw many strange comings and goings. As well as her more permanent residents, she took in temporary guests at the request of Mr Tarbush of Lincoln's Inn and gave them a safe, private and anonymous lodging. For her absolute discretion and professional lack of surprise, Mrs Welland was well paid by the lawyer.

A knock on the door late one foggy night, therefore, did not cause more than a raised eyebrow. Mrs Welland happened to have her hands full of sewing, so her son Peter jumped up and said, 'I'll go, mother. You weren't expecting anyone?'

'No. And Mr Tarbush knows we are full up.'

'Oh well,' Peter said cheerfully, 'we can always budge up a bit and squeeze another one in, if it's an emergency.'

Mrs Welland thought how knocks on the door this late were always emergencies, but she didn't say so. She was beginning to think, in fact, that it was all getting too much for her. She was not a young woman any more, and since Mr Welland had died three years ago she was feeling her age, and found the stairs something of a trial. Of course her daughter Harriet helped her, and Peter was a tower of strength – odd to think of him as a tower, she thought, as she watched him cross the shabby, comfortable parlour, but so he was. Poor Peter had inherited her stockiness and her short legs, and though he never spoke of it and was unfailingly cheerful, she knew he felt it very much that he was only five feet two inches tall – and therefore, in his own view, unattractive to women. He had a pleasant face, and nice blue eyes, and rather unruly fair hair, and the sweetest temper in the world, and she thought, even setting aside a mother's partiality, that he would have made someone a wonderful husband. But his self-consciousness about his height meant that he had never even asked a girl to go walking with him. He did not want to risk being turned down, so he never asked. Under his cheerfulness and kindness, he was a shy soul.

He came back in to the parlour, looking puzzled. 'Nobody there,' he said. 'I looked up and down the street, but I didn't see any movement.'

'Some naughty urchin, then, knocking and running away,' Mrs Welland said. She returned to her sewing, but her mind was on her children. Harriet – who had inherited Mr Welland's tallness, which Peter could have done with so badly – Harriet was forty now, hard to believe, and growing grey and thin like a heron. She worked hard, harder than ever now Mrs Welland was finding the stairs too much, and rarely spoke, but Mrs Welland knew she was worried about her son. Boy – as they called him – was thirteen, and turning out clever. He wanted so much to go into the law, but where was the money to come from? The lodging house supported them all, and would go on supporting Harriet and Peter after Mrs Welland was dead, but it would not produce the sums of money needed to put Boy through university; and though Harriet didn't say anything, Mrs Welland knew she didn't want Boy to become a lodging-house keeper in his turn. Harriet wanted better things for him, despite the fact that no-one knew who his father was. No, perhaps she should say *because* no-one knew who his father was. What had happened to Harriet had changed her for ever, from a lively, chatty girl to a silent, unsmiling, thoughtful woman. All through her pregnancy she had been so utterly low and miserable that Mrs Welland had been afraid she might kill herself, and for eight months she had hardly slept for fear of Harriet creeping out of the house at night and down to the river. But when Boy was born, instead of hating and rejecting him, as might be expected, Harriet had suddenly conceived a fierce love and protectiveness towards him, which had never wavered since. It was, Mrs Welland supposed, Harriet's way of getting by. Everyone had to have their handle to grip life with. And she so much wanted Boy to do well. Mrs Welland wondered whether Mr Tarbush would do something for the lad, in acknowledgement of past services – for if it came to it, he owed as much to Harriet's labours as Mrs Welland's. She would ask him. She would go up to his chambers tomorrow, and put it to him. Lawyers famously never gave anything away, but Boy was quick and clever and might be useful to him. No harm in asking, anyway.

'Listen!' Peter said suddenly. They all lifted their heads.

'I don't hear anything,' Mrs Welland said. Harriet shook her head.

'I'm sure I heard something. A sort of scratching at the front door,' he said. He got up and crossed the room.

'Be careful, Peter,' Mrs Welland said, suddenly uneasy.

'Here,' said Harriet, and held out the poker to him. Peter took it, hefted it in his hand, and went out to the front door again. He paused, listening, and then whipped the door open fast. Smell of fog, a little hazy light from the street-lamps, and a bundle of cloth on the doorstep which rolled inwards as he opened the door and subsided heavily against his feet. He looked quickly up and down the street for lurking danger, and then hunkered down over the bundle. It was a tangle-haired woman in a coarse serge skirt, a dirty blouse, and a thin, cheap shawl folded round her and tied behind. He lifted her head to see her face: thin, white, dirty, eyes closed. She seemed to be unconscious, but not dead at any rate. He turned his head to call out for help, when a hand crept out of the bundle and gripped his arm. He looked down. The woman's eyes were open, looking up at him with pathetic urgency, and the thin fingers dug into his arm insistently.

'Don't be afraid,' he said gently. 'No-one here will hurt you.'

'Peter,' she whispered.

He stared, and gently pushed the hair back from the face to stare again, and the world seemed to catch its breath and miss a beat. 'Fanny?' he said in utter astonishment. 'Good God, *Fanny*?'

'Peter,' she whispered again, and the fingers dug harder. 'Don't tell – anyone – I'm here.'

'Dear God, Fanny, what's happened to you? Let me get you inside.' He hauled her forward, ungentle with urgency, into the passage so that he could close the front door, pull the curtain over it, and turn up the gas. 'Mother!' he called, 'come quick!' And to Fanny, 'Was that you who knocked a little while before?'

She nodded. 'Someone coming. Had to – hide.' She drew a shuddering sigh. 'Help me?'

'You're safe now, Fanny,' he said with fierce determination. '*Safe*, d'you hear?'

'Peter, what is it?'

He turned his head. 'Mother, it's Fanny Anthony.'

'Good heaven! Is she hurt?'

'I don't know. Let's get her into the parlour. Harriet, clear the sofa.'

Peter was strong despite his shortness, and Fanny was famine-light. He lifted her easily in his arms, and carried her carefully through, his eyes fixed on her face. She looked up at him with that same urgent appeal, and he felt a murderous rage rise up inside him which determined that someone would pay for this. Along with his short legs, the greatest cause for regret in his life had been that he had never been able to find and kill the man who raped his sister. He didn't speak of it, but it festered; and now it seemed someone had harmed Fanny Anthony.

Mrs Welland shut the parlour door behind them, Peter laid his burden gently on the sofa, and Harriet went to the cupboard for the brandy, kept for medicinal purposes. She handed a glass to Peter, kneeling beside Fanny, and he propped up her head and put the glass to her lips. She sipped, choked, sipped again. 'Don't try to speak. Wait for a moment, until you feel better. Take some more. That's right.' When she had finished the brandy he let her head back onto the cushions, and she closed her eyes, seemingly exhausted by the effort. Mrs Welland pushed Peter gently away so that she could run her hands over Fanny and see if she had any obvious injury.

'Nothing broken. No blood that I can see. The rest will have to wait until we undress her,' Mrs Welland said. She looked at the pale face for a few moments, and then took up Fanny's hand. 'Fanny, can you tell us what happened? Are you hurt anywhere?'

Fanny's eyes flew open. She stared at Mrs Welland in panic.

'It's all right, Fanny, you're quite safe. You're at Mrs Welland's house. You know me, don't you? It's all right, just rest now. Questions can wait until the morning. We'll get you up to bed, and in the morning Peter shall send a telegraph to Doctor Anthony—'

'No!' Fanny cried out with surprising strength, pulled her hand away and tried to struggle onto her elbow. 'No! Don't tell! Don't tell!' She looked round wildly, found Peter's face, and reached out to him in appeal. 'Peter! Don't tell him!'

He dropped to his knees and took her in his arms, and she clung, panting shallowly, trembling. 'Fanny, it's all right, it's all right,' he said, holding her firmly. 'We won't tell anyone you're here.' His mother made a sound and he looked at her over Fanny's shoulder and shook his head. 'We won't tell anyone at all, not anyone, not until you say so. All right? I promise. That's right. Don't be afraid, Fanny, you're safe now.'

Mrs Welland shook her head doubtfully, but said nothing more on the subject. 'We must get her to bed. But where can we put her? We're full tonight.'

'Boy's room,' Peter said promptly. 'Boy can come in with me. It's out of the way.'

'Yes, all right,' said Mrs Welland. She saw the point. Boy had a tiny room at the back of the house, over the coalshed, reached by a separate short staircase that went up from the passage between the kitchen and the back door. No other guests would ever have cause to use those stairs, and Fanny's presence could therefore be kept secret. 'Harriet, can you go and get Boy up and put him in Peter's bed?'

Harriet nodded. 'Clean sheets?'

Mrs Welland looked at Fanny. 'No, don't bother. I don't think we can bathe her tonight. The important thing is to get her undressed and into bed.'

The exchange was soon made. Boy was dragged sleepily complaining from his bed and put into Peter's, Peter carried Fanny up to Boy's room, and then with difficulty detached himself and left her to Mrs Welland and Harriet to undress. They found her desperately thin and dirty, but with no serious injuries, only some abrasions on her back and a number of deep bruises on her arms and legs. Harriet and her mother exchanged a glance over them, and then got Fanny into bed, where she seemed to fall at once into a dead sleep.

'She'd better not be left alone,' Mrs Welland said.

'I'll stay,' Harriet said. Boy's room was so tiny, there wasn't room for anything as substantial as an armchair. Vigil would have to be kept uncomfortably on a small wooden upright chair; but Harriet did not so much as sigh as she made the offer.

'Thank you, dear. I'll relieve you later,' Mrs Welland said, and went downstairs again.

Peter was waiting anxiously in the kitchen. 'Well?'

'She doesn't seem to be hurt, except for some bruises. But what was all that about not telling Doctor Anthony?'

'Mother, doesn't it occur to you that it may have been him who did this to her?'

'Peter, that's absurd!'

'Is it?'

'But we know Philip Anthony – he lived here, for heaven's sake. He's a good man – look at the work he does with the poor! His whole life is dedicated to good works. How could you even think—'

'I don't think,' Peter said, embarrassed. 'Not necessarily. But she said don't tell *anyone*. She begged us. All I say is, wait until we find out what's happened.'

'She is his wife, after all – he has the right to know,' Mrs Welland said doubtfully. 'He must be frantic, not knowing where she is,'

'From the look of her she must have been wandering the streets for days. You don't get into that state in a few hours. Another night won't make any difference to him. Just wait until she can tell us what happened – please, Mother.'

She shrugged. 'Well, I suppose you may have a point. I just hope we don't get into trouble over this.'

'We won't. Is Harriet sitting with her?'

'Yes. I don't think she ought to be left. If she wakes up, she may not remember where she is, and be afraid.'

'No, she certainly mustn't be left,' Peter agreed urgently.

'I'll take over from Harriet when I've had a few hours' sleep.'

'No, don't you bother. I'll do it. You need a proper night's sleep. You go to bed, and I'll take over from Harriet.'

So it was Peter's face Fanny saw when she woke in the early hours of the morning. She looked at him, frowning.

'Hello, Fanny,' he said gently. 'Do you remember where you are?' Her eyes moved over his face. 'Yes, it's me, Peter. Peter Welland. You're in our house. You came last night – do you remember?'

She sighed.

'You must be hungry,' he said. 'I've got some bread and milk here – do you think you could eat a little?' He supported her in one arm while he fed her with small spoonfuls. She ate about half of it, and then turned her face away from any more, so he put it aside and laid her down again. Still she didn't speak, but her eyes never left his face. 'Can you tell me what happened?' he asked. She seemed to think for a moment, and then she shook her head, and closed her eyes wearily. 'All right, not now, then. Later will do. You sleep now.' He waited a moment, and then started to stand up, meaning to move the bread-and-milk bowl to a safer place; but as soon as he moved her eyes flew open and she made a sound of alarm. 'No, it's all right,' he said. 'It's only me. You're safe. No-one knows you're here.'

'Stay,' she whispered.

'Yes, I'll stay with you,' he said. Her hand twitched on the blanket, and he took hold of it, and the fingers folded round his. Holding his hand, she closed her eyes again, and was soon asleep.

He sat quietly, watching her slow breaths. 'I won't leave you,' he said to her sleeping face. 'I promise.'

For two days Fanny slept while the life of the house went on around her. Every so often she woke and obediently swallowed the food that was spooned into her, and then slept again. Mostly it was Peter who sat with her. Once she woke and found him asleep, sitting on the floor with his head resting on his folded arms on the bed, snoring just a little; she smiled, and went to sleep again.

On the third day she woke to find Harriet there, and was glad of it, because she needed to use the chamberpot. Afterwards Harriet said, 'Do you think you could stand a bath, now?'

'Yes,' Fanny said, and then becoming aware of herself, 'Yes please.'

Patty, the maid-of-all-work, helped Harriet bring up the bath and the water, and then went away and brought back a suit of clean sheets and stripped and remade the bed while Harriet helped Fanny bathe. Afterwards, Harriet dressed her in a clean night-gown and helped her back to bed, where she leaned back on the pillows weakly. 'Are you hungry?' Harriet asked. Fanny nodded. 'I'll get you some breakfast.'

The word kindled something in Fanny's eyes. 'Breakfast? Not slops?'

Harriet considered her for a moment. 'You must be getting better,' she said, and went away down the stairs.

A while later, Peter came up with a tray. 'Harriet says you're asking for proper food instead of slops. What do you say to eggs and bacon?'

He helped her sit up, and then laid the tray across her knees. A sizzling dish of eggs and bacon, and fresh bread with thick butter, and coffee. Peter looked at her expression, and smiled. 'Well, that is a good sign. A person who can look at food like that is not about to die.'

'Did you think I was going to die?' Fanny asked shyly.

'Maybe just a bit, at first. But I think you're round the corner now.' He was going to leave her to eat, but she said, 'Stay with me,' so he sat down on the little hard chair that his bottom knew so well by now and watched her eat. When she had finished, he moved the tray away, and said, 'Do you think you can tell me now what happened to you?'

'Tell me first,' she said, 'have you told anyone?'

'That you're here? No. Mother thought we ought to, but I said until we'd heard your story we wouldn't know who you needed protecting from.'

'Thank you,' she said with great relief. She closed her eyes, and he thought the revelations were to be postponed again, but after a moment she opened them and said, 'I've run away.'

'Run away?'

'From home. From my husband.'

'Ah,' he said.

She looked at him part anxiously, part defiantly. 'Do you hate me now? Do you think I'm a bad woman?'

'Of course not,' he said automatically, for his mind was working. 'Fanny, did he make those bruises on your arms?'

'No,' she said. 'No, of course not. He never hit me. That was—' her mouth trembled, 'that was someone else.'

'Why don't you tell me all about it, from the beginning,' he said. He guessed the bruises belonged to the worst part, and that she would come better to it chronologically

So Fanny told him. She told about her life with Philip Anthony, and he listened with a surprise he was at pains to conceal. Who would have thought the good doctor would be such a tyrannical husband? And yet – he cast his mind back to the time Anthony had lived here – and yet, wasn't he always an uncompromising man, even a cold man? Handsome, intelligent, dedicated to his work – but without that spark of warmth which made charity tolerable to the evangelised? Peter wasn't sure. Perhaps his sympathy with Fanny was colouring his memory. At all events, he could see why a lively, passionate woman like Fanny would find her near-imprisonment with a cold and undemonstrative man intolerable.

She told how she climbed out of the window and took the train to London, and how Charlotte's reaction was that she ought to go back. 'Do you think I did wrong?' she asked Peter anxiously.

'It doesn't matter what I think, does it?' he said.

'Yes. I want to know. I suppose if you avoid the question like that it means you disapprove too.'

'I don't disapprove. You did what you had to do. I think it was unlucky, though. I think it will make things very difficult for you—'

'Difficult!' She laughed mirthlessly. 'No, difficult was living with Philip. Whatever's happened to me since, whatever may happen, I don't regret it a bit. I'd sooner die than go back to him.'

'Really, Fanny? Do you really mean that?' he asked earnestly.

'Yes, really. I thought you must have seen that for yourself.'

He nodded. 'Go on with your story. Tell me what happened next.'

She told him about leaving Charlotte's house, walking through London, staying at the inn, discovering she had

391

been robbed; told him of the queer sense of elation she had experienced when she found she really was destitute.

'It didn't last long, though. I'd had so little to eat the day before, and the pie didn't hold me long. By evening I was so hungry I didn't know what to do with myself.' She reflected. 'I think that was almost the worst time, that first night. I was so hungry, and so afraid. I was too frightened to lie down and sleep. I just kept walking and walking, and, oh, the pain in my stomach! The next morning I met a milk-maid, and bought a cup of milk – it tasted horrible, but I didn't care, I was so thirsty – and then I bought another hot pie, and afterwards I realised I'd been silly because a hot pie just doesn't hold you for long enough. So later I spent the last of my money on a loaf of bread and a piece of cheese, and put it in my bag, and I walked on and in the middle of the day I found a little public garden to sit in. I had some of the bread and cheese, and then I started to fall asleep. I would have loved to, I was so tired, and I didn't feel so frightened in daylight. But then a policeman came by and looked at me, and went away, and then came back and looked again. I suppose he wondered what a lady was doing there. I still looked like a lady then. So I got up and moved on. By the time it got dark I was too tired to be really frightened any more. I slept under a hedge in somebody's garden, and only woke up when a dog came sniffing at me early in the morning.'

'Poor Fanny,' Peter said. 'Didn't you want to go home by then?'

'No,' she said. 'Not once. I was only afraid of being found by someone who knew me, or the police. I guessed he would have them looking for me. That's why I kept walking, walking, walking. And pretty soon my shoes were falling to pieces. They weren't made to take such punishment.'

One thing that abounded in the poor quarters of London were second-hand clothes shops. She had sold her bonnet in exchange for a pair of stout boots, but had had to throw in the change of linen in her bag to make the exchange. Then she had thought that if she went bareheaded in her obviously expensive mantle, she would attract attention, so she had swapped that as well.

'Not for that horrible shawl you were wearing?'

'No, that came later. I swapped the mantle for an old pelisse, and some cash. Not as much as I ought to have had, I don't suppose. I'm sure everyone I traded with rooked me. But I didn't know the price of anything. What a useless creature I was! All my life I've been looked after by other people. I thought I was so smart and clever, and it turned out that I didn't know anything.'

He touched her hand in sympathy, too moved to speak, and she took hold of his almost absently, comforted by the touch without really realising it was there.

That was the third day. After that, her memories began to grow confused. She wandered, never knowing precisely where she was, always tired, always hungry, with only the one thought in her mind, that she must conceal herself from Anthony. Soon, however, he would not have recognised her. She came to know the second-hand clothes shops very well, as she sold her apparel for money to buy food. Eventually she had even sold the pelisse, for a few coppers and the woollen shawl. Soon she no longer attracted notice in the poor streets. Dirty and shabby, she fitted in there. When she slept in doorways, the strolling policemen barely glanced at her. She was safe at last.

'But I didn't know it. I think I was a little crazy.'

Peter pressed her hand. It was enough to drive a gently bred woman entirely and permanently out of her mind, he thought. There must be a vein of toughness in Fanny, to have survived.

Her tale was almost done. She remembered little about the end days. When she had nothing more to sell, she starved; but hunger now had gone beyond the gnawing pain she had felt on the second day. She grew light-headed. She remembered stealing half a sandwich from a clerk sitting on a bench, who had left his lunch-packet open beside him, when he was looking the other way. She had begged at a baker's shop, and been given a stale roll.

'You begged?'

'It didn't seem to matter any more,' she said.

Then one night she was wandering in a very poor street, looking for somewhere to sleep, when a man had accosted her. 'I suppose he must have taken me for a – for a—' She stopped suddenly, her mouth quivering. The hand that was holding Peter's gripped spasmodically. 'He wanted me to – do something. When I refused, he grabbed hold of me. I struggled to get away and he – he *laughed*.' There were tears in her eyes now. She looked at Peter, but not as if she saw him.

'Yes,' he said. 'I know.'

'He said I wanted to really. I struggled and kicked at him, and tried to get away—' She turned her head sharply from side to side, reliving the moment; her hand was hurting Peter's, her other hand was balled into a fist, softly beating the bed. 'He kept saying – pretending he thought I wanted – oh, the *beast*! The *beast*!'

'It's all right,' Peter said meaninglessly. 'It's all right.' His heart was cold with horror. It was like history repeating itself.

'He was pushing me against the wall and pulling at my skirt—' She stopped with a sob, and the tears slid over her lower lids.

'It's all right, Fanny, you don't have to go on,' Peter said. 'It wasn't your fault.'

She shook her head, not wanting to be stopped, needing to tell it all now. 'I thought I was going to die. He was so strong. I was helpless. And then another man came along. I don't know who he was. He shouted something, and the first man looked round, and the second man said, "She doesn't look willing to me. Let her go." And the first man swore horribly at him, and let go of me with one hand to fend off the other, and the second man grabbed his arm, and then I gave a desperate shove, and I got away. I ran down the street. I heard them shouting at me at first, but I don't think they chased me. I ran and ran. I couldn't stop.'

She fell silent. So she had got away – had she? He wanted to ask, but could not, did not dare – but he thought it must mean she got away before the worst happened. She was trembling all over now with the emotion of reliving the horror. He stroked her hand between both of his, and waited for her to calm down.

'And how did you find your way here?' he asked at last.

'I don't know. I was just wandering. I don't really remember much about it. It's just that suddenly I recognised where I was and I thought of you all. I was just by Gray's Inn. I thought I was dying, and I thought if only I could get here, I could die peacefully. Your mother wouldn't send me away. I didn't want to die all alone. So I came here. Then I got afraid. I thought that Philip would be bound to suspect I might come to you, and be having the house watched. I hung about for ages in the street, watching to see if anyone was around. And then just when I plucked up courage to go and knock, someone came down the road. But I don't think it was anyone. They went straight past. And after they'd gone I came back again, but my legs wouldn't hold me up any more. I fell down and couldn't get up. I couldn't even knock. I thought I'd just die there and never get to see you, and, oh, it was awful! And then you appeared, like a miracle. How did you find me?'

'I heard you at the door.' Peter felt weak from hearing the story, as if he had suffered everything with Fanny. How had she survived? That was the miracle. 'Do you remember the date when you left home?' he asked at last.

She told him. 'What's the date now? How long have I been away?'

'Three weeks,' he said.

She looked at him for a long time, and then sighed. 'Is that all? It feels like half a lifetime.'

'Three weeks can be a lifetime. Fanny, have you thought how worried they must be for you?'

She began to tremble. 'No,' she said,

'Those who love you. Think of their agony of mind.'

'No!'

'I don't mean that you should go back. I wouldn't want you to do anything you didn't want to. But just a letter, just a note to say you are alive and safe—'

'*No!* You mustn't tell anyone! He'll find me, he'll take me back! Don't tell, swear you won't tell, oh please!' She was in tears now, and he hastened to soothe her. She rocked and mourned. 'No, no, don't tell, don't tell, don't tell!'

'It's all right, Fanny. I'm on your side, don't you know that? I won't do anything until you say so.'

Later when she was dozing and Patti was watching her, he told his mother and sister the story as Fanny had told it to him. They listened gravely.

'Poor creature,' Mrs Welland said at last. 'Who would have thought Doctor Anthony could treat her so badly that she'd run away? And leave her child behind, too.' Harriet nodded to that point. 'But the question is, what are we to do with her?'

'What do you mean, Mother, do with her? She stays here.'

'For now, of course, dear,' Mrs Welland said. 'But she can't stay here for ever.'

'Why not?'

She lifted her hands helplessly. 'Well, dear, she doesn't belong here. She's a married woman, with a husband and a home and a child.'

'Which she has left because she couldn't endure them.'

'Her mind is unbalanced at the moment by her experiences. When she's more herself, she'll want to go back.'

'I don't think so. You haven't heard her, Mother – she's afraid of him above anything. Could anything but the worst extreme drive someone like her to run away – and more than that, to stay away? She really was willing to die rather than go back to him.'

'Nonsense,' said Mrs Welland firmly. 'She came here, didn't she? That was because she *didn't* want to die. Peter, her poor family must be mad with worry.'

'Yes, I know, but I promised her we wouldn't tell anyone.'

'Peter!'

'Not yet,' he pleaded. 'Give it a few more days at least. Let's see how she feels in a few more days. If you tell Anthony she's here, he'll come straight away to fetch her, and I'm afraid the sight of him will turn her brain entirely.'

'Peter's right,' said Harriet abruptly.

'Oh, very well,' Mrs Welland said at last, but she looked worried. 'Just a few more days. But sooner or later, you know, she'll have to go home.'

Peter nodded. 'We'll cross that bridge when we come to it,' he said. He was quite sure she would never want to go home, but he was satisfied with the ground he'd won, for the moment.

*   *   *

Sibella and Benedict stood by the paddock rails up at Twelvetrees watching as Cooper lunged a nice-looking young black horse.

'He's got beautiful action,' Benedict said. 'A real daisy-cutter. And look how he carries his head – dead centre.'

'Yes, he's beautifully balanced,' Sibella agreed.

'Cooper! Let's have him round the other way. See, he's just as good on either hand. That will make a very fine hunter.' He turned and regarded his wife indulgently. 'So what do you say, Sib? Would you like him? Shall we break him to side-saddle?'

Sibella could hardly believe her ears. 'I should love to have him! But are you sure? He must be worth thousands!'

'Of course I'm sure,' Benedict laughed. 'Do you think you're not worth thousands to me?'

'But the stud is a business. Are you sure you can afford just to give away the assets like that?'

'I'll let you know when the bailiffs come for me, love. But he can be your Christmas present, if it really worries you.'

She sighed with pleasure, watching the black's buoyant, springy trot. 'You're so generous to me. Thank you, darling. He'll make a marvellous hunter.'

Benedict nodded, smiling. 'And it's time you had a really good horse. Perhaps it will help to take your mind off whatever's been worrying you.' She glanced quickly at him. 'Did you think I hadn't noticed? You've been very absent for the last few days. *Is* there something wrong?'

'I've been wondering about Mary.'

'Oh,' said Benedict, and his smile faded.

'What is the matter with her?' Sibella asked. 'I see from your face that you know. She's been so quiet lately – almost depressed. It isn't like her.'

Benedict sighed. 'It was something I hoped to avoid, but it crept up on me. I ought to have realised.' He told her about Mary's questions about the Morland Place inheritance.

'Oh dear,' said Sibella. 'That puts the cat among the pigeons.'

'I suppose I didn't want to have to think about it,' Benedict said in self reproach. 'That's why I hadn't got my answer ready. I had to say something when she asked me, and I probably expressed myself clumsily, and upset her.'

'You didn't tell her about—?'

'No, of course not!' he said quickly. 'But you see, she knows that she's in every way suitable to be mistress of Morland Place—'

'And she must know you think so too.'

He nodded. 'So all that's left for her to believe is that I am denying her on account of her sex.'

'But boys inherit before girls. That's the way of the world. She must know that, too.'

'Yes, but she's steeped herself in family history. Grandmother left the estate to Mama, not my father.'

'But your mother left it to Nicholas, not Sophie, though Sophie was the elder.'

'Sophie was married and gone away long before the question arose. I suppose I've been hoping the same would happen with Mary. I didn't allow for her enquiring mind.'

'And her hungry intellect. She needs something to do,' Sibella said. 'Helping to run the estate would be just the thing. I suppose you can't—?'

'I wish I could,' he said miserably. 'I want it more than anything. But she's not—'

'Not a Morland.' Sibella lapsed into silence, thinking savage things about Benedict's first wife. That woman had done so much damage! How she hated her! And how jealous she was that Benedict had loved her first, so much that he had never even noticed Sibella. Sibella was his wife now, and she knew he was happy with her; but Rosalind the unworthy had had him first, and nothing could ever change that.

'Well,' she said at last, 'it will resolve itself in the end. She will marry and go away, and that will be that.'

'She says she won't. She's adamant that she will never marry.'

'Darling!' Sibella was amused. 'She's only sixteen years old.'

'But her mind is much older. You know she's like a grown woman.'

'Yes, in her mind. But not in her emotions. She's still very young to marry. But one day she'll suddenly see someone she fancies, and fall in love, and that will be that.'

'I hope so,' Benedict said doubtfully, and lapsed into a thoughtful silence.

Cooper halted the colt in his circles and called him in, rewarded him with a titbit, and led him over to the rails. 'He goes a treat, sir,' he said. 'Smooth as silk. And when he's learned to get his hocks under him, I think he'll have a fair turn of speed.'

The young horse approached them with his ears forward and they made much of him, while he ran his soft, enquiring lips over their hands and sleeves.

'You beauty!' Sibella said, stroking his cheeks. He blew into her palms and then reached up gently to nibble her hair. 'Now, my boy, that's not hay!' Then the thought came to her. She resisted it for a moment, because she hadn't liked the look of a horse so much since her dear old Rocket; but she really did love Mary. She took a deep breath. 'Benedict, why don't you give him to Mary instead? A new horse to school will give her an interest, something to occupy her mind. It will cheer her up.'

Benedict saw the force of the idea at once, but then his face clouded. 'I can't ask you to give him up. You like him, I can see that.'

'I do like him, but he's not mine yet, so it isn't a question of giving him up. And poor Mary needs him more than I do.'

Benedict hardly argued, as Sibella noted with a pang. But she was not one to regret a good impulse, and parted from the colt with only a concealed sigh. 'You're very generous,' Benedict said as they walked back to collect their mounts and ride home. 'We'll tell Mary about it when we get home, and bring her over to see him this afternoon. I can't wait to see her face!'

When they got back to Morland Place, a telegraph message was waiting for Benedict. It was from Fenwick Morland, saying that he was in England again on business for his father, and begging to be received at Morland Place at the earliest convenient date.

Mary went quite pale when she heard it read out. She clutched her father's sleeve and said, 'Papa, you will invite him? If he's in London he could be here tomorrow, if you telegraph back straight away. Oh please, Papa, *please*! Ask him to come as quickly as he can!'

Benedict looked at her in surprise, and noted the eyes bright with urgency, the lips tense with eagerness. He patted her hand, and said, 'I don't mind asking him to come, if you'd like him to. He was a pleasant enough young man.'

Mary didn't say anything, but her face was a communication in itself as she reached up and kissed his cheek in mute gratitude. Benedict met Sibella's eyes across Mary's head, and Sibella gave a tiny shrug. Then Mary was dancing away, wild with happiness, kissing the dogs and rushing off to tell the servants the wonderful news. They could hear her singing in the kitchen passage.

'Well,' said Benedict. 'Is that what it was all about?'

Sibella said nothing. She was as surprised as he was, and the only coherent thought she had was that now perhaps there'd be no need to give Mary the black colt. What was that saying about virtue bringing its own reward?

While Sibella was dressing for dinner on the first evening of Fenwick's visit, Mary came into her room with something in her hand.

'Mama, please may I wear this at dinner?'

Sibella turned from the glass. 'The locket?' Mary nodded. 'I'd forgotten about that.' Sibella looked at her for a moment. In her dress of white muslin, she looked almost bridal. Her hair was coiled around her head like a crown of twisted gold rope, falling in three long ringlets from behind. Her cheeks were flushed with excitement, her eyes bright, and the neck and shoulders which rose plump and bare and beautiful from the lace bertha were not a child's.

'You do seem to need some ornament,' Sibella said.

Mary took that for permission. 'Thank you,' she said fervently, and presented the locket and her back to her step-mother so that Sibella could fasten it on.

'You still like him, don't you?' Sibella said.

'Yes,' said Mary.

'As much as before?'

'Oh, more!' Mary turned, and Sibella read the excitement and hope and doubt in that flushed face. 'I thought he wasn't coming back. All this time, and no word from him. He didn't even write!'

'It would have been most improper for him to do so,' Sibella said. 'A young man can't write to a girl he's not engaged to.'

'I didn't know that,' Mary said humbly. 'I thought perhaps he'd fallen in love with someone else, and it was dreadful. I thought I'd never even know.'

Sibella nodded in sympathy. She had seen the man she loved go off and marry someone else – but how much worse it would have been not to know, to spend your whole life waiting and wondering.

Mary went on. 'And then when he arrived, the moment I saw him, I knew that I hadn't been mistaken. And today, when we were all walking up to see the mares – you know we got a little way ahead of you and Papa?'

'Yes, it was noticed.'

She ducked her head shyly. 'Yes. Well, Fenwick was telling me about Twelvetrees – his Twelvetrees – and the horses he's breeding there. And he said there's one young horse, the best and fastest of the new crop, but with such a gentle nature, it would make a perfect lady's horse. He said – he said he thinks of breaking it to sidesaddle in the hope that it may be mine.'

'Did he indeed? And what else did he say?'

'That he dreams of showing me over every inch of the plantation, the woods and the river, and the place where the ducks breed, and the flower garden his mother has begun, and the avenue of limes. Oh Mama, I so want to see it!'

'You're very young, Mary dear.'

'*You* know I'm not,' she said eagerly. 'And you know I can't marry anyone else. Oh Mama, can't you tell Papa so he'll understand? I love Fenwick, and I always will. There's no sense in making us wait any longer. He wants to marry me and take me back with him. *His* father agrees – we only need Papa's permission.'

Sibella felt sad. 'I can't persuade him. He will make up his own mind.'

'But you are on my side?'

403

'It isn't a question of side,' Sibella said. 'Everyone wants what's best for you—'

'*This* is best for me!'

'But America's so far away. We should miss you so. *I* should miss you.'

'But I'm not your daughter,' she said hesitantly.

'Georgie and Teddy and Henrietta aren't your children, but you love them. Won't you miss them?'

'Yes, of course! But—' She sought understanding in Sibella's eyes. 'It's different, isn't it?'

'Yes,' said Sibella. 'It's different.' They were silent a moment. 'Is Fenwick going to ask your father tonight?'

'He wanted to, but I said I must do it.'

Sibella nodded. 'It will come better from you.'

But in the event, there was not much telling about it. Benedict came into the drawing-room and found Sibella sitting in her usual chair, Fenwick, looking handsome in his dinner-dress and faintly exotic with his tanned skin, standing by the chimneypiece, and Mary sitting on the sofa gazing at Fenwick with her whole heart in her face. When she saw her father standing in the doorway, she jumped up and ran to him, flung her arms round his neck, and pressed her hot cheek silently against his. Over her shoulder he met Sibella's eyes and saw the message in them.

He set Mary gently back from him, and looked at Fenwick, and said, 'I suspect you've been making love to my daughter, sir.'

'I love her, sir. We want to be married.'

'Then we had better talk about it,' Benedict said.

Sitting up in bed, Sibella watched her husband walking about the room, preparing himself for bed. She had expected much more anguish than this; he seemed distracted, but not bowed or defeated.

404

'What made you change your mind?' she asked at last.

He was a long time answering. 'She has her heart set on him,' he said at last

'She's very young. She may change her mind.'

'Do you think she will?'

Sibella thought carefully. 'No. I was playing devil's advocate. I was about her age when I first fell in love with you – in fact I think I was a little younger. But I didn't expect you to capitulate so easily.'

'Capitulate? Is that how you see it? But she's waited two years. More importantly, *he's* waited two years, with God knows what temptations all around. He's proved his constancy. It would be cruel to keep them apart any longer, just to test them.'

'But it's such a long way away. We won't be able to keep an eye on her, to make sure she's happy. How will we manage without her? How will you bear not to be seeing her every day?'

Benedict stared into the fire, and the moving light threw the lines into relief, making him look older than his years, and more tired. 'I feel as if it was inevitable. I think I've known for a long time that she couldn't marry any of the local boys – and since she asked me about Morland Place, I've been wondering how any marriage in this country could satisfy her. She's like a great strong bird shut up in a cage too small for it. I think she needs a bigger stage than any England can provide her with. Adventure in a new land – somewhere she can spread her wings without breaking them on the bars.'

'I suppose if she stayed here, sooner or later she would find out the truth.'

He looked up at her. 'I don't know. That must have been on my mind too. Perhaps it's best for both of us if she goes away, right away.'

Sibella saw how the conflict of loving her and not being her father was pulling Benedict apart, hurting him far worse than she had imagined. And if Mary stayed, it was inevitable that they would hurt each other. This was an answer to the problem, a compromise. Let her have some other kingdom, if this one couldn't be hers.

Oh, but America was such a long way away! 'I shall miss her,' Sibella said. 'I love her so dearly.'

And that was when Benedict finally broke. She held him in her arms for a long time, and he sobbed against her neck like a child, for the child he loved so much, who had never been his.

BOOK THREE

Journey's End

I remember the bulwarks by the shore,
And the fort upon the hill;
The sunrise gun with its hollow roar,
The drum-beat repeated o'er and o'er,
And the bugle wild and shrill.
And the music of that old song
Throbs in my memory still.

Henry Wadsworth Longfellow:
My Lost Youth

CHAPTER SIXTEEN

Charlotte remembered Cavendish's description of Balaclava very clearly when she and Oliver arrived in the
yacht *Doris*. It didn't look much like a summer resort
now, after a month of occupation by the British army:
twenty-five thousand men, of whom probably twenty-two
thousand at any one time had diarrhoea. The pretty
villas had been reduced to ruin, some deliberately to
make room, some by sheer carelessness. Fences and
doors had been ripped out for firewood, windows broken,
gardens trampled, vines and climbing roses torn down
and their supports broken up, trees cut down or uprooted.
There was rubbish everywhere, bits of wood, broken
wheels, boxes and spoilt bales, ordure, and heaps of
offal from the animals slaughtered for food. The army
had gone back and forth, up and down, and what had
once been the village street was now a wide, trampled,
heavily-manured track, like a hideous gash torn by giant
claws.

The inlet was jammed with shipping. On the side away
from the harbour the hillside came down to the water
almost vertically, and at its foot the still surface reflected
the green and grey cliff face and the blue sky above. On
the harbour side, whatever water could be seen between
the jostling hulls was thick with bobbing refuse, and the
smell in the landlocked, airless bay was awful. As the *Doris*
glided slowly in, a yellow-brown scum of human ordure
shifted about her bows; Charlotte looked over the side

and saw a dead dog floating serenely by on its back with it stiff legs in the air.

It took some time to manoeuvre into a berth. Captain Christie, the port master, didn't wait for them to tie up before he came on board to welcome them.

'I shall probably have to move you quite soon,' he said after exchanging civilities. 'We're very short of stone jetties, and there's a load of shot expected tomorrow. I can put you up at the far end by the *Hawk* when the steamer there goes out – you'll find it quieter there anyway. Have you much to unload? There's plenty of lighterage, but getting anything large or heavy over the side is difficult, as you can imagine, with the hulls packed so close together. I'd advise you to get anything bulky off while you can.'

'We have nothing large except the horses,' Oliver told him. 'For the rest, it is just personal gear. But I'd be glad to get the horses onto *terra firma* as soon as possible.'

'You'll be billeting at Headquarters, sir?'

'I imagine so,' Oliver said. 'Where is it, by the way?'

'Up on the plateau, halfway between here and Sebastopol – about five or six miles away. Lord Raglan took over a country villa, with plenty of large outhouses, so you'll have stabling there.'

'And the Light Brigade, Captain?' Charlotte said. 'Where shall we find them? I'm eager to see my brother, Lord Blithfield.'

'The Cavalry is up on the plateau near Kadikoi, your grace, except for the 11th Hussars and the 17th Lancers, who are further up towards Sebastopol, camped on the Heights.'

After further discussion it was decided to get the horses off at once, while they had the use of the stone jetty, but to leave the other gear on the yacht until they knew what they would need. The captain knew of an empty stable in the village, and said that he would send up a messenger to show it to them. 'Do you have a bottle of brandy in your stores that's get-at-able, sir?' he asked apologetically.

Oliver, in some surprise, said that he had, thinking perhaps the captain wanted rewarding for his information; but the captain explained that the stable had been seized by the engineers, who had put a padlock on it. 'Any kind of shed is in short supply, and possession being nine-tenths, as they say, a bottle of brandy is the minimum price that will get the key from Major Wilkes. He'll never give it up otherwise, not without an order from General Airey, which could take days – not much use when you want it for tonight. My man will do the business for you, if you entrust the bottle to him.'

Oliver grinned. 'So that's the way things are done out here, is it?'

Christie smiled too. 'Do you see the *Clarissa* over there, sir? She was sent out by Lady Eagleton and a committee of charitable ladies to sell comforts to the troops at cost price. But I guarantee you that anything you buy from *Clarissa* will cost you more than the same article at the Maltese shop in the village. There is always someone who will make a profit out of war.'

While the horses were unloading, Oliver and Charlotte walked up to introduce themselves to Mr Filder, the Commissary-General, with whom Christie said it was important to have a good understanding; and then on to the Post Office to make the acquaintance of Mr Angel, the Post Master General, a man of enormous importance and power amongst so many people far from home. Angel was full of gossip, and they lingered quite a while, until someone stuck his head round the door to say that Lord Raglan and his staff had just ridden in to the village. They hurried out to intercept him.

'Ah, Southport! Glad to see you! You made a quick

411

passage.' The kindly, one-armed old gentleman turned in his saddle to bow to Charlotte. 'Your servant, ma'am. Come to see the fun, hey?'

'Yes, sir, and to be useful, I hope. My hospital experience is all at your command.'

'Oh, ah, yes – your hospital. Heard great things about it,' Raglan said rather vaguely. His mind was evidently on other things. 'Now then, duke, do you know everyone? General Airey you've met, of course. Adye, my adjutant – Tommy Steele, my secretary – ah, and here's Calvert, head of the Intelligence Department. Calvert, your reinforcements have arrived, eh, what?'

Calvert shook hands with Oliver, his quick, dark eyes comprehensively scanning him and tucking away the information in the files of his brain. 'Very glad to see you, your grace. There's a lot going on in our department – prisoners and plenty of deserters to question, to say nothing of the disaffected locals and the Turkish spies. Your background knowledge of political and Court circles will be invaluable.'

'I hope I may prove worthy of my hire,' Oliver said.

'There's someone in our department I believe you know – Cattley, our chief interpreter? He says he made your acquaintance recently in Kiev.'

'Yes, indeed. I shall be glad to see him again.'

'You'd better come up to Headquarters with us when we ride back,' Raglan said. 'The French are up to something – movements to the north-east, beyond the river. Wouldn't be surprised if we saw some action soon. Adye here will fix up your billet.'

The party rode on, except for Colonel Adye, who dismounted to talk to them.

'The *French* are up to something?' Oliver queried.

Adye smiled. 'Slip of the tongue – he means the Russians. You must remember his lordship spent all of his young manhood fighting Napoleon's armies. He can't get used to the idea that "enemy" and "French" are not synonymous terms. It can be a bit awkward when we have conferences with the French commanders.'

'I imagine so,' Oliver laughed.

'Steele and I have to be ready to cough loudly to cover up for him. I'm sure the French staff think we all have consumption over here! Now then, as to your arrangements. You have brought horses with you, I hope?'

'Yes, they're being unloaded now.'

'Thank God for that. We've lost so many, what with the long march and the shortage of water; and now we've been sent nothing but barley for feed, and you know cavalry mounts can't live on barely. Still, we're trying to get that remedied. There's plenty of hay, but the problem at the moment is getting it brought up from the harbour. We're dreadfully short of draught animals, and the road up to the plateau is very steep.'

'Yes, and unmade, I see,' Oliver noted with a shake of the head. 'It won't last very long as it is, Adye. When the rains start it will be a sea of mud.'

Adye spread his hands. 'I know, but what can we do? We're desperately short of men. We haven't a single pair of hands to spare for road-building. We've got the whole exposed flank to guard, gun emplacements to build to cover the Yalta road and the approach to Balaclava, as well as our share of the siege line – and digging the trenches is hellish difficult. The soil up there is only about eighteen inches deep in some places, and then it's solid rock. We've had to build up rather than down, with defensive walls, and you know how time-consuming it is filling sandbags and gabions. The French are all right, of course,' he added, not without bitterness. 'They've got perfect soil on their part of the line – their trenches practically dig themselves – and plenty of manpower to

413

do it, with us guarding their flank for them. And to add to our troubles there's a dozen deaths a day from cholera, and thirty or so falling sick. I tell you, there isn't a sound set of bowels in the entire army – I beg your pardon, ma'am.' He recalled Charlotte's presence with a start.

'It's quite all right, colonel. I nursed cholera in London all through August. There isn't much you can say that would shock me.'

He bowed. 'Things aren't all bad, however. We've made ourselves pretty comfortable up at Headquarters, and there are plenty of good stone outbuildings, so we can keep the horses under shelter. The human quarters are a little crowded, however: you know how Headquarters staff seems to expand day by day.'

'Of which expansion we are an example, I take it?' Oliver said with a laugh. 'Don't worry, Adye, we don't mean to turn anyone out of his bed. We've brought out tents and camp-beds and everything we need on the *Doris*.'

'Good for you, sir,' Adye said. 'I'll see what I can do about getting your gear up to the plateau. You'll need draught animals of course – I wonder if Maude of the Horse Artillery will lend us a team?'

'We can sleep on the yacht for the time being, if it's easier for you, and ride up to Headquarters each day.'

'I think you'll find you need to stay up on the plateau. It's a stiffish ride, and takes up a deuced lot of the day. No. I'll find you a bed in one of the cottages all right, but you'll probably have to sleep your servants in tents. You'll want a soldier-servant too, I suppose? I know of a good fellow – Watson, his name is. He looked after Colonel Forster, who's had to go home through ill-health, so he knows what to do. I'll have a word with his lordship and fix it up.'

'Thank you. You think of everything.'

Adye grinned. 'If I did, I'd have brought out a huge supply of horseshoes and nails, and made my fortune. The tracks are so stony the nags are always shedding shoes. I hope yours are sure-footed. But you're coming back with us now, aren't you, so you'll discover for yourself what I mean.'

'I'd like to visit my brother as soon as possible, colonel,' Charlotte said. 'I understand the 11th Hussars are in a different camp from the rest of the cavalry?'

'Yes, they're between Kadikoi and Headquarters, a bit further out than the rest of the Lights.'

'I'll go there, then,' she said to Oliver, 'while you're busy at Headquarters.'

The road up from the village was indeed very steep, and already deteriorating into a mire, though the weather so far had been dry. It was thronged with an unending stream of men and officers, in uniforms and civilian clothes of all sorts, on foot and mounted on every kind of animal from cavalry charger to ox; and carts in every stage of dilapidation, loaded and unloaded, labouring up and jouncing down.

The air was much fresher up on the top, away from the stink of the contaminated water, and a pleasant light breeze stirred the horses' manes. As they rode higher, Charlotte turned in the saddle to look back down at the bay, and the calm, sparkling water beyond, where a few British ships showed their comfortable presence. From here, everything still looked beautiful, the only evidence of the army being the neat rows of white tents of the Guards' and Heavy Cavalry camps, quite picturesque from a distance.

The camp of the 11th Hussars and 17th Lancers presented more white tents, lines of tethered horses, the exercise ring, and the hurdles and bales which had been erected to practise jumping. Someone must have seen Charlotte coming, for as she rode in, Cavendish came rushing out to greet her, to lift her from the saddle and squeeze the breath from her in delight.

'Charley! Darling old Charley! I'm so glad to see you! I knew we should never keep you away!'

'I couldn't wait to follow you, of course. The difficulty was persuading the Government to find a job for Oliver,' she teased.

'Everyone in the camp wants to meet you. You can't think what a novelty you are! Duberley of the 8th Hussars has his wife with him, and very dashing she is on horseback, and always in demand at dinner-parties. But she's only a plain Mrs, not a full-blown duchess. I shall have to think very carefully who to invite to dine with us tonight.'

'Am I dining here?' Charlotte asked, amused.

'To be sure,' Cavendish said, opening his eyes wide. 'And Oliver too. What else would you think of?'

'I rather supposed Lord Raglan might want Oliver at his table.'

'Oh well, then the Chief will have to have him *en garçon*. The ties of blood, you know! I can't be denied.'

The other officers crowded round, eager for introductions, and Charlotte shook hands what seemed like a thousand times, and received compliments, and chatted, and laughed at jokes, and felt that now she must know what it was like to be royalty. But at last Cavendish claimed her back and escorted her to his tent.

'Shouldn't I pay my respects to Lord Cardigan?' Charlotte asked.

'Oh, the Old Man don't live up here with us,' Cavendish said carelessly. 'Didn't you see his yacht down in the bay? Lord Raglan gave him permission to sleep on it one night when he wasn't feeling well, and he's stayed there ever since. He only comes up when he has to. He likes his comfort, and it's a long ride up to the camp. Here's my tent – what d'you think of it? Famous snug, ain't it?'

It seemed very comfortable, with a neat camp-bed, folding chairs and tables, a wash-stand, clothes stands and trunks and boxes, and his favourite saddle on a rack in the corner. 'Saddles are as hard to come by as horses,' he explained. 'I prefer to keep mine under my eye.' Charlotte was seated in the most comfortable chair, and Cavendish's servant, Parry, brought her a cup of chocolate.

'So tell me, why are you up here, away from the rest of the cavalry?' Charlotte asked when Parry left them.

'To keep the Old Man and Lucan apart. They can't even be civil to each other now, so Lord Raglan sent us up here, which is a damned shame – it's such miles from anywhere. I must say, Charley, we haven't had much fun of it so far in this war. We're never allowed to do anything. The Cossacks are always riding about, taunting us from a distance, and we're not allowed to chase 'em off. We're not even allowed to go out on scouting expeditions. It makes the men damned discontented. They blame the Old Man, of course, especially now he don't sleep with us up here; but he has his orders from Lucan, and Lucan has 'em from Raglan. And Lord Raglan don't want us to dirty our nice pretty uniforms.'

'Poor Cavendish! And you so wanted an exciting charge or two, didn't you?'

'You can laugh, Charley, but the situation is damned uncomfortable. When your commanders have no respect for each other, it goes down the ranks, and discipline suffers. My troop are all good fellows, but I can't stop 'em talking slightingly about the earls when they hear them snapping at each other. And some of the junior officers are as bad. That fellow Nolan I wrote to you about – he's got a bosom-bow in the 17th called Morris, so he's always visiting him and hanging around our camp. They call the Old Man the Noble Yachtsman, almost to his face – right out loud, no matter who's listening.'

'Oh dear, I do see how that must be awkward.'

'Well, it is. The two of them sit and spout about how the campaign ought to be organised, and how the cavalry could win the whole war on its own if only it was allowed – you never heard such stuff! They say the Old Man and Lucan know nothing and ought to be sent home.' He shook his head. 'Nolan thinks himself a cut above everyone else because he's a staff galloper. It doesn't bother me, but he ain't even civil to the Old Man. Talks to him like an inky – it makes the Old Man go purple. I nearly came to blows with him the other day.'

'Good God – with Lord Cardigan?'

'No, idiot, with Nolan! He was blackguarding the Old Man as usual, and I told him it was pretty poor sport to talk like that behind a man's back, and he said he'd say the same in front of his face, and I said I was sure of that because I'd heard him doing it, and if he did it again in my hearing I'd be pleased to give him a thrashing.'

'Oh Cav, no!'

'Well,' Cavendish said, 'the Old Man's been damned decent to me. He may be a Hyde Park soldier, but Nolan's no better. Anyway, I shall like to see which of them stands up better under fire. I doubt it will be that dancing dago! I don't know how Airey sticks him, for Airey's as good a fellow as ever lived.'

To take her brother's mind off his ills, Charlotte told him the home news, and produced the letter she had brought from Alice, which contained little but a description of her own nervous ailments and the sleepless nights she had had over young William's recent illness.

'What's all this about Baby?' Cavendish asked in the middle of it. 'I can't make out the writing.'

Charlotte looked over his shoulder. Alice's writing, she thought, resembled the tracks of a spider that had staggered through the inkpot on its way home after a splendid night out.

'I can't make it out either,' she said at last, 'but be assured it was nothing but a cold and a sore throat. Mrs Phipps naturally convinced Alice it was the putrid sort, and drove her into a frenzy about it. But I sent over my own good Doctor Brown, who looks after my children, and he said it was nothing at all, and sure enough William was better in a day or two.'

'I wish Mrs Phipps would go away, or go abroad, or marry again, or something,' Cavendish said moodily, 'then Alice might be a different person. You don't know how lucky you are, Charley, to have a husband you can talk to and share your thoughts with. Someone you can trust.'

'Our love was tested and proved over a long period,' Charlotte said carefully. This was delicate ground.

He looked at her. 'You mean that I married too hastily, I wouldn't listen to anyone, and now I'm paying the price. Oh, it's all right, I know I must put a brave face on it and be loyal, and I shall. I shan't say anything to anyone but you. But just this once, Charley, let me speak my mind! Six months away from home have given me time to think – too much time, really. I was a fool, and I shall pay for it for the rest of my life. I shall never have the sort of love you share with Oliver. If it weren't for little William—'

'What then?'

'Oh, nothing. But I tell you one thing – when I get home again, I shall get rid of Mrs Phipps, one way or another. And if anyone ever asks for my advice, I shall tell them to be a great deal more careful who they marry than I was. It's a sentence to life imprisonment.'

'Oh Cav, I'm so sorry,' Charlotte said.

He patted her hand. 'Never mind. I'm a grown-up now, Charley, and I must take my medicine. But tell me, is there any more news of Fanny?'

'Nothing when we came away. But Mama promised to telegraph if anything were heard, so I have made sure Mr Angel knows we're here.'

'It's a queer business,' Cavendish said. 'How does Anthony take it?'

'He was very upset. I can't make him out, you know. He must have behaved very badly to drive Fanny to run away, yet I can't help feeling he really loves her.'

'Marriage is a tricky thing,' Cavendish said profoundly. 'The more I see, the more I wonder anyone ever gets it right.'

After that they turned to other subjects. Cavendish took her to see his horses, Rowan and Bracken, and told her in minute detail of everything that had happened to them since they left England. When dinner-time approached, a message was sent up to Headquarters for Oliver, to say that Charlotte wanted to dine with Cavendish, and that a tent was available in the 11th's camp for the night. Oliver sent a message back saying that he could not join her, having too much to do, but that if she was happy to stay where she was, he would dine and sleep at Headquarters and come and fetch her in the morning. The soldier-servant, Watson, had indeed been assigned to Oliver, and he was charged with the duty of going back down to the harbour to bring up their night-gear.

'Famous!' Cavendish said when he had read this. 'Now we can settle in for a really jolly evening.'

A select band of fellow officers was invited to dine with Charlotte. Cavendish asked her to take the head

420

of the table, and placed on one side of her an old friend, Colonel Lord Desford, who had courted her in London when she first came out, and on her other side a very witty young captain called Archibald. Everyone was eager to entertain her, and the talk was lively. Charlotte was agreeably surprised by the quality of the food they ate, too, having had a vague, half-formed idea that soldiers, like sailors, lived on hard-tack and salt pork. Cavendish regaled them with gravy soup, potted shrimps, fried liver and bacon, a shoulder of mutton, pancakes with quince preserve, cheese, and a beautiful dish of rosy red Crimean apples.

Afterwards the gentlemen asked permission to smoke, and begged that Charlotte would not leave them too soon; so the front of the tent was thrown up to form a canopy, chairs were placed under it, and the officers lit their cigars and sat smoking and talking while Charlotte gazed out at the still night, at the enormous stars that hung in the autumn sky, and the firefly camp-lights below. But though everyone was reluctant for the evening to end, they did not sit late, for there would be an early start in the morning: the cavalry had to turn out in parade order an hour before dawn every day. So they bid her goodnight, and walked away, their soft voices and laughter receding into the darkness. Cavendish showed Charlotte to the guest-tent, kissed her, told her to sleep as late as she liked, and went away.

Norton was there, laying out the night-things, and big with news, which she had had from Watson on the long ride up from the harbour. The reason that Oliver had been detained at Headquarters all day was that a Turkish spy had come in with news which the Intelligence Department was trying to evaluate. He said that twenty thousand Russian infantry and five thousand cavalry were approaching from the east with the intention of attacking

Balaclava and taking the Yalta road – known locally as the Woronzov road because it led to the country villa built by that same Woronzov who had been Ambassador to the Court of St James and was Sidney Herbert's maternal grandfather.

The news presented Lord Raglan with a difficulty. There had certainly been movements of some kind going on for several days, but the report of an imminent attack was precisely the same as a report three days ago, which had come to nothing. On that occasion Lord Raglan had marched Sir George Cathcart's 4th Division down from the Heights and turned out the cavalry, and they had stood to all day for nothing. The 4th Division had then been marched back up to camp, arriving in a state of exhaustion; and the cavalry had remained on alert all night, with the result that Major Willet of the 17th Lancers had died of exposure.

'So Lord Raglan doesn't want to turn the men out again on a wild goose chase,' Norton concluded. 'There's so many sick that those who are fit are doing double duty, and everyone's worn out, and Sir George Cathcart was furious, they say, over last time, and his men are on trench duty tonight. So his grace and Mr Cathcart and the other intelligence gentlemen have been busy all day questioning all their informants over whether it may be true this time.'

'They seem to have concluded that it wasn't,' Charlotte said. 'There's no alarm been given.'

Norton nodded. 'That Watson said the Turks are terrible liars, my lady, and that they bring in false reports in just for the sake of spending some time in the comforts of the village.'

'Well, I don't know that one can blame them for that,' Charlotte said sleepily. It had been a long and exciting day.

*　　*　　*

The cavalry trumpets woke her with a start, and for a moment she didn't know where she was or what was happening. It was still dark, but there were lights moving about outside, and the sound of eager whickering from the horse lines reminded Charlotte of what Cavendish had told her, that the cavalry had to turn out an hour before dawn. On the other side of the tent Norton was still fast asleep, nothing but a bit of her nightcap showing above the blankets, for it was bitterly cold. The clear evening last night had brought a chilly night. Charlotte slipped out of bed and went to the door to put her head out cautiously. By the moving lights she could see that it was foggy; she could smell it, too, for there was a hint of the sea in it. Dark shapes were moving back and forth, buckets were clanking, the horses were stamping and snorting at the prospect of breakfast, and a smell of wood-smoke and a distant, red flicker showed where the banked fires were being roused. There was no alarm here, only normal morning activity. She shivered and hurried back to bed.

She slept through the sounds of the cavalry riding out to morning parade; but was woken by what sounded like a distant door banging. But there could be no doors in a camp full of tents. She sat up and listened. Yes, there it was again – a heavy, distant boom. Norton stirred and got up on one elbow, peering gummily at her mistress.

'Oh my lady, what was that?'

Charlotte flung back the covers and swung her legs over the edge of the bed. 'I've never heard it before, but I think it must be cannon,' she said.

Norton's eyes widened. 'D'you think it's the Russians?' she whispered, as though they might hear.

'Someone's firing at someone, that's for sure,' Charlotte said. 'We had better get dressed.'

'D'you think we're in danger here, then, my lady?'

'*I* don't know,' Charlotte said, half exasperated by the question. 'But there is a war going on. We have to be ready for anything.'

She dressed in her riding habit, and Norton was preparing to do her hair when a messenger arrived with a letter from Oliver at Headquarters. It was brief and to the point. 'The Russians are attacking Balaclava. Lose no time but come up here as quickly as you can. Don't wait for breakfast.'

Norton's eyes grew enormous as Charlotte read her the note. She might have been down there now, on the *Doris*. 'If the Russkies get through, they'll take the ship and everything – all your clothes, my lady, and the stores and the medical stuff and everything.'

'They won't get through,' Charlotte said. 'You had better plait my hair for quickness' sake. Hurry up, we'll miss everything.' If the Russians did get through, and take Balaclava, she thought, the loss of the *Doris* would be a minor problem.

The road up from the harbour ran through a ravine, rising steeply for about a mile, and debouching at last onto a wide open space, called the plain of Balaclava. It was an area of about three miles by two, almost rectangular, and fenced in all around by steep hills. The surface of the plain was not flat, but broken by hummocks and hillocks, and bisected along its length by a hog's-back ridge, along the top of which ran the Woronzov road. This ridge the British called the Causeway, and it effectively divided the plain into two valleys, which they called the North Valley and the South Valley. To the west, the plain ended in the almost vertical six hundred foot escarpment of the Sapouné Heights, the edge of the plateau before Sebastopol, on which the Headquarters camp was situated. From the edge of this escarpment therefore, it was possible to look down on the plain as onto an amphitheatre, and see clearly right down both valleys.

A half circle of redoubts had been thrown up on the south side of the Causeway, armed with naval guns brought up from British ships, to command the road and give some protection to the approach to Balaclava. It was the Russians firing on these redoubts which had been the sound which woke Charlotte the second time. By the time Charlotte reached the staff group up on the Heights, daylight had come, and it was possible to see the huge Russian force which was advancing in two columns from the north-eastern corner of the North Valley towards the Causeway and the redoubts.

'My God, my God,' Charlotte exclaimed to Oliver, 'there are so many of them!'

'We calculate about eleven thousand,' Oliver said, without removing his glasses from the sight, 'and I count thirty-eight heavy guns. That's about half the force we know was gathered beyond the river. The rest must have swung round and be coming in from the north.'

'And who holds the redoubts?' Charlotte asked.

'Turks. About a thousand altogether.'

'A thousand? But someone must be sent to help them.'

Oliver lowered his glasses. 'It's not possible, my dear. All the infantry is up here on the plateau, in case this movement is a diversionary tactic to draw us off while the Russians make a sortie from Sebastopol. It would take two hours at least to get a division down there. By that time the Russians would have overrun them.'

'But is there no-one down there?' Charlotte asked, watching with fascinated horror the ant-like advance of the grey army.

'There's Sir Colin Campbell's Highlanders, who were

left to hold the road to Balaclava; and the Invalid Battalion, who were on camp duties; and the cavalry and Horse Artillery.'

'And can't they help the Turks?'

'They have to hold Balaclava. If we lose Balaclava, we lose our supply line and our communications,' Oliver said grimly. 'The Turks will just have to do the best they can – poor beggars.'

In the growing daylight, they watched as the Russian infantry and the heavy guns attacked No 1 Redoubt. The Heavy Brigade and the Horse Artillery were making a feint along the Causeway to try to distract the Russians, but this feint was soon halted by heavy fire from the Russian guns, which destroyed a whole troop of Horse Artillery. After some resistance the No 1 Redoubt stopped firing, the Russians scrambled over the ditch, and the little figures of fleeing Turks were seen issuing from the rear and running towards the harbour road. The Russians brought up some field-pieces to No 1 and opened fire on No 2, and the Turks there immediately fled, to be followed almost at once by those from No 3 and No 4. Now only No 5 and No 6, which were well up towards the Heights and therefore useless for the defence of Balaclava, were in British hands. The army's lifeline was in the hands of the five hundred Highlanders of the 93rd, about a hundred Invalids, and the cavalry. While they watched, the Highlanders, formed up across the road to the harbour, managed to hold up some of the fleeing Turks and form them up on the flanks, but how long they would stay there was problematic.

The chilly, foggy morning was brightening; as the sun rose, it sucked up the mist, and soon it shone from a sky of cloudless, deep autumn blue. It was still, perfectly clear, warm but fresh. The green hills and the higher crags in the distance were etched in lovely clarity, laid with shadows of deep indigo, and buzzards wheeled in sweet silence over the ravines. Beyond to the south and west the tranquil sea curved, sparkling, shading from navy-blue to silver on the horizon, dotted with little toy ships. It was such a beautiful day, it did not seem possible that real war was going on down below in the valley. It was like being in a box at the theatre, looking down at the action on a stage with a pretty, painted backdrop. The air was so still that tiny noises carried with miniature clarity: the clink of bits, the clash of swords, the scrape of a hoof on stone. Charlotte heard the red-pantalooned Turks shouting as they scrambled back towards Balaclava, waving their arms in panic. She heard the crisp orders barked at the Highlanders, bright in their scarlet coats and flashing red and white stockings. And she saw, with relief, the cavalry withdraw from the path of the Russians, and take up a position on the Highlanders' left. The day was so clear that she could easily pick out the 11th from the others; those with glasses could pick out individual officers, and were doing so in little cries of interest – 'Ah, there's Lord George Paget!'; 'Look, that's Hercules Morris!'

The rest of the Russian force had now appeared, taking up a position on the Fediukine Heights, the steep hills that closed in the North Valley on its northern side, and positioning its artillery to be able to fire down into it. The main Russian infantry was establishing itself at the far end of the plain behind its heavy artillery; its cavalry, perhaps about four thousand strong, moved in a square block along the North Valley. It now became obvious that this was no diversion from a sortie from Sebastopol, but the real battle. Lord Raglan gave orders for two infantry divisions – the 1st and the 4th – to march down from the Heights to the plain to engage the enemy infantry. Charlotte, seated on her horse just a few yards from Lord Raglan, was able to overhear everything that went on. The galloper who went off with the order was soon back with a message from Sir George Cathcart to the effect that his men had only just come in from the trenches and were too tired to move, and reminding the Chief of the false alarm three days ago. Sir George was evidently in a testy and uncooperative mood. Several more messages had to be exchanged before he reluctantly agreed to move his division.

Meanwhile Raglan was alarmed at the position of the cavalry. Lord Lucan had positioned them quite correctly so as to be able to come to the aid of the Highlanders, and to attack the Russian infantry on its flank as it advanced.

'No, no, not unsupported. What would the Duke say? To attack like that without infantry support – too dangerous,' he muttered. 'What d'ye say, Airey? Can't sacrifice my whole cavalry division at this stage.'

'They could attack the flank and then withdraw, my lord. Harass and confuse the enemy.'

'But if they engage, they will have nowhere to withdraw to. They will be pushed back towards the harbour. They will be trapped. No, no, I cannot lose my cavalry. Adye – an order to Lord Lucan: "Cavalry to take ground to left of second line of Redoubts occupied by Turks."'

Captain Duberley, of the 8th, who was on Head-quarters duty, was sitting to the other side of Charlotte, with his wife, whom he had summoned up to see the battle as Oliver had summoned Charlotte. On hearing this order dictated Mrs Duberley muttered, 'Lucan won't like that. He's wild for action, and every time he offers to attack, Raglan calls him off.'

'He was well-placed this time, too,' Duberley commented. 'Now it is all on Campbell and the Highlanders.' He shook his head. 'Balaclava's lost. Thank God you came up when I sent for you.'

428

'It's murder,' his wife said indignantly. 'Five hundred men, against the whole Russian cavalry?'

'Campbell won't flinch. They'll sell their lives dear, you can depend on it.'

Suddenly a large detachment of the Russian cavalry which was advancing down the North Valley wheeled left, rode over the Causeway and bore down on the 93rd. The Turks who had been formed up on the flanks broke and ran; the Russians cheered, and charged with greater enthusiasm at the Highlanders. It was usual for infantry to receive a cavalry charge formed into squares, as they had at Waterloo – a battle in which, strange to reflect, Sir Colin Campbell had served with great distinction; and here he was, almost forty years later, with the whole defence of the British base in his hands. But whatever the lessons of Waterloo, there was no time to form squares now. The 93rd faced the Russian charge in a line only two men deep.

It had its advantage: every gun would tell. There was a crackle of sparks from along the line, followed an instant later by the rattling sound of the volley. Russians fell, horses veered away, the charge wavered. A second volley: the charge was halted. The thin red streak of Highlanders swayed forward, eager to come to grips, but though the watchers did not hear the command to stand still, they saw the effect. The Highlanders fell back into line, and fired a third perfect broadside of a volley. Such discipline in the face of overwhelming odds, such horribly telling fire, disconcerted the Russians; they wavered, wheeled, and rode back over the Causeway to rejoin the main force in the North Valley.

When the Turks had broken and run, Lord Raglan had despatched another order to Lord Lucan, to send the Heavy Brigade under General Scarlett to the aid of the Highlanders; but because of the time it took a galloper to get from the Heights to the plain below, the attack on the 93rd had been repulsed before the Heavies could reach them. The Dragoon Guards, the Scots Greys and the Inniskillings were still trotting in formation towards Balaclava with the Causeway on their left. Then suddenly the main body of the Russian cavalry came over the Causeway and bore down on them.

From above it was a terrifying sight. The Russian cavalry, numbering about three thousand, was a great swaying mass in grey uniform coats; they had the high ground, and would be charging downhill. The Heavies numbered only five hundred; not only would they have to charge uphill, but the ground over which they must advance was broken, and made further hazardous by the ruins of a vineyard and the remains of the old Light Brigade camp, through which the left wing had to pick its way.

General Scarlett, with unwavering courage, calmly dressed his lines, holding back the centre and right to the pace of the left wing until they were all on clear ground, then fussily dressed his lines again, as if they were on a parade ground back in England and no enemy within a thousand miles. The Russian cavalry, unnerved by this display of *sang froid*, slowed its charge, losing its advantage; seemed, to the watchers above, to be riding more and more slowly the nearer they approached the Heavies, reluctant to engage these horsemen who didn't even have the decency to be afraid. Then the General stuck up his arm, his sword flashing like a semaphore in the sun, and the Heavies charged. The blood-curdling yell of the Inniskillings and the chilling 'moan' of the Greys as they crashed forward stirrup to stirrup rose up to the Heights. The bright speck of colour that was General Scarlett hit the grey front line of the Russians and disappeared, and then the two forces met. The Russians were almost at a standstill when they received the brunt of the charge. The grey mass seemed to cave under the impetus; but still they outnumbered the Heavies by so much that it did not break.

The Heavy Brigade seemed to be swallowed up; but those with glasses cried out a commentary to those without. The British, mad with all the pent-up frustration of their inactivity until now, were hacking and slashing within the body of the Russians, their howling battle cries rising like the roaring of the sea. The body swayed this way and that, heaving like sea; and then it could be seen that the heaving was not all on the spot, but was moving backwards, uphill. The Russians were giving ground. Lord Lucan gave the order for his reserve, who had been almost foaming with frustration, to charge, and with a wild yell they hurtled headlong at the Russians, hitting their right flank and splitting them as axe splits a log. The whole mass of Russian cavalry seemed to burst into splinters as they turned and fled, scattering to save their lives, and a great roar went up, every British voice cheering as one. Charlotte found herself cheering with the rest. Around her the staff were shouting, throwing their hats in the air, clapping their hands. There were tears on many faces; General Canrobert, who had joined Lord Raglan at the escarpment, was weeping with Gallic openness as he shook the hand of everyone within reach and uttered choking congratulations. Even Lord Raglan, famously serene in all circumstances, had to fumble his handkerchief out of his plain blue pocket and blow his nose briskly before he was able to summon a galloper to go down to the plain with the message 'Well done, Scarlett!'

Down below the Heavy Brigade was at a stand, blood-soaked to the shoulders, trembling with reaction, while the officers moved here and there, reforming it into the squadrons which had been broken up by the action. The Russian horse were in full retreat, streaming away up the Causeway and up the valley to the safety of their own guns and infantry.

'Damme, they're getting away,' said someone behind Charlotte. 'Why don't Cardigan get after 'em?'

But down below the Light Brigade, five hundred yards further up the valley from the Heavies, sat its horses, formed up to precision, as it had sat throughout the action, motionless while the Russians fled unmolested.

CHAPTER SEVENTEEN

One evening about a week after Fanny's arrival at Mrs Welland's, the family was sitting in the private parlour, engaged in their separate activities. Mrs Welland was darning stockings, Harriet was mending a sheet, Peter was doing the accounts, and Boy was engaged with the Trojan War and the inexplicable conduct of Achilles. Mrs Welland had furnished Fanny with some sewing to do – shirt-cuffs to turn – but she was not getting on with it very well. The needle was idle in her fingers for long periods, and her eyes were more often fixed on the flames than on her work.

When the clock struck ten, Harriet put aside her sewing and stood up to go and put the kettle on, as she always did, and Mrs Welland laid down the stocking she had just finished and said, 'Fanny, I think we ought to talk a little about what you mean to do.'

Fanny turned from contemplating the fire and said with a sigh, 'I've been thinking about nothing else.'

'I thought so,' Mrs Welland said. She added with a gentle smile, 'If poor Peter depended on you for his shirts, he would go about the city bare-backed.'

'Mother!' Peter protested, flushing a little.

'I'm sorry,' Fanny said. 'I ought to be doing more to pay you for my keep.'

'Nonsense, Fanny dear. You had a dreadful experience, and you need time to get your strength back. I don't mean

433

to suggest that you're anything other than welcome here, and for as long as you like.'

'But I can't live on your charity. It's very wrong of me,' Fanny said with a worried frown. 'The difficulty is, I don't know what to do.'

'Don't you think the best thing would be for you to go back home?'

'I have no home,' Fanny said.

'*This* is your home,' Peter interrupted quickly. 'Isn't it, Mother? Tell Fanny she must look on this as her home now.'

Mrs Welland turned to look at him. 'I don't think you ought to answer for Fanny on such a serious subject. Fanny, have you thought of what you are risking? Of what you would be giving up? Home, fortune, your child – your position in society. You shouldn't part with them lightly, for once gone, you can never have them back.'

'Fanny hasn't done it lightly – how can you think so, when you remember what she's suffered,' Peter said indignantly.

'Peter,' Mrs Welland warned, but Fanny interrupted. 'It's quite all right, Peter knows my mind is made up. It was made up before ever I came here. I have thought about it from every possible angle, and there is nothing in the world that would make me go back into that prison.'

'But my dear, even if it was as bad as you say, don't you think Doctor Anthony will have – I can't say exactly "learned his lesson", but don't you think he would be kinder to you, after the shock of having lost you?'

Fanny shuddered. 'You don't know him as I know him. If he once got me back, he would make doubly sure I never escaped again. He wouldn't think of it as punishing me, of course – but he'd punish me just the same, and call it protecting me from myself, or something of the sort. People like him can always find excuses in morality and religion for doing bad things to other people.'

Mrs Welland was distressed. 'But he isn't like that, Fanny. I couldn't have been so deceived in him for so long. Recollect he lived here, in this house. I was daily witness to the good work he did, in the most difficult circumstances – works of pity and kindness to the poor.'

'Perhaps to *them* he is all you think, but to a wife—' Fanny paused, trying to find moderate words that would not alienate Mrs Welland. 'Perhaps there are just some people who should never marry.'

There was a silence, until Harriet came back in with the tea-tray. Then, while her daughter was setting the things out, Mrs Welland said quietly, 'At all events, you must tell him that you are safe.'

'No,' said Fanny quickly, and her look of alarm was unstudied.

'You may think he doesn't care for you, but he must be dreadfully worried. And Fanny, think of your poor aunt, and your step-father, and all the rest of your family.'

Fanny looked stricken. 'Yes, I do think of them. Henry and Aunt Rosamund and Charlotte. I hate to think of them worrying. But I must keep hidden.'

Peter spoke. 'I understand why you don't want to write to Doctor Anthony, but why not a note to Charlotte? No, listen to me – you needn't put the direction on the letter. Just a note to her to say that you are alive and well, and in a safe place, and wishing to remain hidden. She can relay that information to your husband if she thinks fit, but she will have no way of knowing where the letter came from.'

Fanny was still doubtful, but Mrs Welland persuaded

her at last. 'It is the very least you should do, in kindness to those who love you.'

The tea was poured and handed, and Harriet resumed her place.

'All very well,' she said, 'but what *is* Fanny to do?'

'Stay here,' Peter said quickly.

'But for the future. When she is strong again,' Harriet said. She looked at Fanny appraisingly. 'She will want something to do.'

'Oh, there's no difficulty about that,' Peter said airily, but his eyes directed towards his mother were anxious. 'There's always more to do here than people to do it, you've said so yourself, Mother. How often have you complained that you can't keep up with all the work? Fanny can help in the house in return for her board and keep – can't you, Fanny?'

'I'd be willing to do anything, if I could stay,' she said, looking from face to face doubtfully, afraid of being turned out. The world outside seemed to her uniformly hostile, divided into the back-streets where she might be raped, and the thoroughfares where Philip Anthony might see her and recapture her.

'There you are, Mother. Another pair of hands to sew and darn and make beds and help in the kitchen. Why, in a week or two, you won't know how you ever managed before she came.'

Mrs Welland's sharp eyes drew a great deal of information from the quick glance that scanned the faces around her. Fanny was terrified of being turned away. Peter was falling in love with her. Harriet doubted Fanny would ever be much use about the house. Boy was wondering if he would ever have his own room back. There was a great deal to be considered, but Fanny's fear had the first call on her heart. She lowered her eyes and said serenely, 'I'm sure you're right, Peter dear. And of course Fanny must stay. But you will send a note to Charlotte, won't you, Fanny – as Peter suggested?'

'I'll help her write it,' Peter said eagerly. 'And it can be sent tomorrow, and then you don't need to think about it ever again, Fanny, if you don't want to.'

'Thank you,' Fanny said, and her profound relief was in the two short words. She drank her tea slowly, and when she put the cup aside, she did not pick up her work again, but sat with her hands in her lap, looking into the fire. Harriet noted this as she reached for another sheet from the work-box, and shook her head a little. Fanny, she thought, was not going to save anyone much work that way.

By the time Jemima and John returned from their wedding-trip, Aglaea had become Mrs Underwood and departed on hers. A letter was waiting for Jemima when she got back, explaining that with due regard for their great age, Aglaea and Mr Underwood had decided to marry very quietly, with just two witnesses and no parade of any sort, and that Aglaea knew Jemima would understand and forgive her for not waiting until she got back to tie the knot. Jemima did understand, but she was disappointed. Weddings ought to be joyous occasions, shared with the people who loved you, and there seemed something a little pinched and unsatisfactory about the thought of two people walking to the church and making their vows to no-one but the clerk and the spiders.

'You've changed your tune, Mrs Anstey,' John said, amused. 'When I married you in front of the whole Anstey clan and its various septs, you cried down the hullabaloo and were adamant that the best way to get married was to have no-one there at all.'

She smiled at him indulgently. 'But what did I know

437

about marriage then, my dear Mr Anstey? I was as ignorant as a green girl.'

'You looked a little like Anne Boleyn on her way to the block, I must say,' John noted. 'Made me feel shocking guilty.'

'Have I made it up to you now?' she asked, stepping closer.

'Have *I* made it up to *you*, is more the question,' he said.

She turned her face up to him. 'How can you even ask?'

She had gone through the first week of her honeymoon in a state of benign shock. That there could be such kindness in a voice, such gentle care in a pair of hands, such deep pleasure in touching – most of all, that she could feel so utterly *safe*, had been such a revelation to her that she wondered how the afterlife was going to be able to compete. John's presence seemed to wrap her round, even when she was not immediately in his sight. She felt as if she had formerly been alone and naked and shivering on a storm-blasted plain, and suddenly found herself transported into a cosy firelit parlour. The bliss of being safe and loved had only one drawback, the fear of waking to discover it had all been a dream. That troubled her very much at first; but every time she did wake, there was John close beside her, ready to prove to her that it was no dream, but reality – and finding great satisfaction, it seemed, in the proving.

The physical thing was nothing like she had expected or feared. As John had promised her, it soon came to seem quite natural, so that she no longer associated it with anything she had heard or had hinted at. It became a private thing between her and her husband quite unconnected with what anyone else might or might not be doing. She liked it because it was a way of demonstrating her love for him, his for her; and there was a power in it – great enough, after all, to create life itself. But best of all she liked lying in his arms in the dark and talking. They spent many hours like that. It felt so safe, she believed she could say anything she wanted, that he would never disapprove or misunderstand. 'If we ever quarrel,' she said once, 'we must go to bed like this at once. We could never stay at outs with each other like this.'

'Why should we ever quarrel?' John said.

'People do.'

'Not us,' he said with confidence.

She enjoyed her honeymoon very much, enjoyed the experience of doing things with someone who was not only her husband but her best friend and the companion, given the whole world to choose from, of her choice. Aunt Aglaea had not been much of a companion – there in body but rarely in spirit. Jemima had never understood what went on in Aglaea's mind, and she realised anew how lonely she had been, and how silent her life. It took a little while to break down the barriers of habitual silence, and at first John had to solicit her opinions, for it did not occur to her to give them unrequested. But she was not dour by nature, and her true self bloomed under the warmth of his interest. By the time they returned to York, she was almost ready to be an Anstey.

John had rented a house in Clifton, not far from her childhood home, and there they removed with the three children. They were a little shy of Jemima at first; and when the shyness wore off, they went to the other extreme and grew bumptious; but the adjustment was made after a few weeks and they settled down to be snug and happy. John had reasoned that Jemima would find her new state less unnerving if she had plenty to do, so although his allowance from the family firm was

439

generous, and Jemima's fortune was considerable, he arranged that they should live in a small way, without too many servants. Two nurses, a cook-housekeeper, a man, and a housemaid were all they started off with, and running the house and overseeing the children, together with making and receiving the expected visits, gave the new Mrs Anstey no moment to worry about anything.

Harry and Celia paid an early visit, and with them they discussed the extraordinary events at Morland Place.

'The whole thing is so hasty, so sudden,' Celia said. 'I can't understand it. I do hope—' She could not say, I do hope there's nothing wrong about it, but the thought was in the air.

'Oh, I'm sure it's a love-match,' Harry said quickly, to cover his wife's near-solecism.

'But how could Mary be in love with a man she's only met once, and years ago?' Celia said.

'Only two years,' John pointed out.

'But she was a child then. And besides, why must she be marrying a foreigner and going quite away out of England, when there are plenty of men in Yorkshire she could have married? I don't think,' she added with all the feeling of a disappointed mother, 'that Mr Fenwick Morland, agreeable as he is, ought to have preference over young men that Mary has known all her life.'

Harry met John's eyes, and they exchanged an amused look. 'But Aunt Celia, plainly Mary didn't fancy Arthur, and that's all there is to it.'

'I wasn't thinking particularly of Arthur,' Celia said with dignity.

'No, but it does seem strange,' Jemima said, coming to her rescue. 'Uncle Ben was always so devoted to Mary, and then suddenly he's sending her off right round the world with a man who's almost a stranger. What do you think of it, Uncle Harry?'

'It may seem odd,' Harry said, 'but I believe both Mary and the young man are very much in love, and when attachment of that sort comes into it, there's nothing more to wonder at.' He felt, on the contrary, that there was a great deal to wonder at. Benedict's attachment to Mary was of such an order, and Mary's abilities were so remarkable, that Harry had believed he would make her heiress to Morland Place after all. As Benedict's man of business, Harry knew the secret of Mary's birth, and appreciated Bendy's dilemma; but equally he knew that Morland Place was Bendy's to do with as he pleased. Yet Bendy had not only consented to the marriage, he had made a settlement on her that Harry thought was on the thin side of generous. Of course, it was always difficult to realise assets, and in a case like this they would have to be portable for Fenwick to be able to take them across the Atlantic. And Harry had been present when Fenwick protested that he would take Mary with nothing, he loved her so much. But Harry couldn't help the feeling that Mary had been little short of 'cut off with a shilling', and he didn't understand why; for Benedict was obviously as attached to his daughter as ever, and as miserable as possible to be parting with her.

Two theories were widely canvassed, though in guarded terms, amongst those not close to the Morlands: one, that Mary Morland had *had* to get married; and two, that Sibella was jealous for her own children and wanted to be rid of her predecessor's daughter. Neither made sense, though, to anyone who knew the protagonists. All Harry could say for public consumption was that it was a love-match.

The wedding duly took place in the chapel at Morland Place, and given the speed with which it was got up, it did everyone credit. It was confined to close friends and family, and absences made it a very intimate affair.

Jemima and John and Harry and Celia were there, but Aglaea was in Paris, Charlotte and Cavendish in the Crimea, and poor Fanny, of course, was missing. But Tom and Emily came down on the train from London, bringing with them their strange little protégé, the rescued climbing-boy, whom Tom said apologetically they couldn't leave at home. The child seemed very much in awe, and clung to Emily as though she were the only thing that attached him to the world. He was still afraid, when presented with any strange new circumstances, that they were a precursor to his being taken back to his old life. But after six months the memory of Mr Figgis's establishment was fading, and after a while he consented to go and play with Georgie and Teddy and John Anstey's boys. When Tom looked in half an hour later to make sure Tommy was not being teased, he found them all playing railway trains together, with Tommy very much in charge, and regarded even by Georgie as the expert among them, on account of his having just made the whole journey down from London, something none of the others had ever done.

The wedding was simple and very affecting. Mary looked beautiful as an angel in white satin with a wreath of myrtle and white silk roses round her head, and Fenwick's locket round her neck. She and Fenwick looked at each other with such adoration that anyone who had come with doubts left them there. Father Moineau spoke the words of the service in an unsteady voice, and had to stop several times to compose himself. In some ways the parting was hardest for him. He and Mary had shared a deep and tender relationship, and he was an old man: once she went to America it was unlikely he would ever see her again, and they both knew it. The old priest had been in tears most days, walking about with a handkerchief always in his hand, constantly wiping and wiping at his eyes. They had spent long hours locked away together, talking; neither would ever say about what. He had even contemplated asking her if he could come with her, though he knew really it was impossible, even if Fenwick had agreed. But Mary was the last love of his life, and the parting from her was very sharp, as sharp as a killing frost.

By a miracle of endeavour, all the arrangements had been completed before the wedding day; the young couple were to set off for Liverpool on the following morning. Benedict was to accompany them to the boat; Sibella knew he had to have his last moment with her alone, and hoped that Fenwick realised it too. There would be tears the next morning, but everyone was determined to be happy on Mary's wedding day, and there was much laughter at the wedding breakfast, and music afterwards.

'After all, we're not parting for ever,' Mary reasoned as she and her father walked round the drawing-room arm in arm for a moment of private conversation. 'These days it takes hardly any time to cross the Atlantic. I shall come back. *We'll* come back – often I hope. And you must come to us. Fenwick will want your advice about the horses.'

'Yes, I must see this other Twelvetrees,' Benedict said. 'It must be quite a place. I envy you your adventure, Mary. You're not afraid?'

'No, why should I be afraid?' she said innocently.

'Oh, of everything being new and strange, that's all I meant.'

'No, I'm not afraid, just excited. It's going to be so wonderful! A new land, Papa, a whole new land. A vast new land, with everything still to do, no rules, no restrictions – soft clay to be moulded to whatever *we* want it to be.'

'There are always rules, my love,' Benedict cautioned. 'I wouldn't want you to be disappointed.'

'Yes, but not petty, silly ones. Everything in America is on a grander scale.'

'You are an expert already,' he laughed at her.

'I shall be soon,' she said.

He was suddenly sober. 'Write to me,' he said. 'Write often.'

'Yes, I will. And you will write to me?'

'Of course.'

'I shall miss you all so much, Papa, and Morland Place and everything.' Her eyes were suddenly too bright.

'I shall miss you,' he said. 'I love you so much, my Mary. I wish—'

'Yes, Papa?'

'Oh, nothing. You're marrying the man you love, and that's the best solution all round.' And then he changed the subject. Nothing must spoil her wedding day.

In the afternoon a professional photographer arrived to take portraits of the young couple. It had been arranged by Tom, and Benedict was struck by the thoughtfulness, and wondered that it had not occurred to him to arrange something of the sort; but his emotions had been in too much turmoil to think of such details. The photographer took a portrait of the young couple alone, and then of the couple with the bride's parents, and one of the whole wedding-party, carefully arranged in rows, some standing, some sitting on sofas and chairs brought out for the purpose. It was fortunately a dry, bright day, and the Long Walk seemed a very suitable place to take the likenesses, with the walls of Morland Place in the background. When his girl was gone, Benedict was going to be very glad of those photographs.

And then, when everyone else was going back indoors, Benedict asked the photographer for one more portrait, of him alone with Mary. It was thus that he wanted to remember her, not on Fenwick's arm.

Paris was enjoying fine weather, too, and Mr Underwood was enjoying it in the company of his sister and looking at the shops. Aglaea was in the Louvre, making sketches of some or other famous painting – he didn't know which. He had never realised there were so many galleries and museums in Paris – altogether too many for comfort. He was an educated man, a cultured man, but his feet and his head had had enough of walking round and looking at things. Aglaea seemed to need to visit every one, and stand looking for an inordinate time at every picture; and when she had exhausted looking at them, she went back and copied details from them. He was beginning to realise what he had only glimpsed dimly before, that the artist had a different way of looking at things from the ordinary mortal; and that genius took up an awful lot of a person's time.

He had been touched when she insisted that Mrs Pownall should come with them on their wedding trip; but he began to think now that she had done it deliberately to provide him with a companion while she was busy; and the drawback to that was that it had meant she knew beforehand that she would be busy, and that she would not want him hanging on her sleeve while she was. That suggested to a man in love not only an unseemly degree of calculation, but a detachment of mind that did not square with unfettered passion.

Mrs Pownall had enjoyed the trip enormously so far. She had never been abroad before, and everything about the trip, from the trains to the French chambermaids, thrilled her. And she had another cause for pleasure. She had supposed when Frederick married Mrs Morland that she would be pushed from the centre of his world to the

445

far rim, and might even slip off altogether; but on the contrary, Mrs Morland seemed not to want to disturb the *status quo* at all, and now here she was enjoying a holiday in Paris with her dear brother on such terms that there might almost never have been a marriage at all.

'Oh, Frederick, only look at that darling hat! But look at the price! How can they think of charging so much?' Mr Underwood explained, not for the first time, that it was priced in the local currency, and translated for her. 'Oh, but that is not so very much after all!' she exclaimed. 'Why in the world would they want to make it seem more, by putting those silly what-you-may-calls on the ticket? If they put it in guineas, they would sell it right off.'

Mr Underwood explained again, patiently, that the majority of people in France habitually calculated prices in what-you-may-calls, and were also so lost to all common sense that they habitually spoke and even thought in French. Mrs Pownall thought it was very silly. 'English does very well for us,' she said dismissively, 'so what should they want more?'

Next week they were to go to Florence, Mr Underwood thought, as Mrs Pownall pondered over the hat and wondered if she – or rather her brother – could afford it. There were an awful lot of paintings in Florence, so he understood, galleries and churches full of them. And more shops, and people not speaking English. His only hope was that Italy would prove irresistibly romantic to Mrs Underwood. So far, she hadn't seemed to anticipate any physical approach from her new husband, and he was too diffident to be able to force himself on her without some encouragement, however passive. A complacent look would have been enough for his love, but Mrs Underwood's looks, when they rested on him at all, were as vague as when she looked at the food on her plate. Only when a painting was in front of her eyes, he thought wistfully, did she seem really to be seeing what she saw.

There had been discontent amongst the cavalry ever since they landed at Calamita Bay, where despite perfect riding country they had not been allowed to go out scouting. At the Alma they been forbidden to pursue the fleeing Russians; and since arriving at Balaclava they had had nothing to do at all. Lord Raglan's statement that he meant to keep the cavalry in a band-box had been repeated often, passed from trooper to trooper, and like a rose thorn was working deeper into the flesh day by day. Raglan's problem had been from the beginning that his cavalry force was very small, the horses were in poor condition, and there was little or no chance of reinforcements being sent. He meant, therefore, to use it carefully, and not risk it until the last resort. The difficulty with such a plan was that it was hard to know when the last resort arrived: in any dire situation it was always possible that an even worse emergency was yet to come.

The more intelligent officers appreciated the problem, but even they did not feel happy about it. It was well known that Lord Cardigan blamed Lord Lucan for the inactivity of his Light Brigade, and felt nothing but contempt for him; it was equally well known that Lord Lucan blamed Lord Raglan in just the same way. The brothers-in-law did not speak to each other unless it was absolutely necessary, but they had independently come to the same decision: each determined he would obey the orders of his immediate superior to the letter, just to spite him. Believing that he, the superior, was profoundly and stubbornly wrong-headed, they would carry out orders and let the inevitable consequences fall where they were deserved.

447

So when the Heavy Brigade attacked the Russian cavalry only five hundred yards away from where the Light Cavalry had been sent for safety, Lord Cardigan sat tight. He had been told to keep out of the way and keep safe; until he had direct orders to do otherwise, he would continue as he was. The troopers and the junior officers fretted and seethed, and even Cardigan was heard to mutter discontentedly that 'the Heavies would have the laugh of them' that day. And when the Heavy Brigade sent the Russians fleeing, the sight of those retreating tails was too much for Captain Morris of the 17th Lancers. Since the death of Major Willet he was in command of the regiment; and as both an experienced 'Indian' officer and a friend of Captain Nolan, he considered himself a far greater expert on cavalry action than anyone in authority. He rode up to Lord Cardigan, and said, 'My lord, are you not going to charge the flying enemy?'

It was a question sure to irritate the earl. 'No,' he snapped. 'Our orders are to remain here, on this spot.'

'But my lord,' Morris urged, 'it's our positive duty to follow up this advantage. Do allow me to charge them with the 17th! See, my lord, the enemy is in disorder!'

'No, no, no, sir!' Cardigan barked. 'We must not stir from here! Those are our orders!'

Morris wheeled his horse with a sharp movement of anger; his eyes met those of the nearest officers, Cavendish amongst them. 'You are all witness to my request,' Morris said, and kicking his horse into a canter, he rode back to the 17th. Cavendish saw him thumping his fist against his thigh in fury, and was torn between anger at his rudeness and un-officerlike conduct, and sympathy with his frustration. They had been at their horses' heads since before dawn, and all they had done was to move from one position to another and look on, while others took action and won glory. And now the enemy was out of sight, and the action seemed to have ceased. The view from here was limited by the various hillocks, and the ridge of the Causeway: the only soldiers of any sort in sight were the Heavies, formed up a little further off, with Lord Lucan at their head.

The sun shone down, the shadows shortened, the horses dozed, cocking one hind foot and then the other. Troopers leaned against the saddles chatting in low voices across the horses' backs, smoking their short clay pipes. Officers ate biscuits and apples and hard-boiled eggs; some lit cigars, and the fragrance of the smoke tickled on the clear air. Lord Cardigan sat erect and utterly unmoving on his favourite chestnut Ronald, as if he had learned to sleep with his eyes open. Ronald sighed and lowered his thick ginger eyelashes, and dozed too, his ears sliding slowly to the horizontal, and his drooping underlip trembling with each slow exhalation.

Up on the Heights, the watchers could see the tactical position, a privilege denied to those down in the valley. The Russians had plainly been greatly unnerved by the ferocity of the British and had withdrawn right up the North Valley. They had a battery of guns across the top of this valley, and the cavalry withdrew behind the battery, with the mass of infantry formed up to the rear. They had artillery ranged along the Fediukine Heights with infantry behind them, and they still held the Causeway and the redoubts abandoned by the Turks.

Oliver, joining Charlotte, said, 'This would be a good moment to counter-attack and retake the redoubts. You see how the Russians holding them are in a weak position, separated from the main army. If we attacked, they'd have to run, or be cut off.'

'If we had the causeway, we could fire down on the main army.'

449

'Just so. I see you have a military mind,' Oliver smiled.

'Will Lord Raglan order an attack?'

Oliver glanced over his shoulder to where Raglan was conferring with Airey and General Estcourt, turning frequently to sweep the valley with his glasses, frowning a little, which was not like him. Usually his face was set in a pleasant, calm half-smile. 'I think he would like to,' Oliver said quietly to Charlotte, 'but he hasn't the wherewithal. He ordered two divisions down to the plain two hours ago, but Cathcart thinks he's being put upon and refuses to hurry. I've never seen the Chief so ruffled. Ah,' he added a moment later, 'something's happening.' Raglan called him over, and after a brief consultation he returned to say, 'Raglan's sending a galloper down to Lucan to tell him to retake the redoubts if possible, with infantry support – when it arrives.'

'Does that mean the Light Brigade as well?' Charlotte asked casually.

Oliver was not fooled. 'Raglan thinks the Russians are so disheartened they will give up and run without returning fire if we charge fiercely enough,' he said comfortingly. 'I agree with him. The Russian system of society encourages yielding in its lowest orders, not defiance.'

They watched the galloper picking his way down the steep path from the Heights, disappearing from time to time behind outcrops and stunted trees and reappearing further down. They watched Lord Lucan receive the order, and then move the two forces of cavalry, sending the Light Brigade to a position at the end of the North Valley, and drawing up the Heavy Brigade on the slopes of the Woronzov road at the head of the South Valley. And then all movement ceased.

Half an hour passed, and there was no movement

below. Muttered comments ran up and down the groups watching from the Heights like little grumbles of thunder. 'Why don't he move?' 'What the deuce is Lucan playing at?' 'There goes our advantage.' 'Dammit, the Russkies will be recovering their nerve at this rate.'

'I suppose he's waiting for infantry support,' Oliver said. 'Raglan should have been more specific if he wanted Lucan to attack immediately. His last order was too diffident – Lucan wants absolutes.'

Another ten minutes passed, and then Airey was heard drawing attention to some movement he had seen through his glasses. Comment rippled along the line. Oliver had left her again, and Charlotte was indebted to Captain Duberley for the information, that the Russians holding the redoubts seemed to have decided their position was untenable, and were preparing to retreat; but they had got out rope tackle, and were plainly meaning to take the guns with them.

'The Chief can't allow that,' Duberley said. 'Captured guns are a proof of victory. If they take those back to Sebastopol, the Russkies'll say they licked us, and that will give them all heart. No, no, he must stop them taking the guns, at all costs.'

Charlotte edged closer to the staff group to listen. Evidently Lord Raglan agreed with Duberley's assessment. 'Can't let 'em have the guns, Airey,' he was saying. 'British naval guns – what a prize! Lucan must get after 'em. Take this down, will you.' Airey took up his order pad again, and leaning against his horse, scribbled away in pencil. '"Lord Raglan wishes the cavalry to advance rapidly to the front – follow the enemy and try to prevent the enemy carrying away the guns. Troop horse artillery may accompany. French cavalry is on your left." Oh, and add, "Immediate." Read it back, Airey, that's a good fellow.'

Airey repeated it aloud, Raglan nodded and said 'That'll do', and Airey turned and handed the order to Captain Leslie, the next galloper in line. But before Leslie could turn away, Captain Nolan, who had been standing at Airey's elbow, stepped forward and addressed Lord Raglan urgently. The word 'immediate' had had its effect on Nolan. If the cavalry was at last being sent into action, he wanted his part in it.

'My lord, my lord, let me go! You know I'm the best horseman in the whole of the Crimea: I can make better speed down the escarpment than anyone! Leslie is a good fellow, but speed is of the essence. You must let me go, my lord!'

Raglan blinked at his vehemence. 'Eh? What? Oh, yes, very well, then, Nolan, if you wish. But make haste, make haste.'

Nolan snatched the message from Leslie's hand, his moustaches bristling with eagerness, and flung himself into the saddle.

'Captain Nolan, tell Lord Lucan the cavalry is to attack *immediately*,' Raglan called to him anxiously. Nolan saluted, jammed his feet into the stirrups, wrenched his horse's head round, and plunged over the edge of the precipice.

Probably every cavalryman in the valley below watched the tiny figure of the horseman making its way down the six-hundred-foot escarpment. The track was rough, precipitous, crumbling, and other gallopers had picked their way carefully. But this one was coming down like a madman, slithering and scrambling, the horse keeping its balance by some miracle, perhaps because its feet were never touching the ground for more than a second – safe by virtue of its impetus alone. If it had tried to stop and stand, it would probably have slipped or toppled over the edge.

'What's that madman up to? He's going to kill himself,' Lord Desford said to Cavendish.

'Something must be up,' Cavendish said.

'Urgent orders by the look of it. Perhaps we're going to see some action after all.'

'Not us,' Cavendish said sourly. 'That galloper's getting more action than we'll see today.'

'Good God!' Desford cried as the horse seemed to hang in the air for a moment, before finding a foothold and scraping round a rock. 'Breathe again, boys. I tell you what, I'll lay you odds that's Lewis Nolan. The man's quite insane. I wouldn't be his horse for the hope of heaven. By God, though, that madman can ride!'

The tiny figure reached the bottom, and galloped furiously across the plain towards Lord Lucan, sitting his horse between the two brigades. Nolan reined his horse so hard, the creature almost fell. It stood trembling and blowing from the violent descent, while Lucan read the order carefully, and then looked up, and looked all around, in evident perplexity. He was surrounded on all sides by hills, and there was nothing in sight anywhere but British cavalry. Then he read the order again.

'Stuff and nonsense,' he pronounced at last. 'Cavalry to attack artillery? Perfectly useless! It would achieve nothing. There's no mention here of infantry support. Cavalry without infantry cannot attack artillery. Ridiculous! Why, such a thing—'

Nolan's moustaches bristled, his eyes sparkled. In the various messes he graced with his presence he had pronounced over and over again that the cavalry could do anything, and that with a determined enough charge they could carry even artillery, with no need for the plodding infantry to help. His head went up to its most imperious angle and he cut Lord Lucan short.

'Lord Raglan's orders are that the cavalry are to attack immediately. *Immediately*, my lord!'

Lucan's face darkened at the insolence. 'Attack? Attack *what*, sir?' he said angrily. 'What guns, sir?'

Nolan gave him a look of utmost contempt, and flung out an arm, pointing towards the North Valley. 'There, my lord, is your enemy, and there are your guns.' And he continued to stare steadily at Lucan, as though daring his pusillanimity to object further.

But Lucan merely turned his back on him. He re-read the order carefully, and then shrugged. He had decided on a policy of obeying every order to the letter; and in any case, Queen's Regulations gave him no choice. He rode over to Lord Cardigan. From this position he could see the Russian batteries drawn up across the top of the North Valley, with their cavalry behind them. *Advance to the front* – well, there was the front all right. *French cavalry is on your left* – yes there were the Chasseurs d'Afrique formed up to the Light Brigade's left, on the slopes of the Fediukine Heights. There could be no mistake: this was what Raglan wanted. But it was madness, all the same.

Cavendish, watching Lucan's approach, saw Nolan turn and follow him, and ride to the ranks of the 17th Lancers, where he joined his friend Morris. The two got their heads together at once in excited conversation.

'Now what's to do?' Desford muttered to Cavendish. 'It looked as though that blackguard Nolan was insulting Lucan as usual. I don't know why Lucan don't have him put on a charge.'

'Maybe it is orders for us at last,' Cavendish said. 'But it don't look as though the Old Man liked it much.'

The brothers-in-law were now facing each other and conversing with perfect, if icy, courtesy. Lucan showed

Cardigan the piece of paper, and said, 'Your orders are to advance down the valley with the Light Brigade. I will bring the Heavy Brigade up behind in support.'

Cardigan's pale and popping eyes seemed to bulge even further. He looked past Lucan's shoulder at the Russian line, cleared his throat and barked, 'Certainly, sir. But allow me to point out to you that the Russians have a battery in the valley on our front, and batteries and riflemen on each side.'

Lucan's face quivered slightly in acknowledgement. It was perhaps the closest the two had been in sympathy in many years. 'I know it, sir,' he said heavily. And then he shrugged again. 'But Lord Raglan will have it. We have no choice but to obey.'

Cardigan saluted, his face rigid. Cavendish felt a sick hollow where his stomach ought to have been. He had longed for a cavalry charge, for glory and honour – but this? The valley was long and empty, narrow, steep-sided, like a coffin; and across the end the Russian cannon bristled like teeth. It was insane. It was certain death. Would no-one object? Would no-one speak out with the voice of sanity? But Cardigan was listening to the details of Lucan's dispositions with grave courtesy, nodding silently; then he saluted again and rode across to Lord George Paget, his second in command.

'We are ordered to make an attack to the front,' he said. 'We'll draw up in two lines. You will take command of the second line, and I expect your best support – your best support, mind!'

'You shall have it, my lord,' Lord George replied, but the astonishment was audible in his voice.

Cardigan turned away to order the formation, and Cavendish heard him say in a clear undertone, 'Well, here goes the last of the Brudenells!' And he just had time to think of little William at home, and be glad that he did not have to say of himself, here goes the last of the Farralines.

CHAPTER EIGHTEEN

From the Heights the observers watched the Light Brigade form up in two beautifully dressed lines: the 13th Light Dragoons and 17th Lancers in the first line, the 4th Dragoons and 11th Hussars in the rear, with the 8th Hussars held back as reserve. Lord Cardigan rode out alone in front of his staff, who were out in front of the first line, and in this position of solitary splendour raised his sword and gave the order. In the silence of noon, the trumpet, tiny and far away, sounded the 'walk, march, trot', and the lines of horses moved forward. The Light Brigade was under-strength, from cholera and dysentery, and numbered a little under seven hundred men. The small body of horsemen moved forward in lovely precision, the brilliantly coloured uniforms and gold lace made brighter by the sun, the clinking of bits and ringing of horseshoes on stone heard quite clearly in the stillness of the day.

Charlotte watched, trying to be glad for Cavendish's sake that he was going into action, glad for her own that he was in the second line, which surely must be safer. And Oliver had said that the Russians would not stand a charge, if it was forceful enough; and whatever Cardigan's failings, he was very brave, and would not falter. She had hunted with him, and knew that he went over everything in front of him without flinching.

The Heavy Brigade was moving off now, a few minutes behind the Lights. After the first fifty yards had been covered, the Russian battery at the end of the valley opened fire with a tremendous crash which made all the horses on the Heights throw up their heads and shift their feet. Clouds of smoke billowed up, but the range was too long to expect any effect. And at any moment now the Brigade would right-wheel and head up the Causeway towards the redoubts. Oliver, watching through glasses, nudged Charlotte and pointed, and then relinquished the glasses to her.

'Look at No 3 Redoubt.'

Charlotte looked. The Russians, seeing they were soon to be under attack, had decided to cleave to the better part of valour, and were already running out of the redoubt, heading towards the safety of their own lines. Yes, and there, too, from No 2, the little figures were scrambling away. She felt relieved for herself that there would be no resistance, but hoped that Cavendish would still get enough of a charge to satisfy him.

Then Oliver gave an exclamation. 'What the deuce is that madman doing? Give me the glasses, quickly.'

She handed them over, and saw what he was looking at – one of the riders in the front rank had galloped out of line, and was now riding across and in front of Lord Cardigan, waving his sword and shouting. With the aid of the glasses Oliver could identify him. 'It's that madman Nolan. Now what's to do? I suppose the pace isn't fast enough for him. He wants to charge at full gallop. But the – oh, good God!' A Russian shell exploded to the right of Lord Cardigan in a spray of earth, and presumably a fragment of something more lethal than earth had hit Nolan. Through the glasses Oliver saw the gold frogging on the rider's chest disintegrate into scarlet. The horse wheeled and dashed back through the ranks towards the rear, the rider staying somehow upright in the saddle until it passed the last of the advancing 8th Hussars. Then the horse skidded to a halt, and the body tumbled to the ground like a sack.

Oliver lowered his glasses. 'The first casualty. Poor devil,' he said briefly. 'And there ends all his vaunted cavalry expertise.'

The murmur of comment on the incident died away, and in silence they watched, waiting for the Light Brigade to right-wheel over the Causeway. But it didn't wheel. In beautiful order, at a steady trot, it headed straight along the valley; past the last moment when wheeling was possible, past the last moment when it was possible to doubt what they were going to do.

'What the—!' someone said.

'They're not turning!'

'What's Cardigan playing at?'

'My God, my God, they're going straight at the guns!'

'It's madness! They'll all be killed!'

Charlotte turned to Oliver, her eyes huge. 'Stop them, can't somebody stop them?' He only shook his head slightly. She knew the answer as well as he did. Even Nolan, were he still alive, could not have got down from the Heights and caught up with them in time. A cold sickness filled her. Cavendish was going to die. Her brother. 'Why?' she asked at last, of no-one in particular. 'Why are they doing it?'

Oliver shook his head again, the glasses hanging from his hand. He didn't want to see any more individuals torn up by shells. He didn't want to see Charlotte's brother killed.

After Nolan's death, just at first it wasn't so bad. The guns at the end of the valley ceased firing, perhaps deciding the range was too great; and the Russians up on the Causeway and the Fediukine Heights did not at once open fire, possibly so surprised at the Light Brigade's suicidal action that they could not believe their eyes. Cavendish discovered that fear did not grind in the gut so badly when one was surrounded by other men, and when one had to set an example of unflinchingness. Good old Cardigan, right out in front of them, and far more exposed than any of them, was riding as though on a parade ground, his back straight as a wand. He might be an ass, Cavendish thought, but there was no doubt of his courage. And the horses gave one confidence: they didn't mind where they were going, as long as they all went together.

And then it started. First from the Fediukine Hills, with a mighty crash, and then from the other side, from the Causeway, with a lesser crash and a sputtering noise, the batteries opened fire, and the riflemen opened fire, and shot and shell poured down on the Light Brigade. Cardigan did not flinch, trotting on at the same speed, while smoke billowed and fragments pinged and whined about his head. Cavendish thought, why can't we gallop? Why can't we get it over with? He felt all around him a similar, unspoken urgency, and the horses felt it, too, and their heads went up, and they jostled a little, wanting to break into a canter. Now a squadron of the 17th was cantering, and its captain, riding ahead of them, was coming up level with Cardigan. Cavendish saw the old man turn his head slightly, and then drop his sword, holding it out sideways so that the flat of its blade rested across the captain's chest. He said something to him, and the captain fell back; then Cardigan shouted, his loud, hoarse voice beating the din of the guns. 'Steady, the 17th Lancers!'

Now the guns at the end of the valley opened fire again with a huge, heavy crash, and a rolling bank of smoke immediately obscured them. Was that worse, or better? Cavendish wondered. It was like a wall of fog, obscuring the end of the valley, from which at irregular intervals orange tongues of flame belched out, marking the positions of the guns. The shells struck the earth in front of them, throwing up fountains of earth and stones – out of range, still, but not for long.

Men were dying now, horses were falling – it was the horses' screams which were the worst. The men mostly fell in silence, or with a sort of grunt, as though taking up a strain. There were men gone from his own squadron. 'Close up!' he shouted. 'Close up the ranks!' Further along the line Captain Archibald took up the cry like an echo. 'Close up to the centre!' It was a drill; they had done it over and over again in England. In front of him a shell from the Causeway smashed through two lancers at once; one horse went down, wildly plunging, and brought down the horse next to it. Cavendish and his squadron opened out to pass round the thrashing group, and on the other side closed up again. The din of the guns made it difficult to think anything, or feel anything, which was a blessing. There were loose horses now, and wounded horses, and their instinct, poor beasts, was not to run for safety, but to get back into line. The unwounded horse they had just passed must have got to its feet again, for here it was, crowding Cavendish's gelding Rowan, trying to force its body into line between him and the man next to him, Trooper Davis. Cavendish glanced sideways and saw the animal's head stretching forward almost level with his knee, its eyes showing white, its reins flapping. He was afraid the loose reins would entangle him or his own horse, and shouted, 'Davis, drive that animal away.' Davis turned his white face towards Cavendish and his mouth opened to answer, when a bullet from a sharpshooter hit him, and the middle of his face disintegrated. Flecks of blood and bone spattered against Cavendish's face, making him blink. He had felt the hot sear of the bullet as

461

it passed his cheek – if he hadn't turned his head just then he would have caught it instead of Davis. Davis remained upright in the saddle for a moment, and then tumbled away, backwards and sideways. The loose horse took the opportunity to crowd into line, and Davis's horse, freed of his weight, competed with it, the two jostling so hard they pushed Rowan sideways into the horse on his right.

But the pace had quickened, in spite of Cardigan; they were cantering now. The front rank was within range of the guns at the end of the valley, and nothing could keep them at a parade trot, and the staff officers had to canter too, or be ridden over. Rowan was going easily, pulling lightly, his ears pricked, unafraid of the noise and the death all round him, as long as he felt his rider's legs against his sides and his hand on the rein. The carnage was frightful now, whole groups going down under the round-shot and grape-shot. The front line's formation was so broken up that it was impossible to close ranks again, and with the loss of formation, the natural desire to gallop could no longer be restrained. Someone yelled 'Up the 13th! Come on, boys!' and the charge was on. It was better, Cavendish thought, to gallop and yell. He did not restrain his men; and a moment later he found himself yelling too, while Rowan stretched himself eagerly, racing the horses on either side. He glanced round, caught Archibald's eye, and grinned like a boy on a spree. It was exhilarating, in spite of everything. And then quite suddenly, Archibald wasn't there, though his horse went on galloping without missing a step, as though he did not notice he had no rider.

There were wounded horses all round Cavendish now, trying to press up against him; his overalls and the saddle-cloth were covered in their blood. He pushed Rowan harder, to get ahead of them. The ground ahead was littered with dead men and dead and dying horses, and if Rowan were to stumble he would be lost. Cavendish had lost all sense of time; he no longer noticed the smoke or the noise of the guns; thoughts of his own death had been pounded out of his head. There were no orders left to shout but 'Close up! Close up to the centre!'; there was nothing left to do but gallop madly towards the orange tongues of flame; nothing to think but that it was nearly over, that they were almost at the guns.

Up on the Heights there was dead silence as they watched the Light Brigade ride into death. The parade-ground precision, the way the ranks reformed when a horse or man fell, looked from above like the movements of a mechanical toy; yet they were evidence of a discipline and courage under fire which brought tears to some eyes. The French general Bosquet was heard to say quietly and with great feeling, '*C'est magnifique, mais ce n'est pas la guerre.*' Charlotte looked at Oliver, and then quickly away again. She did not want to see her own expression mirrored in his eyes. A moment later she found he was holding her hand tightly, and she had no idea which of them had initiated the gesture.

The Heavy Brigade, weary from their earlier action, were being left behind, and when the Light Brigade's pace increased to a gallop and they disappeared into the smoke, Lord Lucan called a halt. The Greys and Royals were already sustaining heavy casualties from the crossfire, and the slower pace of the Heavies would expose them even more than the Light Brigade. He saw no purpose in the sacrifice, and ordered a withdrawal out of range of the guns.

Suddenly there was a tremendous boom, as the Russian guns fired a broadside, all twelve of the front rank of cannon firing together. The smoke rose up thicker than ever; and then, suddenly, there was silence. The cavalry must have gone through the battery, and the guns had ceased firing. The silence was horrible. 'What's happening?' Charlotte whispered. 'Are they all dead?' Oliver didn't speak, only pressed her hand. Her ears were flinching with the memory of the gunfire, so that she couldn't be sure if she could hear anything or not. The plain below was filled with dead men and horses, and the living remnant of the Light Brigade had disappeared. There was nothing to see but that pall of smoke, which hung like oblivion over the end of the valley.

The relief of reaching the guns was so great that it rushed through the blood like a surge of alcohol. The last salvo had blown the front rank to pieces – Cavendish didn't see how many survived, but it could not have been many – and then the smoke rolled over so heavily that he did not see the guns until he was almost on top of them. Someone unseen up ahead gave the 'view halloo' and a roar of elation answered it. Now there was fighting, an enemy to slash at, bearded Russians to kill, something to do instead of being passively shot at. A fierce feeling almost like joy surged through Cavendish. A man appeared at Rowan's shoulder, and he killed him, hacked him through the side of the neck; the first man he had ever killed, but he felt nothing about it but the pleasure of action after helplessness. It took quite a wrench to get his sword free – like trying to pull a carving fork out of a big joint of beef. A man came up on his other side, his face a snarl of rage or fear. Cavendish swung his sword over and smashed it into the man's shoulder, and he dropped, screaming, and spouting blood from the severed artery ran up the blade to Cavendish's hand like a tidal bore. There was fighting on every side, the gunners being slaughtered almost casually, in passing, as the Light Brigade rode screaming at the Russian cavalry. Now Cavendish was

464

fighting mounted men; now he was parrying blows as well as giving them. He felt a searing burn on his left arm, high up near the shoulder, and supposed vaguely that he had been wounded, but his fighting fury was so great the pain instantly disappeared as he hacked and killed and drove Rowan forward. The mass of Russian Lancers they were attacking was falling back ahead of them, flinching from the ferocity of the charge, fleeing; but as they scattered, Cavendish saw his men were facing a huge body of Russian heavy cavalry, and behind them the massed ranks of infantry. His fighting fever cooled slightly. Colonel Douglas, in command of the 11th, ahead and to his right, checked his horse and looked round.

'Too many of them for us, boys!' he shouted. 'We can't kill the whole bloody Russian army single-handed. Fall back, the 11th! Fall back!'

They had come in from the right of the line of Russian guns, and now as the Russian cavalry advanced they had to fall back to the left, towards the centre of the action. There were horses there, too – for a heady moment Cavendish thought they had been surrounded, but he saw at the last moment they were British uniforms – the 4th Light Dragoons, and a few stragglers from other regiments – being marshalled by Lord George Paget. Paget looked past the 11th at the Russian cavalry pursuing them, and shouted out in a cracking voice, 'Halt and front, 11th Hussars! If you don't front, my boys, we are all done for!' Colonel Douglas caught his sense and took up the order; the remaining officers of the 11th repeated it to their sections, and the 11th halted and turned to face the enemy, forming up with the 4th. Desford appeared from nowhere, his busby missing, his left sleeve in ribbons. 'Hot work this, eh, Blithfield?' he said cheerfully, taking up his position. Cavendish saw that his own men were quite calm – not afraid, only eager to fight on. 'Come on, you Russkies!' one of Cavendish's troop shouted, taking a step forward. 'I'll give you toco!' Cavendish had to look hard to see who it was, for his face was covered in blood and blackened with smoke. 'Dress your line, Everard,' he shouted. 'Steady, boys, hold to your ranks now. Show 'em we understand discipline.'

'Look at old Ivan, shakin' in 'is boots!' another trooper, Harris, shouted. It was true that the Russian cavalry was advancing in a very hesitant way, even though they heavily outnumbered the British. A quick glance round told Cavendish the group he was now part of was only sixty or seventy strong; but the Russians had outnumbered them all day, and been driven back each time. Now seventy of them had turned to face two thousand Russians. *What would these mad English do next?* was eloquent in the enemy's demeanour. The advancing Russian cavalry gave the impression of a group of boys trying to decide who should go into the headmaster's study first, jostling as they tried not to be in front.

But Everard, who had looked round when Cavendish shouted at him, now saw what was going on behind them. 'My lord, they're attacking us in the rear!' Cavendish looked. A huge body of Russian Lancers was forming up directly in their line of retreat. Now they were surrounded. The horses were exhausted; Cavendish could feel Rowan's sides heaving under his legs. And for the first time he felt the pain of the wound in his arm; but he did not dare look at it, in case the gesture should dishearten the men. He called Desford's attention to the situation, and Desford called out to Lord George Paget. Paget shook his head, looked all around him, and said, 'What the devil's to do now? We are in a scrape. Where's Lord Cardigan? Has anyone seen Lord Cardigan?'

No-one answered. No-one had seen the Old Man since they reached the guns. He had been there when the great salvo was fired, had disappeared between the guns into the smoke, still upright in the saddle and as steady as a church, looking as unmoved as if it were Hyde Park on a Sunday. But he had been several horses' lengths ahead of everyone else when he reached the guns. Probably he was dead now.

'Well, there's no help for us now, lads,' Lord George said. 'We must sell ourselves dear.' He flung out his sword arm towards the body of Russian Lancers cutting off the retreat. 'There's our way, and there's our enemy. Let's see how many of 'em we can take with us!'

A roar greeted his words. The troopers wheeled about, dug their heels into their tired horses' sides, and charged. The Russians were just a few hundred yards away, and for a moment they stood, but as the British came closer, they seemed to waver. Lord George Paget's small group was coming at them from the centre, and almost at once from the Russian left another group of survivors appeared under Colonel Shewell. The Russian left began to give, so that now the front was on a diagonal. Now escape looked possible; if the Russians continued to give on their left, the English could break out that way – the side furthest away from where Cavendish and his section were positioned. But the horses were exhausted and many of the men were wounded; Cavendish's wound ached savagely, his sword arm was so tired he could hardly grip his sword, and Rowan was trembling under him. They rode at the Russians. Those at the far end were yielding, but at this end they were a solid mass, and there was going to be a fight. Cavendish felt light-headed, and swayed in the saddle, but it was physical weakness only – he had gone far beyond fear by now.

'Come on, men, let's get ourselves some trophies!' he shouted, and with a huge effort swung up his sword and waved it in the air.

A roar answered him from his own men, and Harris shouted 'Good old Bliffy!' as Rowan stumbled into a canter. Cavendish fixed his eyes on the man who would take his charge, a man with a great black beard like a spade; and saw the bearded man lower his lance into the operative position. Oh, would you? Cavendish thought, and a formless yell of defiance poured effortlessly out of his lungs as he dug his heels into Rowan to cover the last twenty yards.

Groups of riders and men on foot started to appear at the end of the valley. Captain Duberley's wife, possessed for the moment of her husband's glasses, exclaimed 'What on earth are those skirmishers doing?'

'Skirmishers? Where?' Duberley asked.

The same answer occurred to everyone a moment later, but it was Mrs Duberley who voiced it. 'Oh, good God, it is the Light Brigade!'

A handful of men, mostly wounded, and a smaller handful of horses, all exhausted: now they had to retrace their steps under the flanking fire and over the bodies of their former companions. But at least the fire was only from one side now, for the two squadrons of the Chasseurs d'Afrique which had been formed up on the flanks of the Fediukine Hills now mounted a brave attack on the batteries there, and through sheer ferocity carried them, before being turned back by the massed infantry behind. It gave the survivors a small chance to get back alive.

In a despair past tears, the observers on the Heights watched the Light Brigade make its painful way back down the valley. Most of them were on foot, for those whose horses had miraculously escaped being wounded slipped from the saddle out of compassion for the animals' weariness. As they passed through the fallen, the wounded who could move began to crawl along with them, or called

468

out, and were helped up, and staggered on between two staggering supporters. Wounded horses cried out for help too, but nothing could be done for them yet. Many troopers would not leave their horses, and limped back dragging a bleeding animal slowly along under the fire from the Causeway, keeping it moving by the sheer force of their love.

When it was obvious that the Light Brigade was in retreat, the Headquarters party made its way down into the valley. Lord Raglan was in earnest discussion with General Canrobert, and as soon as the path was wide enough, they beckoned Oliver to join them, so Charlotte was left to ride alone. She was trying not to think, telling herself that it was useless to speculate. She would know soon enough if Cavendish was amongst that small band that was struggling back down the valley. As they got nearer the plain, they could hear short bursts of cheering, and sometimes applause, as each group of stragglers was welcomed like the victors of a race. The Russian guns were still firing from the Causeway, but sporadically. Charlotte kept her eyes and her mind on the Headquarters party. Airey had joined Raglan now, and others of the staff. Oliver appeared to be urging something; Airey spoke; Raglan and Airey looked towards Canrobert; Canrobert shook his head. More talk, a few gestures, an urgent sweep of the arm from Oliver. Then Raglan spoke, summoned a galloper, and sent him off with an order.

After a while Oliver detached himself and held back to let Charlotte catch up with him. 'I don't know why the French commander is called *Can*robert, when it's evident he *can't*,' he fumed. 'The Russians are all in confusion, beaten against all the odds by a handful of our horsemen: now is the time to counter-attack, give them a real licking! If we let them off the hook, they'll get their spirits up again and end by convincing themselves they won the day. Raglan was for it, but the French general said *non*, and that was that.'

'Can't we do anything without the French?' Charlotte asked.

'Raglan is afraid of moving too many men up and leaving Balaclava exposed. Without French support, he won't do more than secure the position.'

'What was the order I saw sent off?'

'To Cathcart, to occupy the No 3 Redoubt that the Russians abandoned. From there they can fire on No 2 and harry the Russians. But they're not going to try and retake the other two redoubts. The bulk of the Russian force has drawn right back out of the valley onto the high ground to the north, and Canrobert seems to think that's good enough.'

'I see,' said Charlotte dully.

Oliver said gently, 'Are you all right? You're very pale. Why don't you go back to the yacht?' She shot him a look. 'No, that was stupid of me. You must see him first, of course.'

'See him – yes,' she repeated vaguely. He saw that she was in a state of shock, and it was not all on Cavendish's account. He knew that he was in an abnormal state himself. His mind seemed to be operating at arm's length from his body, and he had a hollow, strained feeling in his chest, as though he had been out in a violent gale, buffeted by noise and short of air. To have watched the Light Brigade ride through that valley of death was to have burned on the mind an image which would never be eradicated.

The remnants of the cavalry were forming up at the head of the valley, on the slopes of the Woronzov road, for roll-call. The trumpets called them to parade, and they formed up regiment by regiment – so pitifully thin, the lines, and few of the men mounted. The front line of the charge had been the hardest hit, almost wiped out by that last terrible salvo which had hit them almost at point-blank range as they reached the guns. Here was the 13th Light Dragoons, reduced to two officers, two dozen troopers, and eight horses; the 17th Lancers, hardly better off; a trooper sitting on the ground weeping as the farrier prepared to shoot the horse he had coaxed all the way back on three legs. There was Lord George Paget, his face so drawn and white it was like a death's head, in front of what was left of the 4th Light Dragoons; and beyond them, the 11th, their gorgeous uniforms in tatters, their beautiful horses bleeding and lame, if they were not left behind on that beastly plain. There was Lord Cardigan, miraculously unwounded, his pale eyes red-rimmed in his smoke-blackened face, mounted on a dead-weary Ronald, standing before them, the 11th Hussars, his own regiment, his pride and joy.

'Men,' he shouted to them, his hoarse voice carrying easily to that tattered remainder, 'men, it was a mad-brained trick, but it was none of it my fault.'

Someone answered from the ranks, 'Never mind it, my lord. We are ready to go again if we must.' And along the line tired shoulders were straightened, and weary heads were pulled up a little, proudly. It was that pride which made Charlotte begin to cry at last – that stupid, touching, lovely pride that was manlike, and greater than any man, and which took no account of the wounds, the depleted numbers, and the fact that horses, with no intellect to overcome their physical weariness, were drooping at the knees, only staying upright because it was too much effort to lie down.

She sat her horse out of the way, listening to the roll-call, and the tears dried on her cheeks in the little breeze that had got up with the westering of the sun.

The sky was still miraculously clear: it would be another very cold night. The Russian guns had stopped firing; the occasional pistol shots she heard were the regimental farriers, despatching the ruined horses. How hungry the men must be, she thought – they had had nothing since last night, having been standing-to since before dawn, kept from their breakfast by the very first alarm from the Turks in No 1 Redoubt.

She thought of all sorts of things, to keep her mind from repeating over and over what she had seen long before she came within earshot of the roll-call. Cavendish was not there. He was not there.

Dusk fell early, for it was October. Charlotte was in Cavendish's tent, amongst his belongings. His servant, Parry, was there, pottering about, needing something to do. He kept offering Charlotte food and drink, looking at her with wet eyes like a beseeching dog. Inside, the tent had a lonely smell of damp canvas; when the flap was lifted there came in the smell of cold grass and cold dew. Parry had lit a lamp – yellow light heavily shaded; only enough light to move around by, but it made the outside seem darker. She went to the door to look out at the first two stars, very large and polished in the luminous sky, looking as though one might squeeze a cupful of electric-blue juice out of each. The hillsides were in blackness: there had been an order not to light fires, in case the Russians were planning a night attack. Charlotte felt desperately sorry for the hungry men, with nothing but cold rations, hard-tack and their daily rum-ration to ease their sore hearts and empty bellies. No fires out there in the gathering dark, only moving shadows, sometimes crossing the faint glow of an illuminated tent, sometimes cut out against the turquoise of the western sky. The only sounds were low voices, and the rustle of feet in the grass: no sound of horses. So few of them had come back, and those few were too tired to move or whinny: they drooped against their tether-lines, and twitched uneasily in their sleep.

The men were restless with weariness and overstretched nerves, and without fires to focus them, they moved about from place to place, looking for someone to talk to, telling their stories over and over again. Now and then Charlotte left the tent and walked about too, standing quietly at the back of a group, listening to the men without disturbing them; absorbing their judgement of the day.

'T'warn't the Old Man's fault. He had his orders straight out from Lord Lucan. We all heerd him – didn't we, boys?'

'That's right. He had to do it. Like he said, it wasn't none of it his fault.'

A silence; and then a quiet voice, 'We did it, though, didn't we? We charged a battery and took it – cavalry on its own, without infantry – charged the guns an' took 'em! By God, they'll talk about this in years to come! We'm part of history, lads.'

'That Captain Nolan was right in the end, wasn't he? He always said it could be done.'

'Didn't live to see it though, did he, poor beggar?'

'Gor, did you hear the Old Man sounding off about him when he got back? Wanted to put Cap'n Nolan on a charge for mutiny, for riding across him that way. Ole Gen'ral Scarlett had to tell him he'd just rid over Cap'n Nolan's dead body, to make him shut up.'

'The Old Man was brave, though. He never flinched, no matter what. Not even when that salvo knocked old Ronald sideways.'

'Did you see, when that salvo went off? Right in front of me, three horses knocked to smash. I never saw the like.'

473

'I lost my mare, my lovely Deena. She was three quart' thoroughbred, and clever? Same as if she could read my mind. As clever as a Christian, my Deena was, God rest 'er.'

'My good old bay was the same – take a biscuit from my lips with his teeth without never touching me, he could. And he'd foller me just like a dog. Round shot blew his head right off, poor old boy, poor old horse. What'd he do to deserve that?'

They talked softly of the horses, and many of them cried, for the horses could not share the glory, the horses could not help themselves. And far from home, the horses were their wives and children, the tenderness and kindness in their lives, gentle and faithful in a harsh world.

'Warn't no horse never started no war,' one man concluded, wiping his nose and eyes on his ruined coat-sleeve. 'Warn't no horse never hurt no-one neether.'

'And they looks at you, when they'm hurt,' another said, 'so puzzled-like, as if you could make 'em right again—' He had to stop and sniff and clear his throat. 'T'ain't fair,' he said. They nodded, grievingly. It wasn't fair. The carnage amongst the horses had been dreadful. Charlotte crept away.

They came to her in her tent, shyly, because she was a lady and a novelty; and because she was clever and they thought she might have answers for them; and because she was Lord Blithfield's sister, and Bliffy had been a popular officer. They came hesitantly, and found they were not sent away. Charlotte told Parry to distribute the cold delicacies he wanted to press on her amongst the men, but they didn't come for that – or not only for that. They came to tell her their stories, and the stories of the friends who had fallen. And they told her about her brother.

'He was a-fightin' like a tiger, mum – my lady – when

I last see him, when we 'bout-turned and charged the Russky Lancers. He was over to my left, see—'

'That's where the Russkies was thickest. They was falling back on our right, see, but the most of 'em was up on our left.'

'—and Bliffy shouts, come on, lads, he shouts, let's get us a soovy-neer! And he goes at 'em 'ell for leather. A fine brave officer, ma'am, was Lord Blithfield.'

'But did you see him fall?' Charlotte asked, of one group and then another.

'No, 'm. No, my lady,' was always the answer.

'Him and Trooper Everard, and Harris, and Beeton, they was all fighting alongside each other, and they was sort of, like, swallered by the Russkies, if you get my meanin'. The Russky line was like bending round on itself, ma'am, and they like disappeared in a crowd o' Russkies, fighting like madmen.' A pause. 'And that's all I see. I was fighting my own way out, ma'am, and then the Russky line falls back and we rides out clear, and sets off for our own lines, ma'am, never lookin' back. So I don't know what become of 'is lordship, ma'am.'

Nobody saw him fall. But Everard and Harris and Beeton had not come back either. The dead within reach had been brought back, and he was not amongst them; but there were bodies too far away to be brought in, too near to the Russian line, and the Russians would bury those with their own dead, and they would never be named. That was war.

'Maybe they was capchered, miss,' one trooper offered her shyly, like a child offering a flower it had picked; but it was a very wilted daisy, and he knew it.

The others took up the eulogy again, embarrassed by the false offering. 'He was a fine officer, my lady. And everyone liked him.'

'Not because he was soft, though. Very particular,

Lord Blithfield, near as particular as the Old Man. But fair.'

'Always fair. He never took on at you for nothing. Some officers takes it out on you when they're in a bad temper, but not him. If you done wrong, he'd be down on you like a ton-weight, but it was never for nothing.'

'Right, and if some other officer was a-gettin' at you for nothing, Bliffy always stood up for you. Lord Blithfield, I should say, m'lady.'

'An' a fine 'orseman! D'you remember that black devil that Major Freeman bought, and couldn't get a leg acrorst it?'

'Gor, yes, and Bliffy says, he says, look here, Freeman, he says, you won't never get upsides of a 'orse in that frame o' mind, he says. If you goos up to a 'orse expectin' trouble, he says, trouble is what you'll get!'

'An' then he walks up to that mad black thing – showing its whites, it was, m'lady – and he takes a 'old of the bridle and just looks it in the eye, and like talks to it, steady-like, and smilin' – and blow me if the 'orse don't start smilin' back! It's a trufe! 'Is 'ole ears comes forrard and his lip starts a wobblin' – an' then Bliffy swings isself up in the saddle and says walk on, then, he says, quiet like, and the old 'orse goos off quiet as a donkey. Finest 'orseman in the regiment, Lord Blithfield.'

Charlotte listened, understanding that they were giving her the only thing they had to give; but it hurt her, too, because she saw that they were talking him out. They were laying out their memories of him, smoothing them down lovingly, polishing them; and then they would tidy them away, and Cavendish would be gone, completely and for ever; someone in the past tense, like a history lesson.

After a while, they came to her to ask instead of to tell. Exhaustion and hunger had overcome the elation of the victory, and now came the depression of reaction.

'What was it all for, miss? They say it was a mistake – that Lord Raglan never meant it at all. Is that right?'

'Certainly Lord Raglan didn't mean the cavalry to charge the Russian guns in the valley. He meant you to try to stop the Russians taking away the guns from the redoubts.'

'Then – how did it come about? Whose fault was it?'

'It was a misunderstanding; but I don't know how it came about.'

'I see Cap'n Nolan pointin' down the valley when Lord Lucan asks him summink,' another said, and there was a general murmur of agreement. 'Maybe it was his fault?'

'A gen'ral can't blame a capting,' said an older trooper wisely. 'That ain't the way it goos. Lord Lucan give the order.'

'But Lord Raglan give *'im* the order.'

'An' the 'ole Light Brigade was lost.'

There was a silence, and then the first questioner raised his eyes again to Charlotte. 'It were a disaster, miss, wunt it?'

'It was a great tragedy,' she said.

'But it warn't shameful?' he said anxiously. 'There warn't nothing dishonourable?'

'No,' she said. 'It was the finest and bravest thing ever done, and every one of you deserves the highest honour. There was nothing shameful about it.'

They looked pleased, and there was a general shifting and shuffling as they tried to cope with the admiration of a high-up lady; in the course of which movement one trooper knocked against the arm of another, who winced.

'What is it?' Charlotte asked. 'Are you hurt?' She saw, now that she looked more carefully, that the sleeve of his jacket was crusted with blood around a rent in the fabric.

477

'It's nothing, ma'am. Don't you bother, begging your pardon,' the trooper said hastily.

'You've taken a wound, haven't you? Has the doctor seen it?'

'No, ma'am – it's only a scratch. No need to go a-troubling of the medico.'

'Trufe of it is, my lady,' said another man, 'that Turner 'ere is dead scared o' doctors.'

Turner nervously wiped his lip on his cuff. 'I don't want no medico looking at my arm. He'll only want to cut it off. They always wants to cut everything off. I ain't going back 'ome with one sleeve.'

'If the cut turns bad, you won't go home at all,' Charlotte said. 'Let me have a look at it.'

'Don't come near me, ma'am, I'm lousy,' Turner said, backing hastily.

'Lice are nothing new to me,' Charlotte said, advancing calmly. 'Come on, man, I'm not going to hurt you. Don't you know back home in England I have a hospital of my own, for poor folk? I've helped nurse all sorts of people, and most of them were lousy. Just sit down on that stool, Turner, that's a good fellow. You two, help him off with his jacket.'

The other two, grinning widely with the soldier's usual enjoyment of another's discomfiture, thrust the victim ungently onto the stool, and divested him of his jacket. The cloth had stuck to the wound, of course, and Turner let out a yell as they ripped it free.

'Gently, now,' Charlotte admonished. 'You'd better slip your shirt off that side, too.'

She approached the flinching man with steady calm, remembering as she did the story she had just been told of Cavendish and the black horse. If you expect trouble, trouble is what you'll get. Poor Turner's flesh quivered with fear as she laid hands on his arm. The wound was

478

a long sabre-gash across the thickest part of the upper arm. It had bled copiously, and pulling off his clothes had started it bleeding again, but as she pressed the edges of the wound gently, she saw that it was clean-edged, and not deep to the bone.

'This isn't so bad,' she said. 'The best thing for a cut like this is to be bound in its own blood. I'll just clean around it and bandage it for you, and if you can keep it covered and keep it dry, it ought to heal well enough. Parry, just run to the guest tent, will you, and ask my maid to give you my medical kit out of my overnight bag. I suppose there isn't any possibility of hot water, with no fires lit? No, then get out a bottle of Lord Blithfield's brandy – or whisky. Any ardent spirit. I'll use a little of that to clean up the wound.'

In a while she had Turner cleaned up and firmly bandaged, and he went off, pleased with the attention and enduring the chaff of his companions as they walked out into the darkness. Turner had been comforted; and Charlotte found to her surprise that so had she. By a very small amount, the pain of Cavendish's death had been diminished: she had been able to do something to help, and activity was always the best antidote to grief. She realised how dazed with shock she must have been all this while, not to have thought of it before.

A little later, Oliver arrived, from Headquarters.

'You look tired to death,' Charlotte said.

'The casualty lists are in,' he said succinctly. 'Forty officers, three hundred and eighty men – killed, wounded or missing. About two hundred and fifty Turks, too, despite their running away – or probably because of it, since most of them seem to have been struck down from behind. And the French lost about fifty Chasseurs in that attack on the Fediukine battery.' He passed a hand across his eyes. 'It was a bad day. Raglan was recalling the Duke of Wellington's words after Waterloo – that the next worse thing to a battle lost was a battle won.'

'I suppose we did win?' Charlotte asked doubtfully.

'We didn't lose. But the analysis and recriminations are still going on up there over the Light Brigade's charge. I've never seen Raglan so agitated. He quite lost his marble calm – shaking with anger, and waving his stump about like a club. There was the most terrific row between him and Lucan.' Oliver paused reflectively. 'It's hard not to feel some sympathy for Lucan. The cavalry was his passion, and the Light Brigade especially – the finest brigade ever to leave the shores of England, he called it. And his own regiment, the 17th, has been virtually wiped out. I don't like the man, but you could see how he was suffering. And then the first thing Raglan did was to fling an awful finger at him and cry bitterly, "You have lost the Light Brigade!"'

'What did Lucan say to that?'

'He was furious. He said all he had done was to obey the order Nolan had delivered to him in the most pressing manner; to which Raglan replied that he should have used his discretion, and that if he did not approve of the charge, he shouldn't have made it. That was too much for Lucan. Words poured out of him like lava. Disobey an "immediate" order direct from the commander-in-chief? he said. What about Queen's Regulations? What would the fate be of a general who disobeyed such an order? And he said that the whole thing was Raglan's fault, because Raglan up on the Heights had a clear view of the entire battlefield, while he, down below, could see nothing.'

'Yes, I know from what the men have been saying that was true.'

'So Raglan said if he couldn't see anything he ought to have taken steps to ascertain the position, and Lucan said it wasn't necessary because Raglan knew he couldn't see anything from down there, and he knew Raglan knew because Raglan had had to inform him in the order that the French cavalry were on his left. And they shouted at each other for a bit in a most unmilitary fashion, and then Lucan said again that he had simply obeyed an order he was bound to obey, and that he did not intend to bear the smallest particle of blame, and then he stormed out.'

'Oh dear, how uncomfortable.'

'Lucan could make things very unpleasant if he took the argument into public debate, but I expect better sense will prevail at last. It wouldn't do either of them any good, and it would be bad for the Army. After Lucan left, Airey said, "Well, well, these sort of things will happen in war; take the rough with the smooth, you know", and it was left at that. Apportioning blame won't bring the men back.' He looked at her closely. 'How are you bearing up? My love, I've had no chance to say how desperately sorry I am.'

'Don't,' she begged. 'I can't bear words. Don't talk of it – not yet.'

'What have you been doing here while I've been up at Headquarters?'

'Talking to the men, listening to them. And I bandaged one trooper's arm. It made me realise how selfish I've been. No hospital ever has enough nurses and orderlies, and with all those wounded, there must be plenty of work for me to do in the field hospitals.'

'Tomorrow,' he said firmly. 'Not now. I don't suppose you've even had anything to eat yet, have you? No, I thought not. Well, tomorrow you shall roll up your sleeves with the best of them, if it's what you want, but for tonight we are going to follow Lord Cardigan's example, and go back to our yacht for hot baths, dinner, and a comfortable bed.'

She frowned. 'It doesn't seem right,' she began.

'Not right? It seems to me like the best idea anyone's had all day.'

'No, I mean – to go down to all that comfort, when the men up here can't even have hot food, after all their terrible exertions. All I've done is watch.'

'I applaud the sentiment, but will it help any one of them if you stay here and suffer discomfort? Will it put a hot meal in the belly of one single deserving trooper?'

'Well – no, if you put it like that.'

'I do. Even Lord Raglan said, "There's no need for you to share our hardships up here tonight, Southport." So let's get going. It's going to be a damned cold night. I wouldn't be surprised if winter weren't setting in, you know.'

On the following day, the 26th of October, the Russians made a sortie from Sebastopol, which was beaten back decisively, with the capture of a large number of Russian prisoners. This gave the Intelligence Department an opportunity to find out how the events of the 25th had been described and received by the other side. The Russian prisoners, having been told that the British were frightful barbarians and inflicted horrible tortures on prisoners, were relieved and delighted to find they were treated with all courtesy and given better food than they had at home. Gratitude made them garrulous: the difficulty was not to get them to talk but the get them to stop.

What they had to say was what the British staff officers had suspected: that the captured guns had been paraded through the streets of Sebastopol as proof of a great victory. There had been excited crowds in the streets, church bells were rung, an extra vodka-ration was issued to the troops, and there had been singing and dancing and fornication on a grand scale as a result. Admiral Nakhimov had given a celebration ball in the evening, with fireworks, for the officers and the remaining gentry-folk of the town. And this morning it had been announced that as the English were so disheartened over their defeat, an attack was to be made immediately which would entirely finish them off. There had been no difficulty in obtaining volunteers for the sortie, and the four thousand five hundred Russian foot soldiers had been extremely surprised and disappointed at the readiness with which a mere two thousand English soldiers had driven them back.

Oliver asked about English prisoners from the actions of the 25th, but none of those he questioned knew anything for sure, though one man said he had heard there were no unwounded English taken, and that all the prisoners were in a bad way, which was held to be to their credit. He informed Oliver that the General in command had been General Liprandi, and that he was with the Russian forces camped by the river Tchernaya.

Consequently, Oliver suggested to Lord Raglan sending a flag of truce to Liprandi to ascertain what prisoners had been taken on the 25th, and to offer information about the Russian prisoners.

'Yes, very well,' Lord Raglan said. 'I'll send word to Lord Lucan to write a letter – it had better come from him – and send one of his staff up to the Russian line with it.'

'Sir,' Oliver said, 'may I not go myself?'

'You, sir?' Raglan said in mild surprise. 'Why should you want to go – oh, bless me, I had forgotten. You want to ask about your brother-in-law, I suppose?'

'Yes, sir – there is a chance he was among those captured. But also I may be able to get into conversation with whatever officer meets our flag. I don't suppose any of Lord Lucan's staff speaks Russian.'

'I think that very unlikely,' Raglan said drily. 'Very

well, my dear fellow, do go if you wish – but you had better have one of Lucan's aides go with you, or he may feel slighted and take offence, and I've no wish to rub him up the wrong way again. Yes, yes, find out whatever you can. It's imperative we take the town with the least possible delay. The troops are beginning to suffer from the coldness of the nights.'

Lucan chose one of his aides, Captain Fellowes, to accompany Oliver, and the trumpet-major of the 17th Lancers was told off to carry the white flag, tied to the end of his lance. About mid-morning the group came up to the most advanced vedette towards the Tchernaya. The trumpet-major held his instrument at the ready, and the three of them stepped out in the open and rode at a walk towards the Russian positions, sounding the trumpet every few minutes. It was a tense moment. Flags of truce had been ignored before, and even when they weren't, it was always possible for an over-eager or frightened soldier to fire off his gun without orders or by mistake. But when they were about half way towards the Russian outposts, a group of about a dozen Cossacks broke out and came cantering towards them. The Englishmen halted; the Cossacks rode up to within fifty yards, and halted likewise, and two officers separated themselves and came to meet them.

'*Que voulez vous?*' one of the Cossack officers said. '*Anglais?* Eengleesh?'

Fellowes glanced at Oliver, who nodded that he should continue. Fellowes addressed the officer in French. 'Yes, we are English officers. We have a letter from the general commanding the British cavalry to the general commanding the Russian troops on the Tchernaya. Will you take it to him?'

'What is this letter?' asked the Cossack. His companion was staring at them with the blank, helpful smile of a man who doesn't understand a word that's being said. Fellowes gave the import of the letter, and the Cossack said he would go and ask his general, and rode away. The other looked a little disconcerted at being left with them. Fellowes tried addressing him in French, but he obviously did not speak that language. However, he seemed to feel it incumbent upon him to be friendly, and took out cigars and offered them round. Oliver thanked him in Russian, and immediately the Cossack cried, 'Ah, you speak Russian! That is very good!'

'It is a very beautiful language. I am very fortunate,' Oliver replied. Now the blank smile was on Fellowes's face.

'I wish I could speak English. English too is a beautiful language,' the Cossack replied politely. 'Where did you learn Russian?'

Oliver gave a brief outline of his history. The Cossack listened with interest, and then embarked on what was evidently his own life story, which Oliver followed with difficulty, since the man's accent and dialect were very strange. But when he got onto the subject of horses, it was easier, and it was a short step from there to the charge of the Light Brigade on the 25th.

'Ah, such courage!' the Cossack said, his eyes bright. 'Truly it was a privilege to kill such brave men! And kill them we did, in their hundreds, like reaping a meadow full of flowers! I will never forget it! But truly, master, was it not a madness to charge the guns – so few men and so many guns? Only the English could be so mad. You fight like the very devil, and the worse you are outnumbered, the better you like it!'

'Is that what they say in Sebastopol?'

'What do I know of Sebastopol?' the Cossack said, and spat a fragment of tobacco to the ground with expressive force. 'But my people know how to value the courage of horsemen. And General Liprandi admired your men very much – I heard it told. He asked the English prisoners what spirits they had been given to make them charge our guns and cavalry so madly – was it brandy, he asked, or was it rum? And your men said: sir, if we had had a single sip of anything stronger than water, we should have charged your infantry as well.' The Cossack roared with laughter at that, slapping his thigh with the enjoyment of so Russian a joke. 'So the General said: you are brave fellows, and I honour you,' he went on, 'and he sent them up vodka, a double ration for each. Ha!'

'So you did take prisoners?' Oliver asked. 'Are they still at the camp here, or have they been sent to the city?'

But the Cossack seemed to think he had been indiscreet, and would not say any more about prisoners. He asked instead what kind of food they ate in Balaclava, and he and Oliver chatted about neutral subjects until the first Cossack returned, bringing with him an older officer. He spoke excellent French, though he addressed them rather coolly, eyeing their undecorated, plain blue frock-coats doubtfully, as though he thought he had not been sent men of sufficient rank.

Fellowes explained his mission again, and asked after the prisoners.

'We took forty-five prisoners altogether, all wounded, and some have since died. I do not know their names, nor how many were officers. This is all I have to tell you,' the officer said curtly.

'Will you be so kind as to convey this letter from our general to General Liprandi? And I have here also letters from the Russian officers whom we have taken prisoner – will you be so kind as to deliver them?'

The old officer held out his hand and looked at the sheaf of letters, examining the direction on one or two. His expression softened at this evidence of civilised behaviour.

'Yes, yes, very well. Thank you, sir, thank you.' He cleared his throat impressively. 'I will speak to General Liprandi. And if you come again here at the same time tomorrow, I will give you the names of the prisoners who are still alive – and letters from the officers, if they wish.'

CHAPTER NINETEEN

Charlotte woke from the grateful oblivion of sleep to the instant renewal of sick misery. It was as if Cavendish's death had sat by her bedside, hideous and black, like a vulture waiting to feed on her heart. She had no expectations of Oliver's embassy: she would not flatter herself with such empty hopes. She was glad only that there was something useful for her to do today, having learned long ago that work was the best antidote to grief – that if it did not assuage it, at least it blotted it out for a time.

Oliver had to report back to Headquarters, so Charlotte rode up with him, taking with her a selection from the hospital supplies with which she had packed the *Doris*'s hold before they left England. Up on the plateau she turned aside and went straight away to the nearest field hospital. The familiar sounds and smells reached her before she even entered the marquee, and for a moment her heart sank. She wondered briefly whether those who went through life seeking out pleasure had not the right idea after all. But then she thought of Cavendish again, steeled her nerve, and stepped inside.

The wounded men were lying on the floor, some on paliasses, but most of them on the bare boards, which were all that kept them from the bare earth. There was the usual hospital smell of faeces and vomit, together with a strong reek of blood. At the far end was a trestle, on which a soldier lay, writhing like a wounded snake, while a shirt-sleeved man with his back to her bent over him. The two orderlies who were holding the man down stared at her, their jaws dropping in amazement.

'Hold him still, for God's sake. What's the matter with you?' the doctor snapped, and then, turning his head to see what they were staring at, flicked one glance at Charlotte and Norton and bellowed to another orderly, 'Get those bloody women out of here! This is not a raree show!'

'Sir! Sir!' the third orderly said urgently, rolling his eyes in a kind of panicking semaphore.

The doctor turned fully, took in Charlotte's quality, and said abruptly, 'I beg your pardon, madam. But I must ask you to leave. I am too busy to help you.'

'I know you are busy, Doctor—?'

'Harper, ma'am.'

'Thank you, Doctor Harper. I know you are busy, that is why *I* have come to help *you*.'

An expression of impatience and distaste came over his face. 'Very feeling, I'm sure, but this is no place for females, ma'am. And the men here are not fit to be visited.'

'I don't come to visit, I come to nurse. Mrs Norton and I have long hospital experience. You may trust us. We can clean and bandage wounds and splint fractures, we are not squeamish, nor vain, we don't mind dirt and lice, and we do not faint. Carry on with your own work, pray, and forget we are here.'

Harper looked at her for a moment, frowning; and then the soldier on the trestle gave a feeling moan, and he decided, with a shrug, that it was her own fault if she saw something that upset her. He turned his back on her again, Charlotte nodded to Norton, and they got to work.

The men were not all battle-wounded – some were

sick, some had other injuries – one had a rupture, for instance, and one had been bitten by a horse. Charlotte quickly decided the best use of her experience would be to sort out the ones who needed the surgeon's most urgent attention – the ones she could do nothing for – and with Norton set about treating those she could help. After a short while she revised the categories to add those no-one could help: some were so grievously wounded they were just waiting to die, and some were dead already. She had a sudden and clear picture of what it must have been like here last night, with the wounded pouring in and only one surgeon and three orderlies to deal with them.

Harper was fully occupied with surgery, and she decided he would probably not notice, let alone object, if she organised things. She called over the third orderly and set him to removing the dead, with the help of the soldier who had been bitten. He had been lounging near the door, and volunteered his help, eyeing Charlotte with as great an interest as if she had had two heads or a long furry tail.

'Your injury doesn't prevent you from lifting?' she asked.

'Naow, miss,' he said with the accent of the Seven Dials, 'where I been bit, it don't stop me doin' nuffin', 'cept sittin' down. Bugger got me bendin' over to pick 'is 'oof, bit me right in the—'

'Shut your mouth and be decent,' the orderly growled at him, shocked. 'Can't you see these is ladies? Beg pardon, mum, some o' these 'ere sojers is 'ardly better nor hanimiles. Edmunds 'ere ain't got as much sense as 'is 'orse, nor 'alf the beauty.'

'What's your name?'

'Todger, mum, of the Seventeenth.'

'Well, Todger, you and Edmunds can remove all the dead men, and if that leaves any paliasses free, put the worst wounded on them to get them off the floor. Then you can clean up a little, swab up some of the blood and mess. Mrs Norton and I will start bandaging. Have you wood for splints?'

'Yes, mum – over there, in the corner.'

'Very well. It will do for now. Carry on.'

Todger scuttled off, glad to have clear orders, dragging the gawping Edmunds with him. Charlotte was already bending over a young trooper – he didn't look more than seventeen or eighteen – whose face was white and set with desperate pain. Both his legs were smashed below the knee, presumably from a round-shot. Despite her brave words to Doctor Harper, the sight of his wounds made her stomach fall away from her in a sickening swoop; a feeling of despair filled her, of being faced with a task beyond human power. She wanted to run away, and not stop until she was back on the *Doris*; but the boy looked at her, and his lips moved. They were cracked and parched, but she saw the word they framed. *Water.* She saw the canvas bucket in the corner, but could not find a cup. Fortunately she had brought one in her bag. She fetched it and filled it, and held the boy's head while he drank, then laid him down again. He frowned at her, trying to assemble words.

'Is Betsy all right?' he whispered.

'Yes, she's very well,' Charlotte said. His sweetheart, she supposed. The poor boy was wandering in his mind. 'She's looking forward to seeing you again soon.'

'I was afraid they'd shot her. Her leg wasn't broken, then?'

'No, only sprained,' Charlotte improvised.

He closed his eyes with relief, and he murmured something else, which sounded like '—rub her down—'. He was blue about the lips, and judging from the mess beneath him he had bled himself almost dry. She did

491

not think he would last more than an hour or so. He was one of those in the 'beyond help' category. She had to harden her heart and leave him and go on to the next.

Some time later when she was bandaging a shoulder, she became aware of someone standing behind her; and turning her head saw that it was Doctor Harper. His face, she saw now, was grey with exhaustion, all hollows and shadows; stubble was sprouting through the waxy skin of his cheeks and chin; his arms, hands and apron were black with blood.

'There's no ball in this,' she said. 'It seems to have passed straight through, making a considerable wound, but not touching the bone, so I have cleaned it and now I'm binding it. Do you want to check my work, sir?'

He shook his head, and tried to smile, but it was a mere twitch of his moustache. 'No, you are doing a good job. I beg your pardon if I was abrupt.'

'You had every right. You must have been working all night, while I slept in a comfortable bed.'

'It is my job,' he said abruptly. 'It is not yours.'

'When there are not enough hands, it becomes everyone's job. I am quite accustomed to resistance on account of my sex; but I assure you I am as good a nurse as any man.'

'Better, I expect,' Harper said. 'I must admit that I revolt to my very soul at the sight of you here, a female amongst all this—' He waved his hand wearily to indicate the blood and the suffering. 'But I am too tired to argue with you. I suppose if I ordered you out, you *would* argue.'

'Exhaustingly. Do trust me, sir. Mrs Norton and I can do the simple tasks, and leave you free for the skilled work.'

He nodded and turned away, then turned back to say, 'I don't know your name.'

She hesitated a moment, and then said, 'Southport.'

'Very well, Mrs—' He stopped, and his tired eyes widened. 'Oh, good God, not the Duchess of Southport?'

'I'm afraid so. But don't let it put you off.'

By the end of the day, Charlotte knew that she and Norton had made a difference, that without them the suffering would have been worse. It had been hard to bear sometimes. Most of the soldiers bore their pain in grim silence, but some moaned, and sobbed, and one when he was told he must lose his leg shrieked over and over, 'Not my leg! Not my leg!' until at last the words dissolved in a despairing scream. Knowing what that meant, Charlotte had to hold onto the tent-pole as her knees threatened to give way. Her over-active imagination gave her many such anguished moments; but at least for a short time she had forgotten her own grief over Cavendish.

Harper performed amputations and excisions without anaesthetic. He had no chloroform, and stared when she asked him about it, and said simply, 'This is an army field hospital.' She gathered through the course of that day that soldiers were a different race from ordinary men, a sub-species, on whom less concern and compassion was spent than on the horses. Soldiers were expected to suffer and endure. If you pampered 'em, you made 'em unfit for war. It was an attitude that made her angry, but anger was at least useful in keeping her from failing through too much pity. Later she came to understand that Harper was not a cruel man, and was interested in the idea of anaesthesia, and did not, like many of his kind, believe that pain during surgical operations was actually beneficial; but he had never been issued with chloroform, and would not have known how to apply it, even if he had had time. After a battle the casualties poured in so fast that there was no time for refinements, just the quickest amputations that could be performed. And he was short-handed, his assistants both being incapacitated with dysentery.

The boy with the smashed legs died, as did a man with a bullet lost somewhere in his chest, two with grievous head wounds, and one who died under amputation. The patience of the men was astonishing. They complained more about the lice than about their wounds, and were grateful for attention, how ever long they had been waiting. After treatment, the seriously wounded were transported down to the general hospital at Balaclava, and if necessary were put on ships for Scutari. Charlotte was appalled at the callous way amputees were thrown into the unsprung carts to be jolted over the rough paths down to the harbour; every jolt must have given them agonising pain. There was nothing to be done about the roads, of course, and an appeal to the driver to try to pick the smoothest route only got a look of astonished incomprehension; but she did at least persuade the orderlies to move the men more gently, and to wedge them in so that they would not roll about so much. No doubt they were only careful when she was looking, but she could only do her best.

Finding that she and Norton were all she had promised, Harper grew comfortable with them, and treated them almost like men. On her second day, when they were dealing with the wounded Russians from the sortie, who had been brought in by the fatigue parties, he even offered to show Charlotte how to stitch a wound. 'You will be much more useful to me if you can do that.'

Charlotte thought of her grandmother, tending the wounded after Waterloo. Grandmama had stitched wounds. It was good to be following in her footsteps. 'I should be glad to know how to do it, if you would trust me,'

494

'Oh, you can practise on the Russkies,' Harper said. 'If they complain, you won't understand what they're saying.'

And at the end of the day, when she was wondering aloud at how little in the way of comfort was provided for the wounded, he said, 'If you think it is hard up here, you should take a look at the general hospital. Or rather, you should not, because that really is no place for a lady. They have all the cholera and dysentery cases down there, besides the lingering infections and chronic ailments. Fresh battle-wounds are a joy besides the horrors of that place, I assure you.'

'I'm sure you don't mean that,' Charlotte said, and Harper gave her a grimly humorous look.

At the appointed time, Oliver went again with Captain Fellowes under flag of truce to meet with the Russian officer and receive the details of the prisoners who had been taken at Balaclava. There survived thirty-five men, all wounded, he said. There were also two officers. These were – he studied a piece of paper in his hand, and pronounced the names with difficulty – Lieutenant Chadwick of the 17th Lancers, and Cornet Clowes of the 8th Hussars. Both had been wounded by Cossack lances, in the neck and the back, while fleeing after being unhorsed. Here was a letter from Cornet Clowes to his brother officers in his regiment, which said that he was very well-treated and given every comfort the circumstances would permit.

Oliver asked an urgent question, but the answer was quite specific. No, there were no other officers. There had, indeed, been five others, all desperately wounded when captured, who had died of their wounds, but it was not known what their names were. They had been buried in a mass grave with the other ranks.

It was the last hope, and it had been a slight one. Oliver was aware that Charlotte had set no store by it; yet it would be hard to tell her that Cavendish was certainly dead. She had not spoken of him, and Oliver had not seen her shed one tear; but he knew her too well not to understand the symptoms of her silent suffering. She had found her brother late in life, and loved him the more for it; now she would never even know where he lay. His grave would be unmarked and unvisited. Oliver surprised himself with the strength of his own sadness: that pleasant young man had meant more to him than he knew. He vowed then and there that young William, fatherless now, would not be left to Mrs Phipps's mercy.

He was brought back to the present by the trumpet-major dropping his instrument and catching it with a curse as it bounced off his saddle.

'Beg pardon, my lord,' the man said, embarrassed. 'It's the cold, my lord – my fingers have gone dead.'

Yes, Oliver thought, becoming aware of his surroundings, it was very cold. The nights had been bitter for the last week, but this was the first really cold day – a sullen sky, and a searing, hateful wind that went right through you. It was a horrible contrast from the gloriously warm weather in which the battles before Balaclava had been fought, and reminded Oliver of what he knew from his visits to Russia: that though Crimean winters were sometimes mild, when they were not, they were more bitter than anything England knew. And he knew Raglan knew it too, and was hoping that they could get out before winter set in.

But, Oliver thought, it was already too late for that. How would they ever embark the scattered Allied armies with large and hostile Russian forces in such close proximity, unless they were willing to sacrifice the artillery and cavalry in covering the retreat? And even such a sacrifice might not be enough. The Russians had a huge infantry to draw on, and guns that could rain down fire on the ships in the bays while the embarkation was going on. No, he fancied they were stuck here until they reduced Sebastopol – and that, he thought, was not likely to be before winter set in with a vengeance.

Fanny was making beds with Harriet. She was slow and clumsy compared with Harriet, at whose command sheets seemed to waft effortlessly into place, and fold themselves neatly under the mattress. On Fanny's side of the bed, the sheet wrinkled and made itself crooked, and would only go under the mattress at all in great lumps. And this sheet – she recognised it – was one she had mended only the other day, at great expenditure of effort and pain: she had pricked her fingers so often it had had to be washed again to remove her life-blood. Fanny hated this sheet with an intimate loathing; and now it had managed to get a stupid wrinkle in it, right across the bed. She yanked at it ferociously, and heard a rending noise.

Harriet loosened the sheet and examined it. 'I thought you'd mended this, Fanny,' she said.

'I did – you know I did. Look, there's my patch.'

'Yes, I see it. But you have to sew the sheet to the patch, as well as the patch to the sheet, or it's not strong enough. Now it's torn worse than ever.'

Harriet spoke mildly – she hardly ever spoke in any other tone of voice, but the rebuke was like a slapped face to Fanny. She stared for a moment, her cheeks reddening, and then turned and rushed from the room. Harriet calmly removed the sheet and started again. It was hardly any slower making the bed alone than with Fanny's help, she thought.

Peter found Fanny in the scullery, kneeling on the floor

beside the mangle, leaning against its inhospitable flank as she wept into her hands.

'Fanny, what is it?' he cried in alarm. 'Are you hurt?'

The answer was an incoherent splurge of words and tears. Peter crouched beside her and stroked her thin back. He could feel her vertebrae clearly through the cheap cotton of her blouse. 'What is it, Fanny? Tell me.'

'I'm so useless!' she cried passionately.

'No you're not,' he said.

'I am, I am! I can't even make a bed.'

'Is that what this is all about?'

She lifted her teary face from her hands. 'You took me in and you keep me and feed me and I can't do *anything*! I'm *useless*!'

It was difficult for him to argue, because in the sense she meant it she was quite right. Even the simplest housework was new to her, and she was slow and clumsy. Helping with the washing, she got more soapy water on the floor than through the clothes, and had managed to get her apron caught in the mangle and had to be freed with great difficulty and, ultimately, the cutting-out scissors. Buttons she sewed on came off again at first tug, and when she mended things, they came out in lumps and rucks and her uneven stitches came undone again. She could not cook, and when helping in the kitchen she scalded and gashed herself in such style that Mrs Welland had taken her off kitchen duties permanently. And even carrying things to the table she was likely to spill or drop them. Worst of all, to Peter, was to see how her inefficiency distressed her. She was used to commanding and to being waited on and admired. That was what she was good at. At first she had been so glad of her new haven that in the evenings she had sometimes coaxed a tune out of the elderly and infirm piano, and clowned and made them laugh. Now at the end of the day she was silent, exhausted and depressed.

He said, 'But you'll learn, Fanny. It's all new to you. You'll learn in time.'

She gave him a strange look, and then sat down, her back to the mangle and her knees drawn up, and wiped her wet eyes on her forearm. 'Well,' she said, 'at least we agree that I am useless.'

He sat too, beside her. 'Not useless,' he said. 'Just not very good at housework.'

'Look,' she said mournfully, 'look at my poor hands.' She stretched them out and turned them over and back. 'What a sad sight! I used to have such lovely hands. A young man in my coming-out year wrote a poem to me about my hands – a very bad poem it was too, but sincere.'

Peter felt embarrassed. He had written several poems about Fanny since she came back to them. Did she know? Had she guessed? 'Do you like poetry?' he asked, trying to sound casual.

'Oh, what have I to do with poetry now, or poetry with me? I'm a pauper and an outcast and everybody hates me.'

'Don't be silly. Nobody hates you.'

'Harriet hates me.'

'She doesn't.'

'You haven't seen the way she looks at me when I do something wrong – which is every minute of the day.'

'She doesn't hate you, Fanny. She pities you very much. She understands what you've suffered. Of everyone in the house, I should think she understands best.'

Fanny looked at him sideways. 'I've often wondered – well, about Harriet. Her life. How she came by—' It seemed too delicate a question to ask. 'She never talks about the past.'

'She never talks about anything. That's just Harriet. You mean Boy, don't you?'

Fanny nodded. 'One can't help noticing she doesn't wear a wedding ring.'

Peter clasped his hands around his knees and stared at the scullery wall opposite. 'Harriet used to be a schoolteacher. A school for poor girls down near the Seven Dials – poor but respectable. She liked the work, and the girls liked her. She was different in those days. Not talkative – she's never been talkative – but cheerful, you know, and quite like other girls. One of the school governors took a fancy to her and courted her, and they were going to get married, which would have been a great thing for her. But then one day when she was walking home from school – it was winter, so it was dark and foggy – she took a short-cut through a court off the main street. A man—' He swallowed and began again. 'A man grabbed her and dragged her into a doorway onto some stairs, and raped her.'

Fanny put both her hands over her mouth. Her eyes above her fingers were wide.

Peter went on, 'She came home at last. We were worried because she was late, but not terribly worried, because she might have stayed late at school. I was standing out in the street looking for her to come. And she came round the corner and staggered against the railings, and I ran to her, and there was blood all over her face and her bonnet was gone and her clothes were all messed up.' He stopped again.

'Oh Peter,' Fanny said, 'I'm so sorry.' She wished she hadn't asked. It was awful to have made him drag out these terrible memories.

He shook his head. 'It's all right. You ought to know. We don't talk about it, but it's right you should know.'

'It must have been terrible.'

'She wouldn't have the doctor – said we couldn't afford it. The blood was from a cut cheek and lip, where he'd hit her to keep her quiet. She had a black eye the next day. I had to take a note to school to say she couldn't come in. And I sent a note to her fiancé, telling him what had happened. I thought he'd come rushing round straight away, but he didn't come at all. After a couple of days I wrote again, thinking maybe he didn't get the first letter. And he wrote back saying under the circumstances he regretted that all further communication between our family and him must cease.'

'Oh Peter!'

'I wanted to kill him,' Peter said conversationally. He looked so mild and lamb-like, the words were utterly incongruous, but they didn't make her laugh. 'And I wanted to kill the man who did it, but she didn't know who it was, and though I made enquiries, and we went to the police about it too, nothing was ever discovered. She didn't even remember which court it was. It made it so hard to bear that one couldn't do anything about it. My sister – and I couldn't do anything.'

Fanny laid a hand on his arm, not knowing what to say.

'Well, I suppose you can guess the rest. She lost her job at the school – they said it was because she was away sick, but I think it was *his* doing. And then after a while she discovered that she was – going to have a child.'

'And that was Boy?'

'And that was Boy. When she found out she cried and cried for days. It was terrible. We thought she'd never stop. We thought she'd lose her wits. But then she stopped, and washed her face, and squared her shoulders, and started to help Mother in the house. And she's been quite all right since, only silent, the way you know her. And she won't go out, not past the end of the road, and never after dark. But apart from that, she's perfectly all right. And she loves Boy – we all do. She wants him to do well and not grow up like his father – whoever that is.'

He stopped quite abruptly, and sat silently, staring at the wall, following his thoughts.

After a bit, Fanny said softly, 'I'm glad you told me, Peter. I'm so very sorry. I had no idea, of course. But I understand now.'

He lifted his head to look at her. 'But you see now, Fanny, why you can feel quite safe here?' She nodded. 'And you needn't worry about not being very good at housework. You don't have to earn your keep – none of us begrudge you anything. You can stay here for ever, whether you learn how to make beds properly or not.'

Fanny didn't know whether to laugh or cry. It made her want to cry to be so useless, and it made her want to laugh that he so tactlessly tried not to admit she was useless. 'I must do something,' she said. 'I can't stay here and let you feed and keep me for nothing. I shall have to go away.'

He looked alarmed. 'You mustn't leave! No, Fanny, don't think of it!'

'I thought you wanted me to go back to Philip,' she said.

'No,' he said, his cheeks unexpectedly reddening, 'I want you to stay here. And I want you to be happy.'

'I can't be happy unless I can earn my keep,' she said, her thin shoulders slumping wearily. 'Oh, what can I do?'

'I'll find you something,' Peter said. 'Not housework – you aren't made for housework. I'll find some work that you can do to earn money. Trust me, Fanny. Just don't talk any more about leaving.'

'I don't want to leave,' she said. She put her head down on her knees. 'I've no home now but here.'

'Then you shall stay here for ever,' he said. 'Don't be afraid. I'll take care of everything.' And greatly daring he reached out a hand and stroked her hair; tentatively at first, but then as she did not object, with more confidence.

Fanny, so sad, so weary, and so alone in the world, sitting on the cold scullery floor with sore hands and in borrowed clothes, was at the end of all resistance to fate. 'You're very kind to me,' she murmured. She closed her eyes, and after a moment, leaned into his caress.

'I'll take care of you, Fanny,' Peter whispered. 'I'll always take care of you.'

On the 5th of November another battle was fought, on the plain before the village of Inkerman, just outside Sebastopol and to the north of the British position. The battle was fought over difficult terrain broken by steep ravines, and in thick fog, so the action was fragmented and it was hard to gain an overall view of what was going on. There was a further confusion in that the British soldiers turned out in greatcoats, which were much the same colour as the Russian's grey coats, and all merged into the treacherous fog. The losses on both side were very heavy: in the English Army some two and a half thousand killed and wounded. Charlotte and Norton laboured in the field hospital all day, where Harper now took them so much for granted that he was momentarily surprised at the surprise of his assistant, Cottesloe, who had come back on duty, dragging himself from his sickbed at the call of duty.

Cottesloe, a gingery, pasty-faced young man, made paler by his recent tussle with dysentery, looked shocked at the sight of women in the tent, and hastened to bring his chief's attention to them and offered to chase them away.

'What? Oh, no, Lady Southport and Mrs Norton are trained nurses. They know what they are doing. Just leave 'em alone, Cott, and come and hold this leg. Todger, can't you stop that man screaming? Well give him a tot of rum. And for God's sake clear up that mess, before I slip on it.'

Charlotte and Harper had now developed a system: as the wounded were brought in, she classified them into hopeless, desperate, and not so bad. The first two categories were laid out on one side of the tent, and Harper and Cottesloe saw to the desperate, and as many of the hopeless as they had time for; the not so badly wounded were put on the other side, and Charlotte and Norton dealt with them. Norton, once she had got over her reluctance, had become very quick and dextrous at stitching, so much so that her fame had spread, and those soldiers left to Charlotte's needlework eyed her with misgiving and asked if they couldn't wait for Mrs Norton. Charlotte, having now passed beyond any limits of squeamishness or doubt, was prepared to dig out bullets, too, if they were not too deep in, because to wait for Harper or Cottesloe to do it meant that an otherwise lightly wounded soldier could not be bandaged and moved out, and space in the tent was precious.

Most of Harper's work seemed to be amputations, and Charlotte never quite grew reconciled to it. She felt the terror and agony of the soldiers very much, and though she never looked, she heard, and shook. She sometimes had to hide her face and bite hard on her arm or sleeve for a moment before she could go on, when some wretched victim's terrified sobbing rose above the background noises of the tent. It was such an appalling and wasteful brutality. In the normal way of things, back home in England, two out of three amputees died, of shock or infection; here it was likely to be more. But there was no time to try to save the limbs, no time and no chloroform and no skilled surgeons. Army medicos were butchers, as she was discovering, but that was in the nature of their trade. A sensitive man would never have survived to be even of so limited a use. So here in the field anything that was badly smashed came off, and with no anaesthetic, the best Harper could do for the men was to be quick. He seemed sometimes to work almost in his sleep, cutting, sawing, suturing; then the pallid Cottesloe tossed the discarded limb out through the rear flap onto the growing pile behind the hospital tent, and the limp victim was replaced with the next.

On the 6th, in the late afternoon, the funerals were held of two generals, Cathcart and Strangway, who had died in the action. Afterwards Lord Raglan made a round of some of the hospitals. It was a sign of his particular compassion that he regularly made these visits, both to the field hospitals and the general hospital in Balaclava, and the men appreciated it very much, and spoke of Lord Raglan with respect and affection. The general officers, Charlotte had noted, did not visit their men when they were sick or wounded. It was not customary, nor thought necessary. They regarded their men, she sometimes thought, less as sentient beings than as crude ammunition.

Raglan was very much surprised to find Charlotte at her labours, and was inclined to be severe with Harper for having allowed it. Charlotte stepped in to defend him.

'Indeed, Lord Raglan, Doctor Harper did try to send me away, but I was quite un-sendable. Only consider, my lord, how much there has been to do, and how few to do it. You must allow me to be of help where I can.'

'But my dear duchess, I had no idea, no idea at all! This is not women's work! Sick-nursing, perhaps – but even that is only fit for women, not for ladies. The sights – the horrors – ladies are too delicate for such things, ma'am –

and to mix with common soldiers! No, no, I must insist you come away at once. Does Southport know you are here? I'm sure he does not know what you are about, my dear.'

'Of course, sir; did you think I would do anything my husband didn't like? Do recollect, my lord, that I have frequently done hospital work in England—'

'Yes, yes,' Raglan said, becoming, for him, quite agitated, 'but surely, ma'am, you only supervised the efforts of others? And it was not like this! Civilian hospitals are different. This is war, ma'am, and quite beyond anything any lady should witness.'

'Nevertheless,' she said gravely, 'I must do what I can. Look at these poor fellows, my lord. They have done their duty so bravely. Would you deny them the help I can give?'

'But it is not *your* duty,' Raglan said stubbornly.

Charlotte stuck her chin up at him in return. 'After the battle of Waterloo, as you no doubt remember, my lord, my grandmother tended the wounded with her own hands in just this way – and with the Duke of Wellington's full approval.'

Airey, standing behind Raglan and witnessing it all with amusement, said, 'There we are, then, my lord. When her grace invokes the Duke, we are done for! And besides, what ladies set their mind on, they will have. We men cannot hope to prevail against determined ladies.'

'Hmph!' said Raglan, unconvinced. 'I remember your grandmama very well, ma'am, and she was as stubborn as a – well, the Duke had no choice but to let her have her way in the end.'

'Just so,' Charlotte said with a smile, laying her hand on his arm, 'so it's much better not to waste energy arguing, don't you think?'

'It will look well in despatches,' Airey mentioned in

Raglan's ear. 'Female nurses are all the rage at home. Besides – you remember, sir, that instruction we had from the Cabinet Office last month?'

'Eh? What's that?'

'From the Duke of Newcastle, that they were sending out a party of nurses to the Bosphorus – Sidney Herbert's pet scheme. You remember, sir, we were asked to give Miss Nightingale every assistance.'

'Miss Nightingale?' Charlotte exclaimed. 'So she is to come after all?'

'With a party of forty nurses,' Airey said. 'Should be in Constantinople by now, if they had a reasonable passage.'

'Lord Palmerston asked me to lead that party,' Charlotte said, 'but I declined because I was coming here with my husband.' She turned to Raglan. 'You see, my lord, that my being here is fully endorsed, albeit indirectly, by the Cabinet.'

'But Constantinople is not the Crimea,' Raglan said, 'and Miss Nightingale's nurses are women, not ladies. And besides, their duties will be to make slops and messes for the sick, and mend sheets, and so on. Not – not this!' He waved his hand expressively round the tent. 'However, I see you will not be persuaded. I don't like it, I must tell you. I don't like it at all. But if you will stay – is there anything I can do to make your task easier?'

'Thank you, sir, only do what you can to ensure the wounded have the quickest possible passage to Constantinople. Oh, and, if it is not too much trouble, could you have the amputated limbs removed from the back of the tent? Some of them have been there since the battle of Balaclava, sir, and it is not sanitary.'

Raglan blinked a little, and seemed embarrassed that she should have to ask such a thing. 'Oh, assuredly,

assuredly. I will see to it. A party of Turks, Adye, to remove those things as soon as possible.'

When the staff officers had left, Harper looked at Charlotte curiously and said, 'That's as close to an endorsement from Lord Raglan as you're likely to get. You've got your way. I can't understand, though, why you should want to do it.'

She returned his gaze steadily. 'Probably for the same reason as you – because I *can*. God knows I don't like it here! I hate the pain and the mess and the awful, awful *waste* of it! But I can't stand by and do nothing – and if you made me, it would break my heart.'

A slow smile curved Harper's lips. He was a plain man without beauty or distinction in his features, without even youth, for he was past forty and his moustache and close-cropped hair were greying; but when he smiled, Charlotte thought only that they had laboured – side by side, if not together – in the same cause, and that was beauty enough.

'You're a strange creature,' he said. It was not the way a humble medico ought to address a duchess, but somehow, there was no offence in it. 'Thank God for you, though. Ah, what's this coming in now? Shot in the trenches, eh? Oh, on fatigue party. Wandered too far from the others, I suppose. You men seem to think the Russians are out there having picnics. No, my lad, I'm not going to take your arm off, not this time. The bone is broken, but it's a clean break, lucky for you. This lady will dress and splint you. Yes, it's a lady! Lord, how you stare! Have you never seen a lady before? Well, perhaps not one like this, so I can't blame you. It does tend to take your breath away, the first time you see an angel.'

In the afternoon of the 7th the flood of wounded had slowed to a trickle, and Harper insisted that Charlotte

508

and Norton went off-duty. He was going himself as soon as Cottesloe came back from escorting the wounded down to the harbour. They needed little urging. More even than rest or food, Charlotte was longing for a bath. They fetched their horses from the lines and rode down to Balaclava, to the welcome luxury of the *Doris*, where Charlotte insisted that she would look after herself. It was ludicrous, she said, that Norton, who had worked all day as hard as she had, if not harder, should propose to maid her at the end of it. Norton, who had been thinking all the way down the hill of a mustard-bath for her aching feet, was glad to obey.

Oliver, having been sent a message at Headquarters, joined Charlotte for dinner: mock-turtle soup, local fish – rather bony but with a pleasant flavour – a salad dressed with oil and vinegar, mutton cutlets, boiled turkey with cabbage, and rice pudding with preserves.

'Enjoy it,' Oliver said. 'Especially the greenstuffs. Fresh food is going to be harder to come by for the next few months.'

'So we are wintering here?' Charlotte said.

'There's no doubt of it. There was a council of war at Headquarters this morning, with the chiefs of staff of both armies. Raglan wanted to attack the town this morning, while the Russians are still reeling from the battle. From what the prisoners tell us, they must have lost about fifteen thousand men on the 5th, and some deserters say that the Russians are very disheartened not to have dislodged us. A decisive blow against the town now could carry it. But the French wouldn't hear of it. Canrobert said we must wait for reinforcements, and confine ourselves to defensive action, and nothing anyone could say would persuade him otherwise. So we are to initiate no new action for the present.'

'Couldn't Lord Raglan act without the French?'

Oliver shook his head. 'We've only about sixteen thousand men fit for duty now. So Sebastopol stands, and we stand with it. One or two of the generals asked if we could not evacuate, but that's impossible: the Russians may be slow, but they wouldn't let us leave unmolested. So Raglan has given orders for the hutting of the troops. They can't stay all winter in tents. The ships are being sent out tomorrow to bring suitable wood and materials for making huts. And warm clothing and boots are ordered, too. The uniforms the men came out with were most impractical – besides having gone through a great battle.'

'Yes, they're coming into the field hospital looking like scarecrows,' Charlotte said. 'Rents and patches everywhere.'

'Fortunately there are about four thousand Russian corpses lying out there on the field of Inkerman – all wearing good Russian greatcoats and good long Russian boots,' Oliver said.

'I don't like to hear you speaking so cynically,' Charlotte said.

He shrugged. 'This is a beastly war.' He stared reflectively into his glass for a moment, then made an effort. 'And what has my charming wife been doing all this time? I haven't seen you for three days.'

'I'm sure you know perfectly well what I've been doing,' Charlotte said gravely.

He grinned. 'You put poor Raglan in quite a fret. Ladies in field hospitals? Whatever next! But of course once you had brought the Duke of Wellington into the argument – rather hitting below the belt, wasn't it, my love?'

'Did you hear about the party of nurses that have gone to Constantinople?'

'Yes, they arrived on the 3rd, I understand. I don't

510

envy them their task. Conditions in Scutari are vile, and they won't be welcomed by the medicos: their having been sent out by the War Office is being taken as an insult and a criticism. John Hall was grumbling about it today. He thinks Miss Nightingale is a spy sent out by those who have denied him promotion.'

'He's Chief of Medical Staff, isn't he? Harper has mentioned him in passing. I haven't met him.'

'If I were you I should take good care not to. Which brings me to the point, my love – you are safe enough up at the field hospital, now that the Chief has given his blessing, but I warn you against going into the general hospital at Balaclava. Hall is a woman-hater and a disappointed man besides. Of course, he's only a medico, and not even a gentleman, but even Raglan thought better of telling him what you were doing up on the plateau. If you were to put your nose round the door of one of his preserves, all hell would be let loose.'

'But might he not come up to the field hospital?'

'In the highest degree unlikely. He rarely goes abroad. But you will be going home soon in any case, I imagine.'

'I hadn't really thought about it,' Charlotte said. 'I thought we would all be going before winter set in.'

'Once the hard weather comes down there'll be no more action, and a lot of the general officers will go home. There will be nothing for you to do. It will be very unpleasant here, too, and I do wonder about the supply situation. It seems very precarious. Poor old Filder has only three clerks to help him supply the whole Army – and one of those has only got one eye!'

'Will you come home too?'

'I hope so. But whether I do or not, you will want to be at home, to comfort your mother and Batchworth.'

'Yes, and to see after little William. We can't let Mrs Phipps have him.'

'So you will go, then?'

'Yes, very well, as soon as things are back to normal at the field hospital. Cottesloe doesn't really know what he's doing, and the other assistant, Sankey, is still ill. I can't leave poor Harper so exposed. He's a good fellow, you know, Oliver. And from what I've gathered, good fellows are few and far between in the Army Medical Service.'

'Just so. Doctor Hall is a fine example – a wooden-headed brute, and as spiteful as an adder.'

'I don't like to leave you, though,' Charlotte said abruptly.

He laid his hand over hers. 'I don't like you to leave me either. But I wouldn't have you here through the winter. Cattley knows the Crimea very well, and he says all the signs are that it's going to be a very hard one. As cold as the nights are now, they will be ten times worse before spring.'

'As cold as the nights are now – shall we go to bed and keep each other warm?'

He smiled. 'How could I refuse an invitation like that?'

When they were in bed together he took her into his arms, her head on his shoulder, and stroked her hair tenderly. Loving her, he knew her every movement and gesture and pause; he knew that now at last she wanted to speak about Cavendish, and he waited patiently for it to come. Though he had every advantage over her, of sex, of birth, of standing, of education, it would always be she who shaped their lives together, she who held the power. Yet in a perverse way, this fact only made her the more needy, and his protection of her the more imperative.

At last she said, 'I keep thinking, you see, that it was all a mistake; that he died for a mistake.'

'You could say the same of everyone in this war.'

512

'But that only makes it worse!' she cried. 'That means all the deaths have been wasted.'

'Death is always a waste,' he said.

'But sometimes necessary, to bring about a good.'

'Perhaps,' he said. 'But I don't think wars are ever about good, in that sense. They are about territory, and territory is about trade, and trade is about money. We got into this war to stop the Russians getting hold of Constantinople, that's all.'

'Oliver, don't talk like that. You don't really believe that, do you?'

He paused, thinking it through. 'I think that war is a left-over from primitive times. When two tribes fought each other for a piece of hunting ground, food and survival were directly at stake. But it's an absurdity in these modern times, with steam-ships and railways to speed us about the world, and telegraphic communication to let us know what everyone is doing and thinking in the blink of an eye, that we're still lining up men on an irrelevant piece of ground to see which side is stronger. That's no way to decide modern issues. It's an anachronism we haven't managed to shake off. And now that we have modern weapons, rifles and artillery and mortars, we can inflict such terrible damage on so many.'

'That's not how Cavendish felt. He was so excited and proud when he started for the war, to be fighting for his country.'

'Yes, the words *are* exciting. I felt it too, in the beginning. But I think we civilised countries are all too old to be playing boys' games any more.'

'Is that what killed Cavendish? A boys' game? Then it really was for nothing.' She broke off, tearfully. 'Why do you say these things to me?'

'I swore when I first fell in love with you always to tell you the truth.'

'And what is the truth?' she asked resentfully.

'That he was brave, and honourable, and noble, and he died a noble death. But I don't believe that a death's being "for" something makes it easier to bear. You are too intelligent to delude yourself about that. And you're too generous to begrudge him your grief.' He held her tighter. 'Darling one, I know how hard it is for you. I know why you work so hard and spare yourself nothing.'

He felt her giving. 'Oh, Oliver,' she whispered, 'I loved him so much.'

'I know.'

And then the tears came, like the relief of rain after a long, oppressive day. She cried awkwardly at first, as one not accustomed to it, finding it painful to let go the strong control she had always kept over herself. But he held her quietly, not trying to comfort or soothe, but simply accepting; and then she allowed herself to cry. She cried for her dear and lovely brother, and for all the dreadful, piteous suffering she had witnessed. She cried until she had no more tears, and was left emptied and exhausted, resting against the strong quietness of her husband.

After grief, love seemed to come naturally. She was emptied, and he was there to fill her. He began simply by kissing her brow and stroking the damp hair from her face, as one would comfort a child. But then she turned her mouth up to him for kisses and he felt her stirring against him, and his scalp prickled with the intimation of passion. Since the birth of the twins, he had been very careful, not wishing her to fall pregnant again; but Charlotte had forgotten by now, as women do, the pains of childbirth. There was something both magnificent and touching to her in a strong man's losing all control in her arms. She wanted that; she wanted to feel her power over him, to ease her powerlessness over death. She wanted to possess him, knowing that she possessed nothing else of certainty. Their passion grew; and when the moment came and he tried to draw back from her, she drew him hard against her, kissing him with such intensity that he could not resist. She felt the surge of his life in her, and was filled and comforted and made whole again. Then a wonderful warm languor came over her, as though she had come to the end of a long and difficult journey; and before he had even withdrawn from her, she was sliding down darkly, softly into sleep.

CHAPTER TWENTY

Charlotte fully meant to go home, but on the evening of the 8th a torrential rain started, which went on without pausing for two days, turning sleetier day by day. Because of the nature of the terrain, the British trenches did not drain properly, and many of them were soon filled knee-deep with icy slush. The men on trench duty were continually scrambling out of the trenches to get away from it and restore the feeling to their feet, and once out of the shelter they were exposed to Russian fire. A dismal procession of dead and wounded came down from the trenches every day, to add to the other victims of the rain: men suffering from exposure and frostbite, and an astonishing variety of injuries caused by slipping in the mud. One man came in with a broken pelvis and crushed rib-cage where an ox had lost its footing and fallen on top of him; another lost an eye through slipping and falling on a tent-peg.

The road up from Balaclava to the plateau had been turned into a river during the rain, and now it was a knee-deep slough of mud and manure in which wheeled vehicles sank helplessly. Everything had to be taken up and down by pack animals, which were still – as they had been from the beginning – in short supply; and even they had the greatest difficulty in making the ascent. Coming down to the *Doris* on the 11th, trying to pick a way for her horse through the ruts and potholes, Charlotte passed a pair of loaded mules coming up who were stuck hard in the mud, their eyes rolling in terror, sunk to their hocks and sinking deeper with every agonised attempt to drag themselves out. She remembered Oliver's remarks about the road when they had first arrived. Of course, there had never been the manpower free to do anything about surfacing it; but with winter coming on, she wondered how in the world they were going to get food and fuel and fodder up to the plateau in sufficient quantities to keep the army from starving.

On the 11th and 12th reinforcements arrived at Balaclava, a thousand men from the 67th and 97th regiments, adding to the problems of the commissariat, and bringing with them a fresh influx of cholera, dysentery and accidental injuries; and Sankey, Harper's other assistant who seemed to have been recovering, died. Charlotte could not leave yet, even though she was very worried about the horses. Up on the plateau there was virtually no grazing, and without sufficient pack animals, not enough fodder was being brought up to sustain them. Cavalry mounts could not be used to fetch their own fodder, because they had to be ready for action at any time. The troop horses were getting very thin and weak, and in desperation to fill their bellies they nibbled at anything within range – tether ropes and leather straps and even, when tied up together, each other's manes and tails. The troopers, when not on duty, scoured the hillsides for anything the horses could eat, even scraping lichen off the rocks. Charlotte did what she could by staying up on the plateau with Norton – they used Cavendish's tent now when they did not go down to sleep on the yacht – and sending her groom down, leading her own and Norton's horses, and Cavendish's other horse, Bracken. With three led horses, her groom could fetch up enough fodder to feed her four and some of the troop horses, but it was a dreadful journey to have to do every day.

But if things were bad, they were soon to get worse. On the afternoon of the 13th Oliver rode over to the field hospital to see her. 'Cattley says there's a storm coming. The wind is getting up and the glass is dropping like a stone, and he thinks it will be a bad one. The Black Sea is prone to hurricanes at this time of year. So you'd better sleep at Headquarters tonight. Those tents won't provide much shelter.'

Charlotte was too much preoccupied with her work to do more than acknowledge his instructions; but when she left the hospital tent in the afternoon she found it prematurely dark, and as she stepped outside the force of the wind pushed her off-balance so that she staggered into Norton. The sky was a lowering mass of black clouds, and there was a threatening, briny smell in the air. 'Good God, where did all this come from?' she said to Norton.

'The wind's been getting up all day,' Norton said. 'Didn't you hear it beating on the canvas?'

Charlotte was greeted at Headquarters with the same eagerness as when she had first gone to the cavalry camp. Men confined together for a long period come to know each other's conversation by heart, and a newcomer – especially a handsome woman – is always welcome. She and Oliver dined at Lord Raglan's table: pea soup with bacon; caviar, which one of the deserters had brought in; smoked ham with pickled cucumbers; roasted chickens; and a pudding with plum preserve. Charlotte was always faintly surprised that working all day amidst such horrors she never lost her appetite. In her honour some of the best wine was got out – sherry, hock and champagne – and the conversation grew merry, avoiding, by unspoken consent, the subject of the war. But after dinner one of the younger officers, a fair, boyish-looking subaltern called Lindsay, was persuaded to sing for them unaccompanied. He had a sweet, true tenor, and in the newly reflective atmosphere that he generated, Charlotte was made aware again of the aching of her heart, which daily labour of the hospital allowed her to ignore. She had to rest her face in her hands to hide the tears; but everyone was remembering someone they had lost. Soon the party broke up and the company retired to bed in a subdued and thoughtful mood.

Charlotte and Oliver had to cross the yard between the farmhouse, where Raglan lived, and the subordinate cottage where Oliver had been allotted a tiny room. As they stepped out the black wall of wind hit them, and they staggered backwards; the door was snatched from the hand of the officer holding it and slammed back violently, missing the head of the man following him by a fraction of an inch.

'That was a near thing, Williams,' someone said. 'It would have been too bad if you escaped death from that shell up at the battery yesterday, and then got decapitated by a domestic door.'

'Ah well, a miss is as good as a mile,' Williams said lightly. 'At least I shan't have to shave tomorrow.'

Charlotte and Oliver struggled across to the cottage, holding on to each other tightly, leaning at a perilous angle. The wind battered against their ears, and every now and then something whirled past them, too quickly to be identified – some debris, or bush, or branch probably. They were glad to get back indoors, to the comparative quietness. Oliver's room was small and bare, but the walls were thick, with only one small window high up, so they were as safe as it was possible to be. It was very cold, however, and they hurried to get into the narrow bed and hold each other tightly. For a while Charlotte lay, enjoying the warmth of Oliver's arms and listening to the wind howl outside, and then she fell asleep.

She was woken by a tremendous bang. She opened her eyes. It was pitch dark and bitterly cold. She felt that Oliver was awake too. 'What was that?' she whispered.

'I don't know,' he said. They listened. The wind was howling more loudly than ever, and there was another sound added to it, a rhythmic rattling and thudding somewhere nearby. After a moment Oliver released himself from her arms, got up and went over to the window. Charlotte heard him exclaim under his breath, and then he was hurrying back, getting in beside her, icy even after so short an exposure. 'It was the shutters being ripped off. One of them's hanging by one nail – that's what's banging. It'll go in a minute – yes, there it goes.'

'The wind's worse, isn't it?'

'Yes, and it's as black as Newgate knocker out there. I can't see a single star. There'll be rain or snow with it before morning.'

'The poor horses,' she said. 'They've no shelter at all, not even a tent.'

She slept again, but uneasily, half waking at every sudden sound; only falling deeply asleep again towards dawn. When she woke in the morning, Oliver was out of bed and dressing. The wind was screaming past the unshuttered window, and her heart sank: somehow she had thought of the gale as something belonging to the night; she had expected, illogically, that the morning light would dispel it.

She started to get up, and Oliver, looking over his shoulder, said, 'You may as well stay there.'

'But I must get down to the hospital,' she protested.

He gave her a grim smile. He knew why she was so desperate to keep working. 'My dear girl, you haven't the slightest chance in the world of getting there.'

'Is it really that bad?'

'We shall be lucky to keep this roof on,' he said.

'But what about the men? Their tents will be blown away.'

'Doubtless they will, but we can't help them. It would be impossible to stand upright out there. All any of us can do is stay inside and wait until the wind drops. You'll have to resign yourself to inactivity, my love, hard though that is.'

The inactivity was dreadful for Charlotte; her unoccupied mind at once filled with thoughts she had been at pains to bury. Her brother, her only brother, was dead, his life thrown away in a pointless action which had been a stupid mistake. And all morning the wind screamed in counterpoint to her tormented thoughts. Every time it went up a pitch Charlotte thought it couldn't get any higher; and every time it did. Sometimes it fell away a little, prompting hopes that it was easing off, but the lulls were temporary. It was, as Oliver had said, impossible to go outside. From the window Charlotte saw objects whirled by – tents, kettles, branches, barrels, camp-beds, a ceremonial drum – some regiment would be deeply unhappy about that – and other things unidentifiable. Even if one could stand up, one would run the risk of being knocked down and killed by flying debris.

And still it grew worse. The sky was black, lending a strange twilight to the nightmare. During one squall, part of the roof of Lord Raglan's house was ripped off and disappeared, and the contents of the room below it were scooped out as if by a giant hand, sending aides scrabbling about after flying papers. A tree went whirling past, uprooted whole – probably the rain had washed away the earth that held it. Charlotte saw an ox cart, with two oxen still harnessed to it, go by backwards, the oxen with their legs braced being dragged along the ground resistlessly, their eyes wide with helpless fear, and the sight made her cry. What of the horses? What of the men? What

521

of the sick? Could the field hospital have survived when the roof of a solid farmhouse could not?

At last in the middle of the afternoon the wind began to fall, abating from a hurricane to a mere gale; and then it began to snow.

The destruction was appalling. There wasn't a tent left standing on the plateau. During the worst of the wind, the men had sought what shelter they could, crouching behind boulders or walls if they were lucky, lying down in hollows in the ground if they were not. Now they rose up shakily, frozen, wet and hungry, and surveyed the devastation. Tangles of debris lay where the wind had dropped them, rapidly taking on a covering of snow. An apathy of despair was over the Army. Clothes, food, furniture, camp equipment, all were smashed and scattered, and the men were left with the tattered, mud-soaked clothes they stood up in. They stood silently, with nothing to say to each other, poked hopelessly at heaps of debris, stared almost in tears at some broken object they had picked up out of the mire. If a child in a tantrum had smashed a box of toy soldiers with a hammer and scattered the results about the nursery floor, it could not have been a more comprehensive ruin of an army.

Loose horses were everywhere, driven helplessly by the wind for miles, as their regimental brands showed. Some stood apathetically and were easy to catch; others, terrified, or desperate for food, would not be approached. There was hardly a single waggon left fit to drive. None of the men had eaten since the night before, and it was doubtful when they would eat again; and night was coming on, and it was freezing.

As soon as she could leave Headquarters, Charlotte went to the cavalry camp. Oliver went with her, not liking her to go out alone. They found the camp by the men wandering around little heaps of debris, for there was nothing else to mark it. Cavendish's tent was gone, and most of his possessions were either missing or destroyed. His trunk remained, being of solid oak, only half sunk in the mud, and his favourite saddle, soaked and hardly recognisable, and a box of tinned food which had been too heavy to be whisked off by the wind. Her groom's horse had been recaptured and was tied up with the troop-horses, all of them gathering a white coat of snow; but Bracken was gone. It could only be hoped that someone would find him and bring him back. He carried the regimental saddle-brand, but he was a fine horse, and brands could be altered; and if he crossed the Russian lines the Cossacks would have him for sure.

From there they went to field hospital. The hospital tent was just a few ribbons of soaked canvas and some splintered poles. The wounded were in pitiful case, soaked to the skin, without a blanket to cover them; and many of them had been blown or washed off the duck-boards which had formed the floor of the hospital and were lying half-buried and helpless in the mud. Nobody seemed to be doing anything about it. Todger was there, walking about in an ineffectual way from one man to another, waiting to be told what to do about this disaster beyond his comprehension. Harper had gone down to the harbour the night before and it would be hours more before he could get back up, and Cottesloe and the other two orderlies were nowhere to be seen.

'Todger, where is Mr Cottesloe?'

Todger turned at the sound of her voice, and a look of unutterable relief came over his face. Here was someone at last to take the weight of responsibility from his shoulders. 'Oh m'lady, thank Gawd you're here! The wounded is all wet and the 'orspital is all blown to bits and the blankets gorn. I dunno what to do for 'em. There's Baxter there bleedin' again, and two of 'em are dead, and Foster says 'e can't feel 'is feet.'

'Very well, we'll do what we can,' she said, trying to calm him, 'but where is Mr Cottesloe?'

'I dunno, m'lady. I ain't seed 'im.'

'What about Hay and Biggs?'

'I seed them somewhere abouts, m'lady – a-lookin' for salvage, I think.'

'Very well, go and find them and tell them to come here at once – quickly now!'

'You'll need more help than that,' Oliver said. 'These men ought to be taken down to Balaclava.'

Charlotte made a helpless gesture. 'I know, but even if the road is passable, what can they be transported on? There are no waggons.'

'Very well, the regiment will have to provide labour. I wonder who's in charge here? I'll go and find an officer and get him to detail some men to help you.'

Oliver found a Major Quainton trying to organise salvage operations.

'Oh good Lord, I'd forgotten about the hospital,' the major said when Oliver put his request. 'Why aren't the medicos seeing about it?'

'Harper is down in Balaclava and Cottesloe is not to be found, it seems,' Oliver said. 'The orderlies on their own can't manage. I need a fatigue party of your men to rig some sort of shelter for the wounded before they all die of cold – if you please.' He had no direct authority over Quainton so he had to put it in the form of a request; though as a duke and a member of Headquarters' staff, his request ought to have carried the weight of a command. But Quainton had other things on his mind.

'I'm sorry, sir, but I can't spare any men. You see what there is to be done here. The men have got to have some sort of shelter tonight.'

'So have the wounded,' Oliver pointed out.

Quainton stepped aside and lowered his voice. 'Look here, your grace, you know and I know that most of the wounded are going to die anyway. They are not my responsibility. My duty is to active men, who can be saved, and who will be needed if the Russkies attack again. I'm sorry, but you must excuse me.'

A young lieutenant at his elbow spoke up. 'Sir, you could spare a couple of men, couldn't you? Let me take two men and see what I can do. You know that dreadful fellow from *The Times* is somewhere about,' he added almost in a whisper. 'Wouldn't it just be jam for him, if it got out Lady Southport was tending the wounded all alone?'

Quainton's eyebrow climbed his forehead in exasperation. 'Was there ever such a plagued army in the history of man?' he fumed. 'As if everything else isn't bad enough, to have that damned spying blackguard Russell parroting about us in the papers! Why don't Raglan send the bounder home? Oh, very well, Fisher. Very well, your grace,' turning to Oliver, 'I suppose we can't let them lie there in the mud. Fisher here will come and see what he can do about it.'

Between them they managed to get a shelter rigged, and the wounded moved onto the duckboards so that at least they were out of the freezing mud. There was nothing they could do to dry their clothes. There wasn't a dry blanket anywhere to be found, and no possibility of lighting a fire, for though there was plenty of broken wood around, it was all wet through. Charlotte had doubts about many of the wounded seeing another morning. She chafed their hands and feet – those who had them – and piled on anything she could find by way of covers. Oliver found a bottle of brandy buried in the mud, miraculously unbroken, and they distributed that, a mouthful each to try to warm them up.

By then it was dark, and bitterly cold, and Oliver insisted that she return to Headquarters with him. She didn't want to leave the wounded, but he pointed out that there was nothing more she could do for them, that it was not her responsibility, and that if she made herself ill she would be even less able to help. 'The orderlies can do anything there is to do. They're used to hardship, and you aren't. Come, my dear, I insist.'

He had hardly ever insisted on anything in their life together, and she obeyed meekly.

The next morning reports came in of something very alarming. The hurricane had not only swept the land, it had lashed the sea to a frenzy. Twenty-one of the ships riding at anchor outside the bay of Balaclava had been sunk or driven onto the rocks and smashed to bits; eight more had been badly damaged. It was a disaster. The cargoes of the lost ships had included winter clothes and boots, hutting materials, food, and the desperately needed fodder, all of which were now at the bottom of the ocean or scattered, sodden and ruined, on the beaches. But the loss of the ships was even more serious: transport ships were in any case in short supply, and everything consumed at Balaclava had to be brought there by sea.

The men on duty during the night in the trenches and the outlying vedettes had suffered terribly. Dozens were carried into the camps paralysed from cold; several had been found dead at their posts. And twenty-four of the Royal Artillery horses had died, and thirty-five cavalry mounts. The 17th Lancers was down to nine horses.

Charlotte went back to the hospital. Several of the wounded had died in the night, but the numbers had been swelled by the men brought in frozen. Todger had news for her that he was eager to impart: Cottesloe had been found.

'Found?'

'Dead, m'lady, dead as a 'erring. Lying out in the snow, 'e was, about a 'unnerd yards from the edge of the camp. Gawd knows 'ow he come there. Blown be the wind, I wouldn't wonder. 'E 'ad a gash acrorst 'is 'ed, m'lady.'

'Hit by flying debris, perhaps. Poor man.'

At noon Harper arrived, having started up from Bala-clava before dawn. He stood for a moment staring at the ruins of the camp. 'Man proposes, but God disposes,' he said.

'I am so glad you are here,' Charlotte said. 'Cottesloe is dead.'

'Have you coped all alone? I dare say you performed miracles to reach even this state of chaos.'

'How are things in the harbour?' Charlotte asked anxiously. 'We heard that many ships were damaged and some sunk. I don't suppose you noticed whether the *Doris*—'

'Is afloat and undamaged,' Harper interrupted. 'I thought you would want to know, so I took the liberty of making enquiries before I came up.'

'Thank you,' Charlotte said. 'She's full of stores – amongst them medical supplies.'

'Yes, I know.' Harper said. 'My enquiries were not entirely disinterested.'

'I think the best thing I can do, now you are here, is to go down to the harbour and see what we can bring up that is most urgently needed,' Charlotte said.

'Be prepared,' Harper said. 'It's something of a mess down there.'

Oliver and Charlotte rode down together, taking two horses to act as pack animals when they came up again. Harper had not told the half of it. Balaclava had been sheltered from the worst of the wind, but still it presented a shattered face, with dead branches, twigs and leaves scattered everywhere, tiles missing from roofs, trees uprooted. The ships rolled uneasily in the last of the swell, many with broken stays and broken yards. One ship which had pulled her anchor was beached on the wrong side of the bay with her nose to the cliff. The quayside was in utter confusion: broken boxes and barrels, pieces of wood, split flour-sacks spewing sodden flour caked into lumps like gigantic fungi; dead horses, sheep offal, rotting vegetables, pieces of frayed rope, splintered spars and torn canvas, ruined bales of clothing and split and soaking bales of hay, all lay jumbled together, scavenged amongst by pi-dogs and lean rats.

The surface of the harbour had been churned to a yellow broth of filth and excrement, and floating on its surface was a hideous collection of amputated legs and arms, many of them still clad in their sleeves and trousers. Lord Raglan had ordered a fatigue party of Turks to remove the heap of limbs from behind the hospital tent, but he had not told them what to do with them; so with the insane logic of the peasant, the Turks had dumped them into the harbour, out of sight being out of mind. Charlotte felt a kind of hysteria rising in her. Wasn't that just like the Turks? Wasn't that just like Raglan? And wasn't that just, above anything, like this war?

The weather continued vile, constant rain interrupted only by flurries of snow. Every morning brought in new casualties from the trenches, not just bullet wounds, but men with paralysed limbs and frostbitten extremities. Cholera was also on the increase again, as well as dysentery and fever. The victims filled the field hospitals, where there were no facilities for dealing with them; it was only with the greatest difficulty that any of them could be taken down to Balaclava, because of the state of the roads. From Balaclava they were put on transport ships for the military hospital at Scutari. Short as that journey was, one in ten died in transit: the transports were not designed as hospital ships. But many more died in the general hospital in Balaclava before ever embarking, waiting for the transport to become available.

Food, fuel and fodder continued in short supply up on the plateau, because of the difficulty of getting it up from the harbour. As for clothes, the men clad themselves in anything that would give them protection. Those who still had blankets wrapped them round over their greatcoats, securing them with the belt, when they went on night guard. Strips of blanket doubled and wound turban-style replaced lost caps, and mess-tins were favoured headgear in the trenches against the hazards of Russian riflemen. Uniforms were patched with bits of cloth taken from dead comrades and dead Russians: all the regiments were taking on a harlequin look. And the prohibition against beards in the ranks had had to be abandoned, since there was neither water to shave in nor razors to shave with. The beards did at least give some protection from the cold, though men coming in from the trenches in the morning often had long icicles hanging from them, and found that they could not open their mouths until they had got to a fire to thaw the hair out. As she passed amongst the patched and hairy scarecrows who now formed the British Army in the East, Charlotte sometimes thought of the bright regiments she had seen parading so smartly though London on their way to embark. She thought, bitterly, of Cavendish in his absurdly gaudy Hussar uniform, riding his chestnut charger in Hyde Park, all blue and crimson and flashing gold. All the gilt was gone now; even the officers were patched and shabby, except those who had had parcels from home.

Russian corpses were harvested for their boots, their greatcoats – which were thicker and better than the British ones – and their knapsacks, which were greatly prized. Each Russian knapsack contained a 'housewife' which was now the only source of sewing-needles and sewing-thread; and the knapsacks themselves were cut up to make leggings and to patch coats. Some of the men put long stockings on over the remains of their tattered trousers, filled them with rags, and gartered them with strips of knapsack. Others made leggings from sheepskins, horsehides, canvas or even sacking – anything that would make another layer to keep out the cold.

The lack of boots was a terrible trial. Everyone's original footwear had fallen to pieces, and the replacement boots were at the bottom of the sea. Those who had not been lucky enough to scavenge Russian boots wrapped their feet in whatever they could find, but it was often no more than sacking filled with rags, which could not withstand twelve hours of night duty in a trench filled with water. More than once Charlotte unwrapped the rags from a soldier's feet and found the blackened toes falling off with the wrappings. And the man would generally look surprised – for just a moment before he looked horrified – and say, why, I didn't know it was so bad, I never felt nothing.

The soldiers were enormously stoical, both about hardships and wounds. They came from a class that had survived appalling hardship even to arrive at adulthood, and they could endure sufferings that would have killed a man accustomed to soft living. Charlotte could understand the attitude of many of the field officers, who were against 'spoiling' the men with comforts, thus making them too soft to face up to the pains and dangers of battle. But, she thought, there should be moderation in everything. A hard life did not need to be cruel, and proper medical facilities would surely be a benefit: so many seasoned soldiers were being lost through sickness and infection – far more, ten times more, than from battle wounds.

She discussed these things with Harper as they worked – a little desultorily, since they were not often side by side for any great length of time, and since he rarely contributed more to the conversation than a grunt of agreement or otherwise. But she felt that he was listening, that what she had to say interested him and provided him with a new and welcome stimulation – for his job, she thought, must be as monotonous as it was hard. She told him about Doctor Snow's 'proof' that cholera was a water-borne infection; she talked to him about anaesthesia, which he had never encountered and hardly read about – washed, as he was, into the medical backwater of the Army. He asked her what the death toll was from its use. 'There have been deaths,' she admitted. 'Snow says that sometimes people go off quite unexpectedly, and it's impossible yet to say why. But it's a small number, and the benefits are far greater. With amputations, for instance, the survival rate is greatly increased once the drain on the patient's strength of the pain and fear is removed.'

'We are accustomed to say that the pain is a stimulant, and helps recovery,' Harper commented.

'But the proof is in the numbers,' she said eagerly. 'How many do you lose through amputation? Four out of five?' He nodded. 'Using anaesthesia that is reduced to one in two, almost one in three – and I believe if only we could conquer infection, we should save them all.'

He gave a little shake of the head, as if to say that infection, like the poor, was always with them; so she told him of the experiments Doctor Reynolds had been following, of hand-washing and trying to eliminate the 'seeds of disease'.

He cast her a little look, which she took to be reproachful.

'Of course,' she said quickly, 'in a situation like this, you have problems not dreamed of in civilian hospitals. I suppose in the Army you must always be operating under extreme conditions.'

He said, 'Hand-washing is certainly out of the question here. And there's no time after a battle.'

'Just so. But Reynolds – and some other doctors he writes to – is experimenting with various solutions, in the hope of finding one strong enough so that simply dipping the hands and instruments in a bowl of it will be enough to kill the seeds.'

He grunted. 'Wishful thinking.'

'That's what was said about anaesthesia ten years ago,' Charlotte pointed out.

One time a soldier came in asking for the bandage on his arm to be replaced as it was coming loose. Charlotte asked him when he had got his wound, and he said at the Alma.

'Surely this is not the same dressing that was put on after the Alma?' she asked. The soldier seemed surprised by the question. If a man was fit for duty, there was no provision for further visits to the medico, and the wound being in his left arm, he had been reckoned able enough. When she unwrapped the bandage, she found it full of maggots – two pints, at least, she reckoned, as they dropped to the floor in pale lumps like cake batter. For the soldier's sake – he was watching her face for reassurance – she controlled her instant desire to spring back with an exclamation of disgust. Maggots were a feature of hospital life, like lice, but for sheer volume this surpassed all previous experience.

'How is it, miss?' the man asked anxiously; and when she made herself look more closely, she saw that round the edge of the wound, there was pink and shiny healing skin.

'Pretty well,' she said. 'You'll do.' And the maggots, she noted, as the picked them out, were not attached to the healthy new skin, but to the necrotic tissue at the centre. Later, to Doctor Harper, she said, 'I wonder if we do the right thing in removing the maggots from wounds? It occurs to me that they can distinguish between dead and living tissue to a delicate degree that would be impossible for us. Perhaps their eating habits, though disgusting to us, actually promote healing?'

Harper thought about it as he continued working. 'Perhaps,' he said at last. 'But it needs research.'

'Yes, when I get back to England,' she said, 'perhaps I'll suggest it to someone.' She was encouraged by his receptiveness – he never condemned her ideas out of hand; and as an army surgeon he was not at the forefront of medical advances, and could be expected by nature to be conservative, even hidebound. She had gathered from many sources that a resistance to new ideas was practically a requirement in the Army Medical Service; and she was sensible enough to realise that it was quite possible he listened to her because what a woman said didn't matter – though she didn't *quite* believe it was that.

One day Charlotte was picking her way along the quay towards the *Doris*, her mind fixed on the prospect of a bath, when she saw a newcomer who had just disembarked from a steamer stop and look around him with the usual expression of disgusted disbelief. Charlotte stared for a long moment, unable to believe her eyes; and then he saw her, and his eyes widened too.

'Charlotte!'

'Benedict, Cousin Benedict! What are you doing here?' She put a hand out to stop him embracing her. 'Don't touch me, I'm lousy.' She noted his expression. 'I'm sorry, does that shock you? You will not be so nice when you've been here a while. It happens to the best of us.'

'I'm sorry, that was clumsy of me,' Benedict said, 'but it was a shock – such words, and from you, of all people. I shall try to adjust my expectations. But I didn't think you'd still be here. I made sure you would have gone home by now.'

'There's too much to do. The doctor in the field hospital where I'm helping has lost both his assistants, and it will be weeks before replacements reach us from home. But I mean to go when things are more settled.'

'I heard about Cavendish,' Benedict said. 'I'm so very sorry. It's a terrible loss.'

She turned her head away. 'Don't talk of it, please. I do my best not to think about it – that way I can still be useful.' She made herself smile. 'Tell me instead what *you* are doing here. Not merely sight-seeing, I hope?'

He slipped his fingers inside his coat and struck an attitude. 'I am here at the particular request of the Queen and the Prince!'

She looked suitably impressed. 'The Queen asked you personally?'

'Well, there's a team of us,' he admitted, 'but Her Majesty was gracious enough to say she thought I was especially suited to the job.'

'What job?'

'I'll tell you how it was. The Queen and the Prince and their children stopped off in York in September on their way to Scotland, and took lunch in the Station Hotel. Naturally enough, since I'd been so closely involved in the railway and the hotel I was presented to them. Well, actually I had already been presented, in the

November of fifty-two, at the Photographic Exhibition,'
Benedict corrected himself. 'But they were kind enough
to remember me, and we chatted about photography and
railways and the war and so on, and that's what gave rise
to the great idea.'

She guessed it. 'Ah, you've come to take photographs!
I suppose you heard about the previous expedition? Poor
Mr Nicklin and his assistants disappeared with all their
equipment when their ship went down during the hurricane. Captain Hackett, fortunately for him, was on shore
at the time.'

'Yes, I heard about the hurricane when we called in
at Malta. And I knew Nicklin slightly, poor fellow. But
that's not what I'm here for – though the Queen and the
Prince *are* very interested in seeing photographs from the
Crimea. The whole nation is, if it comes to that.'

'Then what are you here for?'

'I've come with an engineering team, to survey the
ground for a tramway up to the plateau.'

'Good heavens! At last someone is taking our plight
seriously!'

'Yes, the papers are full of it, and the Queen and the
Prince were concerned that there didn't seem to be much
sense of urgency about getting on with the tramway. So
given my railway experience, they asked me to join the
party as their personal representative, to report the truth
to them, and push things along as much as possible.' He
looked round him in frank amazement. 'I see they were
right to be worried.'

'Oh, you don't know the half of it yet,' Charlotte said.
'But, look, I see your companions are waiting for you. I
suppose you must be off to petition Mr Filder for quarters
and rations?'

'I suppose so. What sort of quarters are there in this
place?'

'You'll know soon enough,' she said with grim humour. 'Better you don't anticipate. But come and dine with us tonight on the *Doris* – will you?'

'With pleasure!'

'A new face and new conversation are coin of the realm here,' she said. 'You will be petitioned by everyone in Balaclava, so don't forget you are promised to us!'

It was several days before Charlotte saw Benedict again; then she met him at Headquarters one morning. She asked him how he had been getting on.

He shook his head. 'Things are dreadful here, far worse than I imagined. The reports in *The Times*, you know – I thought they must be exaggerated. Now I see they were no more than the truth. I looked in at the general hospital in Balaclava yesterday. You never saw such sights! Have you been there?'

'It's not thought politic. Doctor Hall hates female nurses,' Charlotte said. 'He doesn't like civilians, either. I wonder you escaped alive.'

'But does no-one care about those poor sick men?' Benedict said with rising outrage. 'Nobody seemed to be doing anything for them!'

'No-one can be spared for the job. There's a desperate shortage of labour. The men are having to do double-duty in the trenches as it is, because so many are off sick.'

Benedict wasn't ready to accept that argument. It always seems to human nature so much more likely that someone somewhere is to blame. 'But those poor fellows are lying in filth, Charlotte! The floors are awash, the sheets filthy – the stench is appalling!'

'What do you expect? Hundreds of people are tramping in and out every day from quagmires of mud – how can the floors be kept clean? Thousands of men are suffering from cholera, which means vomiting and diarrhoea, in a place where there are no sewers and very little clean water. How are sheets to be washed without water and without anyone to wash them? And if they were washed, how would they be dried? Our brave correspondent, Mr Russell, does not address himself to these questions. It makes a better story, of course, to depict everyone above the rank of corporal as a heartless, soul-less tyrant.'

'I see I've touched on a raw spot,' Benedict said. 'But frankly now, do you think it need have been as bad as it is?'

'Perhaps not. But can't be as confident as Mr Russell where blame lies. Certainly this campaign was not well thought out, but no-one knew what they would find here until they arrived, and by then it was too late.'

'I don't know how you stand it, working in a field hospital.'

She sighed. 'It wouldn't be so bad if it weren't for the cholera. That disheartens the men far more than hardship or pain or danger.'

'I suppose there was nothing that could have been done beforehand to guard against the cholera,' Benedict said, a little grudgingly. While reading the newspapers it had been enjoyable to denounce the senior ranks of the army for incompetence. As Charlotte said, it made a better story. 'But tell me now,' he went on, 'what's being done to shelter the men for the winter? I've been riding about this morning, and I didn't see any preparations anywhere. Surely they don't mean to leave them all winter in tents?'

'The order went out weeks ago for huts to be built,' Charlotte said. 'But the materials were lost when the hurricane sank the ships. Now even if the stuff were available it couldn't be got up to the plateau.'

'Well, then, why don't the men build turf shelters, like the navvies do when they're in open country?'

'I don't suppose anyone's thought of it. Do you know how they're made?'

'Of course. I've seen a thousand of them – built one myself at home this summer for Georgie and Teddy to play in. Nothing could be simpler. It's just a hole in the ground, really. You dig out a hole about three feet deep, and whatever size you like – twenty by ten is a good living size – and then you build a wall of stones round the inside of the trench, taking it up to about two feet above the ground. Then you pile the earth you've dug out up against the stones all round on the outside, and pack it tight in a sort of embankment. Then you put the roof on.'

'And how do you make the roof?'

'With planks, if you can get them. But if you haven't anything better, you can do it with brushwood, supported on branches. Then you plaster the roof over with earth, and you're done. It's quite snug, especially when you get a fire going inside.'

'A fire? Where does the smoke go?'

'Out of the doorway – eventually,' Benedict said with a grin. 'But you can't have everything. And they used to say wood smoke was good for the lungs.'

'Have you mentioned this to anyone but me?' Charlotte asked.

'Do you think I should?'

'I think you should, and this very minute. I'm sure if anyone had thought of it I'd have heard it mentioned. Go straight away and talk to Lord Raglan, or Airey, about it. I'd lay odds that you'll be giving instructions on turf-hut building within the day. I suppose it will depend on the terrain,' she added. 'Some of the regiments are camped virtually on solid rock. I don't suppose they'll be able to benefit. But if it keeps even some of the men from the weather, you will have done us a great service.'

*   *   *

538

On the 1st of December, Lord Lucan reported officially to Lord Raglan what everyone had long known, that the division of cavalry was no longer capable of active service. Raglan ordered them to move down into the valley by the village of Kadikoi, where they would be more sheltered, and there would be a better chance of getting fodder to the horses. With so little hay, and only barley for feed, the horses were in a terrible state, thin and weak, their manes and tails nibbled to stumps, and great bare patches in their coats. Every day several went down, never to rise to their feet again. Orders were given for temporary stables to be built for the horses at Kadikoi, but there was little chance of getting the materials up to do it before spring.

On the 2nd of December Lord Cardigan, who had been spending more and more time on his yacht, handed in his resignation to Lord Raglan, on the grounds of ill-health, and was given permission to retire to England immediately. It was a pitiful end, Charlotte thought, to all the Hyde Park dreams of glory. She was at Headquarters when he left there for the last time, and he stopped to say goodbye to her very kindly, and said he hoped to see her and Southport at Deene when they returned.

'Doin' good work, Southport,' Cardigan said to her, nodding. 'Not my field, intelligence. Army needs brainy coves like him, though. Good feller.'

'Thank you, my lord.'

Cardigan laid a thin hand briefly on her arm. 'Damned sorry about Blithfield,' he said again. 'Taken it hard, I can see. Not lookin' too rosy. Ought to go home, m'dear.'

'I will, sir, when things are more settled.'

Though there was no regular action, there was a steady trickle of wounded, mostly pickets being shot by their opposite numbers – they were always potting away at each other to relieve the boredom of the night – and

539

soldiers on trench duty; and every day or so there would be a Russian sortie, or an attack on a Russian position. But that trickle of injury was as nothing to the overwhelming flood of sickness. Cholera broke out again with renewed virulence in the first week of December, and together with dysentery, fever, erysipelas, frostbite, exposure and gangrene, was draining the Army of its life blood. Eighty to a hundred men were dying every day, and ten thousand were in hospital at any one time.

At least Benedict's navvy-huts were providing some relief. The idea had been enthusiastically taken up, and with the usual ingenuity of British soldiers they were always adding variations and refinements. Benedict inspected and marvelled, and was warmly welcomed as the author wherever he went. The wife of a corporal in the Light Division gave birth in a turf hut, and named the child after Benedict in gratitude, much to his amusement.

A couple of clear, frosty days enabled the railway team to complete their survey, and they were ready to go home. 'I shall be very glad to leave, I make no bones about it,' Benedict said to Charlotte on the day his departure was announced. 'How anyone can stay here a moment longer than they have to, I don't know. Don't you long for home?'

'I don't think about it,' Charlotte said. 'I have too much to do.'

'But I thought your medico had a new assistant now?'

Charlotte gave a mirthless smile. 'Oh yes, one. Stebbins has arrived. He knows nothing, he's as ham-fisted as a ploughman, and he finds any excuse not to be there when he's needed. And he drinks. I think we did better without him.'

'You aren't looking well, you know. Why not go home and let someone else worry about it all?'

Charlotte only shook her head. She did feel unwell, and every day left her more tired, but she had gone beyond thinking rationally about it. It seemed that she had always been here, and always would be. A sense of unreality born of weariness and over-stretched nerves kept her rising from her bed every day and going to the hospital like something laid down on rails. The hospital stores she had brought out with her were exhausted, and there seemed to be no drugs or supplies available through the hospital purveyors, not so much as a spoonful of arrowroot for the thousands of deranged bowels on the peninsula.

That night she said to her husband, 'Oliver, I was thinking, couldn't we send the *Doris* to buy medical stores? With our own money, I mean. It seems to be impossible to get anything through the purveyors, and it fills me with despair to see men suffer and die, for want of a little opium or quinine. And since the hurricane, we haven't even things like basins and bedpans and scissors and stump-pillows. They could all be bought at Malta.'

'My love, it is not—'

'Don't tell me it is not my worry, or my duty, or my responsibility!' she snapped. 'I am here, I see these things, I can't shut my eyes to them!'

'Very well,' he said calmly. 'I won't tell you what you know is the truth. I will tell you, however, that if you bypassed the purveyors, not only would the medical staff be incensed, but so would most of the general officers. You are here on sufferance, you know. There are many already who dislike your *meddling*, as it seems to them, though they won't say so if they think I might hear them.'

She whitened. 'Meddling!'

'Professional soldiers dislike civilians on principle. It's axiomatic that civilians cannot understand Army matters, and the Army is jealous of its own affairs. They don't like outsiders telling them they can do things better. Lord Raglan gave you permission to help in the field hospital, but you perhaps don't realise that he only manages to square it with his field officers by letting them think you merely visit the more picturesque of the wounded and talk kindly to them. If it were known what you really do, Raglan would be put in an awkward position. And if you proposed to supply the deficiencies of the Purveyor's Department—' He shrugged.

'So I am to sit by and let men die, to appease the pride of a few self-satisfied, arrogant, heartless blockheads?'

'My love, don't rail at me,' Oliver said mildly. 'I am only telling you the truth, unpalatable though it may be to you.'

'And to you?' she challenged.

'I've never disguised that I dislike your being exposed to that sort of thing. I know what you do is good and valuable, but I wish you would let someone else do it.'

'There isn't anyone else.' A feeling of enormous weariness came over her. She turned away, putting her hand to her head. 'Oh God, even you are against me!'

'Not against you,' he began. 'Never that.' But he broke off as Charlotte suddenly swayed and staggered, cheese-white. She felt the blood leave her head and thrust out her hands helplessly in the swooping darkness, and as Oliver caught hold of her she vomited, simply and suddenly, surprising them both. He supported her while she retched several times, bringing up nothing but a little clear fluid. Then he helped her over to the bed and sat her down, crouching before her and rubbing her hands anxiously.

After a few moments the colour, such as it was, began to return; but studying her in those few minutes he saw how thin her face had become, how shadowed her eyes, and he blamed himself for being too liberal-minded. The time had long passed when he should have exerted a husband's authority, for her own good. Behind these thoughts lay a darker fear, which wound silently round his heart like a cold snake. *What if she took the cholera? What if she died?*

Her closed eyes fluttered open; she drew a deep, shuddering sigh; she looked at him, as utterly weary as a child kept too long from its bed.

'Charlotte, tell me – are you ill? If you love me, don't hide the truth. I must know. Is this the first time you've vomited?'

'No,' she said, and added quickly, 'but it isn't cholera.'

'How can you be sure?'

'No diarrhoea.'

'How many times have you vomited?'

'That's the first time today.'

'Today?'

'I did it yesterday evening, and the evening before. I suppose I should have taken more note of it, but my mind was on other things.'

He scowled. 'You don't seem to be taking this very seriously. Until you know what it is—'

'Oh, I think I know what it is,' she said. And suddenly she smiled, a tired but happy smile that he remembered from other occasions.

'Evening sickness?' he said slowly. It took some women that way, in the evening instead of the morning.

She nodded. 'And a certain event has not taken place. I had forgotten, but it is overdue, and with me—'

'Charlotte! Charlotte! Are you sure?'

The fun that had long been missing from her eyes returned. 'It strikes me, my lord,' she said severely, 'that you don't know your own strength.'

He was puzzling. 'But when? Oh! On the *Doris* that evening when you—'

'When I cried, yes.' She studied him. 'Dearest, I know you didn't mean to do it, but you are pleased, aren't you?'

He couldn't bear the shadow of anxiety in her eyes. 'Oh yes, yes, of course I am! I love our children, I would be glad to have a dozen, if it were not for the risk to you. I love you so much. I'm so afraid of losing you.'

'I'm not afraid. It feels right for this to be happening. Cavendish dying – it sounds silly, but I feel as though God meant this, to comfort us.'

He kissed her hands, in silent tribute. Then he said, 'But this changes things, you do see? You must go home now. It is not possible for you to go on risking yourself here.'

'Yes,' she said. 'I do see that.' She felt disappointed, and at the same time relieved. The thought of returning to civilisation, and sleeping in clean sheets, and eating whatever she liked, and being free of lice, was like a dream of heaven. She was failing in her duty to the sick – but not of her own choice. It was not her fault. She was being invalided out. God had decided for her. 'I shall be glad to go.'

She found Harper in the store-tent alone, and was glad of it. He turned as she came in.

'I've come to say goodbye,' she said.

He nodded. 'I heard a rumour last night. Word travels quickly where there's so little talk about.' They stood facing each other, silent a moment. He said, 'So you will go. Why?'

'I'm pregnant.'

'Ah,' he said.

Not to any other man would she have spoken so baldly of something so intimate; no other man, she knew, would have taken it as she meant it: not as immodesty, merely truth without disguise. They had worked so closely together, had spoken to each other so rarely; knew each other so well, and knew about each other so little. He was forty-eight, his father had been a country doctor, he had joined the Army Medical Service in 1826, he had never been married. That was all she knew about him, a small assemblage of bare facts, as plain and grey as himself.

'Your husband goes too?' he asked.

'No,' she said. 'He's needed here, more than ever. I wish he could come home with me.' That was an understatement. The love that had brought her here rather than be parted from him was going to make the parting tomorrow almost unbearable. But she wouldn't come between him and his duty.

And now she must say goodbye to Harper. She had strange feelings for him, closer and more intimate than, on the surface, their relationship warranted. But they had built something here together, and had learnt to communicate in silence; and perhaps she had been closer to him than anyone else had ever been. 'I have some things in my medicine chest,' she said. 'Just a very little opium, quinine, and arsenic. I was saving them in case I needed them, but it seems selfish now. I will give them to you.'

'You may need them on the voyage.'

'I can get more. And I have a sewing-kit. There isn't much thread left, though.'

His lips twitched, as though he might smile, but there was no smile in his eyes. 'You have become quite a bonny stitcher.'

'Not as good as Norton.'

'Yes, the good Mrs Norton. I shall miss her.'

'Yes,' Charlotte said.

There was a nerveless silence. 'I shall miss you,' he said.

She drew in a breath. Suddenly his face seemed very close and very clear, as though a fog or a veil between them had been lifted. Such a plain face, grey-pale and lined, nothing handsome or even remarkable about it. Brown eyes, pouched and lined with tiredness, meeting hers as they always had, direct, expressionless. Cropped hair, going grey all over, so that it looked dingy rather than distinguished; a grey moustache, not the luxuriant whiskers of general officers, but a small tired thing that seemed as though it hadn't the strength to grow any larger.

She put out her hand, meaning to shake his; but he took hold of her forearm instead, and then the other one, and then, she hardly knew how, but by the consent of both, her lips were laid quietly against his. His were cold and closed, the lips of a man who had hardly ever kissed, but she felt his hands on her forearms holding her hard, and all communication was in them. It was natural, she thought, for a doctor, even an indifferent army doctor, to express himself through his hands. He was a man with mediocre skills doing a vile job as well as he could under appalling conditions; compassion deadened, hope, ambition, even satisfaction long gone. He was a plain, taciturn man whom nobody very much had ever loved; but in that moment she felt the whole essence of him, and loved him. And then they parted, without surprise or embarrassment, and his hands were removed, and the sense of him with them. It had lasted the merest moment, a kiss without history or future, something that existed in isolation in the moment that contained it, and was instantly gone, leaving no residue – except perhaps a

small pocket of kindness in a cold place, which had not
been there before.

'Goodbye,' she said.

'Goodbye,' he said.

And she went away.

CHAPTER TWENTY-ONE

England, grey, damp and mild; London, sooty and cramped. They seemed fantastic to Charlotte. How could so many people cram themselves into such a small space? And the horses – how fat they looked, even the cab horses!

Ungar's face wavered wildly, as he tried to reconcile butlerish imperturbability with the expression of sufficient welcome to the mistress. Mrs Collins had no such difficulties – she beamed and sobbed simultaneously, while the maids lined up behind sniffed moistly and the men coughed and shuffled. Then upstairs and into her mother's arms. Rosamund and Jes, pre-warned by the wonder of the telegraph system, had been waiting in the morning-room, with Lady Turnhouse. Charlotte was so tired and confused she expected for a moment to see her grandmother there, and Papa Danby. Across her mother's shoulder she smiled wearily at Lord Batchworth, and he smiled back out of a chasm of loss. Rosamund still had Charlotte, but Cavendish had been Batchworth's only child.

As soon as the first hugs and words were spent, Rosamund rang the bell, and Miss Frogmore, waiting for the signal, came in holding Venetia and Olivia by the hands, with two maids behind carrying Henry and Marcus. They all seemed to have grown so much in twelve weeks. Olivia was shy of her, Venetia busy and anxious, Henry all smiles and complacency, Marcus wriggling to get down and run about. She kissed them all, and then kissed them all again for Oliver, and wanted to hold onto them tightly for the newly learned fear that something might snatch them from her.

It was good to be home, in a clean, dry place, no mud, no lice, big fires in all the grates. Breakfast was heavenly – oh, the delight of fresh bread, and coffee, and soft, golden buttered eggs! Then to her room, to bathe in as much hot water as she wanted, and fresh clothes. And there was her own dear bed, with clean sheets on it, practically smiling at her. Norton had acquired a terrible cold at Gibraltar, where half the fleet seemed to be in port and sneezing, and retired to bed forthwith. Charlotte longed to follow her example, but there was too much to do, too many people to see. Everyone wanted to ask her questions, hear her views – express their sympathy. They needed her more than she needed rest and solitude.

She had to go and see Alice and endure her grief, which overset the frail equanimity Charlotte had built up in herself at such cost. Alice seemed listless, fidgety; stopping halfway through sentences, getting up and wandering about the room. She asked Charlotte for an account of how Cavendish had died, and then could not listen to it, broke into awful sobbing, working herself into an hysteria. Mrs Phipps rang the bell, and a middle-aged, capable-looking person came in, whom Mrs Phipps addressed simply as 'Nurse'. Charlotte did not miss the accusatory glance that Nurse threw at Mrs Phipps as she took Alice away, as if she blamed her for putting Alice into a fret, though in this case Charlotte could absolve her.

When they were alone again, Mrs Phipps sat for a moment in unaccustomed silence, her eyes bent on the floor, her lip pulled in under her teeth in an expression of anxiety. Charlotte studied her, and saw how the artificial brightness of her cheeks and hair was dimmed, her face lined, her eyes ringed with tiredness. She looked her full age, in a mourning gown of plain cut and unadorned. Had she really had an affection for her son-in-law? She seemed at least to be regretting her past conduct, for she spoke now, without her old affectations, and said, 'I am sorry you should see Alice like that. She has been quite overset by Lord Blithfield's death. Indeed, we all have. I don't need to tell you, your grace, how easy it was to love him.'

'That woman you addressed as Nurse—?'

'Mrs Olwyn is her name. She came highly recommended, and she manages Alice very well.' Mrs Phipps bit her lip. 'I'm afraid it fidgets Alice to be with me when she gets into one of these starts. Nurse has the knack of calming her.'

'Let us be clear,' Charlotte said, 'is Mrs Olwyn an insane-nurse?'

Mrs Phipps lifted haunted, guilty eyes. 'She *has* nursed such people,' she conceded, 'but she specialises in nervous cases. She has excellent characters from all sorts of eminent people. And Sir Wilmot Frayne says that there is no reason why Alice should not recover completely in a month or two. She is of a naturally high-strung disposition, and the shock and grief of bereavement—' She stopped, and looked at the ground again. 'I don't know what we shall do,' she said in a low, lost voice. It seemed a comment surprised out of her, and Charlotte found herself feeling sympathy, quite against her will, for the woman. She had only done what she thought she must to survive, after all; and there was no doubt that she was feeling it now.

'You have no need to worry,' Charlotte said. 'You will all three be taken care of. You must know that Lord Blithfield's Will makes ample provision for Alice and the child; and we would never see you want.'

'Thank you, your grace,' she said. 'But it wasn't money that I was thinking of. How will we go on without him? And how will William grow up without a father?'

'I have a suggestion which might answer that,' Charlotte said. 'My mother and Lord Batchworth would be glad to have the use of this house again. It would seem to me to be the best arrangement all round if you and Alice were to come and live at Southport House. There is plenty of room for all. Alice can be taken care of, and William can be brought up in my nursery with his cousins, which I'm sure you agree would be best for him. And you may have your own apartment, as Lady Turnhouse does, and be quite private if you wish.' In acknowledgement of her new softness towards the untoothed dragon, she did not make any mention of the economy it would represent.

Mrs Phipps seemed humbly grateful, and Charlotte accepted her thanks and said, 'I know Lady Turnhouse will value your company. She was very attached to Lord Blithfield, and needs someone to talk about him to.' If the two dowagers, she thought, could keep each other occupied, Alice could be more quickly brought to a stable state of mind; William could have companionship and, when Oliver returned, at least a surrogate father. And Charlotte would have done her best for her brother.

It was a sad homecoming, and every new encounter emphasised the bitter loss. Cavendish was gone, and taken some of the warmth from the world. But Charlotte saw what comfort the grandchildren gave, and did not delay telling her mother and Jes about her hopes of increasing the brood.

'It's early days yet, of course,' she said, 'but I am sure in myself.'

Rosamund counted. 'An August delivery, then. But is Oliver happy about it?'

'Oh yes. He didn't mean me to risk it again, but he loves his children: he said he'd have a dozen if it suited me.'

'You aren't afraid?'

Charlotte shrugged. 'There's danger in everything. If those weeks in the Crimea have taught me anything, it's that you can't be parsimonious with life. Besides, I had no difficulties with Venetia and Olivia. I don't anticipate any problems with this one.'

Rosamund nodded, and was ready to encourage this happy state of mind. It was in no-one's interest to point out that Charlotte was thirty-two now, not a girl any more. Rosamund had been thirty-four when she had Cavendish, and she'd almost died of it. And Cavendish had almost died, too: she had got him through his childhood by the skin of his teeth, reared him to manhood against all the odds. And now, after all that, she had lost him to a pointless action in a needless war. The waste of it was the bitterest part of loss. She had always protested against his going into the cavalry, and had always been assured that there was nothing to fear, England being locked into a seemingly endless peace. Well, Cavendish had died doing what he wanted to do; but she had made him out of her own flesh and her own heart's blood, and no-one had asked her whether she was ready to give him up.

Rosamund had Fanny's letter to show to Charlotte, and that was good news too. It made Charlotte feel almost light-hearted to be released from having to fear that Fanny was dead and believe that it was largely her fault. The letter was short.

Dear Charlotte,

I am writing to tell you that I am safe and well, so that you do not worry about me any more. Do not try to find me. I am never going back. I leave it up

to you whether you want to tell Philip, but please
tell Henry and Aunt Rosamund not to worry any
more. I'm sorry about everything, but this is for the
best, really.

Your loving,

Fanny.

There was no direction at the top of the page, of course,
and no date. It had been written in good quality ink but
on common paper, so there was nothing by which to trace
it back.

'I knew Fanny's hand, of course,' Rosamund said,
'so I opened it. I was going to write to you, but then
your telegraph came that you were coming home. I took
the liberty of writing to Henry at once. He has been
most dreadfully cut up about the whole thing. I didn't
communicate with Anthony – I thought you would want
to decide about that.'

Charlotte read the letter again. 'It's good to know that
she's safe,' she said. 'But she doesn't trust me, you
see. She doesn't say where she is. She thinks I would
betray her.'

'Perhaps it isn't that. If you knew, and Anthony asked
you, it would be harder to refuse to tell him. And I
don't know but what he mightn't be able to force the
information from you – a husband has legal rights over
his wife.'

'I don't suppose he wants her back now,' Charlotte
said. 'He has her money and the child.'

'But he must have loved her once,' Rosamund said.

'I think he did in a way – perhaps still does. But it's
not the way that takes any pleasure out of her company,
or wants *her* to have any pleasure. He's better off without
her, and I suspect he knows it, otherwise why has he given
up the search for her?'

'You don't know that he has,' Rosamund said reason-ably. 'Until this letter came, we didn't know that she was still in London.'

'She may not be,' Charlotte pointed out. 'A letter can be posted by anyone. It could have been carried to London from anywhere in the country.'

'It's odd,' Rosamund said. 'Someone must be sheltering her. Why haven't they persuaded her to go home, or at least to come back here?'

Charlotte shook her head. 'It's a mystery.' Why, indeed, would a stranger shelter her, and feed and keep her for nothing? 'Well,' she answered her own question, 'perhaps it isn't for nothing. Perhaps she's got herself a position, or work of some kind.'

'Fanny, work?' Rosamund said. 'She might teach in a school, I suppose.'

'If she's teaching in a school in London, we ought to be able to find her. It might take time to enquire at all of them—'

'But should you try to find her?' Rosamund inter-rupted.

Charlotte stared. 'How can *you* ask that?'

'What would you do with her when you found her? Bring her back?'

'No – no, not against her will, of course. But surely, to find out if she's safe and well—'

'She says she is. What purpose can finding her achieve?'

'To know where she is. I need to *know*!'

'It's for yourself, then, not her. Dearest. I want to know, too – of course I do! But she says, don't try and find me. Don't you think, in all her unhappiness, she has earned the right to be left alone?'

Charlotte shook her head, not in negation, but in bewilderment. She was afraid Fanny was unbalanced, for her actions seemed so extreme, her fear and hatred for

Anthony out of proportion. And if she was unbalanced, she couldn't be happy, and might be in danger. But if Rosamund thought she should be left alone, Charlotte distrusted her own opinion. She wished Oliver were here. Oh, for so many reasons, she wished Oliver were here!

Tom and Emily had begun to leave their mark on the house in Upper Grosvenor Street. It had taken a while for Emily to overcome her diffidence, but she had at last begun redecorating and refurnishing the house in a more modern style. Charlotte was shocked at the first sight, and almost resented it, for it was still to her her grandmother's house, in which nothing had ever changed in all the years she had known it; but she made her reason overcome her instinctive prejudice, and complimented Emily on her taste.

Emily was pleased, but was more eager to fetch her to see little Tommy, who presented a very different aspect from when she had first seen him. He must have grown two inches, she thought; and filling out with good food, and clean and neatly dressed, he looked much less ugly and unappealing than before. But the biggest difference, Charlotte thought, was in his expression. He was not cowed, sullen or defiant any more, but cheerful and alert, and his affection for Emily was evident. He remembered Charlotte, and was shyly pleased to see her, but he had obviously no regrets that he had parted with her for a mess of sausages.

Afterwards in the strangely transformed drawing-room, Tom asked her eagerly, 'What did you think of the boy?'

'You've done marvels with him. I wouldn't have known him for the same.'

'He's clever, don't you think?'

'He answered my questions very sensibly,' Charlotte said.

'Of course, he is utterly ignorant at the moment,' Tom said, 'but he learns quickly, and he's catching up at a wonderful rate, considering where he started from. I think he has abilities that will surprise us all one day.'

Charlotte smiled. 'I fancy there's a little partiality at work here.' She did not miss the quick glance that Tom and Emily exchanged at her words, but could not interpret it. There seemed a tension in the atmosphere. 'Have you decided yet,' she asked, looking from one to the other, 'what you're going to do with him?'

'Yes, we've decided,' Tom said. He didn't continue, and his face had an odd look of suppressed emotion, but which emotion she couldn't fathom.

'Well?' she said at last. 'Am I to know, or is it a secret?'

The Westons exchanged another glance, and Emily said, 'No, it's not a secret, but we thought you might not – understand.'

'Approve,' Tom amended.

'We've decided, you see, to adopt him as our son.'

It was not much of a forewarning, but just enough to stop Charlotte making any exclamation, and to have her reply of 'I am so pleased for you' come out fairly readily.

Tom shook his head. 'I can see you think it's strange, but you don't know him as we know him. He has such an affectionate heart, and is so ready to learn and eager to please. And when you think what a start he had—'

'My dear Tom, and Emily,' Charlotte said quickly, 'I do you all possible credit. Nothing could be more worthy than to rescue a child from such pain and degradation. It's not strange at all – except in the sense that there's far too little of that sort of practical benevolence.'

Tom looked put out. 'Practical benevolence be damned! The fact is I took a fancy to the child, I don't know why.

There's no rule about it, you know. And since we don't have a boy of our own—'

'But you may,' Charlotte said quickly, glancing at Emily in apology for broaching so delicate a subject. 'Have you considered the effect on this boy if you should have a child of your own?'

Emily, her cheeks unusually red, said quietly, 'Of course we have considered. But we've been married almost six years, and I'm not a young woman.'

'I'm sorry,' Charlotte said. 'I shouldn't have asked. I am very happy for you both – and particularly for the child. Have you begun the proceedings?'

'Oh yes, it's all in hand,' Tom said. 'The natural mother has disappeared from her last known direction, which makes things easier in some ways. But we don't know his date of birth, even approximately – of course, he has no idea—'

'He didn't know what a birthday was, poor child,' Emily put in.

'So we have to give him a nominal one. I thought April the first would be appropriate. After all everyone will think the adoption is an elaborate joke on my part.'

He said it lightly, but Charlotte could see that underneath it was a sensitive subject to him. Somehow or other, he had conceived a great attachment for this plain and common boy, and every slighting comment or look the unfeeling world directed his way would wound him. Well, she thought, if the boy could engender that much love so quickly, there must be good in him.

'No-one will think it a joke,' she said firmly. 'No-one whose opinion matters a groat. I think it's perfectly splendid. I shall look forward to introducing my children to their new cousin as soon as possible.'

Tom smiled gratefully. 'I have to confess he's already paid one or two visits – though I saw to it Lady Turnhouse wasn't around! I have to tell you Tommy's a firm favourite with Venetia already. She seems to think she found him.'

Charlotte laughed. 'That's Venetia!'

Emily added, 'Olivia, on the other hand, didn't recognise him at first, and when she was reminded about the incident, she somehow got it into her mind that he lives in the chimney permanently. She thinks him a terribly romantic figure.'

Charlotte couldn't decide quite what to do about Philip Anthony. That he ought to be told about Fanny's letter she had no doubt, but how to do it was another matter. It seemed unduly cold and dismissive to write to him; but to go and visit him herself seemed extreme for so little news. It was Rosamund who suggested she delegate the task to Henry Droylsden.

'He's on the spot. And as Fanny's step-father, he is the closest concerned with her, after Anthony.'

'But wouldn't he mind?'

'I think he might be glad of an excuse to confront Anthony,' Rosamund said, 'and satisfy his curiosity about one or two things.'

Henry Droylsden had run the mills firstly for Fanny's mother, then for Fanny herself, taking a salary as manager, though he had done far more than his salary's worth for love of them both. But when on Fanny's marriage the mills had become Anthony's property, Henry had resigned and Anthony had put in his own manager, a man recommended by Henry. Henry had wanted in any case to retire from active work, and enjoy the company of his second wife, who had brought him enough wealth to make the salary unnecessary; and he had felt, too, that his position might give rise to awkwardness if he retained it, by dividing loyalty and responsibility uneasily between two men.

So he had moved gracefully from the foreground to the background of Fanny's life, and, being himself very happy in his marriage, had assumed Fanny was too, and thought that seeing less and less of her was a natural consequence of their relative situations. Fanny had been at pains to protect him from any knowledge that she was unhappy (which was probably just as well, since there was nothing he could have done about it) so the news that she had run away broke upon him with the suddenness of a thunderclap. At first he had wanted to break Anthony's neck; but now that Fanny had sent her letter, he was able to make an appointment to see Anthony with reasonable self-control.

Anthony received him in the business-room of Hobsbawn House, a large room off the vestibule just inside the front door, which added to the impression that Henry was being allowed to penetrate only the minimum distance into Anthony's life. Henry was prepared for the coldness and suspicion, knowing from Rosamund how Anthony blamed Fanny's family for her behaviour; he was not prepared for the evidence in the doctor's face of grief and anxiety.

'I have come to bring you good news,' Henry said as soon as they were alone together, to relieve the anxiety as quickly as possible. Anthony waited impassively. 'A letter has been received from Fanny. She is not dead, as we necessarily feared. In fact, she says she is well and safe.'

Something glimmered in Anthony's eyes. Henry hoped it was joy, but it looked more like anger. 'What do you mean, sir, a letter was received? By whom? Where is it? Show it to me.'

'I haven't it with me,' Henry said. 'She wrote to the Duchess, asking her to pass on the news to you.' It was a tactful lie. 'The Duchess didn't want to write to you because it seemed too impersonal, so she asked me if I would come and tell you face to face.'

'I am obliged to you,' Anthony said with a minimum of gratitude.

'Fanny asks in the letter that no-one try to find her. She said her only purpose on writing was to tell us all she was safe, so that we wouldn't worry about her any more.'

'But where is she?'

'No-one knows.' Henry saw an expression of distaste in Anthony's eyes at what he believed was a lie. 'There was no direction on the letter. She is evidently at pains to hide herself.'

'I don't believe it,' Anthony said baldly.

'Please don't doubt my word,' Henry said dangerously.

Anthony blinked and looked at him as though he had been elsewhere in his thoughts. 'Oh, I don't,' he said absently. 'I absolve *you* from the conspiracy.'

'Thank you,' said Henry with an irony that escaped the other man.

'Indeed, you have no reason to wish to deceive me. I do you the credit to believe you have proper views on marriage. They have told you what they wish you to know. But they know where my wife is, all right. They are hiding her from me. How else could she have remained concealed?'

'You are mistaken. Please believe me, they do not know where she is. Good God, man, don't you think if there were any chance of finding her I would have gone there like a shot? Fanny may be your wife, but she was my daughter long before that, and I love her dearly.'

'I love her too,' Anthony said starkly, and then put his hands over his face. 'Where is she?' he said from behind them.

Henry hesitated. 'What happened between you?' he asked at last. 'Why did she run away?'

Anthony didn't answer. After a moment he removed his hands and gave Henry an utterly weary look. 'I have decided to remove to Norfolk,' he said. 'My estate there needs my attention.'

'And leave all your good works?' Henry said in surprise.

'I have done my duty. Let someone else take over the burden from me. I have my son to think of. Manchester is not a healthy place to bring up a child, and I should like Lionel to grow up where I grew up, and know the place and the people he is to inherit one day.'

Henry said politely, 'I am sure you know what is best for you and the child. You mean to remove there permanently, I collect?'

Anthony looked round the room, but not as if he saw it. 'Oh yes. I shall not come back here. It has unhappy memories for me.'

'What will you do with the house?' It was perhaps an impertinent question, but it was Fanny's home and birthplace, and had been Henry's home too, for the short, happy time he had been married to Fanny's mother.

'It can stand empty,' Anthony said harshly, 'until it falls down. A fitting monument to a ruined virtue.' He looked at Henry sharply. 'I will find her. She will be found and brought back to me. And I will make sure she does not run away again. That is another reason for going to Norfolk. I can keep better control of her there, where there are fewer temptations.'

Henry's heart sank at the grim picture the words called up in his mind. Yes, in the remoteness of north Norfolk, far from any members of her family, Anthony might well keep his wife a prisoner, and no-one would know what happened to her. What lengths would wounded pride go to? They must all, Henry thought, do anything they could to make sure Fanny did not fall into his hands again. But where *was* she, and how was she supporting herself? The information that she was safe and well did not begin to answer the questions that troubled Henry.

The reports in *The Times* had had their effect. When Parliament resumed in January 1855, public opinion was so inflamed about the sufferings of the soldiers and the poor administration in the Crimea that questions were asked, a confidence vote forced, and Lord Aberdeen obliged to resign. By popular request, Palmerston became Prime Minister, Panmure went to the War Office, and a Commission of Enquiry was put in train. But from Oliver's letters, Charlotte concluded that the commission had been formed too late, that the worst of the privations were already over.

'The cold is bitter, almost beyond belief,' he wrote early in February. 'The thermometer went down to ten degrees, but it is so still, one does not feel it as much. But the men all have plenty of warm clothes now, most of them are hutted, and soon all will be. So don't believe what you read in the papers. We had a copy of *The Times* today in which it stated that none of our men were hutted, and that we had had to borrow twenty-five thousand greatcoats from the French, which is simply not true. I don't know how such lies start. Canrobert sent Raglan two sheepskin coats – perhaps that is the source of Russell's "facts"!

'On the twenty-ninth of January the first party of navvies arrived to begin building the tramway, so the last of our troubles should soon be over. But in any case, the road up from the harbour is now more often frozen than not, which makes the going not so difficult. A party of nurses arrived on the same day. Raglan was pleased to note these were "women" and not "ladies" and acceded to their request to help in the general hospital, where you may be sure Hall does not let them do more than prepare invalid foods and roll bandages! They asked to be allowed into the field hospitals, but Lord R refused with a shudder.

'A spy we sent out has come back from Sebastopol to say the Russian soldiers are suffering very much, that they have no fresh meat and only black bread to eat, that they have no medicines and no doctors, and supplies are not reaching the city because of a lack of baggage animals. Also that cholera has broken out, with hundreds dying every day. You cannot believe everything they say, because they try to please you, but when correlated with other reports, one can get an approximation of the truth.

'Now I have some news for you which I hope will please you. Your brother's horse, Bracken, has come into my possession! It was this way: I was riding down from Headquarters when I came across a group of sailors leading a very nice-looking chestnut towards the Naval Brigade camp. They saw me looking and stopped, and when I asked where they had it from, "We found him, your honour," they said, "but he's yours for a pound." I have to tell you that this is not uncommon – the jacks are getting a name for collaring stray animals, which they take back to camp and "take care of" until claimed – for which care they demand a fee. And if not claimed, they sell them to the highest bidder.

'But then I noted that the chestnut had a crooked race and a white coronet on the off-fore, and remembering that Bracken had just such markings, I demanded a closer examination and found deep in the thick winter coat the 11th brand next to a "B" for "Blithfield". I questioned the jacks pretty sharply then, and they said they found him wandering by the river. My best guess is that he strayed so far after the hurricane that he was caught by a Cossack patrol, and has been in their possession ever since, until he somehow broke free from his tether and headed homewards. When they found him he had on a Cossack bridle with the bit removed, which is how they tether them during the night. The jacks sold the bridle in exchange for the rope he was wearing when I first saw him, so I cannot verify it, but it seems likely. You may comfort yourself that Cossacks are good to their horses – certainly he seems very fit. I gave the sailors a sovereign and Bracken now shares Victor's duties, and his stall.'

In early March Oliver wrote: 'We had a telegraph that the Tsar of Russia had died – no reason given, but we were assured it was no rumour. The troops grew very excited and supposed peace would instantly be declared. A Polish deserter said it is being kept secret in Sebastopol until the late Tsar's brothers arrive to bolster spirits, but that it is leaking out. Lord R wanted to mount an immediate attack on Sebastopol at once but Canrobert said can't, and that was that.

'The tramway to Kadikoi is complete and being extended towards the plateau. It has made all the difference that was expected. The weather is milder too, and the men in much better health. Spirits are good, and whenever you visit a camp you find men off-duty playing football or running races or skylarking. You will remember how it was in November and December! You would not know it for the same army.

'And old friend arrived on the 8th – Roger Fenton, the photographer who provided me with the excuse to visit Kiev, if you remember? He has come with two assistants and a waggon and three sorry-looking horses he bought in Gibraltar, but no mules, the lack of which he will soon feel! But he is an agreeable fellow, and makes himself pleasant wherever he goes, and with letters of introduction from Prince Albert he won't find himself short of dinner-invitations. In fact Lord R seated him next to Lady George Paget at table last night – universally accepted as the place of honour! Bosquet has collared him for tomorrow night. They all want their portraits taken, of course. The photographic waggon is besieged wherever it goes.

'General Simpson is to join us as Chief of Staff. He is a decent fellow, I am told, served in the Peninsula and was wounded at Quatre-Bras – all of which endear him mightily to Lord R. We are winding up the clockwork to begin the new campaign next month, and please God it will be brought speedily to a conclusion, so that I can come home to you. I envy Paget almost to killing point that he has his wife here with him. It grieves me that I cannot be with you during this time, though you assure me you are well. Don't exert yourself, or allow yourself to worry, and take Abernethy's advice in everything, and be sure to rest and eat properly, and above all write to me very often to assure me all is well. If I were less needed here, I should be home like a bird, but what we know in advance can make the difference of thousands of lives.'

Mr and Mrs Underwood finished their wedding-trip in Venice, where they went in February for the Carnival, and with Mrs Pownall they arrived back in Scarborough on a wet and windy day in March. First and last the trip had cost a great deal, but there was no doubt that Aglaea had enjoyed it, and her sketch books and the canvases she had covered while she was away required a separate carriage from the station. The agent from London who had wanted her to exhibit in 1851 had been in correspondence with her and was eager for her to have a show in the autumn, with as many subjects from the wedding trip as she could work up in time, and as he had forecast great interest and huge sales, it seemed likely that the honeymoon would actually show a profit in the long run.

Aglaea had agreed to the exhibition, largely to stop Mr Moncrieff from bothering her about it, and as she lost interest in a painting as soon as it was finished, she agreed with Mrs Pownall that they might as well be sold as not. Mrs Pownall had enjoyed the wedding trip hugely, and having learned to shop in three languages, was belatedly coming to think of Aglaea's strange activities not as embarrassingly unfeminine and faintly indecent, but as the entrée into a world of fashion and excitement. The exhibition would be opened by a private view to which everyone important would be invited, and which perhaps even the Queen would attend. Aglaea would be sought by every hostess in London, and – if Mr Moncrieff knew his business, which he appeared to – would become absolutely the latest shriek. Mrs Pownall foresaw for herself an autumn in London of soirées, crushes, dinners, balls, private boxes, promenades, shopping, driving about, and being lionised as the sister-in-law and general interpreter of the wonderful new artist – for of course Aglaea, being so unworldly, would need Mrs Pownall at her side on every social occasion. Perhaps, Mrs Pownall thought in her giddiest moments, they would even move to London permanently. Scarborough could hardly contain so important a talent indefinitely!

While Mrs Pownall dreamed her dreams, Aglaea settled in happily to Underwood House, admired her new studio, unpacked her sketch books, ordered new canvases, and set to work. The honeymoon had opened her eyes to worlds of possibility, and she was revising the opinion she had held for so long that those who sought inspiration abroad were merely lacking in vision, and that Scarborough contained everything anyone would ever want to see.

She was glad to be back, and her mind was furnished with enough to keep her busy for a year or so; but after that she felt she might well want to make another trip to a new country. She barely noticed Mrs Pownall's new appreciation of her work and excitement about the exhibition. Mrs Pownall was always chattering about something, and Aglaea had long ceased to listen, just as those living next to a railway line cease to notice the trains. Mr Underwood did not impinge on her thoughts at all. At her request, the room next to her studio had been furnished during their absence with a bed, which the other two assumed was in case she needed to rest during her spiritually exhausting labours – a day-bed, in effect. The illusion was helped by the fact that she had had moved into it from her old home an arm-chair, a bureau, a table, and various items of sitting-room furniture. But after dinner on the first day home, she excused herself to her husband and sister-in-law, saying that she was very tired, and retired to sleep in the 'day-bed' alone.

Mr Underwood felt humiliated, which led in turn to a surge of anger. He had Mrs Underwood's bags taken to the marital bed-chamber, and her clothes unpacked and hung away in the spaces previously occupied by the first Mrs Underwood's effects. He hinted to the servants that his new wife had slept in the other room that first night for undefined reasons to do with her work, and the next day, when a housemaid assured him that Mrs Underwood was at work in the studio, he went along there to tackle her.

She was laying out a sketch, and it took him some minutes to gain her attention; but when he had it, he asked quite sternly if he could speak to her, and sagely led her into the next room, out of sight of her work. He sat her down in her arm-chair, where she composed herself, hands in her lap, to wait for him to speak. He walked up and down a few times, and then faced her and began.

'Mrs Underwood, you are my wife.'

'Yes, Mr Underwood,' she concurred pleasantly.

'Do you know what that means?'

'Yes, my dear,' she said, still pleasantly, with no overtones of guilt or embarrassment, but perhaps with a faint shade of puzzlement, as if he had asked her if she knew what a canvas was. It put him off.

'You are my wife, and I am your husband.'

'Yes, my dear,' she said, and to help things along she added, 'The one usually follows from the other.'

This was not going well. He shook his head, and walked up and down again. 'I don't think you do understand.'

'Oh I do, I assure you.'

'No, I don't think so. You see, when two people marry, their lives change. There are certain things husbands and wives do together. I have no wish to embarrass you by referring to them directly, but—'

'Oh, you don't embarrass me, Mr Underwood,' she said. 'Pray, be perfectly frank with me.'

'Frederick,' he said, with a little tremor in his voice. 'Can't you call me Frederick when we're alone?'

She considered. 'Do you know, I don't think I can. I have thought of you for so long as Mr Underwood—'

'That is what I complain of,' he said passionately.

'Oh, do you complain, my dear?' she said in mild surprise.

'You still think of me as Mr Underwood, not as Frederick – not as your husband! Aglaea, you slept in here last night!'

'Yes, my dear?'

Anguish overcame shame. 'Husbands and wives are supposed to sleep in the same room!'

Her eyebrows went up. 'Only amongst the lower orders. People of our station do not do so.'

'Who told you that?' he asked, exasperated.

568

She smiled. 'Really, Mr Underwood, I have been married before!'

'And did you sleep in a separate room from Mr Morland?'

'Yes, of course.'

'Always?'

'Except for one time when he had a dreadful nightmare, and he asked me to stay with him in case it came back.' She looked a little embarrassed to be telling him this. 'But of course I returned to my own room before the servants got up.'

Underwood passed a hand over his eyes. 'On that occasion,' he said slowly, making one last desperate effort. 'On that one occasion when you stayed with him, did you—?' She looked enquiring. 'Did you—?' He couldn't think of a way to phrase it.

She tried to help. 'If you want to ask me, did I get into bed with him, I have to say that I did. He was very distressed, you understand. He was like a terrified child.'

'But did you – I mean – did anything else happen?'

'The nightmare didn't come back, if that's what you mean. He slept quite quietly.'

'He slept. You didn't – he didn't—?' But it was no good. Her innocent, vague, enquiring look told him pretty much what he had come to suspect through the long, wearisome weeks of his honeymoon. And what the devil was he to do about it? If she was as utterly innocent as he was beginning to suspect, how could he now, at this late date, make any changes? He should not have allowed her to establish a pattern of behaviour during the honeymoon, because they would now be all the harder to break. And yet he *couldn't* allow things to go on as they were.

'Aglaea,' he said slowly, 'you and I have been sleeping in the the same room, in the same bed for some weeks now, have we not?'

She looked a little uncomfortable. 'It is different on one's honeymoon. I understand that. Even Mr Morland and I—'

He stepped across the room, took her hands, pulled her to her feet, and enfolded her in a firm, almost rough embrace. He kissed her for a long time, eliciting nothing but surprise, but she did not try to pull away from him. That at least was hopeful. He felt that masterfulness was his best tactic. He removed his lips, but continued to hold her, and looking down into her face he said, 'Mr Morland is not your husband now. I am. You know, don't you, that it is a wife's duty to obey her husband?'

'Yes,' she said, with a slight shudder which, in his state of turmoil, he missed. She had heard those words before, and they had unhappy associations for her.

'Very well, then. Tonight, and every night until I give you leave to do otherwise, you will sleep in the same room with me, in the same bed with me. That is my express wish – my command. Do you understand?'

'I will do as you wish, of course,' she said, looking up into his eyes with a puzzled frown, 'but – no, I don't understand.'

He drew a deep sigh, happy with the ground he had made. He knew now where his mistake had been, and what he had to deal with. 'You will, in time,' he said. 'I promise you.'

'That's right,' Peter said, looking over Fanny's shoulder as she sat at the desk. 'You're doing beautifully.'

'But I'm so slow,' Fanny said, removing her tongue from between her teeth and looking from the original document to her own copy.

'It takes practice, that's all. No, that's "consideration", not "considerate".'

'I didn't know there was any such word.'

'Never mind, just copy exactly, even if it makes no sense to you. You'll soon learn the different phrases that come up.'

'But how will I do when you're not here to tell me spellings? Is that one "f" or two?'

'"Affidavit"? Two.'

'It looks like one. This writing is so terrible!'

'That's why copyists are needed. Full stop there. That's right. And Mr Loveday liked the sample of your handwriting very much. If you copy this right, I can get you a thirty-six folio tomorrow.'

'Get me a—'

'Never mind,' Peter said, looking at the little dark curls that nestled at the base of Fanny's bent head, which the spring sunshine through the parlour window was burnishing. He would like to kiss every one of those curls, and then that lovely white neck, and – he pulled his mind back hastily from the brink. 'It's work, that's all you need to know. Oh, this was a good thought of mine!'

'It's much better than helping in the house, at least from my point of view,' Fanny said. 'I don't mind ink on my fingers nearly so much as blisters.'

'From Mother's point of view as well, because it's cash in the hand, and cash is always harder to come by. I only wonder I took so long to think of it.' Naturally a lady born like Fanny wouldn't be able to do cleaning and cooking, but she could read and write, and if Peter could earn good money scrivening, so could she.

'I do hope it will earn me some money, so that I can start paying your mother back,' Fanny said.

'Oh, it will. Law-copying's the best paid, because one word out of place can cost a fortune in the courts; and if you can say you are experienced at it, you will get preference when it comes to giving out. Everyone specialises these days.'

Fanny gave him a quick glance. 'Why would anyone give me this thirty-six folio you speak of, then? I'm *not* experienced.'

He smiled. 'Because Mr Loveday knows me, of course; and he knows I will look over you at first, to make sure.'

'Then you will be doing the work, not I. And while you are overseeing me, you can't do any copying of your own.'

'Oh, your apprenticeship won't be long,' he said airily. 'That's "chattels" with an "e-l" not an "l-e".'

'As long as it means I can earn my living,' Fanny said, 'I shall be happy. But are you sure your mother really doesn't mind my staying here?'

'Not in the least, I've told you so. Are you happy here, Fanny?'

'Yes, I am,' she said. 'There – finished! You had better check my work carefully, teacher!' She smiled at him, pushing the copy towards him. He ignored it, pulling out the chair next to her and sitting down on it sideways, facing her.

'What is it that makes you happy?' he asked seriously.

She had spoken lightly, but now seeing his serious face, she considered, and answered, 'Being away from Philip. Having everyone be so kind to me. Playing games together and singing together and playing the piano and – all the things we do together in the evening.'

'Yes? And what else?'

'Being free,' she said thoughtfully. 'Yes, I know it sounds silly, but when I was a rich heiress and when I was a well-to-do wife, there were so many things to think about and be afraid of. When I was robbed of my last forty pounds at that inn—'

'Yes, remind me to go back and kick that landlord good and hard and get it back from him,' Peter interrupted belligerently.

572

She laughed and touched his hand. 'Bulldog! Watch-dog! But seriously—' She removed her hand just as he was about to take hold of it – 'when that happened. I felt strangely as though a weight had dropped from me. I had nothing, so there were no decisions to make any more. Wealth is fine in its way, but life without it is simpler. You just stay alive, or you don't, that's all. When I think of the things that used to make me out of temper – ridiculous things, like getting a rain-spot on a bonnet, or somebody who ought to have curtseyed to me waiting for me to curtsey first – I can't believe I stuck it so long.'

'But you wouldn't want to be destitute and homeless again. You don't pretend that was fun.'

'No, of course not. But – food tastes better, now I know what it is to be hungry. And I love getting into a warm bed, knowing what it's like to sleep in a doorway. I never appreciated it before. And kindness makes me almost want to cry, now I've known cold-ness and cruelty. *You* are so kind to me, Peter. You take such pains. I didn't want you to think I didn't notice.'

Her eyes met his earnestly, and then something she saw in his face, or something in the air between them, made her blush. Now he did take her hand. He had long dreamed of such a moment, and had planned to the last syllable the thrilling, overpowering speech he would make, that would entrance her with its eloquence. Now with her hand quiescent in his, he said, 'I love you, Fanny.'

She was silent for a moment; then she said, 'I am a married woman.'

'I know. Do you think I don't know that? It's damna-ble.'

'Yes, and it always was, and I don't love him, but

573

it doesn't alter the fact that I am married, and there's nothing I can do about it.'

He turned her hand over and looked down and traced a pattern on her palm with his other forefinger. 'You didn't say – I mean, your first reaction wasn't entirely—' He coughed slightly. 'It was to the point, but you didn't say if you cared for me.'

She looked at him, and thought of the men who had courted her – gay, handsome, titled, rich; men who had flirted and danced and flattered and amused; men who were superb on horseback and men who danced like angels and men who knew exactly what to do in any social situation and could get a cab in Piccadilly on a rainy afternoon at four o'clock just by lifting a finger. She thought of her fiancé Tom Cavendish, the handsome, popular rattle who had backed out of the engagement when Charlotte jilted Oliver and it seemed Fanny would not be able to ally him with a duke; and she thought of Doctor Anthony, handsome as a Greek hero and clever and good, who had taken her money and locked her up in her own house.

And she looked at Peter, flushed of face, not young, not handsome, not dashing, with his tufty fair hair and his short legs and his work-worn hands and his shabby clothes. Who would find such a man attractive? Who would take his love seriously? But her heart was bumping along like a pony trying to keep up with a horse, and when she thought just for the fraction of an instant of kissing him and having his hands touch her, she got a falling-away, quaking feeling in her stomach that she hadn't felt since her coming-out days.

'Yes, I care for you,' she said. He looked up then, and folded both his hands over hers, like someone taking possession of a gift. She drew a shaky sigh. 'But what's the use? Philip would never let me go. I can't even ask him to, without telling him where I am, and I'm not going to do that. You can't ask me to do that.'

Peter gathered himself to say something dangerous, and he said it very carefully. 'Does it matter about Philip?'

He saw she understood him. Her eyes searched his face, her thoughts exploring here and there.

He went on, 'I hope he will never find you; but if he does, I won't let him hurt you, or take you away. You do believe that, don't you? I may be short, but I'm strong. And in any case—'

'Yes. I believe you.'

'What I'm saying is, I will always look after you, and it doesn't matter to me if we are married or not. I can't think of anyone it would matter to – unless it matters to you.'

She reddened, but she was not flinching from the idea. She was considering it carefully, logically. 'Your mother,' she said.

'Not her.'

'She wanted me to go back.'

'Because she thought you'd be happier, that's all. I dare say she would prefer me to be properly, legally married to you if it were an ideal world. But she knows the circumstances. Given the way things are, she would accept it. She's very practical. Has to be, in her line of business.'

Fanny nodded, but a little doubtfully. He saw she wasn't ready.

'It's too soon,' he said contritely. 'I understand. I didn't mean to press you, Fanny.'

'No, really,' she began, not wanting him to withdraw his hand, which was so comforting and warm.

He smiled. 'Don't worry, I'm not going anywhere. We'll go on just as we are, until you want it to change. And if it never feels right for you—' He shrugged. 'I'll just be your watch-dog.'

Fanny laughed, as he meant her to, and the tense moment was eased. But all that evening, when they were in company with the others, her eyes followed him without her volition, and he felt them, and now and then looked at her in brief acknowledgement. The moment would come; and he didn't think it would be long.

CHAPTER TWENTY-TWO

On the 9th of April 1855 the second bombardment of Sebastopol began. All day the Allied guns poured a torrent of shot into the defences, causing massive damage and appalling casualties among the enemy; and every night, by extraordinary exertion, the Russians under the direction of the engineer Todleben cleared away the bodies and rebuilt the works. The Intelligence Department was able to report that in ten days of the bombardment the Russians lost six thousand men; but the Allies were no closer to carrying the town.

Relations between the French and British staff were becoming strained.

'There's no point in knocking down the defences if we don't rush them afterwards,' Oliver wrote. 'That's out of the primer. But Canrobert won't agree to any sort of attack. In fairness it must be said that the French Emperor continually badgers poor old Bob-Can't with unwanted advice and orders. It seems someone has told Young Boney that Sebastopol will only be taken when it is attacked on all sides at once – a view Lord R rejects – so the French won't engage in any "premature" assault. Lord R of course keeps the peace and is unfailingly polite to everyone, but some of the other senior officers are growing increasingly short with their French counterparts. At a council of war the other day Canrobert opened proceedings with the sonorous statement, "Gentlemen, we are here to take Sebastopol." Lyons said loudly, "Oh, 'that's it, is it?" and there was very unrefined laughter all round, which reduced Canrobert almost to tears.'

The situation worsened in May when the electric telegraph installed between Varna and the Crimea allowed Napoleon to interfere at even shorter notice, resulting in a joint expedition to capture Kertch and cut off the Russian supply-line through the Sea of Azov being called off actually after the troops had sailed.

'Everyone was furious. Sir George Brown and General d'Autemarre almost came to blows,' Oliver wrote. 'And then a few days later Canrobert had the gall to present a wholly new plan of offensive, courtesy of the Emperor, which you may imagine was not well received!

'By the way, we have been honoured by a visit from your old friend, Miss Nightingale, to "inspect the hospitals". When it was announced it caused a great to-do, for her commission appoints her over the "Military General Hospitals in Turkey" and since the Crimea is not in Turkey, Doctor Hall said that she had no right to come interfering in *his* hospitals, and appealed to Lord Raglan to ban her. Lord R had more important things to worry about at the time, and told Hall politely to go away and stop bothering him – and that as Miss N has letters from Panmure she might pretty much go where she pleased. Hall was furious and vowed she should not pass. Miss N duly arrived on the 5th; could hardly have chosen a worse day, for the Sanitary Commissioners had just begun to clean out the harbour. *You* will know what they were dredging up! She began at once to step on toes, for having ridden up to the plateau to report to Lord R and finding him absent for the day, she rode about with her entourage looking at the camps and the batteries. This caused huge excitement amongst the men, who rushed out to surround her wherever she went, cheering wildly. The nurse-haters amongst the general officers complained sourly it was like a visit of inspection from the Queen. However, I don't suppose she meant to make quite such a parade of it, and the next day she disappeared into the hospitals to carry out her "inspection", where I expect she'll find enough to do to keep her out of mischief.'

On May the 19th, the harassed Canrobert begged to be demoted to a divisional command, and was replaced with General Pélissier.

'He is what one thinks of as a typical Frenchman – a little fat man with a waxed moustache and goatee beard, pointed toes and hands that are never still. But we understand he is much more of a match for the Emperor. He is pugnacious and care-for-nothing – his men call him "Old Tin-head", and he addresses them pleasantly as "you bastards". Certainly he seems determined on an active campaign, so we shall see.

'You will have heard, I suppose, about Miss Nightingale's illness. She didn't achieve much, poor thing, in Hall's domain, falling sick, after only a few days' inspecting, of typhoid, which I guess she caught through sleeping on board ship in the harbour, where the stench has to be smelled to be believed. They carried her up to the convalescent hospital at the old castle, where she lies still, but is out of danger, I understand. Lord R went to see her on the 24th, and sat with her an hour, and says she ought to go home to England, but she wants to finish her work and so will be shipped back to Scutari as soon as she can travel. They say she has transformed the hospital there – but then, Hall is *here*!

'General Pélissier is proving his worth, authorising in quick succession a night assault on the defences, and the renewal of the expedition to Kertch. It was completely successful, Kertch and Yenikale captured, and any amount of ships, ammunition and supplies taken. The Navy can now enter the Sea of Azov and harry the Russians from that side. A third bombardment of Sebastopol is planned to begin on the ninth of June, and as Pélissier agrees we must follow this up with an all-out attack (in defiance of Young Boney's order), I hope it may all be over in a month, and I shall be able to be with you again before the baby is born. You *are* taking good care of yourself, I trust? Write to me in a great deal of detail about your exact state of health and looks. I long more than I can say to be with you, my dear love. I find I can hardly be civil to General Estcourt, because he has his wife here and I have not.'

At Abernethy's insistence, Charlotte retired from active life at the beginning of June. 'I won't say it was the whole fault last time, your grace,' he said severely, 'but we don't want to take any chances, and we've the summer weather to contend with too. It would be as well not to put too great a strain on your constitution this time.'

Doctor Snow was more blunt. 'It's the sofa for you for the last ten weeks! Quiet, ladylike occupations only – sewing and reading and such-like.'

'I shall go mad,' Charlotte warned him.

'With boredom? Oh, I think not, with a house full of children and relatives. Nothing wrong with that, but don't let 'em fret you. And don't go near the hospital. It's not a cholera year, thank God, but there's plenty of other things you could catch. Reynolds and Friedman and the nurses can manage without you. I'll keep a weather eye on them too, so you'll have no excuse.'

So Charlotte retired to the sofa. Her protests were really only a matter of form: she was very tired after her exertions at Balaclava, and in low spirits. She missed Oliver, and without his supporting presence the loss of Cavendish weighed heavily on her. She went over and over every memory of him, finding anew every time how much she had loved him, how much sunshine he had brought into her life. She wept for him; and for Fanny, too. They had both always been so gay, so full of the joys of life; without them she felt leaden, a creature of earth, without wings. Lying on the sofa, chatting to her mother or Emily, watching the children play, listening to music in the evenings: these were all the activities she felt fit for. She was not worried about the approaching ordeal of childbirth. Somehow she felt detached from it, as though it was something outside her, ordained by God. Whether this baby lived or died, whether she lived or died, had already been decided, she felt. Nothing she might do or not do could affect the outcome.

Home sometimes still seemed a little strange to her: waking suddenly from an afternoon nap she would think herself still at Balaclava. She read everything she could get hold of about the war, every newspaper and magazine, every account, however fanciful; and over and over again, she re-read Oliver's letters. Closing her eyes, she could imagine herself there. In spring, he said, it was very beautiful, the air as clear as it had been that day in October when the Light Brigade died; but the grass much greener, and every hillside etched against the sky and brilliant with colour: jonquils and hyacinths, carpets of crocus, candytuft and vivid blue squills, buttercups glossy as wet paint, wild orchids and lilies. But as it grew hotter, the flowers and the colour disappeared, and the distant hills became invisible, merging into the hazy sky in one indistinct mass like bright fog. By June the heat was almost as much of a trial as the cold had been in January. In that treeless place, under a white sky, the glare from the ground was so fierce by ten o'clock that it was impossible to keep your eyes more than half-open. When the wind blew, gritty dust filled your eyes, ears and mouth. Work and councils of war had to be got through early in the morning or late at night. It was not until long after sunset that the heat left the land; from dusk to nine or ten at night, the air lapped you, warm and damp, like an animal's breath.

In the heat, the men sweated; stand still for a moment, Oliver said, and flies would walk over your lips, and settle to drink the salt pools gathered in your eye-sockets. And men who sweated were continually drinking water: the cholera returned, a virulent strain which killed in a few hours. Up at Headquarters sickness started to spread amongst the staff, whose health was worn down with the length and hardship of the campaign.

'I remain pretty stout, thank God, though I do not escape diarrhoea – no-one does in this place. But rice water mixed with lime juice and a little salt restores me. But other seniors are not so lucky. Sir George Brown is so knocked up, there is talk of sending him home; Codrington and Buller both have the fever and are out of commission, and poor old General Pennefather is so weakened with dysentery he looks ten years older. And our old friend Filder is very bad. Most worrying of all is General Estcourt, who has cholera and is in some danger. Lord R is very distressed – E is an old and dear friend, as you know. Lord R begins to look very old. This has been a dreadful year for him, but the end, we hope, is in sight. There is to be a twenty-four hour bombardment, followed three hours after dawn on the 18th by a simultaneous attack, by the French on the Malakov and the British on the Redan. It will be a short, sharp struggle, and by evening we shall be seeing the inside of Sebastopol. Lord R has chosen the 18th as the anniversary of Waterloo, which he thinks will be a good omen. I shall be watching from a safe distance, I hasten to assure you, on Cathcart's Hill, with the rest of the "tourists".'

The plan was to cease horizontal fire during the night,

continuing vertical fire to distract the Russians while the troops were moved up under cover of darkness and placed in trenches out of sight. Then after dawn there would be a resumption of the cannonade to destroy and Russian repairs carried out during the night and knock out their guns, and then a simultaneous attack at six o'clock, the signal for which was to be a rocket.

But at half past eight on the evening of the 17th, a despatch arrived at Headquarters from General Pélissier altering the plan. He could not place his men so as to be out of sight of the enemy once it got light, and therefore he had decided the attack must take place at daybreak, before the Russians had the chance to spot them. He doubted the Russians would have made any repairs to their defences by daybreak.

Lord Raglan was furious. To have the plan altered without consultation at the last moment was bad enough; but to attack without the planned reducing fire was to endanger the whole undertaking. Of course the French could not hide their assault troops: as always, there were too many of them! They put ten times as many men in the field every time as the British, and suffering ten times the casualties as a result, without achieving anything by it.

'But we dare not risk confusion,' Raglan said. 'Indecision of any sort would be fatal. We must accede to General Pélissier's change of plan. But I tell you, Steele,' he added to his military secretary, 'I do not like it. I do not like it at all.'

No-one slept that night. Watson brought Oliver a cup of tea at half past one in the morning, and at two o'clock he set off with the other observers in the pitch darkness for Cathcart's Hill. It was so black, they could only ride at foot pace, taking turns to dismount and feel their way. It was just beginning to be twilight when they reached the hill. They tied up their horses and went down to join a growing group of spectators sitting on the grass above the batteries, turning field-glasses on the misty outline that was Sebastopol. The batteries were firing hard, and the orange splash of shells breaking showed where the Malakov was, hidden in the murk; the Redan was visible, a black shape with its feet in the white fog.

Dawn had not broken when a shell rose almost perpendicularly from Fort Victoria, trailing a burning fuse behind it like a comet's tail. Immediately a rattle of heavy musketry fire began at the foot of the Malakov. All glasses were trained that way, straining to see.

'It's too early for the assault,' someone said. 'Maybe the Russians have made a sortie.'

Now there was artillery fire as well, and shells; it was obvious a regular battle was being fought out down there in the semi-darkness. And then the sound of Russian trumpets and drums was heard, sending the alarm from battery to battery around what had been supposed to be the doomed city. Slowly the truth dawned on the spectators. One of the French generals must have mistaken the rogue shell for the signal rocket, and had begun the attack. The element of surprise had been lost; and judging by the fire from the Russian side, Raglan had been right and Pélissier wrong about how much the enemy would manage to restore during the night.

There was nothing for it now, no way of calling the men back. Pélissier had to send the rest of his force in to support the premature attack, and Raglan was obliged to send the British in to support the French. But the Russians had been put completely on their guard, and the assaulting troops met withering fire. The Russians added grape on top of roundshot, and the task became impossible. The Allies scrambled up the hill and were beaten back, advanced again and were beaten back; the casualties were appalling.

It was still only eight o'clock in the morning when the failed attack was called off. A wind got up shortly afterwards and blew a dark dust-cloud over the battlefield, mercifully hiding the chaos. Oliver collected his horse and rode back to Headquarters. Gradually the other senior officers and staff rode in, grim and silent. This was not the end to the day that had been envisaged. Oliver went into the mess for breakfast, and was hailed by Manningtree, a young staff officer with whom he had struck up a friendship since Charlotte went home.

'Southport, over here! Come and take a glass of champagne with me. Best thing for laying the dust. Besides, one has to keep up one's spirits somehow.'

Oliver accepted the glass and sat down heavily. 'What a disaster,' he said glumly. 'What a damned awful farce.'

'The one thing we never anticipated was a failed attack,' Manningtree agreed. 'But given the past history of this alliance, I don't know why not. Mountebanks and clowns. It ought to be played at the Hippodrome.'

'Who was the idiot who jumped the gun?'

'General Mayran, over at the Careening Bay. He took a shell for the signal rocket – I suppose you guessed that? But you needn't abuse him – he's paid for it with his life. The slaughter was terrible over there.'

'Any idea what our casualties were?'

Manningtree shook his head. 'But I can tell you,' he said, draining his glass, 'that we lost a damned lot of officers. Where's your glass?' Oliver held it out, and Manningtree refilled it with a shaking hand. 'I tell you what, this damned place is getting on my nerves. I begin to think Sebastopol can't be taken – and why in hell should we want it?'

'Shut up, here's the chief,' Oliver warned, as Lord Raglan came in with Adye and Steele behind him. He looked vaguely round the room, nodding politely to the lounging, grim-faced officers, and then went on through to his office.

'God, he looks old,' Manningtree muttered. 'Who'd be a field-marshall?'

On the 19th a flag of truce allowed the dead to be brought in, and the casualties which had been too far advanced to reach earlier were given relief at last. Some of them had been lying wounded for thirty hours. A large number of deserters from Sebastopol came in, and Oliver was kept busy for the next few days interviewing them. The Russian losses from the 18th had been heavy, almost six thousand killed and wounded; but British losses had been more than fifteen hundred, including two generals, and the French three thousand. And it was all for nothing.

Lord Raglan remained outwardly calm and cheerful as ever, but those close to him could see how hard he had taken it. It was another blow, sustained on an already wounded frame. He had so much to trouble him, and he was losing friends all the time: Sir John Campbell, the most popular officer in the army, had been killed at the Redan; then on the 24th General Estcourt died. Lord Raglan was devastated with grief. He carried on, working through the mountains of paper-work, though it was clear that he was ill himself, suffering from dysentery and pains in the joints. Gently and courteously he insisted that he was quite well, thank you, or that he would be by and by. He died in the evening of the 28th, taking everyone by surprise, perhaps including himself.

'I cannot describe the grief: it can better be imagined than recorded,' Oliver wrote. 'The French feel it as we do: Pélissier and Canrobert wept like children when they looked on that peaceful face. Doctor Prendergast puts it down as "Crimean Fever", which is to say typhoid, but the men say his heart was broken by the events of the 18th.

His successor, Sir James Simpson, is as mild in manner as Lord Raglan, but he does not, I fear, command the same respect. A *Mr* Simpson is not the equal of a *Lord* Raglan, to some of the officers. He seems overwhelmed even by the thought of the task ahead, and I have no confidence in a speedy end to the campaign. I have asked to retire as soon as the present spate of work is over. If all goes well, I should be with you by the end of July, in time for a certain event close to both our hearts.'

The cholera continued to take its toll, especially amongst the newly arrived troops. Oliver said goodbye to more familiar faces: Roger Fenton, the photographer, who had been living at Headquarters for a month, and Mr Filder, the Commissary-General, both went home ill. Oliver was winding up his affairs, Watson was packing, and Manningtree was wistfully calling him a lucky devil, when the news came that Mr Calvert had gone down with cholera. In a few hours he was dead.

Oliver received the news with a resignation born of weariness. He had begun to live, as Charlotte had done, in a dreamlike state of apathy, no longer really believing that he would ever leave this place. Certainly Calvert's death made his own presence essential: Cattley, the chief interpreter, had died of cholera a few weeks before. On the night of Calvert's death, Oliver got very drunk in the mess with Manningtree, and had to be carried to his bed, where he lay for a moment wanting to cry, before falling into a dead stupor.

The next day he was summoned before General Simpson who addressed him long and eloquently on the importance of the Intelligence Division and his place in it, finishing by begging him to stay on. Oliver listened with a thick head and a heavy heart. He had got drunk last night in mere dumb protest against his fate, because he knew he could not go home.

* * *

As August began, Emily and Rosamund called very often at Southport House – indeed, one or the other seemed always to be there. Charlotte drew no conclusions from this. Parliament was in recess, of course, and in the normal course of events the Batchworths and the Westons would have gone out of Town, but a number of gentlemen had stayed up because of the war, so London had not emptied as much as in other years. She was glad that they were there. She was feeling rather ill, though she had been feeling not-quite-well for so long that she noticed it more as a disinclination to do anything than as a definite malaise. Having Mama or Emily there meant that she did not have to pay attention to Alice, or answer questions of Lady Turnhouse and Mrs Phipps. She could lie on the sofa, doze, read, and stare at nothing in particular, thinking of Oliver, which was all she felt good for.

She did not see Rosamund's and Emily's deep concern, because they hid it from her. Abernethy had told them she must not be worried or alarmed; for that reason Lady Turnhouse and Mrs Phipps had not been told that Charlotte was in any danger, for Rosamund could not rely on their tact. Mrs Olwyn knew, and kept Alice quiet. Norton took Ungar into the conspiracy, for visitors had to be strictly limited. When Viscount Calder arrived in London his presence was not even mentioned to Charlotte lest she should wonder why he didn't call: she had not been told that his father, her uncle Lord Aylesbury, was ill.

Doctor Snow was always cheerful. 'Only keep her quiet, and don't worry her, and we'll get through well enough.' At least there seemed no danger of immediate bad news from the Crimea. The Allies were intent upon sapping right up to the fortifications, and nothing but digging was going on at the moment. As long as Oliver didn't take the cholera, he should not be the subject of any alarming telegraph.

But despite all care, when the moment came it was very bad. Abernethy was called at the first hint, and Snow was sent for soon afterwards, and the two of them remained with the duchess the whole time, as did Rosamund and Emily, one of whom was always in the bedchamber. Even so, they nearly lost her; and after the baby was born, there were two more alarms, before the doctors could say with any security that Charlotte would be staying.

She remembered little about it. She was very ill for a week, and during that time drifted in and out of the present, believing herself most of the time to be still in the Crimea and fretting that she ought to be at the hospital helping Doctor Harper. Those watching over her gathered from her confused and urgent ramblings a little of what her nerves had endured. When she was not talking about the wounded and the sick, she spoke about the cold and the hunger; and the horses. 'The horses, the poor horses,' she would mutter; and Rosamund would say, 'It's all right, they've been fed. They're all right now,' and she would be quiet for a while.

When she emerged into daylight again, she was weak and languid, and lay quietly for long hours, watching the square of sunshine from the window travel over the ceiling and down the wall. They were able to tell her that Oliver was well, and she accepted it without comment, seeming to have no apprehension about him, as she had no interest in the child she had borne. It was a girl, quite strong and healthy, not large, but rather long. 'Another girl,' she said when they told her. 'Oh dear. Lady Turnhouse won't be pleased.'

'But you have two sons,' Rosamund assured her anxiously. 'You do remember them?'

Charlotte gave her a faint, amused smile. 'Of course I do, Mama. What a question.'

'What will you call the new baby?' Rosamund asked, relieved and rather embarrassed.

But Charlotte insisted that it was a matter for Oliver, and would not even give it any thought. Abernethy said she could not suckle the child, so a wet-nurse was found, and the unnamed baby disappeared from sight and mind into the nursery. Rosamund was worried by Charlotte's continued languor, but Snow reassured her.

'She'll be all right,' he said. 'She's taking a holiday from herself, that's all. She's worn out, and no wonder when you think what she's endured this last year, physically and mentally. Just let her rest and feed her up and she'll be almost as good as new in a month or two.'

'I hope so,' Rosamund said. 'I couldn't bear to lose her as well.' She didn't like to enquire into that 'almost'.

On September the third a council of war was held to decide upon a determined attack on Sebastopol. The sapping was complete. The French had got right up to the edge of the defences round the Malakov; the head of the English sap was two hundred yards from the foot of the slope of the Redan, and could not be taken further because they had reached solid rock. It was important to move quickly now: the French were short of ammunition, and the Russians had begun a whole new inner line of defence; and besides, winter was approaching, and no-one wanted to spend another on this wretched plateau. The plan was to conduct a ferocious three-day bombardment to wear the Russians down; and then to attack in force at noon on September the 8th. Noon was chosen as it was known from deserters that this was when the garrisons were relieved, and that the old watch marched off before the new one marched in. For a precious few moments, the guns would be unmanned.

The bombardment began on the morning of the 5th, and there was very little return fire from the Russians, though it could be seen through glasses that there was a great deal of activity in the town, particularly across the bridge from the south to the north side of the harbour. Morale was high again amongst the Allies and confidence strong that this would be the attack which would carry the town; but whatever happened, Oliver was determined that afterwards he would go home. News from home had not told him how difficult Charlotte's labour had been, but he was full of foreboding, his nerves overstretched and his spirits low.

The eight of September dawned grey and blustery, the sea tossing and spatched with foam, the plateau before the town obscured with blowing clouds of dust. It was cold, too – after the recent heat it felt uncomfortably chilly, an omen of what was to come if they did not carry the town today. The artillery kept up a brisk fire as the assault troops quietly moved into the trenches. It was usual for the artillery to cease firing around noon for a few hours because of the heat, and it was hoped that the Russians would assume on this day that the cessation was merely routine, and continue as usual with the relieving of their garrisons.

At noon exactly the French leapt out of their trenches and attacked the Malakov, and so completely were the Russians taken by surprise that within a quarter of an hour it was secured; the Russian general commanding it was discovered still taking his dinner. The attack on the Redan was not so fortunate. The troops had two hundred yards of open ground to cover, and a much steeper slope to climb; the Russians, alerted by the firing from the Malakov, had time to scramble to the parapets and fire on the British soldiers. Grape on top of roundshot went through them like a scythe through wheat. The general commanding was knocked out in the first minute, and so many officers were killed that it was difficult to relay orders to the men who survived. The trenches were clogged with wounded being carried to the rear, which prevented reinforcements being brought up, and the French suffered the same difficulty in their attacks on the lesser defences of the Central Bastion and the Little Redan. By three in the afternoon it was plainly useless to go on, and the assault troops were called off and the artillery fire renewed.

But the French had the Malakov, the most important of the defences, and repeated Russian attempts to retake it were beaten off, with terrible loss to the Russians. When night fell the Russians called off their attack, and an uneasy quiet fell over the scene.

'We lost two and a half thousand, the French seven,' Manningtree said to Oliver, drinking left-handed while his servant bound up his right. 'God knows what the Russians suffered.'

'Are you wounded?'

'Just a flesh-wound. I was nicked by a rifleman when I was leaving the battery. God, it was hot work down there!'

'Let me have some of that brandy, will you?' Oliver said. 'I think we'll take it tomorrow. The Russians will be very disheartened to have lost the Malakov, and their losses must have been near to ten thousand. I wouldn't be surprised—'

'What?'

'Oh, nothing,' Oliver changed his mind. Best not to raise hopes; but all that movement across the bridge meant something. He wondered how long the new Tsar would think it worth pouring men and money into the defence of Sebastopol. It was one town in an incomprehensibly vast country. It was easy to lose sight of the fact that capturing Sebastopol would be more symbolic than of any practical use.

Young Lindsay came in just then. 'I say, have you heard? There are half a dozen fires down in the town.'

'Something caught from our artillery, I suppose,' Manningtree said.

'No, no,' said Lindsay, 'they started all together and quite suddenly. It wasn't us, it was the Russkies. They're setting fire to things.'

Oliver stood up abruptly. 'Where's Simpson?' he asked.

All through the night fires sprang up in the darkened town. There were explosions as arsenals and batteries were blown up, and by four o'clock the city was a sheet of flame. Well before dawn the staff officers, Oliver amongst them, were out training glasses on the town, and first light on the ninth of September showed the bridge over the harbour being broken up, its sections towed over to the northern shore, while the rear column of the garrison could still be seen marching up from the water's edge, proof of how recently they had crossed over. The whole southern section of the town had been evacuated.

Dawn broke. Oliver advised Simpson that sentries should be posted to stop the allied troops getting into the town to plunder, as there would certainly be other explosions to come. Simpson was grateful for the hint. He had been suffering from the debilitating Crimean dysentery, and it was hard to concentrate even on a victory when one's mind was on lower things. A cordon of sentries was placed round the town, and all day it burned, and frequent explosions shook the air.

Interviewing some of the Russian wounded, Oliver learnt that Russian casualties over the last action were at near fifteen thousand; that the evacuation to Simferopol, to the north of the city, had been planned over a week ago; and that the new Russian commander-in-chief, Prince Gorkachov, had submitted to the Tsar the opinion that it was no longer worth trying to hold on to Sebastopol. So, thought Oliver, the victory had been given, rather than won; but no doubt there would still be rejoicing in England. Simpson's would be the name on the roll of honour: it was a pity that poor old Raglan had not survived just three months longer. But now, oh now, they could go home. The Russians would surely accept peace terms, and the madness could end.

Sebastopol burned all through the day and night of the 9th, before the flames died down for want of anything to consume. On the morning of the 10th it could be seen that nothing but blackened ruins remained, except for one huge barrack building near the Dockyard Creek, which, it was supposed, must have survived by accident. The first thing was to secure the town, which was done by a regiment of the Buffs under Colonel Windham. Oliver and two others from his department were attached to Windham's party, and thus it was that he first set foot in the town he had camped outside for so long. The devastation was complete, ruined and burnt buildings, great holes and shell-craters in the roads, and the usual depressing debris washing gloomily up and down the shore.

Early in the afternoon a steamer put off from the northern shore, flying a flag of truce. A thin and elderly officer came ashore, together with two subalterns, and walked stiffly up to bow to the reception committee. When he came closer, the stiffness was explained by a bandage clumsily wrapped around his knee; and Oliver noticed how pale and shocked he looked, which gave a clue to how bad things had been inside the city for the past few days.

The officer gave his name as Stepanobsky. 'Is there one amongst you who speaks French?' he asked courteously in that language. 'I deeply regret my inability to speak English.'

Oliver said, 'I am happily able to speak either French or Russian, sir, whichever is more convenient to you.'

'Thank you, sir, you are most gracious.' Stepanobsky bowed, and continued in Russian. 'I have come with a request in the name of humanity, which I am confident, from what I know of the courtesy of the English nation, you will see your way to granting.'

'I hope I may do so, sir.'

'You will have noticed the Dockyard Barrack yonder, which we left unfired in our retreat. We have been using it as a hospital, and we were not able to remove all our wounded on the night of our evacuation. I have come to ask you, sir, to allow us to remove anyone still alive. Technically, of course, they are prisoners of war, but you will perhaps not wish to be troubled with the care of them when you will have so much else to do.'

'Wounded?' Oliver said. 'How many, sir?'

Stepanobsky spread his hands. 'A thousand, two thousand, I cannot say with any accuracy.' His eyes were haunted.

'*Two thousand*?'

'But I doubt whether more than a quarter will still be alive. They were the worst wounded, whom we could not move, and as you have not been into the barrack before now, they will have been without any medical attention, food or drink for nearly two days.'

'Good God!' Oliver said; his imagination supplied too readily what the scene would be inside the building. It was the work of a moment to explain to Windham what was wanted, to summon up a fatigue party, and to send a messenger haring back to camp for a medical team.

Stepanobsky had brought two surgeons with him, and a fatigue party of his own, to carry survivors to the steamer. He was grateful to Oliver for the speed of his reaction. 'The English are a gentle, courteous people,' he said sadly. 'It is the greatest pity that we should find ourselves on opposite sides.'

'I agree, sir. I have always been treated with the greatest kindness when I have been in Russia.'

'May one ask how you know Russia?' Oliver told him, and his face lit. 'But of course, I knew Lord Turnhouse when he was Ambassador! I was attached to the Imperial court, and met him several times. And you are his son? I fancy I must have met you, sir, in 'forty-one or 'forty-two, at a reception in the Admiralty. You won't remember, for you were quite a young man, but I am sure it was so.' Oliver made a courteous answer. It underlined for him the absurdity of war, that this pleasant old man who had once shaken his hand should now be his enemy.

The fatigue party and Windham's aide arrived at a run, and they all hurried off towards the Dockyard Barracks. In a few minutes they were pushing open the doors onto a scene Oliver knew he would never forget. The men were laid out in rows on the ground, head to foot, covering the whole floor; stacked as neatly as firewood, except where they had crawled or writhed out of position in their agony. The stench was not to be imagined – a combination of blood, sweat, faeces, vomit and putrefaction – nor the sound, a low rolling moan, the clamour of hundreds of men in agony. It was a cool day outside, but within a ghastly heat had been generated. Oliver felt a cold sweat of horror spring out all over him, and his stomach rolled helplessly. Of the three men immediately before him two were plainly dead, one missing an arm at the shoulder, the other missing half his face; and bracketed between them was a living man, who met his eyes with the blind and terrified look of an animal, all humanity gone from his expression in the two days he had lain in agony in this charnel house.

Beside him, Oliver could hear Windham's aide sobbing; the fatigue party were pale with horror. The wounds of the victims were appalling – as Stepanobsky had said, it was the worst wounded who had had to be left – and many of then had evidently undergone amputation. Most of those were dead. But some of the wounds were old, and where they were unbandaged they rippled with maggots.

Stepanobsky was evidently as shocked as Oliver, though he must have had an idea of what was here. He gave rapid orders to his fatigue party, and Oliver did the same. Then Oliver said, 'Is this the only room, or are there others?'

'I do not know, sir. I regret I do not know.'

'Then I suggest we make a search,' Oliver said. Together he and the Russian stepped through the carpet of devastation towards a pair of doors. They opened onto another large area, equally crowded. A man lying near the door rolled onto his side and let out a great sob of relief, clamouring in Russian for water. 'Later, my poor fellow,' Stepanobsky said. 'Help is coming.' The man's chest, neck and face were a mask of crusted blood, but whether his or another's it was impossible to tell. They passed through to another room, and found it stacked to the ceiling with coffins – there must have been two hundred of them. Oliver supposed them to be empty, but Stepanobsky shook his head. Not awaiting occupation, he said, but awaiting burial.

At a quick count, Oliver reckoned there must be fifteen hundred or so bodies in the rooms they discovered, and two in three were dead. But the worst horror was yet to come. A door in a corner previously unopened gave onto a staircase.

'Where does this staircase go?'

'To the cellars. Store rooms.'

'We had better look,' Oliver said. They descended carefully in semi-darkness, and as they turned the corner of the stair the smell rose up, thick and sweet. Oliver fumbled out his handkerchief and tied it across his nose and mouth – it helped a little. The cellar was not built completely underground: it had a row of arched windows with vertical bars which he realised he had seen from outside, at ground level out there, but here at the top of the wall, touching the ceiling. These gave light onto a vaulted cellar, with arched bays where perhaps wine or grain or ammunition had once been stored. Now the cellar was filled with decomposing humanity – there must have been five hundred or more bodies, all displaying ghastly wounds, some old, some recent. The heat and closed atmosphere down here had accelerated the putrefaction – many of the faces were silvery with it. Oliver was about to retreat when he heard a voice whisper in English, 'Love o' God, help us. Help us!'

His head snapped round. 'Who spoke? Is someone alive here?'

Stepanobsky looked at him. 'I did not hear anything.'

Oliver stared into the gloom, looking for movement. 'Is there someone alive there? Speak!'

A sob answered him, and a cracking voice said, 'English, over 'ere. English, sir, over 'ere. Oh Gawd, don't leave us!'

Now he saw in one of the bays a man propped up against the wall, saw the head move, saw a feeble movement of a hand. 'I'm coming,' he said.

'Thank Gawd, thank Gawd,' the man jabbered. 'English, English.'

Oliver picked his way through the corpses, trying not to tread on them, afraid his foot would sink in and trap him like a quicksand. He was not entirely rational, in a panic to get out of here, his every animal instinct fighting with his human control. But the sobbing voice called him, repeating desperately, 'English, sir, English,' as if laying a trail along which rescue might come to him.

When he reached the bay, he saw that the man was minus a leg, the remains of his trouser-leg wrapped round the stump for a bandage, his upper body clad in the torn remains of a coat through whose filth a memory of British red showed.

'In God's name, who are you?' Oliver asked.

'English, sir. English.'

Oliver made an effort to speak clearly and calmly. 'Yes, poor fellow, I know you are. I am the Duke of Southport, of the Army Intelligence Department. Sebastopol is in English hands now. You are rescued. What's your name and regiment?'

'Oaks, sir, o' the Thirty-third,' the man croaked eager to tell his tale, as if he thought the vision before him might fade before he had established his existence to a witness. 'Took on sentry dooty, 19th of March, year of Our Lord eighteen-hunnerd-fifty-five. Shot in the leg, sir. Brought 'ere I dunno when, jus' afore the firin' started, from the prison 'orspital. They's all dead down 'ere now, 'cept this bloke, sir. I kep' 'im alive sir, a-talkin' to 'im.'

Oliver looked. A man with a bandage round his head, lying very still on the floor beside Oaks. 'I'm afraid not.'

'No, sir, 'e ain't dead sir. 'E's warm. Don't leave 'im be'ind, sir, please, sir! Love o' Gawd, sir!"

Oliver bent closer, touched the cheek. Yes, life lingered there. The man was unconscious. He was wearing the filthy remains of a shirt and civilian trousers, was bearded and moustached like a Russian. 'Of course we won't leave him. We'll get you both out.'

The horror of this place was making Oliver's legs tremble. He went up the stairs as quickly as he could and found a fatigue party, obliged them to come down with him immediately, to take out these two survivors and search for any others amongst the dead. 'They must be got out first,' he insisted. 'Then search the cellar.'

He saw Oaks rescued – crying now with relief – and ordered the other man brought too, and then himself had to get out, into the open air and the comparative sanity of ruined Sebastopol. While he was still drawing deep breaths of the charcoal-smelling air and feeling his hammering heart slow to normal, two orderlies came out and stopped beside him with the bearded man on a stretcher.

'Beg pardon, sir, but what should we do with thisere feller, sir? Is 'e to go wiv the Russkies, sir?'

Oliver turned. 'Yes, take him to—' he began, and then stopped, his breath gone as if he had been punched in the stomach. The wan sunlight was falling on the face of the man, illuminating it enough to distinguish the features for the first time. Bearded, haggard, but unmistakeable, below the dirty bandage was the face of Oliver's brother-in-law, Cavendish.

CHAPTER TWENTY-THREE

'It was a miracle, sir, a miracle,' General Simpson said, shaking his head in wonder.

'It was the most remarkable chance,' Oliver assented.

'It was no chance,' Simpson said sharply. 'God led you there on purpose. You were His instrument. Those men were not intended to die.' Oliver bowed his head, not wishing to argue, though he might have asked why, if God meant Cavendish to be found, He didn't have him found immediately after the battle. But he knew that the answer to that would be: don't question the ways of the Almighty, sir. 'I hope you have given due thanks to the Almighty for His great mercy, Southport?' Simpson went on.

'I have indeed, sir.'

'And now you will go home. Well, I don't blame you. No, no. I shall be going myself, as soon as Lord Panmure releases me. My health is not what it was, you know.'

'I know, sir.'

'Aye, aye,' Simpson agreed, 'and you've been here longer than me. Well, I hope that puir young man survives the journey.'

'It will be healthier for him aboard the yacht, at any rate, than in the general hospital,' Oliver said.

'Missing a year,' Simpson said thoughtfully. 'It would be a great thing to know what has been happening to him.'

That was something which exercised Oliver a great deal on the way home. How did Cavendish come to be in that place? If he was taken prisoner, wounded, after the battle of Balaclava, why was his name not on the lists? Who had taken care of him? What had become of his uniform? And how had he come by the wound on his head?

That last was the mystery. Prendergast, the Head-quarters doctor, had examined Cavendish when Oliver first brought him back. He was pitifully thin, indescrib-ably filthy, and covered with sores, had evidently been suffering from diarrhoea, and had an infected wound on his upper arm, and a number of other wounds on his thighs and forearms, typical of cavalry wounds, which were healed or healing. These, presumably, were the trophies of the battle. But under the bandage he had a gash on his temple which Prendergast thought was much more recent. He probed the area gently and concluded that the skull was not fractured, which was a blessing. The odd thing, he remarked, was that there was another gash, much older and almost healed, on the other side, a long furrow which might have been the grazing wound of a bullet.

Lying in his bunk on the *Doris*, walking about the deck, helping Dinsdale take care of Cavendish, Oliver wondered about those two wounds and what had hap-pened in between. Cavendish did not come fully to his senses, though he sometimes half-woke, muttering, rolling his eyes under the half-closed lids, moving his hands feebly as though trying to perform some task. His physical condition was so poor that Oliver knew quite well Dinsdale didn't think he would survive the journey; but Oliver was satisfied he had made the right choice. In any hospital Covendish would have been carried off by some disease within days. Here at sea the air was cleaner than anywhere on the land – as witness the better general health of sailors than soldiers – and he was being transported as quickly as possible towards the best care he could receive.

The task Oliver shared with Dinsdale was merely to keep him clean and try to get a little nourishment into him when he was wakeful.

A telegraph sent ahead of them ensured there was an ambulance-waggon waiting at the dock to take Blithfield home to Southport House. London looked fantastic to Oliver, cramped beyond belief; the air foggy, smelling of horses and soot; unpleasantly cold and damp. Oh, but he was glad to be back! By the time they reached Piccadilly, it was Balaclava which seemed like the dream. The narrow harbour, the steep road up to the plain, the hills and escarpments, the plateau dotted with camps, the distant shape of Sebastopol – the views which month after month had been engraved on his mind's eye now had the flavour of delirium about them. A distant, strange, obscure place, a seaside resort in a foreign land – what had he been doing there? What had any of them? They had sewn the plain with dead men, as numerous as corn-seed, and burned the town. The town would grow again, but no crop would grow from the men.

They pulled up before Southport House. The door opened, there stood Ungar with two footmen, ready to direct the moving of Lord Blithfield into the house. Oliver stepped down from the carriage, but before Ungar could do more than lift his forefinger, someone had come past him, running down the steps, a woman in a grey gown. And then his arms were full of Charlotte. Neither of them spoke. Across her bent head he saw Ungar's face trying not to look shocked at this public display. Oliver held her tightly against him for a long time, and then put her back to look at her; and saw what they had not told him by telegraph or letter, how nearly he had lost her.

Charlotte brought Abernethy down to the drawing-room where the family was gathered to hear his opinion.

'His condition is very poor. The lack of food and clean water and proper care have brought him so low that the lesions in his skin will not heal. He needs careful nursing, and feeding up. But he cannot be fed when he is unconscious, and he is unconscious for much of the time. I wish I could say otherwise, but the prognosis is not favourable, I must confess.'

'Is it because of the head wound?' Rosamund asked.

'It's hard to say, your ladyship, whether his insensibility is caused by the head wound, or merely by bodily weakness. Only time will tell.'

'But if he recovers his health, will he recover his wits?'

Abernethy didn't like brutal questions. He hemmed, and looked about him, and said at last, 'Blows to the head in that region can cause loss of memory. But again, only time will tell. The key to his survival must lie in careful nursing.'

'He shall have that,' Charlotte said.

'I know it, your grace,' Abernethy said. 'He could not be in better hands.'

Alice, who had been sitting on the sofa twisting a damp handkerchief round and round in her fingers, suddenly cried, 'Why do you talk to her? I am his wife. *I* should nurse him.'

The interruption was so unexpected that no-one spoke for a moment. Then Abernethy gathered his professional tact together and said, 'My dear Lady Blithfield, the sick room is no place for a lady.'

'Why not? If I'm a lady, *she's* one too.'

'But my dear ma'am, you are too delicate for such worrying sights, such fatiguing labours—'

Alice jumped to her feet. 'I'm not delicate. I'm stronger than her. She's just had a baby. Look at her!'

Mrs Olwyn said firmly, 'That will do, now, Lady Blithfield, dear.'

Charlotte met Oliver's eyes across the room. She was pale and thin and worn-looking. Oliver's eyes said, *she has a point*. Charlotte said with a hint of impatience, 'You haven't any experience in sick-nursing, Alice. Norton and I will take care of him. You can trust us.'

'Indeed you can,' Abernethy said emphatically.

'That's right,' Mrs Olwyn said. 'You want dear Lord Blithfield to get better, don't you? Then leave him to those who know best.'

But for once Alice was stubborn, staring from face to face round the room with unexpected defiance. 'I want to nurse him. I know you're very clever,' she said to Charlotte, 'and I know you know all about nursing, but *he's my husband*. I want to help.'

Charlotte took pity on her. She always had sympathy with those prevented from doing what they reasonably wanted. 'Of course you can help nurse him, if you really want to,' she said. 'Do you think you can bear it?'

'Yes,' Alice said, more firmly than her expression warranted. But there was determination in that silly face, and Charlotte wondered what she might have been like with a different upbringing.

If Alice had the best right, in theory, to nurse Cavendish, Rosamund, as his mother, had the next best right. But it was Charlotte who took charge, and Charlotte on whom most of the burden fell. Oliver knew this was by choice, but he still could not help remonstrating.

'You must not knock yourself up,' he protested. 'I see how it will be. But you are not strong, remember. Let Norton or your mother do more.'

'Norton does her share and more. And Mama is not well either. You know she can't sit for long at a time with her arthritis.'

'Then let Alice do more.'

'I can't leave him with Alice. She doesn't know what to do. In fact, supervising her only adds to the work. But I couldn't deny her.'

'Well, then, get in a trained nurse to help you.'

'Leave him with a hireling?'

He shook his head in exasperation. 'You're making excuses. What is there to do for him most of the time?'

She looked at him with desperate appeal. 'Let me be, Oliver. I must be with him. Later, when he has turned the corner, I promise I will do less. But for now—'

'My love,' he said gravely, 'you must prepare yourself for the possibility that he will not recover.'

It was kindly said, but her expression hardened and she drew back from him. 'He will,' she said.

He left it at that; but he was worried. Endless vigils and snatched meals would not help a constitution which had not yet recovered from a dangerous confinement. But there was no way to keep her from what she felt she must do. Everyone helped as they could; but shortly after Cavendish was brought home, Lord Aylesbury, who had been ailing for many weeks, died, and Rosamund and Tom, with their spouses, were called away to Wolvercote. Charlotte hardly noticed their absence, or took in the death of her uncle, though she had been fond of him. Her world had narrowed to one room, one person in one bed. She hardly even noticed that Oliver was not home very often.

Being released from his commission in the Crimea had not ended Oliver's involvement with events there. His observations and opinions were important, and he was continually being summoned to Horseguards, the War office and by various members of the Cabinet. He went twice to Windsor, and was asked to write a report for Prince Albert on various aspects of the war – a time-consuming business, since Prince Albert's appetite for detail was known to be prodigious. In addition there were several Parliamentary enquiries going on regarding the supply and condition of the army before Sebastopol, and the conduct of the war. He was frequently summoned before committees to give his views, and then summoned privately by senior members of the Government and the Army and asked to change them. Poor Filder was being given a very rough ride, for the senior soldiers and politicians involved in the débâcle were gentlemen, and it was not possible for one gentleman to criticise or blame another; but the Commissary-General was not regarded as a gentleman, so it was obviously much more convenient to make him the scape-goat. Oliver felt bound in justice to do his best for Filder, but it was difficult to make people who had not been there understand what things had been like at Balaclava during that first winter. It was even more difficult to make anyone in the Army appreciate that the organisation of that venerable institution left anything to be desired.

Oliver gave it as his opinion that no individual was to blame for the hell that Balaclava became: the system made it impossible for order and efficiency to reign. Responsibility was fatally divided between different departments, which had no co-ordination between them, and too few clerks to carry out the work. Moreover what the officers and administrators in the field required had always to be authorised by the relevant department at home in England, which had no idea what conditions prevailed and had its own private agenda to work to. Filder, for instance, with a staff of only three, was responsible for supplying food, fuel and clothing to the entire army in the Crimea, but he did not control the transport nor the finance required for purchasing them. The regimental officers might order what their men needed, but the Commissariat was responsible directly to the Treasury, which might or might not grant the expenditure; and the Port Admiral had to provide the ships to fetch the goods, which he might or might not see fit to do.

The Secretary *for* War decided military policy, which the Commander-in-Chief in the field translated into action; but the Commander-in-Chief could not initiate any measure involving finance without the approval of the Secretary *at* War, the army's paymaster. Clothing was provided by the Commissariat, but uniforms were designed and approved by the Adjutant-General. Arms were the responsibility of the Adjutant-General, but ammunition came under the Master-General of Ordnance. The men's daily rations were supplied by the Commissariat, but if they were too sick to eat rations and needed invalid food, that had to be ordered by the Purveyor, who was responsible to the Medical Department. Moreover, both Purveyor and Commissary could only order goods which were on pre-issued lists of acceptable supplies; if they purchased anything not on the lists they were held personally and financially responsible to the Government. This ruling killed initiative and prevented unforeseen circumstances being effectively dealt with. The difficulty of getting supplies up to the plateau, for instance, had been aggravated by the lack of baggage animals; but the commissary could not purchase the large number of extra mules needed because the Treasury would not authorise the extra fodder for them.

But as he gave his evidence and his opinions to the various committees, Oliver felt curiously as though he were writing on the sand just along the tide mark; he could almost see his words being washed away even as he spoke them. The same attitude he had met with in the Crimea was at work in England. Soldiers were a breed apart. Men and officers alike endured horrific dangers and hardships – that was the nature of war. The men were brutes, and needed to be, to endure. Any attempt to mitigate hardship would make the men soft and reduce the efficiency of the fighting machine. That eight out of ten of the deaths in the Crimea had been due to sickness and disease rather than battle injuries was a pity and a waste of manpower; but men, even officers, were replaceable. What must not be injured was the spirit, integrity and traditions of the finest, most effective, and longest-established army in the world. All this fuss over Balaclava was just civilian-talk; and it was axiomatic that civilians could not understand the ways of the soldier.

For a long time Charlotte thought Cavendish would die. Or rather, she refused to think it, but the thought was there, just behind her line of sight, like something threatening in the shadows. There was so little to do for him, only keep him clean, dress his sores and wounds, watch him while he slept, attempt to feed him when he woke. If only there were some way of feeding him while he slept, she felt they would have got on. He was so desperately thin and weak, his body hadn't the strength to heal itself. He came up from unconsciousness from time to time, though he never seemed fully awake. His eyes would half open, he would turn his head, sometimes murmur a few words, or moan a little. In those moments Charlotte did her best to introduce nourishment into him, arrowroot, port wine, meat jelly; and she would talk to him, trying to bring him back to himself. But he was like a man floating just under water, never breaking entirely through the surface. Her fear was that he would sink further down, out of her reach entirely.

The worst time came when he had been home about three weeks, and he developed a fever. Norton was very grave; Charlotte herself did not know how his emaciated frame could survive it. She didn't understand how he could have caught it despite her great care, and racked her brains for some sin of commission or omission. Abernethy said it was just a fever of debility, caused by the infected wound in his shoulder, but that did not comfort her. She had claimed him as her own to nurse, and her care had failed him.

There was no sleep, no rest. Rosamund, in mourning for her brother, hovered in anguish and watched her son slip away. To have lost him once was terrible; to lose him a second time was unendurable. The damp weather made her joints ache and her hands near useless. Batchworth sat in the library hour after hour unmoving, unable to think, unable to pray. Emily did her best to keep the house going, and offered to spell Charlotte whenever she wished, but Charlotte could not leave the bedside. She sat looking at his face, listening to his breathing, and said softly, over and over again, 'You will not die. Do you hear me, Cavendish? You *will* not.'

Now and then Oliver came and stood behind her, and laid a hand on her shoulder. She drew strength from his presence. They both knew their life together must be suspended until this crisis was resolved one way or the other. They had not even had the new baby Christened; Charlotte had hardly laid eyes on it since Cavendish came home. But that touch of Oliver's hand said that whatever happened here, that part of her life was safe, would not be touched or spoiled.

But the fever broke at last, and Cavendish slept. Abernethy allowed himself to be cautiously optimistic: it was, he said, a healthy sleep, a good sleep, unlike his previous restless semi-consciousness. Charlotte slept too, yielding her vigil to others. Cavendish slept for twenty hours, and then woke fully for the first time, opening his eyes and staring about him. Charlotte was again at the bedside, and leaned over him eagerly, smiling. 'You're awake,' she said gently. 'You've been away a long time. How are you feeling?'

But his eyes passed unrecognisingly over her face. He looked around what he could see of the room, and frowned. He did not seem to know where he was.

'Do you know who I am?' she asked; but he didn't answer. Her heart sank. Abernethy had warned that he might suffer from loss of memory. To have him back from death, and not to have him back, would be too cruel. She left him for a moment to call Norton to bring food and send a message for Abernethy. While she waited she talked quietly to Cavendish, but he made no sign of hearing or understanding her. When Norton arrived with a bowl of chicken broth, they propped him up between them and fed him, and he took it eagerly, like a little bird, but silently; and when they laid him down again, he stared up at the tester blankly, his eyes moving a little from side to side as though he were following a distant action.

Abernethy came and examined him. 'He is with us in body but not in spirit,' he said. Cavendish had not spoken or looked at Abernethy directly, his eyes focused elsewhere, an occasional frown passing over his face at what he saw in that invisible world. 'He has sustained a great shock, and I believe his mind is not healed yet. He will not come back to himself until it is.'

'But *will* it heal? *Will* he come back?' Charlotte said urgently.

'God knows,' Abernethy said.

'What can we do?' Rosamund asked.

'Feed him up, make him stronger. Perhaps when his body is stronger, his mind will be able to mend. That's all I can suggest.'

November came. Cavendish's condition improved. He was awake much of the time now, and took nourishment well, and his infected cut was beginning to heal at last.

Abernethy was pleased with his physical progress; but still he gave no sign of recognising anyone or knowing where he was, and he had not spoken, though sometimes he muttered in his sleep. Rosamund seemed pleased with his physical strength, and spoke cheerfully for the sake of the others, particularly Alice; but alone with her husband at night she shed bitter tears; and as the days passed, Charlotte, too, began to give up hope that Cavendish would come back to them. She tended his body and put food into his open mouth, but he was a blank piece of paper on which no Cavendish was writ, and the loss was almost worse than his death would have been.

And then one day when she was spooning rice pudding into him and thinking about something else, he made a strange sound. She thought he was choking, and looked at him, startled, the spoon arrested in mid-air. He moved his hand, frowning, watching it as he lifted it from the bed and deliberately took the spoon from her hand. 'I can feed myself,' he said. His voice sounded creaky from unuse, but it was perfectly comprehensible.

Charlotte drew a breath that was almost a sob. 'Of course you can,' she managed to say. 'Shall I hold the bowl for you?' She positioned it before him and watched as he pushed the spoon into the rice, rather deliberately as if he had never done it before, but then automatically put his other hand up to steady the bowl against his own pressure. Frowning with immense concentration he loaded the spoon and moved it slowly and carefully to his mouth, and then dropped the spoon back into the bowl and let his hands rest while he chewed and swallowed.

'You're very weak,' she said, 'and no wonder. But don't worry, your strength will come back to you in time, now you've made the beginning.'

She had spoken to him so often without reaction on his part that despite his having spoken his first words, she did not expect a response. But he frowned at her and said, 'Charley?'

She stared at him, and her hands shook so much she had to put the bowl down. 'Cavendish?' Her voice trembled. She could feel her heart pounding. 'Do you know who I am?'

''Course I do. But what are you doing here?'

'Where's here, my dear?'

He looked around him, puzzled. 'I don't know,' he said at last. 'Where am I?'

'Home, in England. In Southport House.'

He shook his head, plainly bewildered. 'How did I get here?'

'You were wounded, and we brought you home. Don't you remember?'

'I remember—' A long silence. 'No, it must have been a dream. I don't know. I don't know.' He sounded fretful, and she didn't want him to be upset.

'Never mind, it will come back to you. You've been ill a long time, and everything will seem confused to you for a while. The important thing is that you're home and safe.'

He nodded doubtfully, and let his eyes wander round the room again. 'I don't know this room,' he said at last.

'It's the yellow bedroom, on the same corridor as my own room. I don't suppose you've ever been in it.'

'I don't like the wallpaper,' he said. It was an inconsequential remark, but it made her cry and laugh at the same moment, and she had to take a strong grip on herself not to fall into an hysteria.

From then on his recovery was more rapid, as his natural strength helped his body to heal. Very soon he was complaining about 'slops' and demanding proper food; soon after that he was wanting to get out of bed –

though he found himself bafflingly weak when he tried, and was glad after a circuit of the room to get back into bed. His memory was slower to recover, and Abernethy warned them against allowing any great shock to unsettle him, in case the wits he was regaining fled again. But Christmas after all was a time for rejoicing, when they had not expected it to be.

There was a great deal for him to take in, for he had lost a large piece out of his life. He had no idea how long he had been ill, or even what year it was. Charlotte had not even been pregnant the last time he remembered seeing her, and now here was a new little niece, whom they were calling Augusta after the month of her birth, for want of anything more significant to name her for.

'Poor little thing,' Charlotte said, 'she's been dreadfully overshadowed in her life so far. I must try to make it up to her when she's older.'

Alice was so glad that he remembered her at all that she was all silent smiles and tender tears, a combination which touched him unexpectedly and did a great deal toward attaching him to her again. He was quite bewildered, however, at the sight of his son William, whom he had last seen as a five-month-old baby, and who was now a lively, stocky, fair-haired toddler of approaching two-and-a-half. William did not know his father any more than his father knew him, but he was polite, if wary, towards the stranger in the bedroom, and then went off cheerfully to forget him and play with his cousins again.

The year 1856 began; Sir William Codrington replaced General Simpson, who came home to nurse his unsound bowels in comfort. Codrington had plans, and Palmerston was ready, with British public opinion behind him, to give the Russkies a damn' good thrashing before the troops came home; but the French had had enough of the Crimea, and Emperor Napoleon had the liberation of

Italy in view as his next claim to immortality. Negotiations began between France and Russia for a settlement, and the Peace was signed in Paris in March. Cavendish by then was physically almost recovered, but there were still large gaps in his memory, especially about the war.

It was mostly to Charlotte that he spoke. He still found too many people around him tiring and distracting, and it was her patience that led him through what he did remember, up to the beginning of the charge of the Light Brigade at Balaclava.

'I remember sitting in the sunshine, fretting that we weren't allowed to do anything,' he said. 'And I remember Nolan coming down from the Heights like a madman with the orders. What happened to Nolan?'

'Dead,' she said. 'Killed at the beginning of the charge.'

'Do I remember that? I'm not sure. Dead: I suppose I must get used to that answer. The Old Man's dead too, I suppose?'

'Lord Cardigan? No, far from it. He got back from the guns without a scratch and went home a hero. He was fêted up and down the country. Everyone wanted to hear his account. His memoires sold thousands of copies in the book shops. And an outfitter even had the woollen jacket he wore in the evenings copied and called it a "cardigan". He sold thousands of them, too.'

'Good God,' Cavendish said blankly.

'Do you remember the charge at all?'

'No. Only starting off, and thinking, "This is it, we will all be killed." After that, just confusion – the noise, and people falling. And the horses – oh my God, the horses!' He shuddered and closed his eyes, and a while later asked, 'What happened to Rowan and Bracken?'

'We don't know about Rowan. Either he was killed or taken by the Russians in the battle. Oliver brought Bracken home on the same ship with you, but he got sick almost as soon as he arrived, and we had to have him put down, poor fellow.'

'Ah,' said Cavendish; and he didn't refer to the horses again.

As to what happened to him between the battle and waking up in England, he could give no information. He remembered nothing, just a vague confusion of shapes to which he could put no meaning; and trying to think about it made his head ache alarmingly. Charlotte could only surmise that the old wound in the head had been got during the battle, and had made him unconscious and lost him his memory. How he had lost his uniform and his identity was a mystery. Oliver suggested that perhaps he had been left on the battlefield for dead, and stripped by a scavenger, and later been discovered still to be alive and taken into Sebastopol to be nursed. The second blow on the head he might have come by in any of the bombardments. Someone had given him the minimum of care to keep him alive, that was certain; and someone had put him with other wounded prisoners for safety in the Dockyard Barracks; but Cavendish remembered none of it.

As Charlotte had done before him, he began to read everything he could get hold of about the war, to fill in what he had lost. He was shocked by the news that the charge had been a mistake, and of how many had died; even more shocked by the end the cavalry had come to, up on the plateau during the winter. But mostly that was for the horses' sakes, rather than through any feeling that there had been terrible mismanagement. While he was recovering, there was public discussion going on over what happened during the terrible winter, prompted by the publication of Sir John McNeill and Colonel Tulloch's 'Inquiry into the Supplies of the British Army in the Crimea', and the results of other commissions of enquiry. But Cavendish dismissed the debate with a shrug. He was a soldier at heart, and like other soldiers felt that hardship, however severe, was the fortune of war. In the same way, he accepted his own injuries, and the loss of his memory. 'Some men come back without a leg,' he said once, when Charlotte was commiserating with him. 'At least I still need two boots to be properly dressed.'

But though he was a soldier at heart, he told his mother that he was selling out. 'I expect you'll be glad. I'm sorry I went against your wishes and gave you so many grey hairs.'

'You aren't doing it for my sake, I hope?' she said. 'You know mothers are always in terror for their children's lives. If you lived in a padded box and I had the only key, I'd still worry about you.'

He shook his head. 'The Army's finished for me now,' he said soberly. 'Abernethy says I will make a full physical recovery, but that I ought to be careful about getting any more bumps on the head. So I don't think I had better take part in any more cavalry charges.'

'Does he think you will get all your memory back?' she asked.

'Perhaps, in time. It doesn't matter to me,' Cavendish said. 'I don't much care about the bits I've missed – except that it's confused and jumbled, and I don't know what's real and what's a dream. If I ever do remember,' he said lightly, 'I dare say I shall be glad to forget again in a hurry.'

She reached out and took his hand, and he stroked it gently, frowning in thought. 'But I don't regret it, Mama – except the trouble to you and Papa. Is that wrong of me? I wish it had turned out otherwise, but I don't regret it.'

'That's the best way to feel about one's life,' she said, from a depth of experience.

One day in April Cavendish suddenly asked Charlotte, 'What happened to Fanny? Did you ever hear anything more?'

'No,' Charlotte said. 'We had that one note from her, saying that she was well and safe and that we must not look for her; after that, nothing.'

'And Doctor Anthony? Have you heard anything of him?'

'He went to live in Norfolk and took the child with him, where he is still, for all I know. He doesn't communicate with me, though he may still be searching for Fanny. Perhaps one day he will divorce her, and then she may be at peace.'

'At peace? Unfortunate phrase. Do you think she's dead?'

'No,' Charlotte said thoughtfully. 'I don't now. I think she's hiding, that someone has taken her in, and that she's found a measure of happiness. I hope it's so, anyway. I think if she were in great trouble we would have heard from her.'

'Hm,' Cavendish said non-committally. Then, 'Poor Fanny! Of all people. She was always so merry and care-for-nothing. Who'd have thought the doctor would turn out such a dragon? And to think you nearly married him yourself once, Charley.'

'Nonsense, I never did. There was never anything between me and Doctor Anthony,' she said quickly, and changed the subject. But later, when she was alone, the thoughts came back to her, of the first time she had met Anthony, at the supper table at Mrs Welland's, and how fine and handsome and good she had thought him. Well, so he was, in his way; but goodness ought not be so narrow it squeezed the life out of anyone, or so long-sighted it could not see what was under its nose. And it seemed to be true of Doctor Anthony that he cared only for people he was not required to love; loving Fanny, as Charlotte now believed he did, he yet could not care for her.

And then she thought again of Mrs Welland's house, and wondered suddenly whether Mrs Welland knew anything of Fanny. Might not Fanny have gone to Mrs Welland – that kind, motherly, familiar person – for help? She must have happy memories of Lamb's Conduit Street; and it was there that she had met Philip Anthony. Ah, but perhaps that was the very reason she would *not* go there? Afraid of discovery as she seemed to be, would she not avoid any place connected with him? And surely if Fanny had gone to Mrs Welland, Mrs Welland would have contacted Charlotte? Still, it was perhaps worth asking. She made a mental note to send Norton with a message, and promptly forgot about it.

But a week later she was driving through Russell Square on her way home from the hospital, and passing the end of Theobald's Row, the thought came back to her. She rapped on the roof, and the carriage stopped.

'I am just going to step up to Mrs Welland's house, and ask if she has heard anything of Fanny,' she said to Norton.

'Wouldn't you like me to go, your grace?' Norton asked. She generally remembered Charlotte's proper honorific when she was doing something Norton disapproved of.

'No, no, it's all right,' Charlotte said. 'I'm plainly dressed enough not to put them in a pelter.' She was always plainly dressed when she went to the hospital. 'I'll walk from here, so as not to take the carriage into the street. I don't want to let anyone who might be watching know that I have an interest there.'

'You think Doctor Anthony may be watching the house?' Norton said.

'Not in person, so you need not look as though you thought I'd lost my wits. But he was very determined to find her, and he has plenty of money now, you know. He may have agents looking for her still.'

Norton nodded grudgingly. 'It's possible, of course.'

'Thank you for that ringing endorsement. Wait here, then. I don't suppose I shall be very long.'

She put her veil down over her face and stepped out down Theobald's Row. It was afternoon, going towards dusk, and there were no great crowds about, just enough people so that she did not look conspicuous. She felt a little foolish about her mission, for she was quite sure now that Mrs Welland would know nothing, and indeed might feel slighted that Charlotte had not thought to address her on the subject until now. Besides, Doctor Anthony had been her lodger long before she knew Charlotte and Fanny, and she might be expected to take his side, and believe like him that Charlotte had led Fanny astray. Well, well, she had come thus far, she might as well ask. But as she turned into Lamb's Conduit Street, she saw a man lounging against the wall almost opposite Mrs Welland's door. He was a rough-looking fellow in no-coloured clothes, hands jammed in his pockets, a kerchief round his throat, a battered hat pulled down over his eyes, and a clay pipe sticking out of the corner of his mouth. There was nothing different about him from a thousand other loungers to be found around the streets of London, but the fact that he was standing just there, apparently looking in the direction of the one door that interested her, made her nervous. Her clothes were plain, but they were not poor, and a veil might not be impenetrable to professional eyes.

He had not glanced in her direction yet. Without altering her pace, she turned left into the alley which led to the lane which ran behind the houses on that side. She had never been into the garden at Lamb's Conduit Street, but in reason there ought to be a gate into it from the lane.

If she could work out which was the house, she could go in that way and knock at the back door. Turning into the lane she observed that the houses did have gates; they also had high walls, reaching to just above her head-height, so she wasn't able to see more than the top windows, not enough to recognise a house by. All she could do was to count the houses and try to work it out. When she came to the one she reckoned was right, she tried the gate in the wall, but it was locked.

'Bother,' she said aloud. It was frustrating to be so close; but there was no help for it. It was probably a silly idea anyway; surely Mrs Welland would have written if she had anything to tell. Charlotte was about to turn away when she saw a little further up the lane a wooden box, which must once have held fruit or some other produce. Perhaps some child had been playing with it, or it had been thrown out for firewood. At all events, it would give her just enough height to see over the wall, and perhaps there would be someone inside whose attention she could attract. She looked up and down the lane, but she was alone; and feeling half foolish, half adventurous, she dragged the box back to the wall and stepped onto it.

There was someone in the garden. It was not much of a garden, in fact, just a bare patch with a washing-line strung over it, and along the sunnier wall a row of last year's bean-stalks, bleached and insubstantial like the ghost of summer past. Beneath the washingline a woman stood, taking the washing down and folding it into a basket at her feet. She was wearing a plain brown dress of cheap material, with a big, coarse, blue apron over it, and her uncovered head had brown curly hair pinned up for neatness and convenience rather than fashion. A servant, Charlotte's eyes told her, passing beyond the woman to the windows of the house; and then, finding no-one looking out, coming back to her.

She opened her mouth and took breath to call when the woman began to sing. In a breathy, small, but sweet soprano she sang, 'On Richmond Hill there lives a lass more bright than Mayday mo-orn, whose charms all other maids' surpass—'

Charlotte jumped off the box in a hurry, her heart pounding. The voice went on undisturbed, singing the old, innocent song. Charlotte knew that voice as well as she knew her own. The dark-haired woman was Fanny.

Leaning against the wall, Charlotte went over and over the image that was now imprinted on her mind. There was no doubt about it: Fanny's profile, Fanny's small nose and full lips, even the shape of her head and the way her hair curled over her temples – Charlotte knew every bit of Fanny too well to be mistaken. And stretching up her arms to the washing-line, she had revealed an outline under the blue apron also too familiar to be mistaken. Fanny was pregnant, quite heavily pregnant. But she had been away from Anthony for eighteen months now. Charlotte stared the knowledge in the face. Fanny had formed another attachment; and in spite of the fact that she was a married woman, with little prospect of ever being free to marry, she had – she was—

Pregnant! Charlotte leaned against the wall, her mind running round and round in surprise like a squirrel on a wheel. And living at Mrs Welland's! Which meant that Mrs Welland was helping to conceal her, not only from Anthony, but from everyone. How long had she been here? All along? Charlotte felt angry and hurt that she had been allowed to worry so long, and mourn so long for her cousin, with nothing more than one brief note to say Fanny was not dead. Was it from here the note had been sent? Had it, perhaps, been at Mrs Welland's urging that even so little of a comfort had been vouchsafed to Charlotte?

And then from inside the garden she heard someone call, 'Fanny!'

'Yes?'

'Come and have some tea. You mustn't tire yourself.'

'Oh, don't fuss over me, you bulldog!'

Charlotte recognised the voice: it was Peter Welland, Mrs Welland's son; and the exchange between the two was familiar and affectionate. Now the last piece fell into place. Charlotte gathered herself together and walked back along the lane towards Lamb's Conduit Street. Now she knew everything, except why Fanny had disgraced herself, given up her respectability, become a fallen woman. Peter Welland? It was amazing. He was a pleasant man, she remembered, but nothing out of the way; not handsome or clever or distinguished or rich. Just kind.

Just kind. Charlotte thought of Fanny's life with Philip Anthony, thought of her own judgement on it – how terrible it must be for Fanny never to have known the warmth of married love and tender physical affection. Was that not answer enough? Peter was kind, and that was the one sort of man Fanny had not tried being in love with. And if she could never marry him, might she not decide that it didn't matter to anyone but themselves? And might not Mrs Welland – tolerant to a fault – agree with them? Who, indeed, was it hurting, but Fanny's immortal soul? And might not a merciful God find it in himself to forgive a little sin for the sake of increasing the sum of human happiness?

She turned out into the street. The lounger had gone away – she saw him slouching up the road and turning into Guilford Street. Not a watcher after all. Fanny was safe. Charlotte hesitated. She could go and knock at the door now, confront them, greet Fanny, have the whole story at first hand. She tried to imagine Fanny's face when she walked in on her; and what she saw was not joy, but dismay. Who could it serve to find Fanny out? She had sounded happy, singing at the washing-line, and when she called back to Peter. Soon she would be a mother. It was long past too late to change anything; and if Fanny had wanted her to know, Fanny would have found a way to tell her.

She walked on. Fanny had found a measure of happiness, as she had hoped she would. Let it be, now; let her have her life. The carriage was waiting, the footman jumped down to open the door and deal with the step, she climbed up beside Norton, and the door was closed behind her.

'Well, your grace?' Norton asked. It was growing dusk, and quite dark inside the carriage, especially as Charlotte had not lifted her veil. 'You weren't gone long. I suppose they hadn't heard anything.'

'No, nothing at all,' Charlotte said lightly. She felt the carriage dip to the left as the footman climbed up, and then the coachman cracked his whip, the horses took the collar, and they moved off into the traffic, homeward bound.